THE CRUEL GODS
THE END OF TIME

TRUDIE SKIES
fantasy author

TRUDIESKIES.COM

Content Warning

THE END OF TIME is an adult fantasy book that contains strong language throughout and content some readers may find distressing, including religious criticism, sexual themes, gore and execution, and scenes of abuse and torture.

For a full list of content warnings, please visit:

TrudieSkies.com/The-Cruel-Gods-Content-Warnings

For the civilians of war, past and present. For every innocent caught in the
battles of cruel leaders playing god.

You lived, you loved, and you will be remembered.

We must never forget.

Domain Map

DOMAIN CROSSINGS
XII
XI
I
X
II
IX
III
VIII
IV
VII
V
VI
PHANTASY
KRONOS
MEMORIA
EVENTIDE
JUNIPER
RAPTURE
HEARTSTONE
OBITUARY
SOLARIS
TEMPEST
ARCADIA
WITHERYN

PART ONE

0

Sometimes dreams can be confused with reality. How do you know if you're awake or lost in a dream?
Here are a few checks you can perform to tell the difference:
Check your environment: are there any distortions?
Test your abilities: can you suddenly fly?
Eat a snack: does a strawberry bonbon taste like chocolate?
Read a book: has the text stayed the same?
—Reverie, Am I Dreaming? A Mesmer Guidebook

THERE WERE ONCE TWELVE.

A perfect, symmetrical number. The twelve domains slotted within the hours of a clock in harmonious union. Twelve gods who forged a Covenant bound by the laws of logic and time. That design was meant to bring balance to the universe, to provide a fair and just series of guidelines. Only my Father understood what justice truly meant. Only He could unite the twelve and govern with a firm hand. Only He understood the necessary sacrifices.

Through His vision, He witnessed the end of it all.

By His hand, the Covenant was broken.

And so the twelve became nine.

My fingers grazed the smooth marble of the Council table as I strode around it clockwise, each step a tick or tock. It had been months since I last graced the chamber among the gathered ambassadors. In that time, so much had changed. The various segments that represented the domains had shattered—the clockwork design no longer whole. Eventide had been wiped clean, though that was no loss. The Vesper had always been a dark blight on Chime's streets.

Solaris, too, no longer marred the chamber, though the Glimmer's demise was part of Father's design. Regrettably, I'd not been present to witness Gildola's fall. Gloria had been a valuable ally in keeping the baser domains in check, though that was no longer necessary. I felt no modicum of mercy or pity for the Glimmer. They had threatened Father's rule. Now, their unholy tools would become ours.

I paused beside Phantasy. Their absence surprised me. Who would have ever expected the Mesmer capable of subtle rebellion?

More domains would be wiped from this map in time. Father had seen it.

He'd shared those visions with me as I'd slept, cradled within His cosmic mind during the rest my mortal toil had earned me.

Yet my path had not ended in death.

Upon His benevolent hand, Father had stirred me from my slumber, and I'd awoken once more not to serve as His saint, but as His holy warrior.

His redeemer.

The Council chamber had long been my battleground of choice. That was the Diviner way—to rule by the swipe of a pen, not a knife. Violence was an ugly affair reserved for lesser mortals, yet there was violence in words. A simple command could take a life. Damn a soul. Control a city. Destroy an entire domain.

I rested my palm above the skyline of Kronos—my rightful home—and waited for the seconds to pass.

Tick.

Tock.

One by one, the ambassadors returned to this neutral ground at the behest of their gods. Though the chamber was warded against godly interference, that too was a reflection of the Covenant—a guideline, rather than a fixed rule. The gods could have answered Father's herald directly, but chose to send their voices instead. In the wake of Solaris's destruction, I understood their desire for caution.

The eight remaining ambassadors took their places around the table. They appeared much the same as when I'd last stood among them, though none seemed at all surprised by my presence. I met each of their eyes. The familiarity was gone. Through these mortals' eyes, the gods stared back at me, observing. The ambassadors were no longer mortals with free thought or will, but vehicles their gods chose to inhabit.

As my Father chose to inhabit me.

The clock struck twelve.

IT IS TIME. Father's voice echoed in my mind.

I tugged at the cufflinks holding my shirt in place. A mortal gesture, yet Father could not abide disorder, and neither could I. When I spoke, His words passed through my lips, blessing my mortal voice. "The Covenant is broken. Corentine has awakened. What has begun cannot be stopped."

"About damn time!" Dandelion exclaimed. The Leander ambassador had never been one for taming his opinions, a fact that had not endeared him to me, but now it was his master—Lionheart—speaking through him. "The Covenant was a pointless exercise. An inconvenience at best. So let's not beat around the bush." He stretched back in his chair and placed his feet on the table above Rapture. "Three gods down. Valeria, Gildola, and now Mesmorpheus, that old fool. Corentine desires revenge? Let her take it. The crazy bitch deserves her shot. Those who can't handle her aren't worthy of their domains." He grinned, exposing his fangs. "I have no fear for mine."

"Trust you to hunger for blood," said Erosain. The Ember ambassador eyed Dandelion's feet with utter disdain, though his feminine movements channeled his inner mistress, Edana. "I've had all the time in the universe to enjoy my playthings, and I've yet to grow bored. I have no interest in war, nor do I have any desire to play with the ashes Mother Dear will leave in her wake."

"Then you understand what is at stake," I said. "Corentine will come for your domains. Her agents of Chaos will rip them from you—"

"Corentine may be the reason we're all here, but you struck that match. You never had any intent of uniting us against Chaos, did you?"

The question was for my Father, but it was my tongue that answered. "I stand before you now."

"And we answered your call," said Hazelhearth. The Umber ambassador sat still, as stoic as the tree Unghard had left behind in

Heartstone. "To lose one of our own is to cut off a healthy branch. Lose too many, and we *all* wither. That is what the Covenant stood for—a union to bind our roots. Corentine is part of those roots."

"The root is diseased," I said, choosing the metaphor Unghard would appreciate most. "She will not accept an olive branch."

"Then what is your plan to save Chime?"

"I have no intention of saving Chime."

Father's words resonated with a sudden finality.

YOU WILL ACHIEVE WHAT OTHERS COULD NOT.

I failed you once, Father.

I would not fail again.

"This is the turning of the tide?" asked Aberforth, the Amnae ambassador. He'd been an outspoken critic of the Diviner, despite the similarities our domains shared. "Everything returns to its primordial oil. We join you once more in your new world, or perish with the old? We swam through those rivers once. We need not swim them again."

"We can create the next iteration," said Corvus, the Zephyr ambassador. The other ambassadors exchanged curious looks. Zyclone rarely spoke, not even through their mortals. "An upgrade free from the extreme moralities of dusk and dawn and frivolous dreams—"

"*Frivolous?*" Sonata's shrill voice cut through the room. The Seren hovered above the segment for Arcadia, their tiny wings trembling despite the being speaking for their god, Serenity. "Frivolity is what brings the stars to life. Mesmorpheus at least understood that. I enjoy this existence. I enjoy my domain, my mortals. As the laws set forth over a millennium ago no longer apply, then *I* say a change of leadership is in order. You've had your time, Dor." They chuckled at their own joke. "Now it's ours."

"As much as I am *loath* to agree with that flying mop," said Dandelion, "it's every soul for themselves." He leered at Erosain sitting beside him. "I'll take what's yours. I'll treat your mortals *really* good."

Smoke blew from Erosain's nose. "Try me."

The ambassadors bickered among themselves and exchanged veiled threats. All except for Willow, the Fauna ambassador, who remained silent and dispassionate. Her face was blank. Her soft-brown antlers twitched, the only indication Faen's presence had joined us at all.

THE GODS HAVE GROWN COMFORTABLE IN THEIR DOMAINS, Father said. *THEY DO NOT REMEMBER WHAT IT MEANS TO EXPERIENCE HARDSHIP.*

They are not worthy of your love, Father.

THEY WERE ONCE MY CHILDREN, AS YOU ARE MY SON. A FATHER'S LOVE REMAINS FOR ETERNITY, EVEN IF MY CHILDREN STRAY. IT SADDENS ME SO FEW CAN BE REDEEMED.

THE REST WILL BECOME LOST TO TIME.

Hazelhearth stood, the motion cutting through the chatter. "We will do what is right by our mortals, as we have always done. Is there a place for my mortals in your new world, Dor?"

I bowed my head. "There is a place for those who obey the laws of time."

Zephyr were the world builders. Umber were the peacekeepers. They fit within Father's divine plans.

The others did not.

"Morana?" I prompted.

The Necro ambassador had stayed characteristically quiet. Her face remained veiled, hiding grotesque lesions—a gift from her god. "We desire a Chaos mortal. Then The Nameless One would be willing to negotiate."

"That can be arranged." Having the Necro on our side would be welcome.

When the time came, the streets of Chime would bleed.

I'd tried to rid Chime of Chaos, but not even I could cleanse the city of sin's taint.

Once, the twelve had been thirteen. Chime had been Babel, the domain of Chaos. Father knew the remaining gods remembered those early days, even if their mortal vessels could not comprehend it. When the thirteenth had betrayed them, He had taken Babel and repurposed it into a domain where, should conflicts arise between the gods, they could settle their disputes fairly. Over time, He had changed Babel to match His own design.

The hourglass shape, the clock tower, the brass steamworks—all of it came from His machinations.

He'd named it Chime, for the strike of a clock tolling its beginning.

And now its end.

This domain had served its purpose. A new world needed to be built.

Could its mortals be saved? Were they worth saving? Only I, as Father's redeemer, could judge them.

"You have one hour to make your choice," I declared. "Join me in Dor's new world or perish with the old, as Gildola, Valeria, and Mesmorpheus have perished before you. At the turn of the next hour, this amnesty shall be lifted. Those who stand in the way of time will be abandoned to it." I lifted my hands, palms up in a gesture of peace.

A bubble of time enveloped the Council chamber.

In the blink of an eye, time sped forward with the thrusting momentum of generations over generations, condensed to this one singularity my Father spared me from. The gods would be aware of time's passage, but their hosts could not escape. Their skin withered, aging as the seconds ticked past. Their mortal bodies crumbled away, their bones turning to dust above the rusted facade of the twelve domains.

A reminder of which power ruled the universe.

A message for what it would do.

In the silence of the chamber, I pulled a fob watch from my inner waistcoat pocket. The brass was marred, the glass cracked and damaged. The watch no longer worked, caught between the hours of twelve and one. At the thirteenth hour. This had been Quentin's watch, gifted to him on the day of his creation.

Now it served me as a reminder of what I'd lost.

Of what must be done.

"I will find you, Miss Arkey. I will rend your soul and every last Chaos into oblivion."

Oh *shit*!

The dream cast me out into a void of pretty stars, only it hadn't been a dream, but a vision. A warning.

The ambassadors had met within the Warden embassy in their fancy Council room, and recently. Their gods had argued and taken sides. The Umber and Zephyr had chosen Dor's side, which made them a threat. Though what scared me more was Dor's proclamation.

He wouldn't just let Chime die. He would destroy it himself.

I couldn't let that happen.

What was worse, was I recognized the Diviner from my vision, but couldn't place him. I'd witnessed the Council's meeting from his eyes, but his voice had been distorted, his thoughts muddled by Dor's influence. Some part of me knew him. Knew to hate him.

Unfortunately, it seemed he knew me, too. Though when so many gods and would-be gods wanted my head these days, it was hard to keep track of each threat.

The miasma of stars merged with the night sky, and I appeared on a cloud. An actual pissing cloud. It floated above Central Station around the clock tower, and I was eye level with its massive clockface. I'd escaped that thing once, when my crazy twin sister had dragged me inside and introduced me to the mother I'd never known I had and certainly didn't need. Corentine remained imprisoned behind it, along with my other chaotic siblings. Jinx too. Maybe even Quen.

I'd wanted to look inside to see if my partner really was trapped in there with the rest of them, but this was ridiculous. How had I even gotten up here? More to the point, *how* was I on a cloud? They didn't appear in Central like they did above the Golden City. I gave my cloud a squeeze. It bunched in my grip, as soft and squidgy as cotton buds. Shit. How did one ride clouds?

A chill wind ruffled my hair and nightgown—why was I wearing a nightgown?—and my cloud floated away from the clock tower to the Silver Suite opposite. I faced it, and my heart caught in my throat.

There was Quen as I knew him, pacing his apartment with an agitated expression.

Food lay discarded on his dining table. An open bottle of pink wine spilled over the side. Gods. This was the night I'd run from his apartment.

The night he'd kissed me.

How had I traveled back in time to this moment?

"You walk through dreams and still don't recognize them for what they are, daughter?"

That voice howled through the wind.

I glanced over my shoulder and could have screamed. There, floating on another cloud, was a woman almost identical to me.

Oh, well, that explained the god-damn clouds. All that time inside the Mesmer's temple hadn't yet prepared me for the absolute nightmare my evenings were turning into. I pulled a clump from my cloud and tasted it. Cotton candy. Lovely. "Why are you in my dreams?"

Corentine lazed on her cloud in a silver dress, as though she'd always been free, as though she weren't currently strapped to a metal chair that turned her godly powers into energy that powered the city below. "You entered *my* dreams."

Did gods even dream? Apparently. "Then why in god's name are you dreaming of this?" I gestured toward Quen's apartment. He'd dug out his pistol from somewhere and cradled it with purpose. By the next evening, he'd be spending the night in Grayford as a prisoner of the Godless while donning a pair of fluffy pink gloves.

The Godless. Gods. I'd lost them, too, but I'd get them back.

I'd get them *all* back.

"Your subconscious brought me here. I merely followed."

"I didn't invite you, though while you're here, do me a favor and let Quen out of the little prison you and Jinx have him locked inside. The poor boy's been through a lot."

Corentine plucked a ball of fluff from her cloud and examined it. "Why should I? I enjoy his company."

"All right, let me put this another way. Release Quen, or I'll be forced to break inside that clock tower and shove another fucking tube up your arse."

Corentine chuckled. "You carry such rage, daughter."

I ground my teeth. "You don't know the half of it."

"Oh, but I do." Her cloud floated closer to mine until she was only inches away. "Your rage is misguided. You've got no allies. You've got no one to help you. You can't even access the power buried inside you. How do you expect to rescue your beloved from his tower when all you have... are dreams?"

Dreams were all I had, yes, but a dream was all I needed.

A dream to end the reign of gods on *my* terms.

A dream worth fighting for.

Mesmorpheus had believed in me enough to grant me their power, and while I certainly hadn't expected to find myself wandering inside Corentine's dreams, I'd experienced something else. A vision of Dor's plans. I may not have much against Corentine and Jinx and the army of Chaos they were about to unleash against Dor's own forces, but I had knowledge.

And I had self-respect.

"This must be your dream, because you're dreaming if you think you'll ever see your freedom again. Tell Jinx I said hi." I snapped my fingers, and the scene faded to black, casting Corentine from my mind.

In the void of my unconsciousness, tiny specks of color sparkled within the dark. Thousands of stars. These were the many souls of the Mesmer— my Mesmer—now connected to my mind. They dozed in a permanent state of sleep, apart from the three brightest stars I'd left in the land of the living to watch over me, assuming they hadn't gotten up to any mischief while I napped.

All the Mesmer drifted in my head. All of them except for Reve.

From somewhere, I became vaguely aware of the clock tower chiming the next hour. The signal that Dor's amnesty was about to lift and the real show would begin.

I'd always fancied myself an actor, but *that* had been a dream.

Now it was time to enter the final act.

I

In order to protect the domains from the threat of Chaos, Father ordered that the Wardens shut down the Gate. This was not broadcast to the Council and their ambassadors at the time, due to the irrational nature of our own acting ambassador, Q. Corinth. We could not have anticipated the gods would take their mortals' safety into their own hands and recall them from Chime. Ultimately, the result is as desired. Control of Chime has now reverted to the Diviner. We remain the city's protectors and gatekeepers.
—P. Bezel, *An account of the 'Gate Closure' Incident*

THERE CAME A TIME in every young Diviner's life when one's god would sit them down and explain who they were meant to be and what they were born to do. We were prepared for this meeting as well as one could be prepared to converse with one's own god, though naturally, the event bred outrageous speculation that only served to feed a young Diviner's fears and overactive imagination.

It was meant to be a joyous occasion. A milestone to be celebrated. One entered that room a boy and left a man with the knowledge their entire path had been set out for them. For some, it came as a relief. Why worry about the future when it was set in stone? For others, it became a test of faith, to trust their god knew what was best for them.

For others, it came with the heart-rending realization their life was not their own and never had been. We weren't supposed to admit that, of course.

When my time had come, Dor had made my path quite clear. I was a Warden. I would serve him in that capacity and be blessed with the tools to do so. My destiny was to answer his call and assist his voice whenever necessary. He didn't care if his voice used and abused me in the process.

I remembered leaving that meeting shaken.

I remembered the defiance that came after.

And then I fell. Physically, into the clock tower, and metaphorically. From that day onwards, Dor did not abide any disobedience. My fate was set.

Or so I had thought.

I sat now inside the same clock tower that had cursed me. I had died once more—tossed into the aether and churned through it—only to be reborn not as a Diviner, but something else entirely. Something new.

Something impossible.

But hadn't I lived the impossible? Breathed it?

My skin was no longer the pearly metallic sheen of a Diviner, but the silvery-blue tones of Chaos. The passport tattoo of the domains inked on my arm was no longer present, erased through rebirth. In my reflection in the clockface glass, I *looked* like me, though my ears were now pointed, my hair was a shocking white rather than silver, and my eyes had turned aether blue, hidden behind the spectacles I still needed to see. My teeth felt no different when I ran my tongue over them. Saints, I still possessed my own thoughts and feelings, and sadly, my memories, but what did that mean?

My inner philosopher wanted to understand the hows and whys. To ruminate on what aspects of my soul were Diviner, and which were Chaos.

On what exactly made me... *me*.

Who owned my thoughts? My soul?

I DO, drawled the feminine voice inside my head.

And therein lay another impossibility. Dor may no longer lay claim to my soul, but another god now did. A god who, only a few months ago, had remained hidden and unknown.

Corentine.

YOUR MUSINGS ENTERTAIN ME. I'VE NEVER KNOWN A MORTAL TO SPEND AS MUCH TIME IN THEIR OWN HEAD AS YOU DO.

A Diviner's formative years are spent inventing conversation in one's head while avoiding it with the general populace. I won't apologize for bad habits.

I DON'T REQUIRE YOU TO. IT'S REFRESHING TO HEAR THE THOUGHTS OF A MORTAL WITH SUCH LIVED EXPERIENCE.

Perhaps that was my path—to study and gather a lifetime of knowledge through my exploits across the domains in order to entertain the god of Chaos.

Corentine's laughter echoed inside my mind. *YOUR PATH IS TO SEE TO DOR'S DESTRUCTION. WHY ELSE WOULD HE KEEP YOU ON SUCH A SHORT LEASH?*

If that were true, and Dor had foreseen this outcome, then why not smite me and be done with it? He'd had ample opportunity. Instead, he'd brought me back to act as his voice for a few weeks of misguided hilarity as I traipsed across the domains, making bargains doomed to failure.

Though no. I'd attempted to unite the domains, but Dor's command had been a ruse. Dor had used me for his own ends—to mark which gods would betray him and then to strike first, starting with the Glimmer.

I'd been nothing more than his kept Warden, forever committing foul deeds in his name.

HE UNDERESTIMATED YOU, BUT I KNOW EXACTLY WHAT YOU ARE, QUENTIN CORINTH.

Which is?

MY DARK WARDEN.

A shiver ran down my spine. I'd not intended to escape the clutches of one mad god to become bound to another, though Corentine and her mortals were the best chance of delivering Dor's downfall. He wouldn't stop at Solaris. Which domain would fall next?

And which poor sod would he name as his voice to accomplish it?

"Elijah?"

I physically recoiled at that name. "What?"

"Are you all right?" asked Joe, whose expression was a mixture of concern and weariness for the crazy man sitting beside him. I could have laughed. Weren't we all crazy now?

"Apologies. I, ah, lost my train of thought." Or rather, my train had derailed and crashed into an orphanage full of Fauna pups with no one to save them.

Overactive imagination indeed. Diviner men never grew up, did we?

Joe shuffled uncomfortably where we sat on the cold metal floor of the clock tower. Since we'd both unceremoniously joined the ranks of Chaos, we'd bonded over our shared predicament. He was a pleasant chap for an ex-Glimmer, a good conversationalist, which, really, this place needed, alongside a tea station and a working toilet. The other Chaos largely ignored us, except for Jinx, who I wished would ignore us.

Things could be worse. Jinx had at least provided clothes, presumably since the sight of flapping male genitalia was starting to grow old. The trousers were a tad too big, whereas the shirt didn't fully button at the top, but between the pair of us, Joe and I had created some semblance of normality. We'd even commandeered a corner of the room, which we'd blocked off with old copies of the Courier for privacy.

It wasn't the height of luxury, and the dry air stunk of sweaty musk, but one needed to make the best of things.

"I was thinking of prospective names," Joe said. "You don't like Elijah? Too Diviner?"

I cringed. "I knew an Elijah, once. It's your choice, of course."

"Oh right, the old ambassador, Karendar." He rubbed the white stubble growing on his chin. We were both looking a little unkempt. "I've always gone by Joe. In my head, it was short for Joseph. But it's close to my older name, like this... reminder I can't quite shake off. Now I have this body, it feels the right time to change. Though, should I even consider a Glimmer name? Do I need something more fitting? What do you think of Seraph? Too Seren?"

"It's a brave new world. It doesn't matter if your name is Seren or Diviner. Choose whatever calls to you."

"Say it out loud, please."

"Seraph?"

He mused for a second. "No, I'm not sure about that one."

The makeshift paper door to our little newsprint fort ripped open, scattering the headline from only a week ago: *Outrageous! Tea Prices Rise Again!*

Ah, those were simple times.

Joe crossed his arms and scowled. "What do you want?"

Jinx leered over us in the form of a Glimmer. Her golden skin radiated like a beacon inside the clock tower, and paired with the red gowns she liked to don, she really did play the part well. There was a certain irony in her preferred persona, and I often wondered if she'd deliberately chosen to mimic the rivals of the Vesper. Though Jinx likely related to the Glimmer's unique brand of cruelty.

That twisted smile was all Jinx, but her face? Those eyes?

I couldn't bear to look at them for long.

"I've got a surprise for you," Jinx said.

"Is it a cup of tea?" I asked. "I'm gasping."

"I wasn't talking to you." She nudged Joe's leg with her shoe. "Get up before I smite your arse."

Joe shot me an alarmed grimace, but did as he was bid—what choice did he have, when Jinx had become his own personal god? I dragged myself to my feet and followed, bracing myself for whatever madness I was about to become privy to.

I'd been trapped inside this clock tower for a week now, and I was only aware of the passage of time due to the giant clockface that dominated the far side of the room. Another reminder I wasn't Diviner anymore.

Light danced across the ceiling. In order to protect the clock tower from Dor, the Chaos trapped inside it had summoned aether-powered shields. They did an impressive job of deflecting Diviner, and indeed any of the other domains, but maintaining such shields on a twenty-four-hour cycle took its toll. It was little wonder the Chaos mortals were too tired to bother with idle chitchat.

Though as my vision adjusted to the flickering lights, I realized it wasn't the Chaos mortals maintaining the shield—in fact, they were nowhere to be seen—but rather a group of six shrouded women gathered before the clockface. Their bodies and even faces were hidden by thick cloaks badly tailored from sackcloth.

Chaotic energy spilled from their raised hands. Their skin glowed golden.

Oh, saints have mercy. They were Glimmer.

The one standing in the middle stepped from the summoning circle and lowered her hood.

"Gloria," I blurted.

The ex-ambassador appeared the same as I'd known her in a Glimmer form, but her eyes were now the silvery-blue of Chaos. Real fear lurked in those depths. "Corinth." She looked me over, taking in my new appearance as a child of Chaos. I expected a quip, some comment on how Dor had failed and I'd been foolish enough to be caught in Corentine's clutches, but no. She remained silent. Defeated.

Joe stood beside me, his posture stiff. "What is this?"

Jinx wrapped an arm around Gloria's shoulder, and the poor woman flinched. "A gift. You see, I realized something. Why make my brothers and sisters sweat to protect this damn clock tower when I have my own workforce, right here? The Glimmer weren't shy about forcing other mortals to toil for them. I thought I'd give them a taste."

"By running your own workhouse?" I said.

"An eye for an eye. Isn't that Glimmer justice?"

I clenched my fists behind my back. While I could appreciate the irony, I'd wanted to end workhouses for good, not bring them back as a form of torture! Forcing Glimmer into servitude wouldn't right their wrongs.

"Gloria and her friends here will keep us all safe," Jinx continued. "Day in, day out." She shoved Gloria aside and produced a cane from thin air, as though it had materialized out of nothing. I swallowed a lump in my throat. The Glimmer often used such canes to 'motivate' their workers.

Jinx handed it to Joe. "And you're in charge of keeping them in line."

Joe dropped the horrid thing, and it clattered against the metal plating. "I—What? Why me?"

"Because I've seen your memories. Yours. Gloria's. I think you deserve a little payback for all those years spent inside a workhouse. Aren't I a generous god?" Jinx picked up the cane and held it out. "If they get tired and start whining, give 'em a whack or two. Show them who's boss. Shit, give 'em a whack if you're bored. I won't judge you. Go on," she urged with a bloodthirsty eagerness. "Give it a try."

Joe hastily stepped back, bumping into me. "What—What do we do?" he whispered.

"Do?" I whispered back. "We do what Jinx says. The Glimmer deserve every ounce of suffering they get."

"You don't truly believe that?"

Of course I didn't. I bent my head close. "You lived under a kind and benevolent god. You remember what it took to appease her."

He nodded, understanding dawning in his eyes.

"Brightwell," Gloria pleaded. "Please, Brightwell—"

"My name is Joe." He eyed her with contempt. "You heard Jinx. Get back to your work."

"You can't do this! You can't force us to—to debase ourselves! I refuse!"

Jinx watched on with amusement. "Gonna take that, are you, Joe?"

Joe's clenched fists shook.

I snatched the cane from Jinx's hand and slashed it across Gloria's face. A line of blood splattered the metal grating.

Gloria staggered back, a hand to her cheek, and stared in pure shock.

"Do as he commands," I simply stated, and passed the cane to Joe.

Jinx smirked. "I always knew you were a real bastard, Corinth." She snapped her fingers. "With me."

I hurried after her as she marched to the clockface window. "Is it really necessary to bring Glimmer into this?"

"You tell me." She pointed outside.

I stood on tiptoes and strained past the large VI to the city I once loved, now silenced and caught in its death throes. A city built on deceit and suffering.

Central Station stretched below us. While I couldn't see what state the Gate was in from this angle, there was no missing the forces surrounding it. Diviner. Hundreds of them, all dressed in the black-and-bronze uniform of the Wardens. Among them were a couple of Guardians—immortal clockwork automatons.

They hadn't arrived through the Gate—from what I'd overheard, that had been powered down as soon as Solaris had fallen. A smart move on Dor's part. They couldn't risk letting *anyone* through. So then where had

Dor's forces come from? With the shielding around the clock tower, the elevator from the Golden City was effectively cut off. Though I supposed that still left the Undercity.

Beyond them, toward the waiting area of the station, was a group of Umber Wardens. A few Zephyr were also hammering away at various panels and contraptions around the station. Some looked to be defensive shielding devices—aether-powered tasers and the like, which I'd helped construct as ambassador.

"Unghard and Zyclone have joined Dor," I said, as though commenting on the weather. Really, it came as no surprise. They'd always been Dor's allies.

But that meant the other gods hadn't bent yet.

"Your eyeglasses still work, good for you. Our shield is the only thing stopping those fucks from breaking in here, but we can't shield the entire tower. They've got the Gate and station locked down, but the tower's interior is ours for now. What's their next move?"

"I couldn't possibly fathom Dor's intentions."

"You were his ambassador, so don't fuck with me."

For all of a bloody month! "Corentine has seen my memories. She's witnessed every interaction I've ever had with Dor."

"I'm not asking for your memories. I'm asking you to tell me what Daddy Dor's likely to do next. Come on. Use that imagination of yours." She poked my forehead. "You think like them."

I swatted her off. "I've since ceased being one of them."

"Miss being a prissy little Diviner know-it-all, do you? You know what Dor's done. Don't tell me you still want to bend over backwards and offer him your arse?"

"I hold no love for Dor. Though, you know, nothing lubricates the imagination quite like a drop of tea—"

"If you don't start talking, I'll throw you out that window."

"Am I your ally or your prisoner?"

"That's up to you and whether you'll tell me what Dor's planning."

I bit back a sigh. There was little hope for civilized conversation when Jinx had me metaphorically by the throat. I only wanted one cup of tea. Just one.

Fine. I had nothing better to do than speculate. "Dor will demand loyalty from the other gods, if he hasn't already. He'll work on eliminating those who refuse his rule, either by dangling the threat of Corentine, or… well, the gloves are off. I suppose he doesn't need an excuse now the Glimmer are gone."

"No shit. Tell me something useful."

"He has the Umber and Zephyr on his side. The Umber are loyal to a fault; I doubt you'll win them over. They're Dor's muscle. They'll do the heavy lifting. The Zephyr care not for society, but they'll see your occupation of the clock tower as an insult, and they'll focus their efforts on breaking in. Given their history and knowledge of the clock tower, they're your biggest threat, I'd say."

She chewed her thumb. "What do you suggest? We kill the Zephyr first?"

"Perhaps you should try your hand at diplomacy." If such a thing were possible. "Try and make allies with the domains Dor rejects."

"You and my dear sister tried that. Didn't work out, did it?"

It would have, if Dor hadn't been planning our failure from the start. "It's easier to stab someone in the back if you smile at their face."

"Wow, Corinth! I didn't expect you to be so devious."

Neither did I, but needs must. "You won't defeat Dor alone. You need fighters—Leander or Ember would do the trick, and they're not interested in Dor's rule. You also need someone to match the technical brains of the Diviner and Zephyr. Amnae would be an obvious choice, but good luck getting them to risk themselves. Necro are technically minded—the body is another type of machine, after all. You could try to strike a bargain with them. More importantly, you need absolute bastards to do your dirty work. Glimmer make excellent lightbulbs, I'll give you that. But they're not useful for much more."

"Say I buy your reasoning—how do I get the gods' attention?"

"With a show of power. Prove you and Corentine are a viable alternative to Dor, and that *does* mean playing nice and not coming at them with murderous intent."

"A show of power, you say? How do you fancy a trip downtown?"

The gleam in her eye concerned me. "You're letting me out?"

"I'm taking you for a walk." She jabbed a finger at my chest, forcing me to shuffle back until I was pressed against the clockface window. "Try to escape, and Mother will snap your soul back here quicker than a Mesmer falling asleep after scoffing a bag of sugar."

"Yes, ma'am."

As though on some unspoken command, the tiny door that led outside the clockface window opened, and in popped one of the Chaos males—Lucky, I believe—in the form of a Zephyr. I'd not spent much time in the chap's company, partly because he looked identical to Chance, the Chaos male I'd been forced to abandon in Kronos.

Despite what the great Seren poets may say, death and rebirth wasn't enough to absolve the sins of one's past.

"Everything set?" Jinx asked.

I followed her to the door. "Set for what?"

"You'll see. Lucky will fly you down. Don't cause him any trouble, or he'll drop you." She changed form to a magpie Fauna, allowing her red gown to collapse in a heap, and then she flew out the door.

Lucky opened his arms with a disgruntled groan.

I peered past him to the open door. "Is, ah, is there another way down?"

"I push you out," he said with a voice that lacked the candid charm of Chance.

Heights really weren't my favorite, and the wind was already whistling rather menacingly by the door. I glanced over my shoulder. The Glimmer were still lending their power to the aether shield shimmering around us, though their limbs were getting a little wobbly. Joe gripped the cane so tight, his knuckles looked ready to pop.

I didn't want to leave him, but also, I didn't want to leave Jinx to her own devices. Not when opportunities to stretch my legs were few and far between.

Awkwardly, I climbed into the arms of Lucky, who did his best to sigh, tut, and roll his eyes as his feathers smothered me in a tight embrace. I'd never been quite this intimate with a Zephyr before, though I supposed finding feathers in unfortunate places was no different to bedding a Leander and plucking stray fur from between one's buttocks the morning after.

"Please be gentle, it's my first time," I said.

Lucky's beak scowled in the only way a beak could. He carried me across the threshold, and my grip tightened on his arms. Wind ruffled his feathers. One of them came loose and flew into my mouth—I spat the damn thing out!

Saints. We were up damnably high.

I didn't get a chance to scream.

Lucky leaped off the platform, my heart plummeting with him as he took to the skies.

I buried my head in his chest with one eye looking up at the clockface. The time was nearing one o'clock. As we fell further and further, the hand of the clock grew smaller.

Lucky hadn't yet opened his wings.

"You're going to fly, aren't you?" I yelled.

He either didn't hear me or ignored me outright. I strained in his grip and stared down.

Oh gods, I wish I hadn't.

Central rushed up to greet us with alarming speed. This was typical— invite me out for a little fresh air and allow my feeble mortal body to decorate the streets below.

I'd died twice now. Dor had yanked my soul into the aether, which felt rather like a taser zapping me down to the core of my very being.

And then Kayl had taken my soul.

That... hadn't hurt at all.

If anything, it had been a rather pleasant experience. Like falling into a soft, comfortable bed when one was drunk, with cheerful voices echoing from the party carrying on beyond the walls.

This? This would hurt.

As we neared my eventful demise, Lucky's wings finally flung open, and he swooped down to a green patch that was Meridian Park.

Jinx waited for us on a bench, already back to her Glimmer form and wearing a different red dress. Where *did* she get them from?

We landed with a soft bounce. I staggered from Lucky's arms and hacked up spit and bile into the nearest bush.

"Nice trip?" Jinx asked.

I wiped saliva from my mouth. "Quite pleasurable. Let's not do it again."

Meridian Park remained eerily empty, though piles of clothes were still scattered about from when the gods had recalled their mortals. The Wardens hadn't bothered to clean these up, then. For shame.

Jinx patted the bench beside her. "Take a seat."

I did so, keeping a polite distance. "Are we hosting a picnic? I do enjoy a good scone."

"We're hosting something. Now I've got the Glimmer taking care of the clock tower, we're free to cause a little chaos across the city."

I wrung my hands in my lap. "Like what?"

"Like fuck shit up. What time is it, Time Boy?"

The bench had an excellent view of the clock tower. The aether shield continued to swirl around the clockface, obscuring the hands. "Almost one."

Mere heartbeats later, the clock struck the hour.

A singular *dong* echoed through the city with the mourning cry of a death toll.

The hairs on the back of my neck stood on end. I could taste the static of aether in the air. The presence of Chaos.

Seconds ticked by in painful agitation. The silence of the park—of the whole damnable city—was suffocating.

And then light flashed above the clock tower, near the top plate where the Golden City resided. An explosion followed. Metal shards and debris rained upon Central Station. Saints, it reminded me of when the glass elevator came crashing down that first time Chaos had been unleashed.

I squeezed my eyes shut, remembering the visions that had once plagued me. In this new body, I'd yet to receive a single one. A small blessing I didn't deserve.

I took a breath and opened my eyes. "What did you do?"

Jinx was examining her nails. "Blew up the entrance to the Golden City."

"I don't see what that will achieve—"

"How else do I get a god's attention?"

"With a telegram? What god answers to an explosive—"

As I said the words, a fiery portal opened out on the green before us.

Now that was a rare sight!

Lucky swore, and dove out of the way.

The portal was circular in design, about the height of an Umber, and shimmered with the same radiant power as the Gate's portal. Only, the edges sizzled with a bright red flame that had burned a charcoal imprint into the grass.

Beyond the portal lay the volcanic skyline of Rapture.

It seemed Edana was willing to make contact.

I expected the Ember god to send her ambassador for this unlikely meeting. But no. The man who stepped through was the last mortal I'd expected to face again.

"Sinder," I breathed.

When we last crossed paths, I'd shot him in the head. The second time, in fact, that I'd shot him. The first had been an accident. The second was to prevent the Wardens from capturing him, imprisoning him with an aether collar, and then submitting him to a soul-destroying device. At the time, I'd regretted my actions despite their necessity, but since then, I'd learned of his plot to betray Kayl to Jinx, all for the sake of revenge against the Glimmer—a plot Jinx had happily bragged about.

If I still retained my pistol, I'd have shot him a third time for good measure.

Jinx stood. "Easy, Corinth. Sinder's a friend."

Sinder looked positively revolted at being categorized as such. His lips churned until he finally spat the words out. "I'm here as a messenger on behalf of my queen, Edana." He avoided my eye, addressing only Jinx. "My queen extends an invitation to you and you alone. She states she recently met with Dor, and has information regarding the gods' intentions." He stepped aside and gestured to the portal. "I wouldn't keep her waiting."

"I'd advise not traveling alone," I quickly interjected. "I know Edana. Bring me with you, and I can negotiate on your behalf."

Jinx flashed me a grin. "Do you really think I need you or your advice?"

"You asked *me*—"

"To see if you'd try and fuck me over. I wasn't born yesterday, Corinth. I know how to start a revolution."

All this had been some foolish *test*?

Jinx swaggered toward the portal and draped a casual hand over Sinder's shoulder. "Remember those times Corinth shot you? Want a little payback?" She whispered something into his ear.

Sinder met my eye. "With pleasure."

I rose from the bench. "Wait—"

Flame flared from Sinder's fists. I thrust my hands up in a futile shield.

Searing agony tore into my flesh. I screamed myself hoarse, yet no sound came from my tortured throat. The heat burned away all sound, all feeling, until my soul fell into cool darkness, and then I felt nothing at all.

I floated once more in a blissful void. The moment stretched for eternity.

Until something yanked me forward. Dumped me once more into harsh reality.

I sucked in a sharp, strangled breath.

"Oh gods, are you all right?" Joe spoke above me.

I lay naked on my back on the cold metal floor of the clock tower. My entire body trembled, my heart hammering in my chest.

"Take my jacket." Joe wrapped it around my shoulders. "You just... appeared out of thin air."

I sat up and pulled my knees close to my chest. It was cold. So horribly cold. Without my spectacles, everything blurred.

This death had only lasted seconds, and yet they were among the worst few seconds of my existence. The pain and fear turned to seething rage.

What purpose does setting me alight serve? I yelled at Corentine.

YOU ALLOWED DOR TO TAKE AND TORTURE ONE OF MY CHILDREN. CHANCE NO LONGER RESPONDS TO MY CALL. NOW, THE SLATE IS CLEAN.

You had Jinx kill me for revenge? There was nothing I could have done for Chance, and yes, it was likely Dor had ordered his soul obliterated. That was on me, I'd admit it, but I didn't appreciate a baptism by literal fire.

I BROUGHT YOU BACK HERE, DIDN'T I? BE GRATEFUL.

Grateful! I examined the skin of my arms. I'd felt it melt from my bones, and now it simply tingled. Death was becoming a habit I did *not* wish to repeat. Jinx slitting my throat would have been preferable to burning alive!

AND LEAVE EVIDENCE FOR THE WARDENS TO FIND?

Since when did Chaos care for logic? Arguing with the god of Chaos wasn't logical either, but I wasn't Diviner anymore.

ARE YOU READY TO SERVE ME, QUENTIN CORINTH?

I glanced across the room to the machine plugged into the wall.

To the woman strapped within it.

I gathered whatever mismatch of clothes I could find, including a spare pair of spectacles, dressed, and stepped before Corentine. The thirteenth god, the god of Chaos.

The machine was the same soul-splitting device the Diviner had devised to split a mortal from their god. The same device that had split Jinx from her twin. This version of the device had an altogether different use—to imprison a god and bleed aether from her very veins, effectively turning Corentine into a power source for Chime.

It was disgusting. Depraved. And yet Diviner had occupied this city—this domain—none the wiser to the cruelty that provided energy, entertainment, and comfort.

I'd been oblivious. Had played a part in Corentine's imprisonment.

I pressed my hand against the aether shield that kept her bound. It pulsed under my palm and flickered with the image of twelve individual chains. One for each god of the twelve domains. It would take all twelve of them to break the shield and free Corentine, but of course, none of them would willingly dare.

Their souls were the key. They were what Jinx fought for.

Gather all twelve souls, and this nightmare would end.

I couldn't claim to understand what Jinx or the other Chaos mortals had gone through, but I could sympathize. We were all products of our gods.

MORTALS SUFFER, YET MORTALS DID NOT EXIST BEFORE DOR. NO ONE AGED OR DIED. IT WAS DOR WHO IMPOSED THE RULES OF TIME, WHO INSISTED THEY MUST SUFFER SO.

CHAOS COULD END TIME'S HOLD. YOU COULD. WHERE DOES YOUR LOYALTY LIE?

You saw what I did to escape Dor. He deserves his comeuppance. I'll serve as your Dark Warden if that's what it'll take to stop him, but my service comes with conditions.

NAME THEM.

For one, I serve you, not Jinx. I'd appreciate the courtesy of not being murdered or maimed. It wasn't rude to request a little respect, and I still had my dignity, damn it. *Secondly, a blasted cup of tea wouldn't go amiss.*

Corentine sounded amused. *YOU WOULD DENY JINX. WOULD YOU DENY MY OTHER DAUGHTER?*

I met Corentine's gaze. Those beautiful aether eyes. Strapped to that chair, the great god couldn't move or so much as communicate in any physical way, but in her, I saw Jinx.

I saw Kayl.

It was never Kayl who broke my fall that day thirteen years ago. It was never Kayl who offered the salvation I sought.

It was you.

2

WANTED
THE SERVANT OF CHAOS
AKA KAYL ARKEY, ANNE ARKEY, YUDA MANN
Described as female, six feet tall, curvaceous, short hair above the shoulders, silver-blue eyes that glow. Often changes appearance between domains. Last seen wearing the disguise of a Mesmer.
Once acting ambassador for Chaos on the Warden Council. Target background includes knowledge of the Undercity and target therefore possesses cunning. Approach with extreme caution. Do NOT allow Chaos close enough to touch. Advise attacking from a safe distance with tasers.
—Unknown, *Internal Warden Memo*

THE WINDOWPANES OF THE café shook.

What the shit was that?

I instinctively ducked into the nearest alley and pressed against the shadows, even if I couldn't merge with them. It sounded like an explosion at the clock tower, though not in Central Station—why in god's name did it sound like it came from the sky? I peered around the alley corner and gazed up. Smoke drifted from where the clock tower connected with the upper plate over Central, where the Golden City began.

Shit. I had no idea what that meant, but things blowing up generally weren't a good sign.

The vision from my dreams indicated whatever amnesty there had been between the gods was now over. And since the gods had decided the rules no longer applied, that meant any sorry soul still left in Chime would soon be caught underfoot by warring deities and their immortal slaves. Sorry souls such as myself.

As though I'd gone and manifested my own doom, footsteps tapped down the street. I slunk further into the alley as two Diviner Wardens paused by the entrance.

"Did you see that?" One of them pointed to the sky. "Should we head back?"

"Orders are to keep searching," said the other.

"We've searched all week and found nothing. They're not here. I bet they're in that bloody tower."

"Father says they're here, so they're here. We keep looking."

The Diviner huffed, and their footsteps carried on. I clutched my satchel close to my hip and counted the seconds until the street was clear. I didn't want to use my new Mesmer abilities and risk alerting the Wardens if I could help it. Especially when they knew what they were searching for.

In the week I'd spent skulking around the Market District of Central, the only other mortals I'd encountered were pissing Wardens. Society had effectively collapsed, but they couldn't give it a rest, could they?

Besides their ridiculous patrols, the streets were vacant, save abandoned clothes scattered here and there—the only evidence of a mass exodus from Chime.

The placement of a handbag or a pair of shoes told a tale of what each mortal had been getting up to when their gods had zapped them away. Shoppers hunting for a bargain or running errands. Mortals stopping for a slice of potato pie and a cup of tea. Half-eaten scones and cold coffees remained where their owners had left them. Stores hadn't been locked, yet they hadn't been looted either.

Chime was empty. Her mortals whisked away with the snap of divine fingers.

I distinctly hated it.

It was the chatter, the laughter, the sights and sounds of mortals living their best lives, despite being beholden to their gods, that created the energy of this city.

All that had been snuffed out in an instant.

Would I ever get my home back?

I carefully stepped over the piles of clothes as I traversed the cobblestone streets. Above, smoke drifted across the skyline of Central, though the clock tower continued to shine like a second sun. It didn't matter what was happening over there when I had my own problems to deal with here, not that I could get close to the clock tower anyhow—the place was crawling with Diviner.

The one advantage of this situation was I could pillage whatever I needed from the local stores—food, clothing, drugs for the ever-growing headaches my Mesmer charges were giving me. But I still needed to be careful of watchful eyes and not leave a trail.

I circled the block a couple of times to be certain before returning to Flint's Fine Ales, an ex-Umber-owned liquor store. Who would have thought Umber sold alcohol? Apparently, their green thumbs made it easier to grow hops.

The Mesmer wanted to camp out in their candy store, because of course they did, but that was too obvious of a hiding place, and I'd almost had a run-in with a snooping Warden the other day. Besides, Flint's store had a cellar.

Their brandy wasn't too bad either.

I knocked on the front door in our agreed pattern before entering.

Cosmo immediately bounded over and practically screeched. "Mama! Did you remember the strawberry bonbons?" They reached for my satchel.

I cringed. "Keep it down. There're still Wardens about."

They slapped a hand over their mouth. "Sorry. I forgot." Their eyes welled up. Gods. The last thing I needed was for them to start crying.

"It's all right. We all forget sometimes." I'd certainly like to forget we were being hunted by Wardens and the god of time, but sadly, the drugstore didn't stock the Vesper mushrooms I'd need to escape reality, and I wasn't ready to drown my sorrows just yet.

I placed what I hoped was a comforting hand on Cosmo's shoulder and steered them past shelves full of spirits, liqueurs, wines, mixers—and everything else I'd need to host a party once all this was over—and behind the counter to a storage room that led to the cellar.

Cosmo descended the stairs as I carefully closed the hatch above. A few oil lamps lit the room, creating a cozy atmosphere. It wasn't too shabby, really. The cellar was full of barrels and casks, but there was plenty of room underneath for the four of us. I'd gathered enough cushions and cloth from the nearby stores to build a comfortable fort where we could eat and sleep in peace, and that was all we needed. At least for now.

I'd hoped the Wardens would have gotten bored of their patrols and given us an opportunity to move on. Mesmorpheus had left me with the gargantuan task of bringing down the gods and saving Chime and the domains, that arsehole, and I'd spent the past week just ensuring our survival. How was I meant to plan when I didn't get a chance to think?

Even my pissing dreams were exhausting.

Harmony would have devised a plan by now. Dru would know how to take care of the Mesmer's needs. Sinder would have already cracked open the wine. And Vincent would be busy painting our next flier, his delicate pale fingers stained with ink.

And Quen? He owed me another game of billiards.

Damn it, I *would* get them back. All of them. And then we'd have the piss up of a lifetime.

I wandered further into the room, and my foot kicked an empty bottle. One of the bottles from upstairs.

Rather belatedly, I realized I was missing two Mesmer. "Where's Celeste and Castor?" I picked up the empty bottle. Red wine. A decent vintage, by the looks of it. "*Please* don't tell me they drank this?"

Cosmo stuffed a fistful of bonbons into their mouth. "Celeste said she wanted to try it, and then Castor tried it, and he offered some to me, but it tasted yuck."

For fuck's sake! Celeste was supposed to be the sensible one! I'd left them here because Mesmer didn't drink—or at least, I'd never seen a drunken Mesmer before. I rubbed my forehead. "Where are they now?"

"Are—Are you angry with me?"

"No, Cosmo, I'm not angry." I was bloody livid. "But I need to know where they went in case they run into Wardens."

"They—They wanted to find a bakery. Because that's what you do when you drink wine, or so Castor said. You eat bread and cheese."

They'd gone to find a pissing bakery? Gods, I wished I were drunk enough to laugh.

These Mesmer would be the death of me.

"Right. Stay here, keep the hatch down. Don't open it to *anyone*, you understand? I'll find them."

Cosmo was barely listening as they plumped themself down onto a cushion and helped themself to more bonbons. "Yes, Mama."

I really wished they'd stop calling me that.

I kept my composure until I was back on the store floor and then let out the largest sigh of my entire life. Mesmorpheus had granted me their power, but it came with a burden: the entirety of the Mesmer. Most of them were content to sleep in my subconscious, tucked away in the darkest reaches of my mind, and thank the gods for that. I couldn't let an entire domain of Mesmer run riot. All slept except for the trio who were *supposed* to help me.

But instead of helping me fix problems, they were causing them.

Celeste? I called into my mind. Part of playing god meant I had an uncanny awareness of where the Mesmer were at all times, and I could sense her and Castor nearby. I wasn't sure if telepathy was part of the deal, but it was worth a try.

MAMA! Celeste yelled back. *YOU'VE LEARNED TO TALK! OUR PAPA ALWAYS SPOKE IN OUR HEADS, TELLING STORIES ABOUT THE STARS—*

You don't have to shout. I winced at the voice rattling inside me. *Are you at the bakery? Can you barricade yourself inside until I get—*

WE MADE A NEW FRIEND!

Oh shit. *Hold on, I'm coming!*

I closed Flint's store and made a run for it. The bakery wasn't far, only down the road. If the Wardens had found them, then there was no point in being subtle.

I could have snapped them to safety, but doing so was technically the same as killing them, and I'd promised I'd only resort to that in dire situations.

This situation wasn't completely dire yet. It could be salvaged.

Shrieking echoed down the street. I upped my pace until I neared the bakery—an ex-Glimmer-owned store, judging by the gaudy beige fixtures. There weren't any Wardens lurking as far as I could tell, but figures moved beyond the window, and that awful screeching was pure torture.

I slid against the window and peered inside.

No one was being tortured. Celeste was *singing*!

I burst inside the bakery. Celeste was drunkenly spinning around the tables and warbling some nonsense about stars with the tone of a choking Amnae. In the corner, poor Castor was hunched over a chair and vomiting his guts out, which really clashed with what I'd hoped to find inside— freshly baked bread and sugar cookies.

A young Fauna girl with red hair and a bushy fox tail was patting his back and comforting him.

Celeste staggered to a halt. "Oh, Mama, you made it!"

The Fauna girl dropped to a crouch as though ready to fight or flee. "Another Mesmer?"

I blinked away my own shock. "Why—How are you here?" I closed the door behind me and pulled the curtains across the windows, to be on the safe side. "The gods recalled their mortals. There's no one left."

"You're here, ain't you?" The Fauna girl drew a dirty handkerchief from her oversized jacket, which hung comically over her shoulders like a cloak, and handed it to Castor. She must be between thirteen and fifteen; it was hard to tell by how skinny the poor girl looked. All her clothes were scavenged, likely from the piles left behind.

I forced Celeste to sit before she hurt herself. "Well, that's a long story, but I asked first. Are you alone?"

The girl straightened. "Who wants to know?"

She must have come from the Undercity. She already had the street smarts needed to survive somewhere like Grayford or Sinner's Row— though perhaps not the sense to avoid screeching Mesmer.

Looting a bakery wasn't a bad idea. Most of the fresh goods had turned stale or moldy, but they stocked ingredients to make more.

The kitchen door opened, and out scurried a smaller boy, also dressed in ridiculously oversized clothes. His skin was covered in gray fur, and his nose twitched with little rat whiskers. "I found cinnamon buns—" He stopped dead in his tracks.

I waved cheerfully. "Are they still fresh? I'm starving."

The boy exchanged a nervous glance with Fox Girl.

I raised my hands in a reassuring gesture. "It's okay, I don't mean either of you harm. I was searching for these two." I sat Castor down as well. While Celeste was happily humming away and staring at the bakery menu, poor Castor looked as though he'd been dragged through his worst nightmares. "Thank you for checking on them, but it's not safe around here. There are Wardens everywhere."

"We know," said Fox Girl. "But we ain't scared of no Wardens."

The girl stood defiantly. I liked her already.

"If you need food or supplies, then you'd be safer scavenging from homes over at City Rise. There're no mortals left to occupy them. Or you could let me help you. I have a base." Of sorts. "And I'm no fan of Wardens either. My name's Kayl."

"You look like *her*," Rat Boy squeaked, and hid behind Fox Girl.

"Like who?"

Fox Girl pulled a crumpled piece of paper from her jacket and held it up.

It was a Warden-issued flier warning the Diviner to be on the lookout for the servants of Chaos, and included an almost perfect likeness of my own face, only the artist rendition had me grinning like a maniac with far more teeth than was physically possible. There were smaller images of me too in the guise of a Diviner, Glimmer, and Mesmer.

Sadly, it was me, and not Jinx, for they'd included a list of my known monikers including my short-lived career as Ambassador Kayl Arkey.

Me? A servant of Chaos? Oh, they could piss right off!

"You're Arkey, aren't you?" Fox Girl said with sudden eagerness. "You're the ones the Wardens are after."

It would just be my luck to get ratted out to the Wardens by a couple of Fauna children. "Well, I—"

"That's her!" Celeste squealed on her crash back to reality. "That's our Mama!"

"I'm *not* your bloody mother!"

"Are you fighting them?" Fox Girl took a few tentative steps closer and looked me over. "The Wardens? We heard 'em talking about you. They say you can change faces and eat souls. They're scared of you."

"They have good reason to be scared. I'm terrifying."

"I'm scared of *them*," said Rat Boy. He wrung his hands. "They—They have these metal monsters, and they snatch you away in the night—"

"Snatch who away? Are there more of you?"

"Freddie!" Fox Girl clipped Rat Boy around the ear. "Remember what Wolfy said?"

Rat Boy—Freddie—rubbed his reddening ear. "But it's *her*!" He turned back to me with a shy grin. "We've got a base where we hide from the metal monsters, but it's Fauna only. Mesmer ain't allowed."

Gods. How many Fauna had been left behind in Chime? And why?

I needed to meet with them. Not only to find somewhere safer than the Market District, but also because a group of angry Fauna could be the allies I so badly needed. Assuming they weren't all children, anyhow.

"You know, I grew up in Grayford. I worked in the soup kitchen there for a time, and my friend and I—" I almost choked on the memory of Dru. "We helped lots of Fauna who needed it. I'm offering my help now. My friends here may be a bit hopeless." I patted Castor on the shoulder, and he groaned. "But what the Wardens say about me is true. I'm their worst nightmare."

The door handle of the bakery rattled.

Shit. We'd been found.

I placed a finger over my lips. Fox Girl and Freddie copied the gesture, remaining still and silent.

Celeste erupted into a fit of giggles.

Oh my fucking god, I was going to murder her.

The door burst open and slammed against the wall. I grabbed both Celeste and Castor's wrists and yanked them down behind the table. I glanced at Fox Girl and Freddie. They stood with their mouths open in shock, their bodies frozen in time.

Shitting shit!

"Gather the Fauna," ordered a Diviner Warden. He casually stepped into the bakery as though kidnapping children was a common occurrence.

Another two Wardens entered behind him. Each carried an aether collar. Shit. They were going to collar Fox Girl and Freddie and then do *what* with them?

I had my hand over Celeste's mouth. We were trapped with our backs against the bakery counter. There was a chance the Wardens would take the Fauna and leave without spotting us, and then we could sneak out through the kitchen. But neither Celeste nor Castor were in any state to make a run for it.

Nor was I prepared to leave the Fauna in the Wardens' hands.

"I don't feel so good," Castor whispered. He was rocking back and forth; his dark Mesmer skin had turned an almost pale Vesper purple.

"Don't you bloody dare!" I whispered back.

He lurched forward and made my day considerably worse by vomiting all over a Warden's boots.

The Warden leaped back. "What the—"

His eyes locked with mine.

"It's—It's *her*! It's Chaos!" He whipped out a taser from his belt.

Shit!

I kicked a chair at the Warden. He tripped over it, and the shot blasted a smoking black dot into the table, firing off a fizzle of sparks. Another shot landed near my head from another Diviner coming in from the side.

Celeste broke free from my hold. "Oh look! More friends!"

"You're not helping!" I yelled.

I'd depended on the trio when using my newfound Mesmer abilities, but this time, I would need to do it alone. I let a miasma of sleepiness drift across the bakery.

The Diviner slumped over, instantly falling asleep, their tasers clattering to the floor. Thank the gods for that.

Fox Girl and Freddie unfroze and looked around, confused.

"Are you two all right?" I asked. "You—"

Something pounded against the wall, and the whole thing collapsed.

I flipped the table over into a makeshift shield as brick and plaster flew. A cloud of dust filled the little bakery, making it hard to tell where the Fauna were, and if they were safe. Their tiny coughs were a relief.

"Watch out!" Fox Girl exclaimed from somewhere behind me.

A brass hand lifted the table and threw it against the counter, flinging teacups and saucers through the air.

I scrambled to my feet as the teacups crashed around me, smashing into sharp ceramic shards. My elbow painfully scraped across a bit of jagged brick.

And then a terrible sound rang throughout the bakery. The tick-tock of a clock.

One of the Diviner's clockwork Guardians stood on a pile of debris. An immortal. Its entire body was made of brass and clockwork parts, which clicked and whirred with menace. Its head tilted toward me, faceless and blank.

"Run!" I yelled.

Freddie transformed into a rat. His clothes collapsed into a heap, and his tiny body wiggled free and ran to the freshly made hole in the bakery wall.

Fox Girl hesitated, her brown eyes darting between me and the Guardian.

MAMA! Celeste screamed inside my own head. She and Castor were huddled against the counter, their arms wrapped around each other in fright.

But the Guardian wasn't interested in them.

It marched toward me, knocking tables and chairs out of its way. Shit!

The thing towered over me in height. I skittered back until I was pressed against a wall that hadn't been conveniently knocked down. If I'd still been inside Flint's store, I could have thrown wine at it or something to slow it down, but I didn't think a stale pasty would do much.

My boot accidentally kicked an abandoned taser. My Mesmer powers would be useless against an immortal, and they held no soul for a Chaos to rend, but perhaps their own weapons could be turned against them.

I snatched the taser and fired it at the Guardian's chest.

Sparks bounced off the bronze plating of its abdomen, but still it advanced, the cogs and gears happily ticking away like some demented Diviner toy.

"You shouldn't even be in Chime, you bloody piece of scrap!" I tossed the taser at it, which it swatted to one side.

And then it lunged.

I tried to dive under it, but it moved with immortal speed, slamming into me with such force, it knocked the air from my lungs.

Its metal hands clamped around my neck.

The damn thing lifted me off my feet, and I frantically swallowed air. I tried to prize its brass fingers free, to kick at its torso, but nothing so much as affected it.

Shit! It was going to wring the life from me!

I had Mesmorpheus's soul buried deep inside—could I even pissing *die*?

"Autumn!" Freddie called from the wall. He'd doubled back and was cowering behind a brick. "What are you *doing*?"

Fox Girl—Autumn—pounced at the Guardian. Her claws dug into its metal and tore through its plating with an awful screech. Honestly, I admired the balls on her, but she would get herself killed!

I tried to shoo her away as best I could while the Guardian had me in its grip. Autumn either ignored me or failed to translate my flailing.

She leaped from its legs onto its back and scratched furiously at the Guardian's head.

The Guardian reached behind with its spare hand.

Autumn leaped over it and landed on its wrist where it held me tight.

"What do I do?" she yelled, her brown eyes wild.

"Your—hand," I gasped. My chest heaved with pain, my vision starting to go black. "Give—your hand!"

She didn't hesitate in offering her hand.

I grasped it tight, and let go at the tingle in my palm.

My entire body shrank even smaller than a Seren. I gasped in a mouthful of air as I slipped from the Guardian's grip. My clothes fell around me, and I landed on all fours.

I quickly examined my paw—a paw! I had gods-damned paws! Black fur completely covered my skin except for fleshy pink beans on my paws.

The Guardian stared down at me. I didn't think a being made of clockwork parts could be confused, but it certainly looked like it.

Autumn transformed into her fox body, which was a luscious red-brown compared to my black fur. "How did you do that? How—"

"Never mind that!" I said with a mewing voice. "We need to go!" I sprinted between the Guardian's legs and ran for the hole in the wall. I'd owned this new Fauna body for literal seconds, and yet running on all fours came to me as naturally as cursing.

"What about them?" Autumn pointed her nose at Celeste and Castor still huddling against the bakery counter.

Sorry, I called into my mind. I'd promised not to snap them into the aether, but in their state—and my state—it was either this or allow the Diviner to take them. I searched within myself and found their essences loitering on the edge of my subconscious. With a pull, I yanked their souls back inside me.

Their bodies faded instantly with a poof of air, leaving their clothes behind.

"Did—Did they *die*?" squeaked Freddie beside me.

"They'll be fine, but we won't be unless we run!" I said.

The Guardian was already stomping toward us, shaking the foundations of the building.

"Follow me!" Autumn said.

She led the way out of the bakery and dashed down the cobblestone streets of the Market District as Freddie and I kept up. We turned into an alley, then another, zipping in and out of the streets until we'd left that dreadful ticking behind, only to be replaced with our rasping breaths.

Autumn paused beside a sewer grate. "Down here."

I sniffed at the opening and fought the urge to gag. My new body came with a heightened sense of smell, and it didn't like whatever was down there. "You're hiding inside the sewers?"

"Not exactly." She slipped on under as Freddie followed.

I angled my head at the opening. My whiskers—I had whiskers?— indicated I should be able to squeeze through. Autumn had managed it well enough. But I didn't want to get my new paws dirty.

It wasn't the worst place I'd found myself, and right now, things weren't about to get magically better. The Wardens knew I'd been hiding in the Market District, as they'd suspected—their thoughts would have alerted Dor.

Which meant Flint's Fine Ales was now off-limits.

We needed a new place to hide, and beggars couldn't be choosers.

I slipped under the grate into a dark, dank tunnel. I didn't need Vesper eyes to navigate, as my new Fauna body handled it with ease. The cold metal beneath my paws was a little slippery, but again, it didn't prove a challenge. Why had I never become a Fauna before? No wonder Jinx liked playing with their form—they were absolutely brilliant at everything!

Freddie had run on ahead, but Autumn paused and waited for me to catch up.

"There're loads of tunnels underneath the streets," she explained as we headed further underground. "Sewers, piping. They all go down to the steamworks."

That made sense. Our plumbing and energy had to go somewhere. But the tunnels here were so small. Too small for a Zephyr mechanic to fit within. Someone had to maintain these tunnels, and I doubted any Seren would be up for the task.

This was dangerous and dirty work reserved only for the lowest citizens at the bottom of Chime's social ladder. Lower than even the Vesper. Chime's forgotten mortals.

"You're both from the Undercity?" It wasn't unusual for Fauna to be born within the slums or on Sinner's Row. That was the fate for most young Fauna.

"Nah, we ran away from Juniper."

"Why did you leave?"

Autumn slowed her pace, her wary brown eyes on Freddie ahead. "He ain't from my clan," she whispered. "I only call 'im my brother to make life easier, but he ain't got no one. My clan—they killed his family. Then my ma, she said—she said to be a woman, a real Fauna, I needed to eat 'im too."

I came to a halt. Had I just heard her right? "You had to *eat* him?"

"It's what we do when we get older," she said without breaking her stride, and I sprinted to catch up. "But I hid him," she continued. "And we came to Chime. I won't let anyone hurt 'im. Not my ma, not any stinking Wardens."

Gods. I'd read something once about Fauna maturity rites involving cannibalism, but I'd thought that was an exaggerated tale meant to keep mortals away from Juniper. How could anyone force a child to eat a younger child?

It should have come as no surprise. That was what the gods did. They inflicted their perverse fetishes on the rest of us mere mortals. So many Fauna came to Chime illegally, seeking asylum, for a reason.

I could only hope Autumn was leading us to the Fauna who didn't make a meal out of other mortals. Unless it involved eating the rich. That, I could get behind.

Water dripped overhead, echoing around us, and we carefully leaped over streams of foul sewage that stunk of shit. We entered a sharp-edged hole in a rusted pipe and followed that into another tunnel, and then another, until I became completely lost in a maze of moss-ravaged pipework all leading down, down, down.

An entire labyrinth hidden in the darkest reaches between Central and the Undercity.

Mama! A voice called into my mind. *Where are you? What's going on?*

Oh shit, I'd forgotten Cosmo! *Are you safe where you are? Are there any Wardens?*

I don't know! I could sense their growing panic from all the way down here.

"We're home!" Freddie called. He disappeared through another hole, but this one was marked by a torn cloth covering it like a curtain.

Mama? Cosmo prompted.

Being a god was such an inconvenience. *I'll get back to you.* I tucked their thoughts into my subconscious, ignoring them for now, and stepped beside Autumn.

"This is it," she said. "You can't ever tell anyone 'bout this place, or Wolfy will get you." She shot me a warning look and followed Freddie through.

What I entered was *not* what I'd expected.

The room was a huge cylindrical cistern the width of the clock tower. Running water cascaded down the sides in various waterfalls, though it looked clear, and didn't smell at all of sewage. Healthy green vines coated much of the metal wall where oil lamps glowed between thick piping, highlighting a makeshift campsite below.

Hundreds of tents and other shelters had been built along the inside and into the cistern wall itself. It resembled a compact version of Grayford and its night market, full of homes and market stalls hidden under a patchwork of rainbow canopies.

And everyone wandering between the tents was Fauna.

Most retained their half-animal upright form and wore clothes. Many others were naked. Animals of all types were either resting or engaged in the activities of a thriving community.

This place hadn't sprung up overnight. It must have existed here for years. A whole secret community of Fauna living separate from Chime's rule.

But *how* were they here? Why hadn't their god recalled them, as every other bloody god had?

SHIT'S STARTING TO HEAT UP

I'D ALWAYS WANTED TO enter Rapture and see what the fuss was all about.

I stood in the fanciest damn cloakroom I'd ever seen. There were no windows, just burning brazier lights along the walls, a fluffy plush chair, a mirror, and a magical portal leading back into Chime.

The portal closed behind me, but not before giving me an unfortunate whiff of Corinth's burning body. Nasty, but he'd return safe and sound to the clock tower where he belonged.

HE WILL MAKE A FORMIDABLE ALLY, Mother said. *TREAT HIM AS SUCH.*

We don't need him. I'd managed this far without Corinth. The last thing I needed was a busybody like him ruining my day.

HE IS OUR KEY TO DEFEATING DOR.

Pfft.

WE WILL USE HIM FOR AS LONG AS HE IS USEFUL TO US.

If you say so, Mother. Corinth belonged to Chaos now, which made him one of us. Part of me wanted to make him pay for every shitty thing he'd ever done in Dor's name, and that list was *long*, but... Corinth wasn't Dor. He was as mortal as the rest of us.

If anyone deserved eternal suffering, it was Dor for making Corinth do those shitty things. The difference between Corinth and, let's say, Gloria, was Gloria got off on being the shittiest mortal ever.

"Welcome to Edana's palace," Sinder said with a mock bow.

Speaking of traitors. "Where's the fun at? I heard this place has everything."

"It does. But you're here by invitation of my queen. I'm to escort you to her chambers."

"You're back in her good books? Congrats." I knew his past intimately from when I'd lived inside my dear sister's head. Edana had cast him out, sent him to the Glimmer for a fun holiday in their workhouse, and he'd come out fucked up enough to betray the only family who had ever cared for him, in exchange for a little revenge.

Couldn't say I blamed him. Gildola had it coming.

Sinder stiffened, his shoulders going rigid. "My queen is aware of my history with the Godless." And with my sister, though he didn't say it out loud. "And of my assistance to you. She thought I'd be more palatable company than Erosain."

Erosain was an arsehole, so Edana was right there. "Your queen isn't worried I'll rampage my way through Rapture and take her soul?"

"My queen is a god. She fears nothing." He opened a marble door etched in gold and gestured for me to enter.

I stepped through into a golden hallway lit with more fancy brazier flames. The Ember sure liked it hot. On one side were mirrors—Ember apparently loved staring at themselves, too—but the other was made of glass, offering a window into Rapture. The urge to run over and press my nose to the glass almost overwhelmed me. Almost. I wasn't Kayl. I had some fucking self-control. But from where I stood, the row of colorful casinos was visible, along with the river of magma and lava waterfalls that flowed slowly down mountains across the horizon.

It looked *hot*. And yet, in my Glimmer body, I didn't feel the heat, nor smell the ash and brimstone. It made sense, when the Glimmer also breathed with the power of the sun. They'd be right at home here, if they'd ever summoned the balls to visit Rapture.

Sinder led the way down the hall. He'd not said a single thing about my Glimmer form, though he'd been speaking and walking like he had a stick up his arse the entire time.

"Am I making you uncomfortable?" I asked. Wearing a Glimmer's face tended to make most mortals uncomfortable, but Sinder couldn't bear to look at me.

He gave me a bewildered look. "What do you think?"

"I let you kill Corinth, didn't I? That must have felt good."

He huffed, and a line of smoke twirled from his nostrils. "Was that even necessary? I hold no affection for Corinth, but that's a nasty way to send someone back to their god. Aren't you worried he'll tattle to Dor?"

"Relax. He's on my side now."

"Your side? Did you take his...? No, I don't want to know. Whatever happened to Corinth is none of my business, though..." Sinder's shoulders sagged. "You promised you'd help free Vincent."

"Give me a chance. The Nameless One is on my to-kill list, don't worry."

"And what about—" He paused, and swallowed, as though carefully choosing his words. "What happened to Kayl?"

I stopped and stared him down. "Oh, suddenly care about her, do you?"

Flame flashed in his eyes. "You said she'd be safe. That the Glimmer wouldn't hurt her."

Why should he care? He'd been the one to betray her! "Golden Girl Gildola is gone. The Glimmer are mine. Show a little gratitude. I gave you what you wanted, didn't I?"

"Did the Diviner take her? Central was crawling with Wardens—"

"You think I'd let the Diviner keep my sister? They don't have her, and I don't know where she is. So long as Corinth remains with me, she'll come crawling out eventually."

Sinder looked relieved and carried on walking.

Maybe it should have pissed me off, knowing I'd done so much for Sinder and he only cared for my dear sister. But I possessed a god's soul now.

It put things into perspective.

For once in my life, I had power—control—and the opportunity to shake this universe. I'd given Kayl every chance to join me, to achieve the one goal of the Godless together: bringing the gods down. And she'd practically spat in my face each time. I'd even saved her precious Time Boy.

Wasn't that good enough for her? What would it *take*?

YOU DON'T NEED HER, DAUGHTER.

But I did, that was the worst thing. I needed her—or the souls she carried, anyhow. If I was to free Mother from the clock tower, I'd need the gods' souls—all of 'em—including the two Kayl now had. Valeria and apparently Mesmorpheus.

And I'd also need Edana's.

But as Corinth had said, it would be easier to face the other gods if I had a few allies on my side, and then I could take their souls later. With only one soul to my name, I wasn't much of a threat—*yet*. Sunlight could burn, but that taste of power wasn't enough.

I needed more.

Lying and conniving came easily to me. It was the one skill I had learned from Kayl. Despite everything, we weren't very different, only I wasn't afraid to take the next step and destroy my enemies.

We reached the end of the corridor and another fancy golden door. Edana sure liked to show off, but I wasn't that impressed.

Sinder grabbed the door handle and paused. "I'm sure I don't need to warn you how to behave around my queen, do I?"

Corinth said I'd need bastards as part of my new army. Maybe I should hire Sinder. Bastards didn't come much fresher than him. "Leave her to me."

The doors opened to a penthouse lounge. It was a marble room with a floor-to-ceiling windowed view of the strip, and was full of golden furnishings, marble statues, and bejeweled vases—the kind of useless tat a Glimmer would appreciate. Steps led down to a square couch and piles of pillows, all gathered around a blazing firepit.

Edana, god of the Ember, lay sprawled on one side of the firepit. She took the form of her mortals, with bright red skin, black horns speckled with gold paint, and glittering golden lipstick to match. The curves of her tits and thick hips were barely hidden by a thin golden gown, which wasn't long enough to cover those large thighs.

Fuck me, she was gorgeous.

But what surprised me most was the naked man seated next to her, a golden goblet in his hand. Not so much a man, but a statue. A white-marble statue that blinked and breathed with the uncanny movements of a mortal. Next to him, Edana looked practically chaste, as he hadn't bothered covering his damn stone cock.

Now what was Serenity, god of the fucking Seren, doing here?

Edana sat up slowly, the silk folds of her gown shifting enough to flash me her cunt. "Welcome, child of Chaos. I've heard much about your exploits. Join us." She waved a delicate hand at a tray with wine and a bowl of grapes. "In this room, you are safe."

I was safe in any damn room I deigned to enter. Now to take a lesson from Kayl's playbook on spying; acting like a complete slut.

Edana may be beautiful, but I was shit hot, too, and *fuck* did I know it.

I sauntered down to the firepit and made myself comfortable on a cushion, lifting my own gown so my golden legs were on full display. "I didn't think gods could visit each other's domains."

"Gods can do as they wish," Serenity said, his voice light and feminine. "But to enter another domain without invitation places you at the mercy of that domain while leaving your own vulnerable."

"So what is this? An orgy?"

He smirked over the rim of his goblet. "It can be."

Edana slapped him playfully on the arm. "Business before pleasure." She turned her smoldering eyes to me. "We are aware of who you are and which god you represent."

We didn't need to bother with pointless introductions, then, which suited me fine. "Then you're aware of what I can and will do."

"Corentine deserves her freedom."

Huh. We'd jumped right into spouting shit.

THEY DID NOTHING WHILE I WASTED AWAY IN MY PRISON.

I know, Mother. "Seems awfully convenient that it's only now you believe Corentine deserves her freedom. She's been trapped for millennia."

"What is a millennium to a god?" Serenity said. "We see time differently—"

"Corentine would disagree."

"Corentine spent most of that time sleeping. That was the agreement Dor put in place when the Covenant was first written—that she would not be hurt—"

"Had you popped around the clock tower for a visit, you would have seen for yourself Dor was talking shit."

"And break the very rules meant to keep us out of Chime?" Serenity set his goblet down. "We were not to know the truth. I regret the part I played."

"You didn't care then. You only care now because Dor has gotten sick of you all."

Serenity sucked in a hissed breath. *Oh, was I frustrating him? Too bad!*

Perhaps I wasn't handling this 'play nice' shit as well as Corinth would, but who could blame me for feeling a little pissed off?

Gods were entitled fuckers who thought they could get what they wanted.

I wasn't so easily won.

"Could it be the gods have awoken to Dor's manipulations?" Serenity continued. "We didn't foresee Corentine's return, but as she did then, her presence stirs chaos. And we welcome it."

"Chaos represents passion," Edana added. "Freedom. Imagination and creativity." She raised her glass at Serenity. "All the qualities our own domains thrive on. Dor threatens to stifle the influence of Chaos. That impacts all mortals. We've seen the future he would birth, and we want no part."

This is where they offer to hold hands, sing songs, and forget the past.
THEY DO NOT DESERVE MY FORGIVENESS.

No. They deserved our vengeance, and we'd have it. But right now, I needed to be patient. I'd spent years trapped inside my sister's head as my mother remained trapped inside that fucking clock tower. We could wait a little longer.

If I was going to bring down each and every domain, I'd need allies to get there.

And they needed someone to protect them from Dor.

DOR SEEKS CONTROL. THAT IS WHY HE IMPRISONED ME, AS I COULD NOT BE CONTROLLED. THOSE WHO REBEL WILL FACE HIS WRATH, HIS SOUL-DESTROYING WEAPONS OF DESTRUCTION. HE WILL NOT CARE. AND HE WILL NOT STOP. HE HAS ALL ETERNITY.

Then we need to be smarter than a Diviner. I considered helping myself to a glass of wine, but who knew what Edana had poisoned it with. "Tell me more about Dor's plans."

"Earlier this day, Dor held a meeting for the remaining ambassadors," Edana explained. "He made it clear he intends to war against Chaos, and those who do not rally to his cause will be deemed traitors to time. Unghard and Zyclone have already joined his side."

I knew that. I'd seen their gathering forces myself. "The rest?"

"Anima and The Nameless One remain neutral. They will wait to see which side gains the upper hand. Faen has no interest in war, and will likely side with the victor once the dust has cleared. Lionheart wishes to act independently, and will try to take on Dor himself. He's a blundering fool, but a fool and their soul are soon parted."

"And so you two have come together."

"We stand against Dor. The Diviner have never cared for my mortals, and those deemed unworthy have fallen. Valeria. Gildola—"

"Chaos took those."

"They were weak. But do not fool yourself—Chaos would never have gotten so far if Dor hadn't allowed it."

I resented the implication that couldn't win this ourselves.

That we needed them.

"We mean no offense, my love," Serenity said. "Dor manipulates to his own ends. Should we have chosen to ally with him, he would have found some reason to set Chaos on our path eventually. You aren't a weapon to be used by him, nor by us. But together, we can end his reign and create a new era."

Here it came. I crossed my arms. "You're gods. Why don't you kill each other?"

"Gods have been fighting ever since the dawn of time. Not even Chaos can destroy a god's soul, but merely distribute their energy."

Was that true? *We can't kill the gods permanently?*

THE AETHER OF THE UNIVERSE IS NEVER FULLY DESTROYED, ONLY RESHAPED AND REMADE. WHEN WE TAKE THEIR SOULS, WE WILL EVISCERATE THEM BEYOND RECOGNITION UNTIL THE MEMORIES OF THEIR EXISTENCE BECOME FAINT ECHOES IN THE FAR REACHES OF THE STARS. THEN, AND ONLY THEN, WILL THEY BE FORGED INTO SOMETHING NEW.

THIS IS THE GIFT OF CHAOS. THE GIFT WE SHALL OFFER OUR BRETHREN.

The gods still needed us to do their dirty work, then? Useless arseholes. "What do you propose?"

"A partnership," Edana said. "We know Corentine desires her revenge. We can help her with that desire."

I WILL SEE THEIR END.

Soon, Mother. "You're willing to fight on the side of Chaos?"

"To form a coalition of chaos where we are granted the freedoms Dor once granted us. In exchange, I offer my mortals to serve at your will. They will burn your enemies."

"My Seren will be at your disposal," Serenity added. "They may not fight quite like the Ember, but they make excellent spies. I've already placed my mortals in key locations throughout Chime to gather knowledge. I know Dor operates a base within Timefall Estates in the Golden City, and the steamworks are now under his control. He's focusing on the clock tower. With the Zephyr's aid, he hopes to recapture it."

I'd like to see him try! I'd already blown up the top entrance into the tower, which left only the bottom for them to crawl up. With a couple of Ember in my pocket, we'd burn any Diviner out. "If you can open portals into Chime, then why don't we hop on over to Kronos and end this right now?"

"I've tried, my love. I sent my mortals into Kronos, and Dor caught every one of them. Their souls did not return to me."

"Dor is no fool," Edana said. "Gods know when interlopers enter their domains. Most will have defenses in place to prevent invasion, as I now do. But Dor... he has methods of capturing mortals. Of taking their souls and turning them against us."

The soul-splitting machines. *What happens to a soul's energy if it's cut in half?*

IT NO LONGER EXISTS IN THIS UNIVERSE.

That was comforting.

"There is one more thing, my love," Serenity said. "One juicy morsel of information you'll appreciate. It can be yours, if you agree to our coalition."

"Fine. We can even come up with our own secret handshake. Now spill."

"One of my spies reported a compatriot of yours imprisoned within Timefall. A Chaos male."

Chance.

Fuck, it had to be Chance.

My brother was still alive, and those fucking Diviner had him!

CHANCE IS LOST TO ME. HIS SOUL IS NO MORE.

They'd already shoved him into their soul-splitting machine. That meant the Chance left behind was little more than an empty shell. But I wouldn't let those fucks toy with his mortal body and use Chance like a slave.

I'd get him back, and then I'd make them pay. I'd make them *all* pay. "That's where this all ends—with me destroying Dor."

"And you will," Edana said. "To do so, we must remove Dor's allies and advantages, starting with Unghard and Zyclone. Going after Dor now would only lead to our failure."

I dared a sip of the wine. The fizz popped in my mouth with the tang of berries. "All right. We'll take it slow. When do we begin?"

"We have all afternoon to plan and scheme, though now..." Edana rose from her seat, allowing her gown to slip from her shoulders, cascading in a shimmer until it completely fell in a sprinkling of soot, leaving her naked before me. "I grow tired of discussing business."

Fuck, she was so damn *hot*.

Slowly, so gods-damn slowly, Edana slid beside me, her touch setting my guts aflame. She smelled amazing, too—her perfume made my head spin, sweet like vanilla. Her chest pushed against mine, and her lips traced my ear. "Would you like me to go lower?" she whispered.

I wasn't my sister. I wasn't a slut for any whore who flashed their tits in my face, but fuck, I needed this. I *wanted* it.

DO NOT LET THE GODS TEMPT YOU WITH THEIR WILES. YOU ARE BETTER THAN THAT, DAUGHTER.

If Kayl could fuck whoever she wanted, then so could I.

"Get on your knees," I ordered Edana.

Flame burned in those dark eyes. Had she ever been bossed around, least of all by a mortal? She'd better get used to it.

Serenity sat on my other side and ran a stony hand along my cheek. I nudged him away. "Nuh-uh. I don't do cocks."

In the blink of an eye, his perfectly chiseled male body was replaced by a female one. The curves were a picture of porcelain perfection, as though a piece of art had stepped from a Seren gallery. "Is this more to your liking?"

I nodded, suddenly finding it hard to breathe as Edana pushed my legs apart.

And her lips met mine.

Fuck!

This was what I'd been missing out on for my entire mortal life!

They were toying with me. Attempting to win me to their side in the hopes I'd spare their pathetic lives. It would have been so easy to touch them back, to yank out their souls for a moment of pleasure.

Instead, I let them use me as I'd use them.

And gods, I'd enjoy every moment.

4

*Of all the domains who struggle to integrate into Chime, it is the Fauna
who suffer most. Their animalistic natures are at odds with civilized society.
Most Fauna just don't understand the need for social rites and rules.
Unfortunately, this often results in a messy run-in with the Wardens,
especially when public urination or defecation is involved.
While my colleagues have proposed greater educational reforms, I believe we
should seek to work with a Fauna's natural instinct, not against.*
—Q. Corinth, *Warden Dossier on the Fauna*

IF THERE WAS ONE thing I knew about the Fauna, it was that they had no
worries regarding nakedness. It came with the territory, I supposed.
Swapping between animal and half-animal forms meant clothes became a
pain in the arse, something I'd come to understand myself after switching
between Seren and other forms. It meant most citizens of Chime viewed
the Fauna as either degenerates or objects to be sexualized. It was why so
many Fauna found a home on Sinner's Row within the brothels and cat
cafés, or found themselves abducted into Glimmer-owned workhouses to
save them from their sinful temptations—or protect the rest of Chime
from sinful temptation, anyhow. At least they didn't have to worry about
that anymore.

To a Seren, nakedness was art. To an Ember, nakedness was the
beginning of a good time. To a Diviner, nakedness was a scandal.

But to a Fauna? It was simply nothing.

And that was why no one so much as batted an eye at the mass of naked
bodies *everywhere* within the Fauna campsite. Clothing wasn't a necessity.
At my Fauna height, I couldn't see much besides everyone's ankles—or
paws or hooves—nor did I want to look up and get an eyeful. As much as I

longed to return to a more sensible height, I wasn't ready to get that comfortable with a bunch of strangers just yet.

Autumn had already switched to her half-animal upright form, and the sight of a naked girl as young as her worried me. There were enough perverts in Chime. But no one seemed to notice or care, and a group of naked children were frolicking underneath a waterspout.

"Come on!" she called.

"I hope you're taking me somewhere with decent food," I said.

We wove between the collection of ramshackle stalls and tents. They reminded me so painfully of Grayford. Each had been constructed from a patchwork of scavenged material and colorful cloth, and each bore personal touches that made it more homey. Some tents were decorated in ribbons, others with mosaics made with chips of discarded ceramic and pieces of shiny metal. Trinkets covered a few stalls. Snow globes and other trashy souvenirs, just like my old home.

Perhaps some part of my soul was Fauna. Or was collecting shiny objects a symptom of growing up in the slums?

My nose picked up familiar Grayford scents—chestnuts and spices. A Fauna with a long black and white face and snout like a badger was roasting chestnuts over a firepit as another with spines for hair—actual spines, like a damn hedgehog—added them to bowls of golden curry. Oh gods, yes, I needed that!

Ember knew how to make their curries *hot*, but I reckoned a Fauna curry would have bite.

Sadly, Autumn beckoned me past. We stopped outside a tent decorated in fairy lights, arranged similarly to how I'd decorated my old hanging tram back in the depot. A raggedy older wolf-man stood leaning against a pole outside. His fur was a dark gray, though parts across the left side of his face and shoulder had been scorched away, leaving burn scars, and he was missing his left eye.

This one had seen battle. Thankfully, his nakedness was hidden inside a kilt.

"Oi, then," the wolf chided Autumn. "Where have you been now, dragging in stray cats? I've half a mind to tan your hide!"

Autumn butted him playfully in the arm. "I found the woman those Wardens have been after, Wolfy."

He looked me over. "A Fauna?"

I sized up Wolfy, though the effort twinged something in my neck. "I'm not a Fauna—not technically—"

"Show him what you did," Autumn said, her bushy tail swishing with excitement.

"Here?" I asked.

"Uh-huh."

I was about to get comfortably naked with a bunch of strangers sooner rather than later, though it wouldn't be a first.

I reached inside to where Mesmorpheus's energy resided, nestled snugly between all the other souls I'd ever stolen, accidentally or otherwise, and gave it a metaphorical squeeze.

My height suddenly shot up as I swapped my Fauna form for a Mesmer one. Getting naked in front of strangers wasn't embarrassing, but I found myself on all fours, which was a compromising position at the best of times. Thankfully, my dark purple Mesmer skin hid the heat burning across my face rather well as I stood on my more natural two legs.

Wolfy openly stared at me, and he wasn't the only one. A group of Fauna had gathered around and were pointing and whispering.

I doubted it was due to my natural beauty. They mustn't get many naked Mesmer making a visit, or likely any guests at all. "I don't suppose you have a robe or something I can borrow? There's a bit of a draft."

Wolfy opened the curtain to the tent. "You better step inside. Autumn, wait here."

Autumn pouted. "Aww, but I want—"

"You did good, but this is boring adult business. We'll catch up later." He ushered me inside.

I stepped into an office of sorts with a desk taking up most of the tent, surrounded by makeshift bookshelves stuffed full of worn books and scrolls, as messy as my old hanging tram.

Shit. It was an ambassador's office. A makeshift embassy.

But the woman seated at the desk wasn't the Fauna ambassador I'd recognize from my own jaunt as an ambassador. Instead, she was a cat woman with fluffy white ears.

She blinked at me with golden feline eyes. "Fuck me, that's a first," she began, her accent a posh version of an Undercity lilt. "There're still Mesmer in Chime? We thought everyone 'ad gone. Everyone except those bloody Diviner."

"I could ask you the same. How are Fauna still here?"

"It's her, Trix," Wolfy interrupted. He handed me a robe and passed Autumn's copy of my wanted flier over to the cat woman. "I saw her change from a Fauna to—to this. Autumn brought her here. Said they'd been attacked by Wardens."

Cat Woman—Trix—examined the flier and then gawped at me. "*You're* Arkey?"

I tied the robe around my waist and dipped into a curtsy. "So they call me."

"They call you the god of anarchy, is what."

How flattering. I'd spent so many years trying to hide my nefarious past, and now everyone knew who I was. "My name's Kayl, and I have a few questions of my own."

Wolfy patted his fluffy chest. "I'm Wolfsbane. Named after the plant."

Trix shuffled some papers away off her desk and gestured to a rickety chair. "Take a seat. Wolfsbane, get us some tea. Extra cream."

Wolfy—Wolfsbane—bowed his head and left us alone.

I tucked the robe underneath me to avoid catching my arse on a splinter. "To whom do I owe this pleasure?"

"Name's Trixie Tomcat. Perhaps you've 'eard of me? Singer, dancer, and proprietor of Tom Cat's Café, the fanciest cat café in all of Chime." She leaned back in her chair and rapped silver painted nails across the wooden desk. "Born and raised on Sinner's Row. That was 'ome, until this calamity 'appened."

That explained why this fancy cat was so remarkably well dressed and well groomed for a Fauna. Soft cream fur covered her skin, matching a classy dress straight from a Golden City boutique. Two pearl earrings dangled from her cat ears, and even her makeup was on point, despite the shabby surroundings. She was the sort to be sitting on top of a pile of cushions in the Golden City, not wallowing in the gutter.

This kitty was no stranger to decadence. "You're the big cat in charge?"

"Damn right I am. Someone needed to step up when everything fell apart. This is my town, and my Fauna."

"Wouldn't Faen have something to say about that?"

"Faen doesn't give two shits about us. When mortals started popping out of existence left and right, we remained behind."

Unfortunately, that made sense. "Your ambassador, then."

"She's dead. Don't right know what 'appened to 'er. She and a bunch of other ambassadors went to some meeting at the embassy and never came back."

Shit. I knew what had happened to her. That Diviner, whoever he was, had reduced her to dust. Of course, gods could bring their ambassadors back, if they cared to do so, which I guessed Faen didn't.

"Willow was useless," Trixie continued. "We didn't need 'er then, and don't need 'er now. The Diviner are still 'ere. And our scouts 'ave spotted Umber—"

"Scouts such as Autumn? Sending children—"

"Course I don't bloody send children. That girl's as wild as any newborn pup. She does as she pleases, despite the old wolf's best attempts at taming 'er. Freddie chases 'er tail. Loyal boy, that one. Our scouts didn't report any Mesmer, though, yet you're not only a Mesmer on 'ere." She tapped the flier. "You can turn into one of us. What else can you do?"

In the flier, I wore the colors of Chaos, Diviner, Glimmer, and Mesmer, but since I'd first yanked Lady Mae's soul clean from her body all those weeks ago, I'd taken other souls and worn other faces. I'd not intended to steal souls—I wasn't my sister—and therefore couldn't transform into every domain, but I had a few to my name.

Which would impress this fancy cat? I searched inside for the few disparate souls in my collection—a Glimmer or Diviner was quite the change from a Mesmer, but I didn't want to completely spook the woman. That, and if I turned Diviner, she may decide I was some sort of spy.

I pushed their souls aside and instead reached for one a Fauna would appreciate. Whiskers had been a shitty Leander I'd beaten in an Obituary arena. With a simple flick of his soul, I grew fur again, only this time I remained upright on two legs instead of four.

Trixie sprang to her feet, sending her chair clattering backwards. "'Ow the *fuck* do you do that?"

I examined my claws. "I'm one of those Chaos mortals your scouts have probably heard of." If they were any good at scouting, anyhow. "The ones locked inside the clock tower. The Diviner aren't too fond of us, either."

"Because you can steal souls." Trixie sat back down. "That was all the talk of the town some weeks back. Rumors of electrical monsters in the tunnels. We'd been 'iding underground in our dens when that attack 'appened on Central. We 'eard it all the way down 'ere. Is that 'ow you can turn Fauna?" Her eyes narrowed. "Did you steal a Fauna's soul?"

"No. I can transform into any domain through touch. I don't steal souls from mortals who don't deserve it."

Trixie shook her head. "Where's this fucking tea?" she muttered. "Figured you weren't a real Mesmer, since I've never known one to remain this damn lucid in a single conversation. You know what 'appened topside? Where is everyone?"

I quickly explained the events of the past few weeks—how Chaos had become free, how some Chaos mortals really *did* want to steal souls, and that the clashing forces of both chaos and time had led to the loss of the Vesper, the Glimmer, and technically the Mesmer. I couldn't entirely blame the Diviner for the mass exodus of Chime's citizens. Jinx held some responsibility there.

"War's coming," I said. "In fact, it's already here. Anyone left in Chime will feel Dor's wrath."

"The Diviner can't reach us 'ere—"

"Chime is built from Diviner and Zephyr tech. Of course they can." That they hadn't yet was more likely due to the Diviner underestimating the Fauna and not considering them a threat. Their loss.

"Some of our scouts 'aven't returned." Trixie leaned back in her chair. "And anyone else topside gets taken."

"Taken?"

"By their 'ulking clockwork machines. The embassy's empty. So's the correctional facilities. And the Gate's been off for days. Where the fuck are they taking my mortals?"

A shiver ran down my spine. I didn't want to assume the worst, but Diviner sure enjoyed dissecting mortals and putting them through soul-splitting machines. Could they be doing that to any stray Fauna they came across? To what end?

Like the Vesper, the Fauna were treated like second-class citizens, even when society had fallen apart.

There wasn't much left of the Godless—just me, in fact—but helping mortals was what we did. Usually to escape their gods, though a god's apathy for their mortals was a unique sort of cruelty, one inflicted by a god who didn't care for their mortal's well-being. I wouldn't let these Fauna be used and abused by Diviner, nor would I let them be forgotten.

All right, I was one Godless against a whole line of gods. But this was my operation. I was the last line of defense between mortals and their gods, between Diviner and their ambitions, and between Jinx and *her* ambitions.

And Quen. I was the only one left to rescue him from Corentine's clutches.

If I was to rescue him, I'd need a small army. This was my chance to build one. "If Diviner have been taking Fauna, then they'll know about this place. They'll have scanned their recent past and found it, which means you're all in danger. Help me, and I'll help protect your Fauna. I'll find out what the Diviner are doing to them and put a stop to it. I promise."

"We 'elp *you*?" She eyed me curiously. "What could you possibly need from us?"

"I have some Mesmer who need shelter. I also need somewhere to lie low—"

"'Old on. With the Gate closed, we don't 'ave enough resources to feed everyone. There's no fresh grain coming in from Solaris or fucking anywhere. We're stretched thin enough as it is."

"The Diviner will still be eating, and they have the Umber on their side. We can take what we need from them."

"You and whose army?"

"Your army." I met her stare with my own. "You've got mortals with claws and teeth."

"Chime is the playground of the Diviner. It's their city—"

"Not if I have anything to say about it."

She crossed her arms. "*They* can control *time*."

I switched my form to Diviner. Before she could properly grasp what her eyes were seeing, I brought time to a halt and casually sat on the corner of her desk, then let time slip back to the present. "So can I."

She near enough jumped out of her fur. "Gods fucking save us! If you don't want to steal souls, then what *do* you want?"

"Would you believe me if I said I wanted to end the reign of gods?"

"You sound like one of those Godless."

"Funny you should mention that—"

The curtain opened, and in came Wolfsbane with a tray of tea. He almost dropped it at the sight of me wearing a Diviner's face. "Are we good?"

Trixie rubbed a claw under her chin. "Ain't that the question." She sat back in her chair and watched as Wolfsbane poured the milkiest tea I'd ever seen—Quen would be appalled. "We've carved our niche. I don't care for what you or the Diviner plan for this damn city, but I care when my mortals are 'urt. Whatever use you may 'ave for us, we're not Leander. We don't fight for thrills. We fight for necessity."

"I understand—"

"Do you?" She flashed a fang. "These are *my* mortals."

So the fancy cat was overly protective. Good. She had something worth fighting for. "I won't put your mortals in harm's way if I can help it, but you know the Diviner will. I have a plan for taking them down."

"We ought to hear her out, Trix," Wolfsbane urged, handing her a cup and saucer.

Trixie took a sip of her milky froth. "All right. What's your plan?"

Okay, I didn't have a plan as such.

Without Harmony to guide me, the only real plan I had was to find the one man in Chime who could come up with an *actual* plan. I needed my partner back.

Quen would know where to hit Dor the hardest.

"There's a man who knows what the Diviner are doing with your mortals, and he's currently trapped inside the clock tower. I need help getting him out."

Trixie set her teacup down. "'Ave you seen the state of the clock tower recently? It's Chime's largest fucking streetlamp."

I held up my hands. "I know I'm asking a lot—"

"A lot!"

"We need him." *I* needed him.

"I need to feed my Fauna. What's the damn rush?"

I sank back into my rickety chair and bit back my exasperation. "He's likely being tortured and subjected to his worst nightmares inside that place." It wasn't something I wanted to dwell on, but this was Jinx we were talking about. Her hatred for the Diviner reached greater depths than mine. Who knew what horrors she'd been unleashing on Quen while I'd been prancing around the Market District, wasting valuable time. "And he's... important to me. As soon as we get him free, we'll have a plan to save Chime." Assuming his time spent locked inside the clock tower hadn't sent him insane.

Gods, I hoped we'd reach him before Jinx could do real damage. Quen had suffered enough at the hands of his own bloody god, let alone mine.

"Sounds like you don't 'ave a plan at all. I'm not risking any of my Fauna on some suicide mission—"

"I'll do it. I'll help," Wolfsbane offered. "If it'll make a difference. Risking this has got to be better than risking my tail scavenging for scraps."

Trixie sighed. "Listen. I didn't get to sit my arse in this chair because I fell for every stranger's sob story. You scratch my back, and I'll scratch yours."

A bargain was better than nothing. I leaned forward. "What do you have for me?"

"Like I said, we need food. 'elp us secure our next meal, and you'll get your army. But if you break my trust, then we'll get a meal out of you and your Mesmer. Deal?"

I didn't fancy becoming dinner, and Cosmo would never let me hear the end of it, but I fancied my chances—not that I had many choices left. "Deal." I held out my hand.

Trixie shook on it, and I allowed my form to switch back to Fauna before letting go.

"One of us is going to regret this," she muttered over the rim of her teacup.

Oh, she wasn't wrong.

I couldn't tell if my sinister reputation was due to Jinx's or my own attempts to defy the Diviner. Either way, it came with some perks, namely a large private tent within the Fauna's secret camp, which came with its own bed and wardrobe. It may not be the Grand Hotel back in Central, but it sure beat squatting inside a liquor store.

Wolfsbane left me as I gave myself a good look in the mirror.

Oh, you had to be kidding.

I was a pissing *cat*!

My new cat ears twitched. They were a soft, fuzzy black to match the rest of my fur. Fauna could switch between full animal and half-animal upright forms, the latter of which at least allowed me to put on some clothes. Like my Leander form, this cat form came with a tail. Luckily for me, Wolfsbane had left me with a suitable change of clothes—a breast band and a pair of leggings with a necessary hole in the right place for my tail to slip through. It wasn't an outfit I'd be caught dead wearing in civilized society, but if I was about to go hunting for food, then at least my minimalist clothing wouldn't get caught on anything.

Really, the Fauna needed a better fashion line.

Once I'd slipped on a pair of flats, I reached inside myself and found the trio.

In a blinding flash, they appeared in front of me.

"We're sorry, Mama!" Celeste wailed, and threw herself at my feet.

"Can you forgive us?" Castor pleaded with his hands clasped in prayer.

Cosmo sulked. "*I* didn't do anything wrong."

"I've never tried wine before!" Celeste was full-on ugly crying now. Honestly, it was a little sad. "It tasted like fruit sours!"

"Give over." I pulled Celeste up. "You shouldn't have gotten drunk and wandered off, but it all worked out for the best. We have allies, and they'll keep you safe when I can't."

"They won't eat us, will they?" Castor asked. "I heard Fauna eat other mortals."

Cosmo clutched a hand over their heart. "They're going to *eat us*?"

For gods' sake. "No, Cosmo, no one is going to eat you." Not yet, anyhow.

"What if they get hungry? What if—"

"They wouldn't make very good allies if they ate us, would they? Now, I need you three to stay here and be good. I promised the Fauna I'd help them out."

"Will you be safe?" Celeste wiped her cheeks clear.

"This is me we're talking about." By the look Celeste was giving me, she considered that statement a bad thing. "There are some clothes in the wardrobe. If you're lucky, the Fauna may have some candy around here." Though I doubted it.

I stepped out of the tent to give them privacy, and for my own sanity.

Wolfsbane waited outside, chewing on a rib bone. The slight whiff of cooked fat made me nauseous and curious at the same time. This Fauna body of mine wanted meat, but who had that rib belonged to? I didn't dare ask.

"Bit sensitive, your Mesmer," he said.

"They've been through a lot." A hulking monster of a Fauna walked by—I couldn't even name the creature whose form it took, but it was almost as large as my tent and had a sharp horn on the top of its leathery gray skin. "Try not to scare them. They're a bit skittish."

He followed my eye. "Don't worry. Beatrix is an herbivore."

"That's good to know."

"We'll keep them safe so long as they don't go wandering into anyone's dreams. We know what Mesmer are like."

I crossed my fingers behind my back. "They'll be on their best behavior. I promise."

And if they weren't, I'd wring their bloody necks myself.

Wolfsbane handed me a small drawstring bag.

"What's this for?"

He gave me an odd look. "Is this your first day as a Fauna?"

"Actually, yes."

He tossed his gnawed rib aside as Autumn and Freddie ran over. The two Fauna children were much more at ease here among their own. Autumn carried that arrogant confidence only a teenager could possess, while Freddie beamed with the toothy grin of innocent youth.

I could have sworn we had a couple of Fauna children like these back in Grayford, but my memory failed me now. Dru would know. She could name every face that had ever come to the soup kitchen in search of a hot meal. It was one reason I loved her. She'd made time for everyone. Even a godless heathen like me.

"You're going topside without me?" Autumn pouted, her eyes flicking to the bag in my hands.

"Nothing exciting," Wolfsbane said. "A little scouting."

"I can scout—"

"Fewer tails wagging in the air means fewer for the Wardens to grab." He patted Autumn on the head. "I need you here to protect our new friends—"

"Babysit, you mean."

"They can be a handful," I said. "I appreciate you watching over them."

"They're part of our pack now, and kin watches kin. Put that on." Wolfsbane gestured to my bag. "Use it to carry clothes and anything else you need when you switch forms."

He strode on ahead, and I hastily followed him on a tour of the campsite. On the way, he pointed out where the Fauna ate, slept, shit, and planned their revolutions. There were so many different types of Fauna here, it was like I'd abandoned Chime entirely.

We paused beside the tunnel that led out of the campsite, where a waterfall of sewer water cascaded down the overbearing metal walls and afforded us a little privacy.

Wolfsbane went over the plan. "We'll sniff out a suitable source of food. Then we'll send the rest of our scouts to make supply runs."

"How much food do you have?" I'd walked past happy-looking Fauna and bustling stalls grilling meat. Nothing that indicated hard times, considering the circumstances.

"Not enough. These tunnels connect to Central Station." He gestured to the exit behind me. "We would take what we could from their deliveries—from Solaris, Heartstone. Even Witheryn, when the Necro brought in meat. But now the Gate has shut down, nothing is coming through."

Deliveries had to be coming in from somewhere. Tea and biscuits wouldn't last long with the Diviner. "What about your temple? Is there anything left there?"

"No. The Diviner cleared everything out, and we dare not return. Too many Wardens sniffing around. We managed to catch a couple, after taking one of their tasers. But a Diviner can only last so long."

"I'm sorry—you caught a Diviner? And did *what* with them?"

"Grilled them with light seasoning."

Oh my god. The rib Wolfsbane had been eating... Shit.

It shouldn't have surprised me. Autumn had practically warned me Fauna diets were as fucked up as Necro ones. Fauna likely knew how to keep a mortal alive enough to chop off whatever bits they could feast on, as the Necro did... I really didn't want to think about it any longer than necessary. "When I said I'd help you find food, I want to be *very* clear I'm not helping you eat mortals. You... don't need to eat meat to live, do you?" Like a Necro needed blood or they'd go feral?

Wolfsbane shrugged. "We don't need to. Some of us prefer it."

Thank the gods for that. "Right. Let's think about our options, then. We can't return to the Market District, as they'll be expecting us. What about Sinner's Row?"

"Closed off. It's been barricaded against entry. There're vertical tunnels leading up to the Golden City, but that's quite a trek, even for us. We've barely scouted it out—enough to know there are no mortals left there, either."

Not even the Golden City had been spared the gods' purge. "You say the Gate has been switched off, but do you know that for certain? Could they be powering it on in spurts during unsociable hours, maybe? How else would Diviner and Umber be getting into Chime? They're not using the elevators. They must be using something." A portal of some kind? Mesmorpheus had managed to create their own portal into Chime, so it must be possible. "You'll hate this, but we need to head back to Central Station. We need to find out what they're doing."

It helped I had my own ulterior motive for wanting to scout out the station. An ulterior motive named Quentin Corinth.

Wolfsbane scratched his scruffy beard. "Trixie won't like it."

"Trixie doesn't need to know. But if we succeed, she'll get all the cream she wants."

The old wolf grinned, exposing his sharp fangs. "You're the right sort of trouble, Arkey."

Wasn't that what I always said?

V

The order to evacuate Chime came at exactly 17:30, half an hour after Solaris fell. By then, the other domains had vanished from the city altogether, leaving only Diviner. I assisted with the crossing of civilians into Kronos as Wardens were told to remain in Chime and await further instruction from our Father. I believe this operation could have run smoother with better efficiency. A half-hour delay could have resulted in disaster. The death of Ambassador Corinth at the hands of Chaos has left us vulnerable. I have appealed to our Father for a replacement and submitted my own candidacy for the role. However, Father has stated women are not designed for positions of power.
—P. Bezel, *An account of the 'Gate Closure' Incident*

CLANGING REVERBERATED THROUGH THE clock tower. As the elevator's top entrance, which hosted the platform for the Golden City had been destroyed thanks to Jinx's explosion, the Wardens had renewed their efforts to attempt a siege via the bottom entrance on level with the Gate.

With the amount of hammering, it almost seemed they were attempting to knock the entire blasted tower down. Their activity was a constant headache, even if I couldn't perceive it from my vantage point by the clockface window. Every now and then a Zephyr would fly past and test the aether shield by zapping it with a taser and noting down the reaction. They were plotting, and that did not please me one jot.

All I could do to pass the time was merely observe them and help Joe keep our workforce of Glimmer motivated, lest they slack in their duties and our shield drop.

Should that happen, then we'd all be in trouble, regardless of how our cursed souls had ended up in this predicament to begin with.

Jinx joined me by the window, fresh from her visit to Rapture. Her golden skin looked more radiant than ever, and there was a definite spring to her step.

"How did your meeting with Edana go?" I asked.

"Wouldn't you like to know."

"Yes, that's why I asked."

"I had the best fuck of my entire mortal life. Not that a Diviner would know anything about pleasure." She leered. "Do Diviner even know what they're doing? I bet you just lie there and exclaim, Oh *my*, I have arrived!"

I squinted over the rim of my spectacles. "Diviner make generous lovers, actually. By controlling time, we can slow pleasure and 'arrive' precisely when we choose." The less I knew about Jinx's love life, the better for my own sanity, though perhaps this would allow her to release some of that pent-up frustration she would otherwise unleash on the rest of us.

"Sure, and that's why Diviner are known for their sexual prowess, and not for their incredibly thrilling conversations about timekeeping." She peered over the edge of the window at Central Station below. "Noisy fuckers. How long do you think it'll take 'em to break in?"

"Technically, your aether shield should keep them out indefinitely. But with Zephyr and Diviner minds working on advanced aether technology, your guess is as good as mine."

"Oh, go on. Have a guess."

"Well, by my calculations—"

"Never. The answer is never. You know why? 'Cause I'll fuck them up first." She pushed from the clockface, her expression the same troublesome smirk Kayl tortured me with whenever she was about to drastically ruin my day. "How about you start making yourself useful around here?"

Anything would beat staring woefully out the window. "What do you have in mind?"

"While those fuckers are busy banging their heads against the wall, we'll find their secret base and destroy it."

"They have a secret base?"

"Up there." She pointed above us to the Golden City. "Your old Warden mates are up to their tricks again—stealing mortal souls. My spies think they've got a whole bunch of those soul-splitting machines just waiting for us."

"And you think I can help dismantle them? They were Elijah's—" The name caught in my throat. I cleared it away like a disgusting lump of phlegm. "They were my predecessor's pet project, not mine." A horrid thought occurred to me. Would Jinx want them for her own use? "I don't know how to configure them, so don't even ask."

"Relax, Corinth. It's your playmates who love splitting souls in half, not me. I want them turned into molten metal."

"Then you need an Ember."

A flash of light flickered in her eye. "Don't even need that."

"Then what do you need me for? Should I enter the Golden City, there is a chance I may be spotted by a Warden, and then Dor will learn of my untimely resurrection."

"I thought you'd want to stretch your legs. Are you that keen to spend time with a bunch of Glimmer?"

I glanced over to where the Glimmer stood in their little prayer circle, their arms outstretched as they concentrated hard to keep the shield going. Joe had them working in shifts, so as not to completely exhaust them, but he didn't let up, either. Did the Glimmer still pray, despite their god's demise? Did Jinx now receive their prayers in Gildola's stead? Did Jinx, in turn, terrorize them telepathically?

I returned to the question. "I simply don't wish to be recognized."

"We'll paint you a fake mustache. You don't want the chance to run off and join Daddy Dor?"

"If the Diviner knew I was still alive, they'd collar me, strap me to a table and start cutting out my organs to try and understand how I've become Chaos." I shuddered. "I won't give Dor that satisfaction."

"Then let's get going." She strode across the room with purpose.

I jogged to keep up. "To *where*?" It was difficult hiding my exasperation when Jinx bounced from one eventful plan to another while keeping me in the dark. I resented not being privy to schemes where Dor was concerned. How was I meant to assist when she kept me on such a short leash?

DON'T POUT, Corentine said, her voice amused. *MY DAUGHTER'S MIND IS ONE OF A KIND. TO UNDERSTAND HER, YOU WILL NEED TO TRUST HER.*

Can I trust her to not *kill me this time?*

CAN SHE TRUST YOU? SHE HAS YET TO UNDERSTAND WHO YOU ARE, QUENTIN CORINTH.

What does she expect me to prove?

SHE HAS WITNESSED ONLY SPARKS OF WHAT YOU COULD BE. WHAT SHE WISHES TO SEE IS YOUR TRUE CHAOTIC SELF. EMBRACE IT. UNLEASH IT.

Being reborn as Chaos hadn't automatically prepared me for leading a chaotic existence—at least not yet. Perhaps I needed to give it time.

"We're heading to Timefall Estates," Jinx announced cheerfully, as though we'd been invited for tea and scones. "We're paying your predecessor's home a visit."

Despite Jinx blowing up the entrance to the Golden City elevator, there was a gap large enough for a Zephyr to fly through. Unfortunately for me, that was my mode of transportation as Lucky pulled the short straw and carried me all the way to where Chime's aristocrats made their home. Or had done.

Like Central, the Golden City had been abandoned, with only expensive gowns, tailored suits, fancy hats, and parasols left behind. It had been some time since I last took the glass elevator up, and to see the plaza now, abandoned and showing distressing signs of neglect...

It felt rather vindicating.

"There's no Diviner," Lucky said with that gruff charm I was beginning to like. We'd taken a breather outside the Golden City's shopping arcade, and he was right. There wasn't a single soul in sight. Not even a Warden.

"Doesn't mean there's no one watching." Jinx sat perched on a streetlamp, still in her magpie form. "So, Time Boy." She clicked her beak at me. "Which way?"

"You can hardly describe me as a 'Time Boy' when—"

"Which. Way?"

I held back another sigh. "To the north, past the Academy. There should be a carriage we could commandeer—"

"No need. Lucky will take you."

Lucky scowled with absolute delight at being volunteered.

Jinx spread her wings. "Remember; if you lead us astray or even think of betraying me—"

"You'll bite me, pluck out my eyes, burn me alive with scalding tea, et cetera."

"In that order."

With that settled, I reluctantly climbed into Lucky's arms, and we took flight.

I'd never seen the Golden City from above before, and despite my trepidation, I had to admit it was quite the sight. The sun shone overhead on this beautiful afternoon, casting a sparkling shine across the city's golden buildings, so reminiscent of Solaris. Though as the Academy's sprawling campus came into view, my chest ached with sudden sorrow.

Other than the wind, it was deathly quiet. The Academy was the heart and soul of the Golden City—to me, at least—and it had beaten with an energetic pulse since silenced. No frantic footsteps as students hurried to their next lectures. No passionate debates between the scholars from the School of Philosophy. No banging and commotion from the School of Engineering. The Academy had been my life for much of my formative years, and now... now it was nothing.

I'd have never admitted it then, but the Academy was a home for the Godless. A sanctuary where students could expand their worldly knowledge, mingle with other domains, and dream of a future away from their gods. It was a place where I'd dreamed of a future that would have been mine, had the gods never existed.

Would Chaos reopen these doors to the free thinkers who sought its secrets?

Or would they deem it a relic of Chime's sordid history and destroy it?

I didn't want to ask.

Lost in my mourning, I almost missed the approach to Timefall Estates.

Lucky brought us down beside a section of the brass fence obscured by foliage. Jinx switched back to her Glimmer body, complete with crimson dress. Not exactly the type of clothing for engaging in espionage—she stood out, for one—but who was I to tell her what to do?

I crouched within the bush and observed, despite how futile I thought the exercise.

Jinx had brought us here for a reason, thus I expected Timefall to be crawling with Diviner. But like the rest of the Golden City, it appeared empty, though with one core difference. The streets weren't littered with clothing. The Diviner here hadn't been zapped back to Kronos, at least not straight away. They'd had time to gather their belongings before abandoning the place.

"Looks empty," Lucky said, confirming my thoughts.

"Are you surprised?"

"Shh," Jinx hushed us both. She covered her mouth with both hands and made an odd cooing.

Flapping wings gusted into our bush, and I almost jumped in alarm! I stuck my head out, expecting another Chaos in a Zephyr form, but no. What landed on the ground before me was a Seren, of all mortals. Perhaps the only Seren left in Chime.

Not just any Seren. Oh dear gods, I knew this one.

His deep blue skin and jet-black hair made him resemble a tiny Vesper with wings. We'd unfortunately crossed paths many years ago during my tenure as a Warden. Some Seren used their natural singing ability to engage in criminal undertakings, and this was one of them—a scoundrel and thief who'd begun his career extorting money from innocent victims before aiding an ex-Warden Necro during a murder investigation that turned bloody.

"Nocturne," I blurted.

The Seren grinned. "You still remember me? How quaint."

Jinx groaned. "You idiots know each other?"

"I arrested him at least twice," I said.

"Three times," Nocturne confirmed. "You had it in for me."

"You aided and abetted a known murderer! Where is Gast these days?"

"Every damn mortal got sucked out of Chime by their god, so take a wild fucking guess, Mr. Dark Warden—"

"*Don't* call me that—"

"All right, shut it." Jinx stood between us. "Nocturne is working for me—"

"I prefer Noct, if you don't mind."

Jinx glared at him. Oh, I wished she'd give him a good kick.

"Please don't tell me we've struck a bargain with Serenity?" I asked. The world must have gone mad if I was being forced to work alongside this criminal!

I raised my brow at Lucky, hoping for a little backup, but he was too busy scratching his beak and looking thoroughly bored like some sullen teenager.

Jinx brushed a golden hair from her shoulder. "As I said, Noct is working for me. We need eyes and ears over Chime, and who better than Seren?"

Nocturne snapped the suspenders over his chest. "Spying and gathering intel is my thing. Even you'd vouch for me, Mr. Dark Warden." He winked.

"Tell me what you've learned," Jinx ordered, before I had the chance to object.

Nocturne gathered us in a close circle, and his voice dropped to an overly dramatic whisper. "I've been scoping this place for days. It was crawling with Diviner until yesterday, and then bam! They all vanished. Not seen or heard a soul since."

"Vanished how?" I asked. They hadn't been taken by Dor, otherwise there would be evidence scattered about. "Did you see a portal?" Dor had never summoned a portal to transport Diviner for as long as I'd been alive, but since the Covenant had shattered, there wasn't anything to stop him from opening one.

"Nah, I saw some of 'em gathering inside this big building. Overheard 'em saying they were under orders from some guy they're calling the 'Redeemer.' They seemed plenty frightened by him."

The Redeemer? That sounded like a title Dor would bestow, but it wasn't one I recognized. No, that was more of a Glimmer-based term I vaguely recalled from one of their sermons.

None of this felt right.

"Sounds like a trap," Lucky said. He'd been paying attention after all.

"What do you think, Time Boy?" Jinx asked.

This was why I'd been dragged back to this place of adolescent misery—for my knowledge of the estate and expertise of all things Diviner. "They'll have aether sensors at the gates and various points throughout the estate. The moment you cross that fence, they'll know Chaos is in. So yes. It's likely a trap."

"Sensors *you* devised. How do we shut them off?"

Ah. So that was the *actual* reason I'd been dragged here. "I didn't design them; I merely facilitated their creation—"

"And I want to facilitate their destruction. Tell me how."

"Why are we even here? The estate is empty. The entire blasted city is empty. Dor's forces are focused below, on the clock tower. What do you plan to do, burn down an empty estate for laughs?" If Dor was creating portals to ferry across Diviner as well as his allies, then it didn't make sense to do so from here, not when they didn't have access to the elevators.

They would be creating such portals either in Central or within the Undercity. Being here was a waste of time.

"It's Chance."

I searched her expression for a lie, some trick. "I—What?"

"Tell him," Jinx ordered.

"I saw one of you lot inside with the Diviner—a Chaos male," Nocturne said. "Looked like that brute over there." He eyed Lucky. "And he weren't no prisoner, either. There was something off about him. Something wrong."

"It's Chance," Jinx repeated. "The Diviner still have him, and they're using him. I don't give a fuck if it's a trap. If Chance is there, we're getting him back."

Saints preserve me. The last I'd seen of Chance, he'd been getting his guts rearranged on a Diviner operating table. I'd been forced to leave him behind in my escape, with the hope my ex-bodyguard Ben could save him. But if Chance was here, then... What had become of Ben?

Stupid, stupid man. Of course I knew what had become of Ben. I'd known it the moment I abandoned him in Kronos.

He'd made that sacrifice for me. For Kayl and Ilona.

"I'm sorry," I said. "They'd already submitted Chance to the soul-splitting device. Corentine knows this—there won't be anything left of—"

"We're getting him back." Jinx's hardened stare gave me little choice but to acquiesce.

If the Diviner were using Chance as a puppet, then I could understand Jinx's desire to rip him from his captors' hands. I could understand the desire to come all this way just to destroy this estate and all Dor's foul machinery.

It was my fault. I'd allowed Chance to suffer this fate.

Jinx had brought me here to atone, and atone I would. "The sensors are powered by a generator further within the estate. It can be switched off, but we'll trip the sensor before we reach it."

Jinx slapped Nocturne's back, and he almost fell to his knees. "Good job we have a spy on our side, then, huh?"

Wonderful. We were placing our fate in the tiny hands of a swindler.

I relayed a series of directions to guide Nocturne through the estate and destroy the generator. I'd be more worried about him flying into a trap if I didn't know he wasn't capable of singing his way out of one. He was, after all, a menace to society, which was a useful skill now that society no longer existed. Once the sensors were down, we'd be free to search the estate.

All in all, I'd seen Wardens arrange company picnics at Meridian Park with greater strategy, but whenever I voiced my objections, Jinx silenced them. Never mind I boasted years of investigative experience.

She didn't trust me, that much was obvious.

Honestly, there wasn't much hope of finding Chance, let alone saving him, but if there was the slightest possibility Dor held him here, then I had to act.

I owed him as much. And I needed to earn Jinx's trust.

We sent Nocturne on his merry way. Some time passed before he returned triumphant.

"Sensor's down," he said. "Had a quick fly around on the way back—didn't see aught, 'cept inside that big building I warned you about. Something's in there, maybe your friend. I'd bet my mother's wings."

"Take us there," Jinx said.

Lucky remained on guard outside Timefall Estates as Nocturne flew overhead, guiding us toward this ominous big building. For a man of his stature, a 'big' building could be anything from a schoolhouse to a workshop, though a workshop was the likely option for storing soul-splitting devices.

I held my breath as I stepped over the threshold into Timefall.

As it had in so many visits before, time seemed to shift when crossing that invisible barrier that separated the Diviner from the rest of Chime.

The estate hadn't changed. The streets were impeccably clean and organized in neat lines, everything placed logically. Its architecture didn't hold the personality of Central's brick and brass homes, or even the Golden City's veneer, despite the bronze railings and window frames that adorned the perfectly square and symmetrical buildings. Back then, I would have described Timefall as characterless. Now, in my Chaos form, I could see it for what it truly was.

Lifeless.

As dead as paused time, where nothing new was born and nothing changed.

Jinx strode beside me, her gaze wandering across the estate with contempt. "You used to live here, huh?"

"A long time ago." Before the Academy, before I joined the Wardens and chose an apartment on Central with the excuse I wanted to be closer to HQ, closer to the Gate. Closer to the beating pulse of Chime's society.

"Doesn't look like much."

I supposed not. Many of these buildings looked the same, yet I knew those I passed—the library, where I'd read engineering books about Chime's trams. The church, where I'd once prayed for guidance over my Academy application. And the dormitory, where I'd bunked with other lads my age who struggled to hide their growing sinful nature from the masters, who thought masturbation was a sin worthy of a caning.

Memories as clear and blue as the Golden City skies.

"So," Jinx said, once again punctuating the silence. "Do you still want to fuck my sister?"

I almost tripped over my own blasted feet! "You wish to discuss this *now*?"

Jinx shrugged. "I want to know whose side you're on."

Truly, the maddening realities of Chaos meant I was subjected to the most random of tortures at the most inopportune of times. "I care nothing for Kayl."

"Really? The fact you keep avoiding looking at me is proof you're talking shit."

"Perhaps I feel some modicum of guilt. I used Kayl to free myself from Dor, nothing more."

"Sure. Though you were eager to shove your tongue down my throat when we met in Grayford."

I turned to stare at her arched golden brow. "You've seen my childhood home. I'm a man who was forced to grow up in a domain that discouraged forming intimate connections with others, as well as with a curse that left me touch-starved for the vast majority of my adult life. I'd return the affections of a dead tree if its withering leaves touched me first."

"I did try to warn my sister you were nothing more than a selfish bastard."

"She's Godless. She should have known better." The words tasted bitter on my tongue, but they were the truth.

I'd brought trouble to the Godless's door. Just as I'd told Walter I would.

But here I was. A Godless of my own creation.

With Chaos, I'd finally have a chance of realizing a world I'd once dared to dream of. A world without gods, without sin. A world that would be anathema to the pious. We'd already destroyed the Glimmer. It was possible.

Once again, I'd found myself lost in memory, and my feet had absentmindedly walked without realizing where they—and Nocturne—were leading me.

"This is it." Nocturne gestured at the building before me.

I came to an abrupt halt.

"Recognize it?" Jinx asked.

I swallowed a lump, my throat suddenly dry. "This is—*was*—Ambassador Karendar's home." The last time I'd returned here, he'd forced me to my knees, his belt...

No. That was one memory among hundreds I refused to indulge.

"You're up, Corinth," Jinx said.

I adjusted my spectacles. "Are you quite sure you want us to walk right into a trap?" It had to be a trap, with Chance as bait.

"I want *you* to walk right into a trap. You'll go inside, find Chance, get the fuck out, and then I'll burn this place to the ground."

Of course. Why risk their lives when they could risk mine instead?

Every nerve in my body wanted to refuse. To risk having my soul snapped back into the clock tower and doomed forever rather than step inside that damn building and face whatever horrors Dor had left behind.

To face memories I'd tried so sodding hard to bury.

But I needed to do this. For Chance.

"I'd feel more comfortable if I had a weapon," I said.

"Where's that stiff upper lip? You're Chaos now. You can take souls." She slapped me on the back. "Have fun."

Wonderful. Simply wonderful.

I took a breath and headed for the last building in Chime I ever wanted to enter. The door was unlocked. Where once, the mournful notes of a piano would welcome me, now silence reigned. With some trepidation, I stepped inside.

This house had always been hauntingly empty, and that hadn't improved. When I'd become ambassador, I'd been offered this sprawling space as my new lodgings—to bring me closer to Timefall and the Diviner under my command. I'd declined for obvious reasons, and expected some other pencil-pusher to do something with the place. But no.

It hadn't changed one bit.

An umbrella waited by the coat stand. The bookshelves were still full of its previous occupants' reading material. The wine cabinet was still stocked with whiskey.

The piano remained in the center of the room, holding it together.

Coffee wafted through the air... No, that was my overactive imagination at play.

I quickly scanned the room, but truly, I was alone. Someone *had* been inside—the shelves were free of dust and wear, as though time here had paused after the owner left. The lawn was still perfectly tailored. I took a few hesitant steps forward. A glint of brass shone on the piano top. A fob watch.

As I grew closer, my heart began to flutter.

Saints.

It was *my* fob watch!

I leaped the last few steps and snatched it. No bells alarmed. No fire fell from the ceiling. I ran my thumb over the familiar marred brass and popped it open. The glass was still cracked, as it had been for years. The hands caught between twelve and one, stuck permanently at the hour of my fall.

This watch had been inside my pocket when Kayl took my soul. Which meant the Diviner must have recovered it. But why bring it here?

Why, gods curse it, leave it in this house? On top of this damnable piano?

I frantically spun. Jinx had to be wrong. There were no soul-splitting devices here. Nor evidence of Chance's presence. I could tear through every room, but I knew I wouldn't find a single thing. Whenever Elijah had... *entertained* me, it had always been here. Inside this room. In front of this piano. Never in his chambers.

He'd fucked me here. Forced me to my knees, my hands bound, my back bleeding.

"You've sinned tonight. You know how Father feels about sin."

The fob watch shook in my hands.

For all my talk of affection, Elijah had been the first to love me. To touch me. Those delicate fingers had caressed and hurt in equal measure.

I'd clung to his affirmations, because I'd needed his approval more than that of my own god.

I'd needed him to profess his love. To believe I could be saved, despite all my sins. He alone could absolve them. Only a mortal man could grant another mortal that right, for only a mortal could understand what it meant to sin.

Though, there had never been anything mortal about Elijah Karendar, voice of our father. Not when Dor spoke through Elijah's lips.

Even now, standing in this room, my legs threatened to buckle, to prostrate me through sheer muscle memory. If Dor found me here wearing the face of Chaos, would he attempt to save me, still? Would he send another Elijah to bring me to my knees in search of absolution?

Dor had owned every inch of me, had dictated my very breath. What freedom I'd since gained was as fragile as a thread. I couldn't lose it. I couldn't go back to *that*.

Gods. I had to get out of here. I had to get *out*!

I stumbled back and tripped over my feet. My hand shot out and slammed on the keys of the piano with an awful *dong* as I steadied myself.

Something buzzed above my head.

A Diviner Warden aimed a taser at my chest. Another stood by the doorway. Two more came in from the back.

I've got company! I yelled at Corentine with the hope she'd relay my warning to Jinx and Lucky.

I dove behind the piano as more shots fired. Time rippled around me. The Diviner were attempting to slow time as they advanced. Had they recognized me? They must know Chaos mortals wouldn't be affected by time manipulation?

I risked a peek and made eye contact.

Bugger!

Dor would surely have witnessed my arrival from their perspective, would know I'd come back from the dead, except...

There was no life inside their eyes. Each of them continued to shoot their tasers in quiet unison with no pattern, no strategy, no communication between them. None of them were using pistols, though on second glance, they carried aether collars attached to their belts. Some also carried odd helmets, though I didn't recognize the design.

Saints. They meant to capture whoever trespassed here alive.

This was the trap.

The front window smashed open. Jinx leaped inside and reached for the nearest Diviner.

"They don't have souls!" I cried out.

She grabbed their neck. One touch would have torn out their soul, leaving their body to crumple to the ground, but I was right. The Diviner simply turned around and placed the barrel of its taser against Jinx's abdomen.

Her eyes opened wide. "What the—"

The taser went off, and she collapsed to the floor, her limbs spasming.

Another Diviner was on her in an instant and wrapped a collar around her neck, cutting off whatever powers she could have used to fight back.

MY DAUGHTER! Corentine screeched into my mind.

I couldn't reach her. More Diviner were pouring into the room from outside. Five. Ten. Fifteen. Gods save us, there were so many of them, and none possessed a damn soul! Their shots continued to aim closer to my spot crouched beside the piano.

They had me surrounded.

"Nocturne!" I yelled for all my lungs were worth. "Sing, damn you!"

I clasped hands over my ears and waited for the Diviner to fall. A soft lullaby hummed from the direction of the broken window. Nocturne's vocals were muffled by my fingers, yet the melody was soothing enough to almost entice me to let go of my hold. His dulcet tone had worked on numerous unfortunate souls across Chime.

But the Diviner weren't reacting. Because they didn't have souls.

Oh saints. Seren song was useless against them!

I didn't get time to utter my warning. A taser hit Nocturne square in the chest. He fell through the window and landed outside.

Lucky then flew in through the open doorway, and the Diviner all moved as one to follow him with their tasers.

This was my only chance!

I scurried to my feet and ran past them. Jinx was still conscious, barely. I rammed my shoulder into the Diviner looming over her and sent him sprawling.

"Get up!" I pulled Jinx to her feet. "Run!"

Half-dazed, Jinx stumbled after me. I kept a tight grip on her wrist as I dragged her toward the door. Some of the Diviner noticed my attempted escape, and I barreled through them, shoving them out of my way. A taser shot out, and I yanked another Diviner to me, letting him take the hit.

"Lucky," Jinx gasped.

I glanced back.

The Diviner had shot him down and were collaring him. There were so many of them, they swarmed him like a pack of blood-starved Necro.

Then they placed the odd-shaped helmet around his head. On top was a singular red button. One of the Diviner pressed it.

Aether tore through the room in a single pulse. Lucky lay still; the fight completely gone from him. No. Gods no. That vacant look in his eyes...

That helmet was a soul-splitting device. A sodding portable one!

Once again, I'd damned a Chaos male to a fate worse than death.

I didn't stop running.

Jinx tried to jerk free, but I refused to let her go and dragged her from House Karendar. I stepped over a pile of clothes—Nocturne's clothes, I vaguely realized. Serenity must have yanked his soul clear to safety at the first sign of trouble. Clever. At least then, the Diviner couldn't rummage through Nocturne's past.

"Fucking *stop*!" Jinx kicked at my shin, but the effects of the taser left her uncoordinated. "I'm not leaving Lucky behind!"

"We can do nothing for him." I marched her through the streets of Timefall until we reached the brass railing. I shoved her into a bush, and she fell flat on her buttocks.

She grabbed at the collar. "Get me out of this," she seethed. "I'll burn this place to fucking ashes."

"No, you won't."

She was on her feet in an instant, all weakness gone. She grasped my shirt and slammed me into the railing. The metal dug painfully into my spine.

"Don't tell me what to do, you miserable fuck! You left Lucky behind. *You!*"

I sucked in a breath. "I only had time to save one. Would you rather I left you?"

"I came here to find Chance, not to lose another one of my brothers—"

"Which was a pointless, stupid endeavor—"

"Are you calling me stupid?" She ground her teeth, and her grip on my shirt tightened. If it weren't for the collar, I'd be dead by now.

"I didn't say *you* were stupid." The words tumbled out of me, leaving me tongue-twisted. "But your actions are. You can't risk everything for the life of one mortal, especially if you get caught in the process—"

"I'm literally Chaos."

"Dor knows that. Remember, he is the god of logic, and it doesn't take much to out-logic beings of a chaotic nature. You cannot afford to let him use that against you. If you wish to defeat him, then you need to think like a leader, and that means not taking unnecessary risks, but making sacrifices for the greater cause—"

"I don't need a lecture from the likes of you. What have you ever sacrificed for the greater cause?"

"The Godless, for one. My decisions damned Dru, Vincent, Joe, and more. I made those sacrifices for what I thought was the goal to unite the gods—"

"Fuck you, and Fuck Dor!" Flame flashed in her eyes. "Fuck everything those fucking Diviner have ever done. I want my vengeance!"

"I'll help you get it, if you'll let me." I held up my hands in a placating gesture.

Slowly, I reached for the collar around Jinx's neck. She tensed, but tilted her head back, allowing me access. These collars had been designed to respond to my thumbprint. I wasn't sure if they'd still work after I'd been reborn as Chaos—if my fingerprints remained the same, or if Dor had changed the collars' design. He'd certainly seen fit to produce them en masse.

I slipped my thumb under the collar, grazing her skin. The collar popped open with a click. Thank the gods for that.

"You're a big fucking arsehole." Jinx slammed her palm into my chest, and I fell backwards into nothing.

Actual nothing.

Oh wonderful. She'd killed me again.

I floated once more within the twinkling aether between life and death, where time meant nothing and eons passed with a spark and a flutter. Truly, death wasn't the worst part of dying at all. It was being remade that got you.

It was moments like these that I thought of Reve and the many deaths he'd inflicted on himself just to find this moment of peace. Did the soulless find peace? It horrified me that Dor would so brazenly take the souls of his own mortals and use their bodies to set a trap for Chaos. Would Jinx go back and burn them all? I wanted her to.

But more than that, I wanted her to stop acting so—so chaotic.

I needed her to stop Dor.

She didn't seem to need me. Perhaps this time, I'd remain dead, and leave the fate of mortals and gods to someone else. Though as I thought the words, something yanked my soul forward, and I opened my very alive eyes to the glaring lights of the clock tower.

I sat naked once more on the cold metal.

How many deaths and rebirths could a mortal endure before they went mad?

YOU DID WELL, Corentine said.

Well? We lost Lucky and almost got caught by Diviner.

THEY HAVE TAKEN ANOTHER OF MY CHILDREN. I CAN NO LONGER SENSE LUCKY'S SOUL. WE WILL HAVE OUR VENGEANCE.

Where's Jinx? Is she safe? I'd ruined any hope I had of proving myself to her.

SEE FOR YOURSELF.

"About time you woke up." Jinx stood above me, holding a spare pair of spectacles. "Look, you're right. I shouldn't have risked everything trying to save a mortal who's lost his damn soul. But it pisses me off, you know? I can't..." She drew a breath, and her golden cheeks flushed red. "I can't let the Diviner get away with what they've done."

I put on my spectacles. "I understand." More than anyone. "I'm sorry we lost Lucky, but I *will* help you get the vengeance you seek, so long as you allow me my own."

"Fine. Get dressed, would you? I've brought you a little something." She gesticulated toward Joe, who was standing next to a dining cart complete with its own tea station—a pot of steaming hot water, two teacups and saucers, a milk jug, sugar bowl, and an entire plate of bourbon biscuits.

Beside it was a chair and a pile of clothes. A freshly pressed tan suit. Where had she stolen this from? Timefall? Resting on top of the jacket was my fob watch.

I picked up the watch and cradled it in my hands. I must have looked a state, standing here naked, staring at a simple fob watch.

This was the closest to an apology I'd ever get from Jinx.

Joe poured himself tea. "Would you like a cup?" He looked as stunned as I felt.

Fuck, did I need a drink. "I'd be delighted."

I got dressed and sat down for my first cup of tea since escaping Kronos. Returning to Timefall had drained me worse than death, but at least the soulless there wouldn't tattle and send their memories of my existence back to Dor.

There was nothing left for me with the Diviner.

My new life began now.

6

*You heard that clanging? I swear to god, somethings down there, under the
station. No, it's not the bloody Undercity, it's like it's... between here and the
Undercity. It's not the elevator. Course it's not the pipes.
Pipes don't sound like that. Like... footsteps.
I'm sure I've heard breathing. But there's no one left in Chime?
It's haunted by lost souls!*
—Anonymous, *overheard in Central Station*

I LEFT THE MESMER trio behind with strict instructions to behave, though
if they pissed off our new hosts and got themselves eaten for the privilege,
then they only had themselves to blame.

For the first time since everything had gone wrong—again—I actually
had a plan of sorts. It felt satisfying to be moving, to be doing something,
and running through grimy dark tunnels was part of my repertoire. Sure, I
was running with a mangy wolf who probably could eat me if I pissed him
off, but that wasn't much different from sneaking into a deadly asylum on
Witheryn, or breaking into a Glimmer workhouse, or getting shot in a riot,
or the many other fun adventures I'd undertaken against Harmony's
advice.

Oh, Harm. I wished she were here to see the hoops I was jumping
through to get her back. But first, I needed intel. See? I wasn't rushing into
danger. I was being *smart*.

My new wolf friend waited until we'd left behind the noise of the Fauna
campsite before bringing us to a halt.

"So, baby Fauna. Show me what you can do." Wolfsbane undid his
kilt—I quickly looked away before I got an eyeful—and I heard, rather than
saw, him shove it into his own drawstring bag. "No need to be modest.
Fauna don't choose mates based on appearance."

That was just as well. I turned back, and he'd transformed into a shaggy gray wolf. He looked even more intimidating with those sharp fangs, massive paws, burn scars, and missing left eye. Gods. No wonder the Wardens didn't let beasts like this prowl around Central.

The drawstring bag was wrapped around his back. Ah, I understood now. He could carry his kilt around with him no matter his form.

And now his expectant eye waited for me.

Did the old wolf want me to strip in front of him? Fat chance! I turned my back and slipped off my leggings and breast band. Better an eyeful of my arse than elsewhere. Once I'd shoved my clothes away, I wrapped the drawstring bag around my waist and transformed back into my smaller cat form. It wasn't ideal for carrying a bag around, but it would do.

Though at this height, Wolfsbane towered over me. I nearly toppled backwards trying to meet his gaze. "Can't Fauna transform into other animals?" There had to be something more useful than a bloody cat. "How do I do that?"

"Most Fauna stick to only one or two forms comfortable to them. To change, imagine the animal inside that you wish to unleash. It comes naturally to us."

Right now, I wanted to be something a little bigger than a cat. I imagined myself taller, and something shifted. My height grew, but didn't reach Wolfsbane's eye level. When I looked down, I still had cat paws. "What am I now?"

"A lynx." He flashed his fangs. "It'll do."

He ran on ahead, and I chased after him. He led the way back through the various tunnels and pipes, taking me through the guts of Chime. We made considerably faster progress than I had with Autumn and Freddie, and Wolfsbane's knowledge of Chime's hidden pipework meant he knew where to leap, which path to take, what dangers and pitfalls to watch out for.

In my Fauna form, traversing the pipes and platforms became second nature. My paws were padded and meant for running and leaping. My sharp claws were designed to grab and cling. Every form I'd ever changed into as Chaos had felt second nature to me. How had Quen ever expected me to choose one for the rest of my mortal life?

Eventually, the pipes began to go up, and jumping from one vertical platform to another burned in my legs.

"Can we take—take a breather," I gasped.

Wolfsbane didn't look impressed. "Fauna don't get tired."

"Well, I pissing do!" I plonked my arse down next to a thick metal pipe. "Do any of these pipes go directly into the clock tower?"

"Yes, but they're too dangerous."

"Why, what's up there? Diviner? Chaos creatures?"

"They're electrified. Tends to fry the fur."

That was one way to keep interlopers out. "Do all Fauna travel around via these bloody pipes?" It would explain why I'd rarely seen them on the Undercity elevator.

"Not all. Fauna can be... territorial. We find a dark den and claim it for our clan and kin. Though things are different in Chime. We can't piss on a lamppost and make it ours."

I snorted. "No, I'm sure there's some rule about that in Chime's Handbook." Though Fauna had a reputation for being ungovernable for a reason. "But don't let something as bothersome as Diviner etiquette stop you."

Wolfsbane grinned. "We don't. But we follow what our clan leader says, and in Chime, that's our ambassador. Or was. With her gone, Trixie fills that role. She knows how to manage a menagerie, and that's what we are."

"Give yourselves credit. You're more than that."

"With Trix, we could be. Enough lazing, cat." He nudged me with his nose. "Take a smaller form. It'll be lighter to move."

I didn't want to argue, so I changed back to my smaller cat. Nor did I want to admit it *was* easier to navigate the various platforms once we got going again. My body wasn't built for physical activity—at least not this sort. It was a Mesmer's body, all right. Built for plentiful naps and all the candy I could stomach.

An absolute age had passed when my paws touched down in something wet, slimy, and stinking. We'd reached the sewers.

Wolfsbane leaped across a series of crates left behind as a makeshift platform to avoid most of the damp. "This leads directly to Central Station."

We couldn't get much closer than that.

He paused outside a gutter grate. "This male you wish to rescue—is he like you?"

I supposed Quen was. Though really, I wasn't even sure what Quen had become. "It's... complicated. But you can trust him."

"I'm still not convinced we can trust *you*. Here's how this works, cat; we take smaller forms and scurry along the gutter. Wardens don't always look down. For years, they've never noticed us watching them, learning their security patterns. They thought Vesper were Chime's biggest thieves... The best thieves go unnoticed."

Shit, he was right. No one paid attention to Fauna. They'd really mastered the game. "You can get us into the station undetected?"

"Yes, but follow my lead. Their security patterns have changed since the Wardens took over. Stay low, and stay inconspicuous."

"Don't worry. I know how to play spy."

He shot me a suspicious look. Did I really have that sort of face?

He shrank, turning from a wolf to a tiny mouse. "Your turn," he squeaked.

I imagined myself at his height and felt myself shrink, but I was still taller than him.

"Smaller," he said.

"I'm bloody trying!" But no matter how hard I imagined myself as a tiny thing, I remained at the same height. "What am I?"

"No larger than a kitten. It will have to do."

With that, I followed him out of the gutter, jumping rather awkwardly up and then crawling through on my belly. We emerged next to a bench— *my* bench! The one with the broken streetlamp where Quen and the Godless would meet to scheme. What an odd coincidence. Wolfsbane and I scurried underneath it and waited.

Sadly, the streets weren't as empty as I'd expected.

Wardens patrolled the perimeter of Central Station, both Diviner and Umber. But the scene before me made my breath hitch.

Vines stretched across Central Station, from the ground to the upper walls and windows, covering everything in thick green roots and turning the station into a jungle. They blocked off all access into the station itself, and by extension the Gate and clock tower. Even from my crouched position at ankle level, there was no missing the vines curling around the clock tower in a tight hold, as though trying to strangle the life from it.

It was a web of greenery, a natural shield that rendered the Gate useless, which meant no one was going in or out of the domains. At least they were safe from Jinx.

The thickest roots were at the bottom, also blocking off access to the Undercity elevator and thwarting any attempt to get in—or out—of the clock tower. Umber Wardens tended to their handiwork, despite the damage they caused around them. Stray roots tunneled their way under Central's cobblestones and left cracks no Warden would have allowed only weeks ago. They were a serious trip hazard, for one. Where was the health and safety committee when you needed them?

This was the true terrifying picture of Diviner and Umber working together. A prison of overgrown weeds choking the life from the city.

Above, vines crept up the clock tower but couldn't quite penetrate the shield surrounding the clockface. It still glowed with pulsating aether energy like some damned second sun. That definitely had enough force to fry one's fur.

"See?" Wolfsbane's whiskers twitched. "There's no way to get inside."

Not easily. But it was aether that sparked above us. Chaos energy. It might repel the Diviner or the Umber's fancy vines, but it wouldn't keep me out.

But I wasn't here to launch my daring rescue attempt yet. "The Gate's off. I doubt they're powering it on with that many damn vines stretched across it. Let's get inside the station and take a look."

Wolfsbane led the way, and we skittered across the cobblestones in stops and starts, pausing behind the cover of the gutter, a lamppost, a trash can, until we edged closer to the station wall. I'd admit it was much easier to get around when smaller. Darting between shadows as a Vesper had its drawbacks, but as Wolfsbane had said, the Wardens rarely looked down.

We slipped through the iron bars of the front gate.

Gods. Central Station was barely recognizable. The vines were even more prominent here, stretching across the station concourse, and they smelled pungent, too, like freshly cut grass. Had the Diviner used time manipulation to grow them faster, or were Umber this powerful when given free rein? The vines truly covered everything.

The only space that seemed free of wandering plants was the waiting area, which instead had been converted into a storage space full of crates and barrels. The Fauna's much sought supplies. Though as these were gathered out in the open, there wouldn't be any easy way to break inside them and pilfer what we needed.

It wasn't just Umber and Diviner occupying the station, however. A whole group of Zephyr had taken over the tourist information booth and were using it as some sort of makeshift research base. The Wardens had put the station to use. In fact, the only part of the station that remained the same was the tea stand, which Diviner Wardens were loitering around, nursing a hot cup, because of course they were.

So where were the Wardens traveling in from? Did one of the inner private waiting rooms hide a secret portal?

I signaled for Wolfsbane to follow. Thankfully, the number of roots everywhere made it easy to crouch between them and sneak about, and I headed for the private waiting room doors.

Before I could inch any closer, a Zephyr came bumbling out, their wings taking up the entire doorway.

"Secure the perimeter," they trilled. "Chaos is inside the station."

Oh shit! They knew I was here. Fuck, I was a pissing idiot. I'd forgotten all about the bloody aether sensors Quen had set up, and here I'd gone and set the damn things off!

I was the worst spy. The absolute worst.

I doubled back and hid under a particularly large leaf that had sprouted near the tourist information booth.

"What's going on?" Wolfsbane whispered.

"They know I'm here." As I said the words, a whole line of Diviner Wardens stomped past, their thick black boots crunching over the Umber's roots with a complete lack of respect. My presence had cleared out the tea stand. Maybe we could steal some coffee and make this trip worthwhile; gods knew I needed some.

"Then we need to go."

What? We'd only just gotten here! "They're distracted. Now's the time to find something interesting—"

"And risk your fur? Now's the time to retreat."

"I thought the big bad wolf would be a little more daring, or did your balls shrink when you became a mouse?" They likely had, physically, which opened a whole new world of genital possibilities I probably shouldn't be thinking of right now. "How *do* Fauna choose their mates, if not by appearance?"

His mouse ears twitched at the sudden change of topic.

"Look," I said. "They're searching for me. I'll go be their distraction, you go search the waiting rooms. Find what we came for, and we'll meet down below."

"What will you do?"

I glanced up at the clock tower. "Put on a good show."

I imagined myself with wings. The drawstring bag slipped from my waist as my form changed shape.

And then I took to the skies.

Flying as a bird, or whatever form I now wore, was so much easier than flying as a Zephyr. Back then, I'd glided on my wings and hadn't bothered with the effort needed to flap them. But this smaller body took no effort at all, and dare I say it, flying was a thrill?

Below, Central Station shrank, turning the Wardens into little dots busying themselves. No shouts or screams followed me. Perhaps they hadn't noticed a bird taking a leisurely flight across the skyline, though my route went straight up.

Gods, I hoped I hadn't doomed Wolfsbane to being captured, but fuck it, I needed to know if Quen was here.

Shit. I'd escaped the clock tower once, and now I was willingly planning to break in again. Corentine may be unable to personally hold me hostage, but I'd bet my Chaos siblings would be waiting for me to walk into their trap.

As would Jinx.

That was what she'd be expecting, wouldn't it? That I'd be stupid or desperate enough to come after Quen. She wasn't wrong. But perhaps by walking into the trap I'd surprise her into letting her guard down? No, I was likely overthinking it.

As I neared the clockface, static from the aether shield tickled my feathers. I pushed through it, and drifted outside the large glass window.

And there, directly opposite me, stood Quen.

I wasn't sure what I'd expected. Jinx? My Chaos siblings? But gods! It *was* Quen!

He wore a tan suit, a new bow tie around his neck, his combed-back hair now shockingly white to match the silvery-blue coloring of Chaos, and a clean pair of brass eyeglasses perched on his nose. And he held a cup and saucer.

I was here to rescue him, and he was drinking pissing *tea*?

"Are you seriously drinking tea?"

I don't think he heard me—the glass was too thick—but his eyes widened at the sight of me, and he choked on his tea.

Kayl? he mouthed as he spluttered and wiped his chin.

Oh shit.

Mortals gathered behind him. Glimmer. There were bloody Glimmer inside the tower! Had Jinx brought them back, as she'd brought back Joe? For what reason? To build an army of Glimmer? That was just what I needed!

A pulse of energy rippled around me, and my form switched to Chaos.

Shit!

I fell instantly with a scream lodged in my throat. With no wings and nothing to grab on to, my naked-arse body could do nothing *but* fall! I didn't have a Fauna soul inside me—without touching another Fauna, I had no way to transform back and fly to pissing safety!

Great. Not only would I fall to my death and splatter the streets of Central, but I'd gone and ruined my rescue attempt after finding Quen—again!

And I'd flash an entire legion of Diviner my tits while doing so.

The Diviner. Of course! I could slow time!

I swapped to a Diviner form and cocooned myself in a bubble of time. It slowed my descent, and I found myself floating gracefully like a feather. No splatting necessary.

"It's the god of anarchy!" a voice shouted beneath me.

Oh great.

The Diviner had finally noticed me. Or rather, they'd sensed me fucking with time.

Fluctuations spasmed around me, and my fall dipped and bobbed. They battled against me as time jerked all over the place. They wanted me to go splat, it seemed, though that wasn't part of my plan A, B, or C.

They aimed their tasers at me and fired.

I switched back to a Chaos form and threw up a shield. "Will you give it a rest!"

Their taser strikes bounced against my shield, and I fell again, my fragile mortal body about to smash against the ground.

Something collided with me, knocking me off center.

"Take my paw!" yelled Autumn in her fox form. What was she doing here? Shit, she must have followed us through the bloody tunnels!

I grabbed her arm and instantly changed form to a Fauna. I didn't need to fly—my cat body allowed me to land safely on all fours.

Right in the middle of a circle of Diviner Wardens. Shit.

They pointed their tasers at me and Autumn. "Stay where you—"

A fluffy blur pounced at the Wardens. In his wolf form, Wolfsbane tore through a Diviner—his claws ripped through the man's shirt and chest, causing him to collapse and howl in utter agony—and then Wolfsbane quickly leaped on another, his teeth sinking into their silver flesh. Blood splattered the streets, but it wasn't mine.

The Diviner panicked. One aimed their taser at Wolfsbane as another tried to stop time.

I switched to my Mesmer form, suddenly erupting in height, and summoned a hypnotic miasma. The remaining Diviner instantly fell asleep and crumpled to the floor in a mangled heap of bloody wounds.

Shit, Fauna did *not* play around.

"Get this off me!" Autumn yelled.

Vines had crept across the cobblestones and were now wrapping around Autumn's back leg. She clawed and bit at them, to no use. The vines were too thick.

Footsteps stomped across the street. Umber Wardens were headed our way.

Wolfsbane tackled the vine with his fangs and gave it a shake, and I tried pulling at it, but the damn thing didn't come loose. The vine writhed in my grip with a mind of its own.

"It's—It's getting tighter," Autumn grunted. "Get it off!"

Something cracked with a sickening snap.

Autumn screamed. Her entire leg went limp.

Shitting shit! If Wolfsbane's sharp teeth couldn't penetrate it, then what could? Fire? I didn't have pissing fire—Wait. I did!

I swapped my form to Glimmer and let sunlight burn in my hands. The vine sizzled and finally retracted, flailing as it scuttled back to the Umber controlling it.

"You couldn't have done that before?" Wolfsbane snarled.

"I forgot I could."

"We'll talk about this later. We need to run!"

I didn't need to be told twice. I patted his head and swapped back to my Fauna form. Wolfsbane grabbed Autumn by the scruff of her neck and practically carried her as he led us away from Central Station into the nearest alley.

We paused in the shadows to catch our breath. Wardens ran across Central. Some looking for us, others attending to the mess Wolfsbane had left behind.

Wolfsbane gently lowered Autumn, and the poor girl's leg sprawled out awkwardly. Gods, I wanted to be sick just looking at it.

"I think—think it's broken," Autumn whimpered.

"What were you doing here?" Wolfsbane asked with quiet anger. "I left you with the Mesmer for a reason."

"I saved you, didn't I?"

"You wouldn't have needed to if Arkey hadn't flown off and—"

"Is someone hurt?" whispered a croaky male voice. "I smell... blood."

We slowly turned to a Necro standing at the entrance of the alleyway. Shit. None of us had heard him approach. Which shadow had he crawled from, and what was a pissing Necro doing here? Had The Nameless One sent him to spy?

This one wore the same black suit as most of his kind, his pale skin gray in the alley's dim light, though he didn't look familiar to me.

Wolfsbane bared his fangs. "Back off."

"Is your pup injured?" The Necro cocked his head. "We can heal her."

"I said *back off*." Wolfsbane let out a low growl.

"Our apologies. If you are ever in need of our assistance, you know where you can find us." Hunger flashed in his bloodshot eyes, and he gave me a knowing look. Shit, he recognized me, or his master did. For a moment, I worried he'd jump us, but the Necro bowed and then backed out of the alley.

"Trix will need to know what happened here," Wolfsbane said.

Great. What a fucking mess this had turned into.

Are you okay, Mama? Cosmo asked. *We're worried.*

It's all good. It wasn't good at all. *Everything worked out fine.*

I'd almost ruined our new partnership with the Fauna, but it hadn't been a complete waste of time. I now knew for sure Jinx was holding Quen captive and wasn't torturing him at least. And I knew she now commanded her own army of Glimmer.

But I didn't know what to do next.

Shit. I really didn't know.

VII

The city's prestigious clock tower is as ancient as the Gate. Built to rest atop the Gate's arch, the clock tower serves a few functions; to connect Central with the Golden City above, provide transportation between the two via the glass elevator, and also provide energy and plumbing to the Golden City. It is a marvel of Diviner and Zephyr engineering, the greatest construction the city will ever see. It has lasted for hundreds of years and is destined to last much longer. Without the tower, there can be no Gate, and thus no Chime.
—H. Bezel, *History of Chime's Clock Tower*

THE WARDENS WERE QUITE animated. Even from my view from the clock tower's window, there was no mistaking their movements—typical kettling techniques for riots. Except there were no mortals left in Chime to contain.

Only two mortals could have gotten them so agitated. Unfortunately for the Wardens, they both looked the same. Jinx had left the clock tower on her own errand, so I'd assumed the chaos below was her doing.

How wrong I was.

Footsteps tapped the metal flooring behind me in a pattern I'd grown accustomed to. The confident stride of a woman who knew her worth in the world and wouldn't stop until every mortal and god knew it, too. The kind of woman who would shake the very foundations of the universe, of chaos and time, to make a point.

The type of woman who would be the death of me. Multiple deaths.

Women were never satisfied, were they?

Jinx leaned against the edge of the window and examined her fingernails. "What's fucked them off?"

"It was Kayl."

Even I'd been surprised to see Kayl literally fly up here—I'd practically spat out the first proper tea I'd had in weeks! I hadn't known what fate had befallen her when I was reborn as Chaos, and I couldn't possibly fathom her intentions now.

Jinx eyed me. "And?"

She studied me—waiting for me to slip up and damn myself in some manner. Jinx likely knew of Kayl's presence here, and of the Wardens' reaction, which was why she'd returned.

This conversation was merely a test, though I had nothing to hide. "She flew up in the persona of a Fauna—a black bird. She couldn't maintain it, and fell back down, where I assume the Wardens attempted to capture her and failed." Failed, because they wouldn't be organizing a search otherwise.

"A Fauna form," Jinx mused. "She's not the soul-stealing type."

"Which means there must still be Fauna left in Chime," I confirmed. "Most likely within the Undercity."

"My sister always knew where to find the party."

"Kayl has the Wardens riled. If I were you, I'd use this to your advantage. Strike while they're distracted."

"How? The Gate's still off."

"The Gate's power routes through the clock tower. Unless Dor physically destroys the tower, the Diviner don't have full control over it."

"The Zephyr do."

"Then you destroy the Zephyr."

She turned to me with a smirk. "Is that what the Dark Warden would do?"

I bristled at that name. "It's what you'll do if you want to remove one of Dor's advantages. Take the Zephyr, and you'll gain whatever technology you'll need to defend against the Diviner. As for the Umber, your new allies will make short work of them."

"You really are a conniving traitor. Is that all it took to turn you? A fresh suit and a cup of tea?"

The tea she'd given me was serviceable at best, but when one was absolutely parched, even the blandest of teas became the nectar of the gods. "It's wonderful what a little morale can inspire for motivation. Though— forgive my Diviner metaphor—you're wasting time."

"Unlike my dear sister, I don't hop from one disastrous plan to another." The look in her eye dared me to mention Timefall, but I leashed my tongue. "Tell me, Time Boy; how do we destroy the Zephyr if the damn Gate is down?"

"I thought that was obvious. We turn the Gate back on."

"You gonna walk on over there and ask nicely?"

Really, now. Did I have to spell it out? "Thirteen years ago, I fell into this very tower. Even in my injured state, I was able to access the inner controls of the tower and redirect power." In doing so, I was responsible for the birth of the woman standing before me. "The same panel can be used to reroute power to the Gate, if the Wardens haven't gotten inside and cut the cables yet. All it would take is a burst of aether."

"Can I trust you to get your hands on those controls and not sabotage me?"

"Are there any other trained engineers in this room? You've kept me here for a reason, for my knowledge of the Diviner and for my stunning intellect." I flashed my most disarming smile, though alas, she didn't appear disarmed. "I can operate the tower and get you through the Gate, but you'll only get one shot. Once the Diviner realize what I'm doing, they'll cut *all* power, and you won't get another chance."

"You wouldn't be using this as an excuse to get back to Kronos?"

"Entering Kronos now would be suicide, even for you. Though as much as I've enjoyed my stay here, I'd rather not prolong it for eternity. Variety is the spice of life and all that. You'll need to force time forward if you want to hit Tempest, and so you know, Tempest is *not* a domain to trifle with."

"Too late." Jinx tapped on the clock tower's glass window.

The Wardens were already regrouping, having given up their chase. With that minor distraction settled, the banging resumed as Zephyr returned their hammers to the tower. Worse, vines were growing around the bottom half of the tower, visible even from where I stood. Saints. The Umber must have been growing them all this time.

They were going to encase us within a living prison made of bark and leaves. Or at least I assumed that was their plan. Clearly, they didn't yet know we had Glimmer on our side, and Ember potentially, who'd make short work of an Umber's handicraft.

To burn an Umber's roots would hurt them deeply. Dor wouldn't care.

"I *could* use my dear sister as a distraction," Jinx said. "She'd come back for you. Maybe I should dangle you out the window."

"Then Dor would become aware of my resurrection and ruin whatever element of surprise you have." Which we'd damn well almost lost in Timefall. "Kayl would also come for the Godless, and you have at least one of them on your side."

"Sinder? He's not her favorite heathen right now. Besides, she'd only get in my way. If anything, I need her as far away from the clock tower as possible. Can't risk her getting caught."

I cocked my head. "You still care for her."

Jinx snorted. "As if. But if she dies, I lose whatever souls she's carrying. Souls Mother needs. No, I think you'd make a much better distraction."

"You want to show your hand so soon?"

"I want to show Dor what he's lost."

"You'll earn his wrath—"

"Good. Angry, vengeful gods make mistakes. When the Diviner lay their eyes on *you*, they'll be tripping over themselves. You're my secret weapon." She patted my cheek.

I grabbed her wrist. "I'm not yours." My ire snapped taut, burning through me; an emotion I'd rarely felt as a Diviner, but now suffered in abundance as Chaos.

I wanted to defy her. To scream and wipe that foul smirk from a face I once deemed beautiful. My anger was misplaced, but the sickening dread filling my gut could no longer be quelled in this body, nor did I wish to contain it.

The freedom to feel came with a cost no Diviner dared pay.

"Careful, Corinth." Her eyes flicked to my hand on her wrist, but there wasn't concern there. Merely amused curiosity. "I could cut you into pieces and throw those at Dor instead." She had me by fair means or foul, and she knew it.

I sucked in a breath and released her arm. "We want the same thing. To end Dor."

"Then prove it."

Dor had taught me to fear. To despair. To await a fate I could only escape by shredding my mortal soul. Facing that—returning to *that*... I couldn't risk it.

I couldn't.

I WILL NEVER LET DOR CLAIM YOU AGAIN, Corentine said. *YOUR SOUL BELONGS TO ME.*

When Dor learns you have me... There will be no going back.

DID YOU INTEND TO HIDE INSIDE THIS TOWER FOREVER?

Honestly? Wouldn't that be nice? To have a moment where I could breathe, for once?

I COULD GIVE YOU ALL THE MOMENTS IN THE UNIVERSE. BUT DOR WILL COME FOR US. YOU WILL NOT BE SPARED HIS VENGEANCE. IF YOU ACT NOW, IF WE DEFEND THIS TOWER, YOU CAN BREATHE A LITTLE LONGER.

Even now, I continued to hurtle to my doom, didn't I? But Corentine was right—the longer I delayed the inevitable, the more time Dor would steal for himself. I couldn't abide that, either.

"Fine. I'll dance for Dor. But once we open Tempest, you're on your own." I'd no intention of returning to that blasted domain. "You better act fast before the Umber completely entomb us."

Jinx smirked at my acquiescence, though I wasn't doing this for her. "Don't worry about the Umber. They can wrap their pretty flowers around our tower if they want. In fact, I'd like them to think we're helpless and cowering inside. And then..." She placed her palm against the window. "Then we'll prove them wrong."

Despite my insistence on *not* wasting time, Jinx proved remarkably patient for a being made of chaos. We waited until night. Between the bouts of fitful rest and rounds of tea, I joined her by the clockface as the Umbers' vines grew closer and closer, squeezing the tower in an unnatural choke.

Their vines slowly pierced the Glimmer's aether shield and spread across the clockface. Leaves had already jammed shut the door by the window, effectively locking us in. Soon, a curtain of greenery would hide the clockface itself. Then we'd no longer have a window to the outside world, a means of being privy to Dor's movements.

Some part of my soul that remained Diviner cringed at the vines wrapping around the clock hands and rendering the clock tower mute. For generations, the clock tower had kept time for Chime's citizens, as it had for me. So many of my days had been spent gazing up at the sheer magnificence of the clock tower to ground me. To know it would always stand there, forever watchful.

Ironic that Dor himself would destroy such a tribute to the Diviner, Chime's most iconic monument.

Only one last *dong* would ring out across the city, one final dirge to toll Chime's death.

And then chaos would truly reign.

The hands groaned as they struck quarter to seven in the evening, and I finished off my lukewarm tea.

Joe came to my side, his eyes going wide at the twitching vines. "Has Jinx lost her mind? More than usual, I mean? We could burn them." He glanced to where the Glimmer, including Gloria, were gathered, their arms still outstretched, and pouring blood, sweat, and tears into the aether shield. Joe had kept them going without needing to whip motivation into them. Whatever he'd said to them, they'd taken it to heart. "Why aren't we?"

"Because this is my show." Jinx swaggered into the center of the room, dressed up as though going to the theater. With society's collapse, we'd certainly have front-row seats. Her crimson gown and matching heels held all the glamor and glitz of a Glimmer. "Corinth, with me."

I set my teacup down, and ran fingers through my hair, straightening it as best I could. Death and rebirth had negated the need to shave, leaving my chin smooth and stubble-free. With my new suit, I looked the part.

My hand instinctively went in my pocket and ran a soothing thumb over the markings of my fob watch.

Jinx had been planning this for days, hadn't she? I was merely her pawn.

I followed her across the room as Joe and the Glimmer stared. A giant round hatch spanned the wall at the far end of the room opposite the clockface, normally sealed by an electrical current that could melt skin from bone. But the Chaos of the tower had managed to cut the supply weeks ago. Now, the hatch simply acted as a barrier between Corentine's children and any interlopers who may try to break inside.

Tonight, the hatch opened.

One of the other Chaos, a small girl named Flux, waited for us on the other side. "Panel's charged and ready to go."

"You know how to operate it?" I tried to hide my surprise.

Jinx rolled her eyes. "You said blast it with aether, right? How hard can it be." She strode ahead, her heels tapping against the metal walkway that led further into the clock tower.

I hurried after her, my grip on the railing tight as the platform wobbled precariously underneath me. "If you're not careful, you could risk a surge—"

"Relax, Corinth. Flux knows what she's doing."

Arguing further would be pointless. Chaos mortals may be made of aether, but did that translate into the intricate knowledge of mechanics? One could only hope.

The clock tower's interior was a dark and claustrophobic corridor that would have been terrifying to navigate if Jinx didn't quite literally light up the space with her glowing golden skin. As we ventured further into the center of the tower, I began to remember the details.

This was where I'd fallen as a child.

I REMEMBER YOU, CHILD OF TIME, Corentine crooned. *YOUR CRIES WOKE ME.*

I'm sorry for ever disturbing you.

DON'T BE. THANKS TO YOU, I WILL SEE MY VENGEANCE.

What a legacy I could never have hoped for.

"Here." Jinx stopped by a railing.

The corridor opened to the inner shaft of the clock tower. I carefully gazed down. It was wide enough to fit the entire Undercity elevator plus the storage elevator attached to the back. It normally wouldn't travel up this far, but it had the potential to deliver wares all the way to the Golden City—or it once had.

The tower's inner shaft was an oppressive column of darkness, with only the occasional glaring red emergency lamp to light up the thick brass. From this height, I couldn't even see the bottom.

Ah. The predicament became clear. "You can't expect me to drop down there? Unlike you, I have no means to fly."

"You don't need to fly. You just need to fall." She grabbed my shirt and flung me over the railing.

I reached to grab the metal, but the momentum of her force gave me no chance. A scream tore from my lungs as I plummeted, harsh gravity pulling me to my doom for the umpteenth time in my damn mortal existence!

The emergency lamps flashed as I fell. I squeezed my eyes closed and readied myself for another plunge into the aether. Goodbye, cruel world.

And then I landed on a cushy surface, like a large balloon. The air whooshed from my lungs.

Something bounced beside me. "How did *you* ever become known as the Dark Warden?" Jinx asked.

I rolled onto my back and opened my eyes. "Honestly, I have no idea." My goodness.

I sat up, adjusting my spectacles, which had somehow managed to remain on my head. Jinx's Glimmer light lit up the bottom of the clock tower—or at least the platform level with Central and the Gate. The tower continued into the depths that led to the Undercity, but it was impossible to see, as I sat on a buoyant web of vines.

The Umber had infiltrated this far.

Jinx waited by the maintenance door. Vines had wormed their way through whatever gaps existed in the hinges. With enough pressure, they could burst it open, which was Jinx's intent. "You ready for the spotlight?"

Carefully, I stood, the vines a little wobbly under my shoes. "This reminds me of my Academy graduation. Should I have prepared a speech?"

"You want to hold their attention, not send them to sleep."

Oh, how she wounded me. I may not be an orator, but I could write a damn good speech. Sadly, my contribution to this operation wouldn't be printed in a yearbook.

LET THEM SEE WHO YOU ARE, QUENTIN CORINTH. WHO YOU'VE ALWAYS BEEN.

Jinx pressed her hands against the maintenance door and let the power of Gildola flow through her. I shielded my eyes as blinding light flooded the clock tower, followed by smoke and the acrid taste of burning wood and metal in the air.

She shoved the door open, and then stepped aside. "Have fun."

I was sure I would.

I trod over the writhing charcoal mess of the vines and maintenance hatch and stepped over the threshold into my new destiny.

A line of Diviner Wardens already waited for me, tasers and pistols loaded and aimed at me. Their silver eyes like an ocean of aether lamps amid Chime's nightlife. Their very moods shifted from apprehension and anxiety to shock and confusion.

Did they recognize me? Their old comrade in arms? A fellow Warden? Diviner? Their ambassador for a brief spell? Or did my appearance alert some base instinct? I looked Diviner—like one of them—though I clearly was not.

"Is... is that Clive from the tea stand?" one of them asked.

My god. Did no one have any respect? Tossers, the lot of them.

I lifted my chin. It was time to engage in a little amateur theatrics. "It is I! Quentin Corinth, the Dark Warden! Tell your god I have returned. *Dor!*" I bellowed for all I was worth. "Do you hear me, you inglorious bastard? I have returned!"

The Diviner were stunned into silence.

Aether buzzed around me. Was the Gate already coming back on? But no. The aether wasn't coming from the tower or from the Chaos nearby.

The sky cracked.

QUENTIN! Dor thundered above. Aether static hissed around the clock tower, and his giant silver eye materialized over the station. *WHAT HAS CORENTINE DONE?*

Corentine cackled inside my mind. *HOW DOES IT FEEL TO BE BETRAYED?*

The Diviner before me gasped. Many clasped their hands in muttered prayer to the god's gaze floating in the sky. Others fell to their knees in reverent worship. This level of devotion was beneath the Diviner, and more akin to the Glimmer's antics. But then most Diviner weren't blessed with one's god suddenly appearing above them like some spectral clockwork eye.

I could only tut at their pathetic display. "Such dramatics."

Though, my bravado was entirely for show. The sight of Dor floating there made my knees weak, and my heart was thumping hard enough to send me back to the aether.

Dor was *here*. In Chime, my home. He could pluck me from it. He could take me.

All at once, the Diviner collectively stopped their worship. They composed themselves, and their weapons once again aimed at me.

Oh bugger.

I threw up an aether shield as their tasers fired. I'd never summoned a shield before—it came instinctively and deflected their charged shots.

More shots collided with my shield in a peppered barrage. My back was to the Gate, but if they forced me to retreat, we'd never get a chance to open it!

I dug my heels in and thrust my fists out. *Anytime now!* I called to Corentine.

Air whooshed behind me, ruffling my jacket, as the entire tower surged with energy. Swirls of pink and blue aether danced in the air, lighting up Central Station and the many silver faces staring in wonder and abject horror.

Then the Gate burst to life, burning through the vines covering it. I risked a glance over my shoulder.

There was Tempest. Its night sky was dark and brooding, crackling too with electrical storms, which fit the mood of its mechanical god.

Jinx needs to move, now! Before Dor realized Tempest was in danger.

Shouting filled the station. The Diviner writhed as they pushed against my shield. Oh, they knew.

Something slammed atop my shield.

My legs buckled, and I fell to one knee with a gasp.

STOP THIS, QUENTIN! Dor commanded. Saints! His palm pushed down, squeezing my shield as though attempting to pop it. *STOP THIS AND REPENT!*

Sweat ran down my brow. My shoulders and spine screamed beneath the increasing pressure, until I felt sure I would snap in half. I couldn't hold this for long!

Where was Jinx? Had she already made it through?

Dor slapped my shield, and this time I couldn't hold it.

The shield popped out of existence, and I fell forward onto my palms, panting.

His hand reached for me.

No! I wouldn't let him take me!

But instead of grabbing me, his fingers floated above my head and wrapped around the arch of the Gate.

In the blink of an eye, he yanked on the arch. The Gate's portal flickered and then blipped out entirely as Dor pulled the Gate to pieces.

Saints, no!

The upper arch remained attached to the tower, but the curved side of the Gate fell in a pile of useless bronze cogs and debris.

The Gate had stood here in the heart of Chime since the dawn of time, and Dor had so callously ripped it apart. Perhaps he could repair it, but Chaos couldn't.

He'd damned us.

QUENTIN, he said again, this time with the quiet fury of a father disappointed in his sullen son.

I dragged myself to my feet as the Diviner surrounded me, their tasers primed and aimed at my chest.

It was over before we even stood a chance.

Kill me, I urged Corentine. *Before he takes my soul. Please. Kill me.*

Anxiety crawled under my skin, tugging at my muscles and bones to run. I'd rather die a thousand more deaths than return to Dor's clutches.

I'd rather see each domain burn.

SPOKEN LIKE TRUE CHAOS, Corentine crooned. *YOU'VE PLAYED YOUR PART WELL.*

We've failed.

HAVE WE? THIS IS THE BEGINNING.

Commotion came from further inside Central Station, beside the waiting area, as a Zephyr ran out, his wings flapping. "It's Tempest!" he squawked. "It's under attack by—"

Flame engulfed his entire body in a single *fwoof.*

More flame burst above the station and rained on the unsuspecting Diviner. They scrambled out of the way, their tasers moving from me to the source of the attack.

An entire group of Ember had appeared out of nowhere. They were dressed in a uniform of black leather, straight out of a burlesque theater. Some concentrated their fire on the Diviner while others took aim at the vines and roots tangled around the clock tower.

Their flame lit the station in a display of charred flesh and screams.

The Diviner regrouped. Time shuddered to a stop, trapping the Ember.

With time paused, they'd be easy pickings.

I leaped at the nearest Diviner and grabbed his neck. His skin tingled under my palm. The odd sensation resembled the soft touch of a feather on one's skin, or the teasing kiss of a lover's lips. My own skin changed from the silvery-blue hues of Chaos to the more natural silver of a Diviner. And… There. In the back of my mind, I could feel the itch of time. Knew it was exactly six minutes past seven.

I'd become Diviner once more.

The pressure in my skin built into a static shock that zapped through my fingers. To touch another mortal had always been a traumatic experience, but this was entirely different. No longer did I brace for the death of another, but more… a rebirth.

The Diviner collapsed into a heap, his eye sockets empty.

I'd taken his damn soul.

With my Diviner abilities restored, I thrust time forward. The Wardens had taken down a handful of Ember, but now they spun on me, aware I was blocking their progress.

Time shook in fits and starts, but in those gaps of reality, the Ember continued flinging their flame, none the wiser to the battle of time playing out around them.

Blood dripped from my nose. There were too many Diviner. I couldn't take them all!

The Ember fell, one by one. Their bodies collapsing in spasms. More mortals for the Diviner to take and do with as they wished.

And here I stood, alone. One defiant man against an entire army of Wardens.

Against the forces of time.

As it had always been.

IS THIS ALL CHAOS CAN MUSTER? Dor asked. *PITIFUL. CORENTINE'S ALLIES HAVE LITTLE FAITH.*

The Diviner laughed.

"Actually, this is all we needed," said Jinx. "It's called quality over quantity, you clockwork cockhead."

I spun and gaped.

Jinx stood in her crimson dress beside a glowing red portal—the same fiery portal Sinder had stepped through in Meridian Park, only now it showed Tempest's burning skyline—burning, for the very sky itself was full of smoke and fire.

My god. What had Jinx done?

She brushed ash from her dress with painful nonchalance. "While you fucks were pissing around here, we paid Tempest a little visit. Seems Zephyr can't scream for help when they're on fire. Maybe Daddy Dor should have paid attention to his own allies."

The sky thundered once more as Dor reached for Jinx.

She wagged her finger. "Nuh-uh! You don't get to turn up to the party late!" She grabbed my wrist. "You're my plus one." She winked.

"What are—"

Jinx yanked me into the portal.

*QUEN—*Dor's voice cut off as the portal closed behind us.

VIII

*On putting a report together of the remaining gods, let's begin with our
Father's allies. The Zephyr god, Zyclone, remains elusive. No mortal has
ever communed with them directly, except for their ambassador, Corvus.
Any arrangements made with the Zephyr must go through Corvus.
Thankfully, the ambassador is amenable to most requests.
Zyclone doesn't appear to have any particular goal or need, unlike other
gods. They seem content to tinker with their technical projects. Leave them
with their devices, but promise them a new toy or two, and they're appeased.*
—P. Bezel, *Personal Report on Zyclone*

I STUMBLED FROM THE relatively peaceful quiet of Chime's streets into the howling wind of Tempest. Oh, how I delighted in returning to my favorite domain.

The world beneath my feet lurched. Whatever portal had brought us here had disappeared into the night. I grabbed the bow of a boat—we were on a sodding flimsy wooden dinghy! There was nothing beneath us—no platform, no larger airship, just air and impossible gravity. I clung to the side for dear life as Jinx stood, swaying slightly with the boat's rhythm and apparently unbothered by the sheer oblivion below us, a hand at her brow as she examined the horizon.

The drop wasn't the most terrifying sight.

We floated within the middle of a cursed battle. Blazing airships ranging from tiny flying yachts to hulking metal galleons filled the skies, their hulls lit up in flames. Smoke fought the clouds for dominance.

Good gods.

Most of Tempest's ships clustered together, tethered by the walkway, but this was now to their detriment as fire spread between ships, eating through them like a Mesmer at a candy store. Even the walkway flapped into nothing as it disintegrated into cinders.

Yet Zyclone's fortress remained. The largest airship of Tempest's fleet overshadowed the rest like a dark blot in the sky. Small dinghies like ours flew around it, carrying Ember doing their damnedest to burn it, too.

Saints. There were so many Ember. Where had they all come from? More portals? Zephyr flew at them, trying to fight them off, but the Ember's flame held them at bay. Cannon fire blasted from the nearby ships still afloat; the roar of their attacks exploded overhead and rang in my ears. Some collided with the Ember, smashing them to smithereens.

In all my years of serving the Wardens, of hunting down criminals, handling riots, appeasing gods… I'd never seen anything like it.

This was war. True, bloodied war brought straight to Zyclone's domain.

I'd thought Eventide's fall was horrific. That losing Solaris was brutal. But this?

This… this was pure chaos.

ISN'T IT BEAUTIFUL? Corentine crooned.

Ash was so thick in the air, it made my eyes water, and I choked on the dry taste of death. "Dor's destroyed the Gate!" I yelled at Jinx, though my croaking voice was barely audible over the crackle and screeching of burning ships.

"We don't need the Gate," she yelled back.

"Then why did I risk my damn soul?"

She withered me with a look that said I was a bloody idiot.

Because once again I'd been bait. With the Gate gone, Jinx needed the Zephyr more than ever in order to traverse the domains—though clearly not, if Edana was willing to open portals and ferry her mortals across. They'd dangled me in front of Dor as a distraction to begin their true invasion of the domains in earnest.

"Why am I here?"

"Because the Zephyr have locked themselves inside their shitty fortress and we can't burn our way inside. Oh look, here's our scout."

I followed her gaze. A cluster of flying shapes made their way over to our boat. From this distance they appeared like Zephyr. But they were in fact Seren. Even Seren had been dragged into this madness, and Tempest's turbulent skies were no place for them.

At the center of the mass of wings was the familiar Vesper-like Nocturne. Wonderful. Could this get any worse?

"Ahoy!" Nocturne called out with a jolly wave. His dark blue skin was marred by soot, yet he spoke with such cheer, as though this were merely some exciting adventure. "We meet again, Mr. Dark Warden!"

I gritted my teeth.

"Report," Jinx snapped.

Nocturne landed on the bow of the boat and rolled his shoulders, letting his wings stretch and then relax. "We've examined the fortress. It's locked up tighter than an Umber's arse. Ain't no getting past their bulkheads. Best we managed was singing our way to the hangar, but they caught on to that trick quick enough—they're wearing ear protection now."

Jinx turned to me. "How do we get inside?"

"Why do you presume I'd have the faintest idea?"

"Because you're buddy-buddy with their ambassador."

"Oh yes, ambassadors are well known for placing their trust in one another and sharing their domain's secrets." Though it was true—I considered Corvus a closer acquaintance than most of the ambassadors I'd had the pleasure or displeasure of dealing with. He was a good conversationalist with many interesting stories, even if he came across a little odd. Though, my relationship with him remained purely platonic. We'd shared a drink or two, but we'd never progressed to sharing a bed.

Ambassadors certainly spilled more secrets when pounding one's arse raw. Zephyr, however, weren't the type. I certainly didn't see that changing now Corvus's domain was on fire.

Another Seren flew over to our group. "Diviner have arrived!" he gasped. Sweat beaded his brow, and his wings were a frantic fluttering blur. "Dor's opening portals!"

Saints. This battle was turning into a nightmare.

"Gather the Ember," Jinx commanded. "Burn anyone who crosses over through a portal. Don't give them a fucking chance."

My throat tightened. The horror must have appeared plain on my face, for Jinx smirked in my direction.

"Don't like it? Then help me get inside their damn fortress. I know they're hiding Zyclone in there. The quicker they give up and accept their fate, the fewer of their mortals I'll have to burn."

"You want me to negotiate their surrender?"

"That's what you ambassadors do, isn't it? Sit around drinking tea, talking shit, stabbing each other in the back. So go stab, and do it quick, before Dor decides he wants in on the action."

Since when had I been volunteered as the new ambassador for Chaos?

SINCE NOW. YOU CARE FOR THESE MORTALS, AND DON'T LIE. IF YOU WISH TO LIMIT THEIR SUFFERING, THEN CONVINCE THEM TO STAND DOWN.

Why should they? As far as they're concerned, we're the invading force!

DOR IS THEIR TRUE ENEMY. HE USES THEM, AND WILL DISCARD THEM LIKE THE REST. WE WILL SAVE THEM.

By murdering them?

BY FREEING THEM.

Freedom came at a terrible price.

THEN HELP THEM PAY IT.

What Corentine expected of me was too great a demand to ask of Corvus and his mortals. To surrender to Chaos would be unthinkable to him, and yet if he didn't, he would only drag out this unnecessary conflict.

To make these difficult decisions came with the role of ambassador. Would Zyclone see the logic in it?

Though Jinx was right. We had no time to waste. I had to act now.

"Take the boat," Jinx said, as though she'd read my mind and the conclusion I'd come to. "And take Noct with you."

"Why *him*?" I shot Nocturne a glare. "I'd have better luck on my own."

"Because if your boat blows up, you can at least take a Seren form and fly out of here, idiot." She placed one foot on the side of the boat and thrust herself up, leaping into the open sky. I watched with awe as she instantly transformed into a magpie and flew off, surrounded by an entourage of Seren.

Sadly, she left behind the one mortal I'd rather she hadn't. "So I've gotta watch out for *you*?" Nocturne snorted. "Fan-fucking-tastic."

"The feeling is mutual," I muttered, and carefully climbed over my seat to the dinghy's engine, my heart fluttering at every unsteady wobble. It was a standard outboard motor with a propellor to cast us out into the wind—the Amnae used similar engines on their gondolas back in Memoria. Nothing fancy, and nothing that would get us moving at an adequate speed. The hull itself was mostly wood with reinforced metal plating. In other words, one blast from a cannon would send me spiraling down into the depths of Tempest's skies.

Jinx really expected me to launch her campaign in nothing more than a flammable dinghy? I'd be blown to pieces before I even reached the fortress!

SHE WILL COVER YOU.

I'd have to bloody well hope so. "Tether yourself." I threw a rope at Nocturne, who caught it. "When the wind picks up, it'll stop you from being blown away."

"If the wind picks up, you mean?"

"It's a definite when." This was Zyclone's domain, and they would soon make their presence known.

Nocturne wrapped the rope around his waist as I yanked at the motor's cord. The little dinghy rumbled to life, and then I was sailing the skies to inevitable disaster.

Burning ships continued to light the horizon with the colors of dusk. Though night had fallen over Tempest, the Ember ensured I'd have no issue with navigation. They flew past on schooners, flinging their flame in coordinated attacks at any nearby Zephyr. The Seren, meanwhile, still flew around the ships that so far remained intact, no doubt gathering and passing on intel.

Jinx had struck first with the element of surprise, but her advantage wouldn't last.

And it didn't. Dark clouds swirled above with the ominous grumbling of an angry god. A moment later, a deluge of thick rain plummeted like a veil, returning the skyline to night. It soaked through my jacket in an instant, the sudden bite of cold giving me the shivers.

Nocturne landed in the boat and elbowed me to one side. "Shove over. I'm not flying in this."

"I told you." I struggled to keep the dinghy steady as the rain battered us every which way. It coated my spectacles, reducing visibility to damn near nothing.

"This is wetter than an Amnae's cunt," remarked Nocturne.

"You couldn't have described the current weather conditions with a less vulgar turn of phrase?" I tutted. "I thought Seren were supposed to be eloquent."

"Did joining Chaos not remove the stick up your arse? Or did it come back when you turned Diviner again?"

"You're rather well informed of what Chaos is and can do."

"I'm Serenity's pet spy. Knowledge is my thing."

"Yes, how did you suddenly become Serenity's favorite?" And favorite Nocturne was, if Serenity had brought him back for another round of mortality. "Surely Serenity must be aware you are a con man and a fraud?" And no gentleman, though to voice that out loud would be taking things too far.

"How else do mortals survive when they catch their god's eye? We make ourselves useful."

We did indeed.

As we flew closer to Zyclone's fortress, more airships emerged from the storm. These were battleships coated in metal and armed with turrets and cannons. An Ember's flame would be useless against them, and the deluge was causing their powers to fizzle out.

The cannons fired, smashing through a dinghy ahead of ours. I ducked as wooden debris soared over my head. Blood splattered my spectacles and was instantly washed away by the rain.

The Ember retaliated. They leaped upon the airship and flung their flame at its crew. Charred feathers burst in the air as Zephyr shrieked in fear and agony. I steered my dinghy past the carnage, the small hull bumping up against burned wood. There was nothing we could do to help either side except reach the fortress as quickly as we could. Though not even the rain could wash away the stench of burned flesh and damp ash.

Nocturne grabbed my arm and pulled himself up. "Oh fuck!" He pointed ahead.

Giant birdlike creatures gathered around the fortress. Falcons, Zyclone's immortal guardians. At least six of the beasts.

One of the Falcons swooped low and caught a Seren in their massive claws. The Seren writhed and screamed to no avail. Those claws ripped the Seren apart and tossed them aside, spraying viscera amid the rain.

Another Falcon snatched an Ember and bit their head clean off, swallowing it whole.

Nocturne still held my arm, his grip painfully tight. "Can't this thing go any fucking faster?"

"I'm trying, damn it!" Strong gusts fought against us. Our engine simply wasn't powerful enough to make it.

A horn blared behind me, and I flinched.

Another airship was coming up, fast. My heart leaped to my throat, but then—

"Is that Jinx?" Nocturne called.

My god, it was! Jinx stood poised on the starboard bow, returned to her Glimmer form and shining like a lighthouse beacon. She'd only gone and commandeered a bloody ship!

The Falcons homed in on her. Ember flung their flame out, causing them to swerve and screech.

Cannons fired from the Zephyr ships, blasting into Jinx's. She stumbled onto the deck, out of my view, but the ship held out.

It fired back.

What followed was a cacophony of explosions as each ship filled the space between them with gunpowder and smoke. Each round of cannon fire rattled my bones.

All attention was on Jinx, the real threat to this domain. She'd created a path for us, and we took it.

Our dinghy eventually bumped up against the fortress. I switched off the engine and reached for a metal ladder leading up to the top deck. I didn't cherish the thought of climbing in this storm, but with the walkways gone, I didn't have much choice.

Nocturne untethered himself from the boat and flew up with relative ease. Show-off.

The boat wobbled beneath me. With a deep breath, I leaped for the ladder. My feet slipped on the bottom rung. Saints! The rain sabotaged my grip, and I hung on for dear life.

"One step at a time," I whispered as I climbed. I'd survived this blasted domain once without soiling myself. I could do so again.

My arms were burning from the strain by the time I made it to the top deck. I flopped over the side, my lungs heaving, and I shrugged off my heavy, soaked jacket, and let it squelch to the floor.

Nocturne hovered out of sight. "I hope you've got a plan, Mr. Dark Warden."

Oh bugger.

The bulk of Zyclone's forces gathered on the deck—warriors kitted out in leather armor and carrying rifles, hand cannons, and even spears. Groups flew off together in a coordinated unit headed straight for Jinx's captured airship. Others were targeting the Ember, who were still attacking smaller ships with their flame, despite the constant rain.

A group of Zephyr had spotted me and strode in my direction. I wore the face of a Diviner, and Corvus likely didn't know of my abrupt exit from Dor's domain. If I could play this right, I'd guarantee myself an audience. "Stay hidden," I ordered Nocturne. "I'll handle this the old-fashioned way."

"With fisticuffs?"

"With diplomacy." I raised my hands in a placating gesture. "My name is Quentin Corinth!" I called out. "Ambassador to the Diviner. I'm here to speak with His Excellency, Corvus, and bring a swift end to this conflict."

The Zephyr warrior at the front—presumably their leader, judging by his bright red feathery headdress and the humongous hand cannon in his talons—cocked his head. "Dor sent you ahead? We asked for his aid, and he sends you? Our ambassador has not informed me of—"

"A change of plans." I forced a smile. "Any Diviner who have traveled in are getting burned alive by Ember. Dor asked me to coordinate his efforts with Corvus."

"Our ambassador remains within our command center. There are too many Chaos mortals in our domain to risk opening—"

"Which is precisely why I must speak with Corvus. Without the information I and Dor can provide, Chaos has the advantage, and your domain *will* fall like Eventide and Solaris. Time is of the essence."

The Zephyr clicked his beak. I'm sure his ego didn't appreciate a Diviner bossing him about, but theoretical information dangled in front of him, regardless of whether I actually had any, would certainly be tantalizing.

"I'm unarmed," I added. "And pose no threat to you or His Excellency."

The Zephyr nodded at last. Perhaps my dripping wet suit and sad mop of hair made me too pathetic to distrust. "Remain in my sight."

I swallowed my sigh of relief and followed him across the deck to the main hangar, my shoes splashing through puddles. More Zephyr ran past. I didn't dare glance back to where Nocturne lurked—if they spotted him, he'd be dead, but that was no longer my concern.

We squeezed into the slim gap between the fortress's large hangar doors and entered shelter. While it remained dry inside the hangar, the chaos hadn't lessened. Zephyr busied themselves—the workshop inside had been replaced with racks of weapons, armor, and cots where wounded Zephyr were receiving treatment.

Saints.

There were hundreds of wounded. Many wrapped in bloodied bandages, their white feathers stained red. Others were missing limbs or even large chunks of their wings. Many more were being treated for burns. Ember burns. The buzzing and clanging of weapons and armor being repaired drowned out their groans. The whole room stunk of oil and antiseptic.

I wiped my spectacles to avert my gaze.

OPEN THE HANGAR DOORS, commanded Corentine. *AS SOON AS MY DAUGHTER CAN GET INSIDE, THEIR SUFFERING WILL END.*

The control panel to the doors were closely guarded. I could quite easily stop time to allow Jinx to take over. But as soon as I started playing with time, Zyclone would notice, and the game would be up. No, it would be better to find Zyclone's control center first.

ARE YOU SO EAGER TO CONFRONT ZYCLONE YOURSELF?

Not at all. But Zyclone had always been an illusive god, hidden behind layers of machinery. If they felt threatened, they'd simply cocoon themself, and further prolong this whole sorry affair, regardless of how many mortals died in the process.

Once again, I navigated the brass corridors of the fortress, only this time, they were full of Zephyr huddled in groups. Smaller, younger Zephyr. Families. They'd come here seeking shelter.

We passed one young female Zephyr cradling an egg in her arms. A crack ran down its side, oozing with a bloodied yellow liquid. Gods.

This was what war between the domains meant. The price of freedom.

The Zephyr warrior led me up the metal stairs toward the top of the fortress. Here, the crowds of Zephyr thinned, leaving only battle-hardened Zephyr standing guard, spears at the ready.

"Wait here," the Zephyr leader commanded.

I did so. He disappeared through a nondescript bulkhead, which clanged shut behind him. Precisely one minute and thirty-six seconds passed before the bulkhead reopened, and out stepped a familiar face—Corvus.

He too was dressed in leather armor. A pair of goggles strapped above his beak made his black feathers even more intimidating. He pointed a taser at my chest. "Corinth. You're supposed to be dead."

Ah. Dor had at least informed his allies of my unfortunate demise. It had been a fifty-fifty chance. "I got better. Before you shoot me, please know I *am* here to negotiate a truce."

He tilted his head. "You're aligned with Chaos."

"My allegiances don't matter—"

"We have no interest in what Corentine has to say—"

"Wait!" I raised my hands. "Please. Let me speak. Put me in an aether collar. You must have one spare, don't you? That will stop any abilities I have."

"Do you think us fools? You designed those collars. We know how they work."

"Then tie my limbs, break my thumbs, blindfold me, whatever it takes. I want to stop this, Corvus!"

NO. IF THEY COLLAR YOU, I CAN NO LONGER REACH YOU.

If I'm to earn their trust, I must do this.

I FORBID IT.

I swore to serve you. Trust me to do so.

Corvus nodded at a guard, who produced a collar.

QUEN—

I yanked the collar from his talons, wrapped it around my neck, and locked it in place before Corentine saw fit to snap my soul into the aether.

The guards squawked, pointing their spears at me, but I didn't care. I sucked in a deep breath.

For this moment, my mind was free of mad, depraved gods once more. I finally had control over my own thoughts. "Thank you."

"Is that really you, Quentin?" Corvus still pointed the taser at my chest.

"Yes—it's a long story we don't have time for, but Chaos stole my soul. You may not have noticed, but they're desperately trying to get inside." If Corentine or Jinx suspected foul play on my part, I'd likely not see the dawn ever again. "Let me help you stop them."

"How? We've got Ember portaling in faster than we can detect and burning down our ships! Entire fleets are gone, including residential ships and hatcheries—hatcheries, Quentin! We're doing all we can to hold them off until Dor can assist, but we'd recently transferred the bulk of our shields into Chime, as Dor well knows!"

Gods. Dor had left the Zephyr defenseless. "I've been locked inside the clock tower the past week and working closely with Chaos, with Corentine and her mortals. There must be knowledge inside my mind that could be of use to you. Zyclone is welcome to dig into my brain and pull that knowledge out."

"Zyclone says you stood against Dor—"

"I was Dor's voice. He is—was—my god. Of course Chaos forced me to act against his interests, and dangled me before Dor. You know me. You know how much I care about Chime, how hard I've worked to stop this war from ever happening! This blasted collar is the only thing that blocks Corentine from my mind, that protects me from—from *her*." I clutched at the collar and squeezed back the tears that threatened to spill. "That I am this—this *form*... it shames me."

"You cannot free yourself?"

"While Chaos claims my soul, there is nothing I can do for the Diviner, for Chime."

"If Zyclone digs inside your mind... it could damage you beyond repair."

I lifted my chin. "If my final act in this universe saves mortal lives, then so be it."

Corvus lowered his taser. "You've always been a good man."

"Then let me die one."

He clicked his beak in sympathy. "Very well. Zyclone will take what they can."

"Then there's no time to waste."

The bulkhead opened, and I entered a circular domed room. This was the bridge of Zyclone's fortress, the command center. Its walls were made of hundreds of screens—monitors that not only acted as windows across Tempest, but that watched over the fortress's interior and exterior. They showed the scenes below deck, as well as the many wounded Zephyr, and Jinx's stolen airship still fighting through a blockade of Zyclone's fleet—the fortress's last defense.

Zephyr in white lab coats manned each of the monitors. Scientists. Engineers. The brains of their domain. They fiddled with brass apparatus and consoles that flashed red and spat out a series of *beeps* and *boops* along with the occasional hiss of steam.

It was altogether a far more advanced technological setup than even Kronos. Where Dor's domain favored clockwork mechanics, Tempest took it to the next level.

Though the oddest part of the command center was the giant metal egg in the middle. An actual egg, taller than me. It filled the room, forcing the Zephyr to step around it. The egg's shiny metallic coating reflected the many screens. Numerous wires protruded from the bottom of the egg and connected to the monitors, feeding into them with humming static electricity.

Could that be Zyclone? Outsiders to Tempest had never met the Zephyr god. Not even me, with my old Warden clearance. Rumor had it Zyclone took the form of a metal bird, not... whatever this was.

And there, standing awkwardly next to the egg, was Doctor Zachery Finch.

"Doctor!" I exclaimed.

Doctor Finch spun. His eyes were wild and frantic, his feathers puffed up. The last I'd seen of the good doctor, he'd been shot to pieces by Diviner during our escape from Kronos. Resurrection hadn't been kind to him— he still didn't possess a set of wings like every other Zephyr, and the poor man's expression held even more paranoia than before.

"Master Corinth? But you're... Oh no. Oh no, no, no. They got you! Why are you here?"

I approached him. "I could ask you the same."

He shuffled back a few steps. "Zyclone needs me. I'm their only mortal who has had experience and, well, *contact* with Chaos."

As Nocturne had said, we made ourselves useful. Mortals could sacrifice their one promised life in service of their god, only to be yanked from their earned eternal rest and forced into a fresh life of servitude. What choice did we have?

Corvus came to stand between us. "Corinth has agreed to let Zyclone examine his mind for any knowledge that could help us defeat Chaos. Assist him."

Doctor Finch's beak fell open. He shook off his nervousness and shuffled closer to me. "I feel obligated to inform you of what this process will entail," he whispered.

I glanced over the rim of my spectacles. "It'll kill me. I'm aware." One couldn't rummage through one's brain without doing damage. Though what would become of my soul? If it returned to Corentine, she'd know everything I'd done here.

She'd know I'd betrayed her.

"But I—I don't understand," he stammered. "You helped me escape Dor—"

"Does Zyclone know what Dor did? About the soul-splitting machines?"

"I—Yes. I showed them everything."

"Yet Zyclone is still on Dor's side?"

"The Diviner aren't the ones burning our domain!" His feathers ruffled again, and he sucked in a deep breath. "But they... they tortured Chance. I don't—I don't know what I'm supposed to think, or feel, or—or—"

"I understand, Doctor." I placed a comforting hand on his shoulder. Truly, no one understood more than I did.

"Did you save her? Ilona?" His words came out so quietly, so soft.

He'd died protecting a small Amnae girl. The daughter of my old Academy professor.

"She returned safely to Memoria." It wasn't what I'd wanted, for Professor Burns had asked me to watch over her, but Memoria was safer than Chime or my company right now. At least until Chaos turned its attention to Anima.

Relief made the doctor's shoulders slump. "Would—Would you like a cup of tea?"

My venture across Tempest had left me parched. Alas. "No, thank you. Now really isn't the time."

He nodded, and then fetched me a metal stool. There wasn't much he could do for my comfort—my clothes were still soaked through—but I appreciated the gesture.

A hush fell over the room. Even the beeps ceased. The Zephyr encircled the egg at a respectful distance as Doctor Finch stepped forward, giving me and the egg space.

I held my breath. I really wasn't sure what to expect next.

The egg cracked.

A jagged line zigzagged down the side of the egg before my very eyes. Would it completely crack open, allowing the god inside to emerge? A piece of its 'shell' fell by my feet with a harsh clang.

I swallowed a dry lump.

Cocooned inside the egg was a bird, all right. A mangled, twisted thing made of skin stretched taut across bone and wings. The feathers were few, as though this 'bird' had been plucked mostly clean, or was a newborn ready to fall from the nest. Its beak was larger than my head and a horrid rusted color. Tubes were embedded in its skin, pumping it with... what? Aether? Or did this being feed Tempest?

It reminded me too much of Corentine strapped to her chair back in the clock tower. Had this inspired Dor and the soul-splitting machines?

I was loath to call this thing a god, but this... this was Zyclone.

I half expected Doctor Finch to shove one of those tubes down my throat, but no. Zyclone's talons reached out to me, through the crack in the egg, and wrapped around the top of my head.

Their dry touch made me shudder.

YOU HAVE LIVED MANY LIVES. A monotone voice that crackled with the static of electricity spoke inside my mind. Zyclone.

Look inside them. See what Dor has done to your mortals—what he will do.

CORENTINE WOULD ASK FOR OUR SURRENDER. YOU ARE HER SERVANT.

No. I came to you to help stop this war before it truly rages across the domains. I am what I have always been—a public servant, in service to Chime and her mortals. If you side with Dor, he'll destroy it.

YES. A NEW CHIME WILL HATCH AND EMERGE. ONE BUILT WITH OUR TECHNOLOGY, WITH BLUEPRINTS FROM THE FUTURE.

And your mortals? What will become of them if Dor defeats Chaos? They'll lose their free will, and then you'll lose your spark—the modicum of free thought your domain requires to invent new technologies.

I HAVE SEEN DOR'S BLUEPRINT. HIS DESIGN FOR MORTAL LIFE ELEVATES THEM. FREES THEM OF THEIR BURDENS.

AS I WILL FREE YOU.

Oh well. That was a short-lived conversation. No point arguing, hrm?

I grabbed Zyclone's talon with one hand, and with the other, I pressed my thumb against the collar around my neck and popped it open.

Trust really was a rare commodity these days.

Zyclone tried to wrench free, but it was too late. That same tingling from before spread through my palm, and I sensed what Kayl and Jinx must have experienced.

Power.

I grasped for that power with desperate need and dragged it metaphorically inside my chest. All at once, my mind was flooded with hundreds of voices. Thousands. Many cried out in fear. Many more begged for help as Ember burned through their flesh, and their pain echoed in my heart, agonizing and raw.

Wings sprouted from my back, ripping through my shirt, as my hands and feet grew talons. I kicked my shoes off, as they were useless now, and admired the feathers that had grown across my chest and arms—white with the blue streak of Chaos.

Oh my! I'd become a Zephyr!

The egg fully cracked open, spilling metal eggshell, which turned to dust. Inside, Zyclone writhed and squawked with a pitiful hacking cough. They were little more than a flailing hatchling who'd never had the chance to take their first flight. They'd depended on their mortals for sustenance, and now I was the one to free them of their burdens.

They stilled, likely aware of their own demise, and let out one final shrill cry.

And then they collapsed into a pile of dust and feathers.

The god of Tempest was no more.

The remaining Zephyr in the room took flight. They fled for the bulkhead as though to escape me. Only Doctor Finch and Corvus remained.

Corvus fell to his knees, his wings cloaking him. "Why, Quentin? We trusted you!"

"I'm so sorry. I had no choice." I placed a comforting hand on his shoulder.

Truly, I'd had no choice.

His body faded underneath my touch, disintegrating into more dust. I turned to Doctor Finch, who wavered on his feet with a look of complete defeat.

"You serve Chaos." It wasn't a question, but a statement. His body faded before I could answer.

No, I didn't serve Chaos, nor Dor. With Zyclone's power flowing through me, I was free of Corentine's influence, free of servitude to her. When I'd been rebirthed as Chaos, Mesmorpheus had planted a dream in my subconscious with clear instructions on how to shield myself from Corentine's reach.

I'd needed a god's soul. Any would do.

And now... I was free. Truly free.

My body, my soul, my thoughts. All belonged to me.

Thunder shook the room. Unfortunately, I had little time to celebrate my newfound freedom. Tempest's collapse was imminent, and with the Gate destroyed, I needed to find a way out.

I ran from the control center and headed back through the brass corridors. They were already eerily empty, stuffed with piles of dust instead of stragglers and stowaways. Running with taloned feet and wings on my back was an altogether odd experience, and my feathers kept clipping the corridor walls and pipes, but I made it out to the hangar workshop.

This, too, was empty. The mournful howl of wind had replaced the clanging of hammers. Rain continued to lash down outside. Could I now control the weather? I'd hated this blasted domain. It was ironic I'd see its end.

I slipped between the hangar doors and approached the deck.

Airships surrounded the fortress in various states of disrepair. Charred debris floated across the skyline along with swirling dust. The Zephyr—my Zephyr—were gone.

But the Ember remained. They stared in horror at the gray clouds rolling across the sky. Thunder boomed around me, lightning flashing across the domain.

One such flash highlighted the glowing golden figure standing atop Zyclone's last airship. "So you've betrayed me, huh?" Jinx yelled. "Always knew you would."

"Perhaps if you hadn't insisted on killing me *multiple* times—"

"Yeah, whatever. Good luck escaping this place. I'll come collect that soul you're carrying when I'm done gathering the rest." A fiery portal opened directly behind her into Chime. She stepped backwards, flipping me her middle finger, and the portal swallowed her whole.

Blast!

I glanced at the Ember, expecting more portals to open and rescue them. But no. Edana snapped their souls straight out rather than risk a portal, leaving only their clothes to float away.

They were going to leave me trapped here!

I bounded across the deck. The Ember were gone. Even the Seren. Behind me, gray clouds were coming in fast, wiping out everything in their path. What would happen to a mortal left behind in a domain of nothingness? Mesmorpheus hadn't prepared me for this eventuality, and they could see the sodding future, damn them!

Focus the lightning! a familiar voice yelled inside my mind.

Doctor Finch?

Gather the lightning into one focal point. It carries enough aether to tear a hole between the domains into Chime. That's all a portal is—an aether-based tear.

It *was* the good doctor! But... *Why would you help me escape?*

Are you with Chaos? Or the Diviner?

Neither. I don't have time to explain, but I'm trying to keep the domains out of their hands!

There was a slight pause. *Focus the lightning, Master Corinth.*

Of course. Aether was merely a type of transferable energy, and lightning was electricity in its raw form. The mechanics were sound. If I could create an aether shield, I could surely gather such energy.

I clasped my hands as though to 'hold' the lightning.

Static aether sparked around my talons, blooming into silvery-blue light.

Oh my gosh!

Build it, then focus it.

I did so, letting the energy build until it formed a large sphere of pulsating light within my hands.

The fortress lurched and began to tilt. Blast! It was falling apart!

There wasn't enough time to gather more aether. I had to hope I had enough for a portal.

The fortress screamed with the clanging creak of a dying world. I threw what aether I had before me. It sparked, and for one terrifying moment, I thought I'd failed.

But then energy tore through the sky, opening a slim gap above Central Station. Sadly, high above Central. I'd not tested my new wings—I really did *not* want to test them—but it was this or a different type of eternal prison.

I ran for the portal.

Something caught my right arm and yanked me back.

I stumbled, almost falling head-first through the portal. Rope wrapped around my wrist, pulling taut and preventing my escape.

"Oh no you don't, Mr. Dark Warden!"

"*Nocturne?*" The Seren had lassoed my bloody arm! "What in god's name are you doing?"

He flew above me, both hands grasping the rope. "Think Serenity would be happy if I let you fly out of here?" he called over the thunder. "Nah. But they'd sure be interested in the little trick you pulled off."

"Why give Serenity the satisfaction?"

"Because Serenity's my god, you knobhead!"

The gray clouds thundered closer. That blithering fool would get us both trapped!

I tried to yank the rope free, but Nocturne kept a strong grip, for a Seren. Fine. I'd drag him through the portal with me. I readied myself to leap through.

The portal began to sputter out.

Oh, bugger me.

It won't hold forever, Master Corinth! Hurry!

I strode for the portal, each step laborious as I pulled Nocturne along. Either the portal would close behind me, leaving him behind, or his self-preservation would kick in and he'd fly with me to safety. His choice.

"Give up!" Nocturne yelled. "You owe me!"

I leaped through the portal. The rope tugged with finality, almost dislocating my damn shoulder.

And then searing agony sliced through my upper arm.

No.

The portal had closed.

It had closed on my *arm*!

Everything became a dizzying blur.

I was falling, I knew that. Wind whipped against my feathers, yet my entire body had gone numb—cold and clammy—and I couldn't feel my right arm.

Gods, I couldn't feel it at all, like it was...

It was gone!

I didn't understand. The upper half of my right arm burned with raw flame, but the other half sparked with aether, as though trying to form an electrical connection that no longer existed, leaving a sickening void.

Because it was *gone*.

I fell parallel to the clock tower, but the night sky, the city lights, Central—it all merged into one terrifying smudge. My wings flared open, more on instinct than anything else. My back contracted as I struggled to maintain altitude.

My wings flapped uselessly as I plummeted, and the sky blackened.

9

It was the worst day of my life.
I'd gone shopping with Dorian as I normally do, and we stopped off at that
cute little teahouse. You know the one that bakes those raspberry tarts? A
minor sin, to be sure, but we couldn't resist them. We'd just sat down with
tea when the screaming started, and then... Everyone began to die in front of
me. They disappeared. One by one. I grasped Dorian, squeezed him tight in
my arms and told him I loved him, and he—he vanished.
We were ordered back to Kronos. They won't tell me anything other than
the gods recalled their mortals due to some unfathomable disaster.
They won't open the Gate. I have no idea what happened to Dorian. I
don't—I don't even know if he's safe.
Am I being punished? For indulging in tarts? Daring to love a Necro?
—Anonymous, *overheard in the Plaza, Kronos*

THE GLASS TUMBLER FELL from my hand and smashed against the floor, shattering into shards.

"Mama?" Cosmo asked. "What did you see?"

"It's Quen!" I yelled, startling everyone in the tiny tent. "He's injured—we need to find him before the Wardens do!" I headed for the flap and nearly walked into Wolfsbane.

"Whoa, what's going on?"

"It's Quen, my partner—he's injured, I need to go!" I tried to slide past Wolfsbane, but the bloody beast blocked my way. "Move it!"

Wolfsbane grabbed my shoulders and forced me to still. "Calm yourself, cat. You think it's wise to rush topside after what happened?"

"I don't have pissing time for this! Quen's injured, he's—"

"You have time to tell me why I'm about to go running into danger for the second time this day." His canine eye stared at me hard until my resolve wobbled.

"He's right, Mama." Celeste took my arm and steered me away from the cloth flap. "Remember what Papa used to say—visions can be metaphors, and you need us to interpret what they mean. What did you see?"

I rubbed my forehead. "It wasn't a metaphor. It's real, and it's happening right this moment."

Since Mesmorpheus had given me their power, I'd experienced visions within my dreams, and now waking dreams—a vision that had struck me so fiercely, I could barely think.

Quen had become a Zephyr. He'd flown so high above Central, and then... he'd fallen.

Something had hurt him terribly, but the vision was vague. It had at least shown me roughly where he'd landed—somewhere in Meridian Park—and if I didn't find him first... Shit. Shitting shit!

The three Mesmer listened intently as I described my vision. After my botched mission to Central hours ago, I'd returned to the little tent the Fauna had given us, to rest, change clothes, and allow Freddie to spend time with Autumn while they patched up her broken leg. In truth, I'd felt too guilty to leave the tent and had wallowed here, until this damn vision, anyhow.

Wolfsbane scratched his chin. "I'm not good with interpretation, but you sure you're not imagining your friend falling from the tower based on what happened earlier?"

Oh, he was good at reading guilt on mortals' faces, wasn't he? "I know what I saw."

"He's got a good point," Castor said.

I crossed my arms. "Look, I know the difference between a vision and a dream." Or at least, I was beginning to learn. "I'm going to find Quen whether you help me or not."

"You're basing a rescue attempt on a dream," Wolfsbane said. "You were almost killed by Wardens, and then a damn Necro showed up—"

"Without Quen, I can't help you, or Trixie, or your Fauna. Do you want to spend the rest of your days hiding from the Wardens and scavenging for scraps until they eventually come flush you out? Or do you want a chance to bite back?"

"I'm starting to think you're more dangerous than the Wardens."

"That's because I am." Though probably not for the reasons he was thinking. I turned to the trio. "Can I trust you to remain here and behave? This is Quen we're talking about. I can't afford *any* distractions."

Cosmo rubbed their nose. "*I* can behave."

Celeste hugged my waist. "Please be safe."

I patted her head. "I'll try."

I really didn't have time to offer more comforts or to find Freddie to watch over them. Quen was out there, injured and possibly dying in a bush.

"What's your plan?" Wolfsbane asked as we rushed across the Fauna campsite and back to the tunnels. "Do you even have a plan? Am I wasting my breath asking?"

"We head back topside and sneak through Meridian Park until we find him." With smaller animal bodies, it would be easy enough to hide within the taller grass, weeds, and bushes at this time of night. It wasn't like anyone was mowing the lawn. My feline eyes made stalking through shadows easier than as a Vesper.

"Do you have his scent?"

"His what?"

"To track him? You're his mate, aren't you?"

"I don't know—he probably smells like tea bags." The only men I'd ever cared for smelled like sex when I was done with them, and not like the men of Harm's old romantic novels—sandalwood or whatever. And yes, I supposed we were mates—friends, pals, partners. Or were we more than that? Why in god's name would Wolfsbane ask? "I'm sure you'll be able to smell the blood."

My throat tightened. Quen's blood.

Once in the privacy of the tunnel, I changed into my smaller cat form as Wolfsbane reverted to his wolf. And then we were racing back through the pipework that led up to Central for the second time today.

I ran as fast as my tiny padded paws would take me. I ran until my lungs burned and my muscles begged for mercy. Every second spent underground was a second wasted. A second where Quen was hurt and alone. A second given to the Wardens, who were no doubt tearing up Central's streets in search of him.

The thought made me want to vomit and scream. I wouldn't lose him again.

I fucking couldn't.

"Why were you looking for me, anyway?" I asked, to try and take my mind off Quen possibly bleeding to death. Wolfsbane had entered my tent rather abruptly. Truth be told, I'd expected Trixie to claw my eyes out after our botched mission, but after the first hour had passed, I'd figured Wolfsbane had failed to inform his mistress of our trip topside.

"Trixie wanted to invite you for dinner."

"To dinner? Or *for* dinner? There's a difference."

He huffed a laugh. "We're not Necro. We don't eat our guests."

"Oh really? Then who do you choose to eat? Wardens are obviously on the menu."

"We eat each other, mostly."

I paused. "You mean that literally, don't you?"

He glanced over his shoulder. "Back on Juniper, we have many clans. Clans war. Those who lose become part of the winner's feast."

Autumn had told me as much. "That's fucked up, so you know."

"We know. Why do you think so many Fauna escape to Chime? Not all of us agree with such practices, but it's part of our nature, our maturity and mating rites."

Part of their mating rites? Fuck me. I'd never accept an invitation from any hot, brooding Fauna to get eaten out. That misunderstanding would ruin any night.

And now I was back to thinking about Quen and the promises he'd made while his soul had occupied my body.

This conversation hadn't made me feel any better.

We entered the familiar set of tunnels that led to the sewers, but then Wolfsbane took a different turn into the unknown. The oily stench of raw sewage followed us throughout, until my feline instincts picked up something… fresher. Dirt and flowers.

We squeezed our way out of another grate and emerged onto a gravel path. The silvery-blue glare of a streetlamp highlighted the bandstand opposite the green. We'd made it to Meridian Park.

It must be a cool night, for my breath misted on the air, but my fuzzy body didn't feel it. Like the rest of Chime, the park remained eerily quiet. Streetlamps lit the pathways, though it was the clock tower that helped ward off the darkness—it was still glowing with whatever nonsense Jinx was up to.

Vines no longer covered the clock tower, but evidence of their existence had been scorched into the tower's sides. What had burned them? The Glimmer?

Wolfsbane sniffed the air. "You smell that?"

"The flowers?"

"Blood."

Oh gods! Quen! "Lead the way, and hurry."

Wolfsbane thrust his nose to the ground and ran. I struggled to match his pace as he darted off the path and headed for the bushes that lined the park. I scrambled underneath brambles to keep up.

My tail caught on a particularly prickly twig, earning a sharp hiss.

Wolfsbane's paw batted my cheek. "Shh. Look." He pointed his nose ahead.

I crouched low on my belly. Lights were on inside the cricket hut. Shit, Wardens? Footsteps crunched along the gravel behind us. Wardens marched in, a handful of Diviner and Umber. They must have seen Quen fall from the sky and had come to the conclusion he'd fallen here.

If they found him first, I'd refuse to let them take him. Not without a fight.

"Where's the trail lead?" I whispered.

"East. Toward the lake."

Shit. The lake was fairly open ground with hardly any bushes to hide in. "How familiar are you with the park?"

"Familiar. Where else do Fauna go to shit?"

The park's groundskeepers really didn't get paid enough. "Get me to him."

Wolfsbane once again led the way across the green, using park benches and bushes as cover. The Wardens were busy organizing themselves, but as we passed the cricket hut, a group left carrying aether lanterns. Great. They weren't complete idiots.

A heartbeat later, the glistening waters of the lake came into view.

Wolfsbane stopped abruptly, and my nose bumped into his arse!

"What?" I snapped, but then the stench hit me.

Blood.

A line of blood smeared across the grass, dotted with the odd feather. Its trail led to a large bush by the lakeside.

Shit!

I didn't hesitate. I ran for the bush, scrambling over sharp pebbles and twigs, and I practically dove head-first inside.

And there, sat leaning against a branch, was Quen.

My Quen.

It was him. Half-naked, his bare chest the silvery-blue of Chaos rather than the pearly shade of a Diviner, and an absolute mess of blood, feathers, and leaves, but he was alive—conscious and alive.

He cradled his right arm, but there must be a trick of the shadow, because it looked...

Oh gods.

Most of his right arm was missing. His elbow, wrist, hand—all gone.

It wasn't bleeding—the blood must have come from the scratches on his chest—as what remained of his arm looked red raw, as though burned. What in god's name had happened to him?

I switched from my smaller cat form to my upright half-cat form.

His eyes opened wide, and he tried to shuffle backwards, his legs kicking uselessly in the dirt. "Stay back!"

Gods, he was scared. Terrified, even. What had my sister done? "Quen, it's me. It's Kayl!" I reached out to touch him, to hold him, and he flinched. What could I say to convince him I wasn't Jinx? "Do you remember when I took your soul? And what you promised me?"

"I…"

"You said if we got through this together, you'd buy me an entire bakery."

The panic in his gaze softened. "I'm afraid I'm in no state to fulfill my promise."

"Well, you better shape up, mister, because all the bakeries in Central are closed. Where else am I supposed to get a scone?"

"Now I know that's you." His lips curved into a half smile. "It's pronounced *scone*."

I swallowed a bubble of joy in my throat—a sob or a laugh or both—and carefully crawled to his side. In my rush to reach him, I hadn't considered being churned through the aether and spat out again as a completely different mortal may have changed him. "Are you my Quen?"

There was a sheen in his eyes. No longer the silver I knew, but the same aether as mine. "Until the end of time." He reached up and cupped my cheek with his uninjured hand. "Kayl." My name came out in a strained whisper. "You found me."

I placed my hand atop his. "Of course I did."

My heart ached at his touch. It damn near shattered. He was my Quen. Mine.

His eyes fluttered, and his touch fell from my cheek.

I held his face with both hands. "Stay with me!" I hadn't come all this way to lose him now!

The bush rustled behind me. Wolfsbane popped his head inside. "We've got trouble."

Oh, we had trouble, all right, for anyone who came within an inch of this bush. I released Quen for a moment and joined Wolfsbane.

Wardens approached, their lanterns flashing across the lake. It wouldn't take long for them to discover the bloody trail Quen had left. It wouldn't be easy to get him out of here, either. He was in no state to flee.

But… Quen was Chaos, now. I'd seen him turn into a Zephyr, a completely mad notion I had no time to marvel over, but if he could change faces as I could, then that was the only way we'd escape this mess.

I gestured Wolfsbane to follow and stirred Quen awake before I truly lost him. "Quen. Don't question me, but this is a friend—a Fauna. Touch him, but if you feel a tingle in your palm, let go." The last thing I wanted was for Quen to accidentally steal Wolfsbane's soul. That certainly wouldn't go over well with Trixie.

Gently, I lifted Quen's uninjured arm and placed his hand on Wolfsbane's head. The old wolf gave me a vaguely threatening look, but remained still.

I swallowed a gasp as Quen's body changed. His limbs shrank as they sprouted feathers, and he curled up into a feathered ball. I scooped his eyeglasses as they fell off his head and he landed on his tattered trousers.

Gods! He'd turned into a fucking *owl*!

For a moment, I couldn't help but stare. My Quen. An owl. His eyes round, as though he still wore his eyeglasses. His feathers a beautiful silvery-white with specks of blue. I quite literally could not believe what I was seeing. Was this how Quen felt whenever I'd changed form? It was no wonder he'd been so fascinated when I became an Amnae!

But even as an owl, he was too big to fit through the sewer grates. "This will sound weird, but can you go smaller? Imagine yourself shrinking. It's strange, I know, but if I can manage it..." I trailed off as Quen instantly shrank into a smaller bird that could fit within the palm of my hand. How had he gotten it so damn fast? "Okay, no need to show off."

"Cat." Wolfsbane growled at me. He pointed his nose at the crunch of footsteps approaching. "I'll distract them. Take your mate and run on my signal."

I patted his head. "Thank you. Don't get caught."

He nodded, and then pounced from the bush.

I gathered Quen into my hands. His left wing was crooked and wrong, but his right wing... Gods, half was missing. He certainly wouldn't be flying like this. "I'm going to turn into a cat and carry you in my mouth." Words I'd never expected to utter in my entire mortal life. "I'll try not to accidentally eat you, but if I do, squawk or something."

"Please don't," he squeaked with his tiny beak.

Oh my god. Tiny Quen was the most adorable fucking thing, and—Okay, *Kayl, focus.*

"My right pocket," he rasped.

I placed him on the ground a moment and rummaged through his pocket, pulling out... "Your watch?" It was the exact same design. Trust Quen to go through death and back and still carry this around with him. I shoved it and Quen's eyeglasses into my string bag—didn't want to forget those—and then transformed back to my cat form.

Quen said nothing as I slowly picked him up with my teeth, carefully trying to avoid his injured wing. It wasn't ideal, but I had to get him as far away from here as possible.

Howling cut through the night. Wolfsbane's signal. I peeked out of the bush.

Wolfsbane had caught the attention of the Wardens. He drew them away, giving me the opportunity I needed. I'd owe him one.

I was about to make a run for it when fire burst across the lake.

Oh shit! Ember!

A whole line of Ember raced across the green and tossed their flame at the Wardens. They weren't going to duke it out here? At *night*? Apparently, they were.

They must be searching for Quen, too.

Time slowed around me. The Wardens had been caught off guard, but in the end, the Diviner controlled time, and not even the Ember could beat that. Except... the Ember were still bloody moving!

"They're Chaos?" I said with my mouth full of feathers, which sounded more like *blair clayos?*

"Jinx must be nearby," Quen squeaked. His tiny body trembled in my mouth.

Of course she'd be bloody looking for Quen! Shit! We had to get a move on.

I crouched and stalked quickly amid the tall grass. Gunfire blasted behind me. The Diviner had resorted to shooting the Ember now, though I didn't dare glance back to see who had the upper hand. Were the Ember part of Jinx's team? I had no idea.

Screams mingled with the gunfire. Gods, I hoped Wolfsbane would be safe.

I made it to the sewer grate, slid inside, and landed in a smelly puddle. Quen groaned at the abrupt stop. I rolled him onto a dry patch as I positioned myself below the grate, claws out, fangs ready, in case anyone followed.

"You're a cat?" Quen said deliriously, his voice slurring. "A black cat."

The question startled me. "Well, yes. Apparently, every Fauna has a default animal form based on personality, and this is mine, if that makes sense."

"It makes complete sense."

"Are you calling me a slut?"

"He's calling you unlucky," Wolfsbane said. I jumped as the wolf squeezed through the grate. Blood and bits of flesh dripped from the fur of his face. "Don't worry, it's not mine."

"That's... good?"

"We best keep moving, if you're able."

No arguments there. I gently retrieved Quen, and then we were on our way back through the tunnels to the campsite.

As soon as we arrived, Wolfsbane created a path through the Fauna onlookers, which was easy enough due to his horrifying state, and I bounded back into my tent.

The Mesmer trio leaped up in alarm, scattering cards they'd been playing with.

"You're back!" Celeste hurried over.

"Is that *blood*?" Cosmo shrieked.

Damn it, I didn't have time for them. I settled Quen atop one of the cots the Fauna had set up as a bed. "Not now, Cosmo." I returned to my upright Fauna form. "Castor, take Cosmo for a walk."

Cosmo's lip wobbled. "But I don't want—"

"Now!" I snapped.

Castor grabbed Cosmo's arm and dragged them out.

Quen remained in his tiny bird form, his entire body quivering.

I crouched beside him. "Quen. You need to change back so I can take a look at you." I was no doctor, but there was nothing anyone could do for him in this form.

A whine escaped his beak.

"It's okay." I bent over and pressed a kiss on his tiny feathered head. "You're safe here."

Slowly, his body grew, his limbs expanding to fill the cot. I sat back on my heels to give him space as the change took. As I'd retained cat ears and a tail, his beak remained, and feathers protruded from his head. A strange mishmash of man and bird.

Scratches and other bleeding cuts lined his chest, likely from crashing out of the sky. He was lucky he'd found a relatively soft landing. But his right arm... Gods. It had been cut off above the elbow. A clean cut.

"Who did this to you?" Jinx? An Ember? I would kill them. I would absolutely *murder* the bloody lot of them.

"A portal. It—It closed on my arm." Quen squeezed his eyes shut and ground his beak. His body shook.

Shit. We'd all heard of accidents when crossing the Gate. That was why the station had barriers. But to lose an entire arm?

I draped a bedsheet over him to hide his nakedness, avoiding touching that arm. He needed a doctor, a healer, *anything*.

Celeste handed me a robe. "Is that... Quentin?"

I gratefully shoved the robe on. "We found him."

"He'll be okay, won't he?"

"Not if we don't get help."

The cloth flap to the tent flew open, and in walked Wolfsbane, back in his kilt and his face wet from washing off the blood—most of it, anyway. Beside him stood Trixie. She wore a different gown, this time in a pink hue, and her feline features did not look impressed.

"You found the man who's destined to save us all." She swaggered closer and then suddenly recoiled. The fur on her head stood on end as her cat ears pricked up. "Wait, are you fucking kidding me? Is that the Dark Warden?"

Wolfsbane stepped to her side, his face bewildered. "How can you tell?"

"'Is scent! You think I'd forget the scent of the only fucking Diviner at Erosain's beck and call?"

Anger rose through my gut. I stepped between them and the cot. "Quen isn't your enemy—"

"'E's a fucking Warden! A Diviner—"

"*Was* a Diviner. He forsook Dor—he's on my side."

"Is 'e, now? 'Cause you're the kind of broad that *'is* type lock away in correctional facilities—"

"Mortals change."

Trixie snorted.

"He's her mate, Trix," Wolfsbane said, like that was supposed to mean something.

"Course 'e is." Trixie rolled her eyes. "Why else would she risk my Fauna's lives to save 'im?"

"Because you need him!" I yelled. My tail was flicking behind me erratically, which only irritated me further. "I don't care if he pissed in your milk. Quen rejected his god, rejected the bloody Wardens. He was the benefactor of the Godless, for gods' sake. He's been working to undermine the Wardens for years. Even if you don't believe a word I say, Quen is still an asset to you. He knows the Wardens, the Diviner. He knows how to protect you from them."

Trixie lifted her nose in a sneer. "'E's not gonna be much use in that state, is 'e? Not even worth a meal. Toss 'im out with the trash."

A snarl ripped through my throat as my claws shot out. "Fucking touch him, I dare you."

I'd come to the Fauna to find an army, but it would take an army to stop me if they threatened my family. I'd lost Dru, Harm, Vincent, and Sinder... Quen was all I had left.

No one would take him from me.

No. One.

For a heartbeat, Trixie stared me down, as both Wolfsbane and Celeste watched in tense silence.

Then Trixie sighed. "Fine, 'e's your mate. I get it. But I'm not wrong. 'E's useless in that state—"

"He needs a doctor."

"Obviously. Wolfsbane? Take a look."

Wolfsbane approached the cot.

"Wait." I held up my hands. "You're a doctor?"

"Is that so surprising?" He raised a fluffy eyebrow. "I understand bodies enough to perform minor surgery. Clans war, and war breeds wounds that need healers. I can mend bones, stitch cuts—"

"All right, fine. Take a look but be careful."

I gave Wolfsbane space as he examined Quen. During our entire argument, Quen had been fluttering in and out of consciousness, so I had no idea what he'd heard, if anything. But he didn't resist as Wolfsbane pulled back his sheet.

"Blood's supposed to stay inside the body," Celeste said with completely inappropriate cheer. "At least, that's what Uncle Vinny taught us."

Gods, I'd almost forgotten Vincent had been passing on his medical secrets to the trio. "Yes, thank you. Can you go check in on Cosmo and Castor? Make sure they're okay?"

"You don't need me here? I can hold a scalpel—"

"We'll manage." I forced a smile. The last thing any of us needed was a Mesmer wielding a scalpel.

Celeste left us in peace. A sharp hiss snapped me back to Quen. Wolfsbane had touched his arm.

"Well?" I asked. "How bad is he?"

Wolfsbane stood back and scratched his chin. "Other than his arm? Some bruised ribs, a few scratches... The man's in shock. The loss of a limb will do that. His stump needs cleaning before it becomes infected. He's damn lucky it cauterized and stopped him from bleeding out, but infection will get him if we don't patch it up."

"What else can you do for it?"

"Do? It won't grow back, cat. It's gone."

"Listen to me; Quen's no normal man. He can recover from this." If Jinx could literally grow limbs after taking the power of Gildola, then surely Quen could do the same?

We hadn't had the chance to discuss what had happened on Tempest, why Quen had suddenly appeared in the sky as a Zephyr, but I could guess.

Even if he had taken Zyclone's soul... he wasn't in any state to help heal himself.

"Kayl," Quen whispered, his voice hoarse and full of restrained pain. "It's okay—"

"No, it's not okay!" There had to be a better way. There had to be!

Trixie shrugged. "This is the best we can do for 'im."

Their best wasn't good enough.

If the Fauna didn't have a doctor capable of fully healing Quen, then I needed to contact the one domain who just so happened to specialize in bodies.

I needed a Necro.

"Keep him comfortable." I strode for the tent's flap.

"Where are you going?" Wolfsbane called.

"To find a healer."

10

Disease is largely unheard of among the domains. Most gods do not allow their mortals to fall sick with illnesses and find such ailments distasteful. A shortsighted belief. Death and disease are the great equalizer.
As all mortals must die, all mortals are susceptible to disease. An illness of the body or mind does not discriminate between rich and poor. It seeks to bless all with its fruit. Through sickness, a mortal appreciates health.
Is that not worth celebrating?
—M. Morana, On Death and Disease

IT WAS THE THIRD time I'd gone running through the pipes and tunnels within Chime's underground-before-the-underground, and I'd be lying if I said I completely knew my way. Wandering around dark tunnels had been a fun pastime in Grayford only a few months ago, and that was a far more dangerous hobby than this. Here, the biggest danger was getting lost. The various tunnels were a complete maze, and my desperate need to get through them as fast as possible only added to my panic.

Every second I wasted in these pissing tunnels was a second Quen suffered. Perhaps I'd been hasty in shunning Wolfsbane's help and going it alone.

Thankfully, my Fauna nose made up for my woeful navigation skills, and it didn't take too much effort to find the sewers. From there, I managed to reach Central. I crawled under my bench and collapsed onto my belly, the cold concrete helping to ease the exertion.

Now how would I find a Necro?

Central Station was suspiciously quiet. The Diviner and Umber had retreated to the station house, licking their wounds, while Chaos remained within the clock tower, which continued to glow. But there were charred vines and blackened bricks everywhere as evidence they'd clashed. Had they fought here after Wolfsbane and I had left? It certainly looked like it.

The Gate was also a mangled mess. Someone had practically destroyed it. Great. Our main means of entering the domains had been reduced to rubble.

It hurt my heart to see Central in such an absolute wrecked state, but this was only the start. More fighting would take place. Gods. It would only get worse.

Once I'd recovered my breath, I crouched low and left the station behind me, heading into an alley around the corner. It may be quiet now, but I didn't want to bump into a Warden patrol. With Quen's life on the line, I had to be smarter about this, for a change.

Necro were spying on Central, likely lurking in the shadows. We'd been jumped by one on our last visit. *If* any Necro remained nearby, they'd sense what I was about to do.

I changed back to my half-animal upright form and redressed, leaving me with my cat tail, cat ears, and *very* sharp claws. I ran one claw down my wrist, hissing at the sting. I wasn't trying to hurt myself, but I let a line of blood dribble down my arm. Any Necro in the area would smell it.

Yes, advertising myself as a free meal was a stroke of genius.

I leaned against the brick wall and counted my breaths. In and out. Blood dripped between my fingers. Had I cut too deeply? Would I bleed to death before a Necro found me? Wouldn't that be amusing?

"You smell so beautiful, sweet thing."

My eyes snapped open. Shit, I must have nodded off for a moment, because a Necro male stood right in front of me—the same one from earlier.

Before I could even scream, he dove for me, his hand grabbing my neck.

"Hush," he whispered.

Static spasmed through my spine, as though I'd been shot with a taser, and my limbs went limp. Shit, he'd paralyzed me! I fell into his arms. He propped me up, his cold hand pinning my neck against the wall, as he lifted my bleeding arm to his lips and began to drink my blood.

There was nothing I could do to get this parasite off me.

He'd kill me, and no one would ever know.

Quen would never know.

The Necro paused and gazed into my eyes. He licked my blood from his lips.

A jolt shuddered through my spine, and I drew a strangled breath. My limbs were mine again. I didn't know whether to scream, cry, or run.

The Necro stepped back with his pale hands raised, giving me space as I collected my composure. "My apologies. I did not recognize you."

I examined my arm. It was stained red where my blood had run, but the cut had disappeared entirely. He'd healed it. "Do you make a habit of eating whoever you come across in dark alleys?"

He looked amused. "Naturally."

Stupid question. I suppose I was lucky he'd recognized me, otherwise I'd most certainly be dead. "I need your master's help."

"Oh? What do you require?"

"I need a Necro's healing skills."

Unfortunately, it had come to this. If I could take a Necro's soul, then perhaps I could heal Quen myself and regrow his arm, except Vincent had described the many years he'd spent learning biology and medicine despite his Necro talents. How would I even begin to regrow a limb? And as my new friend here had proven, I was no match for a Necro.

The Necro cocked his head. "Have you forgotten the terms of my master's bargain, sweetling? They would willingly aid you by returning your dearest companion to your side. Holcroft is an adept healer, is he not? Would he suffice?"

Gods, I'd do anything to get Vincent back. "My situation is urgent. Give me Vincent, and then we'll discuss our bargain."

"I think not. My master's terms were clear—bring a Chaos mortal to our domain, preferably one with your delightful face, and we will return your companion."

"How? The Gate is gone!"

"Bring a Chaos mortal here to this alley, and I'll do the rest. We'll be waiting."

Shit!

How was I supposed to convince a Chaos mortal to take a fun trip to Witheryn? Besides Jinx, I didn't know any of my Chaos siblings. And, well, Jinx was the only one crazy enough to make the journey. At least she had the right face.

Aw fuck, I didn't have a choice.

I needed Jinx for this.

I strode from the alleyway, glancing over my shoulder to ensure my new Necro friend wasn't following. Jinx had taken a Necro form before—could she heal Quen? No. I couldn't trust her, and Quen had been so terrified when I first approached him, when he mistook me for Jinx. I couldn't do that to him.

Nor did I doubt Jinx would refuse to help.

But she'd risk a visit to Witheryn if she thought she'd get a god's soul out of the deal. Mesmorpheus had tasked me with getting there first. Was I ready for this? To face The Nameless One? To steal their bloody soul right under Jinx's nose?

Oh no, I wasn't ready for this at all. I could almost hear Harmony telling me how woefully unprepared I was.

But this was Quen's life at stake.

And so I got undressed, took the Fauna form of a black bird, and flew up to the clock tower for the second time today.

Aether continued to swirl around the clockface, making it difficult to see inside. I couldn't tell if Jinx was in there or if she could hear me, but I had to try.

"Jinx!" I yelled with the tiny voice of a bird. Okay, perhaps this was a stupid idea. "I need your help!"

I fluttered on down to the roof of the tallest town house nearby and swapped back to my half-cat form. The last thing I wanted was to attract the Wardens' attention.

Minutes passed. I didn't know exactly how long, because the clockface was obscured by Jinx's shield.

But then a blur landed on the roof tiles, rattling them.

Jinx stood before me in her Glimmer form, her skin radiating power, her lips painted bright red and curled into a cruel smirk. Just as I remembered her.

"Trouble, sister?"

I swallowed the bitterness that bubbled within my mouth whenever I simply looked at her. "I need help getting into Witheryn."

"Oh really?" She placed her hands on her hips. "What reason would you have to waltz into Witheryn and pay the nice and cuddly Necro a visit? Wouldn't have anything to do with your Time Boy?"

"He's injured and needs a healer—"

"He must be alive if you're standing here. Heard he had a nasty fall. Is he still intact?"

"Did you do it? Is this because of *you*? You fucking—"

"Sure, I'd risk losing the soul he's carrying by letting that idiot die. What do you want me to do, send him a get-well-soon card?"

"If you don't want Corentine to lose her precious souls, then you'll help him *not* die." My words came out through clenched teeth, but Jinx was wasting my time and pissing me off just enough that I'd consider entering a suicide pact with Quen out of spite.

Jinx merely shrugged. "All right, sister. You've got me there. I'll play along if I can bring a friend."

"Fine." If Jinx brought more Chaos with her, then maybe we'd stand a chance. "Meet me in the alley behind Lady Mae's."

I waited for her to take off, which she did in the form of a Fauna magpie, and then I changed back into my own bird. All this form-changing and clothing-changing was growing tiresome. No wonder Wolfsbane stuck to wearing a kilt.

The Necro was still in the alley, waiting with an eerie stillness, as though he'd died and his body had remained in that stiff position the entire time. The smile splayed across his lips sent a shiver down my spine. Those lips had wanted to drain me dry, and the fact they'd touched me at all made me nauseous.

"Where is your Chaos friend, sweet thing?" he asked.

"She's coming. Be patient." Though I had to wonder if Jinx would leave me in the lurch. She owed me nothing. I'm sure she'd find it amusing if I walked my arse into certain death.

But then footsteps echoed behind me. Jinx entered the alley with a familiar Seren flying over her shoulder, and...

"Dearest," Sinder blurted

Rage churned in my stomach. "No. You don't get to call me that. You don't get to speak to me at all." I turned to Jinx. "Why did you bring *him*?"

"I made a promise. And Sinder here is my getaway plan in case things go wrong, which I'm sure they will." Jinx pinched his cheek.

Sinder jerked his head to one side, his nostrils flaring. Did Jinx piss him off as well? Too bad! Though, gods, I'd watched Quen put a bullet in his brain. I'd not expected to ever see Sinder again, and certainly not like this.

Why had Edana brought him back? What did it mean that he served Jinx? Ember had fought against Wardens in Meridian Park earlier. Were the Ember on Jinx's side? The Seren too? I'd not had time to question Quen on exactly what had happened in that pissing clock tower.

"And your Seren friend?" I asked.

The Seren waved. "Don't remember me? I'm Noct. We met in Gast's office—"

"You know each other, too?" Jinx sighed. "Fuck me."

Sadly, I did remember Noct, the tiny Vesper with wings. "Then you're here for Gast? I'm sorry, I never had a chance to tell you—he's trapped in the Asylum." Gast had helped me attempt to rescue Vincent from The Nameless One, but instead of coming back to Chime with Vincent, I'd lost them both to the Necro god. A failure that still filled me with guilt.

"Figures," Noct said without any kind of surprise. "Gast's the type to piss off everyone, so when he never returned, I dug out the good whiskey and waited for the end. Came quicker than I imagined."

"Noct here is my backup," Jinx said with a look that suggested now was not the time for reunions. Though if we found an opportunity to rescue Gast as well as Vincent, I'd take it.

I owed Gast a rescue, a drink, and more besides, but that didn't mean I wanted to drag Noct or even Sinder through Witheryn with me. "When you said you were bringing a friend, I didn't mean an entourage—"

"The more the merrier," the Necro said. "My master welcomes all guests."

I bet they did, which was what worried me.

Did I have time to faff around with my sister of all pissing mortals?

Celeste, I called into my mind. *How's Quen? Is he holding up okay? The Fauna haven't eaten him or anything, have they?*

He's sleeping, but don't worry, we're watching him sleep, Celeste answered. *The Fauna have been good to us. Why would they eat him?*

Never mind, just checking. Hopefully, Quen could hold on until I returned. *If anything happens, anything at all, pray to me.*

A portal opened in the alley behind the Necro, making me jump. It swirled in a circle like a dark void, with black mist trailing off its edges. I still wasn't used to the idea of random portals opening all over Chime, nor the knowledge the gods had always held this ability and had simply refrained due to the laws written on a damn piece of paper.

Beyond the portal lay Witheryn. At this time of night, its skies were a navy blue, clear of snowfall despite the landscape covered in a blanket of white.

"You're heading into Witheryn dressed like that?" Jinx eyed my leather breast band and leggings.

"You're one to talk. A gown? Really?" Besides Sinder, who could melt snow wherever he walked, none of us were decked in attire befitting the climate. But it wasn't like any of us were entering Witheryn for a fun tour, either.

"We have a changing room just beyond the portal," the Necro said. "If you'll follow me, I'll ensure your comfort."

I was pretty damn sure The Nameless One didn't care for our comfort, but they likely wouldn't let us freeze to death before they had a chance to eat us first.

I glanced at Jinx and shrugged.

And then I stepped through the portal.

True to his word, our new Necro companion brought us into the dankest, most dreary clothing store I'd ever entered, where even the dust was frozen. The dresses on offer were all thick, cumbersome, and presented in a variety of shades from black to very very *very* dark blue, but I chose an ensemble that would keep me warm without restricting my movement too much. In other words, no frills.

Sinder went for a similar look, dressing in a basic suit and forgoing any gloves or scarves. He kept his hands free, though the jacket and trousers didn't suit him. They were far too masculine, and not his style at all.

The Seren, Noct, went for frilly cuffs around his wrists and neck. The Necro had to personally tailor space for his wings, but Noct looked rather dashing by the end.

And Jinx... Jinx chose the most outrageous and impractical dress she could find. A dark gown that flowed in multiple layered skirts and lace, as though she were preparing for a funeral. We could have gotten moving a lot quicker if she hadn't insisted on switching to a Necro form and touching up her makeup. Then she put on bloody heels. Heels! In *this* weather? I raised my eyebrow in Sinder's direction as my subtle way of commenting on how ridiculous she was being, before I remembered we weren't on speaking terms.

With that sorted, we squeezed into a carriage together, which took far longer than it should have, thanks to Jinx's stupid dress, and then we were on our way to gods knew where.

"I thought the plan was to burn our way across Witheryn?" Sinder whined. He sat opposite me and next to Jinx, his fists constantly clenching and unclenching around a flicker of flame. "Not take a tour."

Jinx patted his knee, much to his annoyance. "You want to find your lover in one piece, don't you? Do as I say, and we won't need to stitch anyone back together."

Of course Sinder was here for Vincent. He'd made his motives perfectly clear when he betrayed me. I glanced sideways at Noct, who sat next to me and was staring out the carriage window. He'd come for Gast.

Jinx had come for a soul, same as me, but not any soul would do. Yes, it was massively awkward to be sharing a carriage with the two biggest arses of my life. And yes, we were being carted to a place of unending suffering and torture, but the four of us had forged an unspoken truce for now. As angry as I was at both Jinx and Sinder, I didn't wish for their deaths.

I wouldn't wish The Nameless One on *any* mortal.

Snowflakes flurried past as our carriage's wheels churned through the ice and snow. It was too dark outside to see where the Necro were driving us, but the journey was taking damn long. I couldn't keep myself from fiddling with my new coat's buttons or tapping my foot.

"Will you fucking sit still?" Jinx snapped.

"Why don't you come over here and make me? Can you even move in that gods-awful getup?"

"You're just jealous I called dibs."

"Jealous?" I snorted. "When The Nameless One bites your head off, I'll be long gone, and not wrestling with my damn skirts."

"That's all you're good at, dear sister. Running away."

"It's called being practical. You've not lived long enough to know to choose substance over style."

"Like you know anything about being practical. Why don't we ask our mutual friend?" Jinx turned to Sinder, who sat with his arms bunched around his chest.

"Leave me out of it," he muttered. "But Kayl has a point. Do you really expect to fight a god while dressed to the nines?"

"How else would I fight a god? It's called making an impression."

"I don't think The Nameless One cares if your lipstick is on point, darling."

"My *ah-may-zing* lipstick is the last thing that fucker will ever see."

"Can you at least take this seriously?" I said. "You haven't forgotten which domain we're in?"

"Don't worry your silly little head, sister. We've got our friend here to sing the Necro to sleep."

"I'll sing you both to sleep in a minute," Noct murmured.

"Please do," Sinder drawled.

"Don't you dare!" Jinx and I yelled at the same time.

We glared at each other, our loathing completely mutual. To think we'd spent our entire lives together. How had we ever managed that?

"*Do* we actually have a plan?" Sinder asked. "Besides walking into an obvious trap? The Godless at least had an escape plan."

Jinx smoothed her skirts. "The Godless fucked up most of their plans, didn't they?"

"Not all—"

"Right, just the ones my sister was in charge of." Jinx blew a kiss in my direction.

I flipped her off.

The carriage slowed to a stop. Were we here already? Wherever here was. I reached over Noct, pinning him to his seat, as I strained to get a better look out the window.

We'd parked behind iron gates within a familiar courtyard. Shit. They'd taken us to the Asylum. Well, where else would they have taken us?

The carriage door swung open, sending a flurry of snow and cold air inside, which ruffled Jinx's dress. The Necro driver beckoned us out. "We've arrived."

Jinx used Sinder's shoulder to push herself up. "Ladies first." She forced her dress through the carriage door, the layers contorting and then puffing out with a comical *whomf.*

Sinder rolled his eyes and gestured at me. "After you."

I brushed past him with my chin held high.

The last time I'd visited the Asylum had been through the side gate of an abattoir. This time, we were given the VIP treatment as the massive iron doors at the front opened wide, and a group of Necro came out to greet us, headed by the Necro ambassador. Mona? Moron? Something like that.

A lace veil covered the ambassador's face, but she didn't bother to remove it as she addressed us. "Ambassador Arkey and guests. Welcome."

"She's not our ambassador," Jinx said.

Really? I shot Jinx a look. "I'm here representing myself to bargain with The Nameless One."

"Our apologies." The ambassador dipped a polite curtsy. "I am Lady Morana. If you and your companions would like to follow." She swept her skirt to one side as she strode for the door without checking if we'd follow.

Oh, that's right. Morana.

Sinder bent his head close. "What exactly did you offer to bargain with The Nameless One?" he whispered.

"Me, of course," Jinx said. "What else would The Nameless One want?"

Sinder chewed on his bottom lip. What could he say? That it was despicable of me to offer my own sister to free Vincent, as though he hadn't offered me on a silver platter for the same damn reason?

Noct stood next to me, his neck craning as he took in the size of the Asylum. "After everything Gast told me about this place, here I am, helping to spring the sorry bastard. We're not leaving here alive, are we?"

"There are worse things than death," I said.

"Like pairing those heels with *that* dress." Sinder nodded at Jinx walking on ahead, somehow traversing the icy stone courtyard.

Damn you, Sinder. I would have laughed, if I didn't hate him, and we weren't about to walk into my worst nightmares. I glanced at him with a look of cool detachment, and while he tried to appear as nonchalant as me, I'd known him long enough to spot the charade.

Oh, fuck it.

Was I really any better than Sinder, for all I'd done? For what I would do for my family?

We'd need a little humor to survive Witheryn. I draped my hand over his shoulder and leaned close. "I don't know. I think Jinx has the right idea about making an impression when tangling with a god. But *that* shade of lipstick? What would you pick?"

"For you, darling? You'd look glam in anything." Tears welled in the corners of his eyes, and his lower lip wobbled. "I'm sorry. I know I can't take it back, but I'm sorry. I'm *so* sorry, for everything—"

I pulled him into a hug.

He shook against me with repressed sobs before ripping himself away. "This isn't the right time. After everything..." He sucked in a strangled breath. "I'm not—not myself anymore. Edana remade me, and she..." He rolled up his sleeves. Where once his arms had been inked with flaming tattoos to hide the scars the Glimmer had inflicted, now there was smooth red skin. Even the *sinner* tattoo across his collarbone was gone. "Vincent marked me, and Edana removed those marks. I need them."

"Are you fucks coming or what?" Jinx called.

Shit. Sinder had betrayed me, and maybe I wasn't ready to forgive him yet—maybe it would be stupid of me to try—but I couldn't stay mad for long. Not with the Godless. Not when I knew what the gods had put him through.

"We'll get Vincent back." I glanced at Noct. "And Gast."

This was my mistake to fix.

Entering the Asylum from the front didn't make the experience any less terrifying than wading through an abattoir, nor was it any warmer. Even my cat ears and fur couldn't ward off the cold, though the tremor in my hands wasn't from the temperature. Maybe the dark, foreboding walls of the Asylum were comforting to a Necro, but it felt like walking into a dark alley with one's instincts on high alert.

We passed a reception desk, manned by a Necro woman, that only served to carve out some sort of normality, but that was all Necro, wasn't it? Unnatural beauty. An uncanny sense of reality. Everything about them, about this place, screamed wrongness. Still, I kept my footsteps steady, following Jinx as Sinder and Noct trailed behind.

The ambassador swung open a metal gate, admitting us further inside. It clanged shut behind us, trapping us.

Mama. Celeste's voice came through. *Mama, are you there?*

What is it? Is Quen okay?

He's awake. He's asking for you... I think he's hurting.

What bloody timing. I couldn't get back now. *Make him comfortable and get him a cup of tea or something. I'll be back as soon as I can.*

Where are you?

I didn't want to stress Quen further with the truth. *I'm finding him help.*

My cat ears pricked at movement around me. Shit, I remembered what we were walking into. Silver lamps shone pools of light upon the many cells.

Rows and rows of steel bars kept the Asylum's occupants separate from us. Most had been blood-starved Necro, but there hadn't been *this* many mortals. These cells were full.

I squinted, and my feline senses picked up groaning, whimpering, and an awful stench, like a combination of rot, feces, and... charred skin. Oh gods.

There were Ember in these cells. Seren too. Shit. Had the Necro captured them? Had the Wardens handed them over as prisoners of war? They were unconscious, thus unable to pray to their gods for help. This was the worst place for them to be.

"Gah, what is that?" Noct bumped into my leg and almost fell over.

I steadied him. "Don't look at them."

"Could any of these be..." Sinder trailed off. His eyes were darting between the cells, his chest heaving in panic.

"Stay with me." I wrapped my arm around his. "None of these are Vincent."

"How do you know?"

"Fauna senses." I tapped my nose. "I can't smell his scent." It was a gentle lie—I couldn't remember what Vincent smelled like—but my gut told me The Nameless One wouldn't keep his prized possessions in the common cells. No, Vincent and Gast would be held elsewhere.

Warmth flowed from Sinder's skin by way of thanks. It had been so long since I'd last felt his touch, and honestly, it helped soothe the aching cold that had bitten down to my bones. I'd never wanted to return to Witheryn again, but at least I'd done so with a Godless.

We rounded a corner, and my heart began to race. The ambassador was leading us down to where they'd held Vincent.

Shit. Vincent had been trapped here for weeks. He'd been in no fit state when I'd left him. What state would he be in now? Could Sinder handle it?

Jinx continued to march ahead down the stone steps as I dragged my feet. She'd once tried to stop me from running us both into certain danger; now here she was, barreling her way into it. Had taking Gildola's soul really made her that confident?

Gods, not even *I* was that confident. Though I didn't have much going for me—I could put the Necro to sleep, at least.

I peeled myself from Sinder's warmth as we reached the bottom of the stairs and the darkened room at their base. It was empty. No Vincent or Gast strapped to chairs. No torture instruments. No blood splatters. A whole lot of nothing.

"This is anticlimactic," Jinx said.

Cold mist filled the room. It seeped across the floor, rising until it completely obscured my vision and my hair stood on end.

"Sinder?" I whispered.

But Sinder was gone.

In a single blink, I stood back inside that abattoir. Bodies of mortals dangled from the ceiling on meat hooks.

Great. We were fucked. Absolutely fucked.

Why had I ever thought this was a good idea?

I staggered back and bumped into Jinx. "Shit!" I started. "Are we alone? Where's Sinder?"

DO NOT WORRY FOR YOUR COMPANIONS, crooned a soft voice I never wanted to hear again. *THEY WILL BE MADE COMFORTABLE WHILE WE BARGAIN.*

"If you hurt them, our bargain is off!" I yelled.

Chuckling echoed within the mist. The meat hooks swayed, tinkling like a wind chime of the damned.

Jinx tensed beside me. "Enough with the smoke and mirrors act. I'm not impressed."

The meat hooks parted, and there stood The Nameless One. Their form was all black limbs atop a hunched shadow of a body, yet their face... It was Vincent's face.

Shit, I was going to be sick.

YOU CAME FOR ME, DID YOU NOT? The Nameless One spoke with Vincent's voice, though it sounded contorted, wrong. *YOU ABANDONED ME, KAYL. AFTER EVERYTHING WE'D BEEN THROUGH TOGETHER.* The face changed to Gast's. *I TRUSTED YOU, LADY, AND YOU LEFT ME TO DIE.*

"Stop it!" I yelled.

"Are you here to fuck with us or bargain with us?" Jinx called out.

The Nameless One's face changed to that of a random Ember. Thank the gods it wasn't Sinder. *OUR BARGAIN WAS THE FACE OF CHAOS IN EXCHANGE FOR YOUR COMPANIONS. I OFFERED TO SUPPORT DOR'S WAR GAMES IF HE DELIVERED ME A CHAOS MORTAL, BUT HE HAS YET TO FULFILL HIS PROMISE.*

HE WANTS TO KEEP CHAOS FOR HIMSELF. HOW GREEDY OF HIM.

The Nameless One wanted one of us by fair means or foul.

"So my dear sister here promised me in exchange for her Godless buddy," Jinx said. "But as you can see, my sister is flaky. I'll give you a better deal." She approached The Nameless One. "Join me against Dor, and you can have her."

What was she doing? Sure, I'd come here to betray her, but still! "Jinx!" I hissed.

The Nameless One laughed. A hacking, choking sound. *OR... WE COULD TAKE YOU BOTH.*

Chains descended from the ceiling.

They lunged for me. I leaped to one side, the metal screeching as it twisted and turned, writhing as though alive. I searched for a way out, but the entire darkened room was full of hooks and swaying bodies.

The chains wrapped around my legs, binding them together. Shit! I fell onto my palms, my fingers scraping against ice and grit.

I tried to pull the chains off me, but steel curled around my torso, clanking up to my arms. Gods, I was drowning in metal! They tightened, tying my arms to my sides and leaving me utterly bound.

"Jinx!" I screamed.

I couldn't move. I couldn't even twist around to see where Jinx was, if The Nameless One had gotten her too.

Gravity shifted beneath me, yanking me up. In a single blink, the room was empty, and I hung from the ceiling, swinging next to the unconscious bodies of two Necro males—Vincent and Gast?

They were naked, and a sharp meat hook skewered through their pale torsos. Blood dripped from each dark gash onto the floor.

But their faces were gone. Their *faces*. They'd been cut off. Ripped from their skin, leaving only muscle and pulpy flesh.

I belched a glob of vomit, which ran down my chin.

"I'm sorry." My limbs were trembling so fiercely, they rattled my chains. "This is all my fault. I'm sorry."

A shadow slithered in the darkness. The Nameless One.

I flailed, but it was no use. I was trapped, so fucking trapped, and yet I'd willingly walked into this.

I was so *fucking* stupid.

The Nameless One drew closer, my breath misting in the air as they neared. One of their tendril-like black arms slowly reached up and touched my cheek. The coldness shocked me down to my core, paralyzing me.

YOU HAVE SUCH A PRETTY FACE, SWEETLING. They caressed my cheek. So soft, yet so cold, making my teeth chatter. *IT WOULD BE A SHAME TO CUT IT OFF.*

"You—You sick fuck!" I couldn't keep the tears from spilling.

The Necro god caught them, and rubbed them into my skin.

ARE THE DIVINER NOT WORSE THAN US? THEY CUT OPEN MORTALS TO STUDY AND UNDERSTAND THEM. WE DO SO BECAUSE IT IS BEAUTIFUL. THE MORTAL BODY IS A FASCINATING DESIGN. THE ORGANS AND THEIR FUNCTIONS. THE CIRCULATORY SYSTEM. THE SKIN.

YOUR FACE IS THE MOST BEAUTIFUL OF ALL. WE WANT TO WEAR IT.

A trickle ran down my leg. I'd gone and pissed myself.

Gods. I didn't want to die this way.

I'd only wanted to save Quen.

I didn't want to die!

The Nameless One pushed a bony black finger into my cheek. The pressure was dull at first.

Then it burned.

I screamed and screamed, though there was no one left to hear.

Who's the Real Monster?

The Nameless One should be avoided where possible. They have been known to send their mortals to spy on and capture mortals from other domains. Some of these unfortunate individuals are subjected to tests and other barbarities. Not all mortals can be recalled once in their grasp. We do not know how, but The Nameless One has a means of blocking a god's influence, similar to an aether collar. It's worth appeasing The Nameless One, however. The Necro ability to heal should not be underestimated. Though the price of The Nameless One's loyalty comes high.
—P. Bezel, *Personal Report on The Nameless One*

THE ROOM WENT DARK. That wasn't a good sign.

There I'd been, rubbing shoulders with my dear sister as we took turns betraying one another, and then she'd disappeared, leaving me with a bunch of bodies on meat hooks, some spooky mist, and the wailing groans of clanking chains. If The Nameless One thought that was terrifying, then they clearly didn't know me. I'd stuffed bodies inside a watchmaker's back on Chime for fun.

If anything, The Nameless One had more to fear.

I sighed and switched my form from Necro to Glimmer. "I've seen more drama in a Seren play." Though to be fair, the show Serenity's mortals had put on for me while I'd straddled her face wasn't the type of play to make a run in a Golden City theater.

Sunlight shone from my head. This damn dress covered me from neck to toe, so I'd been reduced to a walking candle.

But my light didn't illuminate anything except the stone ground beneath me.

"Seriously, cut the act. I'm bored."

A face appeared within the darkness—with the dead eyes of a female Diviner. It wasn't Penny, but it sure as fuck reminded me of her. It floated before me in a perfect oval.

WE TOOK THIS ONE FOR YOU, said a soft voice. *AS A GIFT.*

I scrunched my nose. "What am I supposed to do with it? Hang it on my wall?"

WEAR IT, IF IT PLEASES YOU.

"No thanks. While we're on the subject, you're not getting my face, either."

Something slithered ahead, illuminated by my light. The Diviner's face wasn't hanging in midair. Fuck. It was attached to The Nameless One's body. Now *that* was creepy.

WE ALWAYS ADMIRED CORENTINE'S SPIRIT. A MORTAL BODY IS DESIGNED TO FOLLOW THE RULES OF TIME. IT IS A LOGICAL SYSTEM BUILT OF FLESH AND ORGANS INSTEAD OF COGS AND METAL, POWERED BY BLOOD INSTEAD OF OIL. A MACHINE MEANT TO DECAY AND DIE. DOR'S IDEAL.

"What's this got to do with my mother?"

CHAOS CHANGES THE RULES. MORTALS ARE NO LONGER BORN AS THE IDEALIZED IMAGE OF THEIR MAKER. THEY ARE BORN WITH VARIATION. OFTEN WITH DEFECTS. THEY ARE PRONE TO SUCH GLORIOUS DISEASES THAT GROW AND MUTATE. THAT BLEED AND OOZE.

CHAOS IS DEFIANCE OF PURITY. IT IS WHAT WE SEEK.

"You're saying you're on my side?" That was the gist of what The Nameless One was rambling on about. The Diviner are boring, Chaos is the best, yada yada. As if I didn't know.

IT IS PLEASING TO FINALLY SPEAK WITH A DIRECT CONNECTION TO CORENTINE.

Kayl really had done a shit job of playing ambassador for Chaos, huh.

"You took my sister, so what do you want with me?" I gotta admit, I was curious.

WE WISH TO SEE CORENTINE FREE. PLEASE. SPEAK OF OUR DESIRE.

Wow, who knew gods could be so thirsty for each other? But no. I didn't believe them for one second.

THE NAMELESS ONE ENJOYS THE CHAOS OF DEATH, Mother said. *THEY WOULD FREE ME ONLY SO THEY COULD PREY UPON MY PHYSICAL FORM. THEY WERE ALWAYS LECHEROUS IN THEIR DESIRES. THEY HAVE NO PLACE IN OUR NEW WORLD, DAUGHTER.*

None of the gods did. Though, if the Necro joined Dor's side, the Diviner would have access to healers who wouldn't care about getting bloody.

That was the fucked-up thing about Necro. They reveled in pain and suffering. Sure, I liked a bit of pain myself, and yes, I was attempting to destroy the domains, but I wasn't *nasty* about it. Not like these fucks.

Screaming echoed behind me. It sounded like Kayl, and *that* sent a shudder through me.

LEAVE HER, Mother urged. *TAKE WHAT IS OWED.*

I can't leave her. She still has a couple of souls we need—

SHE IS A LIABILITY. SHE HAS EARNED HER PREDICAMENT.

Or having her face ripped off? Nah. My dear sister was an idiot who thought she could dangle me in front of a monster to save her precious Time Boy. They'd both betrayed me, and maybe that was worth getting your face chewed.

Truth was, it hurt that my sister—my own flesh and blood—would so easily bargain me away. Who was the real monster?

I'd come here looking for a soul, but I wouldn't let Kayl get eaten. Though this little adventure needn't be a waste of time...

If I had the Necro on *my* side, then that would be another ally against Dor. Would Edana and Serenity approve? Eh, who cared. This was my party. I could invite who I wanted.

"How will you help me fight Dor?"

MY MORTALS WILL MAKE THE DIVINER BLEED.

"Good enough for me. Where's my sister? I want to watch her scream."

Chains materialized in the room, as though a fog of darkness had lifted. And there was Kayl, all wrapped up and dangling from the ceiling as The

Nameless One caressed her cheek. Blood smeared across her face from the god's touch.

Tears ran down her cheeks in silent sobs, and I caught a whiff of something foul.

She'd pissed herself.

In all the years I'd been trapped inside her head, she'd never been this scared. Not when she faced Valeria. Not when I threw her off the steamworks roof. Not when that prick Karendar attempted to destroy our souls, and that...

That had scared me.

That had scared me to *fuck*.

The Nameless One wore a white porcelain mask. *MAY WE TAKE HER FACE?* Their voice was heavy and rasping, like they were getting off on the prospect.

I yanked off my gloves and examined my glowing golden hands. They were shaking. Actually shaking, and it wasn't from the cold or fear.

It was rage. Pure fucking rage, because this unholy bastard had made my sister bleed. Only I could touch her.

Only *me*!

Sunlight burst from my palm, and I blasted The Nameless One. I wanted their mortals for myself, but that didn't mean I needed a middleman.

They screeched an awful wailing that would have been entertaining if my sister weren't dangling from the ceiling. The Necro god vanished, leaving behind a veil of smoke.

I aimed at the chain holding Kayl and shot another beam of light. It took a moment to burn through, and then she fell hard, and landed on her side.

"Seriously?" I stood over her, my hands on my hips. "You couldn't change into a smaller Fauna form and wiggle your way out? I just saved your sorry arse *again*." I grabbed the chains wrapped around her arms and waist and melted through them. Ember flame would have been quicker, but you didn't fuck with the sun.

She rolled onto her knees, her chest heaving with fast breaths. "I—I forgot. Why are you freeing me? You handed me over in the first place!"

"Like you weren't going to do the same to me."

Mist filled the room. I dragged Kayl up. She leaned against me, her body trembling.

I wasn't letting The Nameless One split us up this time.

We magically reappeared inside the Asylum's torture room, or what I assumed to be the torture room, based on the fresh blood dripping down the walls. Another fancy trick designed to scare us. Sinder and Noct were still here, staring at the Necro ambassador in shock, and...

"Gods, no," Kayl gasped.

What a surprise, it was only Vincent! Lovable Vincent. Another member of the Godless family who wouldn't harm a soul, only right now he looked like he was about to murder us. Blood ran down his chest from a deep gash in his shoulder. His pale lips were curled back, exposing *very* sharp fangs. He was naked, too, which wasn't to my taste.

Beside him stood another Necro male who Kayl and Noct seemed to recognize, though I didn't have a clue who that idiot was. Both men watched us with that hungry, bloodshot look Necro had perfected. The look that said they'd not eaten in weeks and we smelled delicious.

I was delicious, so I couldn't blame 'em, but my neck wasn't on the menu. If those sharp fangs came anywhere near me, then these boys were getting roasted.

"Subdue them," Ambassador Morana commanded.

Vincent charged right at us. Too fast for a man who'd once relied on a cane, but that was what going feral did to you.

Light flared from my fists.

"No!" Sinder screamed. He leaped in front of me, forcing me to quickly snuff my light before I blasted a hole through his damn chest.

"Move out of the way!" I yelled.

"No, don't hurt him. I can stop him!" Sinder faced the charging Necro head-on. "Vince, it's me! Sinder! Please, it's me."

Vincent didn't stop. He pounced on Sinder and swept him off his feet. It would have been romantic, if Vincent didn't then sink his fangs into Sinder's neck.

"Burn him, you idiot!" I yelled.

But Sinder didn't because he was, in fact, a fucking idiot.

These bloody useless Godless, I swear.

Sinder's eyes fluttered as he let Vincent ravage his neck. Thanks to my dear sister, I had more knowledge of their intimate relationship than I'd ever wanted, but this was no consensual exchange of blood.

Vincent ripped his lover's throat out.

Sinder collapsed to his knees, his head tilted unnaturally, his mouth wide in shock. His neck was a mottled mess of flesh and blood. Nasty shit. Not even The Nameless One could patch that back together again.

Then Sinder keeled over to one side, and his body faded to dust.

Fuck. He was supposed to be my way out of this damn domain!

I hoped Edana realized what deep shit I was in.

"Sinder!" Kayl tried to do the stupid thing of running into danger, but I wrapped my arm around her real tight.

"He's gone. Don't join him."

She yanked herself from my hold, her eyes blazing. "Fuck you!"

Where had that spunk been ten minutes ago, huh?

Vincent returned his attention to us. Bloodied bits of Ember flesh were caught in his teeth and stained his lips red. Ugh, *so* nasty.

Noct flapped over and hid behind my legs. The other Necro was prowling toward us with that same feral look as Vincent.

"Why aren't you singing?" I yelled at the Seren.

"Because singing doesn't work on a fucking Necro!" Noct yelled back. "They can shut off their own damn hearing!"

"Then why the *fuck* did you come along, you useless flying fuck?"

"For that fucker there!" He pointed at the other Necro.

Fuck this! I fired off a beam of sunlight at Noct's pal. It burned a hole straight through his torso.

It didn't stop him. It didn't even slow him.

Charred lumps of his guts slid down his legs, swinging from side to side as he shambled toward us. How the *fuck* was he still standing?

The wound stitched itself together, his skin mending until it was brand new. Fucking Necro!

Morana chuckled. She'd been standing in the corner and watching this entire time with apparent amusement. "Burn us if you like. It's only flesh."

Only flesh, huh? Let's see how fast they could heal. "Sister, get behind me."

Kayl hurried to Noct's side. She'd seen what I could do back in Solaris.

I may have taken Gildola's power, but it was *my* power now. The power of a god running through my veins.

Aether crackled around me in a shield of light. I raised my arms, allowing it to cover Kayl and Noct. The hairs on my neck prickled as the temperature built. Only now did I regret overdressing. The fabric clung to my sweaty skin, though after the fun afternoon I'd spent with Edana's tongue up my cunt, I'd discovered sweat didn't feel so bad.

I would burn this domain to ash.

Flame erupted in a pretty little circle. The fire's intensity was so much, I couldn't make out the Asylum's stone walls beyond the veil of heat and steam. Ash hissed against my shield, the taste of burned meat and wood in my mouth. Everything was swallowed by the screaming of a newborn star.

I'd become the sun. The most light Witheryn would ever see.

My flame fizzled out. Something cold and wet landed on my cheek. As my light faded, so the dismal cold and dark pressed in. We'd been transported outside, where the snow mingled with falling ash.

No. We were still in the Asylum. The walls had burned down in a perfect imprint of my shield. The brickwork glowed with a line of red.

Two black scorch marks were all that remained of Noct's friend and Vincent, but the ambassador was *still* fucking standing! She stood naked, unsteady on her feet, a patchwork of charred skin, pulpy red flesh, exposed bone and organs that were literally dropping out of her.

Yet she was alive. "Persistent bitch, aren't you?"

"You burned him," Kayl said, her voice hoarse. She was staring at the black mark that had once been Vincent.

"That thing wasn't Vincent, and you know it."

HOW DELIGHTFUL, The Nameless One crooned, their voice everywhere at once. *YOUR ABILITIES ARE PROFOUND. WE SENSE THE TOUCH OF GILDOLA.*

"Show yourself, and I'll give you more than a sense!"

Laughter echoed around me. *WE SIMPLY MUST UNDERSTAND HOW CHAOS CAN EMULATE THE ABILITIES OF OTHER DOMAINS. IF WE CANNOT TAKE CORENTINE, THEN WE WILL TAKE YOU.*

WE WILL CUT YOU OPEN TO SEE WHAT DELICIOUS SECRETS YOU HIDE.

"Jinx," Kayl whispered, her teeth chattering. She edged closer to me until we were rubbing elbows.

"I'm not scared of them," I whispered back.

"I'm fucking terrified," Noct said.

The ground rumbled.

Oh fuck.

Hundreds of naked Necro ran across the snow. Well, mostly shambled. They were a grotesque mass of pale skin covered in boils and blisters and diseases I didn't want to know about. They oozed black and green and red. And they were all blood-starved. Feral.

The Necro who had been locked inside the cells of the Asylum.

I dug my heels in and let the Glimmer's power build in my palms.

Closer they ran, their dirty feet scrambling over the melted bricks and ice. As soon as they neared, I unleashed a wave of sunlight.

It burned through them with a sickening crispiness. Their bodies crumbled to ash.

The Necro behind them shoved past and kept coming.

How would I reach The Nameless One like this?

YOU SHOULD HAVE TAKEN THEIR SOUL WHEN YOU HAD THE CHANCE INSTEAD OF SAVING YOUR SISTER, Mother said. *THIS ORDEAL COULD HAVE BEEN AVOIDED.*

I clenched my teeth. *Now isn't the time for lectures.*

One of the Necro snatched Noct. He cried out as he was dragged into the crowd and disappeared into a sea of writhing pale flesh.

"Jinx!" Kayl screamed. Their grubby hands reached for her.

"Oh no you fucking don't!" I blasted them with sunlight, keeping them at bay.

Kayl at least had the sense to switch into a smaller Fauna form—a black cat. She darted between the Necros' legs as they chased her. I could have done the same, but I needed my Glimmer form to burn them.

More Necro kept coming and coming. A never-ending mass of blood-hungry mortals with sharp teeth. Shit, there were too many!

RETREAT, Mother urged. *THE NAMELESS ONE HAS THE ADVANTAGE. RETURN WHEN YOU HAVE GATHERED MORE STRENGTH.*

Retreat how? I spun, but I couldn't see Noct, and he was my only other way out of here!

Shit. I couldn't see Kayl, either.

Only Necro.

My heart was pounding so hard, it almost burst.

The Gate was broken. There was no escaping Witheryn without summoning a portal back to Chime, and that was the one thing I hadn't mastered yet. Were Gildola's powers not enough? Edana could open portals at a snap of her fingers. Why couldn't I?

Light flared behind me. Oh, thank fuck! My prayers were answered!

A flaming portal into Rapture opened, and out poured Ember. They charged at the Necro, battle-ready, and flung their flame in a collision of fire and ice.

Edana herself stepped through the portal. Wow. I'd not expected her to show up, and yet here she was, sauntering in with gorgeous golden heels and a matching gown, as though arriving for a theater premiere as its main star.

EDANA! The Nameless One shrieked. *THIS IS A BREACH OF THE COVENANT!*

"The Covenant is broken, you putrid worm." She gazed upon Witheryn with a sneer.

And then Witheryn fucking *burned*.

Waves of flame spread across the snowfields, burning through what remained of the Asylum until the sky itself turned bloodred. Edana's mortals continued to blast through the Necro, but still, those flesh-hungry bastards kept coming, as though every single fucking Necro in this damn domain had turned up for the party. Necro grasped for whatever Ember were within reach. Those who couldn't react in time screamed as the Necro fed off them.

Blood and flesh splattered the ground, along with ash and soot.

This was the war the gods had promised.

This was the chaos I'd dreamed of unleashing.

"You're overdressed," Edana commented, as though already bored with the battle.

"This isn't Rapture."

She smirked. "Not yet."

YOU ARE NOT WELCOME IN OUR DOMAIN! LEAVE! The Nameless One raged.

A line of fresh Necro appeared on the horizon. In counter, more Ember poured through Edana's portal. They could fight it out until the end of time, and we'd be no closer to a winner.

Edana had said so herself. A god couldn't kill another god.

They needed Chaos for that.

And I needed my sister. Where the fuck was she?

I left Edana's side and ran between the Ember, narrowly dodging flame. "Kayl!" I yelled amid the howling of fire and bleeding mortals.

"Looking for this?"

Oh fuck.

The Necro ambassador held Kayl by the throat. Both were naked—the ambassador's wounds healed except for the ugly lesions on her face, and Kayl had returned to her bipedal Fauna form with cat ears and a tail. Her head lolled to one side. Paralyzed.

She'd only gotten herself bloody captured.

I summoned a flicker of light in my palm. "You better let her go unless you want your entire domain burning to a barren rock."

"You threaten us with fire, and we welcome it. Flesh is malleable. We thank you for the new test subjects."

Test subjects? "What?"

"You have a lovely face. It would look more beautiful with a lover's touch." She tilted Kayl's head to one side and kissed her cheek.

A red patch spread across Kayl's skin from where the ambassador's lips had touched her. Boils erupted, spreading across her cheek in a collection of sore red blisters.

Ew, what the fuck? "What did you do to my sister?"

The ambassador smiled. "Improved her."

Voices called out behind me. The battle had suddenly come to a stop. Had we managed to burn every fucking Necro? No. They'd vanished into thin air. The Nameless One had recalled them, and I had a horrible feeling it wasn't because we'd been winning.

The Ember gazed around at each other, confused. They held their flaming hands aloft, the only light to push back Witheryn's dark.

One of them coughed.

And then another.

A wave of sickness passed between the Ember as they, too, broke out in disgusting boils. Some collapsed onto their knees, clutching their stomachs in agony. Others scratched at their boils, causing them to bleed and ooze. Their flames spurted out, creating a terrifying light show.

The rest screamed and ran for Edana's portal, coughing and spluttering the entire way.

Edana recoiled. "What have you done to my mortals?"

A GIFT, SWEET SISTER, The Nameless One said. *A DISEASE FOR YOUR MORTALS TO ENJOY SPREADING.*

Edana glanced at me. Her expression remained neutral, but horror filled her dark eyes.

She stepped back through the portal and closed it behind her before the Ember could reach it. Abandoning her mortals to Witheryn.

Abandoning me.

Fuck!

The Ember collapsed where the portal had burned, groaning and crying. Yep, that was about how I felt right now. Why hadn't Edana just killed her own mortals? What the fuck had scared her so damn much?

I turned to burn the *fuck* out of Morana, but then everything went dark.

It was as though The Nameless One had thrown a blanket over me, cutting off the heat of battle and silencing all the screaming and stomping. Cold mist pooled around my feet, and I once again stood alone in utter darkness.

Though the silence wasn't quite complete. The soft clinking of chains surrounded me. It was more jarring than unnerving, but The Nameless One sure loved to pile on the drama.

Gods and their amateur theatrics. "Give it a fucking rest already!"

A SHAME EDANA DID NOT APPRECIATE OUR GIFT. MY DOMAIN THRIVES ON DEATH. THE MORE MORTALS SHE GIVES US TO BLEED, AND THE MORE OF MY MORTALS SHE BURNS, THE MORE WE ENJOY IT.

"You didn't seem that thrilled before."

A MASK, MY SWEET. WE WEAR SO MANY. WE WANTED TO SHOW OUR WORK.

More bodies dangling on meat hooks appeared in the mist. Diviner, this time. Their naked silver skin was ravaged by the same boils, spread across their faces, down their necks and across their chests. Their eyes were wide open, their mouths twisting in silent screams.

Fuck. They were still alive. But how?

Why hadn't Dor recalled them? Why hadn't they used their time manipulation to fast-forward the fuck out of here?

WE SEE YOU HAVE QUESTIONS. THIS DISEASE IS ONE WE HAVE PERFECTED OVER GENERATIONS. IT AFFECTS THE BLOODSTREAM AND INTERFERES WITH A MORTAL'S ABILITY TO USE THEIR NATURAL-BORN POWERS, MUCH LIKE DOR'S OWN TECHNOLOGY. WE KNEW THIS DAY WOULD EVENTUALLY COME.

WHEN CHAOS STOOD AGAINST TIME.

A disease that could stop a mortal's powers like an aether collar? "Clever." Fucked up, though. And dangerous. If that shit touched me, I was in trouble. "How does it spread?"

The Nameless One hummed, pleased I'd even asked. *THROUGH TOUCH.*

The Necro had been all over the Ember, and they'd been all over themselves. "Diviner aren't exactly the touchy-feely types." I doubted Dor had volunteered these poor fucks.

MY MORTALS ARE.

Of course. "I assume there's a reason you're showing me this?"

WE OFFER THIS GIFT TO YOU. SPREAD IT IN OUR NAME. They giggled. *PASS IT TO CORENTINE.*

They really were getting off on this, weren't they? "Where's my sister?"

The darkness abated for a moment, allowing the glow of my golden skin to fall upon a figure dangling from the ceiling. Kayl.

She was still naked in her cat Fauna form, only now she was unconscious, and blood dribbled from the boils on her face. Shit.

Neither of us were ready for the god of death. What had she been thinking, dragging us here to become toys for a sick god?

I'd thought the Diviner were the worst, but the Necro had them beat.

TOUCH HER. TAKE OUR DISEASE AND BECOME MINE.

"Touch me yourself."

They giggled again. *WE WILL TOUCH YOU WHEN YOUR FACE IS COMPLETE.*

When my powers were subdued by their disgusting boils, they meant. The Nameless One wasn't stupid.

If they'd perfected this disease over generations, then they'd probably tested it on multiple mortals across the domains. Necro weren't the only domain that could heal. A Glimmer's righteous flame could do the trick, as I'd learned myself. The Nameless One would have accounted for that.

Would they have accounted for the power of a god?

I touched my sister's cheek. She looked so fragile, dangling from the ceiling, her eyelashes fluttering in obvious discomfort. Kayl had dragged us both into another fine mess, but I didn't mind. Not really. Her brand of chaos was more sporadic than mine.

Itchiness prickled under my skin, and my face broke out in burning blisters.

It felt gross, and it came with a nagging headache and sudden urge to vomit.

I let sunlight spool between my fingers. It flickered out, just like their fire had for the Ember.

The Nameless One appeared before me, their face a perfect porcelain mask. *ARE YOU MINE, SWEET THING?*

Black tendrils wrapped around my shoulder, cold to the touch. They slithered up my neck, caressing the boils of my cheek. Death wrapped around me in a loving embrace and looked me in the eye.

Maybe I was fucked in the head. I should be screaming.

What did I have to fear? I'd become a god.

I grabbed the black slimy thing The Nameless One called a hand, but there wasn't any tug. No tingling at all. What did you know? Their disease actually did block my abilities.

But it hadn't blocked Gildola's soul. It still burned inside my gut, begging to be unleashed on The Nameless One's foulness.

That burning flowed through my blood, slowly boiling me from the inside out. Cleansing me with holy light.

My face began to glow.

HOW IS THIS POSSIBLE?

Sunlight burst from my skin, blazing through my thick gown, leaving me naked and aglow.

The Nameless One screeched, blinded by light. I still gripped their slimy hand, and now, I felt the tug. That tantalizing soul on the other end.

I leeched The Nameless One's foul soul into my own, dragging it into my subconscious as it writhed and screamed. Death wasn't so fun now, huh?

My form changed to Necro. I instantly wiped away the blistering on my face, smoothing over the pain like a good shot of brandy. Though it was a shame I'd had to ruin my fancy outfit.

Voices exploded in my head. The Necro—*my* Necro—were consumed with raging bloodlust and the feral need to feed. Other voices whispered in the dark—Necro huddled in their frozen stone homes, terrified of the fire in the sky, of the hunger that could overtake them and turn them into mindless husks.

I'd free them. I'd free them all.

The Nameless One lifted their mask from their face, letting it fall to the ground with a *clink*. I don't know what I'd expected to find behind it—another grotesque horror? But there was nothing. Nothing but a blank black canvas. The Necro god had taken on so many personas, as Chaos did, but they had no identity of their own. They'd either forgotten what it was like to be a someone—a something—with a name, or they'd never been anything to begin with.

I knew what it was like to have your identity wrapped around another's.

YOU HAVE GRANTED US DEATH, they said in their melodic voice, as though they weren't sad about this turn of events at all. *IT IS RATHER... UNPLEASANT.*

Their body faded into dust. The room disappeared with them, banishing the sorry souls trapped there.

I blinked, and there I was, standing in the middle of the ruined Asylum, surrounded by sick Ember as snow drifted down from the open sky.

And there, lying in a puddle of melted ice, was Kayl.

I ran to her side. Blisters still covered her face. I placed my hand above them and let my new Necro abilities take over. They receded, and the redness of her skin faded altogether. With a little jolt, she awoke with a strangled gasp.

She sat up, and her feline eyes opened wide. "Oh gods. What did you do?"

I followed her gaze. The sky had already turned from black to gray, and the falling snow was now dust.

Witheryn was dying as destined.

The Ember disappeared all in one go, snapping out of reality. Then another portal opened, and Edana stepped through. "You're done here? Good."

"No thanks to you." I scowled and summoned another dress to cover myself with. "Was that a strategic retreat?"

"My presence was a hindrance. By leaving, we tricked The Nameless One into underestimating you. Their mistake."

No, she'd been covering her own arse. Whatever. I'd won, and that was all that mattered.

"What do we do with her?" Edana gestured at Kayl.

Kayl scrambled to her feet. "Take me back to Chime. Now!"

I glanced at Edana. "Do it."

Edana shrugged. Another portal opened, this time into a back alley within Central. It was still night, but the streetlamps showed no Wardens waiting on the other side.

Kayl leaped through before I could even blink.

"Wait!" I called, and passed through after her.

I must have done a great job healing her, because she was stomping through that alley at speed, her cat tail swishing behind her. "I thought you needed a Necro!" I called.

She spun, her feline eyes wild and full of anger. She sure looked a state, naked and covered in a mixture of blood and soot. "Will you give me Vincent? Or Gast?"

Gast? Oh, so that was who Noct's friend was. "You know the deal."

"*What* deal? What do you want from me, Jinx?"

What I'd always wanted. "You and me. Taking on the gods. Together."

Like we were supposed to.

Kayl's face twisted, as though she'd tasted something sour. "You're deluded if you think that'll ever happen."

"Why the fuck not? We want the same damn things! To end the reign of gods and liberate the domains—"

"Liberate?" Kayl snorted. "Is that what you call destroying them?"

"You've seen what Chaos can do. We can recreate the domains, make them godless like you always wanted—"

"While Corentine's still around, they'll never be godless."

Why did she hate our mother so much?

SHE IS LOST TO YOU, DAUGHTER, Mother said. *TAKE HER NOW, WHILE SHE IS VULNERABLE.*

I could take her. Wrap her in chains and drag her into the clock tower.

But I wanted Kayl to come willingly. To admit she was wrong, to say *sorry*, for once. Fuck, I only wanted her to see it my way. "Do you really think you can take on Dor and the rest of those fucks on your own?" I reached for her hand. "Imagine what we could do together, as family—"

"We're not family!" She snatched her hand away. "Sinder—"

"Suddenly best friends again with Sinder? After he betrayed you?"

"You betrayed me, Jinx. You. This is all *you*!"

"Isn't that familiar? Why won't you give me a goddamn *chance*?" I yelled, the words raw.

"Seriously?" She scoffed. "You're unpredictable and violent. Why do you think?"

"You're the one who wants to hurt our mother!"

"We don't *have* a mother! Corentine is just another god who wants to dictate mortal lives. Don't you get that? She's as bad as the rest of them, and you're following in her footsteps."

DO NOT LISTEN TO HER LIES, DAUGHTER. YOU KNOW I ONLY DESIRE MY FREEDOM SO I CAN FINALLY LOVE YOU AS YOU DESERVE. YOUR SISTER CARES ONLY FOR HERSELF.

I knew that. She'd made it perfectly clear. Even if it twisted in my guts. *"We're not family!"*

Then what were we?

"You took everything from me the night you chose to turn your back on our mother." On me. "I *loved* you!"

She hugged her chest and choked back a sob. "Did you hurt Quen?"

Why did it always come back to Corinth? "Wasn't me. But if you want help healing your Time Boy, then you're gonna have to bring him to the clock tower. That's the deal."

"That's not happening."

"You'd sooner let Corinth die a slow, painful death?"

She flinched. "That's his choice. Don't talk to me again." She transformed into a cat and bounded from the alley.

Fuck.

Fuck!

I kicked a trash can nearby, sending it clattering into a brick wall. If a Warden heard me, I'd rip their throat out.

WHY DID YOU LET HER GO? Mother asked.

A fucking good question. *She'll come crawling back.* Kayl always used me to get what she wanted, and there was no way she'd let Corinth die.

She'd come back.

She had to.

XII

ALERT!
WANTED TRAITOR QUENTIN CORINTH HAS BEEN SIGHTED IN CENTRAL. FOCUS ALL EFFORTS ON HIS CAPTURE!
Described as male, 5'5' inches tall, slim, short hair, silver-blue eyes that glow. Once Diviner, Corinth is now under the influence of Chaos and may appear as a Chaos mortal. Last seen wearing the disguise of a Zephyr. Target background: ex-ambassador on the Warden Council. Ex-Warden. Corinth is trained for combat situations and should not be engaged in a one-on-one confrontation. Approach with extreme caution.
He is to be captured ALIVE.
—Unknown, *Internal Warden Memo*

SHOUTING STIRRED ME BACK to reality. I was barely hanging onto consciousness by a thread. My body rested on a cot inside a tent of some sort I didn't recognize. The Fauna had given me something to dull my senses, while the three Mesmer watched over me to check that death didn't completely take me—those three I *did* recognize.

But it was the agony in my arm that anchored me. That wouldn't let go.

"You smell like fear," came a gruff voice—the male Fauna with shaggy hair and a missing eye.

There was shuffling, and I opened my eyes to Kayl.

My beautiful Kayl.

She remained in the same Fauna form as when she left, hastily dressed in a robe. Blood stained her cheek. As she kneeled beside me, I caught a whiff of smoke.

"What happened? Where did you go?" I attempted to sit up, but a dizzying spasm of hot pain kept me pinned.

She took my uninjured hand and brought it to her lips. "I tried to find a Necro."

Saints. "Don't tell me you entered Witheryn? You got lucky the first time you escaped—"

"It's gone." She pressed my knuckles to her forehead, clammy with sweat. "Jinx took The Nameless One. I... I couldn't get a Necro to help you. I'm sorry. I failed."

I ran my thumb across her brow. "It's all right. The Fauna can patch up my arm. Then I can make a new one—"

She sat up and stared. "You can grow one back?"

"Not exactly." I grimaced. "This may sound like madness, but the Zephyr... They're inside my head. They can help me build an artificial arm. One made of cogs and springs. It's not ideal, but... it's better than nothing."

Doctor Finch had helped guide my escape from Tempest, even though it had ended unexpectedly. He had the knowledge to create what I needed.

His voice had been whispering feverishly at the back of my mind ever since I woke. Only the drugs the Fauna had administered finally put the good doctor to rest.

"That arm needs to be cleaned up," the gruff Fauna said. "Before it rots."

"And then he'll be okay?" Kayl asked, her voice a strained whisper.

"Then your mate will heal."

Her hand tightened around mine.

I forced a weak smile. "It'll be fine."

The thought of a Fauna attending to my wounds didn't appeal, but he was right. Even a Necro would have struggled to grow a limb. Injuries like mine needed divine intervention.

There wasn't much of that going around.

"Can you put him to sleep?" the Fauna asked. "Use your Mesmer magic? It will make this much easier and less painful. We'll need to clean and stitch what's left."

Concern knitted her brows. "Won't he wake as soon as you do your thing?"

"Not if you put him in a deep sleep."

"Like a coma? Gods, I've never done that before. What if he never wakes up?"

"I trust you," I croaked, my throat going dry.

"You probably shouldn't. Didn't you imply I was unlucky only hours ago?"

"Black cats can be a symbol of luck."

"And also sluttiness."

"I'm a gentleman. I wouldn't dream of passing judgement."

"Are you both ready?" the Fauna asked.

I settled my head against the pillow. "Yes."

Kayl sucked in a breath. "You better wake up," she warned. "I won't save Chime on my own while you nap for eternity."

"Brew me a good cup of tea, and I'll be right up."

She smiled—such a wondrous thing—as she leaned over and kissed my forehead. "Sleep tight."

Her form changed from the fluffy fur of a cat to the dark nebula of the evening sky. Though, her eyes remained the same radiant silvery-blue of aether no matter what form she took. She placed her hand over my head. Warmth radiated from her palm, sending tingles down my spine.

I breathed out a sigh.

My eyelids fluttered, all too heavy. Kayl vanished from my sight, and then something cool and metal pushed into my remaining hand.

My fob watch.

I let it fall aside. "No." My voice slurred. "You."

Her hand slid into mine, the comfort of her touch a balm against the pain.

And I drifted into oblivion.

I strode through familiar gray corridors.

My feet moved of their own accord in a hurried staccato. Nervous energy hummed through my entire body, my hand twitching by my side where my pistol remained holstered. I'd discarded my usual bow tie, leaving my sweat-stained shirt unbuttoned at the top.

Adrenaline from the riot had followed me all the way here.

And now I needed to make penance for my sins.

Umber and Diviner Wardens saluted as I passed. They were dressed in their black-and-bronze uniforms, while I stood out in a tan suit. Elijah preferred it when his emissaries dressed the part, and today... I needed to act that role more than ever.

I reached the door to the reflection chamber and stepped inside.

Elijah waited by the one-way window, leaning on a table. "You're tardy."

"Apologies, Your Excellency, I—"

"You delay the inevitable. We've already interrogated the woman you arrested in Grayford." He nodded to the glass.

I approached the window and swallowed the lump in my throat.

A Vesper woman was chained to the far wall. Even with her midnight-blue skin, the bruises covering her face and neck were unmistakable. Her bottom black lip was swollen, split red. She glared at the window with a conviction that chilled my blood. There was little chance she could see us, but she knew we were here. Observing her.

They'd *interrogated* her.

"What—What is her crime?" I stuffed my hands into my pockets and ran a thumb over my fob watch.

"She's an apostate, clearly. You'll sentence her."

"To Eventide? We can, ah, we can leave on the next crossing—"

"No." Elijah pushed from the table and approached me. "The incident at Grayford was your mistake, and your mess to clean. Varen has already given his blessing. You will prove your loyalty to me, to our Father."

I blinked, and then somehow, I appeared in front of her. My pistol in my hand, my finger on the trigger.

It shook in my grip.

"Shoot her, Quentin," Elijah urged behind me. "She's nothing but an illegal Vesper. Send her back to her god."

The woman didn't utter a single sound. She continued to stare, accepting her fate, yet those amethyst eyes carried all her anger and strength.

"I can't do this, I can't—"

"This is Warden law. Do you want to be a Warden? Or do you want to spend the rest of your mortal existence behind stone walls? Do this for me. For our Father. Shoot her!"

"*No!*"

I turned my pistol on Elijah and shot him in the chest.

The bullet passed through him, splattering his blood against the pristine gray walls.

"You made me kill her!" I shot him again, catching his collarbone. Again—his abdomen. I shot him again and *again* until my pistol clicked, empty and useless, and I tossed it aside. "I killed her!" I staggered against the wall, the weight of those words crushing me to my knees. "I—I... I *killed* her."

The door burst open.

"Quen!" Kayl ran inside and grabbed my shoulders. "It's okay! I'm here."

"Is this a dream?" A nightmare? "Is that really you?"

She squeezed my shoulder, her nails pinching enough to bite. "It's me. I put you to sleep, but I must have fallen into your subconscious, because now I'm here, wherever here is..." She stood abruptly, her eyes going wide at the Vesper woman. "Who is this?"

I rubbed my nose on my sleeve. "Elvira Byvich." Malkavaan's mother.

Kayl still didn't remember her. Not after Anima took those memories.

A single bullet had pierced Elvira's brain, but her body hadn't faded, nor had the light left her eyes. She remained chained to the wall, blood dripping from the hole in her head, from the wound I'd inflicted five years ago.

"I killed her. After the Grayford Incident." My voice broke. "Elijah, he... he knew how much it pained me to kill those Vesper in the riot. He knew how deeply I regretted it. But that was an accident. This? He ordered me to kill her, and I obeyed." I met Kayl's eyes. "Now you see what kind of monster I am. What kind of man Elijah made me."

I'd been carrying this secret for so long. This unbearable cage wrapped that around my chest and crushed my ribs, squeezed the very breath from me. Punctured my heart.

Elijah had ordered Walter to wipe those memories, to allow the bliss of a temporary absolution. But when Walter had brought them back, I still couldn't face them. I'd thrown myself into work, into avoiding the truth. I owed Kayl this confession. I owed Malkavaan so much more. Yet I'd been too cowardly.

Even now, it wasn't my true self who uttered these words.

Only in a dream could I admit what I'd done.

Kayl's aether eyes glowed, though I couldn't fathom the emotions swirling in their depths. The anger. The disappointment. "Quen—"

"Look at me. Look at who I am. What I've done." I dragged myself up and staggered to the one-way window. Quentin, the Diviner, stared back. Corinth, the Dark Warden. My face rippled, changing from silvery skin to aether blue. Diviner to Chaos.

Did I even recognize myself anymore?

I'd died and been reborn so many times. What if each time, I came back worse? A little wrong? A part of my soul withered, or trapped in the aether?

When Elijah suppressed my memories and forced Walter to rewrite them, that had created new versions of me. New Quens. Each fucked up in their own way. Then when they rushed together, merged as one, I'd become damaged. Demented.

A man who would kill without hesitation. Who would damn entire domains.

Or had I always been that man?

The Dark Warden.

Hundreds of mortals had died because I'd killed or condemned them on Elijah's orders. On Dor's orders. "Eventide is gone. Solaris is gone. Tempest by my hand, and now Witheryn? The domains are warring, Chime is in pieces, and this is all my fault." I faced Kayl. "I wanted to unite the gods. To save mortal lives. And look at what I've done."

"This isn't your fault. Listen to me, Quen. Dor abused you. He used you for his own means—"

"Yet I was complicit. For every foul deed I committed in Dor's name, it was still my finger on the trigger. My actions that caused it."

"Oh, give over! You're a mortal, same as the rest of us. Your god gave you no choice!"

"There was always a choice! I could have chosen eternal damnation, and not—not war crimes!" I leaned against the wall and slid down, curling into myself until my head rested on my knees. Dor had leashed me so thoroughly, I could never truly repent. Now I was free, untethered, ready to be judged for my sins. "My soul is tainted. It... it will forever be tainted."

Tears streamed down my cheeks. Raw emotions cascaded over me in a way I'd never been allowed to feel. "I'm—I'm sorry!" I let my spectacles clatter to the ground as my fingers clawed through my hair. "I'm so, *so* sorry." For this. For Elvira, for Malkavaan.

For Walter. For Ilona. For Ben—innocent Ben, whom I'd left behind. Even Joe, whom I'd abandoned to Jinx's whims when I fled the clock tower.

For the mortals I couldn't save. The mortals I'd failed.

The mortals I'd damned to death and despair.

For Chime. My home, now standing in ruins. Abandoned and loveless.

For not standing up enough. Nor not speaking out enough. For not *being* enough.

For all this and more, I was sorry.

Kayl settled beside me. She wrapped her arms around me, granting me the comfort I surely didn't deserve. I buried my head in her shoulder and let my heart tear itself open.

"I'm sorry," I sobbed into her neck. This wasn't how I'd imagined our reunion.

She kissed my head. "You're allowed to cry."

To cry was perversion to Diviner. A weakness one could never permit. To cry was to admit guilt, to confess. To attempt forgiveness was a foolish arrogance, for only the gods could forgive. It was shameful, and I wallowed in my shame, drowning in the emotions Diviner were taught to bury.

They were here, out in the open of my subconscious. I couldn't contain them anymore. They were no longer mine to control.

"Eternal damnation isn't your burden to bear alone," Kayl murmured as she handed me my spectacles. "You're free to walk your own path now. You don't have a god telling you who you must be."

I glanced up with bleary eyes. "You never served your god. You always fought."

"My situation was somewhat different."

"That's no excuse."

"You're feeling guilty. And? You don't think the rest of us Godless haven't wrestled with guilt? You can't change what's done. The past is in the past. So what now, Quen? What are you going to do about it? What kind of man do you want to be?"

I wiped my eyes clear and shoved my spectacles back on. Elijah's bullet-ridden body remained on the floor of the reflection chamber. This wasn't how he'd died, yet I'd killed him all the same. Did I feel guilt for him, knowing he too had acted under the influence of his god? Could he be redeemed?

Could any of us?

"Can we leave this wretched place? Please?" If this was my dream, then I wanted to be anywhere other than a blasted correctional facility. "Take me somewhere safe."

I blinked and found myself standing in the depot of Grayford.

This wasn't my safe haven, but Kayl's. It remained as it had before the Wardens came through and destroyed it. The brickwork was painted in pastel colors, and vines grew up the walls, adding a natural layer of decoration. The tram sat beyond the platform, lit with cozy oil lamps. I could still imagine the collection of cushions inside, where the Godless would meet to scheme and drink their awful coffee. And above that dangled the precarious swinging tram Kayl had made her private room.

She took my hand and guided me up the metal stairs.

"Oh." She stopped suddenly. "I almost forgot. You don't like heights."

"In light of recent events, I believe I'm beginning to overcome my fear." I brushed past her and hopped inside the tram.

It swayed beneath me. The entire carriage was attached to a hook in the ceiling, and all it had taken to bring it down was an Ember's flame. But right now, it was the only place I wanted to be, for this *was* Kayl's sanctuary. Ergo, it was mine.

If it should snap, then I knew she would be there.

Ready to break my fall.

Kayl puttered around the compartment, examining and straightening the many items cluttering the driver's caddy. They were trinkets. Souvenirs. Objects important to her. Comforters, as my fob watch comforted me.

I sat on a pile of cushions and allowed myself to relax. Fairy lights dangled above, winking with a soft glow. Everything about this room was gentle and feminine. It soothed my heart, wrapping a metaphorical bandage around the wounds I'd self-inflicted.

But I wasn't done bleeding yet. Far from it. "I'm going to destroy Dor."

Kayl paused. She held a tiny plant pot in her hand with a single golden flower—Dru's flower, I realized with a jolt. She carefully placed it on a shelf next to a broken clock and sat beside me.

"You took Zyclone's soul."

"I did. Tempest is no more."

"Then... you know what I'm trying to do?"

"When you split my soul from your body, and I changed from Diviner to Chaos, I traveled through the aether for a brief moment. Mesmorpheus came to me. They granted me a vision of your visit to Phantasy." It was the only vision I'd had since my rebirth. Perhaps my last vision.

Then when I awoke inside the clock tower, I'd known I wasn't truly free. I'd escaped Dor only to become chained to another god. While I didn't fault Corentine's ambitions, nor Jinx's, their intentions were no different from Dor's.

They wanted to take away a mortal's right to choose life and freedom.

Mesmorpheus had gifted me the blueprint for my escape. By taking Zyclone's soul, I'd damned the Zephyr, but could shield myself from Corentine.

My thoughts were my own. As were my actions. I was free to sin and blaspheme as much as I liked. The relief of cursing and criticizing one's god without them metaphorically breathing down one's neck was overwhelming.

I would *never* prostrate myself to another being ever again. Now... Now I would think and feel on my own terms.

I'd taken lives. I'd caused misery in Dor's name, and that... it burned through me with guilt and shame and righteous anger. I may not have saved Solaris or prevented this war, but I'd end it, one way or another. I'd make Dor pay for his transgressions.

The only way I could do better, become a good man, was to acknowledge the part I'd played in all this.

It wasn't an absolution, but I'd baptize myself in Dor's destruction.

If this was my path, then so be it.

"Mesmorpheus left me with this, but I don't even know where to start." Kayl hugged her chest. "They think we can rebuild Chime, but how? Have you seen the state it's in? The gods are already warring, and I... I saw Edana fight The Nameless One. It was awful. Ember burning Necro, Necro eating Ember. It was a bloodbath with no end in sight. How are we meant to stand against gods who have a never-ending supply of mortals they can throw at us, at each other, with no regard for their lives? Against gods who can burn entire domains?"

She rubbed her cheek. Her fingers were shaking.

In my wretchedness, I hadn't noticed her own pain. She'd come back from Witheryn bloodied and diminished. She'd witnessed horrors no mortal should ever face alone.

I hadn't been there for her. Another shameful failure on my part.

I took her in my arms and let her head rest against my chest. "Mesmorpheus left us with quite the mess."

She snorted. "The understatement of the century. They're gods. They can drag this shit out forever. We'll be fighting until we're old and gray."

Only Chaos could stop this war. Mesmorpheus had seen it. I still believed the universe needed the forces of chaos and time to balance each other, but not like this. Not under Dor or Corentine's rule.

The very thought of taking the gods' souls for ourselves sounded so wrong—of going against instinct and damning the domains, as Jinx wanted—but the gods had left us with no choice.

It had come down to this.

"It won't be as easy as knocking on a domain's door and inviting ourselves in for tea," I said. "The gods are aware of what threat Chaos represents. Dor has the Umber on his side. Jinx has Edana and Serenity."

"She's got Gildola's power. The Necro, too."

"And we have the Mesmer and Zephyr between us." Though I wasn't yet sure what that meant, or what that power could do. "Technically the Vesper, though we'll come back to that."

She pulled herself from my chest. "If Jinx gets to the gods first... I've already lost Vincent. I can't—I can't lose anyone else."

Jinx was the real threat. Dor had allowed her to take Solaris in order to remove the Glimmer challenging his rule. He could very well allow her to continue her rampage against the domains. Indeed, that came straight from Dor's playbook—to allow Jinx, and us, to rid the domains of their gods and pave the way for his rule.

He wouldn't even need to betray his own allies if we did it for him.

But with every soul Jinx took, she grew stronger, and soon she'd become impossible to defeat. Though even Dor wasn't foolish enough to give his enemies an unfair advantage. Not unless he had plans of his own.

Besides my own personal reasons for going after Dor, I wanted to save Ben. I *had* left him behind, and if there was any way to free him, I'd take it.

"We're caught in the middle of Jinx and Dor's conflict," I said. "We can use that to our advantage. We undermine them. We find a reason to turn Unghard against Dor, and we convince Edana and Serenity to side with us against Jinx. You've already got the Fauna on our side, which was a stroke of genius, by the way."

"I wouldn't call it that. They know we're Chaos, and that we stand against the Diviner, but they don't know the extent of what we can do... Or what we plan to do. We can't tell them we're chasing after the souls of the gods. I don't want to scare them off."

"Agreed."

"Then, what's our first move?"

There was much to do, much to consider, and time wasn't on our side. And yet...

We sat so close together, our buttocks touched. For all my sins, Kayl wasn't repulsed by my ugliness. How could she forgive me, knowing what kind of man I was? What I'd done? She'd asked me what man I wanted to be.

I wanted to be a man worthy of her.

I stood and hoisted her to her feet. "Dance with me."

"Really?" She wrapped her hand around my waist. "Here?"

"Like so." The hairs on my arms stood on end as I placed a hand on her hip. "Do you remember when I invited you to the ambassadors' charity ball? You threw wine on a perfectly clean shirt."

She took on a wistful look. "How could I ever forget?"

"I'd really hoped you would turn up in one of those dresses."

"Which one? The slutty one?"

Heat rose to my cheeks. "Whichever you would have preferred."

She twirled in my arms, and as she did so, her robe instantly changed into the low-cut purple dress. It hugged her figure so tightly, it truly left little to the imagination. Against her Mesmer skin, she became night itself. "How does it look?"

I cleared my throat. "Wonderful."

My own outfit had changed to the tuxedo I'd worn that night. As I swept her off her feet, I swept my emotions away. For this moment, I wanted to forget the gods, forget Chime.

In my dreams, fate didn't matter.

Music played through a loudspeaker in the depot around us. I hadn't known the sound system still worked here, but this was a dream, and the rules need not apply. It was a slow melody, and together we waltzed in the little space the tram provided. The carriage swayed gently to our rhythm, though the dips and jolts of my stomach had nothing to do with its motion.

"You're the woman of my dreams," I said, before my tongue could even understand the implication of uttering such words. My tongue had always been a traitor to my heart, though in this case, they were in cahoots. "Ah, I mean, in your Mesmer persona. Standing here. In my dreams." *Smooth, Quen.*

She fluttered her eyelashes. "You have such a way with words. And with your feet, too."

"I *am* academically trained. Philosophical dancing is part of the syllabus."

"Is it proper for a lowly Undercity maid like myself to be dancing with a strapping young gentleman from the Golden City?" She bit her lip in such a depraved, delightful way, it sent a thrum through my blood. "Think of the scandal."

"Then we best give the Courier something to be scandalized over."

She leaned close and breathed in my ear. "If we fucked in this dream, would you cum in reality?"

Dear saints, this woman! "Kayl, please. I doubt the nice Fauna currently stitching my arm together would appreciate it if I suddenly stood at attention."

"You started it."

I rolled my eyes. "I *meant* taking on the gods together. Would you do me the honor, Miss Arkey?"

"As partners?"

"With some caveats." Though this time, the caveats would be domain-destroying. Nothing would ever be the same again.

"How could a Godless ever say no?"

A familiar whirring clicked over the loudspeaker, interrupting the music. Our dance slowed to a gentle sway. "I may never be able to hold you like this again."

"You'll still have one hand."

"It won't be the same." I'd lost my dominant arm, and that would be a disadvantage in the battles to come, unless the Zephyr performed miracles.

"If I remember, didn't you say you'd sooner touch me with your tongue?"

I chuckled, my cheeks heating again. "I did say that, didn't I."

My dirty, traitorous tongue.

In the sanctity of my mind, perhaps I could finally admit this one truth...

I desired Kayl.

No, that was too small a word for the way my body and mind craved her company. I'd been forced to deny my feelings under Dor's watchful eye, and then Corentine's and Jinx's, but I couldn't contain how I felt any longer.

I could deny Kayl no more.

Another clicking stuttered above me. This time, it didn't sound like it originated from the loudspeaker, but from all around me. It fell into a symmetrical pattern, a tick-tock...

Like a clock.

The carriage shuddered violently. Kayl stumbled into my arms as the entire depot shook.

"Is this part of the dream?" I asked.

Kayl clung to my jacket. "How should I know?"

"You're the Mesmer!"

"I've only been a Mesmer for the past pissing week!"

Another tremor cracked through the ceiling. Gods. The tram was going to fall!

"Mama?" called a voice from outside the tram. Should I be worried my subconscious was being invaded?

"Celeste?" Kayl took a tentative step toward the carriage entrance. "Is that you?"

A Mesmer stood on the decidedly more secure metal platform outside. One of the three who'd been attending to my physical body. "There you are! We tried going inside your mind, but you weren't there. It was nothing but static."

"Are you here to pull us out?" I asked as the carriage once again shook. The great poets said mortals dreamed in metaphors, and I was sure this particular metaphor wasn't positive. "I presume they've finished putting me back together again?"

"Oh yes!" She spoke with a cheerful, dreamy voice as though oblivious to the tremors quaking through the depot. "Wolfsbane did a great job stitching you up. He's not as good as Uncle Vinny, though—his stitching is far prettier."

Kayl winced at the mention of Vincent. "Okay, can you get to the point?"

"That's right." Celeste touched her chin, her head cocked pensively. "I'm supposed to tell you we're being attacked and now would be a good time to wake up."

"We're being *what*?"

An almighty crack split the ceiling above us.

The ground fell beneath me.

"Kay—" I began to yell, but my words and breath were sucked from my lips as darkness swallowed me whole.

Screaming brought me back to reality this time. My eyes were blurry, partly from being dragged awake, and partly from not wearing my spectacles. I tried to sit up, but a wave of dizziness thwarted me. I slumped back down, banging my shoulder with a painful hiss.

No, not my shoulder. My upper right arm was wrapped in a bloodied bandage. The rest of my arm was gone. Completely gone. Only a round stump remained.

The pulsing agony had been literally cut from my arm, but the residual limb above what was once my elbow still radiated with dull pain. It sodding hurt, and not even a good cup of tea would fix it.

The flap to the tent snapped open, and Kayl bounded inside. "Thank the gods, you're awake." She carefully pulled me into a sitting position. "Can you move? We need to leave. Right now."

I managed to swing my legs off the cot without passing out. "What's happening?"

"Wardens." She sucked in a breath. "They've come for us."

13

Faen is another illusive god. Like Zyclone, the Fauna god rarely communes with mortals, including their own. The Fauna's presence on the Warden Council is barely noticeable. This has been a source of much frustration over the years as Faen simply allows their mortals to run rampant within Chime, leaving correctional punishment in the Warden's hands. Faen cannot be counted upon. When the dust of this war has settled, they alone will continue to exist, unaware a war even took place. To that end, they can be ignored for now. Their mortals are hardly a threat.
—P. Bezel, *Personal Report on Faen*

I QUICKLY HELPED QUEN dress in a spare shirt and trousers Wolfsbane had left behind. They were oversized, but they would have to do, because we didn't have time to piss around.

Wardens were attacking the campsite.

Hadn't I warned Trixie they'd attack when they deemed the Fauna a threat? I didn't think the Diviner were here for the Fauna, though. They'd come for Quen. Which meant I'd led the Wardens right into the Fauna's home.

Though conscious, Quen was unsteady on his feet, and I had to wrap my arm around him to stop him from toppling over.

"It may be the drugs or blood loss, but I thought I'd check—this isn't still a dream, is it?"

I guided him to the tent's exit. "I wish it were."

"And you, you were in my dream, correct? You saw... me?"

"We danced. I wore the slutty dress."

"And it was worth every glorious boc! Observe!" He flapped the empty sleeve of his right arm, which I'd attempted to roll up and had now come loose. "That dress cost a limb!" He giggled deliriously.

"*Focus*, Quen. We still need to get out of here in one piece."

He snorted. "In one piece? Bit late for that!"

Gods, things must be bad if I was the sensible one.

We stepped out of the tent into chaos.

The Wardens had cut a giant hole within the wall of the cistern. A perfect circle that glowed red-hot with molten metal. God knows how they'd made it all the way down here through the pipes and tunnels, but they'd brought Umber with them who carried blowtorches and wore welding masks. If anyone knew these pipes, it would be a group of bloody Umber.

Diviner were marching through, armed with pistols, and not tasers. Shit. They meant business. Some also carried odd metal helmets.

"What are those weird hats?" I whispered.

"Portable soul-splitting devices," Quen hissed. "I saw similar devices in Timefall Estates."

Shit, really? The Diviner had invented easier ways to split a mortal's soul? Great.

A line of snarling Fauna arrayed themselves against the Wardens. A menagerie of Juniper's most dangerous and deadly creatures, as Wolfsbane would have called it. They had the fangs and claws, but against Diviner? They wouldn't stand a chance.

"Go! Hurry, you sods!" yelled a goat-woman with horns, hooves, and flappy ears. She stood outside the main dining tent and waved adults and younger children past. A whole stream of them were running in the opposite direction of the invading Diviner. Paws, hooves, and claws pounded through the campsite as panicked Fauna grabbed what few belongings they owned and ran for it.

"Where are we going?" I called out.

"Service tunnel!" A young squirrel-boy tripped over. Goat-Woman scooped him up before he could be trampled underfoot and held the boy close to her chest. "We're evacuating. Trixie's orders!"

"Where's Trix—" I began to ask, but then the entire campsite went still.

A horrible hush whooshed over the cistern, silencing even the flowing water from the pipes above. The fleeing Fauna were paused in their tracks.

The beasts by the entrance had been caught midpounce, stopping their chance of attack. The Umber, too, were trapped in time, but the Diviner didn't need them.

"They've paused time," Quen whispered.

Shit. They had.

I pulled Quen behind a tent. The Diviner spread out among the Fauna and seemed to be... What? Examining them? Checking them for weapons? I wasn't sure.

Then they drew out those soul-splitting helmets and began attaching them. Other smaller mortals—those in half-animal forms too small to fit a helmet—were instead wrapped in an aether collar.

Shit.

A Diviner approached one of the larger, more intimidating bull-like Fauna. Neither a helmet nor collar would fit him. Instead, the Diviner simply held up his hand.

A secondary pocket of time wrapped around the bull-man.

And I felt it. Gods. I felt time speed *up*.

The bull-man disintegrated into a pile of dust within the blink of an eye, just as I'd once witnessed Jinx manipulating time—and as the Redeemer had killed the ambassadors in my vision. The Diviner had literally aged him to death rather than waste a bullet.

Another Diviner did the same thing to a smaller otter-like woman.

Those they couldn't collar and take, they were killing in so terrible a way.

Shitting shit!

I'd been so caught up in what they were doing, I didn't realize Quen was hyperventilating. I rubbed his back. "Stay calm."

"*Calm?*" His breathing was running ragged. "In all my years, I've never—*never* seen Wardens act in such a manner! This is cruel, it's obscene! We never harm citizens. It goes against everything the Covenant stands for—"

"The Covenant's gone." I shushed him before he got us caught or gave himself a heart attack. "These aren't Wardens dealing with rioters. This is war. They're soldiers acting on Dor's command."

"Dor can kiss my buttocks!"

"Are you still high?"

Quen ran his remaining palm down his face. "Unfortunately, I'm starting to sober. We need to stop them."

"Stop them how? There're at least thirty pissing Diviner out there!" Though, shit, I wasn't against taking them down. I could potentially knock some of them asleep, but they'd already spread out—I wouldn't get them all before they noticed. Besides, I'd end up knocking the Fauna out, too, which wouldn't help their escape.

Quen's skin rippled from Chaos silvery-blue back to his familiar Diviner face. Gods! I'd almost forgotten he could do that. It was Quen as I knew him, though his eyes were still like mine—aether.

"I'll hold them back—"

"No, Quen. You can barely stand—"

"Then I'll bloody do it sitting!" He drew a breath. "Find the Fauna leader. Get them and the children to safety. Save as many as you can."

An overprotective part of me wanted to drag him to safety. To abandon the Fauna to their fate if only to keep Quen safe, especially after I'd gone to such pissing effort to get him back. But that wasn't what a Godless would do.

I'd brought the Wardens here. I couldn't leave the Fauna with this mess.

"Stay hidden. I'll find Trixie, but I'll be back." I squeezed his shoulder on his uninjured side and then slipped from behind the tent.

The Diviner hadn't reached us yet—they were searching the tents further on, no doubt looking for us. But as soon as Quen began fucking with time, they'd find him. I had to be careful and quick.

Luckily, sneaking around was one of my skill sets. It was even easier with a Fauna form. I changed into a cat and climbed out of my robe. My nose had gotten a good sense of Wolfsbane's shaggy dog scent, unfortunately, and I followed it to the main tent.

Both he and Trixie were inside, frozen mid-argument. I changed to my upright form and snatched a robe from the hat stand as time lurched forward.

Quen was already making his move.

"I'm not leaving—" Trixie's mouth dropped open at my sudden appearance. "You! This is all your fucking fault! You and the Dark Warden!" She came at me, claws out. "Fucking Wardens are after you and your damn mate!"

Wolfsbane intercepted her. "Easy, Trix—"

"We can argue who's at fault later," I said as I tied the robe around my waist. Really, where did they get all these robes from? "Diviner are here, and they're pausing time to get at your Fauna. My partner is the only reason we're having this conversation, otherwise you'd already be dead—"

"Fucking Diviner," Trixie muttered. "We'll rip them apart."

"No, you won't. Quen can't hold back time for much longer, not in his state. You need to get your Fauna out of here while you still can."

She bared her fangs. "I don't appreciate you telling me what to do. You've lied to me, endangered my mortals, wounded my kin. Who's to say you're not on the Wardens' side?"

"Because, as you figured out, they're after us. They know we're their biggest threat. Quen and I will distract the Wardens, keep them busy, and buy you as much time as we can to evacuate—"

"This is our 'ome—"

"*Was* your home." I knew I was being a hard-arse, but we literally didn't have time to stand around arguing about it.

"She's right, Trix," Wolfsbane said. "It's over. We run and lick our wounds."

Trixie shoved Wolfsbane aside. Rage flashed in her feline eyes, and for a second there, it looked like she was about to pounce on me. But then her claws retracted. "There's a service tunnel to the south. It leads down to the Undercity. We regroup there, and you better not disappear on me! Blood's on your paws, and you're gonna 'elp me collect."

"Fine by me."

I ran back outside to more screaming. With time resumed, the Fauna had unleashed their attack against the Diviner. Blood and fur flew in the air as massive beasts sank their teeth and claws into whatever unfortunate soul happened to be nearest. Their rage only increased at the sight of their kin in collars.

Sadly, they were my bait. So long as Quen could keep time going, we had a means of fighting back.

Mama! Cosmo yelled inside my mind. *Where are you? I'm scared!*

Ah shit, I'd forgotten my own bloody mortals. *Can you and the others get to the service tunnel? We're escaping!* My godlike senses told me the trio were hiding in a tent further up. Shit! Their tent was surrounded by Wardens. *Hold on. I'll come get you.*

I pressed between the tents and used their cover to sneak through the campsite. The bulk of the fighting was further up, by the entrance to the cistern. Fauna scrambled past my feet in their effort to escape, none of them aware of time sparkling through the air.

A few Diviner had retreated to safety behind a wall of solid Umber, and they were now battling Quen. The Fauna passing me stuttered in their movements. Shit.

Quen couldn't hold out much longer.

I reached the Mesmer's hiding place as a hulking bull crashed through the tent next to me. Moss covered his face and expanded around him. He clawed at it, spluttering and choking as it filled his mouth, his nostrils.

Oh my fucking god!

Umber were manipulating the algae and weeds growing in the cistern. Gods, they were suffocating the Fauna with moss. Others were wrappings weeds around the Fauna's necks, strangling them. I'd never heard of an Umber using their powers this way. Shit. I'd never thought they'd have it in them to murder!

This was war, all right, and apparently it brought out the worst in everyone. What next? Mesmer poisoning mortals with candy made from arsenic? Maybe if I let them.

I switched to my Mesmer form and threw a miasma at the nearby Umber. They collapsed to the metal floor with a heavy *thunk*, instantly asleep.

The bull-man ripped the moss from his face and sucked in gulps of air. "Thank you," he rasped.

I patted him on the back. "Head to the service tunnel. Get as many out as you can."

He nodded, and stomped off.

I slipped into the tent where the trio were waiting with Autumn and Freddie. Those two were good young 'uns for watching the Mesmer for me, but shit, I wished they'd evacuated already with the others.

The trio huddled together. Well, Cosmo was hunched over in fright as Celeste and Castor coddled them as usual. "Mama!" Cosmo wailed. "You took so long!"

"Yes, well, we have trouble. Do you know where the service tunnel is?" I asked Autumn and Freddie. "You need to get there *now*."

"We know the tunnel." Autumn stood awkwardly, her broken leg tied to a splint. Her ears were pricked up, alert and listening for trouble. Unlike poor Freddie, she seemed more excited than agitated. "But it's small. They won't fit inside." She pointed her thumb at the trio.

"You can't kill us again!" Cosmo clung to Castor's hip. "You promised!"

I really didn't have time for this. "It's horrible, I know. But this is an emergency—"

"Can they do what you do?" asked Freddie. "Turn into one of us?"

Technically, they could. I'd rebirthed them as Chaos, after all, and they'd had no trouble switching to their default Mesmer form. Did I really want to see what beasts they'd become as Fauna? I supposed I didn't have much choice. "All right, let's try it, but be quick."

"Does—Does this mean I have to get n-na-*naked*?" Cosmo squeaked.

I resisted the urge to rub my forehead. "Look, I'm your god. I've seen everything anyway. There's no need to be shy."

"You could turn into a cute kitty like Mama!" Celeste smiled at me in that same manic way as whenever she was trying too hard to help. I was not a *cute* kitty.

"Do you think I'll be cute?" Cosmo's eyes went wide.

"The cutest little fluffy—"

"Can you please just do it?" I said, trying not to raise my voice.

Freddie offered his hands.

Cosmo and Castor took a hand each, as Celeste took his wrist. Shit, what if any of them accidentally took Freddie's soul? I hadn't taught them how to correctly use their Chaos powers!

The three of them suddenly shrank, disappearing into their clothes, with Freddie still standing there, his soul intact. Thank the gods for that.

A fluffy white nose poked out of Celeste's trousers. "Am I cute?"

"Am I fluffy?" Castor poked out an identically fluffy white ear.

"My feet are huge!" Cosmo exclaimed.

Freddie helped them climb out of their clothes.

Oh, you had to be kidding me.

The trio had become rabbits. White rabbits! Cute rabbits with big floppy ears and pink noses. I supposed it made sense, for a bunch of timid Mesmer, but the image of them as *pissing rabbits* was sending me places I didn't want to go.

Freddie let out an excited squeal.

"Yes, they're adorable." I held up my hand. "But we have to leave! Can you lead them to safety?"

Autumn and Freddie turned into their fox and rat forms. Poor Autumn's leg slid from the splint, forcing her to hobble, though she managed on three legs. Thankfully, it didn't take much to get the trio going—they were eager to hop along and test their new bodies. I stepped out of the tent first to check it was clear.

An Umber was engaged in a fistfight with the large gray-skinned creature Wolfsbane had called an herbivore. The two butted rock-hard heads, the cistern shaking under their weight. But so long as they fought, we had an opportunity to escape.

"Hurry!" I gestured for the trio. Freddie led the way, with Autumn trailing behind them. They were small enough they shouldn't attract attention. Not when huge lumbering Fauna were tearing their way through the Umber.

Time suddenly stopped.

Shit, Quen!

I ran in the direction of Quen and almost tripped over Autumn. She was headed back in my direction, but why...

Oh fuck.

She was walking backwards. Freddie, too. I glanced to where the Umber and Fauna were fighting, and their movements were going in reverse. The Diviner were rewinding time. Shit!

A white rabbit bounded over to my feet. Celeste. "Mama! What are they doing?"

"It's the Diviner. They're fucking with time." They knew the Fauna were making their escape, which meant the Fauna would be dragged back here for capture or worse, including Trixie.

Freddie walked backwards beside me. I scooped him up by the scruff of his neck and let my Mesmer touch knock him out. He instantly fell asleep in my arms. My powers counteracted the Diviner, at least.

We needed to put those arseholes to bed. "I know I'm asking a lot, but I can't do this alone. I need you three to help me reach the Diviner."

"You want us to go out *there*?" Cosmo squeaked, returning with Castor. "Where the danger is?"

"You stay in the tent with Freddie, Cosmo. I'll come get you both as soon as it's safe. Celeste? Castor? Can I count on you?"

"Yes, Mama!" Celeste booped my foot with her nose.

Castor bobbed his head in agreement.

"We have to be quick." If we didn't act now, we'd never save the Fauna.

I hustled Cosmo inside the tent and left Freddie in their care—they couldn't do much worse than the Diviner, anyhow. Celeste and Castor scattered in opposite directions to attempt to flank the Diviner. I wove between the Fauna now marching backwards to their doom, and sent instructions through my mind so we'd be ready to coordinate our attack.

Gods, I hoped Quen was safe. If those pissing Diviner had touched him...

All right, focus.

We're ready, Celeste said.

I stepped toward a group of Diviner. They turned to me, confused for a second until they realized who I was.

"It's Anarchy!" one of them cried out.

Now!

A miasma fell over the cistern. The Diviner tried to run back inside the tunnels and away from me, but Celeste and Castor had already snuck inside. They transformed from white rabbit to Mesmer, catching them from both sides.

The Diviner collapsed in a heap.

The Umber stopped moving backwards and collapsed with them. Sadly, so did the Fauna. It likely wouldn't hold them for long.

"Wake those you can and go!" I yelled. I crouched beside the bull-Fauna and shook him awake.

He rose on weary feet. "What's going on—"

"Help me wake the Fauna and get out of here!"

He soon snapped to attention and began waking his friends.

I left Celeste and Castor to make their own way and ran for Quen. I almost screamed when I reached the tent and found it empty.

Wait, his clothes were abandoned on the floor.

"Quen?"

"I'm here," squeaked a tiny voice. A little bird wobbled out from under the tent cloth, its right wing missing. "I'm sorry. I couldn't hold it, and then a Warden found me—"

"It's okay, but we need to go. Can I carry you? It'll be quicker." I held out my hands.

He hopped into my open palms, and I gently lifted him close to my chest. "This isn't entirely dignified."

"I'll get you a cup of tea later." Although with the state of things, maybe I shouldn't make such promises.

The Fauna were making their escape fully now as they ran through the campsite. They were sensible enough to give up and abandon their belongings. Things could be replaced. Mortals couldn't. I followed as they scurried between my legs.

I turned around a big tent, and the cistern's metal shell suddenly warped into warm sandstone walls.

What the shit?

"Quen, are you seeing this?" I whispered.

"Seeing what?"

"Shit, I'm having a vision." The walls closed in, overwhelming my senses until my reality bled through the eyes of another.

It had been years since I'd last walked these hallways. My feet tapped the pristine tiles, guided by memory, and the past greeted me with familiar comfort. This had been my home for much of my formative years. The scent of chalk, freshly printed paper, and spilled ink never quite left. Doors lined the hall, each a portal into a domain of learning—to an education that would best serve society. Or they had been, before Chime's collapse.

Two Diviner waited outside the lecture hall where I'd once sat for an exam that determined the course of my future. Though, naturally, my future had always been set, thanks to my Father. His will had brought me to this moment in time.

"They're ready for you, sir," greeted one of the Diviner.

The other opened the door, and I stepped inside.

Where once rows of desks lined the hall, now rows of metal chairs stood bolted to the floor. This room had been converted to my needs, though the lectern remained at the front, as did the chalkboard, filled with a series of mathematical equations. Wires spread from each of the chairs, forming a collective web on the ceiling.

And in each chair sat lesser mortals. Fauna. Ember.

They squirmed, strapped in, with aether collars to keep their powers at bay. I'd ordered them gagged. Fearful mortals had a tendency to scream, yet they would have nothing to fear, had they led a life free of sin.

They were ready to receive my judgement.

Through my holy mercy, they would be redeemed.

Something bit my wrist. The classroom faded, returning the campsite to sharp focus.

"Ouch! Did you just peck me?"

"Stay with me, Kayl," Quen said. "We're attempting an escape, remember? And you were squeezing me."

"Sorry," I mumbled.

"What did you see?"

"A classroom. I... I think it was the Academy." I'd looked into rooms like that one when Quen first brought me to meet his professor. Had I just witnessed the past or the future?

Shit. That was where the Diviner were bringing their captives. They were ripping out their souls, turning them into soulless husks. Slaves to do their bidding. Why bother taking them there if they had a means of destroying souls on the fly?

Unless they wanted to interrogate them first.

But Quen was right. I'd have to worry about my vision later.

I stopped by the tent hiding Cosmo and Freddie, the latter slowly waking, and then we joined the crowd of escaping Fauna.

A badger bumped into my leg. I followed it to the service entrance, and now I could see why no one had brought belongings with them. It was a tiny hatch in the floor. Not even my arse would fit through it. Fauna transformed into smaller animals and took turns to squeeze through. At least that meant the Wardens couldn't follow easily.

Wolfsbane waited by the entrance, ushering mortals inside. "Hurry!"

"I'll have to carry you in my mouth again," I said to Quen.

"*Or* I could ride on your back."

"Oh, that's definitely dignified." And really, I wanted to be the one to ride Quen, but now wasn't the time to indulge those thoughts. I placed him beside the hatch and transformed back into my smaller cat form. "Make sure you hang on tight."

He changed his form to a tiny mouse with a missing right foreleg and straddled me, clinging as best he could.

I waited for the younger Fauna to get in first, and then Cosmo with a sleepy Freddie. Celeste and Castor came with the stragglers—wounded Fauna who limped for the hatch. I readied myself to follow.

Wolfsbane, however, made no attempt to move.

"Are you coming?" I asked.

"I can't leave my kin. I'll secure the hatch behind you and cover it."

"Once we're gone, the Diviner will wake up. You know that, right?"

He stared at me with anger in his remaining eye. "I know."

"Does Trixie know you're throwing your life away?"

He grinned in that wolfish way I was growing fond of. "Trixie understands me. She's my mate."

Oh. Now I understood what 'mate' meant. They were partners, much the same as Quen and me. And the old wolf was going to pull the same chivalrous shit Quen would in this situation. I plonked my arse down. "Then we'll wait with you."

His grin fell. "You'll what?"

"If you want to throw your life away, then fine. Clearly you don't care for Trixie or your kin, because if you did, you'd give them the best chance of survival. And that's by not playing hero."

His fur bristled. "This isn't about me—"

"No? Then you'll put your ego aside and help us escape. You can do nothing for them—" I nodded to the Fauna we'd had to leave behind. "But the rest of your kin still needs you. As does Trixie."

Wolfsbane huffed. "Your mate is a real hard-arse," he said to Quen.

"He's just as bad," I said.

Quen muttered something I didn't quite catch.

I slipped into the hatch and waited as Wolfsbane transformed into a smaller dog and pulled the hatch down behind him with his teeth. It locked us in darkness and silence within a cramped tunnel, but we were free from the Diviner, for now. It likely wouldn't take them long to figure out where we'd gone.

Wolfsbane shoved me with his nose. "Go, cat."

I patted his nose with my paw and then set off after the others, Quen clinging to my neck. A long line of Fauna traveled through the tunnel, all animals of smaller sizes. The Mesmer trio were further ahead in their bunny bodies.

We hadn't saved everyone. Some would be taken to the Academy, of all places.

We'd get them back.

The air tasted stale as we marched in silent order. The patter of tiny footsteps and muttered whispering was the only thing echoing through the tunnel, the atmosphere morose. I couldn't blame them. Twice now they'd been displaced from their home. The cistern campsite had been their version of Grayford—a safe haven now abandoned.

Where would they go next?

Gods, the silence was starting to get to me. "Are you all right up there?" I asked Quen.

"Tired."

He'd lost an arm, so I wasn't surprised. "As soon as we find shelter, we'll rest."

He nuzzled his nose against my neck in response.

It was funny how things had turned out. I'd gotten my Quen back, but everything had changed. Quen wasn't the same Diviner I'd met that day on the Undercity elevator. Gods, he wasn't a Diviner at all anymore. He'd been through so much suffering, and it was all Dor's fault. Every shitty thing to ever befall Chime was because of Dor.

Even Corentine. Even Jinx.

If Quen wanted my help bringing Dor down, I was only too happy to oblige. I needed my partner to stop Dor *and* Jinx. But this war they'd started wasn't just about the forces of time versus chaos, or about saving mortals and ending the reign of the gods.

It was also about Dru. Harmony. Vincent. Sinder.

The gods had taken my family away from me, and I'd get them back. No matter what.

The tunnels opened out as we slowly crept our way through the bowels of Chime. They led onto railway tracks. The Undercity.

It had been too long since Dru and I had walked these tracks. They were still lined with soot, and the air tasted of that rancid oil. Since spending time topside, I'd almost forgotten how dirty and grim it was down here. This had once been home. I hadn't missed it.

The Fauna huddled in groups on the tracks. There was little likelihood of a train coming through, though I couldn't tell which line we were on. Everyone seemed to be waiting for a command, some sort of direction to go. Their attention turned to the fat white cat standing in the center.

Wolfsbane approached the cat, and I followed. I assumed it was Trixie, based on the fur pattern, but as I neared, I spotted a pair of fluffy balls dangling between its legs.

"Oh!" I exclaimed a bit too loudly.

Trixie turned around and scowled as much as a cat could. It was definitely her. "Never seen a pair on a woman before?"

"Actually, I've never seen a pair on a cat before." I'd met plenty of Ember ladies with girlcock, so that wasn't a shock. I'd just been caught unawares, considering I'd not seen Trixie in her cat form.

"There are some things Fauna can't change, not like a Necro can. But every part of me is woman, got it?"

"Say no more."

Her tail twitched in annoyance. "Listen up!" Her voice carried through the tunnel. "Wardens could still be after us, so we've got to keep moving. 'Ead to Tom Cat's Café in Sinner's Row. It ain't ideal, but we'll make room until we can get what we need."

The Fauna mumbled and began a dejected shuffle through the tunnel.

"Didn't you say Sinner's Row was barricaded?" I asked.

"I said it's not ideal, didn't I? The cat café is my property. It's got beds, electricity, running water. We'll need other supplies—food, weapons. More importantly, it's under Erosain's protection, and 'e ain't letting no fucking Wardens in."

"Erosain's still there?" I supposed he didn't want to give up his little slice of Chime. "Why leave in the first place?"

"Because Erosain's a bellend."

"He runs a protection racket," Wolfsbane added. "Since the calamity happened, he's taken over the whole Row."

Of course he had.

"Erosain will let us back in for a price," Trixie said. "Guess we'll worry about the price when we get there."

Great. Was now the time to bring up Erosain's grudge against me? Or that I'd been banned from Sinner's Row?

"We're making a base... in a cat café," Quen whispered. "A brothel."

"Needs must."

"If Erosain discovers us—"

"I know." Maybe he'd not recognize me as a cat and we'd get away with it. He'd certainly not expect Quen to turn up looking like a mouse.

Cries of alarm echoed behind us. Someone was pushing through the crowd in a panic.

"Autumn!" Freddie cried out as he scurried around in his rat form. He ran up to us. "I can't find Autumn. Has anyone seen her?"

Wolfsbane and I shared a startled look.

Shit.

I couldn't remember seeing Autumn go through the hatch. Had her leg gotten her caught?

The Mesmer trio bounded over in their rabbit form. "We thought she was with you, Mama!"

Oh gods no. I suddenly felt sick. "She wasn't with me. I didn't see, she wasn't—"

A growl ripped from Trixie's throat. Before I could even react, she pounced on top of me. Quen fell from my back and landed on his side with a painful squeak.

Trixie pinned me, her fangs bared. "You did this!" she hissed into my ear. "If those Diviner 'ave taken that girl, if they 'arm her—"

"Trix, that's enough!" Wolfsbane barked.

"I let this—this *thing* into our 'ome, and now more of my mortals are gone—"

"I know where they've taken them!" I wriggled under her grip, but gods, she was heavier than she looked. "I'll get them back, I swear to you—"

"You swore the last time, and then you brought the Dark Warden to my door—"

"We'll do all we can to help you," Quen said. He'd managed to roll onto his feet and stood unsteadily. "The Diviner are your enemy. They attacked your home, not me—"

"You're one of them!"

"Do I look like one of them?" His mouse whiskers twitched. "The man you think I am no longer exists. Dor killed him. Defiled him. Who I am now is the man who will wage war against him and his mortals. Are you with me?"

The defiance in Quen's words sent tingles through my gut.

There was my Quen. The Godless's benefactor.

"All I see is a washed-out Warden with one arm, and a disaster with no fucking clue. 'Ow the fuck will the pair of you be any use? In Juniper, we eat the weak."

"Then help us," I said. "We'll take them on together, and you can eat whatever's left of them. The Diviner had no right to strike at you. You were minding your own business, living your lives in a city that didn't give a shit. But things have changed, and this is your city now. Take it back."

Trixie glanced at the Fauna standing in the dark tunnel and watching our interaction with bated breath. I followed her gaze. Did she see what I did? Not dejected mortals, but angry ones. The Fauna stomped their hooves and scraped their claws against the stone.

They wanted this fight. They wanted blood.

"Why would either of you care about us Fauna?"

"Because I grew up in Grayford," I said. "I volunteered in the soup kitchen and gave a meal to every Undercity mortal who came to our door, Vesper or Ember or Fauna. Chime denied you a voice, but I won't."

"Please," Quen urged. "The Diviner took your mortals, and that is my responsibility. You saved my life. Let me repay that generosity. Let me get your mortals back."

"They've got our kin, Trix." Wolfsbane's voice was calm but edged with a tremor of fear in it. "I can't—I can't lose them, not like when..." He trailed off, his expression pained, as though fighting to forget some dark memory.

Whatever had happened in his past, the reminder softened the rage in Trixie's eyes.

She lifted her paws from my throat. "Anarchy? Crazy bitch, more like. We'll combine our clans so long as you deliver on your promises." Her eyes narrowed at Quen.

"You have my word," Quen said.

"We'll see. Though none of us are ready for war. We'll rest, we'll train, and we'll plan. On *my* terms."

"Whatever you wish."

Trixie prowled off, her tail curling around Wolfsbane's leg. The old wolf nodded.

The Fauna began their march through the tunnel to Sinner's Row. A few eyed us with curiosity as they passed. We had a ways to go yet.

The Mesmer trio surrounded Freddie. The poor rat boy was trembling all over, and the guilt ate at me. If the Diviner had taken Autumn, then her soul was in danger, and we didn't have time to waste. But with Quen's injury, we weren't in any fit state to mount a rescue attempt, as Trixie had painfully pointed out.

"This is it." Quen somehow managed to sound imposing even with his tiny mouse body. "This is how we launch our battle against the gods." He sighed. "It's not the most impressive start."

No. We were hiding in the dark with allies who didn't fully trust us. "But it's a start."

He cocked his head. "I remember having to convince you to assist me on a foolhardy mission across the domains, and here I am, ready once more to risk life and actual limb. I daresay you've become a terrible influence. Look at the state of us both."

"Don't blame me, that's the almighty power of Chaos. You know I can't do this without you, Quen."

"What a wonderful coincidence, as I absolutely cannot do this without *you*."

I'd admit, we made an odd pair. The two of us against the gods.

Against the universe.

Had Mesmorpheus been high on some illegal candy when they chose us as their saviors? They must have been, because the situation was completely ridiculous.

Whatever happened next, I'd face it with my partner by my side.

My mate.

I'M UNPREDICTABLE AND VIOLENT

Name: Vincent Holcroft, Necro

Known Affiliations: The Godless, Memoria University, Witheryn Asylum
Vincent Holcroft is another member of the Godless and chooses to operate in
the background. He is the artist behind the Godless fliers. One can assume
he uses his healing abilities for the Godless's benefit, though despite his
obvious threatening nature as a Necro, Holcroft has not been known to show
aggression. He was not captured as part of the Warden raid on the Mesmer
temple. His current whereabouts are unknown, though we assume he
returned to Witheryn with the rest of The Nameless One's recalled mortals.
—P. Bezel, Personal Report on Vincent Holcroft

THIS CITY DISCUSTED ME.

I stared through the clockface window at the Diviner scurrying below like mice. Since we'd rampaged through Tempest, Central Station was a fucking mess. Charred vines everywhere. The broken remnants of the Gate.

It was cathartic, really, watching them scramble back together. In only one painful day, they'd lost two of their most valuable allies—the Zephyr and the Necro.

I hope Dor felt it.

Fear.

I hope he had a big fucking cosmic shit over what was coming for him.

YOU LOST THE ZEPHYR, Mother said.

So what? They're not under Dor's command anymore.

YOU PLANNED FOR EVERYTHING. YOU DIDN'T PLAN ON CORINTH BETRAYING YOU?

I flexed my fingers and let my nails sink into my golden flesh. No, I'd known Corinth would betray me. I'd known every word that spilled from his mouth was a fucking lie. But so long as Dor knew he was alive and running around Chime, Corinth remained my distraction. The Diviner would split their focus to hunt him down. Plus, now that Kayl had found him, Corinth would do a better job of keeping my dear sister alive than *she* would.

YOU PUSHED HIM AWAY, Mother whined. *I COULD HAVE MADE HIM MINE.*

I rolled my eyes. *He was never yours. You don't need another Diviner boy toy, Mother. Not after what the last one did to you.*

CORINTH IS NO LONGER DIVINER.

He wasn't Chaos, either. Not like me. Corinth may have the body of Chaos, but that didn't mean he understood our struggle, that he was one of us.

But he had Zyclone's soul, now. Would he know what to do with it? He'd quickly mastered swapping forms and using aether shields in a way not even Kayl had. If Corinth had any sense, he'd use the Zephyr's talents against the Diviner. I guessed we'd see.

YOU HAVE GILDOLA'S POWER, AND NOW THE NAMELESS ONE. RETURN THEIR SOUL TO ME. BREAK THE CHAIN, AND I WILL HAVE MORE STRENGTH TO AID YOU, TO CREATE MORE MORTALS.

That *was* the plan, but I couldn't part with either Gildola's or The Nameless One's soul yet. Not when I needed their abilities to take down the other gods.

Battling The Nameless One had been close. Too close.

If I was going to end the reign of gods, then I needed to be stronger. Better.

REMEMBER YOUR PURPOSE.

I do, Mother. I'll free you. You know I will. But it'll take time.

I'VE WAITED TOO LONG.

Hadn't we all?

Thirteen years I'd spent trapped inside my sister's head. Thirteen fucking years. Apparently, that counted for nothing.

"You're unpredictable and violent!"

Really? Unpredictable? We were fucking Chaos! As for violent... Eh, maybe I'd overindulged in the odd spot of violence a little when I'd gained my new body, but who could blame me? Being trapped inside anyone's head would send you a bit mad. I'd needed an outlet for all that rage I'd been carrying, and no one deserved my wrath more than shitty Diviner.

But if my dear sister thought I was too *unpredictable* and *violent* to team up with, then I'd show her just how nice I could be.

Starting with my new friends.

I stepped away from the clockface and allowed my form to change from Glimmer to Necro. I snapped my fingers.

Vincent Holcroft appeared on the floor. He lay naked and curled in a tight, trembling ball. Chaos had given his pale skin a blue tinge, though his white hair wasn't much different from in his Necro form.

He glanced up, his aether eyes full of horror. "What have you done to me?"

"You're alive. Reborn as Chaos." Kayl didn't have the power to fix the Godless's shitty lives, but I did. They'd see which sister was better. "Your god is dead. You're welcome."

"But why?" he rasped in that breathless Necro accent. "Why bring me back? Why give me life at all?"

"Because we're family, silly! We may not have met, but I was there with you whenever Kayl was. I know you, Vincent. I know you *very* intimately. Everything you've ever thought, ever dreamed, I've seen." Though most of it was a guilt trip worse than Corinth's, with a whole heap of pining for lost lovers that had Corinth's trademark stamp. The two of them were clichéd like that.

Vincent recoiled, guarding his chest. "I served one god in life. I won't serve another in death."

Bloody loyal Godless. "Don't be like that. I thought you'd be happy. I'm doing what you wanted all along—ending the reign of gods. And you're going to help me." I crouched to Vincent's level. "We'll restart the Godless. You, me. Joe over there." I waved at Joe, who was staring at us in shock. He'd get over it. "And Sinder."

"Sinder?" Vincent sat up. "Sinder's here?"

I knew that would grab his interest. "Not right now, but he's one of my closest allies. I could bring him here. Would you like that?"

Vincent chewed on his bottom lip. I could tell he warred with his conscience. His head was in mine, so it wasn't like he could hide it. But everyone had their price, even a goody two-shoes like Vincent.

"I... I killed him."

Oh, here it came. The crushing guilt and shame that had Corinth's trademark stamp, too. Vincent was teetering on the edge of a complete mental breakdown. How did Kayl deal with it? Alcohol? Tea? No, that was the Diviner way.

"Hey, listen to me." I snapped my fingers in front of his face. "Sinder's not dead—"

"I ripped him apart!" A snarl tore from Vincent's throat. "I fed on him! I—I fed..."

"Don't act like you pervs don't indulge your feed-and-fuck fetishes."

His cheeks flushed. "That's different. It's consensual. I *killed* him. He'll... He'll never trust me again, and he'd be right not to."

Sinder had practically thrown himself at Vincent. That looked like consent to me. "If we're going to toss around dirty words like trust, then you should probably know Sinder betrayed my sister so he could get back at the Glimmer."

He blinked. "What?"

Ah-hah! I knew his buddies wouldn't have bothered telling him the truth. "Sinder was spying for me in the Mesmer temple. He totally sold Kayl out, allowing me to infiltrate Solaris and take Gildola and the rest of her stinking Glimmer." I summoned a ball of light in my hand for emphasis. "He betrayed her. Betrayed what you Godless stand for, all because he hated those Glimmer and wanted every one of them to die, just as the Vesper had."

Vincent's shoulders sagged as he shrank into himself. None of what I'd said was a lie, and he knew his lover well enough to believe Sinder carried such hatred for the Glimmer.

"So you see, there's really no reason to feel guilty," I said.

His head dropped. "What do you want from me?" he said with a strained whisper.

I bit back a smile. "Your unending friendship. I'm raising a whole army of Necro, and I want you to lead them." I needed bloodthirsty killers as well as healers. My Necro wouldn't go feral, but with Chaos powering them, they'd be unstoppable against the Diviner.

"I'm a medic, not a leader."

"Don't sell yourself so short, Vinny. You can learn."

"And what will they feed on? Necro need blood."

I waved to the group of Glimmer powering our aether shield. "There's your meal right there."

Vincent looked horrified. But really, who was better than a bunch of shitty mortals who deserved it? The Godless's own enemies!

This was the start of my new army against Dor. The new Godless. Kayl's version had been little more than a wine-tasting club with a few bright ideas, but I'd make them a force to be reckoned with. Edana and Serenity would gift me Sinder and Harmony. Eventually, I'd go after the Umber and get Dru. All that was missing from my collection was Malk. Poor Malk. No one gave a shit about him.

And Reve, though Reve's soul was long gone to the aether. I didn't need a Mesmer seer to tell me what was coming, and what shit I was about to fuck up.

"Vincent?" Joe came bumbling over. Emotion clashed through Joe's mind, cycling from shock to disbelief, concern, and... lust? Really?

Fuck me. Joe had a crush on Vincent. When had that happened? In the Mesmer temple? I hadn't brought Vincent back so I could play matchmaker! That was Kayl's thing, not mine. But maybe it would cure Joe's whining and give him something to fight for.

Joe's emotions finally settled on anger. "You took the Necro?"

"Damn right I did. This place is gonna get a bit crowded soon. Help our new friend settle in." And maybe put some damn pants on him before Joe got ideas.

I strode back to the clockface.

Joe hurried next to me. "What are you planning?"

"A holiday, what does it look like?"

"You can't drag mortals into your battles—"

"I can do what I want."

"You think we're not used to dealing with gods like you?"

Why did he have to make this god business such a fucking chore? There was no reason to be such an arse about it. Bloody ex-Glimmer. "I'm not asking you to worship me. I'm not even asking you to kiss my cunt. I'm just asking you to help me destroy the gods, the domains, and everything between. Is that really asking too much?"

"You're insane."

I raised a brow. "You've only just noticed?" I gave him a friendly pat on the shoulder. "Listen, we've all got our part to play when the world ends. You keep the Glimmer in line, Vincent looks after the Necro, and I'll do the dirty work." Because, quite frankly, the dirty work was the fun part. "Does that sound fair?"

"What will happen at the end of all this? What will happen to us?"

That was the question, huh. "I guess we'll wait and see."

The choice was Mother's.

I sent him on his way, though I could sense his and Vincent's nagging unease. It was weird, having all these mortals inside my mind with their random thoughts and feelings. I wanted to drown them out for a bit of peace, but I needed to find one particular soul first.

And there it was, languishing at the back of my subconscious.

Mortimer Gast. Noct's friend. Another addition to my team.

With a fresh burst of power, Morty materialized on the floor. He wasn't in the same shriveled, pathetic state as Vincent. In fact, a current of anger rushed through him. Good. I wanted angry mortals.

He stood with his chin held high, his fists by his side despite his nakedness. Nope, Morty didn't have any shame. I liked him already.

"Morty—"

"No one calls me that," he snapped.

"I'm not no one." There it was again. The pining for a lost lover. Not another horny boy on my team! What was I going to do with them? Invite them to Rapture for a night out? "You may not have noticed, but your god is dead, and I'm your god now." I wouldn't explain it all again. He was smart, he'd figure it out.

"You look like her."

"Kayl? We're twins. I'm the smarter one." I flashed a grin. "She fucked you over good and proper, didn't she?" Through his mind, I'd seen their brief interactions. My sister really was a piece of work. "Want revenge?"

"Not interested."

"Really? What if I told you she is responsible for destroying Eventide? That she lied to your face about the Vesper?" I leaned close. "She's the key to bringing them back. Even your Zorya."

He snarled, his lip curling back to reveal what I'm sure he thought were fangs, but without his Necro form, it looked far less impressive. "Don't speak her name."

These men were *so* predictable. "Help me, and I'll save the Vesper. All of 'em."

"You want me to kill your sister? I'm not an assassin."

I'd seen his memories and the fucked-up shit he'd done investigating his 'cases,' so he really had no reason to be acting high and mighty. Especially when I could see his cock. "Nope. Kayl's all mine. What I want you to do is what you do best—play spy. She's hiding somewhere in the Undercity with a group of Fauna. Find them, watch them, and report back on their every movement."

I wanted eyes on Kayl, and Corinth, too.

I couldn't let them get in my way. Nor could I afford to let them escape me.

Morty nodded. "I need my partner to assist."

"Your partner?"

"Noct. The Seren with you at the Asylum. I may have been feral, but I know what I saw."

Morty didn't actually *need* Noct—judging from their history, Noct was nothing but a flying headache—but whatever. "I'll sort it. Now go put some pants on." I was sick of being surrounded by so many damn naked males.

He joined Joe and Vincent, and the three of them engaged in conspirator talk of how awful I was. Either they didn't realize or didn't care I could read their thoughts. Maybe they didn't see me as their god yet, but I was tuned into their thoughts regardless. They weren't stupid enough to betray me, at least.

In time, I'd convince them to like me.

I turned back to the clockface window and stared at my reflection.

My face.

My sister's face.

Thirteen years. Who was I, without Kayl?

It hadn't been *my* life in Grayford, growing up with Elvira feeding me. It hadn't been my heart falling in love with Malk. My body exploring sex with him. My pain, when Valeria took him away from us.

My entire life had been wrapped around hers. *Was* hers.

"*I fucking* hate you!"

I rubbed my cheek where Kayl had slapped me back in the Glimmer temple.

She'd hurt me. Really fucking hurt me, worse than the betrayals. Worse than the rejection. Had she meant it, when she'd said she hated me? When she'd said we weren't family? I'd said shit too. Told her she could die alone, that I was done with her... I hadn't meant it. But how could I make her see that? Fuck's sake, I wanted to *help* her.

Every time we crossed paths, I couldn't stop the anger that burned in my chest. Did I want her to feel a bit of the misery I'd felt when she hurt me? Did I want her to hurt too, if only to see what it was like for *me*?

To see through my eyes, for a change?

The Godless weren't my family. They'd loved her, accepted her, but they'd never accepted me. They forgave her for her fuckups. They laughed and sang and drank wine and did her nails.

I had no one to do these things for me.

Only Kayl.

"*We're not family!*"

YOU DON'T NEED HER, DAUGHTER. ALL YOU NEED IS ME.

All I'd ever wanted was my own family. To be held and loved by my mother. To share that with my sister. I'd loved Kayl. I'd fucking *tried*. We could have been allies. We could have been so perfect together. So powerful. The gods would never stand a chance.

WHEN I AM FREE, I WILL GIVE YOU THE LOVE YOU DESIRE.

That was worth destroying domains for.

Was it mean? That my goal was to personally steal all the mortals Kayl had ever cared for? Maybe. But she'd forced me to do this.

If Kayl didn't want to be my sister, then I'd create my own family.

I'd take the Godless's souls one by one and make them mine.

Maybe then she'd fucking realize how much she needed me.

And I'd finish what we'd started.

PART TWO

XV

TOM CAT'S CAFÉ
You ain't never had an experience like a cat café!
Our Fauna will give you a night to remember. While cat girls are our
specialty, our girls (and boys!) can change into any animal form you choose.
Whisper your deepest desires, and we'll take care of the rest.
Confidentiality is the Tom Cat guarantee!
Book your stay with this flier for a free drink!
—Trixie Tom Cat, *Tom Cat's Café flier*

IT WAS LATE WHEN we arrived at Sinner's Row.

I'd expected the streets to be completely empty. Deserted. But no, Ember stood guard by the entrance, which was now barricaded with scavenged shop signs and barbed wire—defenses against Dor's forces, I'd assume. They'd looked surprised to see an entire army of Fauna marching to their gates, but they knew Trixie. They had let us in with little fanfare and with the promise of a visit later on.

What Ember remained in Chime had taken over the stores. Most of the windows had been boarded up. It was strange to see Sinner's Row transformed into a potential war zone, but Erosain had prepared them, at least.

He understood what was coming.

The aether lights and flashing signs of the main street still glowed, though they blurred into colorful smudges as I winked in and out of consciousness. I'd ridden on Kayl's back the entire journey here. Fortunately, our Fauna guises allowed us to sneak into Sinner's Row undetected. For now, Erosain wouldn't know we'd infiltrated his territory.

The Fauna gathered outside Tom Cat's Café, a once popular Fauna brothel and one of the largest buildings in Sinner's Row, other than

Erosain's own bar. Trixie transformed to her bipedal form, her cat tail swishing behind her, as she produced the building's key. Where *had* she hidden it?

"Welcome 'ome," she said, or words to that effect.

I drifted off again, and when I came to, I was lying on a pillow.

The splash of running water echoed nearby. I sat up awkwardly, still in my small mouse form. At this size, everything towered over me, and I found myself in the center of a rather large bed. My spectacles had been left on the pillow, so I crouched beside one of the lenses to get a better look at my surroundings.

We'd made it inside the cat café, then, for the room was certainly designed for adventurous adults. The walls were decorated in cream floral patterns, with silk curtains pulled across the windows. Soft oil lamps glowed above the gaudy furnishings etched in a fake gold. A large mirror took up the entire wall opposite the bed, and above the headboard were leather fastenings designed for more trusting partners. To the side of the bed was a cabinet filled with empty liquor bottles, massage oils, and a pair of frilly handcuffs.

I'd only ever entered a room such as this when investigating a case for the Wardens and never for more, ah, personal reasons. I was a good boy, and cat cafés weren't my style.

For one, places like these tended to take advantage of the unfortunate mortals forced to work inside them. Though, I didn't believe Trixie to be a terrible host, from what I'd heard during my days working cases in Sinner's Row.

The door to an en suite bathroom opened, letting out a rush of steam. Kayl came out wearing nothing but a bathrobe. Her cat ears perked up. "Good, you're awake. I was worried I'd have to take this bath alone."

"Are we safe? Have the Ember...?"

"We're good, for now." She sat on the edge of the bed. "Trixie says we'll come up with a plan tomorrow. I think we're all too exhausted to worry about it. She and Wolfsbane are divvying up the rooms, and I've got the Mesmer sharing one with Freddie a few doors down. It's an impressive building, isn't it? I've been past it before, but never inside. Anyhow, they've given us this room to share. The vanilla room, they call it."

"Vanilla?" I glanced at the fastenings on the headboard. I dreaded to think what other rooms existed here beyond blasted vanilla.

"I know you're tired, but I've run you a bath. We need to clean you off, and Wolfsbane says I need to keep your wound clean to prevent infection. We did just march through the Undercity, and those tunnels aren't exactly hygienic."

"*You're* going to clean me?" I squeaked. "That's not necessary—"

"Quen. You can barely stand. I'm knackered too, but we're both covered in dirt and blood. A soak in some hot water will do us some good. It's a large tub. Plenty of space for us both." She flashed me a wicked grin.

We were going to share a *bath*? Oh, dear gods. "Be gentle with me, please. I haven't the strength to fight off temptation."

"I promise to keep my hands mostly to myself."

The thought of completely stripping myself bare sent my mouse ears trembling, and I didn't entirely know why. Surely, she'd seen enough of me that I shouldn't feel shy? She'd witnessed the worst, most depraved sides of me and hadn't been repulsed, and yet...

Saints. I'd never felt so wretched. Had never been this weak.

The fight had been cut from me before I'd even had a chance to enter the battle.

If I was meant to protect Chime, how would I achieve it like this? With one blasted arm? How was I meant to protect her?

"Can you manage changing form?" she asked, not unkindly.

I drew a deep breath. Changing from one persona to another had come to me quite readily, even in my weakened state. It was akin to holding my breath until my ears popped, and at that *pop*, I was no longer a tiny mouse, but a Chaos male, my legs sprawling across the bed, my cock flopping over my thigh rather improperly.

Yes, this was the lowest point of my entire existence, and the fact I happened to be lying on a bed that had likely seen more depravity than my own depraved soul did not help.

Kayl reached for my left arm. "Come on. Let's get you sorted."

I groaned at the pains and aches of it all as she helped me up and guided me to the bathroom. It hurt to breathe, to exist, and the site of my missing arm throbbed with the occasional stab of sharp pain that kept me trapped in reality. Whatever drugs the Fauna had given me previously had now worn off, and not even chewing on my lip furiously could distract from it.

The bathroom was a generous size, and the bathtub in the corner took up most of the space, though without my spectacles, it was mostly a blur. It was already half-filled with water, and not a single bubble in sight.

Kayl sat me on a stool first and opened a medical kit. "Let me check your arm."

My heart began to race. "Do you know what you're doing?"

"Not a clue. Wolfsbane told me to clean it and wrap it up good. You're not allowed to get it wet, so we'll have to be careful and keep your arm above water."

"Alas, I'd been imagining a hot tub full of bubbles by candlelight."

"Is that how you spent those lonely evenings in your apartment?"

I'd spent many a night soaking in my tub to ease the welts on my back after visiting Elijah... No, I refused to wallow in those memories. "With a glass of wine for company." What I'd give for a glass right now.

"I'm sure there's a few bottles lying around this place, but none for you, mister. Not while you're on this." She pulled out a small bottle with a reddish-brown substance.

I squinted at the label. Laudanum. I'd come across a few mortals addicted to the stuff back in my Warden days, mostly among Undercity residents, with the occasional Golden City cover-up. It wasn't Chime's drug of choice, not when Vesper mushrooms were cheaper. But the Umber were especially talented at growing bespoke substances behind closed doors. Who would have ever guessed them to be drug peddlers?

These sorts of drugs weren't needed when Necro healers could fix most wounds. Though, sadly, that was no longer the case.

"You get a few drops now." Kayl popped open the stopper and handed me the bottle. "And I'll keep the bottle for when you need it."

"You know, I've never taken an illegal substance in my entire mortal life."

"I believe you. That's why I'm keeping the bottle."

I'd tut at her lack of faith, but with the excruciating pain in my upper arm, it was probably for the best. I let a couple of drops land on my tongue and almost gagged! The stuff was vile, more bitter than tea leaves.

Kayl swiped it from me. "Let me know when you're ready."

I closed my eyes and let the laudanum sink into my bones—the ones that remained, at least. It worked quickly, easing the sharpness of reality into a dull, bearable ache. "Do it."

With painstaking slowness, Kayl examined my residual limb.

Wolfsbane had done an excellent job of cutting away and cleaning the charred flesh above my missing elbow—a master at whatever craft the Fauna touted, a chef perhaps—and then stitching it all together again. Really, it had been fascinating to observe. Wardens rarely suffered such catastrophic injuries.

I bit back a sigh. Gone were the days I'd write my reports.

Those days were far behind me regardless.

Kayl washed a cloth with something smelling of antiseptic and dabbed at my sore skin. I hissed at the sting and clenched the stool with my sole hand, my nails digging into the wood. My thoughts turned to tea, to the wonderful varieties one could find within Sinner's Row, for we'd surely be stuck here for a while until Erosain decided what to do with us.

I so desperately needed a cup. Never mind sodding laudanum.

Did the good patrons of Tom Cat's Café indulge in a cuppa before indulging their fantasies? What if their fantasies involved the perfect brew? Could a paying customer simply ask for a large-breasted wench to pour one out before rubbing one out? Would they have the expertise required to boil to the correct temperature? Add the precise number of leaves? Measure the amount of milk? The number of sugar cubes for that ideal balance between tart and sweet?

Some part of me remained Diviner, didn't it?

"Stay still," Kayl scolded. "You're squirming too much."

I cleared my throat. "Sorry."

She wrapped a clean bandage around my arm.

"Bit tight, isn't it?" I said through clenched teeth.

"Wolfsbane says compression will help reduce any swelling and increase circulation, so deal with it."

"Right you are."

"There." She finished attaching a safety pin to keep it in place. "We'll have to change it throughout the day. We can't afford to let it get infected, not when there's no Necro to..." She glanced away suddenly, guilt flashing on her face. "Let's get you washed, then. Can't have you stinking up the place."

"Not when it's such a fine establishment," I muttered.

Once again, she helped me up. Despite the laudanum, I was shakier on my feet, or perhaps that was because of the laudanum. She eased me into the bath, which had cooled to a comfortably warm temperature. Not scalding enough for tea.

She let her robe drop, revealing her nakedness.

Oh my.

She slipped into the bath before my eyes could settle on any one part of her. I *had* seen her naked before—Jinx, too—but I'd not taken the luxury of observing her nakedness beyond the surface of my thoughts.

Now, I ached to go beyond, to soak in her every detail.

Gods, I *ached*.

The bathwater rose to chest level, but did nothing to hide her breasts. I let my gaze linger on a particularly interesting pattern on the bathroom tiles, one that sharpened the longer I stared. It was figures of Fauna bent in a... Oh. They were fornicating.

That didn't help my predicament at all!

"Keep your arm above the water," Kayl chided as she lathered up floral-scented soap on a sponge. "But try to relax."

"Yes, dear." Every muscle tensed. How could I relax when she sat before me? She leaned so close, and then pressed the sponge against my chest.

Her touch was so soft, so gentle. It reached through the space between our mortal bodies and cleansed my heart.

She set aside the sponge and took my head in both of her hands. Gently, her nails massaged my scalp, and she alternated between pouring water down my back and rinsing my hair. No one had ever held me this way, had ever touched my hair, let alone washed it. Not even my lovers.

Not even Elijah.

I took the sponge and dabbed along her cheek down to her neck. She allowed me that exploratory touch, to cleanse the dried blood that stained her.

Together, we washed away the pains that had brought us here. Rivulets of blood and grime flowed down and mingled with the bathwater.

A tear escaped my eye.

She paused. "Am I hurting you?"

"No." I wiped away the tears with my fist, only to smear suds across my cheek. "I'm sorry, I... No one has ever... cared for me like this." There were no matriarchal figures within the Diviner to kiss away boo-boos. We didn't cry. We didn't dwell on pain. The comfort we sought was hidden in the dark where no one else could witness the shame of it.

"Oh, Quen. You're beautiful, you know?"

Only Kayl could look upon my wretched body and call me beautiful.

Only she could plunge into the depths of my subconscious and accept the darkness within.

I'd often thought myself cursed. Especially when my touch showed me another mortal's death. But Kayl had lifted that curse. She truly was my salvation.

I took her chin and kissed her.

A soft kiss. One born of two wounded mortals finding respite in one another. Her palm rested on my chest, above the flutter of my heart, as she closed the gap between us. The taste of her filled my mouth with a sweetness far greater than any tea or biscuit. While my heart should have thought of a greater metaphor by which to profess my devotion, my mind was too addled to meet the task.

My body wasn't up to the task either, but it begged for more. My cock twitched, disturbing the bathwater with eager ripples, and my greedy tongue hunted deeper.

Kayl pulled back and pressed a wet finger to my lips. "Easy. You're not ready for this."

"Please," I rasped, my chest rising and falling with desperate need. "I want—"

My injured arm accidentally grazed the edge of the bathtub. Pain lanced through my nerves, and I recoiled with a cry.

Kayl tutted. "See? You need time to recover."

"You torture me." And it was torture. Worse than losing a bloody arm!

I was riddled with sin. I craved it. The old masters warned against temptation, yet I'd allowed my previous lovers to lead me into temptation with the promise of repenting later. But now I had no god to repent to, or to beg forgiveness from.

Chaos had changed me. Eroded my patience.

No, I hadn't changed. Chaos had simply freed the sinner within. The man Kayl had unleashed was a ravenous beast that wanted to fuck, to down an entire bottle of whiskey and go urinate on a lamppost.

But to touch her... to kiss her without another presence lurking in my mind and judging my every action... That was a victory.

"I'm not taking advantage of you when you're high," she said.

"You'll take advantage of me any other time?"

"If you're a good boy."

My sad cock deflated. She finished rinsing me, and by the time we dried off and made it back to the bed, I was too exhausted to stand, let alone do much else.

Kayl tucked me into the bedsheets and climbed in next to me. We were both naked, a fact that should have sent my synapses firing, but I was too far gone to appreciate it, or to ruminate over when these sheets had last been cleaned.

"Thank you," I said over a repressed yawn. I turned to my good side, my hand tucked under the pillow. My injured arm still felt terribly sore. Even with the laudanum, sleep would be a different sort of battle.

"I'll help you drift off," she said, as though reading my mind. She switched to her Mesmer form and placed her hand over my forehead. "Hopefully without falling into your dreams this time."

"I don't mind if you visit."

"Then I'll watch over them for you."

My eyelids became heavy, and I gently drifted into the unknown. As I did so, Kayl's nose pressed against my neck.

"What are you doing?" I asked, my voice somewhere far away.

"Checking what you smell like."

"What... What *do* I smell like?"

"Soap."

Soap? I chuckled, and then darkness welcomed me into its soothing embrace.

Oh, bugger *me.*

I strained one eye open to check I was still alive. Every inch of me ached, as though I'd been jogging laps across Central instead of sleeping, and my head was positively pounding. Even death hadn't felt this traumatizing, and that was how I knew I must still be bound to the plane of existence. Something furry stuck to my tongue. Either my parched mouth was full of cotton balls, or I'd taken to licking cat girls in my wildest of dreams.

The bed felt empty beside me. Kayl wasn't in the room, though an oil lamp burned on the bedside table next to a glass of water.

I turned to reach for it, and rolled onto my residual limb.

Agony sliced through my shoulder like hot knives.

"Fucking *fuck* it!" I rolled onto my back and panted. The pain sent black splotches through my vision, and I lay in place, squirming until the waves of torment washed over me and lessened. Only lessened. The pain would never leave me completely.

Was this my life, now? I'd earned my freedom, and my divine punishment was to lose an arm? To suffer the rest of my days?

Jinx had regrown her arms in an instant, and that was without the Necro's ability to heal. I'd never expected the Glimmer to have such power, even if they touted their affinity for birth and creation. Yet Jinx had made it look effortless.

I carried a god's soul inside my chest, and what had that earned me?

We've been examining the workings of your body, Master Corinth, came Doctor Zachery Finch's voice inside my mind. *I believe we can help.*

Wonderful. I'd escaped the clutches of Dor and Corentine only for my thoughts and feelings to be observed by another. My self-pitying hadn't been an open invitation for conversation.

If you'd rather we didn't share our findings—

No, Doctor. I rubbed my throbbing forehead. *Please, go ahead.*

I have experience with amputation in mortal bodies. It is a subject I have studied extensively.

I didn't realize you were a medical doctor?

I'm not. I was hatched without wings, Master Corinth. Naturally, I compared my situation to other Zephyr and those who had lost wings and other limbs through amputation.

Ah yes. How tactless of me. I sat up and reached for the glass of water with my missing hand before my brain caught up and corrected its course. Using my left hand didn't come naturally at all, and I almost knocked the sodding glass over as I fumbled for it. But the water was still cool, which meant Kayl couldn't have wandered far. My spectacles waited beside a round brass object. My fob watch.

We cannot grow limbs, but we are well versed in artificial attachments and prosthetics. It will be easier with you as our subject—we can see the severed nerves that remain inside your arm and reattach them, with Zyclone's soul to power a prosthetic.

I didn't quite understand what the good doctor meant, but then the blueprint of his design bloomed in my mind, and the Zephyr's thinking became mine. With the right parts and a little help, I could build a mechanical arm, one made of pulleys powered by the aether of a god. It wouldn't be perfect, but saints... I'd have an arm capable of bending. Perhaps even lifting objects.

But I'd need to find the metal, bolts, and screws required for such a design, and I doubted even Erosain would have those lying around his vaults.

The steamworks would have what we need, the doctor continued. *Though be wary—the Diviner have stationed men there. What they are working on was classified. Even the Zephyr didn't have clearance for their experiments.*

I appreciate the advice. Could that be where they'd taken the kidnapped Fauna? But Kayl had seen the soul-splitting devices within the Academy, of all places. It would be easier to investigate the steamworks from here, in any case. Quite how we'd reach the Golden City, I didn't yet know.

Nor did I have any plan for how we'd reach the domains and complete the blasted task Mesmorpheus had left us with, not with the Gate destroyed.

We have an idea for that, too, Doctor Finch said.

Another blueprint appeared in my mind's eye, one I wasn't entirely prepared for.

A device to open portals and traverse the domains. A way of finally leveling the playing field. I needed to inform Kayl immediately.

Doctor, you're a genius. As soon as I'm feeling more myself, I'll get you out of, well, myself. And then we could begin the necessary work.

I'd rather remain here.

Why? You'll have to come out of me at some point. Why did that sound *so* wrong?

Silence drifted in my mind, and the good doctor retreated into my subconscious, as though afraid of the topic. I couldn't say I blamed him. To be reborn was a traumatizing experience I knew all too well. We'd come back to the subject another time.

There was much work to be done, and little time to achieve it, but I still possessed a mortal body with mortal needs. Right now, my bladder ached for attention.

I donned my spectacles—almost poking myself in the eye while doing so—and took a few wobbly steps to the bathroom. The pain in my head hadn't lessened much. Unfortunately, Kayl had removed the laudanum from the medical box.

I sighed and took care of business. An ungodly amount came out, though it had been a while since I saw to my own needs. At least here I had some privacy. Poor Joe still needed to contend with Jinx, but there was little I could do to save him, not when I had so many mortals on my list to save, starting with the Fauna. We owed them that much.

And then Ben.

A splash of urine coated the toilet seat. "Blast it!"

"Quen?" Kayl called. "Are you in here?"

"Be right out!" I shook myself off and awkwardly fiddled with the sink.

Kayl waited for me, seated on the edge of the bed. She wore a flowing black dress that suited her dark purple Mesmer skin and the constellations that glittered across her cheeks. "I brought you some clothes." She patted the pile beside her. "Wolfsbane dug them out from the laundry room below and assures me they're clean. This, I borrowed off Trixie." She smoothed her sleeves. "They're hosting a meeting for lunch, if you're up for it. Otherwise, I can bring up some food."

Had I slept that much? I had no idea what time it was. "Lunch sounds lovely."

Kayl examined herself in the mirror as I tackled another challenge: getting dressed.

Pulling up trousers was an effort that tired me far quicker than it should, but wrestling into a shirt was nigh on impossible. I thumped the pillow. "These bloody buttons!"

Kayl glanced at me. "Do you want help?"

I sat and seethed for a moment. She'd deliberately not offered her help until I needed it, and knew I would. I hated feeling this pathetic, but I hated wasting time more. "Please."

She said nothing as she sat beside me and did up the buttons.

"Sorry for being so grumpy." I cringed at my own wretchedness.

"You lost an arm. I'd be worried if you weren't grumpy. But I'm leaving your top few buttons undone, so I can admire your chest hair."

"You wicked woman."

She batted her eyelashes with a playful smirk.

What had I done to deserve her? She kneeled before me to tie up my shoelaces, and the smolder in her aether eyes sent heat flushing through my skin before it curdled into shame. I'd kissed her last night when I was in no fit shape to offer her anything, and she'd been kind enough to turn me down.

How could I ever repay her? I could no longer stroll to the shops and come back with a box of scones and a bouquet of roses. How did one show appreciation during the end-times?

I wanted to talk about last night—to apologize—but instead, my cowardly tongue changed the subject. "We should talk about your vision before we meet with the Fauna."

"Is that really what's on your mind when I'm kneeling before you?"

Another flush of heat burned through me. "It's worth getting our stories straight."

"Business as usual, then." She sat beside me. "What's there to tell? I'm getting visions now. I had one of you falling from the clock tower—that's how I found you. It's some sort of gift or curse passed on to me from Mesmorpheus."

A gift or curse was one way of describing them. I leaned toward the latter. "You said you had a vision of the Academy."

"Right. And the Council chamber as well. That's two visions, now, through the eyes of the same man, a Diviner. He calls himself the Redeemer—he's using the soul-splitting machines to *redeem* souls of their sin by destroying them." Her nose scrunched in disgust. "Does his name ring a bell?"

The Redeemer? Wait. Nocturne had mentioned that name during our botched mission in Timefall. While we hadn't encountered this so-called Redeemer, his motivations were plausible enough—trust Dor to consider a broken soul cleansed of its sin. I rubbed my jaw, which prickled with stubble. "I haven't met the fellow. But if you get any more visions like that one, alert me."

"Who else would I alert?" She stood and grabbed my left arm. "Come on, then. I'm starving."

We stepped out to the main foyer. Tom Cat's Café was a refurbished hotel that had kept the glamor of its previous occupation. The café was far more decorative than most Fauna brothels, with an air of class unbefitting the Undercity. The walls were an Ember red, the furnishings a cheap imitation of those in a Golden City lodging. It spoke of extravagant debauchery on a budget. A carpeted staircase connected the three floors to the main reception and cloakroom. Each door was an entrance to a night of passionate entertainment.

As we walked arm in arm down the staircase, Kayl explained the evacuated Fauna had taken up residence within the various rooms, and they were working on making it more homey, restoring it to its original design as a hotel. It would be a tight squeeze, fitting them all in, but at least they were safe with a roof above their heads.

Kayl led me past the restaurant—which was full of Fauna lining up to receive bowls of curry, by the looks of it—and instead led me to a private office.

Trixie and Wolfsbane were already seated inside on plush armchairs. A generous spread had been laid out on the coffee table, consisting of fruit pastries, bread rolls, jam, slices of cheese and ham—definitely not for my palate—and a steaming pot of tea.

"I thought Diviner were better timekeepers than this," Trixie muttered over the rim of a decorative teacup.

I sank into an armchair opposite. "As I mentioned before, I'm no longer Diviner."

"No shit. Tea's getting cold." She gestured at the tray.

Kayl poured me a cup, and I offered her a grateful smile.

"Good to see you with more color in your cheeks," Wolfsbane said by way of greeting. "You're healing quickly."

I bowed my head. "Thank you for saving my life."

Trixie rolled her eyes. "Let's 'ope you're worth the effort. While you were sleeping, we ran a 'ead count. Fifty, I'm down. Fifty fucking Fauna either taken or killed by the Diviner. So 'ow will you get them back?"

Kayl helped herself to a custard pastry. "I saw where they were taken. The Academy."

"In the Golden City? Why there?"

Kayl gave me a look, and I nodded. Best we didn't keep too many secrets from our hosts.

"They have machines that can destroy a mortal's soul," I said.

I took a measured sip of tea as Kayl explained the soul-splitting devices and what they were likely being used for—to create an army of obedient slaves for Dor. Both Trixie and Wolfsbane looked disturbed by this revelation, as one should.

"Those clock-fuckers." Trixie snarled. "We don't 'ave time to faff around, but we're not exactly equipped for an assault. We've got enough leftover food for my mortals to last the next few days, if we ration it. That arse Erosain is demanding an audience, and I'm 'oping to sweet-talk 'im into lending us aid. Even if 'e volunteers a 'andful of 'is mortals, there's no easy way of getting to the Golden City from 'ere. Not even through the pipes."

I set my cup down and pulled out my fob watch. "I have a plan for that. The gods have the means to create portals into Chime. With a little engineering, I believe I can turn this watch into a portal-creating device powered by aether." I didn't know how much Kayl had explained about Chaos's powers, and the souls we both carried, so it was best to play it safe with my explanation.

Kayl's eyes lit up. "Really? We can make portals?" She understood the implication. Get this right, and we wouldn't need the Gate to enter the domains.

We'd be a step ahead of Jinx.

"With adequate tools I can source locally. Then we can use my watch to travel to the Golden City and reach the Fauna."

Trixie didn't look convinced. "'Ow long will it take you to make this thing?"

"A day, if that. I understand time is of the essence—"

"While you're fucking around, my Fauna could 'ave already 'ad their souls snatched!"

"Dor doesn't rush these endeavors. Any experiments the Diviner inflict upon your Fauna will be done with meticulous and time-consuming documentation. A small boon in our favor. But we shall act with haste."

"All right." Trixie leaned back in her armchair. "If you reckon it can be done, then it'll be done. I don't see what other choice we 'ave. Wolfsbane and I will meet with Erosain this afternoon to strike a deal. We don't just need 'is aid, but 'is protection. The Ember are the only ones keeping the

Wardens out of Sinner's Row. If Erosain decides to kick us all out, we've got nowhere safe to go."

"Would it help if I came with you?" I asked. "Erosain and I were once close."

"You're still recovering," Kayl said. "And who do you think he'll be happier to see?"

"Not you. You destroyed his art gallery and broke his legs."

"Wait, 'old on." Trixie stared between us. "*You're* Nadine Noir?" She groaned. "Of course you fucking are!"

Wolfsbane burst out laughing. "Erosain—he ranted about that for *weeks*!"

"And we're 'iding you in our goddamn café, typical." Trixie shook her head and folded herself a slice of ham. "The pair of you better lie low—"

"This is why you should take me with you," Kayl said. "Erosain knows me, and knows what I can do. I'll offer something he wants."

"And what's that?"

"What does any prick in power want? More power."

I bent my head close to Kayl. "Is that wise?"

"Trust me. I know what I'm doing."

I trusted her, but Erosain was a bastard. "Any action you take against him will lead to his death." I'd seen the visions. He was due a smiting from Edana, and soon.

"And? Do you care?"

Should I care? He was a former lover. A friend and confidante. We'd shared many a night in his bar, discussing Undercity gossip, Warden secrets, all over a glass of wine or whiskey. And yet... "No."

"Then that's decided."

Trixie and Kayl moved on to discussing strategy for their meeting, as Wolfsbane added his thoughts of the logistics of running a cat café turned hotel. I didn't cherish the thought of leaving Kayl to handle Erosain alone, or leaving myself to wallow here while time ticked against us. But rushing to our demise wasn't the solution.

We'd have to take our time on this, as much as it pained me. Unfortunately, I was in no state to fight anyone, be it mortal or god.

And if I was to defeat Dor, then I'd need to think how *he* would think—logically.

I helped myself to a bread roll and applied the jam without Kayl's help, lest Trixie and her wolfish companion think me completely useless.

Whatever they expected of me, I'd exceed it.

I had no choice.

16

Name: Erosain (No known surname), Ember, ambassador for Rapture
Known Affiliations: Edana
Of all the remaining ambassadors on the Warden Council, Erosain is
perhaps the most dangerous and volatile. As ambassador for Edana,
Erosain possesses fire power and a flair for persuasion. For years, Erosain
has been amassing power within Sinner's Row, thus creating a personal
foothold within the Undercity that undermines Father's rule. His last
movements were recorded in Sinner's Row. Though most gods have
abandoned Chime, the Ember remain in operation there and have begun
defensive procedures.
—P. Bezel, *Personal Report on Erosain*

I DIDN'T WANT TO leave Quen on his own, not when he was still shaky and recovering, but Trixie needed my help. With everything that had gone down recently, I needed to convince her I was on her side and had her mortals' best interests at heart. Quen would manage without me for a few hours with the Mesmer to watch over him, or force him into a nap, if need be. I hid the bottle of laudanum, though. Last thing I needed was for the Mesmer to get a hold of that.

Gods. The Mesmer were unbearable when drunk. I couldn't imagine what chaos they'd cause if they got high.

While Wolfsbane checked over Quen's arm and stitches, I found the trio seated at a table in the restaurant with a plate of sandwiches, a jam sponge cake, and a pot of tea. Freddie was with them. The trio had adopted him, and the poor boy looked too dejected to leave.

The guilt sat heavy in my gut. We'd lost Autumn, but I'd be damned if I would let the Diviner keep her. As soon as we had the means, I was marching right up to their doors and kicking them down.

"Mama!" Celeste waved at me. "You sure you can't join us? *Please?*"

"Maybe later. You three try not to cause any trouble."

"They'll be good," Cosmo said. "Or they'll get no cake."

Celeste pouted.

Quen approached my side, a smirk on his lips. "Mama?" he whispered. "Dare I ask?"

Heat filled my cheeks, and I was grateful my Mesmer skin hid it, though it wasn't entirely from embarrassment. Quen stood with his sleeves rolled up—the one to his injured arm pinned to his shoulder, but his left arm was bare, exposing the white fluff coating his skin. With his collar undone and the white stubble now framing his chin, he'd never looked such a mess. No longer the neat and tidy Diviner who'd invited me to his apartment.

No, he looked... Rugged. Masculine in a way that sent my legs quivering.

Calm down, Kayl. "You saw what Mesmorpheus left me with. Thanks to them, I apparently adopted the entire Mesmer. So now they call me their mother."

"That's rather adorable."

"It's rather annoying. I barely understand them half the time, so I just roll with it. Will you be all right with them?"

"They've invited me to their tea party. I've been promised tea *and* cake. Though I'd rather be accompanying you. Erosain is no gentleman, and you'll be walking into his lair when he explicitly forbade you."

Yes, he had made a few veiled threats during our last encounter in Rapture. Seems he didn't forgive me for robbing his art gallery and breaking his legs, but that was no reason to hold a grudge. "He banned you as well."

"Yes, but we have history. I'm sure I could talk him around. What if you're walking into a trap? And Erosain attempts to capture you for Edana? She *is* partnered with Jinx."

Walking into traps was my specialty. "I'll be fine. I'll have an angry cat and wolf with me if things go wrong."

"Neither of whom are trained for negotiations such as this."

"If my plan is to work, then I need you to stay out of sight so Erosain doesn't know you're here."

"Because I'm your secret weapon?" Resentment edged those words, though it wasn't aimed at me. Is that how Corentine had seen him? A weapon to be used?

"Because if it turns into a brawl, then I'll be happier knowing you're not with us. If you're not fit enough to fuck, then you're not fit enough to fight."

A blush crept across his cheeks, and he winced. "Can you say that a little louder?"

"Don't tempt me."

"Are you ready or what?" Trixie called by the reception desk.

I sighed. "No rest for the wicked. Don't let the Mesmer run you ragged."

"It's not them I worry about. Please stay safe." He gave me a peck on the cheek and entered the restaurant.

Gods, I didn't want to leave him. Not when I'd only just gotten him back.

Not when there was so much unfinished business between the two of us.

When he came onto me last night, my resolve had almost cracked, but he wasn't in any fit state to handle me, and I wasn't shitty enough to take advantage. Gods knew patience wasn't my strength.

I wanted him. I wanted whatever it was that burned between us.

But not until he was ready. Physically and otherwise.

Trixie and Wolfsbane waited by the reception desk. The former had changed into a flattering cream dress with a sharp slit all the way to the hip, though her scowl and the impatient flick of her tail weren't so flattering. Wolfsbane, on the other hand, was bare chested and wearing only his kilt. They expected trouble, then. He was another rugged male oblivious to the effect he had on his woman. Trixie and I had that in common.

"He looks healthy." Wolfsbane nodded toward Quen, who was now seated with the Mesmer. "Didn't expect him to be up and about so soon." His quirked eyebrow suggested it was strange, and perhaps it was.

I wasn't an idiot. Quen was handling his injury far better than even I'd expected. Had taking Zyclone's soul helped the healing process? It would make sense. The power of a god coursed through his veins.

"Am I going to regret bringing you along?" Trixie said.

"Most likely." I retained my Mesmer form in case I needed to knock anyone out. Ideally, I didn't want to risk losing my dress. The color suited me. "But would you rather let Erosain discover you've been hiding me?"

"Suppose not." She ran a claw down one of the red curtains. "I lived 'ere for years, you know. This is my 'ouse, but this is Erosain's town. Try not to piss 'im off too much. We still need 'im."

That was debatable. "What if I told you Erosain's days were numbered and Sinner's Row could be yours for the taking?" It would be a whole different atmosphere with the Fauna in charge, and honestly, they deserved something to name theirs.

"We'd 'ave to see if there's anything left worth taking." She pulled a small vial from her purse and handed it over. "Knock the whole thing back."

I examined the bottle full of glittering silver liquid. "How long does this shit last for?"

"Until you piss it out."

"Sounds good to me." I popped open the stopper and downed it in one. I'd expected it to taste bitter, yet it had a cloying sweetness that shuddered through me. Really, I shouldn't be drinking unknown substances, but if I was going to earn Trixie's trust, then I had to place my trust in her.

Wolfsbane opened the door for her, letting Trixie step out onto the main street. I'd not noticed it at first, but his devotion to her was plain, from the way his eye constantly followed her every movement, to the way his body moved in time with hers. His mate.

He beamed with a wolfish smile as I followed.

Sinner's Row had always been a shelter for the depraved. The original home of Godless heathens. Today, I'd claim it as my own.

All right, I had my work cut out for me. Sinner's Row was a mess.

Every store window we passed was boarded up, with broken glass and other debris strewn about the main street. It had never been clean in the way Rapture's main strip was—I doubt anything could be wholly clean in the Undercity—but Sinner's Row had been reduced to a battleground as bad as Central. Okay, maybe not quite as bad. The Diviner hadn't marched through here yet, at least, but by the look of the place, Erosain sure expected them to.

Honestly, it was in such a state, it held the mood of Grayford after the riots, when every mortal had been pinned by a tense quiet.

Ember patrolled the streets like Wardens, only these were Erosain's hired muscle—red-skinned muscle in black suits, carrying pistols and makeshift batons made from broken pipes. They watched us walk by with amused leers. One brave soul attempted a wolf whistle, but stopped when Wolfsbane snarled in their direction.

Trixie strode with a purposeful swagger, her chin held high.

"That must get old," I said. She'd likely be used to such attention.

She snorted. "Erosain's men make it clear who owns this strip, but they know I don't bed fleas."

We made it to Erosain's bar without being accosted. For all their leering, the Ember held some begrudging respect for Trixie and allowed us to pass through. That, and we were clearly expected.

The bar was empty, which wasn't a surprise, though they'd kept the place in good condition and the bar well stocked, despite everything. Ember guards shuffled us into a booth and left us alone. Seemed they would keep us waiting and let us sweat it out. An old intimidation tactic, I'd assume, but all it did was bore me.

Wolfsbane barely fit in the booth and sat hunched over with his arms folded across his chest. Trixie tapped her claws on the table, her whiskers twitching. She had less patience than I did.

"What do you think Erosain wants from you?" I asked. He'd been the one to demand this audience, and he certainly wouldn't offer the Fauna his protection for free.

Trixie shrugged. "'E's never thought much of us, but that's Chime in general. We're the lowest of the low. Lower than even the Vesper were.

They saw us as things that could be bought and used without a say in our own futures. But whatever the fuck Erosain wants, I'll take it. I fought to give my mortals a 'ome. I bent over backwards—on all fours—to provide for them. I'll do it again."

There was an intensity to her feline gaze that hurt my heart. "You should never have been forced to. We had a soup kitchen back in Grayford. It was open to everyone, not only Vesper—"

"What good's a soup kitchen in the long term? One 'ot meal a day won't cut it."

"It's better than ending up in a workhouse."

"Why do you think I offered my mortals a 'ome? I know what the other domains think of us and what we do, but sex work is valid work and safer than those fucking workhouses. I 'elped my girls gain independence. So many cross over into Chime with no idea what this damn city expects of them. Wolfsbane and I, we kept them on the straight and narrow, kept them safe. A roof over their 'ead. No hard drugs."

"And I break anyone who harms our kin." Wolfsbane cracked his knuckles.

"Is that how a big strapping wolf found himself in Sinner's Row?" I asked.

"I was raised in one of those workhouses." His lip curled at the word. "The Glimmer would come to Juniper and take young Fauna cubs. Missionary work, they said. Take the orphans and raise them into good little citizens who worshipped their god instead of Faen."

Shit. I could fully believe the Glimmer would be capable of stealing children for their own perverted practices. "You escaped?"

"I played the good little wolf. I offered to enter Juniper as a tour guide and help Glimmer pick the runts of the litters. Instead, we lured the Glimmer to our clan and ate them."

"You... ate the Glimmer?" Why should that surprise me?

"They tasted sweet." Wolfsbane flashed his fangs. "The Glimmer soon realized their missionaries weren't coming back, though. They came for the cubs. I fought them and earned this." He rubbed the burn scars across his shoulder. "Once they started burning, I... I couldn't stop them. I failed those cubs."

"I'm sorry. The Wardens should have stopped them—"

"Wardens don't do shit," Trixie muttered.

"I came back to Chime," Wolfsbane continued. "To lick my wounds. No one wanted me, so I found a dry corner in Sinner's Row. That's when Trix found me. Gave me a job as a bouncer. I lent her my services—to protect my kin where I could. Trixie's way may not be Chime's, but it keeps our kin fed."

"I get it." I did. The Glimmer workhouses were full of abuse. "We tried to shut those workhouses down." And would have, eventually.

Trixie groaned. "Shit, you really are one of those Godless, aren't you?"

"You've heard of us, then?"

"I've seen your fliers. What a waste of paper. Besides your soup kitchen, did you actually *do* anything?"

I sat up straight. "We defied the gods—"

"A child's goal."

"Not so childish when there are dead gods, is it? Thanks to us, the Glimmer won't be running their workhouses anymore. You're welcome."

Trixie bit her tongue.

All right, the end of the Glimmer wasn't down to the Godless—not directly, anyhow—but we were the only ones who would free the Fauna. Even if the Godless had currently been reduced to me and Quen, though I was working on that.

Once we were restored, we'd solve Chime's inequalities, as we were destined to.

One of the Ember guards approached our booth. "His Excellency will see you now."

We followed him through to the private hallway with glass walls. These allowed Erosain's guests to watch whatever lurid activity was going on in the rooms on the other side, but now those were empty. When I'd first come here all those weeks ago, they'd been filled with Ember putting on quite a show. This was where I'd met Joe, who hadn't been here of his own free will.

It had been one of the few signs of Erosain's true nature as an arsehole. Though really, so few ambassadors weren't gaping arses.

The door at the end of the hall led to Erosain's private suite, and we were swept inside.

It remained much the same as when I last entered—a more intimate version of Erosain's bar, with cabinets stocked full of colorful bottles lit by a line of brazier flame that ran all the way around the room. At the opposite end, another door led through to his famous art gallery, which I'd so thoughtfully ruined during my last visit.

The ambassador himself lay sprawled across a large square couch positioned lower in the center of the room. It encompassed a glass table that gave a view of the lava river miles below.

"Lady Arkey," Erosain announced. He was dressed in his usual tuxedo, a leg draped over his other knee and a glass of sparkling gold in his hand. He made no attempt to rise and greet us, but nor did he seem surprised by my sudden appearance. "I do recall banishing you from my dominion."

"Fortunately, Chime isn't yours."

"Not yet." He sipped from his glass. "Chime is currently anyone's for the taking, and I would be a fool not to throw my hat into the ring on behalf of my Queen, just as I'd be a fool to dismiss potential alliances." His gaze drifted to Trixie. "Welcome back, my dear. I knew you wouldn't leave me for long."

The irritation in Trixie's expression had gone, replaced with a sultry mask as she practically purred. "What can I say? We cats feel at 'ome where it's 'ot."

Erosain sat up and patted the couch. "Join me."

Trixie sat closest to Erosain, with Wolfsbane next to her, and me on the edge in case I needed to make a quick getaway. Erosain's red eyes scrutinized my every breath. He still held a grudge, but at least he was willing to be diplomatic.

Quen had *nothing* to be worried about.

I'd not even asked about Erosain's art collection... Yet.

Erosain snapped his fingers, and an Ember server came over with a tray of drinks. The man placed identical sparkling silver glasses before me, Trixie, and Wolfsbane.

"You're here to talk business, and such talk goes best with a little lubrication." Erosain raised a glass. "To the end of times."

"You couldn't 'ave chosen a more cheerful topic?" Trixie muttered as she sipped from her glass.

"What could be more cheerful? The end brings new beginnings. Ironic, that the future seems so bright when the god of sunlight is no longer with us."

Oh, so that was why Erosain seemed so jolly. With the Glimmer gone, the Ember—and indeed Fauna—could finally rise from the Undercity. That was worthy of a toast. If only the Vesper were still here to share in the good news.

"You have Chaos to thank for that." I sipped my drink. It was strong alcohol with a sharp citrus tang. Tingles ran down my spine, and I suppressed a shudder. Definitely strong.

It probably looked odd for a Mesmer to be drinking, but oh well.

"But not you?" Erosain quirked one of his fake eyebrows. "Chaos rages across Central, clashing with Diviner and Umber. Where do *you* stand, I wonder?"

"Where I always have; with Chime's mortals."

"Is that why you two have formed an alliance?" He glanced between me and Trixie. "And why you're at my door, begging for help?"

I bit the inside of my cheek at the insinuation I'd beg him for anything. "You want allies, Trixie's mortals need food and shelter. Seems like a win-win to me."

"You're acting as an intermediary? Forgive me, but to ascertain trust, I must know your motives, you understand. It wasn't so long ago that you stole from me." His words took on a hard edge. "How do you intend to pay that debt?"

Oh, he hadn't quite forgiven me, had he?

Trixie leaned closer to Erosain. It was skillfully done—the flutter of her eyelashes, the curl of her tail around his shoulder, the hand she placed on his thigh. A transformation from the bossy cat I knew to a playful flirt who preened the ambassador's ego. "I'll settle any debts incurred—"

"No," Erosain snapped. He grabbed her wrist and lifted it from his thigh. "I want to hear how Lady Arkey intends to repay me."

A low growl escaped Wolfsbane. Up to now, he'd been sitting in silence and sipping his drink, even remaining still when his mate draped herself over Erosain's lap. He trusted Trixie completely, but he didn't trust Erosain.

I patted Wolfsbane on the shoulder. A subtle signal to calm down, which he took with a huff. I met Erosain's eyes. "I can offer you freedom."

Erosain blinked at that. "Go on."

What had I told Trixie? That arseholes in power craved more power? I didn't know for sure if that was what Erosain wanted, but it was a good guess. "You know what I am and what I can do. Not only can Chaos take souls, but we can rebirth them. Separate them from their god. I can free you from Edana."

His breath hitched. "Why would I want that?"

"Why wouldn't you?" Wasn't freedom what all mortals craved? "Edana owns your soul, and everything else you are. She alone decides what movements you make, whether you live or die. I could cut your strings, and then Sinner's Row would truly be yours."

"To go against a god would be foolish," he said slowly, as though churning the words and allowing them to sink in.

"And yet oh so easy." I took another sip of my drink. Tingles rushed through my blood now, little bubbles that bounced and popped under my skin.

I caught Trixie's eye and blinked twice.

Erosain released Trixie's wrist and stroked his beard. "A tempting offer. You're right, the price of freedom comes high, but it also charges interest. Why should I trust you to deliver it?"

"Because I help mortals." My words came out slurred. "Excuse me." I covered my mouth and belched. "I think the—the drink went to my head."

I attempted to sit up, and my limbs flailed uselessly.

Wolfsbane took my arm to steady me. "Here, let me help—"

"No, I can manage," I moaned. My dress rode up my thigh as I struggled to right myself. Gods, what an undignified mess I was!

Erosain set his glass down and steepled his slender fingers. "I'm afraid I'll have to decline your offer, Lady Arkey. You see, I have nothing but pity for godless heathens. I belong to my Queen, and she provides everything I could ever want. In return, I'm only too happy to hand over what she wants: you."

Well, I'd given him a fair chance of saving his soul. More than he deserved, really. I flailed my hand in Trixie's direction and accidentally knocked over my glass, spilling the fizzy liquid over the table. "Trix?"

Trixie plucked a stray cat hair from her dress. "We appreciate that you 'elped guide my mortals to safety, but let's not forget it was you who put them in danger to begin with."

My mouth fell open with a gasp. "You're betraying me?"

She chuckled, but it was a dangerous thing, as sharp as her claws. "If it makes you feel better, then we'll call it that."

Erosain patted Trixie's knee. "Don't worry, Lady Arkey. Trixie and her Fauna will be *well* taken care of." The slight leer of his grin implied otherwise. "But first, let's take care of you." He rose to his feet and clapped his hands once. "Escort our guest."

One of the Ember guards grabbed my upper arm and hoisted me to my feet. I stumbled from the couch, my legs unsteady and all over the place. "At least take me for a drink first!" I spat, a dribble of saliva accompanying my words.

Erosain rose to stand before me, his grin growing wider as he stroked his curling fake beard. Pompous prick. "I'd thought an Undercity drudge such as yourself could handle your drink better. I rue the day Quentin dragged you into my bar."

"You poisoned me!" I accused.

"Restrain her arms," Erosain ordered, ignoring me. "Don't let her touch you."

Another guard yanked my arms behind me. They roughly bound my hands in a very ungentlemanly way.

"Rude," I said.

Erosain continued to ignore me. He lifted a key from around his neck and opened the door to his art gallery, only it wasn't an art gallery anymore.

The plinths and art pieces were all gone, leaving an empty room.

And a flaming portal into Rapture.

Erosain waited beside it and swooped in a low bow. "After you."

The Ember guard hauled me forward, and then I was thrust out of Erosain's bar, Sinner's Row, and Chime entirely.

Stepping through a god-made portal from Chime into another domain was no different from using the Gate, and with the Gate now destroyed, it was the most fashionable way to travel. Really, it seemed every god was at it.

We'd entered some sort of posh cloakroom. The decadence reminded me of Edana's golden palace, which made sense. It was surprisingly cool, for Rapture. Erosain had likely dragged me inside the palace, and not some random alternative bar. He led me through a corridor with a window overlooking the strip, wringing his hands with glee the entire way.

The problem with ambassadors was their gods spent too much time in their heads, turning them into miniature versions of themselves—all that cruelty, and a god-complex to go with it.

"S'will smite you, yanno," I said, my voice still slurred.

He glanced at me with a sneer. "My Queen will be delighted by the gift I've brought her. What will she do with you, I wonder? I could suggest many things, though I hope she allows me to watch when she snaps your bones and burns them into ash."

He really couldn't get over that, could he?

After I tripped over my own feet once or twice, we finally made it to the end of the corridor. A couple of Ember standing guard opened large double doors, and I was rudely shoved inside a flashy penthouse suite.

"My beautiful Queen." Erosain bowed so low, his beard brushed the tiles. "My gift to you."

Unlike the throne room where I'd first been introduced to Edana, this was a small, more intimate space without an orgy of writhing mortals in the background. A square couch not unlike the one back in Erosain's bar filled the room, surrounding a firepit.

Seated there was the god of the Ember, as breathtakingly stunning as the first time I'd laid my eyes on her.

"You may leave us," Edana commanded.

Erosain rose from his bow. "She is dangerous, my Queen. Perhaps I—"

"Do not make me repeat myself."

One of his fake brows twitched with mild irritation. "As you wish."

With a snap of Erosain's fingers, the guard released my arm, and then I was left alone with the Ember god.

She rose slowly from the couch, her dress dropping in a flowing cascade of gold. "You are hardly a threat to me in your current state, child of Chaos."

I suppressed a smirk. "Aren't I?"

My form changed from Mesmer to Glimmer. Luckily for me, Erosain's guard had secured my hands with rope and not metal. A flash of sunlight was enough to burn through my bindings. I rubbed their imprint from my wrists once free and then straightened my dress.

Oh, Erosain thought he'd gotten one over on me, but I'd learned ambassadors couldn't be trusted long ago. Fool me once, shame on them. Fool me twice... The vial Trixie had provided earlier negated whatever cocktail Erosain had tried to poison me with. Seems ambassadors shared the same bag of tricks. They probably exchanged notes.

"Hrm." Edana's gaze roved over my transformation. "You do surprise me."

"It's part of my nature." I fluttered my eyelashes. "Though I'm rather offended that your ambassador both poisoned and manhandled me. I would have accepted an invitation without the cloak-and-dagger act."

"And yet the cloak-and-dagger act suits you. Come." Edana gestured to her couch. "Allow me to rectify my voice's insolence."

I sat opposite Edana, the firepit smoldering between us. "So you chose to ally yourself with my sister."

Edana sat with her legs crossed at the knee, her golden dress not covering the beautiful curves of her thighs. "You know the stakes of the game. Dor wishes to destroy the domains that do not serve him. Chaos is the only power to stand against time."

"Chaos doesn't care for your domain, either. Corentine will destroy you all."

"You served as her voice only a short time ago."

"Because I thought Corentine and Dor could put aside their differences for the sake of Chime's mortals." Well, no. Corentine never liked that plan, and it turned out Dor was never going to go along with it either. I'd had hope, for once in my mortal life, and they'd shat all over it. "I see now that they're both a lost cause."

"What do you intend?"

"To remove them and anyone who gets in my way."

"Including your sister?"

"If it comes down to it."

"You may even succeed. You have Quentin Corinth on your side, correct? Does he have the fortitude to stand against Dor?"

There was no point in hiding Quen's allegiance—Jinx would have told Edana about him switching teams from Diviner to Chaos. He didn't know I'd traveled to Rapture, and he'd be livid when he found out. Quen might consider himself a smooth talker when it came to flirting with gods, but he wasn't in any fit state to impress.

Besides, this was my plan—my operation. I wanted to prove to Trixie I still had it where it mattered. And Edana had made it clear she'd wanted *me*, not Quen.

I adjusted my position, giving Edana a good look at my legs. "Quen is willing and ready to face Dor." Almost ready. "We'll take the steps we need to get there. I'm sure Jinx has filled you in on her master plan, but she can't be trusted. When she's finished with you, she'll take your soul, just as she took The Nameless One and Gildola. That's Corentine's plan: to destroy the gods. All of them."

Technically, it was my plan, too, but Edana didn't need to know that. I could take her soul now, but I wanted to keep Edana around for the same reasons Jinx likely did—her mortals would make great allies. They'd shown how ruthless they could be in Witheryn. And with Edana allied to myself, I had someone to spy on Jinx.

I needed to convince Edana to bet on the right sister.

She didn't seem too concerned, but then gods likely didn't concern themselves with threats from mortals until said mortals were ripping their souls out. "Who is to say your goals aren't aligned with your sister's"

Oh, she wasn't a fool. "Because you know what Quen and I fought for. If we lose the gods, we lose their mortals. I've lost enough… I won't lose any more. Work with me, and I'll ensure you and your mortals keep your domain."

"You enter my domain with threats and demands, yet it was your sister who destroyed the Glimmer and freed us from their clutches."

"For her own benefit. Even if you choose to trust her, she can't take on Dor herself. Neither can you. Quen and I are the only ones who can." I swapped to my Mesmer form. "I've seen visions. I know Dor is strapping your mortals to machines and ripping out their souls, and I know where to find your Ember. With your help, we can destroy those machines."

She sat up. *That* had her interest. "You took Mesmorpheus."

"Mesmorpheus gave themself to me. They saw a future where Quen and I would succeed."

"What else have you seen?"

"Join my side, and I'll tell you."

When a god had everything, knowledge of the unknown became true power.

A subtle smile curved Edana's lips. "What aid do you ask of me?"

Here came the demand that would make or break this impromptu meeting and determine whether I'd walk out of Rapture alive. "I want Sinner's Row."

If Edana had eyebrows, they'd be shooting right up, though the surprise lit up her eyes regardless. "To what end?"

"I need a base for myself and my Fauna allies. They've already agreed to fight by my side, but they need food, shelter, and room to grow. We'll work with the Ember there to regain Chime from below. All you need to do is keep Jinx away."

Edana rose from her seat. My heart skipped a beat as she approached. Shit! I'd gone too far!

But she simply sat beside me and placed a possessive hand on my knee. Gods, she smelled *good*. "I have never bedded a Mesmer. While I know you are but a facsimile of their domain, we will reach agreement on this deal if you allow me to explore your Mesmer body and mind at my leisure."

It was my turn to swallow my surprise. If I needed to whore myself out to Edana to protect the Fauna, then I'd pay the price.

Quen wouldn't need to know.

And gods, fucking Edana wouldn't even be a chore, not really. The woman was gorgeous. Though if we could wrap up our business quickly, then I'd be scratching her soul off my hit list of gods first. Then no one needed to be hurt. No one important, anyhow.

I licked my bottom lip. "Deal. One other thing. I want Sinder."

"The mortal who betrayed you?"

The heat was starting to make me sweat. "I need someone I trust— *know*—to deliver messages to you." Which was partly true.

Really, I wanted another Godless by my side, especially after Jinx's threats.

I needed Sinder.

"That can be arranged." Edana's fingers slowly traced up my arm and took my chin. Shit, she didn't intend to fuck now, did she?

I placed my palm on her thigh. Gods, her skin was hot to the touch. "I promise to return once the soul-splitting machines have been destroyed. While they remain in use, we lose mortals and give power to Dor. Let me deal with them, and then I'll be all yours." The longer I waited, the more danger the Fauna were in.

Edana pulled her fingers away with a pout and instead rested them on my shoulder.

The double doors to the penthouse opened, and Erosain swaggered back inside. "You summoned me, my... Queen?" His eyes opened wide at me sitting beside his god in one piece. I couldn't help but flash him a smug grin.

"You will step down from your position in Sinner's Row and answer to Lady Arkey."

Erosain clutched a fist to his heart. "My Queen? You cannot ask this of me!"

"I just did," she drawled.

"She is Chaos! You cannot align yourself with such—such filth! It is beneath you!"

"You insult my guest, Erosain. Apologize."

"I will not!"

My breath hitched.

Edana didn't move. She didn't so much as flinch.

Flame burst from underneath Erosain's feet.

It completely engulfed him. His silhouette writhed as it bathed in dancing red and orange flames. It would have been beautiful, if not for his bloodcurdling screams.

Thankfully, it was over as soon as it began. The flames receded, leaving a black scorch mark on the pristine tiles and twirling smoke.

The ambassador was no more.

Well, I'd tried to offer him a way out. That's what you get for placing faith in a god.

I blinked, and then Sinder appeared next to the dark spot that had been Erosain. Sinder was dressed in similar clothes to the former ambassador—a black tuxedo, heels, and makeup to match, though his dark eyes were wide with fear and the hands he clasped over his stomach trembled slightly.

"Sinder will serve as my new voice," Edana announced.

Oh shit! That was *not* what I'd intended. Serving as a god's ambassador was more of a curse than a blessing, and based on the pleading look Sinder was giving me, he knew it.

Edana summoned a pair of silver keys on a chain and handed them to me. "Return to me soon, child of Chaos. I will be watching."

The message was clear. Edana would watch me and my actions through his eyes.

He'd never get any peace so long as a god filled his mind.

I stood on wobbly legs and strode for Sinder with as much dignity as I could muster. He offered his arm, which I wrapped myself around like it was a pissing lifeline. Together, we left Edana's penthouse and strode through the corridor back to the portal.

"Dearest," Sinder rasped, breaking the awkward silence. "I know you hate me and likely want revenge, but this?"

"I don't hate you. I had no idea Edana would make you her voice."

"Then why?"

I turned my head to look him in the eye. "Because now you can help me fix what you broke."

He swallowed a lump in his throat and nodded.

We passed through the portal and returned to Erosain's bar. Trixie and Wolfsbane remained seated on Erosain's couch, waiting for me.

Wolfsbane leaped up. "You're back!" He eyed Sinder. "And safe?"

"This is Sinder. He's a friend." I pulled myself from his arm and tossed the set of keys into Trixie's lap. "A gift for you."

She held up the keys with a suspicious squint. "For...?"

"Sinner's Row. It's all yours."

Her feline eyes opened wide. "Are you fucking with me?"

"Like I'd dare. Do what you want with the place. Just promise me you'll make it a home for all mortals who need it."

It was a genius plan. The Fauna couldn't remain cramped in that shitty hotel forever. There were too many of them—they needed room, not to mention food and supplies. Trixie could have betrayed me to Erosain, but she'd trusted me, despite everything. She deserved to be rewarded for that trust.

And now we had a defensive base to operate from. Even Quen would be pleased to see Sinner's Row in the hands of a mortal with a heart.

All it would potentially cost was a night with a god between my legs.

XVII

We've been stuck here for a week now with no end in sight. The tea stores are closed, and the rations they're sending in from Kronos are barely sufficient. How is it we run out of sodding milk at three in the afternoon? It's preposterous. Dare I say it? The tea is subpar.
I've complained to my superior, and now I'm being reported to the 'redeemer' over the matter. I hope he can 'redeem' our woeful tea.
—Anonymous, overheard in the Market District

I SAT AT A round table with the three Mesmer. They were practically identical as far as I could tell, with the same shimmering pattern of stars across their faces, the same black suits and neat dark hair; thus they'd taken to wearing accessories to help me tell them apart.

Celeste, the woman among the three, announced her femininity by wearing a tiny pink bow in her hair. Her nose scrunched in concentration as she poured tea from a porcelain pot into five matching cups—three for the Mesmer, one for me, and one for the small Fauna boy, Freddie, whom the Mesmer had taken an overprotective liking to.

The second Mesmer, Castor, took over the tea-making operation by handling a jug of milk. He wore a simple blue necktie, marking his masculinity. I'd witnessed Celeste and Castor holding hands and exchanging giggling kisses; thus I took the two for lovers. An oddity in itself for a pair of Mesmer. I watched the fellow carefully as he poured a decent measure of milk. Nothing too frothy.

Cosmo then handled the sugar bowl. They wore a purple handkerchief in their top shirt pocket and responded neither to he nor she, as though Cosmo acted as the bridge connecting Celeste and Castor. Another oddity, but it worked for them.

"Three or four sugars?" Cosmo asked cheerfully as they scooped out a sugar cube.

"Two will suffice," I said.

Cosmo looked shocked. "Are you sure? Mama has at least three sugars. I can't get out of bed without six!"

"Two is plenty for me—"

"Everyone in Phantasy takes at least three, though four or five or six is better—"

"Think of it this way: the less sugar I take, the more is left over for you."

They mused on that.

I glanced around the restaurant as Cosmo finished serving up the tea. It was midafternoon, and the restaurant had closed their makeshift soup kitchen for now, though Fauna still loitered about the room, resting on dining chairs, or curled up underneath the tables like they were tents. There were too many Fauna to comfortably fill this hotel, and not enough scraps to feed everyone. I could only hope Kayl and Trixie were able to negotiate with Erosain.

There were plenty of empty buildings in Sinner's Row we could take advantage of. It all came down to how generous Erosain felt. I didn't know how Kayl intended to win the ambassador over, considering the animosity between them, and she had declined to fully divulge her plans.

I trusted her implicitly. That didn't prevent me from feeling useless. Negotiating with ambassadors was meant to be my expertise, and instead I'd been reduced to babysitting the Mesmer. Or, they were babysitting me.

Cosmo slid a cup over to me. "Two sugars!"

"Bless you." I grasped the handle with my left hand. The tea sloshed slightly as I lifted the cup with a little too much vigor. I wasn't used to handling objects with my left hand yet—a failure on my part—and I corrected my grip before it could spill.

I took a tentative sip as the three Mesmer watched me with disconcerting smiles, as though I were a critic of some Golden City restaurant and they eagerly awaited my judgement.

Well, I had nothing else going on.

Throughout my mortal years, I had indulged in many cups of tea across the domains. Nothing matched the temperance of a cuppa from Kronos, and I'd mimicked their techniques to create my own satisfactory beverages from the comfort of my apartment. The Diviner may have done many terrible things, but they knew how to brew.

The Mesmer were known for their sweet teas, and I was certain Cosmo must have slipped in an extra sugar cube, for this stung my teeth. But something else was off about it. It didn't taste right. No, the leaves weren't too bitter; the sugar offset that.

Was it the milk?

How honest could I be, when the Mesmer were so keen to impress? I placed my cup down on its saucer and forced a smile. "It's delightful, thank you. Hits the spot."

Cosmo let out a squeal. "We have cake!"

Indeed. The Mesmer had sourced a plate of triangular cucumber sandwiches and an entire sponge cake from somewhere. Likely scavenged from the hotel's kitchens.

Castor carefully cut generous slices for each of us, including poor Freddie. He slid a plate over to me. "Careful, it's sticky."

I didn't make a habit of indulging in sweet treats, though a few biscuits wouldn't have gone amiss. But who knew when I'd get another chance to indulge again in these troublesome times? A little sugar would help me heal—in body and soul. I gave the slice a hearty bite and then wished I hadn't.

Dear gods. The cake was stale. There was no moisture to be found. The blasted thing was drier than a trip to Obituary or a Zephyr's sense of humor.

I take offense to that, came Doctor Finch's voice inside my mind.

You wouldn't, if you were forced to eat this abomination. I swallowed what felt like a brick and then lubricated my throat with more of that awful tea. Were the Mesmer trying to poison me?

They truly had scavenged this cake from somewhere undesirable, and I certainly didn't wish to know where.

I do not detect any signs of poison within your system, the doctor said.

I held back a sigh. Did I need to start explaining the sarcasm of my own mind? *What, exactly, are you observing in my system?*

Your vitals. We can stimulate cellular growth and repair severed connections to your nervous system at an accelerated rate.

It took me a moment to understand his meaning. *You're healing me faster?*

Correct. While we cannot regrow your arm, we can increase your cellular metabolism.

That would explain why my energy levels had perked up. Here I'd thought the laudanum had been performing miracles. Injuries like mine took months to recover from, and adjusting to losing a limb had permanent ramifications. Unfortunately, I didn't have reams of time available to heal or adjust.

Chime was falling apart. The gods were warring. I couldn't afford to wallow when mortals were suffering, or when Fauna were in the hands of the Diviner, potentially losing their souls. When I had no idea if Ben had made it out.

My residual limb still ached, even when dulled with laudanum. Occasionally, spasms of pain shot through my missing fingers, as though they still existed somewhere. I wasn't at my best, and perhaps I never would be again.

The sooner I healed, the better. *Keep doing what you're doing, Doctor.*

A silent acknowledgement passed through my mind.

I took another measured sip of the tea. It really did not taste right. Was the milk off? It likely was, if it had been abandoned in the hotel for over a week. "May I ask what milk you used?"

"Oh!" Celeste fidgeted in her seat with sudden excitement. "We couldn't find any milk in the kitchen, so we asked Gerty." She waved to someone behind me.

"Gerty?" I followed her eye as a large-breasted goat-woman sauntered over carrying a young goat-child.

"Was that enough milk for you, dears?" She gave her swollen breast a squeeze. "There's plenty more where that came from."

Oh, dear gods!

I gagged and spluttered tea down my chin.

The goat-woman—Gerty—sank into a spare chair. "There's naught wrong with it," she chided. "It's fresh!"

"Of that I have no doubt!" I hastily wiped myself clean with a napkin.

"Then what's your bellyaching?"

"I thought it was nut milk!" That was the standard for milk products brought into Chime—almond milk, hazelnut milk, oat milk! Not breast milk, my goodness!

"Nut milk?" Gerty cocked her head. "If you'd prefer that, I can ask Gerry to whip it out. *Gerry!*" she yelled.

"No, no!" I held up my hand. "No, thank you!" While I appreciated the taste of a man's seed, I did *not* want it in my tea.

Saints. What was I doing? Sitting here, drinking god-awful tea, when I could be making progress? I needed materials and schematics for a new arm if I was going to be useful in the battles to come, as well as parts for Doctor Finch's portal-creating device. Wasting my time here wasn't helping either of those goals.

Kayl had left me behind to rest and recuperate, but we didn't have the luxury. Besides, my body was healing at a fast rate. I felt strong enough to gather the parts I needed. If I did so before Kayl returned, then at least we'd be ahead of schedule.

I put my unfinished tea aside and stood. "If you don't mind, I'd like to stretch my legs and go for a walk."

Cosmo frowned. "Mama says you're not allowed to go wandering."

"I'm feeling much better now. A walk always does wonders for the body and mind."

"Maybe we should pray to Mama and ask—"

"That won't be necessary. We wouldn't want to disturb Kayl when she is busy, would we?" Nor would I wish to worry her.

Cosmo picked at a few crumbs of cake on the table. "No, we wouldn't want that!"

"Why don't the three of you have a nap? I'll be back before you wake."

Cosmo clapped their hands. "I love naps!"

I thanked them for the tea and left them to finish off their stale cake.

Where will you find supplies? Doctor Finch asked. *Your allies stated Sinner's Row would not be appropriate.*

No. They may have adequate tools here, but likely not the parts I'd require. There was only one place in the Undercity I'd source them.

The steamworks.

Sneaking out of Sinner's Row required little effort. I simply switched my form to Diviner and paused time, leaving the Ember guarding the entrance none the wiser. It was remarkable, really, how easy it was to simply morph between Chaos and Diviner. I hadn't tried a Zephyr form since leaving Tempest. Sprouting wings would prove rather problematic.

Traveling all the way to the steamworks would sadly prove more difficult.

The Undercity trams weren't running. There was no one left *to* run them. Whatever Diviner were left in Chime certainly didn't wish to provide transport to Sinner's Row, but the power was still on.

There really was no one to stop me from entering the driver's cabin of an abandoned tram and taking it for a joyride.

I flipped on the various switches and coaxed the tram away from the platform by Sinner's Row. There could be more abandoned carriages ahead, as well as debris; thus I took it slow. The controls hummed beneath my touch with a pleasing purr as we rumbled along the dark Undercity tracks, and were thankfully easy enough to operate with one hand.

This had once been my dream. How different would my life have turned out if I'd followed it and become a tram driver instead of a Warden? Dor had given me little choice in the matter, but had the choice been mine... Where would I be now?

Would I still have met Kayl? The Godless?

Would this timeline have ever happened at all?

Should I pray to you, Master Corinth? Doctor Finch asked.

His thoughts startled me out of my own. *No, Doctor. I don't require your prayer or worship, just your cooperation.*

You own my soul. That makes you my god.

Technically, I supposed it did, though I had no wish to claim the title. However, I *had* taken the entirety of the Zephyr, and that made me responsible for them. To that end, I would do my best by them, however that may be.

No one ever listens to me. The good doctor's emotions bloomed through me with sorrow and regret.

I'm listening to you now. Whatever you need, I will do my utmost to assist. Though it would be easier if you had your own body. He'd been born without wings, but as his new personal god, surely that would be simple enough to provide?

I don't want wings. But I... His hesitation gnawed at me, but then the thought drifted in my mind without him needing to utter it.

You feel like you were born in the wrong body?

Isn't that... a sin?

Ben had also confided in me that he felt as though he belonged to a different domain. That he should have been born an Umber instead of a Diviner. Of course, expressing those feelings was taboo. To voice them meant admitting apostasy—that the gods had made a mistake somewhere in your creation.

The gods weren't infallible. Dor had been wrong about Ben, as Zyclone had been wrong about Zachery. *Which domain calls to you?*

I don't know anymore. I thought, perhaps, I may be Diviner. I like to tinker. I work best with my Diviner colleagues. That's why I joined the steamworks and Hector Bezel's team. It was... the only time I felt I belonged.

Again, I sensed his hesitation. *But?*

The Diviner are... cruel.

Memories flashed inside my mind of Kronos and the experiments the Diviner had forced on Chance. Horrifying memories, and all too recent. They'd split Chance's soul. Cut open his guts and rummaged through them to learn how a Chaos mortal worked, as though their physiology was different from any other damn mortal.

Yes, the Diviner could be cruel. They lacked an emotional connection other domains didn't, and that was entirely Dor's design. But mortals from other domains were also forced to commit atrocities in their god's name. It didn't make those domains intrinsically evil. I'd met good Diviner. Good Glimmer.

Without their gods, mortals stood a chance of being better.

Only you can define who you are, I said. *I'll be here to guide you through it whenever you're ready.*

My mind went quiet, though I sensed the doctor's gratitude. When I took Zyclone's soul, it had been partly out of self-preservation—to protect myself from Corentine. It was also to prevent both Corentine and Dor from taking advantage of the Zephyr's technological minds.

But in taking Zyclone, I'd killed Zachery Finch. Twice now because of my actions. Taking care of his mental well-being was the least I could do.

My thoughts returned to the present as my tram exited a tunnel to a dark blot covering the skyline. I'd arrived at the steamworks.

Another tram was already parked by the platform, so I slowed mine to a halt and hopped down onto the tracks. It was eerily quiet except for the ever-present hiss of steam. The steamworks were still active, then. Even with Chime emptied of mortals, the streetlamps and elevators required power.

With any luck, the steamworks would be empty, allowing me to slip in undetected.

Alas. Two Diviner stood guard by the main doors. It made sense for Dor to protect the steamworks from Chaos, though I'd rather hoped they'd have more important things going on.

There would be no stopping time to sneak past these fellows. But as I edged closer, something looked amiss.

They were slumped against the walls, unconscious.

I scanned my surroundings, but we were alone as far as I could tell. These Diviner weren't injured. There was no blood, no sign of a scuffle, yet they were out cold.

One of them twitched. An involuntary spasm. Someone had tased them, and recently.

Which meant I certainly wasn't alone, but who else would be here? Jinx?

Approach with caution, Master Corinth.

Quite. Carefully, I stepped past the unconscious Diviner and entered the steamworks.

The inner reception area was much the same as when I last visited here with Kayl—when I first met Doctor Finch. Only now it was abandoned. Dust covered the waiting-area chairs and the reception desk, but this was the dust of neglect, not the death of mortals.

I took one step at a time as I eased myself into the maintenance corridor. I fully expected to run into another Diviner, but the corridors were empty, with only the hum of aether for company and the occasional clang from the piping.

Where to, Doctor? I asked.

The workshop below. My office had the required parts, but they must have been recovered by now.

Guide me.

With the good doctor's instructions, I made my way through familiar corridors to a metal staircase. This led to the reactors, where steam power was converted to aether. Or so I believed. Since that last visit, I'd learned it was Corentine's energy that powered Chime. The steamworks churned it through the city. Steam was merely a byproduct of this process.

The pipes and walls around me buzzed with energy, and yet I hadn't passed a single soul. There must still be mortals here maintaining the pressure levels—why guard the entrance if not? Yet my path remained clear. It was unsettling.

Someone wanted me here.

Should I have brought a weapon? What would have been the point? I was hardly trained to fight with my left hand, and despite the doctor's accelerated healing, I was, as Kayl had so politely put it, in no shape to fight.

I reached a door that said *Workshop.* It was already ajar.

This felt like a trap, and I was carelessly walking straight into it.

No wonder Kayl never listened to me.

You should run. Doctor Finch's anxiety itched under my skin.

Someone has gone to a great amount of trouble to clear my path. The Diviner? Jinx? *It would be impolite to turn back now.* And I wasn't leaving without the parts I needed. I pushed open the door.

And came face to face with myself.

"Good afternoon, Past Quen," he—*I*—said.

My jaw almost bloody fell off! "Future Quen?" I spluttered.

Is that you? Doctor Finch squawked inside my mind.

It's... complicated. Saints, where could I even begin?

My future self stood in the center of the workshop in the tan suit he'd worn the last time I'd encountered him in the Mesmer temple when he facilitated my rebirth as Chaos. His form was that of a Diviner, though his eyes glowed with pure chaotic aether. He pulled a fob watch from his waistcoat pocket—my fob watch!

Gosh, it took me a moment to realize. He possessed both arms. Did that mean I grew mine back in the future?

"No," he said, examining the fob watch. "At least, not that I'm aware of." He snapped the fob watch shut and glanced at me. "Now listen carefully. We have only twenty minutes to spare, so please keep your inane questions to a minimum."

I bristled. "That's rather—"

"Rude. Yes, and I won't apologize. Time is of the essence." He tucked the fob watch away and then shrugged off his jacket, revealing my old brass pistol strapped to his hip. I wanted to inquire how, but I kept my *inane* question to myself.

This all explained why the corridors had been empty.

How is it possible for you to both exist at the same time? Doctor Finch demanded. I could practically feel his flustered flailing inside my mind.

Somewhere—or somewhen—in the future, time will fracture.

How?

I suspect we'll eventually find out.

My future self tossed his jacket onto a bench, then removed his waistcoat and began to undo his shirt buttons.

"Should I be alarmed?" I asked while trying not to feel alarmed. This was my future self, after all. If I couldn't trust him, then who could I trust?

"Honestly, it amuses me to see you squirm," Future Quen said. "Fear not. If we were to touch—"

"It would cause a paradox."

"Precisely." He pulled the shirt off his right arm, leaving it to dangle half-on.

My heart skipped a beat.

It was a metallic arm with a silvery sheen that could pass for Diviner skin. The metal was smooth enough to be near perfect, though the elbow joint and fingers were clearly artificial. My future self flexed the digits with precision.

A leather strap stretched across his chest and back, holding the arm in place with a simple buckle. He flipped that open, and then gripped the top half of the arm where it merged with his bicep.

With one clean twist, the arm popped right off.

"My goodness," I gasped.

Future Quen carried his artificial arm and placed it on a spare workshop table. There were similar tables dotted around, each piled with tools, cogs, and screws. He gestured to the arm. "Take it."

"You're giving me your arm?"

"I'm giving you *your* arm. You don't have time to gather the necessary parts and test run a blueprint, but you will later in your future. I no longer require it."

"Why?"

"Because my timeline is about to end."

To end? What did that mean?

"It means I can no longer help you or your allies. This is all I can give you. Oh." He drew the brass pistol from its holster and laid it next to the arm. "And this. The chamber's full. You can source more ammunition from Sinner's Row."

I strode over to the table and placed my left hand on the pistol grip. It most definitely was my pistol, but I'd lost it in Kronos. "Where did you get this?"

"Under your bed back in the Silver Suite." He waggled his eyebrows. "You left it unused for years. Just remember to replace it before your past self needs it once more."

That implied I would be falling back in time in my near future.

"Events will happen outside your control," Future Quen confirmed.

"And you can't give me any hint as to what's to come?"

"You know that will affect the timeline." He drew his shirt back across his chest and slid on his waistcoat and jacket, despite his missing arm, with a maneuver that implied practice. "I've witnessed multiple futures. This path will hurt you, but I can no longer help you. You will despise me for allowing the pain to come."

I swallowed a lump in my throat. What horrors awaited me in my future?

Surely I must survive them for my future self to be standing here healthy and mostly whole?

"If there is one piece of advice I can give you, it is this: remain devoted to your god."

Such a declaration made me physically recoil. "I have no devotion to Dor—"

"I'm not speaking of Dor." His lips curved into a smirk.

Kayl.

"You were meant to die in her service," Future Quen said. "And you will die again if you wish to see her rise. I could comment on the self-respect you so badly need, but we both know you've always needed religion, whether that be the Diviner, the Wardens, or the Godless. Well, don't just stand there. Try it on." He nodded to the arm.

How was I meant to even concentrate after that information?

How was I even meant to *breathe*?

I lifted the arm. It was surprisingly light.

"It's molded to fit you and you alone," Future Quen said. "Trust it to stay in place and hold. The Zephyr will need to connect your nerves internally for it to function. Doctor Finch will understand what I mean."

I popped open my shirt buttons with a push from my thumb and then shrugged out of the rest. How was this blasted arm meant to attach to what was left of me? The upper half was shaped like a cup. I gently peeled off the bloodied bandage around my stitches and tossed it aside, then pushed the metal arm up against my residual limb. It slotted into place, the material gripping tight as though forming a suction seal. Oh my.

The strap I draped across my shoulder and pulled tight across my back and chest. It took a moment to fumble the buckle, but it would become easier with practice, I was sure.

We see the connections, Doctor Finch said, excitement running through my veins. *Give us one moment.*

I wasn't entirely sure what to expect, but then...

Agony burned through my arm.

I screamed and collapsed against the workshop table, knocking aside cogs and bolts. It was as though I'd been shocked with aether! Pure electricity zapped down my residual limb, shooting through the fingers that no longer existed. I sank to the dusty floor, panting, as sweat beaded my brow.

Apologies, Doctor Finch said. *We should have warned that the initial connection between nerves may hurt a little.*

A little? It was excruciating!

The pain was replaced with pins and needles. I tried shaking off the sensation, and my fake arm spasmed. Good gods.

I imagined myself lifting my hand, and it rose!

It was moving! I tried wiggling my fingers next, and while there was a slight disconnect between willing them to move and the action, the fact they were moving at all was nothing short of a miracle. "Saints!"

"Greater control will come to you in time, but it won't stop the aches and pains, I'm afraid," Future Quen warned. "Take it off when you don't need it. You're still injured and require rest. Oh, and practice learning to grip. I'd recommend having a jolly good wank, that will soon teach you." He chuckled to himself.

I tutted. "Are you certain you're me?"

He wore a sly grin. "I am the absolute best version of you." He pulled out his fob watch again. "Time's up. Run along, now. You've got a destiny to fulfill."

"In death?"

"My dear boy. Death is only the beginning. Kayl is your god." His eyes sharpened with intensity, and aether radiated from them. "Become the man she needs you to be."

Light burst around his form, shading him in a silhouette of bright blue and pink aether.

And then he was gone.

I pulled myself up with one of the workshop tables and leaned against it.

"Kayl is your god."

Those words tore through me with emotions I couldn't interpret.

Had I escaped two gods to become shackled to another? But no, Kayl wasn't a god, not in the traditional sense. Perhaps my future self was speaking metaphorically and not literally. We were both poets with a flair for the dramatic.

Kayl was Godless. Her path was to destroy the gods, not replace them.

And yet...

If she were to become my god, would I throw myself at her feet in reverent worship? Would I sacrifice myself for a new dogma? My future self knew us both well.

What did that say about me and my depraved desires?

An alarm blared overhead. Bugger. The Diviner must have regained consciousness.

We still require parts for the portal-creator, Doctor Finch reminded me.

Oh gosh! I'd almost forgotten. *Tell me what you need.*

The good doctor guided me around the workshop as I snatched up the tools and parts he mentally pointed out. I hadn't thought to bring a bag; thus I ripped off my shirt and fashioned a container for my freshly stolen goods.

It was awkward to tie my shirt into a bag. My new hand couldn't yet properly grip and made sloppy work. I attempted to lift a screwdriver, and my metal fingers gripped *too* tight, crushing the handle.

My future self encouraged me to hold my cock like this? Gods forbid!

Master Corinth!

The doctor's warning drew my attention to the door.

A Diviner stood by the entrance. "It's the Dark Warden!" he yelled.

Wonderful. I grabbed my pistol with my left hand and took aim.

The shot went wide and caught him in the bicep.

The Diviner staggered back with a scream. I'd aimed to kill, but my left hand was obviously not up to the task, and I didn't trust my new hand not to damage my pistol.

But it gave me the opening I needed.

I slung my makeshift bag over my shoulder, the motion stiff but workable, and then rammed past the Diviner, knocking him down.

A shot ricocheted off the wall, inches from my head.

Two more Diviner ran down the corridor, both in Warden uniforms.

"Don't shoot, you idiot!" one of the Diviner chided their partner. "That's the Dark Warden. The Redeemer wants him alive!"

The Redeemer?

Why did they want me? On Dor's orders?

Regardless of my curiosity, I would not allow *anyone* to drag me back to Dor.

I took aim once more and fired.

This time, my bullet pierced the chap's neck. Better.

Blood spurted from his artery, shooting up the wall in a splash of red. He collapsed in a pile of clothing.

"Stop!" the other Diviner called. He drew a taser.

I charged toward him and swung with my new arm. The hand didn't quite clench into a perfect fist, but the effect was the same. It collided with the Diviner's nose in a sickening crunch, and he collapsed to the ground, unconscious.

"Sorry." I placed the barrel of my pistol to his forehead and pulled the trigger.

There was no missing from this angle, and I wasn't taking any chances.

I took his taser and shoved it into the band of my trousers. It could come in handy. And then I was sprinting back up the stairs and into the main corridor of the steamworks.

The alarm rang in my ears. It was much louder up here, giving me a damn headache. Though no. Everything was aching. My legs, my chest from breathing so heavily.

I leaned against the wall to catch my breath, my lungs heaving. Blood had splashed onto my bare chest. How was I going to explain that?

You're not fully recovered, Doctor Finch said. *Stop running so fast.*

What do you expect me to do? Take a five-minute nap in someone's office and hope the Diviner leave me be?

The Doctor didn't answer.

I pushed away from the wall and continued down the corridor, my pistol aimed at the double doors leading back to reception.

I burst through them, left shoulder first.

A single Diviner stood waiting for me.

"Pendula," I gasped.

She lifted her chin. "Quentin."

Saints. Of all the Diviner I could have bumped into here, my ex-betrothed was the last I'd expected to see. She wore a tan jacket and shirt, her silver hair with its single streak of brass curled in a neat bob, as prim and pristine as when we parted—when I'd shot her with a taser.

Only, the silver skin of her face was marred. She'd had two scars when I left, both inflicted by Dor as a punishment to me; the words *masturbation* and *deceit* carved into her flesh.

But now, new scars glistened on her cheek and forehead. Four more scars cut into her skin.

Deserter.

Traitor.

Betrayer.

Apostate.

These weren't meant for Pendula. They were meant for me.

Was she the Redeemer? Had she been sent to absolve my soul?

I lowered my pistol. "Dor did this to you?"

She crossed her hands in front of her stomach. "Father knows you're alive. That you have... changed. He—He has punished me for your desertion."

That he would do such a thing was obscene. It burned through my gut with such force, I wanted to shoot my way into Kronos this instant.

How *dare* he?

"Penny—"

"Turn yourself in," she blurted. "Return with me to Kronos, and this…" She touched the scar below her left eye, which said *apostate*. "This will stop."

And if I didn't, it would only get worse. "I can't."

"*Please*, Quentin." Her silver eyes were red, rimmed with tears. "If you hold any respect for me at all, then please. Stop this."

It wouldn't stop, though, would it?

I could return to Kronos, hand myself over to Dor, but the punishments wouldn't stop. Dor knew my weaknesses, my sentimentality. He knew dangling Pendula would bait me. Did he watch me now, through her silver eyes?

Did he understand who I was? What I'd become?

Why would he even want my return? To remove a threat to his rule?

Surely, he must know I would come for him. Not yet, not until I was ready.

But one day soon.

Dor would die.

A part of me ached to ask Ben's fate, but he too would become a pawn Dor would dangle before me.

Footsteps echoed in the corridor behind us. Of course. Penny was merely holding me here until I either surrendered or found myself surrounded.

I didn't have time for sentimentality. For mercy. This was war, and it was an ugly thing.

"*Kayl is your god.*"

And she waited for me.

One click of my trigger, and my bullet pierced Pendula's cheek, directly on the A of traitor. I'd been aiming for her forehead, but good enough.

For a heartbeat, her mouth opened in surprise.

Then she collapsed into a pile of dust.

"Apologies," I murmured. I hadn't wanted to send her back to Dor, and perhaps it would have been kinder to steal her soul instead, but I couldn't risk getting physically close.

Diviner burst through the reception doors. Now was the time to take my leave.

I charged past them, slinging my bag of stolen goods to bash them out of the way, and then I was out of the steamworks and running for my freedom. I switched my form to Chaos and tossed up an aether shield to keep their bullets and tasers at bay as I launched myself into the waiting tram. I wouldn't be able to ride it all the way—I couldn't risk Dor learning of my destination—but I needed out of here.

Only when the engine kicked the tram into life did I risk putting my pistol down and sag into a chair. That entire endeavor had left me completely drained.

I flexed my new hand. Somehow, the signals from my brain convinced it this collection of metal parts was real. It didn't register precise touch, but I'd been cursed with a lack of touch since my youth regardless. More remarkably, my new arm remained attached despite switching forms. I'd need to experiment with it to learn my limitations.

Are we the villains? Doctor Finch asked with heartbreaking sincerity.

According to the Covenant, yes.

Though the Covenant no longer applied.

Now that Dor knew I couldn't be controlled, the battles to come would prove more dangerous.

For the first time... I welcomed the challenge.

If I could survive losing an arm and the Mesmer's attempt at a tea party, I'd survive war.

It's Mortal Appreciation Day

Name: Harmony Arabesque, Seren
Known Affiliations: The Godless, Memoria University, The Chime Courier
(ex-editor), the Arabesque Family of Arcadia (disowned)
Harmony Arabesque is the leader of the Godless and the mastermind
behind their organization. Though physically disabled due to a missing
wing, Arabesque has proven resourceful and has previously used her Seren
song to escape the correctional facility. She was not captured as part of the
Warden raid on the Mesmer temple. We believe someone may have tipped
her off, as she was last seen in Central Station during the Gate closure.
Her current whereabouts are unknown.
—P. Bezel, Personal Report on Harmony Arabesque

THOSE DIVINER FUCKS WERE up to something.

I watched them scurry around Central Station from behind the safety of the clockface glass. If looks could kill, I'd have slaughtered them all by now, but even my best glares weren't enough to send them up in smoke. Suppose I'd eventually need to get my hands dirty and do it in person.

Technically I didn't even have to. I had mortals for that.

Mortals who didn't listen to a fucking word I said!

It was lunchtime, and my Necro needed to eat. My Glimmer apparently objected to being a meal.

"Lay a single finger on me, and I will burn you to nothing!" screeched Gloria. She stood in the center of the room and glowed menacingly at the Necro male who'd tried to sink his fangs into her.

"I just want a taste." The Necro leered.

No one really liked the Necro, so I couldn't blame the Glimmer for wanting to avoid them, but really, those sanctimonious tarts had it coming. The Glimmer gave no shits about the Necro except when they could use them to dye their hair or lift their cheekbones, so it was only fair the Necro took what they could from the Glimmer in turn. Everyone needed to eat.

But if the Glimmer started burning all my Necro, then that would be a pain in the arse.

Joe pushed himself between the two. "No one is eating anyone."

The Necro bared his fangs. "I was promised *her*."

Gloria huffed with indignation. Despite being trapped inside this room and forced to power my aether shield, she was still a snotty little bitch. Throwing her to the Necro might humble her a bit.

I strode over to the commotion. "Let the Necro eat."

Joe turned to me in alarm. "What? Wait a mo—"

The Necro didn't wait.

He pounced on Gloria. To her credit, she attempted to blast out a beam of light that would be enough to melt through most mortals. But I was Gloria's god, now. I simply found her soul among the many thousands inside my mind and negated her powers.

"Stop!" Gloria yelled, her hands raised to protect herself.

The Necro flung her to the ground.

Gloria screamed, until his fangs ravaged her neck and she couldn't scream anymore. Blood splattered across the floor. Shit, this was messy business. Had I gone too far? The other Glimmer huddled against the wall, some of them working on the aether shield, others staring in shock. Their fear made my own blood run cold.

Opposite, a group of Necro watched on, licking their lips. Their ravenous hunger burned in my mind, overwhelming the Glimmer's fear.

They said the gods lived through their mortals, feeling everything they did, but *fuck*. Their conflicting emotions and sensations flowing through me made my head spin.

Gloria shook with silent sobs as the Necro straddled her and drank greedily. For the first time in her mortal life, she was powerless.

Torment wasn't as much fun when you were the one being tormented.

"Stop this!" Joe pleaded. His hands twitched, as though he wanted to seize the Necro and pull him off but didn't dare. Instead, he rounded on me. "Please!"

"Why? You think she ever gave a fuck about the mortals she tortured inside her workhouses? I've seen her memories." My voice came out in a snarl. "And she deserves every bit of suffering she gets."

Pleasure throbbed in my mind from the Necro feasting on Gloria, but something about it was wrong it. Utterly vile.

The Necro pushed up Gloria's skirt. I blinked as he undid his trousers and pulled out a rock-hard cock. The fuck?

Revulsion burned through me. It caught in my mouth with hot bile.

Vincent charged across the room. He launched himself at the Necro with his cane in his hand—one I'd left for him to use—and whacked it across the Necro good and proper, beating him until he was forced off Gloria.

They both staggered back, teeth bared at each other.

"She's mine!" the Necro snarled, his lips dripping with Gloria's blood, and his trousers pulled down below his arse with his cock on full display. Ugh.

I regained my composure. "No, she's *mine*." With a single thought, the Necro vanished in a scattering of dust, and Gloria's neck stitched itself into one piece. She was still a mess—her robe covered in blood, and the woman trembling in a puddle of her own piss.

"Clean her up," I ordered Joe.

Joe kneeled by Gloria's side and dealt with her as I turned away.

Gloria deserved her suffering. She fucking *deserved* it.

But Necro were nasty fuckers.

How had I ended up with the two worst domains in my arsenal?

I snapped my fingers and ordered Vincent to my side. He straightened, his expression wary. Pain lanced through his leg, forcing him to place his weight on the cane. That little stunt had cost him.

"The fuck was that all about?" I demanded.

"Necro experience arousal after a feed."

"That's disgusting."

"It's the effect blood has on us."

That gave a whole new light to the feeding and fucking Necro were known for. "Then I can't have Necro males in my army." The Glimmer were already afraid of them, and I couldn't risk that shit happening again. Feeding was one thing, but... I shuddered.

"You're their god, now. Take away their hunger, and this won't happen again."

Summoning the souls I owned was easy, but rewriting their entire biology to remove their dependence on blood? That was a whole different layer of complexity that required a fucking Academy degree or something. "Or you and Joe can come up with a way of feeding them that keeps everyone happy."

In the meantime, I was going to replace every male Necro with a female because those fuckers couldn't be trusted.

I carried the entirety of the Glimmer and Necro in my mind. Thousands upon thousands of mortal souls I could pull out and throw against the Diviner, and yet I couldn't fit them all in this shitty room. I'd deliberately selected my chosen few; the Glimmer for their firepower and stubbornness, and the Necro for their viciousness, but my plans had obviously backfired.

What I needed were loyal minions. Mortals who *wanted* to fight for me.

Something bronze caught my eye. I glanced out the clock tower window.

Fuck.

More of Dor's shitty clockwork immortals had appeared in Central Station. A lot more. And... giant boulders on legs? Were they Umber?

GOLEMS, Mother said. *UNGHARD'S IMMORTALS.*

If Unghard was lending Dor their immortals, then they must be gearing up for round two. This time, they meant business.

I'd never summoned an immortal before. Would possessing Gildola and The Nameless One's souls be enough to create one?

How do I make my own immortals? If I was going up against them, then I'd need something to fight back with.

I NEVER BOTHERED TO MAKE ANY, Mother drawled. *THERE WAS LITTLE POINT BEFORE MY IMPRISONMENT, AND AFTER, I LACKED THE POWER TO DO SO. PERHAPS IF YOU*

UNLOCKED MY CHAINS WITH GILDOLA AND THE NAMELESS ONE'S SOULS, I COULD ATTEMPT IT.

We've been through this. If I'm to stand any chance against Dor or the rest of them, I need Gildola's power to fight and The Nameless One's healing ability.

I STARVE, DAUGHTER. EVERY DAY IS AGONY.

I know, Mother. It pained me to see her strapped to that damn chair, but the quickest way to defeat the gods would be to gather more power to use against them. Otherwise, my mortal form wouldn't stand a chance. *When I steal more souls, they'll be yours. I promise.*

THEN HOW WILL YOU FIGHT AGAINST IMMORTALS?

It was a good question. I could fling Glimmer at the Guardians and melt through their bronze bodies and metal cogs, but the Golems? I didn't know shit about those, and sunlight would do fuck all against stone.

I needed an expert opinion. Edana would be my first go-to—she was the only god so far with experience in battle. Just my luck that I had no easy way of contacting her. *But* I did have a Seren on hand who could pass on a message to Serenity.

Oi, Gast, I called to the Necro private eye I'd sent scouring the Undercity. *Is Noct with you?*

Yes, Gast snapped back, annoyed I'd interrupted the one job I'd tasked him with, which I supposed I had.

I need him to contact Serenity and pass on a message.

Fine.

"Why are all my mortals so rude?" I wondered aloud.

"Because they fear you." Joe approached with a frown. Blood stained his golden hands from helping Gloria, and Vincent sucked in a breath at the sight.

"I'm their god. All I want is a little respect—"

"But don't you see? By threatening them, torturing them, you're no better than any other god. What's the point in giving you their loyalty if they earn pain in return? Trying to rule through fear won't work. We've suffered under cruel gods our entire lives."

I crossed my arms. "What are you saying? That I need to start handing out medals and cake to boost morale?"

"If you want us to respect you, you need to respect us first." Joe thrust his chin out, but the rapid thump of his heart betrayed his bravado.

"Listen to him," Vincent urged. There was no such fear in Vincent's soul, only a bone-tired weariness.

How do I appease my damn mortals? Ruling with a metal fist apparently didn't work.

HOW SHOULD I KNOW? I COULD NEVER OFFER MY MORTALS ANYTHING WHILE TRAPPED INSIDE THIS TOWER. A GOOD SMITING USUALLY DOES THE TRICK.

I didn't want to be Gildola, or any of those other shitty gods. The Glimmer deserved a smiting, but I needed them to work for me, too. Ugh, they were giving me a damn headache.

It wouldn't hurt to try it Joe's way, would it? I'd made him and Vincent my counsel for a reason. They needed to see I was better than the gods.

Better than Kayl.

We hadn't gotten off to the best of starts, but I could adapt.

"Fine." Maybe I didn't have the personal touch my dear sister had—she made this socializing shit look easy—but I'd been in her head long enough to know what worked. "We'll throw a party." I knew just the god who specialized in parties. "You'll love it."

Joe and Vincent exchanged a wary glance.

What? Did they doubt I could pull it off? I'd show 'em a *real* party.

DO YOU HAVE TIME TO WASTE ON SUCH TRIVIAL MATTERS?

I turned back to the window. More immortals were gathering around Central Station. Did I have time for a party? Eh, why not. Dor couldn't destroy everything without me, could he? I was the star of the show.

Though one of the Umber Golems looked oddly familiar. It reminded me of Dru. Another of the Godless I needed to get my hands on.

Gast's voice bloomed in my mind. *Serenity is ready to meet.*

Good. Then let's get this party started.

Wow. Arcadia was prettier than I'd thought.

It had taken a bit of effort to coordinate a fun trip to Serenity's domain, and for some reason, no one was actually keen apart from myself. Transporting a whole group of mortals from the clock tower was easy enough, though. I just zapped them from reality and remade the guests I'd invited.

Apparently, they weren't keen on that either. They'd soon put on a smile.

It was a glorious sunny afternoon on the Isle of Decadence. Arcadia had hundreds of isles, all based around something or other, and this one was the perfect place to hold a party, so Serenity had said. I strode along a stone path between rows of fruit trees and berry bushes with Joe and Vincent by my side and our entourage of Glimmer and female Necro trailing behind. We'd come dressed for the occasion, and I was smoking hot in my red dress as always, though Joe and Vincent scrubbed up well in their matching black suits and grumpy lil faces. Who knew black suited a Glimmer?

"Cheer up, lads. This is going to be fun."

"Why are we even here?" Joe asked. "Shouldn't we be defending the clock tower?"

"Don't you worry about that. I'm giving you the afternoon off to relax."

His doubt echoed in my mind. Even the Glimmer behind us were scanning the bushes for threats. I was giving them a free holiday! This was what Joe had said they wanted. You'd think they'd be happier.

Arcadia was so completely different to dreary old Chime. The air was hot and sweet, like breathing in syrup. Everything looked inviting, even the bushes with their thick juicy red and purple berries. I wanted to snatch a handful and squeeze 'em.

The orchard opened to lush gardens and a wide marble pavilion. I whistled.

Serenity had come through, and how! The pavilion was decorated in bunting and flowers, and inside were rows of tables covered in platters of food—a mixture of fruit, cheese, and crackers for the Glimmer, and what looked to be fine cuts of meat for the Necro.

Between those were miniature water fountains, except the running water was a dark red. Oh, we were going to get shit-faced, all right.

Serenity swaggered from the pavilion, dressed in nothing. Honestly, I was starting to appreciate her female form and the fact she loved to show it off. "Welcome, my love. Is this to your satisfaction?"

"It's perfect."

"Then my Seren are at your disposal." She clapped her hands, and a group of female Seren swooped out of nowhere in a cloud. They were mostly naked, each dressed in only a toga that barely covered them. A few carried harps and got to work creating some ambient music as the rest took their place by the food, ready for instruction.

I addressed my mortals. "Listen up! I know life's hard, but it's about to get a lot fucking harder. We're in a war against the Diviner, and I'm not gonna stop until every one of those fucks is dust."

Gloria snorted. "What choice do you leave us?"

"You've got the choice of either enjoying it or whining about it."

"You want us to enjoy our own imprisonment?"

"Come on, Gloria." I smirked. "We both know you enjoy bringing lesser mortals to heel, so here's your chance. Bring the Diviner to heel in my name. In return, I may even start to respect you."

Gloria scoffed.

I gestured to the pavilion. "Eat, drink, and fuck each other to your hearts' content. Enjoy it, because you may not get another chance. But with every win against the Diviner, shit like this will be your reward."

The Glimmer and Necro muttered among themselves. Joe was rubbing his forehead, clearly impressed with my roaring speech.

"Go on, then!" I urged.

They shuffled on past me and headed to the pavilion as Serenity watched on, amused.

"Do you really think this will win them over?" Vincent asked.

"Why wouldn't it? I bet they've never been invited to a party like *this*." Vincent and the rest of the Godless always hosted their little card and wine sessions, and my party was *far* better.

"Clearly not."

"Look, if it'll make them a bit more motivated, then that's good, right? I wasn't lying. Our fight against the Diviner will get worse."

"Your fight."

"Oh?" I cocked my head. "Were you pretending to be Godless all those years spent painting fliers?"

"The Godless exist to free ourselves of all gods, including you."

"Well, you'll just have to put up with me, won't you? Why don't you go get a damn drink and enjoy yourself?"

Vincent scowled and then strode away to the pavilion, a limp in his step. Arthritis flared up in his joints. I'd assumed that a punishment from The Nameless One, but it was the touch of Chaos. That random spark of imperfection that cursed all living mortals, because without it, mortals wouldn't be mortals. They'd be flawless. Like gods.

I could take his pain. Would he want that? Would he be grateful if I took it away? Or would he whine because I stole his autonomy, just as Joe whined about me rebirthing him as the man he wanted to be?

I *could* ask, but then he'd feel indebted to me and would whine about that, too.

A gift's a gift. I'd ease his pain slowly—subtly—and then he'd be grateful.

Then he'd see I could fix his life's woes better than Kayl ever could.

"Vincent has a point." Joe hadn't joined the others yet. "You won't win loyalty with cake if you threaten them while cutting it."

"Who's threatening anyone?" Was my reputation *that* bad?

Joe held up his hands, his exasperation clear.

"Go get Vincent drunk," I told him. "Maybe he'll fuck you, then."

"Wha-What?" Joe spluttered.

"Oh, please. I know you've got a thing for him, and don't deny it. So now's your chance. Pretty gross being into Necro, but who am I to judge?"

"I'm not 'into' Necro." Joe rubbed his jaw. "Okay, maybe once. I had a crush on a Necro called Greaves who'd bring me male clothes back when I was trying to hide who I was from Gildola. But then... let's say I had an encounter with a Necro I'd not want to repeat and leave it at that."

Now, that was the kind of gossip my sister would kill for. I dove into Joe's memories.

Images of Sinner's Row flashed in my mind. Joe had once gone there in search of a certain private eye who could help him escape the Glimmer. Instead, he'd crossed paths with Erosain, who'd then... Shit. Erosain had drugged Joe and strung him up as a prized possession for the pleasure of Necro wanting a feed and a fuck.

I'd been there with Kayl, inside her mind. I'd witnessed it.

And now I wanted to cancel this party and fight my way through Rapture. Erosain deserved to fucking *die*.

"Do you want to ditch the party and murder the fucks who did that to you? We can slice 'em up real slow—"

"No, no! It's... fine. But, uh, thank you. I'm fond of Vincent. He was kind to me when I first joined the Godless. I wouldn't want to come between him and Sinder."

"I wouldn't worry about Sinder."

"Well, um..." Joe adjusted his necktie. "I best watch over the party."

"You do that."

Joe joined Vincent on a private couch. The Glimmer and Necro had segregated themselves into groups; the Glimmer mostly outside the pavilion and basking in their natural sunlight, while the Necro drank from the fountains. Oh. The red stuff *wasn't* wine. Made sense.

Maybe if they drank some booze, they'd loosen up enough to make friends.

YOU ARE BECOMING TOO FAMILIAR WITH THESE MORTALS, Mother cautioned. *THEY ARE NOT YOUR FRIENDS.*

Maybe. Maybe not. It wasn't like I had many friends—Chance was gone, Lucky was gone, Flux wasn't that talkative, and everyone I'd ever met was through Kayl.

I didn't need her to make my own friends and allies. She'd see.

NO MATTER WHAT GIFTS YOU BESTOW UPON THEM, THEY WILL NOT BE APPEASED. THEY CANNOT BE TRUSTED. THEY WILL BETRAY YOU.

They're my mortals. I'll win them over when they see the benefits of playing for my team. I could make the Godless so much more.

THEY DO NOT DESERVE YOUR FAVOR. YOU WASTE PRECIOUS TIME ATTEMPTING TO ONE-UP YOUR SISTER WHEN YOU SHOULD BE TAKING SOULS.

Relax, Mother. I hadn't come all this way to drink wine and admire the view.

Though it was rather pretty.

I found Serenity inside the pavilion at the back. The god was stretched over a couch, eating a bunch of grapes as two Seren hovered over her shoulder, wafting her with giant leaves. It was a nice breeze. Arcadia wasn't as scorching as Rapture, but it sure made me thirsty.

"Would you like a drink?" Serenity offered. "Normally I have Sonata organize these events, but I rather enjoy getting hands-on. It's been some time since I last entertained guests. With Chime closed, we've had to resort to entertaining ourselves, and that does grow dreary."

I sat on a couch opposite and accepted wine from a Seren. They busied themselves with topping up pitchers and fetching bowls of grapes. It was funny how domains carried on as normal while Chime fell apart. "War isn't exciting enough for you?"

"War? Pah. I have no interest in the fight, but in who steps forth triumphant. There is drama in wins and losses. Poetry that can be inspired by victory or despair."

"Uh-huh." I plucked a grape and shoved it into my mouth. Fuck, I'd never tasted anything so damn sweet. What was it with their grapes? "So we've got immortals in Central Station now. I can't deal with them alone."

Serenity sat up and crossed a leg over her knee. "Diviner Guardians and Umber Golems, I assume? Interesting. Dor is moving forward faster than I would have anticipated. You are aware of how immortals operate, yes? They are vehicles at our disposal. Weapons we can wield when a god needs to make a personal touch without direct interference. Dor means to crush you, that much is obvious. It's rare for Unghard to take such an approach."

"Can you make your own immortals to crush them back?"

"Me? Oh no. I don't sully myself with immortal subjects. My mortals are lovers, not fighters."

"They can sing."

"Our song doesn't work on immortals. They're soulless beings."

"Then they can fly." I crushed a grape in my fist and let the juice flow between my fingers, sticky and warm. "Drop knives from the sky or something."

A flicker of annoyance passed over her stony face. "Do not fret, my love. I shall speak with Edana. We have just the weapon for this particular... challenge."

"What weapon?"

"Why ruin the surprise?" She popped a grape into her mouth and savored the juices. "When the time comes, immortals will clash. Stay out of their way and let them tear each other apart."

I shifted on my seat. I didn't appreciate Serenity keeping me in the dark, but she knew not to fuck me over. If Dor managed to get inside the clock tower, then he'd only come after Serenity and her precious Seren next. "Fine."

Serenity patted the couch beside her. "Why don't you come here, hrm? I went to such great lengths to gift you this afternoon. Let me show you how we relax in Arcadia."

"I want another gift."

"Oh? What do you wish for?"

"Harmony Arabesque."

Serenity's nose scrunched. "Of all my mortals, why that one?"

I knew I was pushing my luck by asking. "Because she's Godless, and I'm building a collection of Godless to annoy my sister."

"You do play amusing games. Arabesque was a disappointment to me—"

"Then you won't mind if I take her."

Again, her eyes flashed with irritation. Serenity had no real desire to appease me, but she would anyway.

Because I was Chaos, and she had no choice.

Serenity forced a smile.

And then Harmony popped into existence before my eyes.

The former leader of the Godless gasped a breath and then staggered backwards, knocking over the grape bowl. She was likely off-balance from the two wings that sprouted from her back, and from being spat out from the aether into a shiny new body. A body without clothes. Naked Seren were weird.

"She's yours." Serenity tutted as Harmony accidentally stomped on a grape.

I grabbed Harmony's arm before she could fly away and yanked her soul clean from her body, which collapsed to the ground, face-first into the remaining grapes. We got a good view of her fluffy wings and bare arse, but at least I didn't have to see her eyeless gaze. That part of stealing souls was always a little creepy.

"You can do what you want with the body. I don't need that."

Serenity curled her lip. "I'll add the wings to my collection." She clapped her hands. "Take it."

A flock of four Seren fluttered on down and hefted Harmony's body, each of them carrying a limb, and they flew from the pavilion.

I waited until they were gone—I wasn't nasty—and then found Harmony's soul floating among the others within my subconscious. Having a Seren soul at my disposal would be useful if I ever needed to sing myself out of a situation, though I'd sooner turn Fauna and bite my way out.

Singing wasn't my style.

With another yank, I pulled Harmony from inside me and rebirthed her as Chaos.

Oh *shit*!

As a Chaos mortal, Harmony stood tall. Real fucking tall! About as tall as me, with legs for *days*. Seren faces were sort of chubby and baby-like, but without that influencing her features, Harmony was...

Stunningly gorgeous.

She was fucking *hot* in that mature way Glimmer were so good at, and I now hated myself for being attracted to the pissing leader of the Godless!

"This isn't happening." Harmony stumbled and fell on her arse. She tried to cover her naked chest, and gave up, instead choosing to glare at me. "Jinx."

Oh, there was so much venom in her tone. "That's me."

"Why am I here?"

"I'm making the Godless fashionable again, and that means you're now part of my team. Joe!" I called. "I've brought you a new playmate."

Joe ran over in that busybody way of his. He shrugged off his jacket and wrapped it around her shoulders as he helped her up. "Are you okay—*Harmony?* Is that—is that you?" He stared at me. "Is that her?"

Harmony clutched Joe's arm. "Joe?"

And then Vincent was limping over, his face as pale as Witheryn's snow. Well, paler. "Harm?"

"We're having a reunion party, apparently," I said. "Go find her some clothes."

Joe pulled Harmony away, though from the defiant glint in her eyes, winning her loyalty from my sister would be a fun challenge.

"Amusing," Serenity commented in a way that said she wasn't amused at all. "But I do grow bored."

I bit back a sigh and sat on the couch beside her. Sure, she had to appease me, but I had to appease her too, for now. I couldn't let her worry about my inevitable betrayal, could I?

That would surely cheer up my new Godless friends.

Dor was making his next move. I still needed to wipe Unghard off the board. That would be *my* next move—reduce Dor's allies and collect myself another part of the Godless team. This time, the prodigal best friend.

That left Sinder, who remained safe in Edana's care. Oh, and Malk, though he was trapped inside Kayl's head. Getting him out might prove a problem.

One by one, the Godless would fall into my hands.

What would my dear sister say to that?

19

There are three levels of alert following an emergency:
Amber: An incident has occurred on campus. Return to your dormitory and
remain inside until given the all-clear by a staff member.
Red: An incident has occurred locally in the Golden City. If you have
residency in Chime, you will be permitted to leave the campus if it is safe.
Black: An incident has occurred that affects the safety of all citizens in
Chime. You may be required to return to your temple for advice from your
ambassador. Be prepared to cross over to your home domain if necessary.
—Faculty Notice, *Emergency Protocols at the Academy*

"WHAT DO YOU MEAN, he's not here?"

I'd returned from Erosain's bar—Trixie's bar now, I supposed—expecting Quen to be waiting for me and ready for the good news, only to learn the trio I'd left in charge of keeping him safe had instead let him wander off. And now no one knew where he was.

The Mesmer were still seated at the table with Freddie, the teapot empty, the cake reduced to crumbs, and they were playing with tarot cards of all things.

"It's not *our* fault," Cosmo sulked. "Papa said he wanted to go for a walk and that he'd be back before we woke from our nap, but when we woke, he wasn't here, so that makes him a liar, not us."

"Do you want me to consult my cards and find him?" Celeste pointed at the deck of twelve cards spread across the table. One from each domain, if I remembered correctly. She flipped the first one, revealing an illustrated depiction of Witheryn. "Oh. Well, the Necro card doesn't *always* mean death—"

"Why does a Mesmer need tarot cards? You can see the bloody future!"

"In dribs and drabs. It's different for us. We see potential futures, but not necessarily futures that make sense. That's why we like the cards—they can help us understand it."

Where had they even found a deck? In one of the hotel rooms? "You know what? Never mind." I rubbed my forehead. Why did being in their company give me headaches? "Wait—did you call Quen your papa?"

"The Fauna say he's your mate," Castor said. "That makes him our new papa."

Heat rose to my cheeks. Did Quen know what he'd signed up for?

A whole lot of chaos.

Unless he was dying in an alley somewhere because he'd gone and wandered off when I'd told him not to. Did he not realize he was still wounded? Fuck's sake! I had no way to find him... Actually, I did.

I sank into the spare chair. "How do I induce a vision?" I had the power of the Mesmer inside me. That had to be useful for something.

"You can't induce visions, silly," Celeste said. "They come and go." She flipped another card, revealing Kronos. "Oh! The Diviner card often means logic, but maybe it's a reference to Papa?"

"Look, I need to find Quen since you pissing lost him—"

"Are you angry?" Cosmo gasped. Their lower lip was starting to wobble.

"I'm not angry, I'm just disappointed—"

"That's worse!" Cosmo cried.

Oh, give over!

"It's quite all right," came Quen's ragged voice from behind me. "Apologies for running late."

I scrambled out of my seat, and my jaw dropped.

Quen stood shirtless beneath his jacket, exposing the white fluff of his chest—with a leather strap running across it, for some reason—and the handle of a pistol peeked out from his trouser band. Blood and soot smeared his cheek, and his hair was a tousled mess.

"Don't worry, it's not my blood."

Right, because admitting that wouldn't worry me. He looked like he'd been in a fight, yet that wasn't what surprised me. "You regrew your arm?"

"Not exactly." He dropped a white bag onto the table—his shirt?—and struggled to shrug off his jacket.

I helped get it off, tossed it onto a spare chair, and then carefully ran my fingers along his new arm. It was metal, the surface cool and sleek under my touch. "You dolt! What were you thinking, running off alone? You went to the steamworks, didn't you?"

He flashed a sheepish grin. "We don't have the time to wait for me to heal. I needed spare parts, so I got them. I assume your meeting with Erosain went well?"

"Don't change the subject." He'd always been a chivalrous arse, but that was going to get him killed. Gods, I could throttle him. "You made yourself an arm?"

He half collapsed into the chair I'd warmed up. "My future self was there. He presented me with the arm." He dug his pistol out and placed it on the table, and then a taser from his back pocket. "And my pistol."

Shit. I didn't know what that meant, but it had to be a good thing, right? I leaned against the table. "Is he—you—helping us?"

"In this instance, yes. But we can't rely on him again. He's heading toward his final destination, whatever that may be." Quen flexed his new fingers. It was an odd sight for sure, but this was what his new Zephyr powers had promised. "Now will you please inform me of how your meeting went?"

"I met with Edana."

Quen sat up. "You did *what*?"

"Oh, so only you're allowed to embark on dangerous adventures alone?"

"Kayl—"

"It's fine, Quen. Edana's on our side. Sinner's Row now belongs to Trixie. She's working out the logistics with Sinder now, who is Edana's new ambassador, by the way."

Quen leaned back in the chair, his other hand gripping the arm tightly as though he was reeling from all this information. "Dare I ask how you pulled this off?"

I bit back my amusement as I related the details, omitting the part where I'd effectively agreed to become Edana's whore. Quen didn't need to know that. Castor got bored and took Freddie on a hunt to find more cake as Cosmo nodded off in their chair and Celeste offered Quen more tea, which he politely declined—which was odd, for him. He must be tired. By the end of my tale, even Celeste had grown bored and decided to escort a sleepy Cosmo upstairs for a proper nap, giving Quen and me our privacy.

Quen sucked in a breath. "Erosain is dead, then?"

"Very dead."

"Can we trust Edana? She's allied with Jinx. She could well pass on information of our whereabouts and actions henceforth."

"She won't. She knows Jinx is only using her." In fact, I'd gotten the distinct impression Edana feared Jinx, with good reason.

Quen quirked a brow. "Edana is no fool, but what's done is done. If Trixie can run Sinner's Row without us, then that's one less thing to concern ourselves with." He relaxed and finally smiled. "A brilliant move, my dear. I should never have doubted you. Though I do wish you'd inform me of your plans."

"*You* were supposed to be resting."

"And *we* are supposed to be partners." He stared over the rim of his eyeglasses.

That judgemental look was meant to put me in my place, and it withered me, all right. He sat there, shirtless, his chest rising and falling, and my tongue felt heavy in my mouth... Gods. Did he ever stop to think of what effect that look had on women?

On me?

I cleared my throat. "Then no more wandering off, mister."

He snorted. "Agreed. We should delay no further." He dug through his makeshift bag of bits and bolts. "With these, Doctor Finch and I can create a device to open portals to other domains. It's best we don't inform Edana of this technology."

No. Edana could make her own portals, but if she learned we could do it ourselves, then that would cause problems. Summoning portals was the one thing the gods had going for them. For now, anyhow. "How long will this take?"

"Half an hour if the good doctor would let me rebirth him, but he's refusing, and states I can manage by myself." Quen sighed. "I'll give it a go. I had hoped for more time to prepare, but..."

I placed a hand on his arm. "Forget it for now. You need to rest—"

"It's not that. We need time to train, to see what our powers can do. We both possess the souls of gods. We need to learn our limits."

"I've been living with Chaos a lot longer than you. I've got some idea."

He glanced up at me. "You're not trained for combat situations. We'll be facing off against actual gods. With a few days, I could at least teach you some self-defense techniques—"

"I'm going to stop you there—"

"Indulge me, please—"

"What makes you think I need you to teach me self-defense?"

He blinked as though it should be obvious.

I grabbed the thumb of his other hand and wrenched it back.

"Bugger me!" He snatched his hand away. "Gods forbid I care for your safety!"

I gave him a pointed look. "You dragged me all the way to Eventide to face Valeria."

"You were under my protection—"

"And I destroyed Valeria." Albeit accidentally. But I'd still faced a god and lived to tell the tale. Not many mortals could claim that.

"All right, you've made your point." He pulled his watch out of his trouser pocket and added it to the collection of shiny objects on the table. "Give me an hour to freshen up and get to work. As soon as this is complete, I want to test it on a visit to the Golden City. Let Trixie know we'll be ready to rescue her mortals."

"Is there anything else I can do to help in the meantime?"

"A cup of tea would be lovely, please. With *actual* milk."

What had the Mesmer done to him when I was away? My poor Quen had been through so much lately.

I bent over and kissed his forehead. "Coming right up."

His cheeks reddened a little, and something flashed in those aether eyes. Hunger.

Was it for me, or for the hunt to come? Soon we'd be taking our fight to the gods themselves, and there was no coming back.

Only with a little nagging did Quen wash the blood from his chest and change clothes. He'd lost the bandage from his wounded arm in the steamworks—another thing I nagged him about—but he insisted he no longer needed it, and his stitches looked healthier.

Then it took over an hour for him to finish fiddling with his pocket watch. Dismantling the tiny pieces with one hand wasn't easy, and he hadn't gotten to grips enough with his new arm yet for it to be of any use. He eventually got frustrated and just popped his arm right off, which was one of the strangest things I'd ever seen in my mortal life, and then I stepped in to assist where necessary. It was a painstakingly slow process that involved three cups of tea and a barrage of swearing—mostly from me.

I'd never claimed to be patient.

Eventually Quen declared it was finished, but it didn't look any different. It was still a pocket watch. The glass was still broken, and the hands remained stuck between the hours of twelve and one. Nothing about it seemed special.

"So?" I asked as I sat on the edge of the table. "How does it work?"

Quen cradled it in his left hand as though it was the most precious item in the universe. "In theory, I should be able to wind the hour hand to the required domain and then use a spark of aether to project a portal to that domain."

"In theory?"

"Engineering is an iterative process. Doctor Finch assures me it *should* work, but I'd rather test it first. We wouldn't want the portal to collapse when we're halfway inside it." He grimaced. "I've only got so many limbs left."

"How long does the portal stay up, then?"

"That is dictated by the minute hand. The hour hand of the watch will determine the domain, and the minute hand determines the duration, up to a maximum of one hour. Naturally, we don't want to leave portals lying around willy-nilly. We also need to be careful when traveling to a domain. The gods will notice us punching a wall through." He pulled himself up from the chair. "But that shouldn't affect travel around Chime."

I followed him as he headed into the center of the restaurant. "How do we travel around Chime if each domain corresponds to the time?"

"I've programmed certain domains into locales around Chime. Since Eventide, Solaris, Phantasy, Tempest, and Witheryn are no longer with us, there's little point in opening portals to those respective domains. There'd be nothing there to open *to*. Thus, Eventide will open to the Undercity, Solaris will open to the Golden City, and Witheryn will open to Central."

"Clever. What about Phantasy and Tempest?"

"I'm saving those as a backup in case things go horribly wrong."

At least one of us was optimistic.

He offered the watch to me. "If you would do the honors?"

"Me?"

"It will be easier to operate with two working hands."

I took the watch and popped it open. "You trust me not to break it?"

"I have every faith in you."

It seemed the Mesmer agreed. We'd gained a small audience of the trio, Freddie, and some other Fauna I didn't recognize. They lounged around the restaurant, waiting for me to either cast magic or make a fool of myself.

"You can do it, Mama!" Cosmo called out.

"The cards are in your favor!" Celeste added.

Castor said nothing, as he was stuffing himself with more cake. Where *did* they keep finding it?

"All right." I bit back a sigh. "Show me what to do."

"Wind the clock to five past four," Quen instructed. "Then use your Chaos form to give it a jolt of aether."

Easier said than done. Time and I had never got on, and clocks were especially prone to ignoring me altogether. Still, I wound the clock and switched my form to Chaos. It had taken being chased out of Kronos to master my aether shielding, and summoning aether to power this thing probably used the same process.

Static crackled around my wrist and the pocket watch. Shit, what if I used too much aether? Would that overload it?

"That's it," Quen urged. "Hold it."

"I am bloody holding it!"

Light burst from the watch. I blinked, temporarily dazzled, and then gasped aloud.

A round portal floated at the center of the restaurant, slightly taller than me. It shimmered with aether just as the Gate's portal used to, and through it was the Golden City's plaza. The streets were empty, but I'd recognize those bronze boutiques anywhere. At this time in the afternoon, the sky shone clear blue.

Quen took the watch from my hand and snapped it shut. The portal remained open, even when he shoved the watch inside his trouser pocket.

"'E did it," said Trixie. I spun, and there she was, standing with Wolfsbane by the restaurant door. "The madman actually did it."

I double-checked Sinder wasn't with her, and thankfully he wasn't. The last thing we needed was Edana learning of our new portal through him.

"Don't get excited yet." Quen picked up a saucer and tossed it through the portal like a child's flying disc.

It collided with a lamppost on the other side and shattered.

He then strode up to the portal and waved his hand through it. "Now you may get excited, if that pleases you." He cocked his brow with a smirk that weakened my knees.

Just when would I have my wicked way with him? Between rescuing Fauna and fighting gods, our schedule was looking rather busy.

Wolfsbane paced around the portal and whistled. "To think the gods could have made portals like this at any time, and only refused to do so because of the Covenant."

"So they wanted us all to believe." Trixie scowled at Quen. "You think you're so smart, don't you?"

I wrapped my arm around Quen's. "That's because he is."

Quen gave me a grateful smile.

Trixie shook her head. "You said my mortals are being kept in the Academy?" She eyed the portal. "This can take us there?"

"Yes and yes, *but*!" I jumped in before Quen could open his mouth. "I already asked Edana to help us. It would look suspicious if we went ahead ourselves."

"Why would you ask a fucking god for 'elp?"

"Because the Diviner are taking her mortals, too." I met Trixie's scowl with my own raised brow. "And the Ember can melt those machines into never being functional again."

"Working with Edana gains her favor," Quen said slowly. "Which will only work in our favor. Especially as you're now in command of Sinner's Row."

"You want me to sit and wait while you do all the work, when it was you who put me in this damn situation in the first place?" Trixie said.

I chewed my tongue to avoid saying the first thing that came to mind, which was *You'd only get in our way*. "Worry about the mortals you have here and let us handle the rest. We'll get them back. I swear it."

Honestly, you'd think she'd be more grateful for the gift I'd given her. Sinner's Row was now hers to do with as she liked. Admittedly, it was in a bit of a state, but nothing a little TLC wouldn't fix.

Trixie huffed. "Then do what you need to do, and do it soon."

As she said those words, the portal blipped out of existence, presumably at the five-minute point.

Quen waited until Trixie and Wolfsbane left the restaurant before collapsing into a chair. His skin had turned clammy again, and his chest rose in shallow breaths. "I only—only need a moment," he rasped. "Then we can launch our rescue."

"Today? Not a chance."

"The longer we—we dally, the greater danger the Fauna are left in."

"You think I don't know that? You're not ready to go up against Diviner."

"The Zephyr are healing me quicker—"

"I don't care. You can barely stand."

He tutted, as stubborn as I was, but I wouldn't be out-stubborned, not when he struggled to pissing breathe.

"Look, I'll dig out the laudanum," I said, "Then we'll get a good night's sleep and see how you feel tomorrow. Deal?"

He rubbed the upper half of his severed arm and hissed. "Deal."

At least one of us was being sensible. Shame it had to be me.

Quen fell asleep as soon as his head hit the pillow. Zyclone's power may be speeding up his recovery time, but he'd still lost an entire limb. Though when he woke the next morning, he had a bit more color to his cheeks and a spring to his step.

Sadly, he wouldn't be dissuaded from launching our rescue, and truth be told, I didn't want to wait either. Not when Trixie kept shooting me scathing looks.

We shared a small breakfast of tea and crumpets in our hotel room and then dug out suitable clothing from the wardrobe. I couldn't go up against the Diviner in a tight black dress, and Quen didn't wish to launch into the fray without a shirt. We made do with what we could find—a simple blouse and skirt for myself, and a tweed suit for Quen.

"This isn't my style," he complained as I helped do up his buttons. He'd screwed his new arm back on and needed a little help getting it through the sleeve.

"Beggars can't be choosers."

"My Seren tailor would faint if he saw me in this travesty. Perhaps we should find a boutique while we're in the Golden City so I can obtain proper attire. I can hardly fight against gods in this awful getup."

"Quentin Corinth!" I gasped with mock shock. "You wouldn't be thinking of looting, would you? Not you, a man of the law?"

His lips formed a smirk. "I can hardly be a man of the law when I commit crimes against fashion."

"I never would have thought you'd be the fashionable type."

"That wounds me deeply. I pride myself on my impeccable taste."

"Oh, so that's why you were drawn to me." I left his top button undone. "Speaking of terrible taste, why does Trixie hate you so?"

"I may have questioned her a few times while investigating incidents in Sinner's Row during my Warden days. It may surprise you to know my past self was a bit of a hard case."

"Really? I'd never have guessed. The Quentin Corinth I met wasn't so bad. What changed?"

"The Grayford Incident."

Yes, that would have done it. The Grayford Incident had been a catalyst for us both. Quen had been imprisoned in a correctional facility and then chose to become the Godless's mystery benefactor upon release. Thanks to his support, I'd established the Godless, met my family. Without Quen, I'd have never made it so far.

He'd sacrificed so much for us. For me. The memories he'd wiped to protect the Godless, the battles he'd fought against his own god. Yet it felt like this was only the beginning.

I rested my palm on his chest, above the beat of his heart. "I'm proud of you, you know."

"For what?"

"For becoming the man you are." My Quen.

Quen placed his other hand over mine, and our fingers interlocked. "What changed... is that I met you. If our paths hadn't crossed on that elevator, if I hadn't dragged you all the way to Eventide... would I have ever questioned Elijah or Dor? Or would I still be serving him now, as he ripped Chime and the domains apart, because I believed such actions justified?"

"Have a little faith in yourself to do what's right."

He lifted my fingers to his lips. "I have faith in *you*. That's all I need."

Again, those eyes flashed with a hunger that set of flutters in my gut. They were filled with a need that went beyond simple lust.

In his company, the domains, the very universe, simply faded away, as though we were two souls stranded in the center, and all the stars of the sky waited for us, and us alone.

But the universe couldn't wait. Not when the Fauna needed rescuing.

Gods. I didn't want to pull myself from Quen's warmth, but it was time I took my place on the stage. "Let's go show Trixie what we're made of."

"Let's."

Quen grabbed his pistol, and then we made our way out of the hotel and back to Erosain's bar, where Sinder awaited us.

"You escaped Jinx?" Sinder said, surprised by Quen's sudden appearance.

"As did you," was Quen's cool reply. "I hear congratulations are in order, Your Excellency?" Quen's tone was free of malice, but edged with sarcasm.

Sinder's nostrils flared. "I didn't ask for this."

"Really, now? There's no part of you that enjoys serving genocidal women? You rather enjoyed burning me alive on Jinx's command."

"Wait, *what*?" I glanced between them. No one had told me about that!

Guilt flashed across Sinder's face. Shit, had he really burned Quen? "She ordered me to. I had no choice! You *killed* me!" Sinder pointed a damning finger at Quen that burned with a single flame. "Shot me straight in the fucking head!"

"It was either that, or let the Wardens take your soul," Quen said. "Though if we're playing tit for tat, you *did* betray Kayl. Forgive me for feeling a little petty. How can I assume you won't betray her again?"

"What loyalty should I hold for Jinx? She killed—" His shoulders sagged. "Vincent is gone. Without him, I've got nothing. Nothing but mistakes to amend. You would understand what that's like, wouldn't you, Corinth? Or did the Dark Warden leave his conscience behind in the aether?"

Quen's left hand twitched beside his pistol.

Great. I didn't need Quen defending my honor, though I wasn't impressed that either of them had kept the simple detail of Quen being *burned alive* from me.

"All right, that's enough out of you both." I pushed between them before sparks started flying. "We've got a job to do."

Sinder shook his flame away, though he didn't take his eyes off Quen. "My queen has a portal ready into Rapture. From there, we'll travel to your destination. She'll want to speak to you both once you're done."

I'd worry about that later.

We headed inside the bar, which was already occupied by Fauna taking advantage of their new station. What would the Fauna do with the place? Something better than what Erosain had used it for, I hoped.

Sinder led us through the back halls to Erosain's old art gallery, where a portal into Rapture blazed, as promised. A heartbeat later, we'd stepped from Sinner's Row to Rapture once more.

A handful of Ember waited in the cloakroom, dressed in black. The same fighters who'd helped Edana invade Witheryn. Having watched them firsthand, I knew they'd be up to the job.

"Where to?" Sinder asked.

"The Academy."

Quen cleared his throat. "If I may?" He turned to address the Ember. "First off, I wish to thank you all for your assistance. We do not anticipate what force we'll come upon in the Academy, but we have reason to believe they are hiding the soul-splitting devices within the School of Art. They could very well be manufacturing said devices within the School of Engineering. Here's the plan; Edana, if she will be so kind, will create a portal inside one of the Amnae greenhouses on campus—I'll provide a detailed description of which. This will allow us to enter the Academy grounds unseen; however, they'll likely have sensors designed to detect us. We cannot afford to waste time.

"Sinder, Kayl, and I will sneak into the School of Art and assess the situation. Once we have determined the level of force, Sinder will signal for the rest of you to follow through the portal. Our priority is to free any non-Diviner mortals we may find there and bring them to safety, including Fauna and Ember. Your target is those blasted machines." He drew a breath. "I want them all destroyed."

"What about the Diviner?" one of the Ember asked. "If they attack—"

"Kill them without hesitation." Quen didn't even blink.

When had he become so ruthless?

And why did it turn me on?

Quen was willing to do whatever was necessary to save the Fauna. Or, more likely, to get back at Dor and the domain that had tortured him for years. I couldn't say I blamed him, but *damn* was it good to see him become the Godless I always knew he was deep down.

"You're reprising your role as Dark Warden after all?" Sinder drawled. "At least it's them and not me."

I shot him a glare. We did *not* need another pissing argument right now.

Thankfully, Quen didn't take the bait. "Jinx and I investigated Timefall Estates not that long ago. The Diviner who attacked us lacked souls. Killing them is a mercy."

"Shit, really?" I said. "Dor's been ripping out the souls of his own mortals? Why?"

"Soulless mortals are willing slaves. They're also immune to Chaos and various other abilities his enemies possess."

Because that was how a god of logic would strategize, I supposed. But to do that to your own mortals? Gods.

"And what if we kill a mortal still in possession of their soul?" Sinder asked.

Quen gave him a look. "Then their souls go back to Dor. Do you suddenly care for Diviner?"

"Not really, no. But I thought we were doing this to save mortals, not damn them."

"We are," I said.

It just may take damning them to save them.

"Then ready when you are, darling," Sinder purred, a murderous glint in his eye.

Gods. We were actually doing this, then.

Our first attack against the Diviner.

It was time for payback.

I crossed over from the dry heat of Rapture into the humidity of a greenhouse, and not just any greenhouse. This had belonged to Quen's

Amnae professor. Quen had once dragged me here to determine exactly who I was. After everything that had happened since then, returning to this place felt oddly bittersweet.

Only now, nature had completely reclaimed the professor's old laboratory. Vines nearly obscured the rows of multicolored jars and bottles lining the walls. They stretched across the floor, mingling with the pipes and wires that fed into the recliners I'd once sat on to explore my memories.

At least the Diviner hadn't repurposed them.

Quen stared at the recliners, likely lost in bigger memories than mine. I nudged him softly, and he shook away whatever thoughts plagued him.

Sinder tried the door. "It's locked. Someone's chained it."

"The faculty or staff, most likely," Quen said. "You should be able to melt through it easily enough. However, before we proceed, I'd like to add an amendment to our plan."

"If you're trying to keep secrets, I have a god in my head."

"I'm aware." Quen pulled the taser from his belt. "I'll need to capture a Diviner, alive. Scanning their recent memories will be the quickest way to determine how many soul-splitting devices they have here, and where."

"That seems risky."

"Riskier than traipsing across two entire buildings? If we're careful, we won't alert any Diviner, and then Dor won't learn we're here."

"And deprive them of whatever *that* is you're wearing?" Sinder eyed Quen's suit.

Quen gave me an exasperated look as if it say, *See?*

I rolled my eyes. "Melt the pissing door."

Sinder fluttered his eyelashes. "For you, dearest." He gripped the door handle. A line of smoke twirled from his hand, and then the door creaked open.

"Proceed quietly but deliberately," Quen ordered.

This wasn't my first time sneaking into a place I didn't belong.

Outside, the Academy campus seemed empty. I don't know what I'd expected.

Both Central and the Undercity had been abandoned, but somehow I'd thought the Academy would be full of Diviner taking advantage of the situation. But no. It was as dead as the rest of Chime with only scattered clothes as evidence anyone had been here at all.

The sun still shone over gorgeous blue skies, and yet the grass across the Academy campus green had grown an inch beyond what was likely socially acceptable around these parts. How scandalous.

No Diviner patrolled. Perhaps they simply didn't expect a sneak attack.

Quen led the way between the greenhouses. He knew this campus better than anyone, and navigated it with ease until we came to a set of double doors leading into the posh School of Art.

A group of six Diviner stood in front of it, exchanging orders, judging by the hushed whispering and anxious gesticulating.

We crouched behind a wall.

"They don't look soulless to me," Sinder whispered.

No, they didn't.

"We'll have to draw them out," Quen whispered back. "They'll patrol in twos. Wait until one is closer. Burn one, and I'll zap the other."

"Why am I doing all the murdering?"

"Because if Dor learns I'm here, that will only complicate matters."

"I could put them to sleep," I offered.

"Yes, thank you," Sinder said. "I'm all for burning our enemies alive and dancing on their ashes, but it's a little crass."

"That's never stopped you before," Quen muttered. "Wait for my signal."

We waited as two of the Diviner in Warden uniforms neared.

"*Now,*" Quen whispered.

I switched to my Mesmer form and created a miasma to cloud the two Diviner. They collapsed to the floor instantly. Quen ran out and dragged one of them under cover as Sinder dragged the other.

"Give me a moment." Quen's face changed from Chaos to Diviner, and he placed his left hand on the Diviner's forehead.

"That's so unsettling," Sinder murmured.

I shushed him.

Quen's eyes fluttered shut. It felt like an age passed before he broke contact and sucked in a breath. "The devices are being held in the classrooms, exactly as your vision foretold." Quen glanced at me. "That's where they're holding the Fauna and Ember."

"That's all?" I asked.

"These are prototypes. They've since moved their operations to Kronos. We've no chance of destroying those, but these..." His throat bobbed. "We must move quickly."

"Shall I signal Edana?" Sinder asked.

"Please. Kayl and I will run on ahead. Remember, our priority is saving mortal lives."

Sinder nodded and stalked back to the greenhouse.

I squeezed Quen's left arm. "Are you all right? You didn't see..." I trailed off, since he didn't need me to spell it out. While Quen's Diviner abilities allowed him to see someone's past, they often gave him horrible visions of their death.

"I'm fine." He forced a smile. "Since my rebirth, I've stopped having those particular visions." He handed the taser to me and drew his pistol with his left hand. "But if we don't act now, those Fauna won't stand a chance."

I didn't need to be told twice.

We crouched. I followed Quen's lead, and on his signal, I put another patrolling group of Diviner to sleep. And then another, until we reached the school's back door.

Quen peered into the hall. "It's clear."

Slowly, we edged our way inside. I remembered this hall from both my vision and the first time I visited here. The classrooms and lecture halls had been busy then, but now an ominous silence weighed on my shoulders. Dust floated in the air, and not the dust of neglect. The dust of dead mortals.

The Diviner must have cleared this space, for there were no abandoned clothes scattered about, but they'd done a piss-poor job, as dust still lingered everywhere as evidence the School of Art had held many students.

I really didn't like how quiet it was. Where were the Diviner patrols?

It felt like a trap.

Like they were leading us in here.

Quen checked every classroom window we passed, and I checked after him. Most were empty, except for one with piles of clothes inside. That was where the Diviner had dumped them in their haphazard attempt to sweep the consequences of their war under the rug.

Another room had a tea station set up, because of course it did.

We came up to another classroom I recognized instantly. "That one," I whispered.

"Two Diviner. One at the front, and another at the back."

"If I try and knock them both out at the same time, I'll hit the Fauna."

"Then I'll take the one at the back."

I nodded.

Quen eased open the door and slipped inside.

It was exactly like my vision. What had once been a classroom full of chairs and desks was now packed with rows of those awful god-splitting machines.

And at each of them sat mortals; mostly Fauna, but also a few Ember.

Shit.

They were conscious, but their eyes were glazed over. Fuck, were we too late?

"Chaos!" one of the Diviner yelled.

Shit, I'd almost forgotten the plan! I summoned another miasma and knocked the Diviner out cold. Using my Mesmer powers came more naturally than shooting with a taser.

A shot went off at the back as Quen dealt with his Diviner.

"Blast it!" he yelled. Another shot ricocheted off the wall. Shit, had he missed?

"You okay?" I called.

Quen leaned against the classroom wall, panting. "Got him in the end. Sorry. Hard to aim with my left hand."

Shit, we couldn't afford mistakes like that.

I turned to the god-splitting machines, and a flash of red fur caught my eye.

Gods, it was Autumn!

I leaped over the snoring Diviner I'd knocked out and ran past the rows until I found her. The redheaded girl with the fox ears was strapped to the chair, her expression dazed.

"I've got you!" I climbed over and began undoing the straps. "Quen!"

"Working on it," he called back.

I got Autumn undone, and dragged her up. "Help me get everyone out."

Together, we pulled Fauna and Ember from the machines. I touched Autumn's shoulder and changed form to Fauna. My cat claws made short work of the various straps, cuffs, and wires as I shredded through them. Anything to get the mortals out of those damn things.

We were halfway through when the door burst open.

"Diviner are on the way!" Sinder called.

Quen ran to the door. "We'll deal with them. Get the Fauna out and melt those blasted machines."

"With pleasure."

I switched back to my Mesmer form and joined Quen in the hallway. He held his pistol in his left hand, pointed toward the footsteps thudding closer. He'd not used his new hand at all. Perhaps he hadn't learned how it worked yet.

"You're not worried Dor will notice you?" I asked.

"At this point, I couldn't give a damn." The sight of mortals strapped into those machines had hardened his expression.

Time slowed around us as the Diviner arrived. They stomped into the hall, a whole group of them, aiming tasers at us.

I thrust my hands out, sending another cloud of sleepy dust. It tore through them, and they tumbled like dominoes.

Quen blinked at me. "Have I ever told you how incredible you are?"

"Once or twice, I'm sure."

Time resumed. The rest of the Fauna ran out of the classroom as Sinder directed them to the greenhouse.

"That's all of them!" Sinder called.

I joined him by the classroom door as the few Ember cast their flame across the machines. Slowly, the horrid things twisted into deformed shapes. The heat blasted my cheeks, yet it was satisfying to watch them melt into useless metal.

Quen tugged my arm. "We're done here."

I followed him and Sinder back outside, where the sky still shone a perfect blue, innocently unaware of the chaos that had befallen Chime beneath it. No Diviner followed us, and that made me suspicious.

This had been too easy. Or was I becoming more paranoid?

I'd almost reached the greenhouse when something flashed in my eyes, and I stumbled forward.

And then everything went dark.

The Guardians lined up with pleasing symmetry. Their heavy brass bodies clanked as they took their positions, the clockwork mechanics of their brains whirring with the soothing rhythm of a ticking clock.

Opposite, the Golems attempted to mimic our symmetry, but immortals made of rock could only manage so much. Unghard watched through their dark, pebbly eyes, as Father watched through mine. This was a joint venture, a partnership to protect Chime. Since we'd lost the Zephyr, it became imperative we stand against the forces of Chaos, united as a single wall to push back tyranny.

Our target was the clock tower, and this time we would not fail.

"Kayl? Are you with me?"

I gasped as my eyes snapped open. My head was resting on Quen's lap— I must have fallen. The air tasted dry, with a hint of sulfur, and the blue skies had been replaced by a red ceiling. We were in Rapture. Quen had dragged me through the portal, or someone had.

"You had a vision," Quen prompted.

I sat up. We were back inside Edana's palace, and Quen had brought me to a couch in her cloakroom. The portal remained, but this time it was open to the Undercity.

Thank the gods, the Fauna had made it to safety.

"It was the Redeemer. He's got immortals—Diviner and Umber ones—and they're planning another attack on the clock tower. We've got to go." I stood on wobbly feet. "We've got to get there—"

"Easy, now." Quen pulled me back down. "We can't fight against a legion of immortals—"

"You don't understand." I grasped Quen's metal arm, and my fingernails dug into his sleeve. "They've got Dru." I swallowed the dryness in my mouth. "One of the immortals is Dru!"

20

I'm scared for my boy. They've ordered him to enlist, but he's not even an adult yet. How is he supposed to fight against Diviner? How are any of us? He's putting on a brave face and says he likes the training, but throwing around fire won't be enough, will it? Gods. I don't know what to do. They won't listen to me when I say he's too young. They just say it's what our Queen wants, so I've got to deal with it.
—Anonymous, *overheard in the Golden Palace, Rapture*

AFTER THIRTEEN PISSING YEARS, I finally understood how a Diviner felt when someone else was wasting their damn time.

Edana had ordered us to report back to her as soon as we'd finished burning the Academy classroom. Quen had informed me the Fauna had been returned safely to Trixie's care, and she would do a head count to see who was missing. And now I sat with Quen on a couch as he politely explained my vision to Edana without revealing I'd been the one to witness it.

I didn't want to wait around and plan, not when I knew Dru was in Chime, ready to be tossed into a pointless battle between gods and their immortals. Unghard had promised Dru would be used to defend Heartstone, so what was she doing here? I'd thought the supposed 'kindest' of the gods wouldn't go back on their word so pissing soon.

It *was* Dru. Even with Dru a Golem, I'd recognize those flowers anywhere.

That vision had come to me for a reason.

Dru needed me.

"Jinx has already informed me of the arrival of immortals in Chime," Edana was saying. "It appears Dor is preparing to launch another attack on the clock tower."

"Does Jinx have a plan in place?" Quen asked.

"I will send my immortals to assist. Serenity also has a plan to drive Dor's attempt back."

"So you can open a portal to Central?" I asked. "And we can go now?"

Edana addressed me. "It would be unwise to involve yourself in the battles of immortals."

"I don't care."

Quen shot me a warning look. I didn't understand why we had to be so damn polite. I could take Edana's soul right now and be done with it, only Quen had decided we still needed her, and I supposed we did. If I had the power to create my own immortals, I certainly didn't know how. How scary would a Mesmer immortal be, anyhow?

"I can put the immortals to sleep," I added.

"Your powers will not work on an immortal. They are essentially extensions of their god's reach."

I knew that. Of course I knew that. But I wasn't going to sit here, slurping fruit juice! I'd asked for water, since running around the Academy had been thirsty work, but of course water was too exotic for Rapture. Normally I wouldn't have risked it, but I didn't think Edana would poison me so soon. Shame I didn't have any of Trixie's anti-shit-ambassador protection potions on hand, but I'd pissed out the last lot.

"This attack doesn't make sense," Quen said. "If Dor wanted to get inside the clock tower, there isn't much that could stop him."

"Jinx's aether shield keeps the Diviner out, doesn't it?" I said.

"But not the Umber."

"What are you saying? This is a distraction?"

"Precisely. Though from what, I cannot fathom."

"Or perhaps it is a demonstration," Edana said. "Meant to draw out invested parties." She gave me a pointed look.

"It's an opportunity," I said. "You say immortals are an extension of the gods? Then I can reach Unghard. Corner one of their immortals and plead my case. We need the Umber to turn against Dor, and this is our chance." If I could speak with Dru...

"What makes you believe Unghard will listen to a being of Chaos?"

"Because I've traveled to Heartstone, and they made my best friend an immortal." All right, our last encounter hadn't ended well, and Unghard had effectively banned me from their domain, but even they had to see that throwing their mortals—and immortals—against Ember would only prolong their suffering.

"Unghard can be reasoned with," Quen added, "if we isolate one of their Golems. Jinx cannot defend against immortals alone. She'll need our help."

Would Jinx need our help? I doubted she'd ever ask for it or be grateful if we provided any. Even if Dor got past Jinx's shield, he still couldn't reach Corentine. The only risk would be to Jinx herself, and, well... that was her business.

But she *did* have the Glimmer and Necro now. If Dor decided to destroy Jinx's sorry arse, that meant losing them. It meant losing Joe and Vincent. I couldn't let that happen.

"Very well." Edana leaned back against the couch. "Though, you will arrive separately from my own mortals. Jinx cannot learn we are in league."

"Thank you," Quen said. "If we may, we'll return to Sinner's Row to gather our allies."

Edana allowed us to leave, so we hurried back to the portal cloakroom. So much had already happened today, but there was no rest for the wicked.

There was irony in going out of my way to help protect Jinx when she'd refused to help me, but this wasn't about Jinx.

It was about Dru.

I kept my mouth shut until we crossed over to Sinner's Row. "You think this is a bad idea, don't you?" I asked Quen. He'd been looking pensive the entire walk back.

"Fighting against immortals? I can think of nothing more pleasant, other than the delightful tea and cake your Mesmer provided me with yesterday. But you're right. This may be a good opportunity to commune with Unghard directly." He scratched his chin with his new metal hand, and then suddenly pulled it back and blinked at it, as though perplexed by the action. "My presence alone could serve as a distraction and divide Dor's attention, but it won't be easy."

"It's not the worst idea I've ever had."

"There was that time you forced me to fight in a Leander arena."

"That worked out well in the end."

He rolled his eyes.

I bumped his side with my elbow. "We laugh in the face of danger."

"I'll stretch to mild chortling." He wrapped his new arm around mine, shuffling it until it felt right for him, though for me, being with him felt right no matter what face he wore or what limbs he needed to replace.

I could always count on him.

And together we'd get Dru back.

"Does this mean you're coming up with a plan? You *always* have a plan."

"Perhaps. I like to think on my feet. It's better than thinking on my buttocks."

"You can call it an arse, I'll let you."

He smirked. "That's generous of you."

Gods. What would that new hand of his feel like squeezing my arse? No, Kayl, bad Kayl. Think about that *later*. "Are you sure you're up for this?" He'd fumbled back in the Academy, though if he was tired, he was putting on a good show.

"I don't intend to go toe to toe with an immortal, if that concerns you."

"Quen—"

"One of the first lessons a Warden is taught during their training is how to assess and deescalate a situation, and that includes knowing which battles are safe to engage in. Trust me."

Famous last words. "You're still recovering, you know."

"I'm aware. But if we're asking the Fauna to risk their lives for our cause, then the least I can do is show up with them."

He made a good point, but I didn't like it.

At least I'd be there to watch over him. This was my fight, and I wasn't running from it.

More of the Fauna filled the main bar, turning Erosain's luxury bar into a lively soup kitchen full of chatter and the clatter of spoons in bowls. I'd wanted to check in on the Fauna we'd recovered. They seem subdued.

Shocked. We'd need help in our fight against the Diviner—that was the whole point of our partnership—but those Fauna needed to recover.

Wolfsbane waved me over from across the room. Quen and I joined him at a booth where Trixie was nursing a cup of milky tea.

"Well?" I asked as I slipped in. "Did we get them all?"

Trixie took a deep slurp from her cup before answering. "That we know of."

"And they're okay? Autumn is okay?"

"She's with Freddie," Wolfsbane said. "He's overjoyed by her return."

That was good, wasn't it? So why did they both look so grim?

"We're grateful," Wolfsbane added.

"But?"

"My mortals are in no state to fight," Trixie said. "We know what's going on in Central, and what you've come 'ere to ask, so don't sugarcoat it."

Okay, I hadn't just rescued her mortals and given her the keys to Sinner's Row to be treated with this level of scorn.

"We only need a handful," Quen said. "A few of your best fighters to help keep the Diviner off my back—"

"You're talking about fighting fucking immortals! Look, we're still falling over our arses 'ere, trying to figure out the problem you've dumped on my lap—"

"A *problem*?" Seriously?

"We need to recover and rebuild. We're not ready to fight your damn wars."

"Tough shit! You think the Diviner will wait for you to get your shit together? We upheld our end of the bargain, so pay up."

Trixie bared her fangs.

"It's all right, Trix," Wolfsbane murmured. "We can spare a few."

"And they'll be safe, will they?" Trixie snapped.

"I've got a plan," Quen said. That quickly? He really did think on his feet. He also remained calm in the face of Trixie's anger. That Warden training was good for something. Though, shit, I was livid.

I understood Trixie's fears and the danger we'd be placing her mortals in, but didn't she see the danger we were all in if the Diviner won? They'd taken the Fauna from right under her whiskers. The only way to stop that from happening again was to fight back, and the fight had already begun.

When the fight was against the forces of time, it would take Chaos to defeat it.

And Chaos didn't wait.

"All right." Trixie sighed. "What's your master plan? I'm not risking my mortals on some suicide run."

"Do you have more tea, with lots of sugar if you can manage it?" Quen asked. "I'm afraid we'll need some flasks."

All right, that wasn't what I'd expected, but Chaos worked in mysterious ways.

We were late to the party.

The portal opened into chaos, and not the fun kind. Quen and I, plus five large Fauna including Wolfsbane popped out around the corner from Central Station, by the old bench that served as my Godless meeting spot. Already the brass Guardians were stomping their way across the station concourse, each step vibrating through the cobblestones beneath my shoes.

I'd taken the chance to refresh myself and grab a drink and cheese sandwich while Quen made his plans with the Fauna, but now we were truly out of time.

The battle was here, and we were willingly entering the fray.

It really wasn't how I'd expected my Godless career to go, though it probably was inevitable. Were we even ready for this?

Quen gestured for us to huddle together. "Here's the plan. Edana will shortly launch her immortals to protect the clock tower. While she handles the Umber, I'll lead the Guardians on a merry chase toward Meridian Park. You all have your flasks?" The Fauna lifted their flasks of incredibly sweet tea. "Wonderful. Use them on the Guardians if you must. The sugar content will slow them down."

"And we're to lure one particular Umber?" Wolfsbane asked. "How do we know which one?"

"I'll know," I said. "Just keep the rest off my back and, I'll handle it."

"As long as you know what you're doing, cat."

Oh, I never knew what I was doing. That was what I had Quen for.

A column of flame burst from the station concourse. The Ember had arrived.

"Remember," Quen said. "If the situation turns dire, retreat to the Undercity." He met my eye. "Stay safe and do nothing foolish."

As if!

Quen patted my arm with a forced smile, and then he was off, leaving me with my entourage of muscular Fauna. He didn't want us to be seen together in case Dor decided to attack us both, but watching him run off on his own hurt my heart.

Would he be safe with so many immortals running around? Where the gods were concerned, anything could happen.

"Come on, then," I said to Wolfsbane.

I jogged over to the station as the other four Fauna changed into smaller animal forms to take position and spy—two smaller mammals, a rat and a hare; and two birds to fly up top. I couldn't remember who was who, so in my mind I'd been calling them Tom, Dick, and Harry. One of them was named Badger, I think. They took the form of a magpie.

I leaned against the station wall and peered through the window.

Shit.

Wolfsbane came to my side. "That's quite a lineup."

He wasn't wrong. Edana's immortals gathered around the clock tower. They were beautiful swirling tornadoes, their limbs pure fire, with two hot-blue eyes marking their face. They twirled in a flaming ballet, a line of defense against the Guardians and Golems who crossed the station concourse.

It was a sight unlike *anything* I'd ever seen before.

Chime had existed for years without a single immortal standing within it. We'd always assumed it was impossible for them to even enter through the Gate. Immortals and their gods were meant to be barred from Chime, and yet here they were. Doing the impossible.

I didn't know what was creepier—that the gods were controlling their immortals like faceless puppets, or that they watched through their immortals' eyes.

Movement caught my attention. Quen had entered the station without getting noticed. Though as I scanned the waiting area and various booths, I couldn't spot a single mortal soul, nor were any Diviner on guard. Because who would be foolish enough to go striding toward a bunch of giant immortal beings?

My heart leaped to my throat as he drew his pistol with his left hand and aimed it at one of the clockwork Guardians.

"Dor!" he yelled. "You needn't send your lackeys to find me. I'm right here."

The defiance in his voice and posture sent shivers through me. He'd come so far from the man I'd met on that elevator. I wished Trixie could see it.

"He's got balls, that one," Wolfsbane whispered instead. "Let's hope he doesn't lose them."

One by one, those clockwork monstrosities faced Quen, the cogs and gears whirring inside their heads the only thing I could hear above my own breath.

And then they reached for him.

Quen bolted, and a trail of hulking brass monsters bounded after him. It would have been comical if it didn't scare the absolute shit out of me, but Quen had a plan to lead them on a chase through Chime's back alleys. Quen knew these streets as well as I did. I doubted Dor did.

As soon as the Guardians exited the station, Edana's immortals went on the attack. The two groups clashed, immortal versus immortal.

The fire-dancers flung flame at the Golems, who launched their heavy bodies at them in retaliation. Stone fists punched through blazing figures, tearing their fiery forms with ease. But as fast as Edana's immortals dissolved, they reformed again, as though the Golems were simply swatting air.

Flame wasn't doing anything to the Golems, either. It simply fizzled against their hardened skin, unable to penetrate. But it kept them occupied, which was all we needed.

"Which one?" Wolfsbane yelled over the *whoosh* of flames and the *thunk* of stone fists slamming against the ground.

"Golden daisies for eyebrows." I strained to see through the window. *Come on, Dru. Where are you?*

Wolfsbane signaled to one of the flying Fauna and got a tweet in response. "We've found it. At the back." He pointed behind the Gate, close to the maintenance yard. Perfect. We could lure Dru out there and separate her from the others.

"Follow me, but keep an eye out from above." I skirted the wall and headed for the back entrance to the station, just as I had all those months ago with Dru when escaping from Lady Mae's café.

When all this bloody nonsense had first started.

I'd expected the maintenance yard to be as unguarded as the station, but my luck had run out. Two Diviner Wardens stood by the iron gate, armed with pistols and carrying those awful soul-splitting helmets.

Great. So much for quickly sneaking in.

I switched to my Mesmer form. "I'll knock them out. Watch out for more."

Wolfsbane whipped off his kilt and readied himself in a pounce. I really did *not* need to see what he'd been hiding underneath, but I'm sure it delighted Trixie.

At least a naked, growling wolf-man would give my enemies pause.

I summoned a miasma and let it float over the Diviner.

They remained conscious.

"What the shit?" I whispered.

With an unnatural stiffness, they both turned to me, their movements entirely in sync as if they too were clockwork Guardians, though much shorter ones.

Shit.

They weren't mortal at all. They were soulless, as Quen had described them.

"They're not mortal!" I yelled. "They're not—"

Wolfsbane shoved me out of the way as a shot blasted past my ear. Another ricocheted off the cobblestones.

"Run!" Wolfsbane growled. He extended his claws and pounced at the Diviner.

Shit!

I scrambled past him and ran into the maintenance yard. The sickening sound of tearing followed, and I risked a glance over my shoulder.

Wolfsbane was ripping the Diviner apart, his claws digging into bloodied flesh. And the Diviner weren't screaming. They weren't reacting at all.

Gods. Why would Dor do this to his own damn mortals?

I sagged against a tall crate and caught my breath.

The yard was full of similar crates. None of them were covered in dust or grime, which meant they hadn't been abandoned here before Chime went to shit. This was where the Diviner were storing their supplies, but I didn't have time to think about that now. We could always return to steal or destroy them later.

I carefully made my way through the maze of crates, watching out for more Diviner.

A tweet whistled above me. One of the Fauna landed on a crate. Badger the magpie.

"It's clear," he trilled. "There's a path to the Gate."

"Thank you. Let Wolfsbane know it's safe."

He clicked his beak and took off.

There was no more time to waste. I hoisted my skirt and jogged toward the commotion at the Gate. Edana's immortals and the Golems still fought, only... groups of mortals now fought with them. Ember versus Umber.

While the immortals wrestled one another in some pointless dance, their mortals were caught in a deadly game of tag. Each side made an attempt at attacking the other and then scrambled out of the way as a Golem's foot crashed down beside them, or a line of red-hot flame scorched the ground.

The immortals gave no consideration to the mortals scurrying around them. Why in god's name were they here to begin with?

"Help me!" came a whimpering cry beside me.

Gods, I almost leaped from my skin! I'd been too busy staring at the absolute nonsense in front of me to notice a young Ember woman hiding behind a crate. The poor thing was shaking from head to toe.

"Please," she begged. "I can't—I can't do it anymore—"

"It's all right. Stay hidden—"

"You don't understand!" She cradled her arm close to her chest. Gods. It was a mangled mess of bruising and blood. "My Queen, no, please! I'm not a coward, I can't—"

She disappeared in a puff of smoke. Edana had reclaimed her.

I ground my teeth. Edana had forced that girl to fight for no gods-damn reason, and then snapped her soul back when she'd been too scared to continue. I'd never asked Edana to bring mortals here, and as soon as I was done, we'd be having words.

I glanced back at the station just as a Golem trampled another young Ember. The lad's screams cut off with a sickening crunch, and his body collapsed into dust.

Why make mortals fight the battles of immortals?

What was the pissing point?

The Golem that had crushed the Ember turned to me, and I swallowed the urge to throw up. Golden daisies. Shitting *shit*. Dru had killed a mortal. Dru, the sweetest girl I'd ever known, who'd give the shirt off her own bloody back just to help another, and she'd squashed an Ember to death.

She probably didn't even realize.

Gods, if she knew, she'd never forgive herself.

Fuck. None of this was Dru's fault. She hadn't killed a mortal. Unghard had used her body, that sick bastard!

I picked up a spanner from an abandoned tool kit and threw it at Dru. It bounced off her forehead with a satisfying clank.

"Oi!" I called out. "Dru! I know you're still in there, and I need to talk!"

Those emotionless dark eyes blinked.

I picked up a screwdriver and threw that next.

Dru batted it out of the air and stomped toward me.

Good. I hoped.

This part of the plan depended on Dru not squashing me to death.

I backed up further as Dru pummeled through the crates like they were paper. Cans of food spilled across the yard, not slowing her one bit.

Shit, for a Golem, she moved fast.

"Dru, it's me! It's Kayl! Your best friend!" I skittered backwards, quickly running out of yard to retreat to. "Remember when we broke into here and took a joyride down the elevator?"

Dru was showing no signs of recognition whatsoever.

"Well, if you're not in there, then I need to talk to Unghard! I know you can see me. Is this really what you want for your mortals? To fight in some pointless war?" My arse bumped into a crate, and I shimmied out of the way. "Dor is using you! He doesn't care for order—look at this place!" I gestured toward the Gate, which still lay in pieces. "Does *any* of this serve Chime? The station is ruined. There's nothing left to salvage."

Dru slowed to a stop. Oh, thank the gods, had I gotten through to her?

Her fist shot out.

Shit!

Her stony fingers clasped my neck in one single movement. I choked down a breath as she lifted me off the ground, my feet kicking at air.

I scratched at her thick wrist, but it was no use.

Dru had me at her mercy.

I pressed my palms against her stone skin. If I could yank out her soul, I could save her, rebirth her. But as I frantically tried to grab hold, there was nothing under my palm. No tingle. Nothing at all.

Because she was immortal. There was no soul for me to take.

"Chaos." Dru's lips moved, but it wasn't her voice. It was Unghard's. "Chime can be reseeded and grown again. You are a weed to be plucked."

"You're—*wrong*," I wanted to say, but my own voice came out in a garbled splutter of drool. My lungs were burning with the pressure of trying to breathe.

How was I meant to get Unghard on my side when they were a fucking stupid pile of rubble?

I was an idiot to think I could get this damn thing to listen.

And now Dru was going to crush the life from me.

My vision started to fade.

Something fluttered past.

Badger the magpie was circling overhead. He dove at Dru and attacked the arm holding me with his beak and claws. If Dru could loosen her grip and let me breathe—

She snatched the magpie with her spare fist.

Oh gods.

Badger let out a desperate cry as Dru's fist crushed him in an instant. *Shit.* Blood leaked between Dru's fingers. That poor bastard hadn't stood a chance.

A snarl erupted behind me as Wolfsbane leaped at Dru's head, his claws extended.

And then he hung in midair.

Someone had paused time.

"That's enough," drawled an annoyingly familiar female voice. "Put Arkey down before she passes out."

Dru's grip lessened. I sucked in air as I slid to the ground and landed in a wobbly heap. My breath hitched, and I spluttered a series of undignified coughs. It took a moment to regain my composure, and when I finally stood on uneasy legs, I stared at the last Diviner I ever wanted to see.

"Pendulum," I said. "What a pleasant surprise."

Her silver eyebrow twitched. "It's Pendula." She pointed a taser at me and shot me square in the chest.

Aether spasmed through me. I staggered back with a gasp and collapsed against Dru's thick leg. "*Shit!*" It wasn't the first time I'd been shocked, and yet it still caught me off guard.

Dru placed a heavy hand on my shoulder, holding me captive. Immortals were immune to time, then, though it wasn't like I was going anywhere.

Had I walked into a trap, or was I just damn unlucky?

The Ember and Umber still fought in the station—this bubble of time didn't reach them—but Pendulum or whatever paid no heed as she casually walked past me and approached Wolfsbane, who still hung in thin air. She was as immaculately dressed and groomed as the last time I'd seen her—when Quen had tased her and made a run for it out of Kronos—but a crazy look filled her silver eyes.

And her entire face was covered in odd words like *betrayer* and *traitor*. Worse, they looked red raw, as though someone had carved them into her skin recently.

Had Dor done that to her? Gods.

But did that mean... she was on our side? Had she betrayed Dor?

Then why in god's name had she pissing tased me?

"What do you want?" I called out, my voice slurring thanks to the taser strike.

"At this precise second, information." She paused by Wolfsbane and placed a hand over his forehead. "You see, Chaos is an anomaly. We cannot see or predict events based around Chaos. Fauna, however, are quite easy to decipher." Her eyes fluttered shut.

Oh, shit! She was scanning Wolfsbane's past! That meant she'd see our base, our planning, everything, depending on how far back she bloody went! I needed to knock her out!

She waggled a finger at me and tutted. "Don't try anything, or I'll rupture his brain."

Fuck!

A second later, she pulled back with a smug smile. Whatever she'd seen had satisfied her curiosity. And that meant Dor would have seen those memories, too.

The Fauna were in danger because of me. *Again.*

"You make interesting allies, *Ambassador* Arkey." She lingered on that title as though I was supposed to care about it. "Undercity dregs do tend to stick together."

"Look at yourself." I wiped drool from my chin, as my limbs had finally stopped trembling. "Traitor? Betrayer? Why serve a god who does that to you?"

Her lip curled into a sneer. "My Father didn't do this to me. Quentin did."

"Quen?" He would never do something so awful!

"These are *his* sins I bear! And I will pay them back twofold. I know he's here, leading our Guardians on a fool's errand. Little does he know he's the fool." She aimed the taser back at me, though it shook in her hand. "You'll ensure his timely surrender."

Shit. She was crazy.

This *was* a trap, and I was bait.

Dor wanted Quen by fair means or foul, but I wasn't letting *anyone* take him.

Though I also had no means of warning him.

Wolfsbane still hung in the air. If I knew Diviner, then Pendula couldn't keep time paused for much longer, which meant his untimely death was mere moments away. If that silver-arsed bitch shot me again, there wouldn't be much I could do to stop it.

I could put her to sleep, but Dru's hand still grasped my shoulder. I was sure she could snap my limbs in half without much effort, and as Edana had so painfully pointed out, my powers wouldn't work on an immortal. My charm certainly hadn't.

What options did I have? I scanned the yard, hoping for some advantage, and—there. The dead Fauna had dropped his flask of tea. It was hardly a weapon against a mortal, but better than nothing.

I yanked myself from Dru's grip, my blouse ripping as I tore myself free and dove for the flask.

A zap from Pendula's taser shot past my head and fizzled against Dru's skin.

I snatched the flask and fumbled the lid as Pendula took aim again.

Would tea damage a taser? I was about to find out. I flung the entire contents at Pendula's face with a wisp of steam.

She screamed and staggered back, her hands reaching for her face.

Oh shit! The tea was still hot! I'd thought it would have cooled by now.

"You slag!" Pendula raged, her face Ember-red. She charged into me and slapped me straight across the cheek, knocking me aside.

I rubbed the imprint on my skin. "Oh, fuck you!"

Something barreled into me *hard*, and I fell onto my hands. Dru had knocked me down and was winding up her arm, preparing to pummel me.

This mission really wasn't going well.

Time resumed. Wolfsbane landed on his feet, confused, and then spotted Dru's fist. He launched himself at it. "Run!" he yelled.

I scrambled out of the way. "You can't stop her!"

Dru's fist collided with Wolfsbane. He flew into a crate, his body smashing it into splinters.

Pendula had recovered her taser and once again took aim. "I'll return you to Kronos, Miss Arkey," she said through clenched teeth. Tea dripped from her now messy bob, darkening the brass streak through her silver hair. "And I will personally see to it your soul is cut to *nothing*."

I raised my hands in surrender. "You know, I wasn't that impressed with my first visit to Kronos. I doubt a second one will change my mind."

"You won't remember the second one."

The ground thudded beneath me.

Shit, had the Guardians returned? Did that mean Quen was nearby? He was in danger if so!

But no, the vibrations under my feet weren't the rhythmic clanging of Diviner immortals, but rather... a stampede.

I turned to the station as a horde of snarling naked Leander charged on all four paws. They leaped at Umber and Ember alike, tearing through mortals with teeth and claws, and clambered over the Golems.

Pendula swung her taser at an approaching Leander whose mane dripped with fresh blood. "No closer, you mangy mog!"

The Leander leaped at her.

Dru's arm swung down and smacked the Leander out of the way, shielding Pendula.

I took the opportunity and ran into the station. Yes, the danger was there, but at least Pendula wouldn't follow.

Where the fuck was Quen?

Ember and Umber were now caught in a three-way fight with Leander. Where in god's name had they come from? And why now?

My question was soon answered—Leander poured out of a large portal that shimmered at the center of the station's waiting area. It was hard to tell the orange desert apart from the many naked Leander, but soon their numbers trickled down.

Another figure emerged from the portal. Far taller than the others and standing on hind legs. A massive flaccid cock hung in plain view.

The three maned heads of Lionheart surveyed the station. Two of them grinned at the carnage already unfolding, while the middle head sniffed the air, as though savoring the scent of blood spilled across the concourse.

I stared dumbfounded. "You've got to be shitting me."

XXI

Lionheart is the most brutal of the gods, and his mortals are no better. They live for the fight, and this war is a playground to them. They cannot be reasoned with. They act on instinct alone. There are positives, however. Lionheart's bloodthirsty nature means he is likely to forgo allies and can be goaded into a combative encounter. As Lionheart has rejected our Father's offer for peace, I suggest we allow him free rein for now and come up with a suitable plan for destroying his mortals.
—P. Bezel, *Personal Report on Lionheart*

SOMETHING WASN'T RIGHT.

I'D run through the streets of Central with a pack of Guardians on my heel, and then my pace had dropped to a leisurely jog. Some habits never died, and as I fell into the monotonous rhythm I'd set when training with the Wardens, so my mind wandered.

Had I always been prone to distraction and wanderlust, or had my rebirth as Chaos revealed this side of me? I couldn't be sure. Discipline took practice, and I was surely out of it.

The Guardians weren't attempting to gain on me, and they had a considerably wider stride than I did. That, and my stamina was sorely lacking since I was still in recovery. This was a chase, but who was chasing who?

I slipped into an alleyway beside the Brick and Briar tavern to catch my breath. Even a simple jog proved exerting and caused me to sweat, though I didn't want Kayl to learn the extent of my current weakness, lest she lock me away in a closet.

What use would I be if I couldn't keep up with her?

A magpie flew overhead and landed on a streetlamp. One of the Fauna. Badger, he went by, due to his fondness for black-and-white animals.

"What's going on?" I called.

"Your lover's trapped." His voice was oddly higher pitched and feminine, though I supposed when one shrank to the size of a bird, so did one's vocal cords. "A Diviner has her."

Blast it! "The Golem?"

"Uncooperative. Hard to tell. The Fauna aren't moving."

Whoever held Kayl had trapped her in a bubble of time. I could sense its rippling effect from here. "I'll deal with it. Watch over the station."

Badger took flight.

Negotiations with Unghard had been a long shot—they'd effectively thrown us out of Heartstone on our last visit, but it had been worth a try. I shouldn't have left Kayl to handle this alone. If Dor got his hands on her…

Sod my recovery. I broke into a run.

Heavy footsteps thumped behind me. *Now* the Guardians were picking up the pace. If I could reach Kayl, I'd blast anyone who got in my way and open a portal back to the Undercity. Sod the consequences.

The bubble of time popped, leaving a ringing in my ears. I skidded out of the alleyway. Fighting was still ongoing in Central Station among the Ember and Umber, only… Dear gods. Were those *Leander*?

I drew my pistol and hid by the station wall. Naked Leander prowled the station on all four paws. Mostly male, judging by their manes. Some were attacking mortals, but most were goading them… Kettling them. I scanned the crowd and caught a flash of dark hair. Kayl. Good, she was safe. As safe as one could be, given the circumstances.

She was staring in horror at something within the waiting area. A portal from Obituary.

Leander charged out, which explained their sudden appearance. But as the tall form of Lionheart stepped through the portal into Chime, my jaw went slack.

The Guardians had paused their pursuit outside the station, observing as I did. Dor hadn't calculated this possibility. Neither had I.

Was *this* Serenity's distraction? Saints.

Ember and Umber ran from the sight of Lionheart, and oh, was he a sight. He stood taller than at our last encounter, towering over even the Golems. I holstered my pistol and wove between the retreating mortals.

Kayl practically ran into me. I pulled her inside the abandoned tea kiosk.

"Quen!" She wrapped her arms around my shoulders in a quick hug. "It's Lionheart!"

"Yes, I see that." A red mark bloomed across her cheek. I cupped it with my left palm, and she hissed at my touch. Someone had struck her, and that lit a fire so fierce in my stomach, I was ready to run back out there and blast the brains of whoever had done it. "What happened?"

"Pendula happened."

My heart caught in my throat. "Pendula's here?"

"She wanted to use me as bait to draw you out. Her face—Quen, it's covered in scars."

Only yesterday I'd shot her in the head. Which meant Dor had brought her back, freshly reapplied her scars, and then ordered her here as a message for me.

It sickened me.

The kiosk shook as a Golem stomped past.

Kayl peered over the counter. "Dru's still out there. She killed one of the Fauna. She killed—" Her voice choked off.

I pulled her back down. "That wasn't Dru."

"I—I know. We need to find Wolfsbane—"

"We're surrounded by an army of Leander. It's best we make a strategic retreat." I pulled out my fob watch. "There's nothing left for us here."

"What about Lionheart? Why's he even here? Let's at least see what he does." She peered back over the counter.

I wasn't expecting much from Lionheart other than what he did best: carnage.

The Leander encircled the concourse and waiting area, trapping mortals and immortals alike. That... was unexpected, but I didn't like where this was going.

"Cowards!" Lionheart roared, his voice rattling the teacups behind me. "I was promised a challenge. Is this the best the gods can offer? They send their immortals to fight their own battles? Pathetic! Are none of you brave enough to face me yourself?"

No one dared move or breathe, and none said a word other than muffled whimpering.

"Then I will test you." Lionheart opened his arms, and the portal to Obituary grew wider. "Mortal. Immortal. You're all invited to a festival of battle. Then your masters will see what they stand to lose."

The portal expanded at a rapid rate.

Mortals screamed as the portal sucked them into Obituary. Leander kettled them, not allowing anyone to escape as the portal devoured mortals and immortals alike.

I pulled Kayl up. "*Now* we're leaving."

"Not without Wolfsbane!" She pointed ahead.

Saints. Wolfsbane was being sucked into Obituary along with the Fauna we'd brought with us.

I glanced behind me, at the station exit. The Guardians were gone.

Kayl ran from the kiosk.

"Wait!" I called.

"I can't leave him!" she cried. "Trixie would never forgive me!"

Blast it! I shoved my fob watch into my pocket and ran after her.

The portal had expanded over the entire concourse now, covering even Lionheart himself, until half the station was full of orange sand and the reddening skies of early dusk.

Shouts carried on a breeze. The familiar cheering and jeers of the arena.

Kayl disappeared inside the portal. I leaped after her.

And staggered into a waiting area bench, bashing my knee against it. "Bugger me!"

The portal had zipped out of existence, leaving me alone in the station.

"No!" I kicked the bench. I couldn't leave her alone in bloody Obituary!

What was Lionheart's plan?

I yanked the fob watch out and wound the hands to eight o'clock. "Work, damn you!"

My metal fingers couldn't grip properly, and the watch slipped and clattered to the concourse.

QUENTIN! boomed Dor's voice above.

Wonderful. Absolutely wonderful.

The concourse shook as Guardians appeared out of thin air. At least twelve of them. They surrounded me in a circle with no escape.

I did *not* have time for this.

I snatched my fob watch and switched my form to Chaos. One burst of aether, and another portal opened into Obituary, albeit a much smaller one. I'd set it to open for exactly thirty seconds.

One of the Guardians swiped at me.

I ducked, narrowly missing its fist as it swept over my head.

And then I dove through the portal.

I landed on warm sand. The portal snapped shut behind me so quickly, it almost sliced my buttocks. I patted them just to be sure, but no, my cheeks were safe. My tweed jacket, however, had been caught at the coattail. What a pity.

Though in this heat, I wouldn't need a jacket.

I transferred the fob watch to my trouser pocket, shrugged off the jacket, and abandoned it to a fate it surely deserved. Then I took stock of the situation. It wouldn't behoove me to rush into danger unlike, *someone*.

I'd arrived in Obituary—that much was obvious—and stood inside one of the locker rooms of the arena. A similar one to when Kayl and I had faced Whiskers. The thrum of the crowd outside crackled with an electric energy that could practically power a streetlamp. Whatever battle Lionheart had planned may have already begun, which meant I had no time to dally.

This time, I came armed with a fully loaded pistol. I could kill at least, oh, six Leander, should my aim hit true. Against hundreds, that would surely make a difference.

I took in a breath and strode for the arena doors.

Yes, I was being oddly flippant about this whole thing. Kayl's life was in danger. Lionheart and his mortals could have already ripped her limb from limb, and my own limbs were performing their own warm-up by trembling erratically.

Of all the damnable domains I could have been dragged into, why did it have to be this one? When I'd expressed my intent to *never* set foot here again?

All right, Quen, you're being dramatic. How bad could it be?

No one guarded the entrance to the arena. Cheers and boos washed over me in a single wave of screeching noise as I stepped out into the evening sun.

It was bad. Oh my gosh, was it bad.

The arena floor was full of Ember and Umber mortals as well as a handful of immortals, surrounded and outnumbered by Leander two to one. I wasn't used to seeing Leander naked on all fours outside the bedroom, yet these combatants were feral, their manes shaking off sand, their fangs snarling and dripping with saliva as they prowled the perimeter, watching and waiting for some invisible signal. Picking their targets— including each other, I noted.

In the center stood Lionheart, as tall as when he'd entered Chime. His golden fur glistened under Obituary's orange sun, and his flaccid cock flapped in the breeze, which was certainly a sight.

This wasn't how gentlemen fought their battles. Even Wardens retained their clothing when wrestling!

The cheering from the arena stands was deafening. Every seat had been taken, the entire arena packed with laughing and jostling Leander, who pointed at the unwilling combatants, a sadistic hunger in their feline eyes. The entire domain must have squeezed into this one cursed arena. Males, females, even children. Entire families had come to watch—or had been forced to, obligated to pay respect to their god. Leander even wandered between the stalls, taking *bets*!

Saints. Some even sold kebab sticks and ales.

This is not good, Doctor Finch whined inside my mind. *In your state of health, I predict a less than one percent chance of survival.*

Yes, thank you for that.

If you die, what happens to me?

That was a good question, and I had no answer other than to *not* sodding die.

I merged with the crowd of mortals. Many were staring in shock at being surrounded by so many Leander. A few looked as scared as I felt. Kayl was here among them, somewhere. If I could grab her and Wolfsbane, we could portal out before the Leander noticed us.

Lionheart raised his hands, and the arena hushed into fevered whispering.

"Honored guests!" He bellowed across the arena, all three heads speaking in unison, and I froze in place. "You have been chosen to partake in my festival of battle! A celebration of strength and skill. Test your mettle against me, the greatest warrior the universe will ever birth!

"The rules are simple. You will fight with the weapons your gods gave you. No blades. No hammers. Your body and your wit. You may form groups or fight alone, but the battle will only end if I can be bested in combat."

Saints. This wasn't a battle—it was a slaughter.

Had Lionheart waited for this moment to pluck Ember and Umber from Chime? Besides the Fauna, they had the power and stamina to last in an arena. Diviner would be no sport. Necro had the feral tenacity, but their healing ability gave them an unfair advantage.

I turned to the nearest Ember. "Pray to Edana," I urged him. "Tell her to recall her mortals *now*."

The Ember, a male, instantly fell to his knees and muttered a prayer. It didn't take long for his eyes to open wide. "She won't."

"Why in god's name not?"

The Ember shook his head.

For intel? Was she willing to sacrifice her mortals merely to observe Lionheart's actions? Or did she simply not care? Her mortals would return to her regardless, but she was damning them to a bloody death.

I couldn't imagine Unghard would put their mortals through the same torture, and yet the Umber remained. They were too stoic, too proud, to run from this challenge.

They were sodding idiots.

"For those wondering, yes, my own mortals have chosen to celebrate this festival," Lionheart continued. "They will challenge me, and I will grant them the highest of honors my domain can bestow—an obituary! Now, let the festival begin!"

The crowd erupted in frenzied roars and howls. Gosh. I'd never seen anything like it!

Immediately, Leander tumbled into the sand, claws already out and slashing at each other. For what? The honor of being killed by Lionheart first?

Ember and Umber huddled in groups. I pushed through them, frantically searching for any sign of Kayl or the Fauna.

A line of Golems stomped past, kicking up sand. They formed a protective barrier around their mortals and readied themselves to face the Leander head-on. Good. Unghard cared that much, at least.

"Quen!" Kayl called. My heart skipped a beat as she came running with Wolfsbane and three other Fauna, though I didn't see Badger among them.

My knees almost buckled in relief. "We need to go before this travesty begins—"

"What about them?" She scanned the arena, concern twisting her features as she laid eyes on the Ember and Umber. "We can't leave them to face this!"

"Edana won't recall them. Neither will Unghard, by the looks of it. We can open a portal, get as many through as we can."

"We can hold off the Leander," Wolfsbane added with a low growl.

"I could put them to sleep?" Kayl suggested.

"You can't knock out the entire arena," I said. "Not with Lionheart watching over us."

"Then I'll fight too." She touched Wolfsbane's arm, and her form switched to Fauna, her black cat ears twitching.

I didn't like it. If she switched between animal forms, then yes, she could avoid any Leander coming our way, but she'd also be naked. The thought of *that* in an arena full of Leander was enough to send my heart panicking again.

It was rude to stereotype Leander as brutish rapists, but the stats spoke for themselves. I could not—*would not*—risk it.

"Kayl, you enter the portal first."

"Quen—"

"This is nonnegotiable." I stared her down over the rim of my spectacles. When it came to stubbornness, Kayl gave it her all, but I didn't care if this made me a chivalrous bastard. I pulled the fob watch out and began winding it to twenty past ten—to the Undercity.

A Leander charged into me and knocked the watch from my hand.

"No!"

It fell onto the sand and was then kicked further into a crowd of Umber, who would surely break it with a single step!

Wolfsbane transformed into a large wolf and leaped at my Leander attacker, teeth gnashing. The other Fauna also took forms suitable for the arena sand—a rhino, a giant snake, and ironically, a lion—and they launched themselves at Leander.

"I'll find it!" Kayl yelled, and she instantly transformed into a smaller cat, leaving her clothes behind.

Blast it! That was entirely what I'd been attempting to avoid!

I drew my pistol and chased after her as she crawled under an unsuspecting Leander. I'd barely had time to train with my new arm or practice shooting with my left hand, and here I was, thrown to the literal lions once more on the whims of a mad god and a madder woman.

A woman who was now a black cat.

A hysterical laugh escaped me before I could clamp it down, but no one noticed my hysterics because the entire arena had descended into madness.

Saints, did I desperately need a cup of tea right this moment, preferably with a drop of whiskey. All I could taste in the air was salt, sweat, and desperation.

Leander fought each other, shredding through flesh and fur. Blood had already spilled, and the crowds cheered for it.

More Leander attacked the Umber, who tried desperately to find life beneath the ground to use in their defense, but there was none. No, nothing but death graced this arid prison.

Ember threw their flame, scorching the fur of any Leander who dared come near. Edana's immortal dancers twirled in pretty spirals of blue fire, melting circular patterns of glass into the sand.

The Umber and Ember grouped together to keep the Leander off their backs.

And then there was Lionheart himself, caught in the thick of it.

The Leander god tore his way through a line of mortals as though they were made of paper. Their screams were sucked into the void of the arena. I swallowed a lump in my throat. Lionheart did not grant a quick or clean death. His claws cut through flesh and spilled blood until his own fur became slick with it.

I wanted to retch, to run, and yet the raw violence mesmerized me and kept my feet locked in place.

"Quentin!" a familiar voice called.

A Leander barreled into me. I aimed my pistol at his head, and he raised his paws in surrender. "Dandelion?"

"Oh, thank the stars, it *is* you!" The ambassador was almost unrecognizable without his black suit and top hat. I'd seen him naked before, yet here, surrounded by so much blood, it jarred me. "You have to help me!" he begged. "Nelle—the Lioness—she is here with her cubs! Please! I cannot protect them alone!"

We'd once tried to rescue the Lioness from Lionheart's clutches, but she couldn't leave her cubs behind. I scanned the arena. "Where?"

Dandelion pointed to a lone female being stalked by a group of males. She stood snarling and snapping her teeth. Behind her were three younger Leander. Juveniles, not quite cubs, but certainly not old enough to stand against full-grown mortals.

Children! Doctor Finch squawked. *We must protect them, Master Corinth!* His panic shuddered through me.

This was a problem I didn't need, yet the good doctor was right. We couldn't leave them, either. "Why is she here? And you?" Dandelion was Lionheart's voice!

"Demoted," he said, his shoulders sagging. "I don't care what Lionheart does to me, but he means to kill her, Quentin! She and her cubs!"

The crowd gasped, and I turned my head sharply. Lionheart raised an Umber above his head and ripped his torso in half. Guts spilled across the god's face like bloodied confetti, and the crowd *loved* it.

The Umber's body disappeared in a sprinkling of dust. Their flesh was made from stone, and yet Lionheart had pulled him apart with ease.

I thumped my chest and swallowed back the burning bile that had suddenly risen.

This was a bloodbath, and soon, Lionheart would run out of mortals.

Then he'd be left with us.

"I've got it!" Kayl bounded over. She'd transformed back into a bipedal Fauna. Her black fur hid most of her nakedness, though beige sand covered it. She thrust the fob watch into my left hand.

Dandelion squinted. "Ambassador Arkey? How are you both here?"

"Long story." I shook the watch, dislodging the fine grains caught inside. "Change of plans." I turned to Kayl. "The Lioness and her cubs are trapped in the arena. We're getting them out."

I would *not* allow children to be sacrificed to this cruelty.

Kayl's eyes hardened, and she nodded. "Then let's go."

She whistled a signal to Wolfsbane, who disengaged from the Leander he'd been fighting and chased after us. The other Fauna broke away and followed.

We ran across the arena, kicking up sand and dodging past the remaining Umber and Ember still fighting for their lives. The dust of too many dead mortals had already joined these sands. We simply couldn't save them all. It was basic mathematics. Logistics.

I hated that my mind thought this way.

I was a Warden. I'd spent my entire life damning mortals to their gods because I couldn't save them all. In this arena, I'd made my choice.

Save the children.

Save Kayl.

Nothing else mattered.

"Save them!" I ordered Wolfsbane, pointing ahead to the group surrounding the Lioness. I bent over, hands on my knees, and sucked in precious air. All this running about was taking its toll.

Wolfsbane leaped at the nearest Leander. The other Fauna followed his lead. The rhino trampled over his prey as the snake wrapped around another, squeezing the Leander until they popped in a shower of dust.

Blood stained the Lioness's mouth. She'd already killed in defense of her cubs, though as we approached, her snarl faded into confusion. "Tiny man?"

She remembered me, then.

Dandelion gathered the cubs in a single protective hug. "We're here to save you!"

"Save us? How can you save us from *that*!" She gestured to Lionheart, who wrestled with one of the Golems. Oh, Lionheart ripped off one of the Golem's arms to more cheers.

"We can open a portal," Kayl explained. "And get you out of here."

"What good will that do? He will bring us back." Tears formed in the Lioness's eyes and she shook her head with frustration. "There is no escape. There never has been."

I'd hoped to portal them out before Lionheart noticed, but she was right. Lionheart was no fool. He'd notice his missing champion. We could take their souls—rebirth them. But how to explain that quickly without terrifying them?

"We can rebirth..." I met Kayl's gaze and read the solution in her eyes. "No." The word came out with a sudden breathlessness.

"Why save only these when we can save them all? This is what we agreed to do—"

"We can't stand against him—"

"We've got no choice! What do you think this is all for, Quen? How long do we wait? How many mortals die and live and die again in the meantime?"

"We're not strong enough yet." *I* wasn't strong enough!

"This is the best chance we have! I'm ending him, whether you help me or not."

I calculate your odds of survival at less than 0.5 percent—

Shut up! I aimed my pistol at the nearest Leander and shot him in the face. He collapsed backwards and faded instantly. My aim was improving.

Booing and jeers erupted from the crowd.

"Diviner!" Lionheart roared.

The entire arena ground to a stop with that one simple word. All eyes turned to me.

Oh, bugger me.

"Now you've done it," Kayl muttered.

I braced myself as Lionheart stomped across the arena. His giant cock swung between those furry, muscled legs, and he whacked mortals aside with the flat of his phallus. One poor sod went flying through the air.

I'm sure such a display was meant to make me feel insignificant, and it was working. I felt ready to soil myself. Yes, I'd died before, I understood the whole rigmarole, but between having my soul yanked out, my body burned alive, or Lionheart ripping off my remaining limbs, I'd rather choose the first two.

My body wasn't ready for battle. My residual limb was already sore at the connection, an unbearable throbbing ache, my metal fingers twitching of their own accord. Kayl had been right—I needed time to rest.

Time no longer cared for what I needed.

"Child of Chaos." Lionheart leered over Kayl with his middle head as the other two grinned. "Interesting. I didn't expect to catch you in my net. Clearly Serenity knew something I didn't when they tipped me off. You trying to steal my Lioness again?"

Kayl rubbed sand from her furry arms with painful nonchalance. "It seems you no longer need her."

"You're welcome to earn her. Though... You stole power from me. Perhaps I shall take you as payment, and you may serve at my feet as my new Lioness. Do you purr in that form, little kitty?"

Boiling rage surged through me, and I pointed my pistol at the god.

He roared with laughter, and the arena laughed with him. "Are you challenging me, Diviner? What a small creature you are. I'll take you both and make you watch as she services my—"

My trigger finger twitched, and my shot hit him in the shoulder.

The crowd gasped.

A trickle of blood ran from the wound, but Lionheart merely rolled his shoulder, and the bullet fell out. "A coward's toy. Can a Diviner fight like a man?"

I was doomed. Utterly doomed. And yet I realized I held one key advantage.

Lionheart didn't know I was Chaos. Even when wearing a Chaos form, it was so like my Diviner skin, the fool didn't recognize the difference.

He knew Kayl could easily take his soul, and would keep her at a distance. For all his ego, he wouldn't risk a confrontation with her. But I?

If I could get close enough, all I'd need was one touch.

One touch to destroy his rotten soul and end this.

I holstered my pistol. "Then fight me. I challenge you to a duel! Man versus man."

Kayl grasped my left arm. "Quen—"

"Trust me," I whispered.

Lionheart gestured for space, and the remaining combatants shuffled back into a circle. I caught Wolfsbane's eye, his expression a mixture of bemusement and disbelief. A bloodied gash stretched across his chest, but thankfully wasn't deep enough to require urgent medical attention. The other Fauna looked weary on their feet. One of them nursed a broken wrist.

They were hurt, but alive.

Dandelion gathered the Lioness and her cubs, and they too grimaced in my direction. Did *anyone* have any bloody faith in me?

Kayl stood with them, and she at least thrust her chin high with a look that exuded confidence. It was odd, seeing her standing there naked and covered in sand alongside everyone else, who were also naked. I felt overdressed as I took position my before Lionheart.

Obituary's sun burned overhead with an angry bronze haze slowly starting to descend. In this early evening, the air was much cooler, yet sweat still tainted my skin, shirt clinging to my back. I wanted to roll up my sleeves, but that meant exposing my metal arm, and that was a disadvantage I didn't want to reveal.

I readied my feet and fists in a boxing stance. Part of my Warden training had involved learning to box. I wasn't any good at it. But wrestling? I wasn't any good at that either, though I had some experience grappling males.

Lionheart shrank from his nine-feet to a more reasonable and sporting seven-feet. He still towered over everyone, except for the Golems.

"I'll take my time with you, Diviner." He huffed at his own joke. "Start by breaking your bones. Then I'll mount you in front of your Chaos. Show her what she can expect."

Such words were meant to rile me, but I imagined him as a three-headed cub and allowed his threats to dissipate. They were rather dull, cliched things.

I'd endured worse horrors than Lionheart.

I could do this.

"All I'm hearing is the mewing of an oversized kitten."

Lionheart snarled and pounced at me.

I braced myself for the impact.

He landed on me, the force equivalent to being run over by a tram. It knocked the wind from my lungs, yet I didn't need to stand, I didn't need to fight back.

I just needed to grab hold.

Claiming his soul should have been as easy as touching his chest with my palm. But there was no tug. Lionheart's fur was so thick, it acted as natural armor.

Saints. Had I completely miscalculated this endeavor?

He slammed me into the sand and sat atop my chest. "Weakling."

"Kitten," I spat.

His claws retracted, and he batted my cheek with his paw, though the force was more like a harsh slap. "Am I a kitten now, Diviner?"

I grabbed his paw with both hands. My metal hand crunched down with strength that surprised even me.

Lionheart's feline eyes widened. "What is this?" He tried to shake his paw free.

I placed the palm of my left hand against the rough leather of his cute little toe beans.

Static crackled around us, and my form changed to Leander.

The tug called to me, begging me to put this cat down, and I followed its compulsion.

"What!" Lionheart roared and yanked his arm up, dragging me with it. He shook me off like I was a snake, but it was too late.

The roar of the arena exploded inside my mind. Every Leander screamed with horror and fear. They didn't understand what was happening, and gods help them, they certainly hadn't asked for this fate, but I didn't care one jot.

Panic erupted across the arena. Leander bolted for the exits in a mad scramble to escape, the crowds clambering and tripping over one another. They wouldn't get far.

In my subconscious, I searched for the Lioness's soul.

It was there. Safe.

And she would never know pain or fear again.

Lionheart staggered in a circle within the arena, pacing like a wounded animal. "You tricked me! Fucking Serenity, they set me up. I'll *destroy* you!"

I examined my left hand, which had now turned into a fluffy paw. "Try it."

He lunged.

The Lioness leaped before him, stopping him in his tracks.

She glanced at me over her shoulder, the eager expression in her feline pupils asking for permission. All the hurt and hatred she'd carried her entire life flooded my mind. Saints, it was so overwhelmingly powerful, all I could do was nod.

She grinned with satisfaction.

And then she ripped Lionheart to shreds. Or what was left of him. Her cubs joined in, kicking and spitting at the flailing Leander god.

He died without dignity, howling like a kitten as the Lioness tore him apart. His flesh and fur turned to dust. None of Lionheart's mortals cared to save him.

Kayl ran to my side. "Oh. My. *God*." She squealed. "Quen, you look so gods-damn adorable right now. We *need* to get you a bow tie."

"*Adorable?*" I spluttered. "I'll have you know I'm fierce!" I bared my new fangs to prove it.

"So adorably fierce."

My new whiskers twitched, and I scratched my new mane. I'd never grown a beard before, but the sensation must be similar. Something felt oddly tight in my trousers. Oh. I had a tail now! My cheeks heated at the memory of helping to dig out Kayl's own tail all those weeks ago.

Dandelion examined his fur as dust fell from his mane. "What's happening to me? Quentin?"

The orange sky turned gray and mortals faded from existence.

The Lioness's cubs huddled together in fear.

I gave them a sympathetic smile. This wouldn't be easy. "This domain is dying. You'll fade out, briefly. Like going to sleep. But I will bring you back. It'll be different from what you are now, but it will be better. Safer. I promise you."

I'd bring them to Sinner's Row. Trixie could give Dandelion and the Lioness shelter, and the cubs could play with Autumn and Freddie. It wouldn't be a perfect life, but I'd do right by them. It was the least they deserved.

The Lioness hugged her cubs, her fur covered in the blood and dust of Lionheart's demise. Dandelion huddled with them. Together, they joined the arena sand, and settled in my subconsciousness.

"What now?" Wolfsbane prodded.

The Fauna were staring at me.

Ah. Yes. Our escape.

I dug out my fob watch. Thankfully, it had survived this trip to Obituary and my scuffle with Lionheart unscathed. I switched my form to Chaos and wound it to twenty past ten.

One quick burst of aether, and a portal opened to the Undercity, on the outskirts of Sinner's Row.

We didn't want the Umber following us inside, after all.

"Everyone, step through!" I called.

Wolfsbane and the Fauna ran through first. Kayl and I guided the remaining Ember and Umber mortals. Edana's immortals had all disappeared, leaving only two Golems.

One of them had golden daisies. Dru.

"Quen," Kayl said, her voice a whisper.

"I'm sorry." I stared up at Dru, though it wasn't her I addressed. It was Unghard. "You can't come with us—you won't fit through the portal, for a start. But I assure you; your mortals will not be harmed."

The Golem regarded me. "You destroyed the root of a godtree. You bear their soul."

"Lionheart was torturing *your* mortals—"

"Yet Chaos toys with the natural order of things. This is what Dor warned of."

"Dor will destroy you next!" Kayl spat. "Or do you think the death of the Glimmer was a coincidence?"

"We have faith in Dor's vision."

The Golem stepped back. A portal appeared behind it with Heartstone's mountain glowing in the evening sun. It enveloped the two Golems, and then they vanished in the blink of an eye.

"Shit." Kayl kicked sand.

Shit indeed. We could do nothing more than return to Sinner's Row and rest. Pins and needles stabbed through my metal arm—it needed to come off.

I stole one final glimpse at Obituary as the empty arena crumbled into nothing.

I'd never wanted to see this blasted domain again, and now I never would.

"Shall we?" I offered my left hand to Kayl.

She took it, and together, we stepped through the portal, leaving Obituary to finally write its own end.

XXII

Love is an illusion.
The Covenant says you have free will.
Then why can't you marry a mortal from a different domain?
Or have children?
The gods dictate who you can love.
And they want your love for themselves.
—Anonymous, *Godless flier*

"YOU KILLED A *GOD?*" Trixie stared at me in sheer disbelief.

"You should have seen him, Trix!" Wolfsbane said with far too much eagerness. "He straight-up challenged Lionheart and ended him! He's a madman!" He whooped a laugh and slapped my back so hard, I almost bloody fell!

Once we'd seen the Umber off, we'd retreated to Erosain's old bar— now Trixie's bar—and relayed exactly what had transpired.

We'd gathered in a private booth with much needed refreshment. Kayl had managed to find a robe from somewhere and was sipping a fruit cocktail while I helped myself to a well-earned hot toddy. Wolfsbane had already downed two pints of ale and was on his third.

While Wolfsbane clearly enjoyed the adventure, Trixie was not as impressed. "All I'm 'earing is you put my mortals in danger. Look at you." She gestured to Wolfsbane. "You're bleeding all over my new table."

Wolfsbane put his tankard aside and rubbed the wound across his chest. "It's only a scratch—"

"And who's gonna tell Badger's family 'e didn't make it back? I fucking ain't."

"I will." Wolfsbane straightened, his mood turning somber. "To Badger." He raised his tankard.

I hadn't known Badger long, and was rather confused how he'd died. I could swear I'd spoken to him before Lionheart launched his attack, yet he'd apparently been squashed by a Golem—by Dru, if Kayl's guilty look was anything to go by. "To Badger." I raised my teacup in toast.

"To Badger," Kayl added.

"We were caught in a bad situation and made the most of it," I said. "I'm sorry for the loss of Badger. I could never have predicted Lionheart would show up." A warning from Edana wouldn't have gone amiss, though perhaps Serenity had also left her in the dark.

"And you killed 'im." The look Trixie was giving me was oddly neutral.

"We're godless," Kayl drawled. "It's what we do."

"Is that your plan? Kill the gods?" *All of them?* was the unspoken question on her lips.

"You bet."

Concern flashed in Trixie's eyes. Kayl likely missed it—the alcohol must be going to her head—but I'd spent years observing others' tells as a Warden.

Trixie feared us.

She feared what we could do.

I finished off my drink. The whiskey burned down my throat and settled into my gut with a pleasing warmth that helped soothe the aches in my arm temporarily. "I think it's best if we retire for the evening. It has been an exhausting day, and we could all do with some rest." That, and I wanted to wash away the sand and sweat from that blasted arena. "But first, I have a favor to ask."

Trixie leaned back in the booth and crossed her arms. "Another one?"

"When we escaped Obituary, I brought some friends over with me. Leander. They need shelter. If you could provide them with lodgings, I would be most grateful."

"More mouths to feed?"

"One of them is a female with three young cubs. They've been abused under Lionheart's rule."

"They fought with us," Wolfsbane added over the rim of his tankard.

"Fine. We'll 'ouse them," Trixie said.

I bowed my head. "Thank you."

Kayl downed her drink, and then we carefully made our way back to the hotel we'd chosen as our base. It wasn't exactly home, but it had beds, and that was good enough.

As Kayl checked in with the Mesmer, I found an unoccupied room and got to business.

It was easy enough to locate Dandelion, the Lioness, and her cubs floating within my subconscious. They were the only Leander I knew personally, and, in Dandelion's case, intimately. I'd yet to rebirth a mortal, since Doctor Finch was appalled by the idea, but these deserved another chance at mortal life.

And perhaps having a small army of Leander on my side would be useful in the battles to come.

Slowly, I dragged their energy out of my mind. They popped into existence with a flourish of aether and stood naked in the room.

Five Leander forged by Chaos. Their beige fur now held a gray tint, and their eyes came alive with the silvery blue I'd grown so accustomed to.

The Lioness fell to her knees and hugged her three cubs tight.

"You... you did it." Dandelion examined his paws. "You brought us back."

I smiled. "As promised. I'm afraid this will have to do for accommodation until we can get you settled, but I'll try and sort you some clothes—"

"Quentin." Dandelion shushed me. "We are indebted, my friend." He yanked me into a crushing embrace.

"It's—quite—all right," I gasped.

The Lioness laughed. "Let him go, you fool, before you kill him."

"He's no tiny man!" Dandelion declared, but thankfully let me go. "He is a legend as tall as a mountain."

I straightened my shirt. "I wouldn't go that far."

"I would." Kayl leaned by the door, still dressed in her robe. She retained her Fauna form with black fur and cat ears, though she'd since cleaned off the dirt and sand. The way she stood posed, her thighs exposed, made her look lithe.

I shook off the heat rising in my gut. "In a fair fight, Lionheart would have pummeled me."

"Take the win, Quen," she chided. My cheeks flushed at the spark in her eyes. *Saints.*

The Lioness stood and took Kayl's hand. Tears rimmed her feline eyes. "How can we ever repay you both?"

"By living a good life," Kayl said. "That's the best revenge against shitty gods."

"That is wise." The Lioness snorted. "Would you meet my cubs?"

The three cubs hid behind Dandelion's legs.

Kayl chuckled. "I think they're a little shy. Maybe in the morning. I've spoken with the Fauna at reception downstairs. They'll fetch you some food, if you're hungry, and we'll work out proper lodgings and clothing tomorrow if that's okay with you?"

"You have our thanks. And please. Call me Nelle."

"Nelle."

The two embraced, and then Kayl was ushering me out of their room to give them privacy. This was all new to them, and it would take time for them to settle into their new lives.

It astounded me that I could give them this. A gift that should have been impossible.

This was what it meant to be Godless.

You saved them, Master Corinth, Doctor Finch said. *I judged you harshly when we first met in the steamworks.*

We all make mistakes, Doctor. Does this mean you're ready to come out of me?

For what purpose? You have your arm. Your portable portaling device. From here, I can continue to monitor your vitals and oversee your healing—

I'm not a project you need to work on and maintain.

Your continued existence is to my benefit. Now that you possess two god souls, we can increase the output of your healing capabilities—

Doctor. I appreciate your concern, but you can't remain inside my mind. I required my privacy, for one thing.

Your internal monologue is of no concern to me, Master Corinth.

We'd see about that.

I followed Kayl into our shared room. Someone must have been inside and tidied, for the bed was made neat and the scent of lavender lingered over the bedsheets. The tiny bar had also been restocked, though with water and bags of peanuts and not whiskey. Alas.

Kayl sifted through the nuts. "Are you hungry?"

I sat on the edge of the bed. "Surprisingly, no. Is that odd?" I *had* devoured an entire god, albeit metaphysically. Adrenaline still ran through my blood, and I wasn't sure if I was riding the exhilaration of battle, or of actually doing good in this blasted world for once.

Or if it was because Kayl leaned over in such a way I could see the curve of her breasts.

I cleared my throat and rolled my metal arm. I'd been wearing it for hours now, and it chafed where it attached to my residual limb. It would do me some good to pop it off and rest my arm.

"I've always had a large appetite," Kayl said. "Is that a Chaos thing—oh! They've got jelly babies!" She pulled out a packet of confectionary and held it aloft like some grand prize. "I thought they stopped making these." She sat on the bed and shuffled next to me, her buttocks rubbing up against my hip, and she opened the packet. "I always loved the purple ones. Gotta start with nibbling the head off and working your way down."

She offered me the packet, and I pulled out a green-apple-flavored Umber shape. "It makes sense. Not, ah, biting the heads off, but what you were saying before. We are beings who can manipulate aether, which takes a tremendous amount of energy. It's only natural we must seek to replenish it."

"So I have an excuse to stuff myself with candy? And here I thought I was a Mesmer after all." She dug out a dark blue Mesmer jelly baby—candy floss flavor—and sucked it into her mouth, leaving a sheen of sugar dust on her lips.

Oh my.

"Do you want another one?" she asked, her whiskers twitching.

"Please," I croaked.

She pulled out an orange Leander and pressed it against my lips. I opened my mouth, and my tongue flicked her fingers.

My trousers suddenly felt tight.

I leaped from the bed and strode over to the wardrobe, shaking my leg in a little hop as I did so. "I really must find better attire. These trousers are *far* too tight, and quite frankly, I could do better than whatever the denizens of Sinner's Row considered fashionable." It *was* rather disturbing to be wearing the outfits of former brothel-goers.

"Well, why don't we take a trip to the Golden City?" she suggested. "Raid their boutiques. I could do with a few new dresses."

"Now? It wouldn't be entirely safe—"

"Where's your sense of adventure? Besides, there's no one there."

"Dor could have Diviner on the lookout."

"At the boutiques?" She raised her brow.

I supposed she made a good point. "You're utterly corruptible."

"Isn't that part of my charm?"

And many other things. Were we really about to raid a boutique? At this time of night? "Do you want to dress first?"

She tightened the robe around her waist. "Why bother?"

Gods help me.

I quickly freshened up in the bathroom, if only to wash away the residue of blood and sand, and then I held my fob watch. I set it to five past four. Solaris for the Golden City.

With a burst of aether, a portal opened in the middle of our room. Through it, the many stores of the Golden City plaza were still lit against the evening sky. Chime's streets may be empty, but power continued to surge, the city carrying on without its mortals to occupy it.

I took Kayl's hand and stepped through. We hurried across the cobblestones of the plaza, my heart pumping the entire way. A fit of giggles escaped me as we took shelter under the awning of a store. Gosh, I felt like a schoolboy again, smuggling biscuits under the bedsheets in my dormitory.

Kayl popped open the door, and then we were in.

She was right, of course. The plaza was empty. Once the store's door was closed, my muscles relaxed. I pulled the blinds down over the window, to be certain. There was still enough light inside to allow us a leisurely perusal.

The store was a Glimmer-owned boutique I must have passed hundreds of times. Luckily, the outfits catered to both male and female. The male side of the room was mostly suits, thank the gods, though it was a poor selection compared to the female side, which was full of skirts, blouses, ridiculous hats, ball gowns, and floral dresses.

Kayl immediately ran to the floral dresses. "Gods. They're gorgeous. Have you seen the price tag on them?" She pulled one from a rack, a pink design decorated in purple flowers, and held it against her hip.

I browsed through the suits, and yes, the cost was eye-watering. "Tonight, they're on a discount."

To steal was theft. A petty crime, but a crime all the same. How many mortals had I incarcerated for what I was about to do? How many gods had punished their mortals for such sins?

If it was a sin to dress well, then flog my buttocks.

It actually *was* a sin to dress well, according to some, but I no longer cared.

"Well?" Kayl called. "What do you think?"

I turned around, and my mouth dried out.

She'd changed her form back to Mesmer and slipped into the pink floral dress. It was modest compared to other outfits I'd seen her wear, and yet it shaped her curves in a manner that set my desires aflame. She gave it a twirl.

"You look stunning."

"I bet you say that to all the girls."

"Only you."

The stars on her cheeks twinkled in a blush. "Let's get you looking fancy. Can you turn Leander again?"

"Why?"

"I want to see what you look like in a top hat."

I playfully rolled my eyes and changed my form to Leander. Fur sprouted across my body, making my trousers even tighter, and a mane spilled down my chest.

She placed a top hat on my head and giggled.

I adjusted my trousers to make room for my tail. "I'm a Leander, I'm supposed to be threatening."

"Trust me, it's impossible for you to be threatening."

"For years, I've been known as the Dark Warden," I muttered.

"Mmhmm." She undid the buttons of my shirt. Her fingers wove through my chest fur, sparking a flutter through my skin. "May I see it?"

"See what?"

"Your cock." She bit her lower lip. "I've never seen a Leander one up close."

My heart bounced inside my chest, somersaulting through a performance of acrobatics, sending heat pumping south.

Are you safe, Master Corinth? Doctor Finch's voice almost made me bloody jump! *Your heart rate has increased quite rapidly—*

I shoved the good doctor into the far reaches of my subconscious. This was *not* a moment I wanted an audience for.

"Quen?"

I made a sort of whimpering meant to be acquiescence.

She smiled, the most beautiful thing in the universe, and her fingernails traced down to my trousers.

Slowly, so painfully slowly, she undid the zipper and pulled them down. My semi-erect cock strained against my boxers.

Then she popped it out.

"Gods. It really is spiky." Her hand wrapped around the shaft, her touch so soft and delicate. I leaned against the clothes railing to steady myself.

Saints.

Pleasure jolted through my core as her hand rubbed against the tiny penile spines my cock had apparently grown. I stared down at it, as fascinated as Kayl.

"No offense, Quen, but I'm not going to fuck you like this." She let out a chuckle, but there was nothing unkind in her tone.

Honestly, having experienced the end of a Leander's cock, I didn't blame her.

My form changed back to Diviner, and the penile spines vanished. "Any better?"

"Much better." Her hand continued to rub up and down my shaft, and I stood fully erect and throbbing against her palm. "Is this okay?"

"Yes." My voice turned hoarse.

Her eyes met mine, the aether inside them aglow. "How do you want me?"

In every way conceivable.

I wanted that filthy mouth of hers around my cock.

I wanted that tongue to commit sins.

And yet I wanted to taste her. Oh, so desperately did I hunger for her with the powerful desire of a Necro.

I should be a gentleman. I should hold back. To crave carnal pleasure was a sin carved into my very soul, yet my entire existence had been curated to reject sin. From the lessons of my school boy days, to Elijah...

I couldn't help craving it. Even Elijah hadn't been enough for me.

But with Kayl it was something more.

I'd lived inside her body, once. Existing with the flow of her movements, the sanctity of her thoughts. Watching from her eyes, feeling the touch of cloth on her skin. I'd drowned in the very essence of her, and its absence had left me bereft.

I needed her. My goddess. I ached for this.

"I want to fuck you on that counter. On the floor. I want to lick your cunt until you scream my name."

Her eyes widened. "Quentin Corinth! That is the most depraved thing I've ever heard you say."

My heart skipped a beat. "Did—Did I go too far?"

"No." Her lips curved into a smirk. "You're perfect." She let go of my cock and wrapped her arms around my neck, pulling me closer until our lips met.

All the stars of her skin exploded on her tongue, flooding me with aether. Igniting my unholy desires.

That was what her touch did to me.

It destroyed me and birthed me a thousand times over.

We broke contact with a gasp for air. "Are you sure about this?" I panted. "I don't want you to feel rushed into it, or somehow obligated—"

"I've never been more sure." She leaned in to kiss me again.

"It might not be safe. What if Wardens are out—"

"Quen." She pressed a finger against my lips. "Shut up and fuck me."

"Right you are."

Kayl tore off my shirt as I tugged down the straps to her dress, desperate to place my mark on her skin. She helped the proceedings along, and we weren't gentle with the poor fabric in our haste to get it off.

As I kicked off my shoes and finished undressing, she pulled gowns and suits from the store's racks and threw them down into a pile. A makeshift bed.

Then we were both tumbling, our naked bodies pressed together on the floor of *Gladys's Golden Finery*.

She leaned back, her smile encouraging as she opened herself to my exploration. For so many years I could never touch another mortal without experiencing their death, and perhaps she remembered that in offering her body.

By gods, it was overwhelming. I'd witnessed her nakedness before; she was truly sublime, but I didn't know where to start. I merely stared down, admiring the shape of her nipples.

"Touch me," she urged. "I'm all yours." She took my hand and placed it atop her breast.

Gosh, it was so *warm*.

Memories surfaced at the forefront of my mind. I'd never touched a woman before, not like this, though it couldn't be that different from playing with a man.

Yet I had a copious number of memories that detailed Kayl's needs.

I'd sifted through Malkavaan Byvich's memories some time ago, and they had been *quite* vivid. While I'd wiped those memories out of respect and privacy for their relationship, Walter had brought everything back. Some days they appeared stark and demanding.

I would take these memories to the aether, but right now, thanks to Malkavaan's previous experience and expertise, I knew exactly what to do.

I bent over and pressed my tongue against her nipple. The first flick sent her moaning.

Musical instruments weren't my forte, and while the Seren would describe foreplay akin to plucking an instrument, to me, it was more like preparing a steam train for departure. Not the most erotic of imagery, but one needed to stoke the engine to the correct temperature, pull on the right handles, twiddle a few knobs.

Kayl responded to my touch. Each feather-like caress of my fingers across her nipples made her writhe. The tip of my tongue licking the sweat from her neck earned a groan. I moved with considered care, slowly dragging my lips and the slight edge of my teeth down, *down*, lingering but never quite reaching where she wanted me.

"Quen," she pleaded.

I glanced over the rim of my spectacles, which were beginning to steam. "Yes, dear?"

"*Please?*"

"Since you asked so politely." I took off my spectacles, placed them aside out of harm's way, and shuffled closer. Precum was already dripping from my cock. In my concentration, I'd barely paid my own needs any attention, but now the need was almost too much.

Gods, I *ached*.

Once more, Kayl opened herself to me. Her mound glistened with wetness.

My tongue pressed flat against her clit and lapped her sweetness.

"Fuck!" Kayl gasped.

This was everything I'd ever imagined and desired. My tongue moved with wide, slow strokes, exploring her inner and outer lips, and then moving back to the bud. I worked my jaw hard, applying firm pressure with rhythmic motions. Kayl groaned beneath me, her hips bucking and twitching.

Her fingers wove into my hair, tightening against my scalp. "Don't stop."

I maintained my pace, and her body arched.

"*Quen!*" Her voice came out in a low moan that increased in pitch and intensity as her thighs squeezed against my cheeks and practically crushed my face.

And then her entire body deflated with a happy sigh.

"How... how the *shit* did you do that?" she said between pants. "I thought you'd never been with a woman before?"

I licked my lips clean and pushed my spectacles back on. "I haven't. Yet." I raised my brow with a satisfied smirk.

She reached for the top hat and threw it at me. "That's for being cocky."

I chuckled and caught it. "I'm a modest man, I assure you."

"Put it on," she said. "Fuck me while you're wearing it."

"As the lady commands." I sat the hat tight on my head and once again shuffled in position, placing my elbows on either side of Kayl's abdomen.

A sharp pain spasmed up my right, arm and I immediately sat up with a hiss.

Kayl sat up with me. "Are you all right?"

I rubbed where my residual arm connected with my metal one. "I'm sorry, it's just... I've been using it all day. I should... take it off." I turned away from her probing stare. I could hardly fuck her while balancing on one arm, and my poor cock began to deflate in agreement.

"Quen. It's fine. Take it off and get on your back."

"But you—"

"I know what I'm doing, so let me. But keep that hat on." A twinkle shone in her eye.

We swapped places. I removed my metal arm, and it came off with instant relief. The skin was so sore and raw around where it connected. Then I lay back against the makeshift bed and shuffled into a comfortable position.

I'd never fucked liked this before. It left me feeling entirely exposed and oddly vulnerable.

Kayl kneeled beside me. To her credit, she wasn't perturbed by my arm and had taken the whole thing in stride. Her hand wrapped around my shaft and gently tugged it back to full hardness.

"You're incredible," I said.

"Me? You're the one who took on Lionheart and won. When I'm with you, I feel like I can do anything, you know? That together we can take on the gods."

She bent down and took my cock into her mouth.

"Holy saints!" Her tongue caressed my head, and those lips damn near sucked out my soul! "Stop."

She did so, looking concerned. "Am I hurting you?"

"No, but if you keep doing that, then no one's getting fucked tonight."

She flashed a grin and then crawled on top of me. "Don't blow your load. I'm not done with you yet."

Saints, she was going to actually kill me.

Goodbye, cruel world. Welcome me to sweet oblivion.

I chewed my lip as she lowered herself on top of me, her slickness accommodating my cock with ease.

Fuck, it fit so perfectly, felt so right.

Kayl began with a slow rhythm. "Is this okay?"

I mumbled an incoherent squeal. The pleasure massaging my cock was indescribable.

How had I been missing this my entire life?

I groped her breast with my left hand, but Kayl was doing all the work as I held on figuratively to reality. It was all I could do to remain conscious as she rode my poor mortal body to the edge of existence.

It became unbearable.

"I'm going to—to—"

"Hold on a little longer," Kayl ordered.

I could do that. I could hold on.

Hold on.

Her breasts crushed against my chest, her hips thrusting wildly, and her lips took mine with sudden desperation.

I couldn't hold on any more.

"*Fuck!*"

I emptied years' worth of frustration inside her.

Years of sin.

She sat up, my cock still twitching inside her. Sweat shone across her body, her hair sticking to her cheek and forehead.

She was the most beautiful woman in all the domains.

My goddess.

I reached up and pulled a lock from her cheek. "Marry me," I blurted.

Another twinkle shone in her eyes. "Was I that good?"

Heat flushed through me as my brain finally caught up to reality. "I, ah—"

"Oh, Quen. You say the funniest things." She cupped my cheek with a smile bordering on pity. "Do we have a connection?"

"We're connected right now."

She hummed, and then pulled herself from me with a wet squelch. "I think we better clean ourselves up and get back to the hotel before Trixie wonders where we've run off to. And you *did* scream rather loud. A Warden may have heard." She glanced over her shoulder and winked.

I watched as she wandered off to gather clothes from the rack.

The post-coitus clarity hit hard. It practically slapped me across the face.

I loved her. Gods damn me for a fool, I *loved* her.

And I'd only gone and asked her to marry me. *You idiot, Quen! You absolute bellend!*

She'd rightly laughed me off, because of course she would.

Because she wasn't *mine*, and deep down she knew what an uncouth, ungentlemanly bastard I really was.

Did I even know what love was? Truly?

Could an emotionally dead Diviner even *understand* it?

All this time I'd been salivating over her like some perverted Leander while her real lover—the love of her life—remained trapped in the far reaches of her subconscious. The love Kayl and Malkavaan shared was more profound than anything a Diviner could comprehend. How could I ever hope to reach those depths? Did I deserve to even try?

I owed it to her, to Malkavaan, to find those memories and restore them.

Instead, I'd pissed over his memories. Taken advantage of them. Fed my animal instincts, the depraved part of my soul that craved sin.

Gods, I felt sick.

I needed to get those memories back. I needed to get into Memoria and claim them from Anima.

Then we could return Malkavaan to where he belonged. At Kayl's side.

And, if she had any mercy in her heart, she'd forgive me for what I'd done.

For I surely couldn't forgive myself.

WHERE'S THE LOVE?

Everything went to shit. Nothing new there.
It started as it always does; with a case. A lady comes into my office. Says she
needs me to spring a friend of hers from the Asylum. Should have known
then it was a bad idea, but there was something about her that drew me in.
Maybe it was the glow of her eyes.
Or maybe the fact her face could change at the blink of an eye.
So I went with her into the last place I ever wanted to return to.
Didn't work out.
I died. Came back. Died again. Nothing new there, either.
Only now... Well. Things are far, far worse.
—M. Gast, from the new personal journal of PI Gast

HUH.

HOW THE FUCK had Corinth found a way to open fucking portals?

I'd watched the battle of the immortals play out from the comfort of the clock tower. Imagine my fucking surprise when Corinth ran past through Central, chased by a whole line of those clockwork hulks of metal the Diviner kept as pets. Curiosity had gotten the better of me, so I'd flown over the station and found my dear sister facing off with a Golem!

Wow, had I been missing out on a party.

It'd been easy enough to take a Fauna shape and spy on them. Corinth didn't even guess it was me.

Then Lionheart had shown up, as Serenity's secret surprise—who knew goading a dumb lion would be enough to get him into Chime—but that wasn't the most interesting part. Nope, that came after, when Corinth pulled a fucking portal out of his arse and stepped through it to Obituary.

Stranger still, I could sense the burst of aether coming from it. A few hours later, I sensed it again, this time coming from above in the Golden City. What else did I find?

Corinth fucking my sister!

Was *anything* sacred anymore?

I threw my hands up. "He's fucking my sister!"

A few faces within the clock tower glanced at me in alarm. A few more mortals skittered away and made themselves look busy. The Glimmer kept separate from the Necro, despite me making new female Necro who weren't quite as handsy as the males. Joe and Vincent were doing a good job of keeping them from fighting, at least, though the party I'd so generously thrown hadn't done much for morale.

ARE YOU SO SHOCKED, DAUGHTER? Mother drawled. *OR ENVIOUS?*

Fuck no, I wasn't envious. Kayl was the one who liked floppy dicks, not me. And well. I wasn't *that* shocked. Corinth had been eye-fucking Kayl since the day they met, and Kayl fell for anyone who gave her the slightest bit of attention. The fact they'd kept up the *'Oh no we mustn't'* charade for so long was more of a shock.

The pair of them had always been dirty liars, even if they'd been lying to themselves.

DON'T JUDGE THEM TOO HARSHLY. CHAOS AND TIME HAVE ALWAYS BEEN DRAWN TO ONE ANOTHER.

We all knew how well *that* had gone.

OPPOSITES ATTRACT, DAUGHTER.

Couldn't say I related.

"Is there a problem?" Harmony asked, her brows raised in a way that suggested *I* was the problem.

She was still in the form of Chaos, though now dressed in a smart casual suit that somehow made her even more hot. Wow, could she pull it off.

Since my party hadn't worked out, I needed someone with leadership experience to become my voice and advise me, and who better than the leader of the Godless? Joe's heart was in the right place, but I was sick of being surrounded by so many men. I wanted a woman's touch. Besides, no one knew the Godless better than dear old Harm. We couldn't let that brain of hers go to waste, could we?

Harmony hadn't wanted the position of my voice. In fact, her reaction had been 'Oh dear gods no,' but it wasn't like I'd given her much choice.

"Corinth is fucking my sister."

"And? This affects you how? It's hardly the scandal of the century, and you've got more important things to worry about."

She may be right, but she didn't have to say it *that* way, geez.

THE PROBLEM WITH THE GODLESS IS THEY'VE SPENT TOO LONG LIVING IN DEFIANCE OF THEIR GODS. THEY'VE FORGOTTEN WHAT FEAR MEANS.

I don't want them to fear me, but respect me.

THAT'S THE SAME THING. A PUBLIC FLOGGING WILL BOOST MORALE AMONG YOUR MORTALS.

Knowing the Glimmer and Necro, they'd both likely get off on it.

What actually bothered me about this whole shitshow wasn't Corinth fucking my sister, but his amazing new ability to create portals. Had he learned that from the Zephyr? He and Kayl had four god souls between them, and I only had *two*.

How the fuck had they gotten ahead of me?

Gast! I yelled at the Necro from inside my mind. *Get back here. I need intel.*

I'm gathering your intel, he replied in a scathing tone. *I can't do that if you send me traipsing back and forth.*

Why were my mortals so damn rude? It was a simple request.

WILL YOU TAKE HIS DISRESPECT, DAUGHTER? NOT EVEN YOUR SISTER WOULD ALLOW MORTALS TO WALK ALL OVER HER. SHE WASN'T THAT SOFT.

Soft? Me? *I'll show you, Mother.*

My mortals *would* respect me.

I ground my teeth and found Gast's soul within my subconscious. One quick yank dragged his arse through the aether.

Light pulsed in the room, and his naked body appeared out of thin air. He landed on his knees with a strangled gasp and then glared up at me.

"Was that necessary?"

I crossed my arms. "Maybe next time you'll answer me with a little more respect."

"Oh, for gods' sake." Harmony snapped her fingers at Vincent. "Can we get some clothes over here?" She shot me an unimpressed look. "You can't keep on killing and rebirthing mortals every time you don't get your way. Keep it up, and you'll inspire another generation of Godless."

Wasn't that the point?

Vincent strode over with a pair of trousers and a shirt for Gast, as though he'd prepared a set in advance. He handed them over, and I didn't take my eyes off Gast as he redressed.

How was that for respect?

BETTER.

"You may go," I dismissed Vincent.

He exchanged a wary glance with Harmony, his thoughts a whirlwind of concern, and then left us alone. Course, Vincent hadn't needed to use his cane since the party, not that he'd noticed.

"Well?" I asked Gast. He was taking his sweet time doing up his shirt. Buttons weren't that complicated.

"You can't take the memories from my mind?"

Technically, I could, but he was the detective—he'd see things differently from his perspective. That, and I wanted to see if he'd lie to me. "I hired you for the job, so deliver."

Gast looked as though he wanted to retort, but thought better of it. "Noct and I traced the targets to Sinner's Row, where we observed." He didn't need to explain his intimate knowledge of Sinner's Row. I'd seen his memories, his past. That shithole was his home. "Arkey and Corinth are based in a cat café with the Fauna. They're working closely together."

I knew Kayl had gotten in with the Fauna somehow. But if they were hiding out in Sinner's Row, they weren't doing it under Erosain's nose. "Where's Erosain in all this?"

"Dead. The Fauna have taken over."

Which meant Edana was aware of the Fauna and likely aware of Kayl and Corinth.

Which meant Edana was a two-timing hussy.

I WARNED YOU, DAUGHTER, Mother drawled.

How dare she betray me before I had a chance to betray her first! That bitch.

"Keep watch over them and pray to me as *soon* as you learn something worthwhile." I gave Gast a pointed look. If he'd come to me sooner with this info, then I wouldn't have been caught off guard by Corinth's damn portal.

He nodded curtly. "As you wish."

I waited until he was out of earshot and then let out a sigh. "Being betrayed sucks arse."

"Some might describe it as cosmic payback," Harmony commented.

"What's that supposed to mean?"

"You *did* betray Kayl."

"Hey, she betrayed me first!" We'd had a bit of back-and-forth with the old betrayal, though really, that was all Sinder's fault. He was a bigger traitor than me, and judging from the images flashing through Gast's recent memories, Kayl had forgiven Sinder a lot quicker than she'd ever forgiven me.

It wasn't like I'd been part of her life for thirteen shitty years, or protected her or anything! Ugh!

"What are you going to do about it?"

"You tell me. You're my advisor. Advise."

Harmony tucked her hands behind her back and rocked on her heels. "Erosain's dead. About time, really. If the Fauna have taken over Sinner's Row, then that's a defensible position. They could hold out there against the Diviner, if the Diviner decide to pay them any attention. It also means you can't touch them."

"I can touch them if I fucking want—"

"Do you want to reveal your hand to Edana so soon? The moment she realizes you know she's betrayed you, the Ember will turn on you. Is that the kind of firepower you want raining down on this clock tower?"

Suppose not. "So I let them get away with betraying me?"

"You play along with Edana's game. See what her angle is."

"You just don't want me killing Kayl's allies."

"Kayl's allies are all in this room, listening to you."

Not all of them. Not yet. I still needed Sinder's soul, and whatever the fuck had happened to Dru. And maybe I needed to catch Corinth somehow. That would really fuck with Kayl the most, and he carried souls I needed.

"Rushing in and causing mayhem is exactly what the gods expect of Chaos," Harmony continued. "So don't be a fool."

"No, rushing in and being a twat is what Kayl would do. Just because we look alike, doesn't mean we are alike."

"You're right." Harmony gave me a cool look. "Kayl is far more pleasant to talk to."

Wasn't I fucking *trying*?

Fuck this. Being inside the clock tower was souring my mood, especially when my own damn mortals kept staring at me.

They saw me as a monster, and I was nowhere near as bad as their gods had been. I wasn't Gildola, or The Nameless One. I'd liberated them—actually achieved something the Godless never had.

THEY SHOULD BE THANKING YOU AND THROWING THEMSELVES AT YOUR FEET IN WORSHIP. WHERE IS THEIR DEVOTION?

Mother was right. Where was the respect?

WHAT DO YOU EXPECT FROM MORTALS? THEY WILL IMPRISON YOU NEXT.

Was that what I could expect from my future? In thanks for me freeing mortals, saving their sorry arses, they'd eventually rise up and lock me away in a clock tower? Turn me into a glorified power source next?

Then what the fuck was I doing?

I headed for the door leading out of the clock tower.

"Where are you going?" Harmony called.

"Out." I switched to my Fauna magpie form, leaving my dress behind, and took to Central's skies. I needed to clear my head and think, and I couldn't do it with her scowling at me.

How had Kayl put up with her all those years? She was *such* an arsehole.

Central was quiet in the evening with no mortals left to hit the pubs, sing rowdy songs, and piss in the street. The city was still lit with all those damn streetlamps everywhere—a waste of energy if you asked me—though from this height, I'd admit they looked rather pretty the way they glittered.

I circled the clock tower and let the wind massage my feathers. Flying was fun. Almost as much fun as getting my clit licked, though thanks to Edana betraying me, it wouldn't be the same. Sure, Serenity was eager, but Serenity creeped me out.

You knew what you got with Edana. Smoking hot sex. Real passion. Fucking betrayal.

The Godless didn't trust me or like me. My own mortals feared me. All that was completely understandable. I hadn't spent all that time in my sister's head to not see how shitty the gods were. That was why it was up to me to destroy them all and save the day.

Maybe *then* they'd respect me. Like me.

But was that enough? The Glimmer and Necro sure as shit didn't act any more respectful since I'd killed their gods.

Maybe they needed more action than what I was giving them. They were bloodthirsty creatures, and I wasn't talking about the Necro. The Glimmer *loved* making other mortals suffer. No, flogging them wouldn't do any good, but handing them the reins? Setting them off on a holy quest to spread a little oppression? Oh, they loved that shit.

So that was my plan. Kayl had made friends with the Fauna, so now I had to go and take her new friends. I'd return to the clock tower and let everyone know by yelling, *All right, you fuckers, we're going to kill another god.*

The party may have been a bust, but I bet they'd enjoy a fun picnic in Juniper.

I wasn't letting Kayl steal the Fauna from underneath me.

IT MAKES ME HAPPY TO SEE YOU ENJOY YOURSELF, DAUGHTER, Mother said. *BUT DO NOT GET CARRIED AWAY. REMEMBER WHAT CAUSE YOU SERVE.*

Like I'd forget. *I'm working on it.*

IMAGINE WHAT WE WILL ACHIEVE WHEN I AM FREE. WE WILL MAKE THE UNIVERSE OURS.

A godless universe. Just as Kayl wanted.

I swooped back around and flew over the station. The immortals who'd rampaged through here had done a number on the place. It was fucking wrecked. The chairs in the waiting area were scattered, and trash had been thrown everywhere. No one remained here—the Diviner and Umber had finally abandoned it, leaving crates and other supplies behind.

There wasn't much point in staying since the Gate was broken in half. But I wanted to make sure they hadn't left any booby traps.

I flew on down to the private waiting room and perched on a windowsill. My magpie eyes were great at spotting movement, but so far so good.

The door had been left ajar, so I hopped on inside.

BE CAUTIOUS.

I'm always cautious.

This waiting room had also seen better days. Clothes were scattered across the couches, and a thick layer of dust coated the tables, magazines, and lampshades. I followed the corridor through to the ambassador suite.

It was empty, except for a collection of discarded teacups. The Diviner had certainly been using this space. Would they return and use it again? Maybe I should leave a few booby traps of my own.

Dor wouldn't give up his attacks so easily. No, they'd break for a cup of tea and a shitty digestive biscuit, and then pick up where they'd left off. Like clockwork.

Without the Zephyr on my side, there wasn't an easy way to rig this place.

If only we still had Chance. He loved tinkering.

Silver flashed behind me.

I flew behind a cushion as a Diviner walked into the room. Alone.

Not just any Diviner. A woman. I'd recognize that perfect stride anywhere, and the neat bob of silver hair with a single streak of bronze that framed her pretty little face.

I leaped up and swapped forms to my Glimmer body. "Penny. What a surprise!" I grinned.

Penny spun and aimed a taser at me. Her silver eyes opened wide. "Jinx?"

Fuck me!

Her face.

The grin fell from my lips. Scars covered her face. Words carved into her skin, covering every inch of her cheeks, her forehead. They were bloody and raw, as though they'd been cut recently.

"Did Dor do that to you?"

Penny's face reddened, and she touched the scar below her left eye, which said *apostate*.

I changed my form to Necro. "I can heal them." One single touch and I'd wipe them away. I stepped toward her. "Let me—"

"No!" She brought the taser back up again. "Don't. If you heal them, Dor will only apply them again."

I clenched my fists beside my hips and seethed. "That sick fuck." As if I needed another reason to hate Dor. "I'll take him down for you."

"I wouldn't advise it."

"No? Got cold feet after we took down Gildola?" I swapped my form back to my Glimmer body. "What do you think? Does it suit me?"

"Yes, though I hardly think that's a compliment." Penny rolled her shoulders, and her composure slid back into place. *There* was that cocky smirk.

The one I wanted to taste.

It had only been a couple of weeks ago we'd conspired to bring down Solaris. Most of the planning had been hers—I'd just had to act my part and convince Sinder to betray my sister. Okay, it had felt a *little* weird working alongside a Diviner, but Penny wasn't like those stuck-up time-keeping wankers. And she was nothing like Corinth.

No, Penny had a flair of Chaos about her, right down to the brass streak in her hair. She was a woman who knew exactly what she wanted and wasn't afraid to destroy a few domains to get it.

And that was fucking *hot*.

BE WARY OF TIME'S CHARMS, Mother warned.

Don't worry, I'm not Kayl. I didn't spread my legs for Diviner.

But that didn't mean I couldn't have a little fun. "I didn't lie when I promised to take down your domain. Unfortunately, we Chaos run on our own schedule. But don't worry. You're still on my to-do list."

"How do you plan to invade Kronos? We've improved our security since our last encounter, and the Gate is no longer operational."

"Where's the fun if I reveal all my plans?"

"What plans?" she drawled. "If I recall, you required *me* to do the thinking for you."

Cheeky cunt. "That's funny." I tapped my bottom lip. "Your domain has launched multiple attacks against the clock tower, and yet we're still standing, and, oh, look at the *state* of this place! Where did your Diviner go? Did they get scared?"

Her eyes narrowed. Was I pissing her off? Too bad! "A strategic retreat is wise when a brutish god decides to grace us with his presence. Make no mistake—we *will* destroy the clock tower." She flashed me a sweet smile. "It's only a matter of time."

"Give it your best shot." I blew a kiss.

Penny fired the taser.

I ducked. The shot fizzled over my shoulder, and sparked against the wall. That wasn't what I'd meant!

She took aim again, and I charged. I rammed into her side, knocking her off her feet, so she landed backwards on the couch.

I slapped the taser from her hand.

Then I was straddling her.

She squirmed, but was only pushing us further up the couch. The poor woman didn't know where to put her hands, and finally chose to place them on my waist.

Her touch shuddered through me, as though her palms were made of aether.

As though *she* were Chaos, and was about to rip out my soul.

I leaned over her, my breasts pressing against her blouse, our lips close enough that I could taste the lingering scent of tea on her breath.

Penny froze, those silver eyes opening wide, her chest rising in rapid gulps. That pretty face turned a delicious shade of pink that made her scars less noticeable.

Fuck, those lips were so plump. Her tongue ran over them in a single lick, leaving a glistening trail of saliva.

"Where's your god now?" I whispered.

She swallowed. "Watching over me, as always."

Diviner burst into the room.

Fuck!

I leaped from Penny while transforming into a magpie.

Three Diviner males had entered the room, blocking the only exit.

"Take her alive!" Penny ordered.

Another taser fired and missed my left wing. The Diviner aimed their shots, but as a magpie, I was a much smaller target. I flew under one Diviner's legs, and the other actually tasered him in the balls! He fell to the floor with a pleasing shriek.

Fucking idiots.

The other Diviner tried to swipe me out of the air.

I waggled my tail feathers and shat on his face.

Okay, maybe that wasn't dignified, but I didn't give a fuck.

Penny had lured me in with her wiles and attempted to trap and capture me.

She wanted *me*!

Maybe it was the adrenaline of being chased, but I couldn't keep myself from laughing, my tiny beak clicking with giggles.

It was *exhilarating*.

I flew out of the waiting room, dodging another pair of idiot Diviner men, who stumbled after me, but I made it out of the station into open skies.

Shouting followed, and then faded the higher I flew.

THAT WAS TOO CLOSE, Mother chided. *WHEN YOU PUT YOURSELF IN HARM'S WAY, YOU ENDANGER US BOTH.*

How was I to know Penny would be there?

YOU HAVE AFFECTION FOR THIS 'PENNY.'

No, she's another dumb-arse Diviner.

THEN WHY DIDN'T YOU STEAL HER SOUL?

I could have.

I could have made her mine.

So why hadn't I?

BECAUSE YOU ARE NO DIFFERENT FROM YOUR SISTER, AND YOU WILL MAKE THE SAME MISTAKES.

That stung. I was way smarter than Kayl. Hadn't I protected the clock tower? Taken down two gods? Negotiated with two others and built a damn army?

YET SHE REMAINS AHEAD OF YOU. SHE HAS TAKEN EDANA FROM UNDER YOUR NOSE. AND NOW CORINTH CAN SUMMON PORTALS.

Mother's disappointment hurt. *I've got a plan. It won't fail.*

THEN FOCUS.

Focus. The one thing I could do that Kayl couldn't.

Everyone thought the stars shone from her arse. No one believed what I was truly capable of. Not Harmony, or Gast, or Vincent, or even Joe.

But I'd fucking show them.

I'd show them all.

24

Can you believe it? The Gate's been down for days, now. I was supposed to receive a custom-bound manuscript from a printer back in the Golden City, and now I have absolutely no way of contacting them.
When is the Gate going to open again?
It was rather odd, though, wasn't it? Never seen the Gate power down like that before. Did you read Aberforth's announcement?
Something about an incident in Chime? Golly gosh.
—Anonymous, *overheard in Mr. Kipler's, Memoria*

WE RETURNED FROM GLADYS'S Golden Boutique with bags full of clothes, as much as we could carry. I'd chosen a selection of floral dresses for myself while Quen finally found a tan suit that fit him, and then I'd picked out a few choice outfits for Nelle. I was sure the Lioness would appreciate wearing something that hadn't been scavenged from a brothel. I'd also packed one of those ridiculous hats with the feathers for the cubs to play dress-up with.

It was gone midnight by the time we were done. Quen ran himself a quick bath while I busied myself filling my wardrobe. The dresses I'd technically stolen were worth hundreds of bocs, but what did that matter when society had collapsed?

Who knew the end of the world could be so lucrative.

They were gorgeous dresses. I'd be the envy of Sinner's Row. The Fauna spent too much time scurrying about naked to truly appreciate fashion. Really, what did they have against clothing? They were missing out. Except for Trixie. She appreciated the finer things in life. Perhaps I should take her on a shopping spree. It might loosen her up a little.

Sinder would definitely appreciate these.

"All yours." Quen exited the bathroom, wrapped in a towel. His silver hair was a fuzzy mess, and I could smell the soap from across the room.

Maybe now I'd get a proper chance to wrap my mouth around that cock.

"Wait up for me." I sauntered to the bathroom and gave him a little shake of my arse and a wink. I needed to freshen up, too. Today had been a *day*.

I'd failed to win over Dru or Unghard, but we'd crossed Lionheart off our list and saved the Lioness and her cubs to boot.

And we were only getting started.

By the time I'd finished washing and preening myself, Quen was fast asleep.

So much for a repeat performance.

I slipped on a silk nighty and climbed into bed next to him. He'd had an exhausting day, so I couldn't blame him. Besides, there'd be time to take advantage of his morning glory.

I snuggled closer to him and rested my head on his left shoulder. "Thank you," I whispered.

For everything.

He'd come so far in the past few days since he'd lost his arm. He was still my Quen, and every bit the man my dreams had wanted him to be. Gods, it had been too long since I last fucked; I couldn't even remember, and I hadn't realized how desperately I'd needed it. Not just the release, but the touch of another. The closeness.

The agonizing wait had been worth it. I'd always known Quen was a sinner, deep down, and the way he'd practically worshipped my body was divine apostasy.

How could a Diviner go through his life with those skills and consider them a sin? What wasted potential. Diviner utterly squandered their gifts.

Gods. Quen had opened the floodgates, and now my horniness was back *on*.

Fuck, I wanted him. I wanted *more*.

But Quen needed his sleep, so I'd have to behave until morning. Gosh darn it!

Sheer luck had brought Quen into my life.

Whatever fate, or Mesmorpheus, had planned for me, I didn't fear it.

Nor did I fear the gods. Dor, or Corentine.

With Quen by my side, I had no reason to fear.

Together, we'd take on the universe, and the universe would shake.

When I woke, the bed was empty.

I rubbed the sleep from my eyes as I sat up. "Quen?"

The bathroom wasn't occupied, and Quen's clothes, shoes, and metal arm weren't here. Was it wrong of me to feel disappointed?

Mama! Cosmo yelled inside my head. *You need to wake up! It's Papa!*

What's happening? Are you safe? I yanked off the sheets and launched myself from the bed. Gods, if something had happened to Quen...

He won't let me have more than four spoons of sugar! He says three is plenty, and that we have to share, but I saw Castor add six spoons to his tea!

What? I sank back down onto the edge of the bed and rubbed my forehead. *Quen is with you? Wait, never mind, I'm coming down.*

I quickly dressed and headed downstairs, where Quen was pouring tea for an audience in the restaurant. The trio were arguing over the sugar cubes as a group of younger Fauna including Freddie sat in awe.

"And thus the perfect cup of tea has been brewed," Quen was explaining. Gods, was he giving a lecture on *tea making*? "Boiling water first, followed by a dash of milk, and then one may add a *reasonable* amount of sugar to taste." Yes, he was.

"Six sugars is reasonable," Cosmo sulked.

Freddie put his hand up. "What happens if you put the milk in first?"

"Why, the very universe itself implodes." Quen shuddered. "I wouldn't recommend it. Now, what is the perfect accompaniment to a good cup of tea?"

The Fauna exchanged glances.

"Two bourbon biscuits," I called out.

Quen finally noticed me standing in the crowd, and his face lit with a smile that sent my heart fluttering. "The amount of bourbon biscuits is, of course, according to taste."

"My ma likes digestives," said one of the Fauna.

"To each their own. Now, everyone help themselves to a cup, but do be careful. It's quite hot."

Quen finished pouring the Fauna tea and then came to my side with a sheepish smirk. "The Mesmer and Fauna aren't well versed in the matter of tea. I thought it my duty to teach them the proper manner."

"Did you now?" I snorted. "You're such a dork."

Freddie came over carrying a cup between his hands. "Is it okay if I bring this to Autumn? She's not been feeling too well since... since she came back."

"Of course," Quen said. "We can always brew more."

"Thanks, mister." Freddie waddled off with the cup balanced carefully.

Come to think of it, I hadn't seen Autumn around. "I should go check up on them."

"Before you do, I'd like to have a private word, if I may?"

"Does it involve me getting on my knees?"

His cheeks flushed red. "Regarding our next moves."

"You're no fun."

"There'll be time for fun when the gods are dead."

He said it with such passion that my knees went weak. "You really say exactly what a woman wants to hear."

He playfully rolled his eyes and then led me to a private larder inside the restaurant's kitchen. It was surprisingly well stocked with packaged and canned goods. They must have restocked with supplies from Sinner's Row.

"Oh!" A shiny orange can caught my eye. "They've got canned peaches!" I reached to snatch one, but Quen took my hand.

"Focus for a moment, please." There was a strain in his voice. Something was bothering him.

I tucked my hands behind my back. "Go on."

"I woke early this morning, as I wanted to test the capabilities of my new arm with Doctor Finch's assistance." Quen flexed his metal fingers as he spoke. They didn't quite move naturally, but his control was improving. "Specifically, to test if it's waterproof."

"Waterproof?"

"It's time I visited Memoria and restored your memories. We need the Vesper back."

"All right. We'll come up with a plan." We needed to target Anima eventually, but Memoria would be one of the hardest domains to crack thanks to the entire place being under bloody water. Anima was also a slimy bastard. They'd fucked with my memories and made me forget my connection with the Vesper. That in itself was worth revenge.

"I already have a plan in place." He took in a breath, as though what he was about to say would anger me. "I'll be traveling to Memoria alone."

I hated being right. "What? No, that's a stupid idea—"

"If we both enter Memoria, then we risk getting caught in Anima's net. I won't endanger your memories—"

"But you'll endanger yours? Haven't you done that enough? Quit your chivalrous shit!"

He winced. "It's precisely because I have gone through it that I know what can be restored should things go wrong. I asked you to trust me when I challenged Lionheart. I'm asking you to trust me again."

I chewed my tongue. Of course I trusted Quen. I trusted him more than I did any man, any mortal, alive. He *had* beaten Lionheart... "I don't like it. If we work together, we stand a better chance of taking down Anima."

"Brute force won't defeat Anima. I know the Amnae, and they require a diplomatic touch."

"You're saying I can't be diplomatic?"

"I'm saying this is my area of expertise. Please let me handle it."

Could I argue with that? The man had studied at the Academy, for gods' sake, whereas I'd literally crawled up from the Undercity as a blight on society. He had the political education, the Warden training, the brains of a Diviner.

Honestly, I often forgot his upbringing was so far above mine, because Quen never belittled me. I never felt less-than in his presence, nor would I ever allow myself to.

But for all I'd studied politics with Varen, and for my brief spell as an ambassador, I could freely admit I wasn't part of Quen's world. I'd tried to drag him down to my level, and now...

Gods, the whole idea left me queasy, but he was asking for my permission, not demanding my submission. I had to trust he knew what he was doing. "All right."

He breathed a sigh of relief. "Wonderful. When I travel through, I'll leave my pistol and fob watch with you for safekeeping."

"Don't you need your watch to get back?"

"If all goes well, I should manage to get back without it. And I'd rather not risk this technology falling into the wrong hands. Should things go awry, then you will have a means of accessing the domains."

"Rescuing you, you mean."

"If it comes to that." He forced a smile. "You know how it works. I'll be leaving on the hour—"

"The *hour*?" I'd only gotten one chance to fuck him senseless, and he was running off to pissing Memoria? Was this because I'd laughed off his random marriage proposal? Gods, I thought he'd been joking!

"Time is of the essence. The longer I dally, the greater the chance Dor will convince Anima to become an ally, and that would make for a dangerous combination. It's best I nip that in the bud before it's too late. And the sooner I restore your memories, the sooner we can bring the Vesper back, and anything else Anima may have taken."

I hated that his words made sense. Quen was doing this for the Vesper, but also for me. God knows what else Anima had done to my mind.

I did miss being a Vesper. It had been my life for thirteen years.

"Do I at least get to fuck you before you go?"

His cheeks again turned that lovely Ember shade. "I'm afraid I need time to prepare. But once I'm back, I'm all yours."

"Promises." Apparently, I couldn't have my cake and eat it too. And now I really wanted cake. The Mesmer must have stashed some around here somewhere.

I let him get on with whatever it was he needed to do and scrounged up some breakfast. Since Trixie had taken over Sinner's Row, the food choices in the hotel's restaurant had improved. I managed to put together a plate of scrambled eggs, plum tomatoes, and toast with melted butter to scoop the tomato juices with. The Fauna had these little sausages cooking on a grill, but god knows what poor unfortunate mortal they'd been made out of.

By the time I'd had seconds, made a cup of tea, found actual coffee, and rescued that can of peaches, Quen was ready.

We made space within the restaurant. Quen had attracted another audience of Fauna, as well as the Mesmer trio, and this time Nelle, Dandelion, and the cubs came down. They wore the clothes I'd gotten them, and the cubs were cautiously trying the sausages.

"Are you off on another adventure?" Dandelion said. "All work and no play, that one!"

"I wanted to play, but apparently adventure is far more appealing," I said.

"Please," Quen said. "I'm doing this for the future of the domains."

"How could you leave this stunning beauty behind?" Dandelion nudged me. "Pah!"

Because this was an act of love for Quen. He was doing it for me.

I wrapped my arms around Quen's waist. "Stay safe. I'll be incredibly mad if you get yourself killed."

He rested his metal arm across the small of my back. "I have Doctor Finch watching over me. He refuses to let me die."

I tapped him on the forehead. "Then I'm depending on you, Doctor."

"I can also communicate via Dandelion, should I run into trouble. Keep him nearby, and he can pass on messages. Try not to fret." Quen cupped my cheek with his other hand and leaned in for a kiss.

I grabbed his jacket and yanked him close; our lips pushed together and opened into something that would make an Ember blush.

Dandelion whooped.

Quen broke the kiss with a breathlessness that made me reconsider this whole thing. But then he was winding up his pocket watch, and a heartbeat later, a portal to Memoria appeared.

Memoria looked exactly as I remembered it. Buildings made of teal and brass pipes lined the tiled streets, and were decorated in shell patterns. Above, water rippled beyond the glass dome, casting wavy light. Memoria was so different from any other domain. It was a wonder it existed at all.

Quen pressed the pocket watch into my palm. "Give me twenty-four hours." He stole one last kiss—a peck on the cheek—and then he strode for the portal.

My heart thumped inside my chest. This was happening too fast. I could run after him. I could leap inside before the portal shut, toss the pocket watch through, and then Quen would be forced to let me tag along.

Someone took my hand. Gods, I jumped out of my skin! But it was only Cosmo.

"He'll be okay," Cosmo said.

"Have you seen a vision?"

"No, but Papa is smart. Not about sugar, but about other things."

I bit my lip as Quen stepped through the portal. There was still time to run, to catch up—

The portal blipped out.

Shit.

A few gasps swept through the crowd watching us. I glanced over my shoulder. Trixie stood by the restaurant doors with Wolfsbane. The old wolf had finally seen to his wound, as a thick bandage wrapped around his torso, though he looked almost sad that he couldn't join Quen in his battle against another god.

Trixie, however, looked annoyed. That expression made me uneasy, though I was sure Trixie suffered from a chronic case of resting bitch face.

Another figure lurked by the door. A tall man in a dark trench coat, the collar turned up so I couldn't see his face. Something about his poise seemed familiar, but I couldn't put my finger on it.

Cosmo squeezed my hand, bringing me back to the present. They were sweet, really. With the amount of sugar they ate, they had to be.

"Come on, then." I slid the pocket watch down my blouse. "Let's go check on Autumn and Freddie."

"We could bring them some sweets?"

"Good idea."

Twenty-four hours, Quen had said. Twenty-four hours. I could manage.

Cosmo led me upstairs to the room Autumn and Freddie were sharing. From what I understood of the Fauna, the pair of them were as close as siblings without being actual siblings. That was a bond I could understand and cherish.

I missed my Godless family terribly. Harm, Vincent, Dru, Reve. At least I still had Sinder. I'd check in with him later and reminisce over a good bottle of wine to help pass these pissing twenty-four hours.

"Come in," Freddie called when Cosmo knocked on the door.

We entered a room much smaller than mine. It held no bed, but instead some sort of tent in the center, made of pillows and bed-sheets. A den of sorts. Maybe beds weren't comfortable for animal shape-shifters.

Autumn was seated underneath it on a cushion, her expression blank.

Gods. I recognized that expression.

Something wasn't right.

Freddie stood beside her, swaying on his feet. "She's been like this ever since she came back. She won't even eat or drink unless I tell her to. What's wrong with her?"

Cosmo held out a light green Fauna jelly baby for Autumn. Lime flavor. "For you."

The fox girl didn't even blink.

"Autumn, try it," I said.

She took the jelly baby and ate it without hesitation.

"See?" Freddie flumped onto a cushion, his rat whiskers twitching.

I kneeled in front of her. "Autumn, can you hear me?"

She stared at me, her brown eyes vacant. Lifeless. "Yes."

"Do you remember who you are?"

"No."

That wasn't a good sign. "Give me your hand."

She willingly offered it. I took her hand in mine and pressed my palm against hers. There should have been a tingle, a pulse of energy I could grab to take her soul.

But there was nothing.

Her soul wasn't there.

Autumn had been so full of life and energy and fire, and that fire was gone.

It was *gone*.

Panic spread through me until it threatened to make me vomit. The Diviner had already split her soul and turned her into a mindless slave, just as the Glimmer had been doing back on Solaris. The other captured Fauna had likely suffered the same fate, and I'd not even checked in with them to notice! Gods, Trixie and Wolfsbane probably assumed they were in shock, not that they'd had their souls *ripped* from them.

Which meant Quen and I had arrived too late to save them. We'd failed. Shitting shit!

Pendula knew. That fucking bitch *knew*. She'd scanned Wolfsbane's memories, she'd seen where we'd made our base and that we'd brought the soulless Fauna back with us.

And I, in my absolute fucking idiocy, had forgotten to warn Trixie.

We were all in danger.

Quen had picked a damn fine time to go running off to Memoria!

I climbed to my feet. "Cosmo, wait here. I need to find Trixie."

I hurried out of the room and then jogged down the stairs to the office Trixie had been using before they moved out to Erosain's bar, praying they were inside. As luck would have it, the light was on. I didn't bother to knock as I burst inside.

"We've got a prob—"

Someone slammed into me, knocking me into the filing cabinet and making it rattle. A cold hand grasped my neck, and an electric spasm shot down my spine. My limbs fell uselessly at my sides.

"Damn right we have a problem," said the man in the trench coat.

"Gast," I gasped.

The formerly dead Necro propped me up against the wall. He'd paralyzed my body, but left my head free to breathe, blink, and speak. The last time we'd spoken, The Nameless One had taken him and Vincent prisoner, demanding I bring Jinx as an offering to release them. I'd had no choice but to leave them behind.

Then his feral form had attacked us in Witheryn, before Jinx had blasted him to ashes.

But he was here. His face still the same pale Necro hue, but his eyes weren't bloodshot, no. They were full of colorful aether.

Which meant Jinx had brought him back, and he was here on her orders.

Great. Just what I needed right now.

"Didn't expect to see me again, did you?"

"I'm sorry—"

"Lady, you left me to die in Witheryn. Apologies won't cut it."

"The Nameless One took you! They wanted my sister in exchange for your release and Vincent's, which I fully intended to do, but then she kidnapped me, dragged me to Solaris, and all this shit in Chime happened. I was coming back for you both."

His eyes narrowed. "Convenient. Shame I know what's really going on."

"Whatever Jinx has told you is a lie—"

"Runs in the family, does it? What do you say, Trix?"

Gast swiveled my body so I caught sight of the desk. Trixie leaned back in her chair, her lips in a tight frown. Noct hovered over her shoulder, his wings a blur. We'd lost him in Witheryn—I assumed Serenity had brought him back, too.

"You let a spy *inside*?" I said, appalled.

"Gast's an old acquaintance of mine," Trixie said. "And a lot more trustworthy. 'E's been filling me in on a few missing details. Like 'ow you and your shitty twin are responsible for every bad damn thing to befall this city. Eventide? Solaris? Gone because of you. And that's your plan, isn't it? 'Op between the domains and fucking destroy them—"

"I'm trying to save the domains from my sister!"

"Is that what you and your mate did to Obituary? You 'saved' it?"

"Jinx wants an end to the domains, to destroy them for good. Quen and I are taking the domains to *protect* them from her—to remake their mortals free from their gods—"

"Jinx took Solaris and Witheryn," Gast explained. "And she 'rebirthed' us. Only, our souls somehow belong to her, now. She reads our thoughts, controls our lives. Tortures us—"

"Which is why I'm trying to stop her!" I said, exasperated. "You've seen how we've brought back the Mesmer and Leander. We mean them no harm—"

"But you gave them no choice?" Trixie's feline eyes narrowed into slits. "Who the fuck are you to decide the fate of an entire domain?"

"The Leander were being tortured by their god. Ask Nelle—"

"So you took it upon yourselves to become their personal savior instead? Is that what you 'ave planned for my Fauna? To eventually invade Juniper and take us?"

"Your god doesn't even give a shit about you!"

"You don't know anything about Faen." Trixie snarled. "Faen offers us freedom. True freedom. They let us live our lives without interference. That means we can't pray for 'elp whenever we need it—we're on our own. No other domain 'as that, and I won't let you take it from us. Whatever Godless future you're offering, we don't fucking want it."

Shit, this wasn't going well.

"You took Eventide, didn't you?" Gast demanded. His voice was calm in that deadly way Necro spoke before ripping your throat out. "You lied to me—"

"I didn't lie—"

"You took the Vesper. So bring them back."

"I'd love to, but I can't."

"Little known fact about the Necro—we can enhance our own hearing. I overheard you and Mr. Dark Warden talking about saving the Vesper. Want to try answering me again?"

"Did you also overhear that he needs to travel all the way to Memoria to do so? The Vesper are trapped in my subconscious. I can't access them. Did Jinx not tell you *that*?"

Gast bared his fangs. "I want the fucking truth! Noct!" He glanced over his shoulder. "Serenade it out of her."

"Fat lot of good that will do!" I snorted.

Trixie covered her ears as Noct flew over to me with an apologetic look. At least he wasn't acting like a prick.

He drew a breath, and then sang the sweetest song I'd ever heard.

Pretty lady, I beseech you so,
Please tell us everything you know,
Help us fix the discord you sow,
Pray tell us, where did the Vesper go?

Warmth flooded my blood, as though I were suddenly drunk on wine and had taken a few Vesper mushrooms on top.

Gods. Noct really was a beautiful creature. The fact his skin was the perfect shade of Vesper blue only hurt my heart, and I shed a single tear.

"I loved a Vesper," I said. "A man named Malkavaan Byvich. He was Godless, and my friends and I called him Malk. He escaped Valeria's clutches and came to Chime as a child with his mother, Elvira. She took me in. I loved her too." The words spilled from deep within me. I barely understood what they meant.

I spoke of my childhood. Of when Malk and I were captured by the Wardens and dragged into Eventide. I spoke of the bargain Quen had made to try and spare him, when Valeria instead took him. Then I detailed the lengths I'd gone to save him.

My Malk.

And I spoke of when it all went wrong.

"I took Valeria's soul. It was an accident. I was trying to prevent Jinx from destroying Eventide, and in doing so, I was responsible. It broke me."

Gast exchanged a glance with Noct. "So why did you lie?"

"I didn't. When Quen named me ambassador for Chaos, I entered Memoria to negotiate with Ambassador Aberforth. He brought me to Anima, who chose to alter my memories and hide the Vesper within my subconscious so I wouldn't have access to Valeria's powers. It means I can't restore the Vesper, like Jinx restored you. Anima made me forget."

The fuzzy feeling in my mind faded, and with it, the knowledge of whatever I'd just spoken. Things I'd forgotten and couldn't quite reach, and yet a Seren had somehow broken beyond those barriers with the sheer magic of their song.

"What the fuck did you make me say?"

Gast rubbed his jaw with his spare hand. "The truth."

"Well. That was a lot," Trixie said.

"You're both idiots," I said. "Whatever you've made me confess will have gone right back to Jinx, which means she'll know I'm here. You've endangered us all."

"She already knows. She's—fuck!" Gast's head swiveled to the door. "She's here!"

Shit.

The door to the office burst open, and in ran Wolfsbane. "We've got—trouble?" He blinked at Gast holding me against a bloody filing cabinet, of all things.

Trixie sighed. "You may as well let 'er go." She gestured lazily at me. "If that's 'er evil twin outside, then we're fucked."

Another jolt shuddered through my spine. Gast released me, and I almost slipped down to my knees in surprise. He grabbed my arm to steady me, an apology in his expression.

All right, he'd screwed with me, but I'd screwed with him first.

"What's happening?" I asked Wolfsbane.

"You won't believe me, but... there's a naked statue outside and it's talking."

Oh *shit*.

"Serenity," Noct gasped.

"You're fucking kidding me?" Trixie leaped from her chair. "The Seren god? We've got the Seren god 'ere?"

I ran from the office to the main foyer. Some of the Fauna watched by the window, trying to catch a glimpse of the street outside. I barged past them.

There was Serenity, all right. This time in the form of a woman and standing in the middle of the pissing street as though she was debating a hot night in a cat café. A whole group of Seren surrounded her.

And standing next to her in that ridiculous red dress was Jinx.

Jinx put her hands to her mouth. "*Kayl,*" she called. "I know you're in there, sister. You better come out right now, or we'll huff and puff and blow this whole shitty building down. You've got ten seconds, so move your dumb arse before someone gets hurt."

25

There are several domains the Wardens classify as 'unsafe' merely to caution mortals from traveling to them unprepared. Juniper is one such domain. While its lush jungles may tempt intrepid adventurers, be aware these jungles are full of dangers—and that's before warning you of the Fauna themselves. Yes, Fauna can appear playful with an innocent sort of charm, but that itself is by design. Don't forget the Fauna have a Necro's taste for meat. Do not turn your back on them.
—Q. Corinth, *Warden Dossier on Juniper*

SHIT, SHIT, SHIT, SHIT, *shit*!

"Ten," Jinx began.

I'd always known this confrontation was bound to happen eventually, but I hadn't expected Jinx to learn of my partnership with the Fauna so soon. Gods, I'd expected the Diviner to be the ones kicking down our doors. Perhaps they were lurking in the shadows, waiting to see how this played out.

Had Edana betrayed me to Jinx? Or could I land the blame squarely on Gast for being the worst pissing private eye in Chime?

"Nine."

Shit! I pushed past the gawking Fauna and fished the pocket watch from my blouse. Quen had entrusted it to me. There was no way I could risk Jinx getting her hands on it. But where could I hide it?

"Eight."

I had mere seconds to decide.

I stumbled through the foyer to a vase holding a bunch of decorative twigs that had been spray-painted gold to fit the décor. It wasn't an ideal hiding spot, but I had little time for anything better. I checked no one was looking and slipped the pocket watch inside, letting it clank to the bottom.

"Four. You're tempting fate, sister."

"All right, I'm bloody coming!"

I yanked open the front doors and stepped outside.

Jinx waited next to Serenity with a whole flock of colorful Seren hovering in the air around them and a small entourage of Glimmer. Some Fauna and Ember loitered nearby, both frightened by the sight of a literal god standing in Sinner's Row, but Serenity looked simply bemused rather than murderous. A haven for sin may be her sort of crowd, though artistically, Sinner's Row was nothing special to look at.

"So this is where you've been hiding, sister."

I raised both hands, palms forward. "You got me."

"Looks like I was too late to grab your Time Boy, but never mind. We'll make the best of a shitty situation." She snapped her fingers.

The hotel doors opened once more as Gast strode out, his hand grasping Trixie's arm, and his face caught in a grimace. Wolfsbane and Noct followed, the former's wolflike features twisting between anxiety and rage.

It didn't take a PI to work out what had just happened. Jinx had ordered Gast to take Trixie hostage, and there was little Wolfsbane could do about it. Poor Noct flew on over to the Seren and joined their little circle, his head dipping as he passed Serenity.

"There," Jinx said. "That's better. Always a good idea to start negotiations with collateral."

"What do you want, Jinx?" I asked.

"The end of the gods, destruction of the domains, yada yada. But right now, what I want most of all is that pocket watch of Corinth's you're hiding."

Shit. Of course she wanted it. "I don't know what you're talking about."

"Don't play dumb, it's boring. I know Corinth can create portals with it. So here's the deal. You hand it over, and no one needs to get hurt. Sound fair?"

Gods damn it. The one advantage Quen and I had, and Jinx was here to sweep it away. If I handed it over, then Jinx would have unfettered access to whatever domain she liked, and we'd have no chance of keeping up, unless Quen could make a spare. But without Quen here, I had no clue if that was even possible.

But if I didn't hand it over, then Trixie, Wolfsbane, and the rest of the Fauna were at risk. Sure, I'd given them Sinner's Row for their own protection, but what use was that now with an actual god standing among us? Serenity and Edana were allies. The Ember wouldn't step in to save them.

And yet, if Jinx entered Juniper and got hold of Faen, the Fauna were doomed regardless.

I glanced at Trixie, who had likely reached the same conclusion, judging by her grim face. "Fuck 'er," she spat.

"Wow, rude." Jinx grinned. "I like you. We'll take you last."

"Look, I don't have it," I said. "Quen took it with him when he left for Memoria—"

"Except, I know you're lying, because I saw him hand it over to you through Gast's eyes."

Yes, I was definitely blaming Gast for this shitty mess. "Well, I lost it."

"That's slightly more believable given it's *you*, but I know you're talking shit. Guess it's time for a demonstration." Jinx's form changed to Necro, for some reason, and she nodded to Serenity. "Go ahead."

"With pleasure," Serenity crooned. "Sing, my little doves."

The Seren began to sing.

I instantly covered my ears. Wolfsbane and the surrounding Fauna went to do the same, but then stone hands broke through the cobblestone street and grabbed their arms, wrenching them back. Serenity's doing. The god was holding them in place and preventing them from protecting themselves.

The singing held no vocals. It began with a hum that slowly turned into a high-pitched whine. I'd heard of opera singers who could hit notes so high, they shattered glass, and it seemed these Seren were attempting the same.

The Fauna shook their heads back and forth, but their groans were lost to the Seren's shrieking. Some turned into smaller animal forms in an attempt to get away, but they remained crushed in Serenity's stone hold, unable to escape.

"Make it stop!" Wolfsbane screamed. He writhed, switching from his half-animal form to his wolf shape, and back again. Multiple changes within the blink of an eye, each accompanied with a scream, a howl.

Gods, I couldn't take it anymore! "Stop it, Jinx!"

But Jinx only smiled.

She either wasn't listening or couldn't hear me. What was it Gast had said? That he could manipulate his own hearing? I glanced at him, my hands still firmly clasped over my own ears. He stood impassive, gripping Trixie's shoulder. She looked horrified, but gods, she couldn't hear Wolfsbane's cries.

Gast had somehow deafened her.

The pitch grew so loud, it was as though a hot knife pierced my skull.

Blood trickled from Wolfsbane's ears.

And then his head exploded.

Oh my god!

Bits of flesh and brain matter flew through the air, raining down on Sinner's Row. His body deflated like a sad balloon, and then faded altogether.

More of the Fauna popped in a similar way, their heads bursting open in a shower of bloody pulp, eyeballs, and teeth.

Then the windows of the hotel shattered, and other windows along the street. Glass rained from above, and I ducked, crouching to avoid any stray shards. I could barely hear anything above the ringing of the Seren's song, and Trixie's garbled screaming.

The singing stopped, and Serenity withdrew his bloodstained stone hands. I slowly uncovered my ears, and yet the buzzing didn't quite leave me, though I wasn't sure if that was the aftereffects, or the sheer adrenaline pumping through my veins.

Jinx's form changed back to Glimmer. "Have I made my point, sister? Now, unless you want the Seren to put on a concert for every fucking Fauna in Sinner's Row, you'll find that pocket watch—"

"You *bitch*!" Trixie snarled. She tore from Gast's hold and launched herself at Jinx, claws outstretched.

Serenity casually snatched Trixie in midair, holding her up by her throat. The god looked Trixie over as she struggled and choked, clearly unimpressed. "What shall I do with this creature?"

"Let her live," Jinx said. "It's more fun that way. As I was saying—"

"Kill them all if you want." I lifted my chin. "You're not getting that watch."

Wolfsbane was dead, and gods, that *hurt*. I didn't want the Fauna to suffer at Jinx's hands, but death was better than being enslaved to her whims.

Shit. When had Jinx become another god to be brought down?

When we spoke of ending the reign of gods, was this really what she'd imagined? Had I been ignorant to who she truly was?

"Okay, sister." Jinx sighed. "I get it. You need a little extra incentive. See, I don't need your shitty pocket watch. Not when I have friends like these." She gestured to Serenity.

Serenity dropped Trixie like a sack of potatoes and waved her hand over Jinx.

A portal opened, but it hadn't opened to Arcadia, or at least the foliage on the other side wasn't like the tailored gardens the Seren so loved.

No, the forest on the other side was thick and dark, with giant tree trunks and leaves. It looked wild. Dangerous.

Shit.

She'd opened a portal to Juniper.

Jinx approached the portal. "I'm paying Faen a visit. Think you can stop me? Then you know how to reach me. See you soon." She blew me a kiss and stepped inside, her Glimmer accompanying her.

The portal snapped shut before I could even think.

Fuck!

Serenity and her Seren vanished at the same time, taking Gast with them, and leaving me alone with Trixie and the bloodstains as evidence the Fauna had lived here.

Trixie stumbled to the spot where Wolfsbane had died, her shoes crunching over glass. She fell to her knees in Wolfsbane's blood and let out a mournful wail.

"'E—'E was my mate!" she howled, tears streaming down her cheeks. "My mate."

I didn't know what to do, what to say. "I'm sorry—"

"No." Trixie stood and wiped her eyes dry. "You don't get to say sorry."

"I—"

"Shut *up*!" She was in my face in an instant, fangs bared. "Everything fell apart when *you* entered my fucking life!" She grabbed my neck, her claws digging into my skin.

"I can bring Wolfsbane back!" I spluttered before she could murder me.

Trixie blinked. Her grip around my neck eased, but didn't leave entirely. "'Ow?"

I sucked in a breath. "If I take Faen before Jinx does."

She released my neck and stepped back, her cat ears going flat. "If you're the only one who can stop your *bitch* of a sister, then I 'ave no choice, do I?" She stared at the bloodstain marring her dress. "I won't let it end like this. Not like this." She choked back a sob and then shook her fur, regaining her composure.

"I'll stop her."

"No, *we* will. You're not entering Juniper alone. You won't last five fucking seconds without me, and I want payback."

I didn't want to endanger Trixie—gods, I was sounding like Quen— but she was right. I couldn't go running into Juniper without a guide. I knew nothing about the domain, so my chances of finding Faen alone were next to none.

Plus, with a guide, I'd have an advantage over Jinx. With any luck, she'd get eaten by a carnivorous plant.

"Then let's go save your mortals."

Trixie's whiskers twitched. "What's left of them."

We quicky changed into more suitable clothing—the standard Fauna leggings and breast band they so favored. Trixie insisted on bringing a flask of water, and rope for some ungodly reason, but otherwise we left the hotel with little—only a string bag to hold clothes and Quen's pocket watch. I'd considered heading into Memoria and fetching Quen, but that would mean needing to find him first. Warning Dandelion wouldn't help. It would only make Quen worry, and I owed it to Trixie to sort this mess out myself.

Jinx was already one step ahead of us. We couldn't afford to waste time.

I changed my form to Chaos and set the pocket watch to ten past two. Juniper's hour. Before I could set it off, the hotel doors burst open, and out came Nelle dressed in a similar outfit to me. She must have taken it from my wardrobe.

I lowered the watch. "What are you doing?"

"You go into danger? I come. Protect you."

"You don't have to do that—"

"You saved me and my cubs. Of course I do."

"Stay. Watch over your cubs."

"And let you get eaten in a jungle and make your tiny man cry? No."

I sighed. "We don't have time for this—"

"Shouldn't the male be risking 'is life?" Trixie said. "Your mate with the mane—"

"He's my brother, and he's useless. He watches over my cubs while I kill." Nelle bared her fangs in demonstration. "They called me the Lioness. I called them meat."

Trixie shrugged. "Good enough for me. The jungle belongs to the cats."

That was lucky, then, since it was about to get three of us.

With a flash of aether, I opened a portal in the main street of Sinner's Row. It wasn't even lunchtime, and yet Juniper looked dark and foreboding. Honestly, staring inside it gave me worse chills than Eventide. At least I knew what to expect with the Vesper. Even the *Traveler's Handbook* warned of the dangers lurking inside the jungle.

Worse things than Jinx, perhaps.

Oh, Quen would kill me when he found out.

I touched Trixie's arm and changed back to my Fauna cat form. I followed her as she stepped through the portal first, with Nelle at my back. There was a chance Jinx was trying to trick me, and would snatch the watch as soon as I entered Juniper, but no. She was crazy enough to actually go after Faen and succeed.

Instead, I was attacked by a humidity similar to Memoria's. The air tasted heavy, with sweet scents that would get a Mesmer drunk. It wasn't difficult to work out why—we were surrounded by trees thicker than the clock tower, flowers larger than a Seren, and massive leaves that blocked out any natural sunlight, as though I were standing in Central with the Golden City plate looming above.

Though the noise surprised me the most. The sky was alive with a near-constant chittering, shrieking, and howling. Gods. No wonder mortals found this domain terrifying.

"This way." Trixie beckoned me to some invisible path apparently only she could see. The entire jungle floor was a mess of overgrown tree roots, dirt, and leaves, with no road in sight. Not even a few rocks to act as a path.

Well, she was right. I'd have no way to navigate this mess on my own. "Do you know where you're going?"

Trixie gave me a sharp look. "You've got our face, but not our instincts. Stay close, watch your footing, and *don't* eat anything."

"Why would I eat something?" *What* would I even eat?

"You seem like the kind of mortal who would put anything in their mouth without sniffing it first."

That was plain rude. Possibly accurate, but rude. Where had this reputation of mine come from? "Fine. Keep your secret delicacies."

"My mate has just died, if you could quit your shit."

"Sorry," I mumbled. "We *will* get him back."

"Too fucking right we will. We're 'eading east." Trixie pointed to a gap between two trees. If it wasn't for my feline eyes, I'm sure it would have looked pitch black. "I prayed to Faen, but they won't acknowledge or answer my prayers. We'll need to 'ead to their temple and attract their attention."

"It won't be as simple as knocking on their doors, then?"

"Faen's temple is 'idden behind impenetrable thorns."

I'd spent so many years warning mortals *not* to pray to their gods and attract attention that it was actually pissing annoying to be chasing after this one. "If it's impenetrable, then that should stop Jinx, surely?"

"Slow 'er down, maybe. I've got a plan to get us through."

Trixie led the way. This was her home, though it was hard to separate the classy cat lady drinking milky tea in her chair from this more feral cat with the permanent scowl. She'd been through a lot in the past few hours, and I hadn't even told her about Autumn.

Gods. I still didn't know how many Fauna I'd lost to Dor's insanity. All of them? I didn't have the heart to bring up the subject. Not when we had to get Wolfsbane back first.

All right, Kayl. Focus.

The trek through Juniper was perhaps the most laborious of my life. It was certainly no walk in Meridian Park.

We'd not brought shoes, which meant I relied on my catlike padded feet to navigate the uneven ground. My toes brushed against leaves, twigs, and slimy mud. Each touch sent a little jolt through my stomach, the sensations so utterly strange. We pushed past so many different types of trees, and not just the thick ones, but spindly ones, spiky bushes, and trees that wept with syrup. Thorns snagged on my string bag. I had to keep checking it for tears.

All the while, we were assaulted by buzzing things. Annoying flies wouldn't stop pestering me and earned a few slaps and a growl. I should have brought that stupid hat.

While I was struggling with the pissing flies, Trixie and Nelle both seemed in their element. Nelle strode comfortably, as though it was the most natural thing in the world. My padded feet may be meant for navigating jungles, but my mortal legs still ached.

"You are lucky," Nelle was saying. "That your god pays you no heed."

"You another Godless like 'er?" Trixie snorted.

"I am now. Most Leander were never worthy of Lionheart's attention, though they would scratch and nip at each other for the chance. And for what? I earned Lionheart's attention. Do you know what it cost me?"

I remained silent. This was Nelle's story, and if she needed to let it out now, in Juniper of all places, then I wouldn't stop her.

"Everything," Nelle continued. "He named me his champion. I was forced to fight in his arena every day. For each battle, he rewarded me in the way males think a woman deserves to be rewarded. He fucked me."

Gods. I knew Lionheart was disgusting, but that... "I'm so sorry that happened to you."

"Have you ever been taken by a god? You cannot say no. You are at their mercy. If I displeased him, he attacked my cubs. I could never displease him. Others, they hissed and spat at me. Jealous fools. Is that the attention you want from your god?"

"I never said I wanted to fuck Faen," Trixie murmured. "But we're Faen's mortals. During this whole shitshow, they've done nothing to 'elp us. Fuck, we couldn't even return to Juniper and escape the Diviner like every other damn domain. They abandoned us. We were forgotten by our own god."

"It's better to be forgotten," Nelle said.

I couldn't argue with her. "I thought you preferred your freedom?"

Trixie spun, blocking the path with her fangs bared. "What do you expect a Godless world to look like?"

"Like Chime. Mortals working together, supporting one another, without the gods dictating our lives."

"You'd do it all alone?"

"You've already been doing it alone, by the sounds of it."

Trixie snarled. Perhaps that had been a low blow.

"My point is," I hurried on before she abandoned me to the flies, "that you wouldn't be alone. You'd have other mortals, and we'd figure it out. Together."

"Chime can't even sort its own shit out. Mortals bicker and squabble. Not even the Covenant could prevent that. I was born in a brothel, but this land is where my blood comes from. It's where my soul belongs."

"Wild and free," Nelle mused. "What I want for my cubs."

The two of them exchanged a glance, and there was a connection between them I wasn't privy to. Maybe they thought I simply wasn't cat enough to understand, but I was Godless. Freedom was all we ever craved.

I trudged behind like a third wheel. The way Trixie had described Wolfsbane as her mate, had cried over him, I'd assumed Fauna mated for life or something.

Something felt off, and it took me a moment to realize what.

The shrieking of birds and animals had stopped. Even the flies had abandoned this place. It was eerily quiet.

I felt myself controlling my own breathing as we stalked further through the jungle. The only sound was the occasional snap of a twig, or the rustle of leaves, which sent my heart pumping. If Jinx was making her way through Juniper as we were, there weren't any signs she'd rampaged through here.

Something nipped at my feet, and I almost screamed.

Nelle was at my side in an instant. She grabbed the stalk of a plant that had teeth. Actual pissing teeth!

"Don't step into that," Trixie warned.

"Good bloody advice!"

She hushed us. "We're here. Faen's 'unting grounds."

That didn't sound ominous at all.

The tree line thinned. Before us lay an entire wall of thorns. Prickly dark gray things as tall as the clock tower, stretching on for eons. This was what Trixie had called impenetrable, and I believed it.

It was one way of keeping intruders out. "Is there a way through?" Even an Ember's flame would have difficulty with these thorns.

Trixie beckoned us on until we reached some sort of red rock. It had been chiseled into a flat slab, with manacles attached.

A stone altar. It hadn't been painted red. It was stained with blood.

What the shit?

Trixie pulled rope from her string bag. "We're offering you as a sacrifice."

"I—What? You've got to be joking!"

"This is the only way to get Faen's attention—"

"By offering me on a bloody platter? No thank you! Is this normal for your domain? You offer living mortals as *sacrifices*?" Gods, I'd thought it horrible when gods demanded tithes and tributes, but this?

Juniper was as bad as the rest of them.

Trixie placed her hands on her hips and scowled. "We don't 'ave a fucking choice! Faen goes through seasons, and right now they're in the season of the 'unt. That means they'll only communicate if we offer a sacrifice. You'll attract their attention, and then you can do whatever the fuck it is you Chaos cunts do."

How much did I trust Trixie? What if she planned to sacrifice me to Faen in revenge for Wolfsbane's death?

Well. She could have betrayed me to Erosain, and hadn't. "I don't like it."

"I don't care." She snapped the rope taut. "Give me your 'ands."

Shit. Was I walking straight into another trap? I had to be setting a record.

I offered my hands. Trixie bound them *tight*. Great. At least she hadn't bound them behind my back.

"Are you sure about this?" Nelle's eyes darted between me and Trixie with an uneasiness that made my stomach churn.

"No, but if I do happen to get eaten, make sure Quen knows."

If this was a trap, then my ability to send mortals to sleep likely wouldn't help, but I still had Quen's pocket watch, assuming I could get my hands free.

"Sit your arse down." Trixie gestured to the altar.

This was such a terrible idea.

I sat on the corner of the stone slab, my string bag still slung over my shoulder, and my bound hands tucked into my lap. If Quen knew what I was doing, he'd throw a fit, or likely sacrifice himself, that arse.

Trixie stood over me and began to chant. "We offer this prey for your 'unt, O Mighty One. Accept this prey. Accept this offering. Accept this abomination."

"Abomination?"

A dark mist seeped between the thorns, and then the jungle went dark. Oh shit!

Something yanked me forward, and when I blinked, the jungle returned, only I was now alone and surrounded by a circle of thorns.

"Trixie?" I called.

A SACRIFICE? A voice spoke inside my mind. It wasn't male or female, but it held an odd purring vibration.

Shit. Faen.

YOU ARE NOT PREY, the voice continued. *YOU ARE LIKE US. EVER-CHANGING.*

An animal form appeared before me. Oh shit.

Faen was like no god I'd ever seen before.

The Fauna god was made of various animal parts. The head of a deer, with massive antlers. The body of a peacock with wide colorful wings. Feet made of a lizard. The tail of a lion. And then those parts shifted and changed, rippling through various animal shapes. In a few blinks, their face had morphed from a deer's to a horse's, an owl's, an elephant's, and then a monkey's. It never stayed the same for long. The constant shifting was maddening, and almost impossible to look at.

Faen was utterly grotesque and yet oddly mesmerizing.

"I can change form," I said. "But not like that."

YOU HAVE HER SCENT.

I knew exactly who Faen meant. "Corentine?"

SHE AWAKENS.

"You're a bit behind the times. I'm here to warn you. Chaos has already taken six domains, and yours is next unless you defend yourself."

THE HUNTER BECOMES THE HUNTED.

Faen's form continued to shift as they prowled around me, and I had to turn on my feet to keep them in view. The way those changing eyes stared left me completely unnerved. If Faen decided I was a threat and pounced, there wasn't much I could do to escape. My hands were still bound.

But... those thorns looked sharp.

Faen suddenly came to a crouching halt and sniffed the air.

I smelled it too. Ash. The gray tree line had an orange glow.

Shit! The thorns were on fire!

Faen roared. It was a terrible garbled scream that changed in intensity and pitch as their face changed. I cringed, unable to cover my ears against that awful sound.

YOU HUNT IN PAIRS! Faen accused.

Jinx. It had to be.

I ran for the thorn wall. If I could cut through my bindings—

Something collided with me, knocking me down with a painful thud. I tried to crawl away, but then a single paw pressed against my spine, pinning me. Faen.

I WILL FEAST ON YOUR ENTRAILS.

Shit! With my hands bound, I couldn't wiggle them free to grab Faen's damn soul. "Let me go, and I can stop her!"

YOU ARE BOTH ABOMINATIONS. EVER-CHANGING, YET YOU CHANGE THE NATURAL ORDER OF THINGS.

That was what Unghard had said. "How is changing forms any different from what you do?"

YOU TAKE POWER FROM THE GODS AND WARP IT. UNNATURALLY EARNED.

Oh. That was what Unghard had meant. I supposed they *would* be upset about losing their souls.

Flame burst from the thorns behind me, the sheer heat too close for comfort. The thorns crackled as they bent into useless soot, the wall collapsing in on itself as the flames spread.

Huh. Maybe an Ember's flame would have done the trick after all.

Sunlight shone through the gap of burned foliage, and out stepped Jinx, her golden skin glowing so bright, I couldn't make out her red dress. A small group of Glimmer glowed beside her, their powers working to burn the thorns down.

Jinx's light dimmed as she leered at me. "Tumbling in the dirt already? Whatever would your Time Boy think?" She pointed her hand at Faen. A burst of light shot at the god.

Faen screeched and pounced at Jinx.

Jinx switched to a Fauna magpie and flew at them.

Shitting shit! I shuffled onto my knees and crawled out of their way. Fire was spreading through the wall of thorns thick and fast as the Glimmer continued their work, though thankfully they ignored me. Oh, I was a pissing idiot! I carried Lady Mae's soul. I switched my form to Glimmer and burned through my bonds.

I was free, but now I was in deep shit. Jinx and Faen were jabbing at one another.

"Silly girl!" Nelle pushed through the thorns with Trixie, who reeled at the sight of Jinx and Faen fighting it out.

"What now?" Trixie yelled.

"We need to stop Jinx!" I yelled back. It was hard to hear over the crackle of the burning thorns.

"'Ow the fuck do you plan to do that?"

I only had one trick up my sleeve. I switched to my Mesmer form. "Stand back."

Trixie grabbed Nelle's arm and pulled her out of my way.

I summoned a miasma. It wouldn't affect Faen, but I could at least knock Jinx out.

Faen shrieked. I covered my ears, my miasma fading. A gust of wind blew around me, and the wall of thorns vanished, taking the flames with it but leaving us exposed to the jungle. The Glimmer spun, frightened.

Shit. We weren't alone.

Eyes blinked in the darkness between the bushes and leaves. Thousands of Fauna in their animal forms, watching us. Teeth flashed, an entire army snarling and gnashing.

"Faen's summoned them," Trixie gasped. She clutched her head with both hands and groaned. "They're calling upon us to... *'unt.*" Her feline eyes suddenly turned predatory, and she licked her lips.

Oh, that wasn't good.

Trixie's claws unsheathed and she pounced at me.

I stumbled back, but Nelle tackled her, throwing Trixie down. "Stop Faen!"

Fauna charged from the trees. Sunlight shone from the Glimmer as they took aim.

Fuck, fuck, *fuck*!

Nelle could handle Trixie, but an entire army of Fauna?

No. I'd dragged her here. I wouldn't leave her to be torn to pieces.

I stood my ground and once again summoned my miasma. It pooled around my fingers in a cooling mist, and I let it spread across my feet. I'd need a wide net to catch the Fauna and Jinx, which meant I'd have to knock out Nelle and the Glimmer, too.

Better that than the alternative.

The Fauna pounded through the jungle, scattering leaves and dirt as they ran on all fours. Lions, wolves, bears. So many of them, each staring with a feral hunger and foaming at the mouth with an unnatural rage.

They were almost on us.

My miasma fell upon the clearing. The Fauna staggered to a halt, confused. And then they collapsed to the ground in one single *thud*.

Oh my god, I'd actually done it! Trixie, Nelle, and the few Glimmer had collapsed with them, bearing only a few scratches. Thank the gods.

Something hot snorted against the back of my neck.

I spun to Faen, who once again loomed above me. Jinx was nowhere to be seen. Had I caught her? Had she escaped?

Or had Faen eaten her?

I held my hands up in a calming gesture. "Look, I'm on your—"

Faen bit down on my right hand.

Agony cut through to the bone. I screamed and tried to pull back, but their mouth clamped around my fingers. A tiger's fangs. The ragged teeth of a shark.

Their head shook from side to side, as though I were some dirty rag to be tossed aside.

I tried to grasp their face, to wrench their soul and stop them, but their form changed so quickly, it was impossible to take hold.

My hand slipped free. I fell back on my arse as blood spurted.

Gods. My hand was a mangled mess of torn flesh. Silver bone shone in my thumb, but my index finger was gone. Completely gone.

Faen had eaten my fucking finger!

Darkness washed over me. I was swimming in nothing, the throbbing pain forcing me in and out of reality. I caught flashes—blood, so much blood, thick and sticky; it made my mouth wet with saliva. Big leaves above, light twinkling between gaps. Vomit running down my chin, my shirt. Wetness across my chest as I cradled my hand.

YOU ARE NOT WORTHY PREY, said a voice from beyond.

It hurt. Gods, it hurt *so* much.

I forced my eyes open. To *see*.

Faen was still there. My blood staining their lips. They would eat me, finish me off, and then that would be the end.

Would I see Quen again?

Or was I about to lose everything?

"Don't cry, sister," came Jinx's voice. "You did your part. Now I'll do mine."

Jinx was here. She was awake. How was she here? How...?

She grasped Faen's tail.

The Fauna god howled.

And then the jungle turned gray.

It was over. The Fauna around me stirred, and they wailed their grief. The end was here, and I couldn't save them.

I pulled my bleeding hand closer to my chest, cocooning myself as dizziness threatened to take me once more.

Jinx grabbed my shoulder, her touch a painful reminder of reality. Her face sprouted black feathers. A Fauna's face.

"Do you think you can end the reign of gods alone? You and I, we were always meant to be together. Let me help you, sister."

I tried to shrug her off, but could barely move without ripples of pain shuddering through me.

"Look at you. It's honestly sad. I saved your ungrateful arse from Gildola, and then The Nameless One, and now Faen. Admit it. You need me."

"No," I whispered.

"So you're just gonna bleed out here while the world ends, huh? Give me Corinth's watch. I'll heal your hand in exchange."

I wanted to scream. To spit in her face.

But gods. It *hurt*.

Around me, the Fauna were already fading. Their mournful sobs were too much.

"My—My bag," I said.

Jinx gently pulled it from my shoulder and dug out the watch. "Was that so hard? Could have saved you a lot of trouble, but never mind. You always were one for trouble." Her form changed to Necro. "Now stay still."

She placed her hand on my neck.

Warmth flooded me, easing the pain instantly, as though I'd gotten high on laudanum. I gasped aloud, sucking in the warm air of the jungle. Above, the canopy of leaves had faded, opening the jungle to wide gray skies that peeled back the darkness.

With each heartbeat, my strength returned. Then my fingers tingled.

Fingers.

Jinx had regrown my missing finger.

I examined it as she stepped back. It had been completely restored, as though Faen had never bitten it off. "Why?"

Jinx changed her form to Chaos and wound the pocket watch. "Because you're my sister."

A portal opened to inside the clock tower. I'd recognize that room anywhere, with its brass walls and pipes. Though how did Jinx know how to use the watch? How long had she been spying on Quen and me? Had Gast been lurking inside Sinner's Row all that time?

Familiar faces stared back from the other side. Joe. Vincent. They looked as shocked as I felt!

And...

It couldn't be. "Harm?"

She looked completely different. Her skin was the silvery-blue of Chaos, and she stood far taller than I'd ever expected, without her Seren wing. But that face was all Harmony.

Which meant Jinx had taken her soul before I'd ever had the chance.

No.

She'd stolen Harm from me.

"That's right," Jinx said with a smirk as she read my expression. "I'm rebuilding the Godless, like I promised. We'll finish what you started. All that's missing is you." She held out her hand. "What do you say, sister? We can take on the universe."

I recoiled.

"Really? This place is about to go *pop* any second. Do you want to be trapped here when it does? When will you learn you can't do this without me?" She stepped through the portal with her awoken Glimmer, expecting me to follow.

I'd have to. She was right. I didn't have a choice.

At least if I did... I'd be back with Harmony and Vincent.

I stood on shaking legs.

"No!" Nelle yelled. Gods. I'd forgotten about Nelle!

She ran past me and leaped through the portal. My mouth dropped as Nelle wrenched the pocket watch from Jinx's grasp and threw it out. It landed on a dead leaf beside me.

"Tell your tiny man I pay my debts!" Nelle said.

And then the portal closed.

Shit!

I scrambled for the watch and held it against my chest. Nelle was gone, lost to me and in mortal danger now she was trapped with Jinx. Quen could get her back, couldn't he? He owned her soul.

I had bigger problems.

The vast gray nothingness was quickly devouring Juniper. Most of the Fauna were gone, and that hurt worse than losing a finger, but I didn't have time to wallow.

I switched my form to Chaos and set the pocket watch to one minute past ten. A portal opened back into the Undercity.

As I was about to step through, a figure shifted at the corner of my eye.

Trixie.

She stood there, her cat ears flat, her arms dangling uselessly by her side, as her home fell to dust around her. I'd promised to help her. To protect her Fauna.

I'd failed.

Her feline eyes met mine. "You sure fucked this up, didn't you?"

And then her body collapsed into ash.

I choked back a sob and leaped through the portal. It snapped shut behind me, plunging me into the familiar darkness of the Undercity tunnels. The taste of soot and oil replaced the perfumes of Juniper's flowers.

Shit. I'd lost the Fauna, lost Trixie and Nelle, and now I'd lost Harmony too. Who did I have left on my side?

Gods. I needed Quen.

I closed my eyes and let myself return to where it had all begun.

In darkness and despair.

XXVI

Another illusive god, for Anima surrounds themself with an impenetrable shield of water. This thus makes them among the most difficult of the gods to reach. Thankfully, I believe Anima is amenable to negotiation. The Amnae share many of our values. It would be of benefit to us to earn their favor, if only to gain their much-sought-after ability to alter memories. In the battles to come against Chaos, such an ability will prove useful.
—P. Bezel, *Personal Report on Anima*

MEMORIA HADN'T CHANGED AT all. That wasn't a surprise.

The Amnae went about their daily life as though they'd forgotten Chime and the other domains had ever existed, and that wouldn't surprise me, either. Though they'd always been happy to open their domain to others and allow other mortals to live and work in their cities—with some caveats—they were also quick to cut off contact with the outside when it suited them. There was no greater motivator to close one's doors than the end-times, I supposed.

Anima was no fool. They knew Chaos would be a risk, and Dor likely couldn't be trusted. Oh yes, mortals often thought the Diviner or Zephyr the smartest of the domains, but wisdom came from the accumulation of knowledge born of an obsession with reading. In short, it came from the Amnae.

Unfortunately, that meant I was the only non-Amnae in the entire city, and that would surely draw attention. Nor could I simply pause time to get around. Anima would certainly notice. I needed a new face, and fast.

It was unlucky the portal had opened so close to the city, and not in a more suburban area. I stalked into an alley behind one of the brass-and-teal town houses, a hand on the taser I'd brought with me. I'd no intent of using it unless necessary—who knew what effect it would have on an Amnae? Their translucent skin was a natural conductor.

The familiar scent of salt water permeated the entire city, but back here, it stunk of grime and seaweed growing between the tiles. Every domain had its dirty back alleys, and this one was no different. I crouched uncomfortably close to a pile of rotting kelp.

Graffiti had been scrawled onto the wall. *Aberforth fondles fish.*

Quite.

An Amnae chap reading the local newspaper loitered by the entrance to the alleyway, lost to whatever article held his attention. Now was my chance.

"Excuse me," I said. "Do you have the time?"

He lowered his paper and stared at me, perplexed. "The time?"

I quickly touched his wrist with my left hand. The change happened gradually.

If I were a scientist, I would have studied how Chaos changed between the many forms of the domains, and thus documented the phenomenon. The scholar within me certainly marveled. It started within, as my lungs adapted to Memoria's humid air. Then gills emerged from my neck, and I drew a garbled breath.

The last of the changes were purely cosmetic. Silvery-blue scales appeared across my skin. My fingers and toes fused into fleshy webbed blobs. Rather remarkably, my metal arm remained attached to my residual limb, and I could still flex it as normal.

How, then, could Chaos switch between domains so easily? Was it through the connection Chaos shared with each god by virtue of Corentine acting as their mother? If another god were to come into existence, could Chaos take on their persona, too?

It is a statistical impossibility, came Doctor Finch's voice. *All energy in the universe originates from Chaos and Time, thus the likelihood of gods being created outside that spectrum would be next to zero. Therefore, any new gods created by either Corentine or Dor would have the same limitations. And given the nature of their relationship—*

All right, Doctor. I should have known my ponderings would awaken a Zephyr's imagination. *These are questions to debate another time.* I had a job to do.

The Amnae fellow dropped his newspaper in shock. "What—What are you?"

"Just a chap on a walkabout."

"But—But—you were *Diviner*!"

"Really, now!" I scoffed while subtly kicking off my shoes. They were suddenly too tight and uncomfortable for my new Amnae feet. "I think you've been hitting the sea salts a little hard. What Diviner would ask for the time?" I picked up his paper and handed it back. "But it's quite all right. I can see you've got enough to contend with." I walked off, leaving him to scratch his bulbous head in confusion.

If anyone else had noticed my transformation, then they'd likely dismiss it as a trick of the light.

I stepped out of the alleyway. Above, water bobbed beyond the giant glass dome, casting wavy colors and light across the busy streets.

Now that I'd acclimatized myself, it was time to enact the next step.

I needed to find Ilona Burns.

How will we find her? The doctor's anxiety bled through our shared connection. *This city is overwhelming!*

Relax, Doctor. I have it in hand. There were many places in Memoria where one could seek knowledge. Libraries, archives, memory parlors. However, I had one goal in mind. Memoria University. Walter had once worked there as a professor, and they kept family records. It would be the quickest way to track down his daughter.

I merged with the foot traffic heading into the main city. While the Gate would be closed, it acted as a central hub for most of Memoria's businesses and academic institutions, thus the University was within walking distance. Steam-powered carriages chugged past. Other Amnae chose to travel via the glass tubes above the city. Those were filled with water, allowing them to swim much quicker than walking. I didn't quite feel prepared to strip and go for a swim yet. Though if all went well, it would happen sooner than later.

My path also brought me parallel to a canal and the gondolas transporting mortals to and fro. That would have been my preferred option, if I had any currency.

Though, I rather enjoyed taking a stroll. It took my mind off other things.

Namely, the woman I'd left behind.

Even a whole domain away, guilt continued to gnaw at me. I'd left Kayl in good hands, or rather paws—Dandelion had promised to keep an eye on her while I was gone. Yet I hadn't needed an entire hour to prepare, and I hoped she hadn't realized I'd been avoiding her. It wasn't so much *her*, as it was my duty to Malkavaan.

It wouldn't have felt right, bedding her again.

Even if her absence hurt me. Even if it ached.

No. I needed to focus on the mission at hand.

Eventually, I reached the main square, which housed the Gate. As predicted, the station was empty. With no Gate to queue up for, there was no need to occupy the waiting rooms and no one to operate the tourist information booths. How would the lack of tourism affect businesses? Yet across the street, the tourist traps and cafés were just as busy with Amnae customers. They'd simply moved on.

I continued along the road leading to the University. It was famed for taking in undergraduates from other domains, so again, I wondered how the lack of admissions would affect their classes. The domains weren't meant to be kept separate like this for great swathes of time. We'd created an entire society based on a mutual exchange of knowledge, culture, and trade. Yes, they needed to protect themselves, but it saddened me all the same.

Though as I approached the University grounds, it didn't look as though they were hurting for students. The campus was swarming with young, eager-looking students. Were they not aware of the dangers outside their domain? Or were they taking advantage of it?

I would have spent my final days holed up reading, Doctor Finch said. *If Zyclone hadn't forced me into their service.*

As much as I enjoyed academia, there was more to life. *Perhaps you should have been born an Amnae, Doctor.*

Do you think so?

We'll soon find out.

Like the School of Philosophy back in Chime, Memoria University was built with a traditional aesthetic. None of this modern brass, teal, and glass that filled the city's town houses, or the seashell cottages of suburbia, but the same coral-like stone that comprised the domain's Gate. Quite simply, it was an ancient coral castle, with turrets that pointed sharply up at Memoria's glass dome. Brass windows and doors had been cut out of the coral and rusted with age. The entire building looked as though it had been plucked from under Memoria's seas, though it wouldn't look out of place in an Arcadian museum, either.

I followed a group inside and headed for the reception desk. An orange-skinned Amnae woman greeted me.

"Good afternoon," I began. "Could you point me to the directory, please?"

"I'm the directory, sir. Do you have a particular query?"

Of course the Amnae stored their directories inside their own brains. They practically had eidetic memories. Though I was hoping to peruse their records privately. "I'm looking for information regarding Professor Walter Burns. I'm a former student of his, you see, and I—"

"One moment." Her eyes fluttered shut. "I'm afraid Professor Walter Burns passed away during the tragic Golden City elevator malfunction on Chime over a month ago. My condolences."

"Oh my. That's... terrible, I had no idea." I had *some* idea. "Do you know if he has any living family members I could pay my respects to?"

"Professor Burns is survived by his daughter, Doctor Ilona Gillian Burns. You're in luck. Doctor Burns is currently on campus."

Doctor? Doctor Finch screeched in my head with sudden excitement. *She's earned a doctorate?*

Calm down and let me think! "Where might I find her?"

"Head to the sciences department." She pointed to a corridor. "You'll find her office next to the faculty staff room."

"Thank you."

Do you think she'll remember us? Doctor Finch asked as I headed down the corridor.

Truthfully, I don't know. I'd been the one to bring Ilona to Kronos on an ill-fated scheme to save Chaos, which had never been meant to succeed. I'd also been the one to help her escape, but the experience had terrified her, and she'd made a run for it at the first opportunity. I wouldn't blame her if she'd wiped those memories, or didn't wish to meet with me. But Ilona was the only Amnae I knew.

And I still owed Walter. I'd promised to protect her.

I've... never been close to other mortals, the good doctor admitted. *I doubt I ever will. But children are precious. Even among Zephyr, they are rare and inquisitive. If there is one good cause in this world, Master Corinth, it is to protect the children.*

On that we agreed. Most gods denied their mortals a childhood, and those who did allow children often abused them. My own father had abused me.

Would I ever have children? It was a desire buried deep within, but what kind of father would the Dark Warden make?

A tragic one.

I passed large lecture halls until I reached the science department. It wasn't hard to find Ilona's office. It was the first one I came to. I knocked politely on the door.

The Amnae girl who answered it was exactly the same as I'd left her. Young, short, with purple scales and a child's innocent gaze because, gods, she was *still* a child, and yet the plaque above her door clearly marked her status as a doctor with a PhD in mnemonics.

Walter would be so proud.

"Hello, Ilona," I greeted with a smile.

Her eyes opened wide. Even though I wore an Amnae form, she recognized me.

"May I come inside?" I prompted.

"Ye-Yes." She opened the door and allowed me into her office.

It reminded me so much of Walter's old greenhouse. Vines and other plants covered the walls around shelves of colorful jars containing concoctions I'd never understand. A single recliner took up most of the room, with a simple bench and scattered notes.

Ilona closed the door behind her and leaned against it. "Master Corinth? Is that you?"

I changed my form from Amnae to Diviner. "It's me."

"You... You've become Chaos?"

"Yes. I'm not here to harm you." I raised my hands in a placating gesture. "I need your help."

Ilona listened with rapt concentration as I explained everything that had happened since we parted ways, including my untimely demise and rebirth as Chaos and the domains that had fallen since.

"Then... you're here to take Anima," Ilona concluded.

This was the test of whatever goodwill I'd earned. She either trusted me completely, or I was about to find myself unceremoniously plucked from Memoria. "I know what you must think—"

"No, no." She waved me off. "I—I'm sorry. I didn't trust you. I was... scared. Kayl, the Chaos woman—she had my name tattooed on her arm. That perplexed me enough to begin searching through my father's records. I found his memories. He'd hidden a backup before his death, because he feared... he understood what was to come. I know everything, Master Corinth. I know you're Godless."

Thank the gods for Walter's foresight. "I need memories Anima has stolen, in order to save the Vesper, but I understand the risks. Can you make a backup of my own memories?"

"Only Amnae can copy their memories. I'm not sure if it'll work on Chaos."

I offered my left hand. "It's worth a try?"

She took my hand, and I once again transformed into my Amnae self.

Ilona giggled. "Father would have loved to see that."

I'm sure he would have gotten a kick out of it. "Before we begin, I have one more surprise. Do you have a spare lab coat at all? For a taller adult male?"

"Um, I can get one?"

"Please do."

I waited until Ilona left the room. *Are you ready, Doctor?*

No, he whined.

None of us are ever truly ready. I found the good doctor's soul nestled in my subconscious and slowly pulled it out.

I understood his apprehension. He'd been reborn once and had hated the experience, and I could attest: it didn't get any easier. But he'd agreed to finally leave my mind for one reason only. Ilona.

Light burst into the room, and a male Zephyr staggered against the recliner. His feathers had the silvery-blue tinge of Chaos, though interestingly, he was still missing his wings.

"Oh no, I'm alive!" Doctor Finch squealed. "And *naked*!"

The office door opened as Ilona returned. "Zachery?"

He whimpered and hid behind the recliner.

I took the lab coat and passed it on. Really now, his feathers hid his nakedness well. If I hadn't transformed into a Zephyr myself, I'd assume they had no genitals.

As soon as he'd put it on, Ilona tackled him in a hug. "I thought you'd died!"

"I did die." His beak softened into a fond smile. "Enough of that. You're a doctor now?"

Ilona let him go and wiped away tears. "You inspired me to finish my thesis."

"Then I will count that among my greatest achievements."

Quentin! Dandelion's voice roared through my mind loud and sharp, making me wince. *We have a problem, Quentin!*

Oh saints. Kayl. *What's happening?*

Serenity came here. They came after the Fauna. I'm sorry. They... they killed your wolf friend.

Wolfsbane? Dread curdled in my stomach. *Are you safe? Is Kayl—*

They've opened a portal to Juniper, Quentin. Nelle, she says she will go with Kayl and watch over her. I can't leave the cubs alone—

Stop her! I yelled into my mind. *Do* not *let her leave—*

They're gone.

"Fuck!"

"Is something wrong?" Ilona asked.

I paced the room. Why would Serenity attack now? Of all the sodding timing! Jinx must be behind this. If Kayl had left for Juniper, then the Fauna were in danger.

Why would Kayl run into danger when I'd *expressly* told her not to?

When I was *here*, risking everything to save her bloody memories?

I had no easy way of returning to Chime, let alone Juniper, which meant I had no choice. My plan needed to proceed, now with haste. "Apologies. We've trouble back home. I'm sorry, but we must expedite matters. Ilona, I know I'm asking a lot of you, but can you please make a backup of my memories? Doctor Finch has kindly volunteered to keep them safe."

She glanced between me and the doctor. "He would need to be Amnae."

"Yes." I turned to Doctor Finch and peered over the rim of my spectacles. "If you could please hurry this up."

He sighed. "What do I do?"

"Take her hand, but if you feel a tug in your palm, let go."

He nodded and took Ilona's hand.

I'd seen Kayl change from Umber to Amnae once, and yet the sight still took my breath away. More so since the change from Zephyr was rather more pronounced. The good doctor's feathers receded into scales similar to mine, and then his beak vanished.

Ilona gasped, and I too struggled to hide my shock. Without his beak and feathers, Doctor Finch was unrecognizable. He was a tall, thin man who somehow managed to look even dorkier than I did, and yet *I* was the one with the spectacles!

He rubbed his jaw with both hands. "I don't have a beak!"

And then he began to hyperventilate. Wonderful.

Ilona sat him on a stool. "It's all right, Zachery. Breathe."

"How do I *breathe*?"

"Slow breaths, in and out."

Such dramatics. I resisted the urge to roll my eyes. My lack of sympathy made me a prat, but while Kayl remained in danger, my nerves were shredded. Between swanning off to Witheryn and now Juniper, did the woman enjoy aging me? Or was it simply a penchant for deadly domains?

Could I judge, when I'd come all the way here? At least Memoria had a decent café.

I reached inside my mind and found Nelle's soul. *Nelle? If you can hear me, are you safe?*

We are safe, came her reply almost instantly. *The jungle is treacherous, but no more than Obituary's desert. I watch over your woman.*

She's not my *woman—*

I keep her alive, like I promised.

I swallowed my sigh of relief. At least with the Lioness watching over Kayl, she'd not get eaten by anything, though I'd be a lot happier if she weren't in Juniper at all.

Doctor Finch finally calmed down.

"I think we're ready now," Ilona said.

"Excellent." I made myself comfortable on the recliner. "Then let's begin."

Ilona positioned herself behind my headrest and placed the suckers of her fingertips atop my forehead. "This will feel a bit odd... but you know that."

"You won't have to read my memories to copy them, will you?" The last thing I wanted was to expose a child to the lurid thoughts and scenes of my recent past.

"No. But I've seen your memories through my father's."

"Oh." Which meant she'd likely seen far worse than my recent past. She'd have witnessed her father's death through my eyes. "I'm sorry."

"I've seen worse."

I let out a nervous laugh. "What could be worse than my memories?"

"Watching my father forget my own mother."

"Ah." Sometimes I should keep my foolish lips closed. I fidgeted in the seat. My residual arm was already aching at the connection between flesh and metal.

"Stay still," she chided.

"Yes, ma'am." Like father, like daughter.

Ilona's fingers slipped *into* my head, and then images flashed through my mind, too quickly to grasp. I gritted my teeth at the dizzying colors speeding through my mind.

"Almost done," she said.

"How fascinating!" Doctor Finch exclaimed. He'd brought his stool over and was seated staring at me. It was rather disconcerting.

The images suddenly stopped, pausing on a scene from my childhood.

My very first memory inside Dor's sanctum. I'd lain naked in the palm of his hand. The sterile white had hurt my eyes, and all I could hear was the tick-tock of a thousand clashing clocks. They'd hurt too, at first, until they'd faded into a soft rhythm that had brought me comfort. Dor had coaxed me awake, his voice gentle. He'd asked me what time it was.

And...

Saints.

I'd answered that it was thirteen o'clock. My very first words. How had I forgotten them until now? That was the day I'd been made.

Ilona's touch withdrew from my head. "All done. I can transfer these to Zachery."

"It's best you remove the memory of you doing so when you're done. I don't wish for Anima to trace this interaction back to you."

"Leave that to me."

"What now?" Doctor Finch asked.

I sat up and stretched. "Now, I deal with Anima."

"Alone?" Ilona's concern creased the ridge of her brow.

"If all goes well, you'll see me again soon."

"If it doesn't?"

"Then you'll be seeing me again soon, though I likely won't remember you."

Doctor Finch wrung his hands. "This is a terrible idea." The suckers of his new Amnae fingers made an awful squelching.

"Yes, but it's the only one I have. Kayl is in danger, and I have no time to dally." I stood and pulled the taser from my belt. "Take this for your protection. Stay inside the university and remain inconspicuous, or as much as you can manage."

The good doctor gawked at me, his new Amnae face showing far more exasperation than his beak ever had. Yes, I did ask rather a lot of him.

"I'll make sure he's kept out of trouble," Ilona said. "We'll come up with a plan."

I patted her shoulder. "Thank you. Stay safe."

"You too." Those Amnae eyes were full of worry. I did so hate to place this burden on her when it was my duty to keep her from harm.

Ultimately, that was my goal.

I left her office and clicked the door shut behind me. It was time.

I'd had twenty-eight years of it—technically twenty, since I'd begun my existence as an eight-year-old boy—and yet time never felt like enough. If I had more time, I could enact a more intricate plan for dealing with Anima. But then Kayl had gone and entered bloody Juniper.

Of all the gods, Anima would be the most difficult to reach. No other god surrounded themselves with an entire body of water. I couldn't simply hunt them down, no. I needed the Amnae to bring me to them.

Ergo, I needed to cause a scene.

I headed out of the university and back to the main square outside the Gate. It was almost lunchtime, now, and the streets were still busy with casual shoppers and café-goers.

My form switched to Diviner as I stopped in the center of a crowded intersection.

A few Amnae stared, but I wasn't interested in their attention.

I raised my hands and brought time to a jarring halt.

The Amnae stopped in their tracks. Some were caught midwalk, others in various amusing poses. Time wasn't a toy to be played with, and yet I could see the appeal. Above, the swell of the ocean had stilled, creating an awful pressure ready to pop in my ears.

I waited an entire minute before releasing time back to the present.

And then I waited a minute more.

The crowd parted, and a familiar figure strode straight for me.

"Quentin Corinth," announced Aberforth.

"Ambassador."

The last time we'd stood so close, I'd wanted to shoot him. Alas, I'd left my pistol behind. He'd effectively blackmailed me, turned Kayl's stolen memories against me, and it had all been for naught. Aberforth was, to put it mildly, an utter bastard. The worst Amnae Memoria had to offer.

"How are you standing here?" he said.

"Gravity, I suppose."

Irritation swept over his face, his blue-tinged gills flapping. "Did Dor send you? Anima did not sense your arrival… nor does he sense the presence of Diviner."

That confirmed what I'd always suspected. While the gods could sense the mortals of other domains entering their own, they couldn't detect Chaos. "No, Dor didn't send me. I'm here of my own volition. I wish to bargain with Anima."

"You invade our domain and demand an audience?" Aberforth sneered. "Your request is denied."

"It wasn't a request." I dove forward and grabbed his wrist.

He tried to pull back, but with a single pulse in my palm, I ripped out his soul.

I couldn't spare the time for the whole song and dance he'd have put me through. Best cut out the middleman and skip straight to the source.

Aberforth's body collapsed to the ground, his mouth open in shock, his eyeless sockets staring up at the glass dome. I'd spit on his face, but he wasn't worth the moisture.

Once again, my form switched from Diviner to Amnae, and I tucked Aberforth's soul into the deepest reaches of my subconscious for now.

Rather predictably, mortals screamed and ran.

Another minute later, a group of large, burly Amnae with broad shoulders appeared from one of the overhead water spouts. They carried bronze tridents and thrust them at me in a vaguely threatening manner.

I held up my hands in surrender. "Gentlemen. I apologize for the unfortunate mess." I nudged Aberforth's head with my bare foot. "Bring me to Anima, and there will be no further incidents. You have my word."

One of the Amnae approached—a fellow with sea-green scales. "Take off your clothes. We swim."

I didn't make a habit of undressing in front of strangers, and yet it was starting to become one. Presumably, they wanted to ensure I wasn't armed. Unfortunately, there'd be no hiding my metal appendage.

To reveal one's nakedness was to make oneself vulnerable. In truth, I was only too willing to reveal parts of myself that society deemed perverse and did not wish to see, both physically and emotionally. To a Diviner, whipping out an emotional willy was far more grotesque. I slipped off my shirt and then began to slide my trousers down. It brought a flash of memory from when Kayl had slid her hand around my prickly Leander prick.

What would she make of an Amnae cock?

Stop it, Quen. Don't go there.

The Amnae strode around me in a circle, and I clenched my buttocks, feeling rather exposed. He nodded, and then led me toward the entrance to one of their glass tubes.

"Can you swim?" asked my sea-green companion.

"Yes, though I'm out of practice." I'd learned to swim during my Academy years in the pool on campus, but such skills were rarely required in my duty as a Warden.

"Then try to keep up." He dove into the tube and swam up.

Right. How hard could it be? I leaped in after him, hoping my metal arm would handle the stress and depths.

As it turned out, it was bloody hard!

Water completely engulfed me, overwhelming my senses. It stung my eyes, muffled my hearing, and left me with a floating sensation reminiscent of flying as a Zephyr—if the sky were thicker, at any rate. My breath escaped in a single collection of bubbles, and for a heartbeat, I exhaled and inhaled in frantic gulps. I was no longer breathing through my nose, but rather, the gills on my neck.

Already, my new companion had swum ahead, though I didn't think he'd abandon me to Memoria's ocean. I was too much of a liability.

My Amnae body was designed for the task at hand. I simply needed to let it work.

Though I'd learned to swim with my arms in a tight breaststroke, my new body preferred to focus on my legs and flipper-like feet, which was just as well. I didn't trust my metal arm to manage with any finesse, but it did at least hold up underwater. My future self must have known I'd make my way to Memoria eventually and had it prepared accordingly.

I swam through the glass pipe, which carried me and my new companions above the city at a dizzying height. It really was like flying above. The flow of the water pulled me through with forward momentum, and soon, the dome above loomed closer.

The pipe flushed me out unceremoniously, my companions following behind.

I stretched in a vastness I'd never experienced before. Saints, it was... freeing.

My sea-green companion beckoned me on, and then I was swimming over the glass dome, my form likely casting a shadow on Memoria's streets. Despite the size and scope of the city, we quickly cleared the glass perimeter and found ourselves level with the rocky underwater coral that kept the city stable.

Down we went. The lights of the city faded behind us, replaced with bioluminescent plant life among the coral and fish that swam by.

We swam into darkness.

The glowing jellyfish soon abandoned us, a trail of bubbles ahead of me the only evidence I still swam in the right direction.

Then my companion came to a halt.

I floated beside him. We'd come far down—there was no natural light left. Oh gods. Had I made a terrible mistake in coming here? I couldn't tell which direction was up. There was no chance I'd find my way back.

The pressure squeezed my chest, forcing my gills to flap erratically in a flurry of bubbles.

I couldn't breathe!

A burning pain struck my chest. This was it. My heart had finally given out.

No. I was still here, floating in nothingness, yet the burning was so acute, I felt it deep inside, where Nelle's soul—

Nelle. Her soul had returned to me. Did every god feel their mortals' deaths as I had? Or did they host so many mortal souls that each death felt like an awkward itch? I delved into my subconscious, swimming through an ocean of souls until I found the Lioness cocooned in aether. Her last memories bloomed in my mind's eye.

Juniper had fallen. Jinx had stolen my fob watch, opened a portal... and Nelle had leaped inside, stealing it back. She'd thrown it to Kayl as the portal closed, securing Kayl's safety while damning herself.

Jinx had killed her—a blast of pure, deadly sunlight.

Oh, Nelle. My emotions clashed—relief that Kayl and my fob watch remained safe, devastation at losing Juniper and the Fauna with it, wrath at Jinx's actions, and pride for Nelle's sacrifice. I'd reunite her with her cubs once I was done here.

But first, I had another god to contend with.

A shape emerged from the gloom. I'd never personally met Anima, but I'd studied enough reports on Memoria to recognize them.

Anima was certainly god-sized. Their entire body loomed over me in the shape of a giant jellyfish. Their head was a bulbous mass of fleshy teal, and purple tentacles unfurled beneath them in a dangerous skirt of boneless limbs with sharp barbs.

No other god enshrined themselves in an inhospitable sanctuary. Perhaps no other god was quite as paranoid.

YOU DESTROYED OUR VOICE, boomed Anima's otherworldly echo inside my mind.

A mere demonstration of what power I possess. And not, say, vengeance for Aberforth once calling Kayl a whore. All right, I *had* demonstrated my abilities by simply being here, but one did not forget these slights, and Aberforth was an absolute knobhead who'd needed silencing. *You see what I have become.*

YOU HAVE BECOME CHAOS. YOU NO LONGER SPEAK FOR DOR. DO YOU SPEAK FOR CORENTINE?

No. I seek a different path, as I did before—to unite the domains against Corentine and Dor. That is why I'm here. To offer a different way.

CHAOS SEEKS TO DESTROY.

I have become Chaos, but Chaos does not control me.

THEN WHAT DO YOU SEEK?

A partnership. You've been waiting to see which side would gain the upper hand. I represent an alternative. Join with me, and you need not fear Chaos, nor bow to Dor's rule. All I ask for in exchange is the return of Kayl's missing memories so we may rebirth the Vesper. I swear to you—your domain will not be harmed.

YOU WOULD BETRAY DOR FOR THIS PARTNERSHIP?

Dor no longer owns my soul, nor do I care for his.

Water swelled around me in discontent, and I feared those tentacles would lash out.

Domains have already fallen to Chaos thanks to Dor's manipulation, I continued. *Do not assume your domain is safe. He cares nothing for your mortals, unlike me. You know me and my reputation—I simply seek shelter and protection for mortals, including the Amnae. Dor's plotting resulted in the death of Walter Burns. He was a mentor to me, a dear friend.* A better father than Dor could ever claim.

VERY WELL. WE SHALL EXCHANGE MEMORIES. Anima held out a single tentacle. An offer of peace.

I had to take it.

I had to trust this was my path.

My future self had led me here, had made it clear where my true loyalties remained—as Kayl's servant. What I chose now was to serve her cause. My future self had presented me with this arm for a reason, had ensured it could withstand the depths of Memoria, had given me the mental fortitude to face Lionheart and now this.

I had to trust in him. In myself.

I slid my left palm around the tentacle. It was soft, squishy, and surprisingly warm.

A jolt of static shot up my arm.

And then a mass of writhing tentacles overwhelmed me.

They wrenched my arm behind my back with such force, I let out a garbled yell of pain.

Fuck!

Another tentacle lashed at my metal arm. I grabbed hold and tried to crush the life out of it.

My arm popped off, ripping the strap from my chest. Anima had sodding well pulled off my arm! I watched helplessly as it sank out of sight, lost in the darkness, leaving me to flail with only my residual limb free.

Stop! You're making a mistake!

YOU DESTROYED OUR VOICE.

Is Aberforth's soul worth risking your entire domain?

More tentacles wrapped around my legs, my torso, squeezing me so completely I couldn't move. My chest rose with rapid gulps of air, but it was no use.

Anima had me.

WE DO NOT TRUST CHAOS, NOR DO WE TRUST DOR. BUT WITH YOU IN OUR GRASP, DOR WILL NEGOTIATE.

No. Oh, gods no.

They couldn't dangle me in front of Dor. Use me as bait. *No!*

Tentacles slithered across my back, up to my forehead. Suckers attached themselves to my skin.

Please! Listen to me!

A sharp barb plunged into my mind.

Once again, images flashed before me with dizzying speed. Recent memories. My battle against Lionheart. My confrontation with Zyclone.

YOU HAVE TAKEN ZYCLONE AND LIONHEART. DEATH WOULD NOT BE ENOUGH FOR YOU.

To protect their mortals from Chaos! I tried to writhe free, but my left arm was still wrenched painfully behind my back, my palm unable to reach any of Anima's tentacles and claim their soul.

My body deflated in their grip. Useless, defeated.

Was this truly what my future self had envisioned?

I felt a door closing in my subconscious. Anima was locking the Leander and Zephyr away, just as they had done with Kayl's memories of the Vesper. Soon, their power would be lost to me, as would their souls. Dandelion, Nelle and her cubs. I'd brought them back to life only to fail them. Doctor Finch's soul would also be trapped in the deepest reaches of my subconscious, and with it, my memories.

Gods, I was a fool to think I could outsmart Anima. That I could plan for this.

And then I felt another familiar sensation.

Of memory slipping away.

Please, I begged.

I squeezed my eyes closed and concentrated on the one face I would refuse to forget.

Her beautiful smile. Those aether eyes.

Kayl.

Kayl. Kayl. Kayl—

My eyes popped open suddenly. "Oh, goodness me!"

I sat up and straightened my spectacles. It took me a moment to gather my bearings. It was early afternoon in my office, and paperwork was scattered across my desk, along with a smudge of spilled ink—my metal arm had accidentally knocked a bottle over. I was still so clumsy with the sodding thing.

Gosh, I must have fallen asleep, though preparing lecture notes could have that effect.

That was right. I was meant to be preparing a lecture on the application of time from a Diviner's perspective. How fortunate the University had so graciously invited me to take up a position as professor. It wasn't how I'd expected to spend my retirement, but after losing an arm in service to the Wardens, there wasn't much else for me to do.

A mind such as mine was wasted back in Chime on a diet of tea and crossword puzzles.

My metal arm ached, as it so often did in Memoria's humid air. I'd need another tonic to ease the pain. Thankfully, my faculty came well stocked.

A knock rapped at the door. "Professor Corinth?"

I gathered my notes into a tidy pile. "Come in!"

The door opened to Doctor Burns. A child prodigy teaching in a similar field to mine. She'd delighted me with her company these past few weeks. Without her, I'd never have settled in quite so quickly. "Done for the afternoon? If you're free, I thought you'd like to accompany me to Bath's Books and Beyond. It's a bookstore around the corner from Mr. Kipler's. You simply need to get out of this office."

"That sounds delightful." I could do with stretching my legs. "And please. Call me Quentin."

As I stood, a note caught my eye. It was a dirty scrawl, a mess of ink that was unfortunately my left hand's attempt at handwriting. Had I written it while napping?

It was just the one word, repeated over and over.

Kayl.

What in saint's name did that mean?

"Quentin?" Doctor Burns prompted.

"Yes. Apologies. My mind has been out of sorts today." I chuckled. "Working too hard."

I followed Doctor Burns out of the sciences department. Students milled about, discussing the upcoming regatta said to be the highlight of the academic calendar. I'd never visited Memoria during the boat races, but the locals liked to complain about the canals being blocked.

We'd almost reached the main doors when Ambassador Brooke flagged me down. A marvelous woman with rouge-red gills, she'd been the one to secure my employment in Memoria, all while stepping into the role of ambassador after the late Aberforth died in a tragic gondola accident. "Professor Corinth? Can you spare a moment? A visitor has arrived from Kronos for you."

A visitor? That was rare. There weren't many visitors to Memoria since travel restrictions were placed on the Gate. "I'll catch up," I said to Doctor Burns, and left her by the entrance as Her Excellency led me back to reception.

It had been many weeks since I last visited Kronos. It was thanks to Father's blessing I'd earned this post. Even in retirement, it was good judgement to make allies across the domains. It was what He would want.

A Diviner stood waiting by the counter dressed, in a sharp pinstripe suit. His bronze hair shone radiant in the light.

My breath hitched as he turned to me. Those brass eyes were as beautiful as the day I first lost myself to them during our Academy classes. "Eli."

"Quentin." Elijah placed a soft kiss on my cheek. "I've missed you."

PART THREE

27

Sometimes our imagination can run away from us. That's okay. Sometimes it's fun. But remember the most important rule: do no harm. Mortals of other domains don't like it when we change their reality. It can scare them, because they're used to experiencing reality a certain way. Always get their permission before engaging them in dreams or illusions. Screaming can hurt your ears, and we don't want that.
—Reverie, *Is this Real? A Mesmer Guidebook*

I WASN'T ALONE. NOT yet.

I hurried on through the Undercity's tunnels and back to Sinner's Row, my bare feet scraping the cobblestones until they were numb. Yes, I'd lost the Fauna, but I still had three Mesmer depending on me to keep them safe. Since Jinx had practically rampaged through the main street and declared me her enemy, I didn't know if that meant Sinner's Row was safe for us anymore. Edana could well turn her back on our deal, and the Ember could be marching on the hotel at any moment, ready to burn it down.

There, tucked within the far reaches of my mind, were the trio. Three bright souls that quivered with nervous energy. They were worried.

I reached out to Celeste. *Where are you? Are you all safe?*

Mama! she called back. *There you are! We're still in the hotel, but something odd has happened. Some of the Fauna have disappeared. They went poof! Like that.*

Some of them? Jinx had taken Faen. They should all have vanished with her.

Freddie's gone. But Autumn's still here. There are some other Fauna in the rooms upstairs but they're not saying anything. It's scaring Cosmo.

Gods.

Autumn's body hadn't faded because she no longer possessed a soul. She'd been left behind, along with the other Fauna we hadn't saved in time.

I sagged against the tunnel, and my breath came out in ragged gasps.

What fate was worse? To be forgotten by your god? To lose your soul? Or to be bound to Jinx?

I'd failed the Fauna so utterly. They deserved better than this. Better than the 'salvation' I'd delivered them. How in god's name would I explain this to Quen?

How could I look him in the eye and confess to how pissing useless I was?

Gods, I needed him. Only Quen could sort out this mess.

Now wasn't the time to wallow in self-pity. I pulled myself from the wall and wiped my dirty hands down my leggings. Now wasn't the time for dignity, either. In my Chaos form and Fauna garb, I felt naked, but I could no longer change into my cat body to make the walk back bearable.

I drew in breath and pushed on.

The last time I'd been racing through tunnels was when I escaped with Quen and the others back to Grayford. When the Glimmer had fucked me over.

When Reve had... died.

Everything had gone wrong then. If Reve hadn't insisted on using that damn machine, would Varen have still betrayed me? Would Jinx still be inside my head?

Would any of this have ever happened?

"Chaos has awakened! Her children bring the end of the gods! The end of Chime! The end of time itself!"

Reve had seen the future. He'd known what I was. And yet he'd still chosen that fate.

Why? Had all this been because of one selfish, suicidal Mesmer? I had the entire domain of Phantasy in my head, and yet the answer wasn't any clearer to me. Every single Mesmer who had ever been born. All of them except for Reve.

Maybe it was as simple as that. He hadn't wanted me in charge of his soul, and considering how shit I was doing, I couldn't blame him.

As soon as I got back to the hotel, I'd get Dandelion to reach out to Quen. We'd then make arrangements using his pocket watch to pull him out of Memoria, regardless. Yes, he wanted to restore the Vesper, but they weren't going anywhere. They could wait.

At least my sense of direction didn't fail me. I didn't have my Vesper eyes, but I managed to stumble my way through the dark based on muscle memory alone. Only after I'd emerged from the tunnel did I remember I could have turned Glimmer, but whatever. The closer I got to Sinner's Row, the clearer the air, until a different sort of scent became obvious.

The scent of corruption—alcohol and piss.

Ember remained on guard by the main entrance of Sinner's Row. They shot me a perplexed look as I staggered past them, but they made no attempt to stop me. More Ember patrolled the streets. The change of leadership from Erosain to Trixie and now back to the Ember clearly hadn't affected them. I supposed this meant Sinder was now in charge. Edana had likely already informed him of the Fauna's fate.

Shit. Even if Edana offered me shelter, Jinx knew I'd made the hotel my base. We couldn't stay here. But where else could we go?

Thankfully, Jinx wasn't waiting outside the hotel doors, ready to pounce. I checked over my shoulder in case Gast lurked in the shadows, spying on me. He probably was, that arsehole. If he hadn't been playing hero, Trixie would still be here.

Why were men like that?

As soon as I opened the door, Cosmo ran at me.

"Mama! You're back! We were so worried!" Tears welled in their eyes, and they started blubbering.

Give me fucking strength. "It's all right, I'm here." I wrapped my arm around their shoulders and steered them into the dining hall. "Where's Dandelion?"

"He's—He's gone." Cosmo sniffed.

"Gone? Gone where?" Shit, had he heard of his sister and decided to come looking for me?

"Like the others."

I entered the restaurant and froze.

Piles of dust were scattered around the room, on the floor and various chairs. Some had abandoned clothes, but there weren't as many garments as the rest of Chime's streets since the Fauna barely wore anything.

But in the middle of the room was one large pile of dust surrounded by three smaller ones and the wide-brimmed hat I'd stolen from the Golden City.

Dandelion and the cubs.

I leaped inside my subconscious and found Cosmo's memory. They'd been standing here and watched as the Leander had faded not long after the Fauna. But that wasn't possible. Quen owned their souls, and he wouldn't have zapped them out of existence unless…

No.

Oh, gods no.

I gripped Cosmo's shoulder. "How do I get inside someone's subconscious? Mesmorpheus could travel between mortal dreams, couldn't they? How do I do that?"

"You can only do that when they're dreaming, silly—"

"Then how the fuck do I knock someone unconscious from here? Daydreams are still dreams, right?"

Cosmo winced. "Mama, you're hurting me."

I let their shoulder go. "Sorry. But Quen's in trouble. I need to get inside his head." I had the powers of a god. Surely that meant something?

I needed to reach Quen. I needed to check that Anima hadn't wrapped their slimy tentacles around him and fucked with Quen's memories! If Anima had locked the Vesper away inside my mind where I couldn't touch them, then they could have done the same with Quen and the Leander.

"It can be done," came Celeste's voice. She and Castor entered the restaurant arm in arm. "But our old papa never did it and told off any Mesmer who did. To force yourself on another's subconscious isn't nice."

"I get that. But if Quen's in trouble…" Gods, if his memory *had* been fucked with, then he may not even realize he was in trouble.

Celeste nodded. "We understand."

"We'll help," Castor added.

I rolled my shoulders and shook the tension from my hands. "All right. What do I do?"

Castor gestured to a couch. "Change to your Mesmer persona and lie down."

I did so, crossing my hands over my chest and letting my dirty, sore feet rest. "Now what?"

Celeste pulled over a chair. "Relax. You'll need to enter a lucid dream state. I'll enter your subconscious to help guide you, and we'll go from there."

"So... I just nap?"

"Yes."

That, I could do. If the gods could be defeated through the sheer power of napping, then I'd have all this chaos wrapped up by teatime.

I closed my eyes.

"Papa wouldn't like this," Cosmo said somewhere above me.

Celeste hushed them.

And then reality faded away.

When I opened my eyes, I was back at the depot.

It was exactly how I remembered it. The tram carriage nestled beside the platform. My room dangling from the hook above. Dru's plant pots by the large arched windows. Vincent's art on the brick walls. I'd recreated this place in my mind when Quen asked for a safe place. A sanctuary. And now my mind had apparently chosen it as my default.

It was home. The only home I'd ever known.

"This is your haven," Celeste said.

I almost jumped out of my pissing skin! She appeared out of nowhere beside me and then wandered off to admire Vincent's artwork.

"Did Uncle Vinny paint these?" she asked.

"Yes," I croaked. A wave of nostalgia suddenly came over me. Would we ever have this again? Me, my family, drinking wine and playing card games?

A peace that was just ours?

"And Reve? He slept downstairs?"

"You know of Reve?"

"Of course. He was our family too. Not many Mesmer make friends with other domains. You accepted him. That's why we accepted you."

"I..." Gods. Reve had been such an enigma, though I was fond of him. Losing him had hurt because he'd been one of us. A Godless. If there was a way to bring him back, somehow, I'd grasp it with both hands. "Thank you. Am I lucid dreaming right now?"

"Yes." Celeste turned from Vincent's paintings and faced me. "You have our old papa's abilities. You can walk through dreams."

"But only if the other mortal is dreaming?" I glanced at a clock on the wall and wasn't sure why I'd bothered. The time was thirteen minutes past one, and I had no idea if that was accurate in a dream world.

It had been early afternoon when I took my nap, which meant Quen was likely still awake wherever he was in Memoria.

"Technically. But you should be able to reach Quentin. You both shared a body, however briefly. That connects you on a deeper level than most mortals. Know that when you enter his mind, it will cause him to lose consciousness."

"He'll pass out?" That wasn't ideal, but I couldn't afford to wait.

"His mind will remain clear."

"Right. How do I do this?"

"Find his essence among the stars and reach out to him."

"Oh, that simple?" The Mesmer had spent a lifetime staring at stars and pondering their meaning, yet the closest thing to stars I'd ever studied was the aether lights of the Undercity plate. Back then, aether lamps used to send my head bonkers. It was only after I learned what I was—pure Chaos—that the migraines stopped.

Hold on—was I onto something? Chaos shared the same aether that powered those damn lights, and Quen was now Chaos. Maybe I *could* find him through the stars.

I wandered out of the depot and onto the tracks that led between the trash piles of Grayford. My memories created a scene I remembered with detail. Ahead were the crumbling buildings of Grayford, but I didn't need to go that far. I stood surrounded by a comforting darkness and stared above.

The lights flickered, twinkling like artificial stars. Silvery-blue with hints of pink. Beautiful aether.

More appeared, as though the real stars of Chime came to join me. Every soul was a star. *That* was the truth the Mesmer held dear. Every soul a star, every soul its own galaxy. Did all mortals have the potential to ascend into godhood?

What would reality be like then?

As I gazed across a ceiling of stars, one drew my attention. Silver with hints of bronze. Quen's soul.

I reached out to it, feeling a tad silly as I did so, but its energy hummed around my hand as I pulled it closer.

And then Quen appeared before me, just as suddenly as Celeste had.

He wore his usual tan suit, the jacket covering his metal arm, dressed as neat and proper as ever. His eyeglasses perched on his nose, not quite hiding the surprise and confusion in his aether eyes.

Thankfully, my dream self had come fully dressed in a neat skirt and blouse. I wanted to yank his lips onto mine, but first I had to be sure. "Are you my Quen?"

"This is the Undercity. How am I here? I was in the University, and then..." He spun, examining his surroundings, before focusing on me. "Am I whom?"

My heart sank. No recognition lit his eyes. "You don't remember me?"

His brow furrowed. "Should I?"

Shit!

Shitting shitty *shit*!

I was going to portal myself into Memoria and shove a fish up Anima's fucking arse! "Quen, it's me." I took a step toward him.

He shuffled back. "I have no idea what tomfoolery this is, ma'am. I assure you I have no perverse affiliations with Mesmer—"

"Quen, you *know* me—"

"My name is Quentin!"

Gods. What had Anima done to him? Wiped his memories of me, or completely rewritten who he was? "Quentin who? Who are you?"

"Who am *I*?" His voice rose hysterically. "Who, exactly, are *you*? Am I dreaming?"

Fucking gods. I'd known some shit like this would happen. Why would he enter Memoria alone when he *knew* this was a potential consequence?

Because he was still a chivalrous arse, deep down.

He'd asked me to marry him, and I'd practically laughed in his face. So what did he do? Run all the way to Memoria on some crusade for my benefit because he assumed I was still mourning the Vesper I couldn't bloody well remember. That was exactly the sort of thing Quen would do—put his life, heart, and soul at risk for idealism.

Could I fault him for it?

Yes. I pissing could, because without him, how were we meant to fight the gods?

I couldn't do this without him. Without *him*. My Quen.

And I was going to rip the domains apart to get him back.

All right. I took a deep breath. I needed to know exactly what Anima had done to him, and why, if I was going to fix this, and panicking would only scare him off. "You first."

"It is impractical for a Warden to share secrets when compromised in a dreamlike state."

"Okay, so you're a Warden."

"Ex-Warden, actually. If you believe you can invade my dreams to steal secrets to use against my organization, then you are sadly mistaken. I'm retired, and any secrets I previously held have been wiped from my memories." He flashed a wry smile. "The benefits of befriending Amnae."

Anima had not only fucked with Quen's memories, but constructed a whole new backstory. Why? What did he want Quen for? If Anima knew Quen was aligned with Chaos, then why not just murder him? "How are you spending your retirement, then? Studying fish?"

"What interest is it of yours?"

"You know, the Quentin Corinth *I* met was a lot politer than this."

His brow furrowed again. "How do you know my name? We've met before?"

"How would you even remember? You've wiped your memories. This isn't the first time, is it?"

He lifted his eyeglasses and rubbed the bridge of his nose. "Apologies. You've caught me at an awkward time, and I still have no idea why I'm here inside this dream. Did we meet during a case? Did I help you?"

I took a step closer, and this time he allowed me to close the distance between us. "You've always been there for me. You know that, deep inside." I placed a hand on his left arm. "Let me help you remember."

The confusion remained in his stare. "I... If I've removed those memories, then it is likely for good reason. To protect myself, or to protect you."

"Protect me from what? What are you doing in Memoria?"

"Nothing untoward. I'm lecturing at the University."

"You're a professor."

"Yes. Teaching mnemonics." He placed his hand on top of mine, his breath hitching at the contact.

I bit my bottom lip. His touch felt so warm, so right.

He'd been gone less than twenty-four hours, and yet I still ached for him.

Anima had gone and ruined *everything*. How the fuck would I get Quen's memories back? By taking on Anima myself? I wanted to scream and cry, but more than that... I wanted to kiss Quen. Right this moment.

"Who are you?" he whispered. "Your name?"

"Kayl."

His eyes opened wide.

And then he vanished.

I stumbled forward, reaching out for the man no longer there. "Quen?"

Shit! I glanced up at the many stars and couldn't see or sense him among them. He was gone. Ejected from my dream. Someone must have woken him from the other side.

"What an interesting turn of events."

Ugh. Just what I needed.

Corentine was leaning against the arm of a scrapped couch, wearing a tight black dress. It still felt odd seeing her face to face when she had *my* face. Jinx's face.

"Why are you here?" I demanded.

"You invited me, daughter—"

"I bloody didn't!"

"All the aether in the universe is mine." She gestured at the blinking lights above us. "You summoned these souls here. I merely followed."

I crossed my arms. "What do you want?"

"Can a mother not desire to check in on her children? Especially those who abandoned me?"

"Perhaps your children wouldn't abandon you if you weren't so overbearing and understood boundaries. Now get out of my head."

"Are you so willing to show me the door when I've only arrived? It seems you and your lover need my help."

"Your help?" I snorted. "If you think this tiny setback is enough to send me begging for you and Jinx, then you underestimate me."

"Anima has stolen Quentin's memories. You're the one underestimating the severity of this situation, daughter. How do you intend to fight Anima? We know what happened last time. You lost your Vesper lover. Would Anima force you to forget another?"

I clenched my teeth. Confronting Anima was far riskier than going against any other god—even The Nameless One, who still left me rattled. If Anima caught me, then... There was a chance I'd forget Quen. Then I really would lose everything.

"All right. You send Jinx, and then Anima can fuck with her memories and make her forget all about *you*. Enjoy wallowing in your clock tower for another millennium."

Corentine chuckled. "Your sister has made me so proud. She's captured the souls of three gods now—Gildola, The Nameless One, and Faen. Each of their powers would be enough to evade and defeat Anima. How would you face Anima with the power of the Mesmer? Can you take the shape of a sea creature like the Fauna? Hold your breath, like the Necro? Or even burn through the glass dome itself like the Glimmer?"

When she put it like that, I did appear woefully unprepared. But the last time I'd accepted Jinx's help, she'd stolen Witheryn and Vincent from under my nose. How stupid did Corentine think I was?

This was my dream, and she was outstaying her welcome. "Oh, fuck off."

The smile was wiped from her lips in an instant, and a madness I'd only ever seen in Jinx's eyes shadowed hers.

And then she was right in front of me.

"Shit!" I staggered back, but Corentine moved impossibly fast.

She grabbed my neck, her fingernails cutting into my skin.

"Get—*off*!" I tried to pry her free, but then both hands wrapped around my neck. They squeezed tight, choking the life from me.

"It's the nature of Chaos to bless me with one competent daughter and curse me with you," Corentine snarled.

She forced me to my knees. It was all I could do to keep breathing.

"What a disappointment you've been." Corentine leered above me. "You and your sister could have destroyed this universe by now, if only you weren't so stupid. But no matter. Your sister will forsake you. She doesn't need you anymore."

I coughed, spluttering saliva onto her wrist, but she didn't let up.

Gods. She was going to kill me in my own dream.

By the glint in her eye, she was enjoying every second of it.

I grasped her wrist and attempted to take her soul, but there was no tug—nothing—because she wasn't technically here.

Celeste! I called out. *Wake me up! For gods' sake, wake me!*

My vision started to go black.

"Don't forget who owns your soul, daughter." Corentine's voice swam around me. "I made you. I can unmake you."

She laughed, a discordant, chaotic sound that drowned me in a sea of stars.

And those two glowing aether eyes burned me to stardust.

I sucked in a strangled gasp of air. "Fuck!"

Castor pinned my shoulder to the couch, preventing me from rolling off and bashing my head. Gods, I must have been flailing, because the poor man's right eye was half-closed. He let up when he saw I was back in control of my limbs.

This was the second time Corentine had invaded my dreams. How was she doing it? Had I left the backdoor of my subconscious open, somehow?

Cosmo replaced Castor as I sat up and steadied my breathing. "Here." They offered me a cup of tea and a small plate of biscuits. "New Papa says tea helps you stay calm in a crisis, but sugar helps me with bad dreams."

Were these even dreams, when they felt so real? When Corentine had been there?

When I'd touched Quen?

I snatched a bourbon biscuit and then another. Dreams were another domain no different from reality, or so my Mesmer instincts told me. If Corentine ever did achieve her freedom, I had no doubt she'd murder me for real.

Whatever her motives, Corentine now knew Anima had Quen, and Quen was vulnerable to manipulation. Jinx could go after them. Corentine had been right about that—Jinx stood a much better chance of getting Quen back than me.

But I had a shortcut.

I cradled Quen's pocket watch in my hands. "How can I take on Anima? I need ideas—crazy ones, even crazier ones. Hit me." If anyone could come up with a plan, it was the Mesmer with their infinite imagination.

There was no chance I'd sit here and do nothing while Quen was trapped in Memoria. I was getting him back, one way or another.

Celeste helped herself to a custard crème. "Easy. With our old papa's powers, you can create a new reality around Anima to manipulate them into doing what you want."

A muscle in my head popped. "I can do *what*?"

"Create a new reality. Like wrapping them in a dream, only you are in control of the dream and can warp it however you wish."

She made it sound so pissing easy! Oh, we can solve all our problems by just creating a *whole new reality*! Why hadn't I thought of that? "Somehow I don't think it's possible to trick a god into stumbling into a dream world." Did gods even dream? Well, Corentine did, but what else could you do when trapped in a clock tower? "Wait, have Mesmer been walking around tricking everyone into dreaming their own reality?" Why did I even ask? My head was aching enough without contemplating the philosophy of pissing reality. That was Quen's sort of thing, not mine.

"No. Our old papa doesn't like us casting illusions because manipulating others is wrong."

"A Mesmer did that once," Cosmo said with sudden eagerness. "Nova. He'd spin illusions and make mortals do whatever he wanted. When Papa found out, they were so mad. Nova was never allowed to leave Phantasy again."

Gods. I dreaded to think what chaos a rogue Mesmer could get up to. Though bending reality could be useful, morality aside.

Then again, maybe taking on Anima myself was too ambitious. Maybe this was one battle I *should* leave to Jinx. I could still travel through to Memoria and bring Quen back. Even if I couldn't immediately restore his memories, he'd be safe.

That was better than nothing, wasn't it?

Fuck's sake. What a stupid position to be in.

Quen had forgotten me. Had likely forgotten our purpose. He wasn't my Quen anymore, not like this, and the thought of never having him again... Gods, it hurt as badly as when I lost Dru.

But Dru was still in there, somewhere. I hadn't given up on her, and I wouldn't give up on Quen. He was still *him*. Still my smart, charming Quen. I'd bring him home, keep him safe, and find the real Quen again. He'd risked everything to find the missing parts of me. It was the least I could do.

I stood from the couch. "I'm going to Memoria."

"Is that safe, Mama?" asked Cosmo, whose lower lip was already wobbling.

I forced a smile. "I'll bring you back a souvenir."

Their eyes lit up. "Really? What kind?"

"Their gift shops sell sticks of rock. Really hard candy. You'll love it."

I rushed upstairs to change out of my breast band and leggings and then made my way to the center of the restaurant, where Quen had previously summoned the portal to Memoria. If I could trace his steps, he'd be easier to follow, or so I hoped.

He'd at least given me a starting point—the University. In an ocean of Amnae, a silver-haired Diviner should stick out.

I swapped my form to Chaos and wound the pocket watch to five past one.

The trio gathered around me. Their apprehension vibrated through our shared bond with nervous energy. While Gods lived through their mortals' lives, I'd never get used to feeling the emotions of other beings. It was both a thrill and a violation. Their emotions were theirs, and I gently placed a mental wall between us. Not to block them out, but to allow them the privacy of their own thoughts and feelings.

I was their temporary god, but that didn't mean I owned them. "Stay safe while I'm gone. If there's any trouble—if anyone other than Sinder enters this hotel—hide and then pray to me, okay?"

"Yes, Mama," the three of them said in unison.

They weren't so bad, truth be told. They trusted me, which was more than the Fauna had managed.

I activated the pocket watch.

For a split second, I sensed the aether as a portal ripped between the domains and opened into Memoria.

And then water gushed into the room.

"Run!" I yelled and turned to leg it, but the wave swept me off my feet. I fell, splashing into what felt like a pool, as if I were back on Arcadia and being dragged out into the ocean.

Another wave crashed over me, pulling me under.

Shit!

I held my breath and tried to grasp hold of the couch, a table, pissing anything! Above me rang the garbled screams of Celeste and Cosmo.

Castor was swimming toward me—how did he know how to bloody swim? He grabbed my arm and pulled me against the wall.

I breached the surface and sucked in a gasp of air.

The entire dining hall was flooded. Water still poured from the open portal, and the levels were rising fast. Teacups and chairs floated past, and... Oh my god. Fish! Colorful stripy fish had swum in through the portal!

"Mama!" screamed Cosmo. They and Celeste stood atop a table that had floated over and gotten itself wedged in the kitchen doorway.

"Stay put!" I yelled back. They were both soaking wet, but safer there than where I was.

"The portal!" Castor said.

Shit, I'd dropped the pocket watch. I hoped it was waterproof. "It'll close in a few minutes." But did we have a few minutes? The entire ocean of Memoria was emptying into the hotel! "The doors! We need to open the doors, drain it out."

Castor nodded and then dove back into the water. He'd always been the quietest one of the trio, and now I appreciated the fact he was the most useful Mesmer I'd ever met.

A moment later, the portal snapped shut, sending one last wave of water lapping around the restaurant.

And then the main hotel doors burst open, and the water surged once more, draining into Sinner's Row until only a shallow pool above my ankles remained.

Shitting shit!

Why hadn't that worked? When Quen had opened a portal into Memoria, it had opened inside the city, not in the middle of the damn ocean! What had I done wrong? Had I forgotten to press the 'don't fuck up' button somewhere?

Edana had said the gods defended their domains against invasion, and there was no better defense than leagues of fucking water. Had Anima sensed Quen attempting to enter their domain and allowed Quen in, while denying me? Or was it simply a case of not being tricked twice?

No way was I getting into Memoria like this.

Something orange bumped into my shin, and I almost screamed, but it was only a fish. A bulbous, slimy orange fish flopping from side to side, its stupid face gasping for breath. There wasn't enough water for it.

"Mama!" Cosmo waddled over, their clothes as waterlogged as mine and they squelched with every step. "What do we do? We've got to save it!"

"Grab a bucket, it needs water."

"Where from?"

"I don't know, the kitchen!"

Cosmo whimpered and ran for a bucket.

It wouldn't survive in the Undercity. Great. I'd gone and committed a war crime against a bloody fish.

I left it to its fate and searched the debris for Quen's pocket watch. Thankfully, it glinted in a pile of soggy biscuits. I shook out the water. The damn thing didn't tick or tock, so who knew if it still worked.

Boots splashed through the remaining water, and I turned. Sinder approached, his eyes wide in surprise.

"I know you like to shake things up, dearest, but this is ridiculous."

I wrung water from my blouse. "Don't start."

"You've flooded the street. How, exactly, did you manage that?"

"It was an accident."

"Does this have something to do with the Fauna? We know they're... missing."

I gave up trying to dry my clothes and let my wet hands fall uselessly to my sides. "It's everything, all right? The Fauna are gone. Jinx took them. And now... Quen is missing, too. And I—I can't get him back." I covered my mouth and suppressed a sob.

Gods, what a miserable day this had been.

Sinder took me in his arms. "I've got you, darling."

I tried to pull back. "Don't, I'm soaking—"

"It's fine." Heat emanated from his skin, warming and drying me. Sinder always knew how to comfort me after a bad day, and despite everything, I needed that—and him—right now. Even if he was Edana's lackey, and anything I told Sinder would go straight back to her.

It didn't matter, did it? Edana would already know Jinx had been here and taken the Fauna. Gods, Jinx was probably watching all this unfold from a rooftop and laughing her tits off.

I'd fucked up. Again.

I couldn't face Anima alone. I couldn't save Quen.

But I still refused to ask Jinx for help.

I pulled from Sinder's embrace, though, gods, it was difficult to do. "I need to speak with Edana."

If I needed to whore myself out to Edana to save Quen, then I'd do it.

I'd do whatever it took.

XXXVIII

"QUENTIN? ARE YOU HURT?"

I went to rub my bleary eyes and smudged the glass of my spectacles instead. Blast. "What happened?"

"You fainted."

Had I? I must have, for I was seated on my buttocks next to the university reception desk and had drawn a crowd of gawking onlookers. How terribly embarrassing! Was it the shock of seeing Elijah here, for the first time in months? Or was the Memoria humidity finally getting to me?

"I'm so sorry." I stood on shaky legs.

Elijah took my metal arm and helped me up. "Let's get you a cup of tea. Is there somewhere we can talk?"

"Mr. Kipler's comes highly recommended."

"I was thinking something more private. There's a lot we need to go over. Your Excellency?"

Ambassador Brooke had been kind enough to clear the area and grant me a little privacy, and now came over and placed a reassuring hand on my upper arm. She was the touchy-feely type. "I've already spoken with the faculty staff and have arranged for a private room. Would you mind if I joined you?"

"Of course not," Elijah replied. "What I have to report also concerns Memoria."

The two ambassadors exchanged serious glances. Should I be worried? I'd hoped to catch up with Eli privately, but I supposed there'd be time for that later. He wouldn't have come all this way unless it was of dire importance.

We followed Ambassador Brooke back inside the university, this time headed for the administration offices and not the science department. The entire way, my stomach fluttered with anticipation. What did I have to be nervous about? Seeing Elijah again after so long? Or was it the dream I'd had?

I would have chalked it up as just an odd dream if the Mesmer woman hadn't identified herself as Kayl. That name meant something. Something so vital, my mind couldn't let it go. But what? I'd have to ask Elijah once we were alone. I didn't believe in coincidences.

Brooke led us into a meeting room already stocked with tea—both herbal tea and the black brew I preferred—as well as digestive biscuits and those little kelp cakes, which were more like sweet seaweed crackers with a hint of sea salt. Actually rather moreish.

Elijah and I made ourselves comfortable as Brooke poured the tea.

I ignored the digestives and went for a kelp cake. "What's this about?"

Elijah sipped from his cup. "What do you recall of the incident in Chime last month?"

What an odd question. "Has something happened?"

"Unfortunately, things have worsened since your retirement. I need to see where you're at before I can get you up to speed."

I knew early retirement was too good to be true. I glanced at Brooke. "Are Warden protocols in place?"

"What we discuss here concerns the future of all domains," Elijah said. "Brooke has a right to know."

Brooke nodded. "You have my discretion and my thanks, Karendar."

Well then. Warden protocol demanded a true and accurate account of events as clearly as I could recall them, lest my time in Memoria had distorted the facts.

I shifted in my seat and placed my metal arm across the table in a comfortable position. I'd lost this arm during the last battle against Chaos. It seemed these battles were far from over.

"It all began two months ago with a spate of murders targeting Diviner across Central. These were no ordinary murders—Diviner were somehow losing their souls, yet their bodies remained as evidence. You ordered me to investigate, Elijah, and my investigation brought me to the Undercity and to a group of heathens known as the Godless." A ragtag group of sinners and other undesirables. "We arrested them, but were too late in discovering they'd been harboring the very creatures responsible for the murders—unholy beings made of Chaos. Not only did they possess the ability to devour souls, but they could modify their physicality to any other domain." Making them the biggest threat to Chime and the domains history had ever seen.

Elijah nodded. "Very good. Continue."

"Alas, one of these creatures escaped capture and ran into Eventide. We couldn't stop them, and their true devastating nature became apparent—they took the soul of Valeria." Of an actual god. "This resulted in Eventide's destruction and triggered an attack on Central Station. We lost many good men, and during the battle, I was severely injured while protecting you. The Wardens eventually regained control and restored peace, though... I'm unsure as to the fate of the Chaos creature. My injury took me out of the bigger picture. Father granted me an early retirement, and I came here to recover and teach."

I'd not given much thought to my sudden retirement. Even with my injury, I still could have continued to serve the Wardens. The new arm I'd been generously gifted by a Zephyr engineer made mobility much easier, though the aches and pains continued even on my good days.

At the time, Elijah had been keen to emphasize I wasn't being discarded, but that my retirement was a reward for my service. Chime needed him, now more than ever. But I'd needed him, too.

Information regarding Eventide's demise and the nature of the Chaos creatures had been hushed to prevent panic among the populace. It was business as usual here in Memoria... Or at least it had been. Last month, the Gate had been placed on lockdown. No one was leaving.

That never happened. Something had gone terribly wrong.

Eli wouldn't be here otherwise.

"What's happened?" I asked again.

Elijah set his cup down. I knew him intimately enough to see when he was bracing me for bad news. "There have been Chaos attacks since. More domains have fallen."

Saints. More domains gone? More gods dead? That couldn't be! "Which?"

"Solaris. Phantasy. Tempest. Witheryn. Obituary. Juniper."

No.

My gods.

That was half of them! "How—How could this have happened? How am I only now hearing of this?" My heart was thrashing against my chest. I stood and paced. "The Wardens exist to prevent this from happening! Entire domains, just... *gone*?"

None of it made sense! Oh, I could understand Juniper falling victim to Chaos, that actually made sense; perhaps even Lionheart, but Gildola wouldn't have been that foolish or reckless. Neither would Zyclone or The Nameless One have been.

And why would Chaos target the Mesmer? That was akin to kicking a child!

The Mesmer... A Mesmer woman had visited my dream, but that wasn't possible if the Mesmer were gone...

Unless.

That hadn't been a Mesmer at all.

"Quentin, sit down," Elijah ordered.

I sat and reached for a cup of tea with my metal hand. My artificial fingers gripped too hard, crushing the handle to pieces. The cup fell and spilled tea across the table. Blast! I still hadn't mastered control of my damnable arm yet. "I am *so* sorry—"

"Don't worry about it." Brooke beamed a polite smile and mopped the spillage with a napkin. "There's more available."

Elijah passed me a spare cup, which I gratefully took with my trembling left hand.

Tea burned down my throat, grounding me in the present. "How did these attacks happen?"

"We underestimated Chaos."

I wanted to laugh at the absurdity of it all. "I assume Anima is aware of this?"

"Anima is aware," Brooke said. "We have protections in place to keep Memoria and our mortals safe."

"Do other domains also have a plan in place?"

"Our priority is that of our mortals and allies," Elijah said.

Our allies. That should have included the Zephyr, surely. Even the Necro. Obviously that now included the Amnae, and likely the Umber.

What were Edana and Serenity doing during this mess? If they had any sense, they'd be throwing themselves at Dor's feet.

"Father needs you," Elijah confirmed at last. That was the reason for his visitation. "We hate to drag you out of retirement, but as you see, the situation requires it."

"Understood." Though... "Why hasn't Father spoken to me regarding this?"

I'd prayed to Father, and heard no response. Nothing.

"I wanted to be the one to break this news." Elijah reached across the table and took my left hand. "And I missed you."

My heart fluttered at his touch. "I'm yours in whatever capacity you need me." Though I wasn't sure what good I could do against an enemy who had destroyed seven blasted domains. At this point, *was* there a way to fight back?

No. I couldn't think that way.

If we didn't stop Chaos, then more domains would fall. It would be the end of everything.

As a Warden, retired or otherwise, it was my duty to protect Chime and her mortals.

To the bitter end.

Elijah squeezed my hand gently. "Then we must return to Kronos as soon as possible."

I turned to Ambassador Brooke. "Apologies, Your Excellency. It appears I will no longer be gracing your halls. If I may, I have some lecture notes to pass on to Doctor Ilona Burns."

"We'll be sad to see you leave us," Brooke said. "We appreciate and thank Dor for looking out for our domain during these difficult times. Before you depart, we do have a situation I was hoping you could assist with."

I glanced at Eli, who nodded. "Go ahead."

Brooke set aside her herbal tea. "Our local Wardens have been investigating a group of revolutionaries in the city, calling themselves the Godless. Sound familiar?"

Painfully so. "I thought we rounded those up back in the Undercity?" I'd been there for the operation when we arrested their leader, a Seren woman named Harmony Arabesque, and the rest of the Godless members. Last I'd heard, they'd been incarcerated in our correctional facility and then carted off to face judgement from their gods.

Elijah sighed. "It appears their ideology has spread to infect other domains. Such heathens are the reason Chaos creatures continue to pose a threat. They undermine the sanctity of the remaining domains and must be dealt with."

I concurred. "How may we help?"

"The Godless recruit new members by inviting their victims for recreational activities, such as book clubs, and then altering their memories to make them sympathetic to their cause," Brooke continued.

"That's... horrendous." I couldn't think of a more horrific crime than to take away one's freedom of thought by manipulating their memories. "I understand your concern. Is Anima unable to locate them?"

"Unfortunately not. They have been careful to remove and alter their own memories enough to avoid detection. However, we may have one lead. We believe one of their main recruiters is Doctor Ilona Burns."

What? "That's not possible. I've worked with Doctor Burns, and she's a dedicated professional, despite her young age—"

"Perhaps her young age makes her more susceptible to Godless propaganda—"

"Honestly, I fail to see—"

"Quentin." Brooke placed her hand upon mine. "Doctor Burns is complicit."

My eyes fluttered closed, and for a heartbeat, everything went dark.

Thoughts raced through my mind.

My eyes snapped back open, and I shook off the strange feeling. "Apologies, I think I nodded off for a second there. What were you saying?"

Brooke patted my hand and returned to her herbal tea. "You were telling me your concerns about Doctor Ilona Burns."

"Oh. Yes, that's right." Gosh, what a long day it had been so far, if my own mind was befuddled. "I believe I have reasons to be suspicious. I know how it sounds—Doctor Burns is a dedicated professor, but her young age does make her more susceptible to Godless propaganda. She invited me to her book club earlier, which could very well be a front. With your permission, I'd like to investigate."

"Will this be safe?" Elijah asked. "I don't wish to risk Quentin's life."

"We'll have our own Wardens on hand to swoop in and take over," Brooke assured us. "All Quentin needs to do is lead us straight to them."

I flashed my most charming smile. "I may be retired, but I've still got it."

"Thank you, Quentin. Karendar." Brooke nodded at Elijah. "We appreciate your support in this matter."

I finished my tea and stood. "Then let's not waste any time."

I knew Elijah and Father needed me, but taking care of this mess first would flush out any residual Godless still foolish enough to defy the Covenant, while also building relations between ourselves and the Amnae. With domains dropping like sugar in a teacup, we needed all the support we could get.

Retirement didn't suit me, anyhow.

Once a Warden, always a Warden.

Doctor Burns waited for me within her office. It was a typical Amnae lab, full of bubbling green and purple potions she required for her research. While memory transference and retrieval was her expertise, I knew a thing or two about mnemonics myself. A bright girl, and she clearly had a bright future ahead of her. Or would have, if she weren't cavorting with heathens.

That was one reason I wanted to help her. She was young. There was still time to rehabilitate and educate her. Honestly, I didn't see the point of punishment in this case.

She was just a child.

"Doctor Burns?" I rapped on her door. "Are you free?"

She placed down a flask and removed her goggles. "Quentin! I was so worried. We saw you faint. Are you all right?"

"Yes, thank you. Nothing to worry about. Listen, I'm being recalled to Kronos. I'm afraid I won't be able to complete my lectures."

Her shoulders sagged. "You're leaving? When?"

"Soon, I suspect."

"Is that why a Diviner was visiting? Who was that? The ambassador?"

"Yes. Things are serious outside Memoria, and the Wardens need my help—"

"But you're retired! They can't demand you leave—"

"I've volunteered." I forced a smile. "I know this is sudden. I'm sorry. If you've got time, I'd like to hand over whatever lecture notes I have, and also visit this bookstore you keep going on about. Purchase myself a souvenir before I leave."

She'd been adamant we visit this particular bookstore. There was a reason she'd been so welcoming, and I doubted it was because she considered me a potential candidate for a club full of heathens. No, as an ex-Warden, the secrets I carried made me a target.

Doctor Burns was an expert in her field. If anyone knew how to dig deep into someone's memories and steal secrets, it was her.

It was a risk I'd have to take.

"Yes! We must!" She quickly shrugged off her lab coat and gathered her belongings. The relief that flashed across her face was so quick, so slight, I would have missed it if I hadn't been observing her every reaction.

I hated that she was a case, now, and not a trusted colleague.

But I'd been suspicious of her since the very first time we met, hadn't I?

Together, we set out for Memoria's main city. Despite the Gate being off, the city was as busy as ever, with citizens and students alike browsing the shops and teahouses. We strode past Mr. Kipler's, and while I would have relished the opportunity to try their tea and cakes, I simply didn't have the time. Cakes were an indulgence I also couldn't afford, spiritually. It was as though Elijah's arrival had reminded me of my true nature.

To indulge was to sin. Even in something as innocent as kelp cakes.

As we neared Bath's Books and Beyond, I became aware of the entourage following us. Amnae Wardens weren't so different from Chime's counterparts. They dressed in plain clothes and did an excellent job of mingling with the crowds, yet to me they were painfully obvious. At least they were on my tail, as Ambassador Brooke had promised.

On my signal, they would move.

But I had to be sure of the ambassador's suspicions first.

"Here we are," declared Doctor Burns as we paused outside the bookstore. We hadn't ventured far—the bookstore was practically opposite the Gate, making it a prime tourist destination, I was sure. "I'd like to introduce you to its owner. They run the book club, and I think you'd be interested in hearing what they have to say."

Oh, I certainly would be.

A tinny bell rang as I followed Doctor Burns inside. Bath's Books and Beyond was what I expected of a bookstore. There were rows of waterproof books—essentially, books printed on or wrapped in a newly invented synthetic material the Zephyr called plastic. The store also boasted a collection of traditional paper-based books inside a glass case to protect them against humidity. This store, like most in Memoria, had water spouts connected to the pipes running across the ceiling, which would pump out mist intermittently.

Across the counter stood a tall Amnae. The store's proprietor, I assumed. Their skin was an odd mixture of purple and yellow stripes with both black and white fins across the ridges of their head. They wore a simple shirt and slacks common to most folk in the city.

"Ilona, welcome!" they greeted Doctor Burns with a garbled voice that sounded neither male or female. "And you must be the professor." They held out their hand to shake. "I'm Laguna, owner of this here joint."

I held up my hands, palms open. "Apologies, I make a point not to touch mortals if I can help it. The hazards of my domain. Please, call me Quentin. How would you like me to address you?"

"Am I that ambiguous?" They chuckled. "Nah, I appreciate you asking. Never been a fan of sir or ma'am."

"Understood. Doctor Burns has been singing your praises."

"Naturally! We're only the best bookstore in town. Do you have a fancy for anything in particular? We're more about selling adventures here than textbooks, but we cater to all kinds."

I actually rather enjoyed reading books. Fictional stories were largely prohibited by our masters during my old school days—they were considered a waste of time. But for a young, impressionable Warden, stories of heroism had shaped my outlook on life. A Warden needed an active imagination to be effective, in my opinion, and nothing served that need better than fiction.

"Could we see your special stock?" Doctor Burns asked. "Quentin is leaving for Kronos soon."

"Oh!" Laguna's eyes widened. "Let me close up early." They locked the store door and swapped the open sign for closed. "Now then, if you'd come this way."

Doctor Burns and I followed Laguna into a back storage room that led downstairs into a cellar, which *did* surprise me. I didn't think Amnae buildings contained cellars.

"We host our book club down here," Laguna explained as we descended a metal staircase. "This month we're reading the *Tales of Lunis Aquaria*. They're a bunch of stories set in imaginary domains, similar but different to ours. Crazy to think other domains could exist out there, you know? With whole new gods and mortals."

"Indeed." Though, such a notion was blasphemous to consider. There were only twelve gods—had been only twelve gods. Saints, the entire system of Chime would need to be reworked once this was over. Losing one god to Chaos was bad enough, but seven?

Seven.

I'd given it little thought because my mortal brain failed to comprehend its significance.

Chaos had achieved the impossible. How could we stand against such a foe?

We came to the bottom of the staircase, and Laguna paused beside a rusted metal door. "Before I let you inside, I ask you keep an open mind." They produced a thick iron key from their slacks and opened the door with a groaning screech.

I braced myself, half expecting a laboratory like Doctor Burns's office or perhaps even a torture chamber, but no. The inner room was cozy, filled with bookshelves, tables with planters and lamps, and even a rug bringing the whole ensemble together. Though, the dank scent of seaweed lingered underground.

At the far end, an older Amnae lady sat in an armchair and nursed a porcelain cup. Beside her was a round glass bowl containing a single fish. How odd. As far as I recalled, it was prohibited for locals and tourists alike to interact with Memoria's fish.

"Is it teatime?" the old woman asked. "I'd like a cup of tea."

"Good afternoon, Doris," Doctor Burns greeted cheerfully. She placed her satchel on the table beside the fish bowl and pulled out a flask. "I've got your brew right here."

"Oh, goody! I need my tea, dear." The old lady—Doris—held out her cup.

Doctor Burns poured a foul green mixture. The same concoction I'd seen her working on in her office.

Saints. They really were altering the memories of innocents, as Brooke had described. "What are you doing?" I demanded.

Doris lifted the cup to her lips.

"Stop!" I strode for the cup.

Laguna stepped in front of me. "It's not what you think—"

"You're poisoning her!"

"It's not poison." Doctor Burns sipped from the flask. "See? The green pigment is from seaweed, to make it palatable for Amnae tastes."

Doris finished her cup. "Is it time for tea?"

I stared, aghast. "If that's not poison, then why is she like this?" The poor woman looked around the room, confused, as though she didn't know where she was. "It's clear to me you've been altering her memories!"

"We're trying to restore them," Doctor Burns stated. "That's what my research is about. Restoring that which was taken by a divine entity."

"You're speaking of Anima?"

"Yes."

That confirmed Brooke's suspicions. Both Doctor Burns and Laguna were apostates. Godless.

"Anima has always demanded our memories," Laguna was saying. "In exchange for our existence. It's the price we pay for our livelihoods, our freedom. But what freedom is there when Anima takes and takes?"

"My own father forgot me," Doctor Burns said. "Forgot me, my siblings, my mother. Yes, I had siblings, once. Anima demanded those memories; made my own mother forget she'd birthed them. They died, neglected. It ruined her life, and mine."

Gods. Could that be true?

"Sometimes they take too much," Laguna added. "On the surface, Memoria looks peaceful. The perfect city to outsiders like you. Amnae who have lost too many of their memories are taken away, locked inside homes where they can't even remember who they are. Mortals like Doris, here."

"Is it teatime yet?" Doris asked.

Laguna smiled, and there was a fondness in it. "Soon. Doris was a regular customer of mine. When she started losing large chunks of her memory, she came to me, frightened out of her wits. The Wardens wanted to lock her in a home, but she begged me to keep her safe. That was the beginning."

"My mother suffered a similar fate," Doctor Burns said. "It's what I discovered when I went through my father's old memories, trying to piece his research together."

"Why are you telling me all this?" I'd not expected them to hand a confession over on a platter, yet here they were, spilling their guts.

"Because you were in my father's memories, Quentin. You're the only one who can help us."

What nonsense! "You have me mistaken—"

"No. There's no mistake." The fire in her eyes was more adult, more Ember, than an Amnae child should possess. "You knew my father. Professor Walter Burns. He taught you at Chime's Academy—"

"You're wrong. I have no recollection of this Walter—"

"Because they've rewritten your memories. The Wardens. Ambassador Brooke—our new ambassador. Yesterday we had a completely different one."

"You're lying."

"They're lying to *you*. You're not the man you think you are, but I can help you remember." She held out her hand. "I can restore your true memories. Trust me."

I recoiled. "Don't you dare touch me."

"*Please*," she begged. Tears welled in her eyes. "I've watched your memories. You... You were there when my father died. When Elijah Karendar ordered his execution. You tried to stop him."

No. I refused to believe it.

Eli would never do such a thing!

Laguna subtly made their way to the door. They were blocking me in.

If they touched me, they could alter my memories. Make me believe their twisted version of reality.

This was *my* reality, and I would not allow them to take it from me.

I ran for the door.

Laguna leaped in front of me. I rammed into them with my metal arm. The action sent a spasm of pain through my residual limb, but had the intended effect—it sent Laguna sprawling.

"Quentin, stop!" Doctor Burns yelled.

"Is it time for tea?" Doris said.

Laguna grasped my leg. I shoved them off, a bit too forcefully, and they fell in a heap.

I didn't waste time seeing if I'd injured them as I scrambled up the metal stairway and around the counter.

The store door was locked. Blast it! Laguna had the key!

I ran to the windows and thumped them.

The Wardens got the signal.

A second later they bashed the door down and flooded inside.

"Downstairs," I said.

I leaned against the counter and caught my breath as the Wardens marched back upstairs with Laguna and a confused Doris in cuffs, and then finally Doctor Burns.

"Your memories are in the ocean!" she called to me. "It's the fish! Anima releases them in the—"

One of the Wardens grabbed her neck. She gasped, and then her eyes rolled back, and she collapsed in his arms.

"What did you do?" I demanded. "We're not to harm her!"

"A factory reset," he grumbled. "Brooke's orders."

"What does that mean? A factory reset...?" But as I glanced at Doctor Burns' face, I was hit by a horrible realization.

She was smiling at me with the innocent playfulness of a child. Drool ran from her lip.

He'd wiped her memories in a single blink. *All* her memories.

Saints.

Doctor Ilona Burns was reduced to a babe. All that research, all that potential... gone.

Brooke couldn't have ordered this, surely?

It was... cruelty, obscene cruelty! Doctor Burns may be an apostate, but she surely didn't deserve such a fate! Would the same happen to Laguna? To Doris? Though in the old lady's case, perhaps it was a mercy.

I'd be having words with Ambassador Brooke, posthaste.

The Wardens escorted me back to their HQ. An odd building compared to the stone gray halls of Chime's HQ, for their building was the shape of a glass bowl. Inside, however, the offices contained the same pitiless bureaucracy.

Elijah waited for me inside Ambassador Brooke's office.

The ambassador sensed my discomfort and immediately rose to greet me. "Quentin. I hear I have you to thank for rounding up the Godless—"

"Ambassador, I must say how disappointed—"

She hushed me and took my hand. Really, Brooke was being rather inappropriate with how forward she...

I blinked. I must have blacked out for a moment, for an odd feeling fell upon me. "Apologies. It has been a long day. What were you saying, Your Excellency?"

"How pleased I am with your support. Thanks to you, the Godless will no longer plague Memoria."

I bowed my head. "Happy to be of assistance. Throw the book at them, Ambassador, and may we never see their kind again." It had been disappointing to discover Doctor Burns operating as an apostate, but justice had been done, and now I could return to Kronos with my head held high.

Brooke glanced at Elijah. "How lucky you are to have such a gentleman in your employ."

Elijah smiled. "Quentin is a gift from our Father."

"Isn't he just." Brooke patted my shoulder. "Why don't you rest for a moment? Help yourself to tea, and then we'll make arrangements for your departure."

I sat beside Eli and poured myself an herbal tea to help steady the slight tremble in my metal hand. All this running about wasn't good for my recovery, and my residual limb ached with the occasional spasm of sharp pain.

There were kelp cakes on offer, but I resisted the temptation.

"I'm proud of you, Quentin," Elijah said.

For the first time since he entered Memoria, we were now alone.

Time hadn't changed him. He was still the sharply dressed man I knew, with his pinstripe suit, neatly-combed-back bronze hair, and stunningly beautiful brass eyes.

It was a sin to love, to lust, and yet...

Elijah meant everything.

"I'm sorry it has been so long," I said, the words catching in my throat. "But I'm glad you're here."

His delicate fingers lifted my chin. "There's much work to be done."

My heart skipped a beat. "I know. I'm with you."

He leaned closer, and then those soft lips were pressing against mine with such force, it consumed me.

"My Quen."

"Until the end of time."

Nausea rose in my gut. It wasn't the sparks of pleasure I'd expected.

Something felt off. Wrong.

I loved Eli. Didn't I?

Yet as he kissed me, my thoughts wandered back to the Mesmer woman in my dream. Kayl. I'd considered bringing the matter to Elijah, but he had enough to contend with. He didn't need to know about the ramblings of my subconscious.

It had only been a dream. Nothing more.

A perverse dream at that. One... I did not wish to recount.

What sort of gentleman was I, that I found myself attracted to Mesmer? That I imagined them with such pleasingly plump buttocks and shapely bosoms? That the aether of their eyes made my cock twitch?

That she would name me Quen, and I rather liked it.

Saints.

On my return to Kronos, I'd purge myself of such sins through worship and prayer. I could not allow myself to fall victim to the temptations of flesh.

Father needed me.

And I needed Him.

29

I got the news this morning. Hazelhearth, she—she turned up on my doorstep. Asked if she could come inside for a cup of tea. Sat me down.
It's my daughter. She's dead.
Hazelhearth said she died in Obituary. Obituary! What was she even doing fighting in Obituary? I knew it was bad news the second Hazelhearth appeared at my door, but... Surely Unghard could bring her back? Bring my precious Tulip back? I've prayed and prayed, but Unghard says mortals only get one life, even though Tulip died fighting for our domain.
They won't bring her back...
—Anonymous, *overheard in Rockwell's, Heartstone*

BROOKE HELD QUENTIN'S HAND *with a possessive touch that grated on me. For our partnership with the Amnae to work, I needed to breed trust between our domains, and only they could rebuild Quentin's mind to match my will.*

"He must not forget his undying loyalty to me," I reminded her.

"Relax." She let his hand go. "He's all yours."

Quentin blinked, none the wiser about this little interruption. "Apologies. It has been a long day. What were you saying, Your Excellency?"

"How pleased I am with your support. Thanks to you, the Godless will no longer plague Memoria."

He bowed his head. "Happy to be of assistance. Throw the book at them, Ambassador, and may we never see their kind again."

Brooke flashed a knowing look in my direction. "How lucky you are to have such a gentleman in your employ."

I forced a smile. "Quentin is a gift from our Father."

"Isn't he just." Brooke patted Quentin's shoulder. "Why don't you rest for a moment? Help yourself to tea, and then we'll make arrangements for your departure."

The ambassador finally left us alone. It was difficult enough dealing with the fawning of some vapid Amnae woman. She had only served Anima in this capacity for less than a day, and was merely her god's vessel, present so long as she served a use.

It was a pity that Quentin killed Aberforth. He was far more tolerable.

Quentin sat beside me and poured himself herbal tea, a foul drink I did not approve of. Still, he was avoiding the biscuits. A good sign. We'd performed this routine so many times over the years—I'd wipe his memories, guide him toward the correct path, and he'd stick with it, for a while.

He'd stray into sin eventually. He always did.

No. Not this time.

We'd begin his rehabilitation as soon as we arrived in Kronos. I'd get him on his knees and make him beg for my belt. Then I'd thrash him until I was certain his will was absolute.

I'd redeem him yet.

"I'm proud of you, Quentin."

His eyes met mine. They were no longer the pure silver of a Diviner, but held the blue taint of Chaos.

"I'm sorry it has been so long," he said, his voice hitching with an emotion I'd need to train out of him. "But I'm glad you're here."

I placed my fingers under his chin and lifted it. Good. He still responded to my touch. "There's much work to be done."

"I know. I'm with you."

I took his mouth. Tasted the very lust I'd known would be boiling inside him. That had always been his particular sin.

When we returned to Kronos, I'd claim the rest of him.

Piece by piece.

"No!"

I pressed my face against a pillow and screamed into it until my voice cracked.

The door opened, and Sinder ran inside the room. "Dearest? What's wrong?"

I let the pillow fall and tried to control my breathing before I completely lost it. "It's Karendar—he's back, and he's got Quen!"

Sinder sank onto the bed beside me. "Karendar? The old Diviner ambassador?"

I nodded, struggling to keep the tears at bay. "I had a vision."

I'd stepped inside my room to get dressed in clean and dry clothes, when I was overcome with a vision and fell onto the bed. It was the same man I'd been having visions of for the past week. The Redeemer. I'd known there was something painfully familiar about him, but it hadn't clicked until now.

Dor had brought the worst fucking mortal back from the dead. Elijah Karendar.

And he'd taken Quen.

Worse, the Amnae *were* fucking with Quen's memories, on Karendar's orders. Shit! They'd made Quen believe he was a loyal Warden again, fighting against the Godless and Chaos. If they brought him to Kronos, Quen would be completely at Dor's mercy, and I'd have no easy way to rescue him.

Quen was their prisoner, and he didn't even know it.

Sinder took my hands and let his warmth soothe me. "Visions don't always come to pass."

"These ones do." They felt more like lucid dreams—like I was there, watching them happen in real time. The visions I'd experienced before had already happened, and I knew, deep in my gut, Karendar was real, that he and Quen were on their way to Kronos, if not there by now.

There wasn't any point figuring out how to get into Memoria or take down Anima. If Dor had Quen, then they could do anything to him— torture, dissection.

Gods. They could strap him to a machine and take his soul. Turn him into a mindless slave. It sounded like that was what Karendar wanted Quen for.

I wasn't ready to face Dor. What was I going to do? March into Kronos and put the Diviner to sleep?

But I had no choice. "We need to get into Kronos."

Sinder groaned. "Darling, you're killing me—"

"Can Edana help me or not?"

"I'm just a messenger. You'll need to speak with her directly, but I'll tell you this—she will not risk a fight against Dor directly without good reason. Right now, Jinx has her favor."

Because Jinx was the competent twin between us. She had the power of the Glimmer, the Necro, and the Fauna, which was a lot more useful than what I had. Gods, even Quen would fare better than me in a direct confrontation—he had the Zephyr and Leander's powers.

What did I have? Hopes and dreams.

"Dearest, is Corinth worth risking everything?" Sinder said it with complete sincerity, yet the audacity of it pissed me off. We were Godless. We helped mortals regardless of the risk. Though, Sinder had never liked Quen. Had never accepted him as one of us, despite being our bloody benefactor.

"Yes. As are you, and Harm, and Vincent, and Dru. I'll save everyone, eventually. But Quen has the souls of Zyclone and Lionheart. We can't lose them." What would happen to those souls if Dor attempted to destroy Quen's? Gods, I didn't want to even think about it.

Sinder sighed. "Right. Throw on something nice, and I'll quickly do your makeup—"

"We don't have time—"

"Trust me. Edana will appreciate it if you put in the effort for her."

Great. The love of my life was being carted off to possible torture while I had to do my pissing makeup so I could whore myself out to save him.

Wait.

Was Quen the love of my life?

When had I started thinking of him that way? Before we fucked? After? When the damn Fauna had gotten it into my head that we were more than partners? Mates?

When the Mesmer had started referring to him as their papa?

After all the times he'd risked his own soul to save mine?

Quen and I had never even discussed what our relationship *was*. We'd sort of... fallen into it. Partly because our gods were doing a terrible job of keeping us apart, no matter how hard they tried.

He'd asked me to marry him. That *had* been a joke. Hadn't it?

Shit.

"Am I in love with Quen?" I voiced the words aloud.

Sinder wore a sympathetic smile. "Have you only figured this out now?"

Aw, fuck. Now Edana would know I had a weakness she could take advantage of. Oh, who was I kidding. She'd probably already known.

I picked out a tight black dress as Sinder helped apply some subtle makeup that brought out the silvery flicker of stars on my Mesmer face. It was ridiculous. Mesmer weren't supposed to have sex appeal.

Downstairs, some of the Ember were helping to dry out and clean up the mess the flooding had caused. They didn't look particularly thrilled at being ordered to do manual labor, but Sinder was the boss now, and they did what he told them.

The trio waited by the reception desk. They'd since dried and changed too, though their hair was still a damp mess.

"You're leaving *again*?" Cosmo whined.

"Quen's in danger. You'll be safe here. The Ember will look after you."

"What about the Fauna?"

"There're still Fauna?" Sinder asked.

"It's... complicated," I said.

"Edana will need to know if you're harboring the enemy—"

"They're completely docile and no threat to you or Sinner's Row." I cringed at my own description, but it was the truth. "The Diviner stole their souls. They're practically dead. Edana will understand that."

Sinder swallowed a lump in his throat.

"We can look after them," Celeste insisted. "We tell them to eat, otherwise they won't."

"It's the least we can do after they looked after us," Castor added.

"Keep them inside, then," Sinder said.

We headed out of the hotel. Sinder accompanied me back to the bar and the portal that would take us to Rapture. I was impressed by how well he was running Sinner's Row and managing a bunch of Ember under his command. But of course, Sinder had many years of management experience from when he worked for cabaret theaters before he became Godless, and from when he worked for Erosain directly as a spy.

"When we meet with Edana, try not to piss her off, dearest," Sinder said as we entered Erosain's old art gallery turned portal chamber. "It'll be me who bears the brunt of her temper."

"I'm not going to all this trouble to piss her off."

"And yet you're a natural."

He made it sound like all I did was meet with gods and give them the finger, which yes, okay, I could see where I got that reputation. But I wasn't Jinx. "Quen's life is on the line. I won't do anything to jeopardize that."

"Naturally, Corinth's more important than I am."

I pulled a face and stepped through the portal.

This was another massive waste of my time.

Becoming god of the Mesmer had revealed the secrets of the universe to me, and I truly understood why the Diviner disliked the Ember so much. It wasn't because the Ember were massive sluts and sinners, or even because Diviner had a permanent clock up their backsides. It was because sluttery took up too much valuable time.

Paint me silver and call me a Diviner, because I finally agreed that wasting time was the biggest sin of them all.

Hopefully one quick slap of Edana's arse would get this over with.

The queen of the Ember awaited us in her penthouse throne room. Perhaps she wanted to set the mood, as the room was once again full of a writhing harem of naked Ember fucking and sucking, just as they'd been the first time I visited Rapture. There were no mortals from other domains, though, which I supposed wasn't a surprise.

I strode between them with my chin held high and Sinder by my side. Unfortunately, my scandalous dress meant I was flashing my knickers at the Ember below me, and they weren't shy about sneaking a peek, those perverts.

Edana watched my approach, her chin resting on her fist. She wore black to match me, her black eyeshadow and lipstick making her look even more dangerous. I had to remember she was a god who could burn me alive if I bored her.

"I grow tired waiting," she said.

Great. I guess I'd need to put out if I wanted her cooperation. "Sorry. You may have noticed there's a lot going on right now."

Sinder shot me a scowl.

All right, I'd try that again. I cleared my throat. "We made a deal that I'd offer myself in exchange for shelter and protection for the Fauna. Since Jinx went and destroyed Juniper, that means you've failed to uphold your part of the bargain."

Oh, now Sinder was glaring at me.

Edana waved a dismissive hand. "I cannot control the nature of Chaos—"

"You could have warned me, distracted her, anything—"

"And reveal my hand? I gave you Sinner's Row and my voice at your disposal, and you squandered these gifts. I have yet to see a return on my generosity." Flame flared in her eyes.

"The way I see it, Sinner's Row barely changed hands. And thanks to me, you replaced your insufferable ambassador with an upgrade."

"Oh my god," Sinder whispered in despair.

Edana snapped her fingers with a flash of irritation. "Sinder."

His spine straightened. "My Queen?"

"Make yourself useful." She pointed to her feet.

A whimper escaped Sinder's lips as he got on his knees and literally crawled to her feet. Gods, I half expected him to start sucking her toes or something, but instead Edana lifted her legs and simply rested her feet on his back, using him as a mortal footstool.

Which she was doing to piss *me* off.

It was working.

She wanted me to throw myself at her feet instead, but I didn't have the time or patience for her stupid games. Truth was, the thought of cozying up to Edana—of offering her my body—sickened me. It might be the price she demanded, but it had nothing to do with physical pleasure.

It was about humiliation and control. It always had been.

And I refused to debase myself further.

Though it wasn't just about me being stubborn. Since I'd realized Quen was the love of my life, that meant something. Loyalty, I supposed. The only man, mortal, or god I wanted touching my body was him. Even if that meant fucking up my chances to save him.

It didn't have to. I could still offer my mind.

I finally sat on the couch before her and crossed my leg over my knee. "We both need things from each other, so let's start over."

Edana looked disinterested. "I'm aware of your price. You would risk my domain for an attack on Kronos when you are woefully unprepared. You were meant to remove Dor's allies, and yet they grow. Anima makes for a powerful partner."

"Anima is a fish trapped in a glass bowl. Their reach only goes so far."

"Yet they managed to capture Quentin Corinth."

I dug my fingernails into the couch fabric. "Then we get him back. Without Quen, we lose Zyclone and Lionheart's power—"

"Then we lose them. They mean nothing to me."

Of course Edana only cared about her own domain and mortals. "If you want to stand against Dor or Corentine, then I think you'll find the Zephyr and Leander are allies worth having on your side."

"They're not worth an attack on Kronos."

"And Quen? He's an asset to you. The one man who can take down Dor. But in Dor's hands, he'll be a formidable weapon the Diviner will use against you."

Edana shifted her feet, and Sinder grunted as her heel dug into his spine. "Without Quentin Corinth, the battle against the Diviner will be... difficult. But I hold no emotional sentiment. Dor, however, will hold him hostage against *you*. That makes you a liability. Especially when you continue to dangle half-baked promises. Chaos is beautiful, I won't deny that, but I can find my pleasure in your twin."

Oh, that thought was disgusting. Not even Jinx would lower herself to fucking a god, would she? Shit, I didn't want to even imagine it. "Jinx might give you a good time, or she might steal your soul, but she can't offer you what I can."

"So far you've offered me nothing."

"I'll show you the future. Right here, right now." That was what Edana really wanted me for. Other than the Diviner, no other mortal could offer her a glimpse into the future and its many possibilities. Mesmorpheus may not have whored that particular ability out, likely for good reason, but I wasn't so shy.

Besides, viewing the future would benefit me, unless I accidentally revealed a future where I betrayed Edana and took her soul. Shit. I hadn't considered that.

By the interest in Edana's eyes, I'd gone and fucked myself over.

Could I fake a future? I was sure the Mesmer seers of Sinner's Row pulled out all kinds of happy fake visions for the satisfaction of paying customers. There wouldn't be many returning customers if they were all doom and gloom. What was it Celeste had said? That I could cast illusions and bend reality to my will?

Fuck it, it was worth a try.

Edana snapped her fingers, and the sexual moaning behind me suddenly stopped. I glanced over my shoulder. Her harem was gone.

"Did you just kill your own mortals?"

"Don't presume to question me. Remember whose domain you sit in."

Now I wanted to create a vision of her choking to death on her own vomit. Sinder flashed me a warning look—the 'don't get us smited' look. Edana was showing off her powers. It seems we'd both gotten bored with this particular game.

I slowly stood. "Where do you want me?"

Edana patted her knee. Really? Could this get any more awkward?

I swallowed my revulsion and approached. To think I'd found her attractive. But there was nothing worth worshipping when it came to the gods. They were ugly all the way through. I lowered myself onto her lap, careful to avoid stepping on Sinder. The only way this could be worse was if Jinx magically turned up to gloat.

Gods, I hoped my luck wasn't that bad.

"I'll have to touch your face," I said. "To show you what I see."

"Then do it."

Honestly, I was surprised she trusted me this far. She really was desperate for some hint of the future.

Part of me wanted to take her soul while I had the chance, but I really would need her help fighting Dor. She knew how to command immortals, and there'd be no greater distraction than a god entering Kronos and blasting it to shit.

I placed my hand on her cheek. Gods, it was hot to the touch, and her strong perfume washed over me, sweet like cinnamon.

Despite living as a Mesmer, I wasn't an expert at this, but I'd entered Quen's dream by touching his face when Wolfsbane needed him knocked out, so I presumed it could be done. And that was ultimately what I was trying to achieve. A dream. A false vision.

"There are different variations of the future. They can change, depending on our choices and actions." At least, I was sure I'd heard Quen or the future version of Quen mention something similar. "I can only show you what the stars wish for us to see." Wow, I even sounded mysterious! Maybe I was born to be a Mesmer. I was a natural at talking shit.

I closed my eyes and let us both fall into fantasy.

When I opened my eyes again, I stood in Central.

The city was destroyed. Completely obliterated. The design was similar to a vision of the future Quen had shown me inside another dream, so it had been simple enough for me to imagine and reconstruct. It turned out projecting my memories and images into locations I could visit was quite easy in the dream world. I'd done it a few times with Grayford, when Quen had astrally projected himself into my mind, or the opposite.

All it took was an active imagination, and I was a natural at that. Was this what Celeste had meant by manipulating reality? Maybe it was that easy.

Edana wouldn't care for a visit to the Undercity, though. No, she wanted something far more dramatic.

She stood beside me, scanning the scene. Cinders smoldered from debris that had burned down. Ashes floated past on the breeze. Above, the Golden City plate was no more—it was gone. Simply gone. The sky billowed with dark clouds and threatened to lash Central's streets with pent-up anger.

The clock tower was also gone. The collapse of the plate above had destroyed it, and it lay in fractured ruins like metal splinters. Glass lay scattered across the station. The remnants of the clockface.

Aether no longer burned in the city. The streetlamps were out. The constant hum of electricity had been cut off, rendering the city dead. Lifeless.

And Corentine was no more.

Only one figure stood in the center of it all. One man in his tan suit, a pistol holstered at his hip, and a pocket watch in his hand.

"Quen," I gasped.

He tucked the watch into his jacket pocket and approached us. "Queen Edana." He swooped a low bow. "You honor us with your presence."

"What has happened here?" she demanded.

"The city is yours, my Queen. It may not look like much now, but give it a bit of elbow grease and we'll have it good as new, so long as you live up to your end of our bargain."

"Which is?"

"To allow mortals to live their lives in accordance with the Covenant."

Edana hummed noncommittally. "What of Corentine and Dor? What happened to the forces of Chaos and Time?"

"They live on within myself and Lady Arkey. They put up quite a fight. Kayl was able to subdue her sister and take Corentine's soul, while I dealt with Dor. We agreed Chaos would be too volatile to be allowed freedom in Chime, but the Diviner could return, should you allow it."

Gods. Was my imagination making this up? This future sounded almost too good to be true.

Quen caught my eye and winked.

He pissing winked!

Shit. This Quen wasn't my Quen, nor a Quen I'd randomly plucked from my subconscious. This was Future Quen. He'd entered my dream, somehow.

Or I'd entered his.

He knew I was fucking with Edana. That arse!

"And the other gods?" Edana asked.

"Dead. Our bargain was with you, my Queen."

Edana nodded, seemingly satisfied with that answer. Too bad for Serenity.

I draped my wrist across my forehead dramatically. "Oh, the stars are growing too faint! I hear the call back to reality!"

And with that, I kicked Edana from the dream world. She'd wake up in a moment, and I'd wake up with her.

But first...

I grabbed Future Quen and yanked his lips onto mine.

He pulled back and chuckled. "Easy now. I'm only a dream."

"Is this the future? The actual future?" I thumped his chest. "I thought I was finally learning to make illusions!"

He rubbed his chest and smirked. "Your illusions are wonderful, my dear."

My stomach fluttered at that simple term of endearment. "I've lost you. In my reality. Does this mean you're safe? Will I get you back?"

His smile faded. "You know the future can change."

"Then help me. Help *us*. Please."

"I can't. Your future is your own."

"You've helped me before."

"And my time is now up. This is a quick stop on my way to my final destination. I'm almost at the end."

"What does that mean? The end?"

"It means this will finally have a purpose." He gestured to the crumbling ruins around us. "Because if it doesn't, and it was all for nothing..."

Shit. "This *is* the future."

"*A* future."

"The bad one?"

"That depends on your perspective. All things must end. From those ashes, a new world may rise."

"*May* rise? You don't sound certain."

"It's the risk we'll have to take. Speaking of, you shouldn't be here."

"You're the one who barged into my fake vision."

He chuckled, and gods, how I missed that sound. I grabbed him again, and he playfully rolled his eyes as our lips met once more. His metal hand slid down my back and landed on my arse. I almost jumped as he gave it a squeeze.

"Quentin Corinth!" I gasped, breaking contact. "When did you become such a filthy boy?"

He waggled his eyebrows. "My dear, I was lost to sin the very moment I first laid eyes on you in the Undercity. It just took a little motivation to draw it out. Now *go*. Save your world, so I can save mine."

My vision became hazy as reality pulled me out of my dream.

"Wait!" I called. "You asked me to marry you. Your past self did, anyhow. Were you joking? Did you mean it?"

He positively beamed. "There's only one way to find out."

And then he was gone. Damn it, could he be any more infuriating?

I reached for him. My Quen. I didn't want to let him go.

He was my world.

I needed to save him.

Reality was all the worse for Quen's absence.

I awkwardly pulled myself from Edana's lap, though she didn't seem to notice. She was too busy lost in her own thoughts. I supposed she hadn't experienced many visions, though they weren't that different from tripping on Vesper mushrooms.

Hopefully our visit to the future would convince her we needed Quen, because without her help, I didn't know how I'd get him back.

Finally, she took in a breath and acknowledged my existence. "That was… enlightening."

"It's *a* future," I said, mimicking Future Quen. "Though if you want that one, then we need Quen. Clearly I can handle Corentine." Though I sure hoped Quen had been making that up, because fuck if I knew how to. "But only Quen can handle Dor. He's obviously the brains of this whole thing."

"Obviously. Very well."

I almost launched off my seat. "You'll help me get him back?"

"On one condition."

And there I went, crashing back down.

"To aid our chances, we must remove the Umber," Edana said.

Okay, I hadn't expected that. "You want me to invade Heartstone?"

"My mortals and immortals have clashed with Unghard's forces, and we remain at a stalemate. Any attempt to invade Heartstone ourselves has ended in failure. Unghard knows when we enter their domain. They erect stone barriers impervious to our flame."

"You think I can get past them?"

"You have a means of entering domains that Unghard may not detect. If you remove the Umber, then Dor loses a valuable ally, and it tips the battle in our favor."

I couldn't argue with that. It would mean delaying my rescue, but facing the Umber and Unghard had to be easier than Dor and his shitty Diviner.

And Dru. I could get Dru back.

Gods knew I needed her help.

Though the next question was… *how* would I take on a bunch of mortals made of stone and twigs? I could bring Sinder with me and burn down the place, but no. Unghard would appreciate a delicate touch. Sure, my last few attempts at negotiation hadn't worked, but I had persistence on my side.

"Be ready to leave for Kronos," I said. "Unghard won't be a problem."

Was it bravado? Arrogance? Or desperation fueling my ambitions?

By the look on Sinder's face, it was most likely madness.

But Elijah Karendar had Quen, and I would do *anything* to get him back. Climb a mountain. Wrestle a god. Anything.

I'm coming for you, Quen. Hold on.

30

Unghard is the second of our Father's allies, and the most loyal. They alone understand the importance of duty and the sacrifices required to protect Chime. Their Umber are also excellent at conflict mediation. Quite frankly, we need their strength. We won't win this war without them.
—P. Bezel, *Personal Report on Unghard*

I RETURNED TO THE hotel to change for the third bloody time. If I was going to be climbing literal mountains, then a black dress and cute heels wouldn't cut it. That, and I didn't think my gorgeous arse would appeal to the Umber, somehow.

The Ember had done a great job of clearing out the bottom half of the hotel, not that the place really needed the effort. Only the Mesmer trio and a few soulless Fauna occupied it now, but the trio liked the variety of beds, and it kept them safe. Edana had promised to keep watch over the hotel in case Jinx decided to fuck with us, and really, I couldn't think of anywhere better for the Mesmer.

Sinder accompanied me and waited with the Mesmer down in the lobby. "If I'm not coming with, dearest, then why did you insist on bringing me along?"

To save him from that bitch. "To keep an eye on the Mesmer. They're a lovely bunch. They'll even make tea for you, if you ask nicely."

Cosmo held up a bucket. "You can help me name my new fish! I'm thinking either Sugar or Sprinkles."

Sinder scratched his upper left horn. "Are you *sure* you don't need me? Entering a domain on your own never worked out well in the past."

"I can't risk bringing an Ember and offending Unghard." I patted his shoulder. "Don't worry, I'll be fine."

He mumbled something I didn't quite catch.

I changed from Mesmer to Chaos and set Quen's pocket watch to five past three for Heartstone. There was a chance Edana was wrong, and I'd open a portal into a tree or something. It couldn't be worse than flooding Sinner's Row.

Thankfully, the watch still worked. The portal opened to the clearing of a peaceful wooded area with trees swaying in a gentle breeze. It looked almost suspiciously normal.

I glanced back at Sinder standing with the trio. "If anything goes wrong, I'll let Celeste and Castor know."

The two of them saluted me.

"Why not me?" Cosmo pouted.

"Because you've got the important task of looking after Sprinkles."

"I like Sugar more."

"Fine, Sugar." I resisted the urge to roll my eyes and stepped toward the portal.

"Good luck," Sinder called, his tone implying I'd need all the luck in the universe.

Well, at least *I* had faith in me.

Oh, you had to be shitting me.

The portal had brought me to the foot of a mountain. It was the exact mountain I needed, at least—from my view in the clearing, I could see the gigantic Heart Tree at the pissing top. How in god's name would I get all the way up *there*?

Yes, I'd said I'd climb a mountain for Quen, but I hadn't meant it literally! The universe was surely testing me.

On the plus side, I *could* get there. Unghard hadn't summoned a pile of rocks upon my head, which meant Edana was right. Punching a small hole into Unghard's domain had gone unnoticed. Either that, or they'd laid a trap around the next tree.

There was no more time to waste. I hoisted my skirt and began the slow trek out of the clearing and to the rather terrifyingly high mountain. For some reason, it brought back memories of the times Dru and I worked in

Lady Mae's kitchen. She'd done most of the work cleaning dishes, but gods, the drudgery had been never-ending.

To work was an Umber's prerogative, so they said, but why were they so obsessed with making life hard?

Still. It was a nice day for invading domains and killing gods. The afternoon sun shone through the trees and warmed my skin against the slight breeze. Insects chittered around me, and the air tasted faintly of moss. It was a completely different atmosphere to Juniper. Where that had been dark and oppressive, as though the jungle wanted to devour you whole, this felt more like a picnic in Meridian Park. It was altogether rather lovely as I strode from the clearing and found myself on a dirt path.

Something rattled behind me. I turned to a steam wagon rolling down the path. Oh, thank the gods! I could get a lift and save my poor soles.

I went to flag it down, but—oh shit! I was still Chaos! That would set off alarm bells for sure.

Perhaps now was a good time to try an illusion. Could they work on someone who was awake? No time like the present to find out.

I summoned a miasma as the wagon neared. The driver, a large gray boulder of a man, slumped over in the driver's seat, asleep, and the wagon slowed to a stop. Perfect.

I climbed up beside him. His eyebrows were big bushy things. Baby blue hydrangeas. I only knew what they were because Dru had once pointed them out in Meridian Park's gardens. I carefully avoided touching them as I placed my hand on his forehead. For this illusion to work, I wanted to channel an Umber face with some authority. I needed a full ride up to the top of the mountain without argument, which also meant changing form to Umber.

The man woke and suddenly sat up. "Ambassador Hazelhearth! What—What are you doing here? Uh, Your Excellency?"

Oh my god, it worked! Now to act like I had a stick up my arse. "I was admiring the roses, why do you think I'm here?"

"I didn't mean to—"

"Do you often fall asleep when driving a dangerous vehicle?"

"No, ma'am! I'm sorry, I don't know what happened—"

"A likely story." Despite sitting next to the man, who was literally the size of a boulder, I managed to look down my nose at him. "Fortunately for you, I've become separated from my own wagon. We can forgive this matter in exchange for a small act of service."

"Oh! Yes, it would be my pleasure, Your Excellency." He bobbed his head in a ridiculous motion that shook the wagon. Umber sure loved serving others. "Is there someplace you need to be?"

"The Heart Tree, of course."

"Of course, of course." He glanced back at his cargo of logs. "Ah, are you comfortable sitting up front, Your Excellency? I don't really have space at the back, but—but I *could* throw out some logs—"

"Here is fine." I made myself comfortable on the hard passenger seat—as comfortable as I could, anyhow. Umber apparently didn't believe in the concept.

The man pulled on the wagon's handle, and the steam engine kicked back to life. We began a slow rumble up the dirt path toward the foot of the mountain. It was faster than walking, so I couldn't complain, but the sooner I dealt with Unghard, the sooner I could rescue Quen.

We rode in awkward silence. The poor man kept fiddling nervously with the wagon's brass knobs and handles, and smoothed down his hydrangeas. I would have asked for his name, but I don't think Hazelhearth would have cared. He made a few attempts at small talk, which I shot down with a simple stare. It was a shame, since Umber were so friendly, yet their ambassador was a bitch. Or maybe she'd just been a bitch to me? The Umber were the nicer version of the Diviner and Glimmer—didn't approve of Chaos, expected everyone to behave and bow and scrape. No wonder they'd become Dor's allies.

If the Umber were going to be stubborn about it, then I had a battle on my hands.

The wagon slowly made its way up the mountain on a path that spiraled all the way around it. Stone homes were carved into the mountainside on each level. From my last visit, I knew the Gate was somewhere in the middle, and above that, Dru's house.

Gods. Would Dru's family still be pleased Dru had been made an immortal now she was fighting in stupid wars? Probably.

Though I was glad not to be climbing the mountain, the wagon was going *too* slow, and I was on a damn schedule. "Can't this thing go any faster?"

"Sorry, Your Excellency. Slow and steady gets the job done, as my pa always says."

"Does your pa work in public office?"

"Um, no—"

"Clearly, since he doesn't value other mortals' time."

He flinched. Maybe I was being too harsh. "I can't really go any faster... That would be breaking the law—"

"I *am* the law." Oh, I'd always wanted to say that!

"Are—Are you sure? I mean, it was a big hoo-hah at the time, what with that wagon running over that poor Glimmer girl—"

"Yes, I remember the incident." Well, I could picture it. "But this is an emergency. I must return to the Heart Tree with haste. You have my permission."

"If you insist." He grabbed a handle. "Hold on tight."

A puff of smoke burst from the steam engine, and the wagon lurched forward.

Shit!

I was pinned to my seat as the wagon took off at speeds I couldn't imagine in Chime—faster than even the tram! I hung on for dear life as it took a corner so sharply, we almost toppled over! I'd asked for speed, but gods.

The wagon was rattling so hard, it vibrated through my bones and made my teeth chatter. Even the logs in the back were bouncing up and down. Gods, if they got out, they could kill someone. As we neared the more populated areas, a couple of Umber had to dive out of the way. Their cursing was drowned out by our dust.

"Sorry!" my new friend called over his shoulder. "Important ambassador business!"

"Watch where you're going!" I yelled as the wagon veered toward the edge of the mountain.

He yanked the wagon straight. "Sorry." He giggled, making his hydrangeas twitch. "This is the most excitement I've had in years!"

His excitement was infectious, but I didn't want him driving us *off* the pissing mountain. I'd not spent my entire life as a Godless to start praying now. "Keep it together!"

"Yes, ma'am."

I grasped his horn and gave it a good honk, just in case.

Though as we drove further up, he was forced to slow the wagon due to the number of vines stretching across the road. Dru had said something about them being sacred. I doubted the Umber would appreciate us running them over.

We'd almost reached the middle of the mountain when I spotted something across the horizon. Smoke. A whole plume of dark smog billowed between trees. "Is that normal?" I pointed it out.

"Fires? Controlled ones are good for the forest occasionally, though... we've got none scheduled."

I suddenly had a bad feeling. Edana wouldn't have followed me to Heartstone, would she? No, she'd said she couldn't.

"Something's going on," my new friend stated.

I followed his gaze. Our wagon reached the outcrop where the Gate was situated, and a massive crowd of Umber had gathered in the station area. Most of them looked concerned and were pointing at the smoke. Shit. That wasn't normal, then. I glanced back and—

Fuck! The forest was on fire. Flames had joined the smoke, and they were moving, cutting a path through the trees with increasing speed. Worse, whoever was doing it was heading this way. To the mountain.

To the Heart Tree.

Jinx. It had to be Jinx. How the fuck had she gotten here? My portal had closed behind me, so she couldn't have followed.

The crowd parted as a woman approached. "Everyone, be calm and return to your homes! Unghard's Golems will protect you."

Oh shit!

My new Umber friend did a double take, and then recoiled as the illusion fell from his eyes. "Ambassador Hazelhearth?"

My luck had run out sooner than later.

The real Hazelhearth looked just as shocked at my sudden appearance in her domain, though to her and everyone else, I looked as I normally did when taking an Umber form—with grayish blue skin and a collection of blue and pink flowers on my brow. The form of Chaos.

A whole group of Golems materialized out of thin air, landing in a circle around the wagon with a collective thud. There were at least six of them. Massive things. Though Dru wasn't among them.

"Chaos!" Hazelhearth shrieked. "Your kind is forbidden from stepping foot in our domain! And *you*, Mason Rockwell!" She pointed a damning figure at the Umber beside me. "You blundering fool. Are you aware of the treason you've committed by aiding the enemy of Unghard?"

My new friend, Mason, scooted as far away from me as he could get. "I'm sorry, I didn't know! Please have mercy, Your Excellency! I've got a wife and two children—"

"Oh, give over!" I said. "I tricked him. Let the poor bastard off, he didn't know any better."

Hazelhearth's eyes narrowed in recognition. "Ambassador Arkey. We don't know how you invaded our domain, but you won't be leaving alive."

How many times could I roll my eyes in one day? "I'm no threat to you. If I were, then he'd have lost his soul by now." I jerked my thumb at Mason. "I'm here to talk, like I've been bloody trying to all this time. Though you've got bigger problems." I gestured to the smoldering trees. "My twin is on her way to burn down your domain and everyone in it." I didn't know for sure it was Jinx, but I was willing to put bocs on it. "Only I can stop her."

The Golems marched toward the wagon. Mason flinched and whimpered, and my own heart leaped to my throat. Having watched them rip Ember apart, I didn't want to be on the receiving end of those massive stone fists.

I stood, somewhat shakily on the rickety wagon, but I mustered as much confidence into my voice as I could. "You harm me, and your domain is done for."

Hazelhearth held up her hand, and the Golems stopped, becoming as still as stone. "Your threats are idle. My mortals will crush you."

"While you're crushing my bones, Jinx will keep on burning."

"We can rebuild."

"I'm sure your mortals won't agree."

"My mortals are made of stone."

Bloody stubborn Umber. "Your souls aren't. And what about the Heart Tree? You're willing to let that burn? I can protect it."

Hazelhearth sighed with exasperation. "Why would you? You're Chaos—"

"All Quen and I ever wanted was to unite the domains *against* Chaos! You're the ones being awkward about it—"

Screaming broke out, and we both turned. Umber ran up the mountain path. Some were carrying children in their arms.

"Your Excellency!" one of the Umber cried. "There's a—a monster! It's burning up the mountain! It—It touched my husband, and he—he collapsed, and his eyes! They're gone!"

I gave Hazelhearth my *I told you so* look. "You can't pummel her. She's got Faen's powers; she'll outmaneuver you. And it wouldn't matter anyway, since she has The Nameless One's power also. She can heal from any wound you inflict."

I'd never seen an Umber blanch before, but Hazelhearth suddenly looked as though she was about to vomit, pass out, or piss herself.

"Your Golems won't stop her," I continued while the woman was speechless for the first time in her mortal life. I'm sure ambassador training never covered these scenarios. "But they can buy us time. Use them to block off the mountain, get your mortals to safety, and get me to the Heart Tree. You don't have a choice."

She regained her composure. "Can you stop her?"

I met her eyes and didn't blink. "Yes."

"Rockwell, fire up that wagon." Hazelhearth gestured for me to shuffle over and then climbed in beside me. "Don't sit there, gawking!" She honked the horn. "Return to your homes and barricade yourselves!"

The crowd gathered their things and ran from the station. To their credit, they organized themselves with considered panic, and not the sort of mass hysteria a mob in Chime would succumb to. The Golems gave them space to evacuate before marching down the mountain to meet Jinx on some unspoken command.

Mason eyed us both warily, but he cranked on the steam engine and we were moving up the mountain, back on track.

Adrenaline and guilt rode with me, my stomach churning. I hadn't come to Heartstone to save it. I wasn't about to become Unghard's savior, but their end. Hazelhearth was finally placing her trust in me, and I'd straight-up lied to her face.

It wasn't a question of saving the Umber from Jinx.

It was a question of getting to Unghard first.

Judging by the smoke growing closer, I didn't have much time.

The wagon flew up the mountain, bumping over the roots without a care—sanctity didn't matter when your world was at stake. We passed stone homes that Umber were busy barricading with thick vines. It wouldn't be enough to stop Jinx, but she likely wouldn't busy herself with random mortals unless they got in her way.

I hated that we were doing this again—fighting over gods. When would it end?

When Dor was dead.

Question was, who would get the kill?

More Umber were also returning to their homes as we approached. How had they learned of the attack so soon? Had they noticed the smoke, heard the panic, and reacted accordingly? "News travels fast here," I commented.

"Unghard has broadcast a warning," Hazelhearth explained through clenched teeth. "All mortals are to seek shelter."

Oh. Good. At least Unghard was taking the threat seriously. No other god had bothered to warn their mortals.

"No, no, *no*!" yelled a familiar overbearing voice. "We can't leave the pots behind!"

"This is an actual emergency!"

"It will be if you break my pots!"

The wagon neared Dru's house. Her parents were arguing outside, over pottery of all bloody things. I didn't want the Smith family to recognize me, but Dru wouldn't be happy to see them getting rampaged over by Jinx.

I reached over Hazelhearth's lap and honked the horn. "Get inside! Your daughter sacrificed everything to protect this domain! The least you can do is sacrifice some damn pots!"

They stared at me, dumbfounded, as we rode on by.

Maybe they'd listen.

As we continued upward, the air grew colder and thinner. Clouds obscured our ascent, and our wagon disappeared into thick fog. I was about to ask if Mason knew where he was going, when we popped out of the cloud and arrived at the peak.

The Heart Tree loomed over the entire mountain. Gods. I'd forgotten how large and beautiful it was. Its leaves twinkled with color, and the trunk had a glittering collection of gemstones embedded in the bark.

Umber surrounded the tree. At least fifty men and women. Some carried weapons I'd expect of a Leander—hammers and axes. Beyond them stood six Golems.

One of them was Dru.

Mason brought the wagon to a stop.

I climbed down after Hazelhearth and followed her. "I thought Unghard ordered everyone to get to safety?"

"They did. These have volunteered to protect the Heart Tree. We are loyal. We'll fight to protect Unghard."

For a Godless, those words were vile, but I couldn't deny the Umber loved their god. Though, they'd be fighting a pointless battle.

"Is the Heart Tree Unghard's soul?"

Hazelhearth gave me a sharp look. "Why do you need to know?"

"So I know what to protect. If all Jinx needs to do is snap off a branch to take Unghard, then that'll make things harder for us."

Some of the Umber exchanged alarmed glances at our conversation. Did they understand the true nature of the threat coming for them and their god?

"The Heart Tree is a vessel. A shell. Unghard dwells inside it."

Interesting, though a little weird. If Unghard's soul was inside the tree, then there must be a way to reach it, other than burning the damn tree down. I didn't think Jinx would have a problem there, but I certainly couldn't start ripping off branches with this crowd. They definitely *would* pummel me.

I could put them to sleep, but that would leave me vulnerable to Jinx. These mortals were the best defense I could ask for.

"Can I speak with Unghard?"

"You may *not* enter the Heart Tree—"

"Look, I need to talk to them."

Vines shot out of the ground beneath me and wrapped around my legs, holding me in place. They still didn't trust me, did they?

I EXILED YOU FROM MY DOMAIN, AND YET YOU PERSIST LIKE AN UNRULY WEED, came Unghard's voice inside my mind.

Yes, that's me. An unruly weed. How flattering. *Maybe now you'll listen?*

THE POWER OF CHAOS TAKES ROOT AND SPREADS. YOU CANNOT BE PRUNED. THE WHOLE GARDEN MUST BE UNEARTHED.

Can you talk properly for a hot pissing minute? Jinx is on her way to burn your pretty little tree.

MY GOLEMS WILL PROTECT ME.

I bit back a sigh. *No. They won't. If you can't stop Jinx from invading your domain, then what makes you believe you can defend yourself? If you think I'm stubborn, then you're not ready to face her.*

YOU CANNOT TRICK ME, CHILD OF CHAOS. DOR HAS WARNED US OF CORENTINE'S TRUE NATURE. SHE HAS GROWN THORNS AND WOULD SEE THE UNIVERSE WITHER AND DIE. UNDER CHAOS, NO LIFE WILL GROW.

I'm not on Corentine's side—

YOU ARE HER VOICE.

Was *her voice, and only to find a solution where mortals could live in peace without their bloody gods warring and throwing their lives away! Obviously that's worked well. Jinx is the one who serves Corentine. I'm trying to stop her.*

YOU WOULD FIGHT AGAINST YOUR OWN NATURE?

Yes! That's what I've been trying to say!

EVENTIDE WAS TAKEN BECAUSE OF YOU.

Yes, but that was an accident, and you have no idea how much I regret it. But Mesmorpheus saw the future. They gave me their soul willingly—

THAT IS NOT WHAT DOR DECLARED. YOU ENTANGLED MESMORPHEUS—

Dor's lying to you. He wants the domains to war so he can remove his rivals—how else could Solaris fall so easily? He'll do the same to you when you're no longer useful to him.

The vines tightened around my calves. *THIS IS DECEIT.*

You're a god, use your bloody brain! All this time you've been sacrificing your mortals to fight for him. Where are the Diviner now, hrm? Your domain is in danger, and where are your allies? No one has come to protect you. Dor would let you fall.

Screaming echoed not far from where I stood. The Umber readied their weapons, bracing themselves for the fight.

The ground rumbled. Stone erupted before me, forming a massive wall that surrounded us and the entire Heart Tree. The Umber gasped in awe. Those who weren't holding weapons fell to their knees in prayer. Yes, it was a fancy trick, but would it hold?

Jinx had made it this far.

WE ARE UMBER. Unghard's voice blasted the mountain peak with guttural rage. *WE WILL PROTECT OUR HOME.*

The Umber cheered with a war cry. Gods, I'd never known them to be so bloodthirsty.

You're only delaying the inevitable! I called out in my mind. *The longer you draw this out, the more your mortals will suffer.*

Unghard either didn't hear or chose to ignore me.

Shit, this was going to get messy. Umber may have skin made of stone, but they still bled like any mortal. Lionheart had shown that.

I wished Quen were here. How would he handle this situation? With more decorum, that was for sure. He was a charmer... and that was why I loved him.

The ground shook again as Dru approached and stood over me. No recognition sparked in her eyes, but she'd apparently become my personal statue.

Then the vines receded from my legs, and I almost toppled.

"Unghard does not trust you, but even they aren't cruel enough to leave you defenseless," Hazelhearth explained.

"Thank the gods for small mercies."

Her lips formed a grim line. "If you can stop your twin, then do so. However, if you betray us..." She eyed Dru. "This Golem will crush your bones."

"That's good to know." Dru wasn't here for my protection, then. So kind of Unghard to personally choose my best friend as the Golem who'd attempt to break my spine when things went wrong.

And they were about to go *very* wrong.

Something pounded against the newly erected wall, and dust rained down. Hazelhearth jumped. My heart ached at the fear on her face. This was a torment I didn't wish on her. On anyone.

A crack splintered down the wall.

"How is Chaos doing this?" Hazelhearth whispered.

Honestly, I didn't know. Had Jinx transformed into one of those large Fauna with the horns and was ramming into the wall? That was the only explanation I had.

SERENITY! Unghard yelled.

What? Oh, you had to be shitting me!

A hole blasted through the wall, and who should step through except Serenity? The Seren god was still in her naked female form and looked rather pleased with herself.

"Floral dresses are still in season, I see!" she said, as though she were popping round for a spot of tea. "Oh, and your garlands, how delightful. I simply must bring some back to Arcadia."

The Umber were staring in shock.

Where the fuck was Jinx?

Shit. This was a distraction!

I turned to warn Hazelhearth as a bunch of Seren flew through the hole. At least fifty of them poured through. Some carried... harps? Oh fuck.

"Shoot them down!" Hazelhearth ordered.

The Umber threw their weapons at the Seren as others gathered rocks and lobbed them.

Some projectiles collided with the Seren, knocking them out of the air. Most of the Seren were small and light enough to fly out of the way. All the while, Serenity stood there laughing. Actually laughing. This was pure entertainment for her.

The Seren strummed their harps and then began to sing.

I immediately covered my ears.

You big dumb rocks, what have you got?

A big dumb rock about to rot.

Drop your stuff and fall to your knees,

We've come for you, so die now, please.

Their melody grated in my ears with a harsh twang I hadn't known harps were capable of. It certainly wasn't their best work.

But the Umber... Gods.

Those who hadn't covered their ears in time dropped their weapons and fell to their knees, as the lyrics suggested.

And then they collapsed into dust.

Shit!

I hadn't known the Seren could literally sing someone to death, either! This was a whole new level of horror I wasn't mentally prepared for.

Hazelhearth looked just as horrified. Her flowers were stood on end, quivering.

Golems stomped past and launched themselves at Serenity.

Who promptly smacked them down with a simple flick of her wrist.

"Now, now!" Serenity tutted. "You forget my domain makes art out of marble and stone. We'll make art out of you!"

Another Golem swung their fist at Serenity, who caught it and crushed it to pebbles. Shit! Unghard's Golems may be immortal, but that didn't compare to the might of a god.

MY TREE! Unghard screamed.

Hazelhearth and I both spun on our heels.

The Heart Tree was on fire.

There, standing naked in her Glimmer form before the smoldering trunk, was Jinx.

She waggled a glowing finger at me. "You're too late, sister!"

Shitting shit! I left Hazelhearth behind and ran for the tree.

Jinx pointed her palms at the Heart Tree's thick branches and shot out bursts of sunlight. Two Golems standing nearby tried to grab her, but she switched form to her Fauna magpie and flew out of the way.

Her flames took hold fast. They burned through the top canopy of the tree, casting down a flurry of charred leaves. The smoke was growing so thick, it tickled my throat and sent me into a coughing fit.

STOP HER! Unghard begged.

It's too late. I can't save you or your tree. But I can save your mortals.

YOU TRICKED ME!

You were doomed from the start! I can't stop Jinx, and neither can you, not with Serenity on her side. Let me inside your tree.

TO TAKE MY SOUL?

It's either me or Jinx. She'll enslave your mortals. Torture them. I won't.

YOU CANNOT DEMAND—

Your mortals don't have time for this. You knew this would happen, just as it has to every other god. So make your choice.

The Heart Tree continued to burn. Those Umber who were still alive had thrown themselves to their knees, begging for help, for mercy, while Serenity pulled apart their Golems as though they were toys.

"Stop!" Hazelhearth screamed. Vines whipped from the ground and lashed at Jinx. It was a desperate last stand.

Jinx pointed her hand at Hazelhearth, and with a single blast, the ambassador was reduced to ash.

Make your choice! I yelled. *You know me. You've seen my entire life through Dru's memories. I have no love for the gods, but everything I've ever done has been to serve their mortals. Everyone says you're the kindest of the gods, and I've yet to decide if that's true. You make them sacrifice themselves for you.*

Now it's time for you to sacrifice yourself for them.

Something green flashed at the corner of my eye.

And then the fire and smoke and screaming were gone, as though they'd been sucked away, and I stood in the center of a grove.

It reminded me of Juniper, except less terrifying. The sky was dark, completely shrouded by leaves. Mist drifted lazily across the soft grass beneath my feet. And I was surrounded by a circle of strange stone pillars. It was otherworldly in a way I couldn't explain.

This was a rare moment of calm, and I greedily swallowed the cool air.

It looked like I'd been transported into the woods, but no. The walls were made of thick bark, not individual trees. One side glowed red with flame, as though someone was trying to burn their way through it. Jinx.

I was inside the Heart Tree.

"Kayl?"

Oh my god! I turned to face Dru waiting in the grove, naked. It was her—all mortal. Her limbs and face at the proportions I knew, the vines of her hair brushing across her shoulder. Her golden daisies fully grown and standing proud.

My best friend in all the domains. "Dru! Is that—that really you?"

"Unghard, they..." She ran fingers through her daisies. "This is the end, isn't it?"

"No. This is the beginning." I reached to take her hand.

Hot air and smoke blew across my face. I recoiled, covering my eyes.

Jinx had burned her way through the bark. Shit! She was inside the grove!

"Nuh-uh, sister!" She pounced at Dru.

"No!" I ran to stop her. Vines fell from the branches above and wrapped around my waist. They pulled me into the air, away from Dru.

What are you doing? I kicked my feet in midair. *Let me save her!*

SACRIFICES MUST BE MADE.

Shit! Unghard was using Dru as bait!

Jinx grabbed Dru's arm and yanked the soul from her.

"No!" I screamed.

Dru's body collapsed to the grass, her eyeless sockets staring at me.

You bastard! I could have saved her! I choked back a sob. I'd only just gotten her back!

And now Jinx had her. No. She'd taken Dru.

What else would she take from my fucking life?

While Unghard dangled me in midair, vines attacked Jinx. She laughed like a madwoman as she tore them free from her limbs and burned them to nothing.

Tears ran down my cheeks. *You can't win this.* My own voice sounded hollow in my mind. *Stop fighting it.*

More vines curled around my abdomen. Would they rip me apart? Kill me? I didn't know if I had the strength to care.

Dru was gone, and Jinx was about to win another god's soul.

Something pushed into my hands.

A giant acorn. A seed?

It glowed with the same iridescent light as the Heart Tree's leaves and hummed with energy. Somehow, I could hear the call of the mountains whispering feverishly from within it. The rustle of leaves. The howl of wind. The echo of rock falling on rock.

The voices of thousands of Umber.

This... is your soul?

TAKE IT.

It was an offering. I'd lost Dru, but I could protect the Umber. Dru's family.

I brought the acorn to my chest and squeezed tight. My palm tingled, and then those voices exploded into my mind. The Umber were scared.

Some still fought with the Seren outside. Others gathered with their families to pray.

SERVE THEM, Unghard said as the acorn disintegrated in my hands.

I will. I promise.

The vines gently lowered me to the grass before crumbling.

Gray leaves fell from inside the grove, completely drained of their beauty. One landed on my shoulder and then faded into dust.

"No fucking way!" Jinx said, standing only inches before me. "You *beat* me? How?"

The trunk of the Heart Tree split in two. Serenity pushed her way through it, her perfect marble skin covered in dirt and dust. "Are we done here, my love?"

Jinx glared at me. "Not yet. My sister has gone and *ruined* my day. Are you so jealous, you had to steal Edana's heart from me?"

Shit. She knew Edana had betrayed her.

"Don't worry." Jinx grinned at Serenity. "I'm stealing it back. Isn't that right?"

"Anything for you, dear one." Serenity gestured lazily, and a portal to Rapture appeared.

Shit! If she went after Edana, then I'd lose my chance to save Quen! That was what this whole pissing visit to Heartstone had been for!

Jinx held out her hand. "Why don't you come with me, sister? We'll see which one of us Edana chooses."

I didn't have a choice. I refused Jinx's hand, but I followed her and Serenity into the portal.

And to whatever madness Jinx planned next.

ALL'S FAIR IN LOVE AND WAR

As god of the Ember, Edana is one of the most dangerous and volatile gods. She possesses a cunning beyond the likes of Lionheart, and a charm that even outmatches Serenity, yet Edana is not afraid to wade into conflicts personally. Nor can she be appeased. It would be pointless to seek negotiation with Edana. Her mortals are anathema to the principles we hold dear. No, with the Umber on our side, we should seek to crush her.
—P. Bezel, *Personal Report on Edana*

I COULDN'T BRING MYSELF to be pissed off at Kayl.

Sure, she'd taken the Umber from right under my nose, but she'd shown some actual initiative for once in her mortal life. I'd gone to all the trouble of recruiting Serenity and breaking into Heartstone. Edana hadn't bothered joining us, stating Unghard's defenses were too difficult, but Serenity had no problem punching holes through rocks. It came easily to a god carved from marble.

Really, I'd thought I had it. But whatever. I'd managed to steal the prodigal best friend instead, so now I could add Dru to my Godless collection. My dear sister didn't seem pleased about that.

She wouldn't be pleased with what was coming next, either.

I snatched a dress from Edana's cloakroom and headed for her penthouse with Kayl skulking behind, and Serenity bringing up the rear in case Kayl tried anything funny. My dear sister really had no choice but to follow, though she said nothing the entire way. No sarcasm. No blaming me for her mistakes. Instead, she looked weary. Glum.

Oh yes, she knew what was coming.

The double doors opened, and we entered Edana's private suite. She was alone, except for Sinder standing dutifully by her side. Edana's expression remained neutral, despite my unannounced visit and me dragging my sister here with me, but Sinder struggled to hide his shock. How had he managed to play spy for me, with a face like that?

"I see you've brought a guest," Edana drawled.

Wow, she was so damn shameless. "I found my dear sister sneaking into Heartstone. Funny, how you didn't tell me, when your voice over there was helping her out." I gave Sinder a pointed look as I made myself comfortable on the couch. "I hate being the last to know."

Thanks to Gast earning his keep, I had eyes on Sinner's Row. I knew Edana was shacking up with Kayl and playing both sides. It wasn't a surprise, really. I understood a thing or two about betrayal.

That Edana was helping Kayl invade domains behind my back was a kick in the teeth, though. And a real big fucking shame. I liked Edana. I liked the way her tongue felt on my clit. The way her fingers caressed my nipples and made them hard. She was everything the Godless admired—a god who truly embraced sin.

Our relationship had a time limit, but still.

I WARNED YOU, DAUGHTER, Mother said. *NONE OF MY CHILDREN CAN BE TRUSTED. ALL THEY DO IS BETRAY.*

Betrayal runs in the family. Kayl lingered nearby with Serenity watching over her. At least I could rely on Serenity, though she was acting smug about the whole thing.

Edana met my eye. "My actions have been to assist you—"

"By helping my sister into Heartstone?"

"I didn't help. I nudged. We needed Unghard down to pave the way to Dor. Your sister was best placed to deal with it—"

"Best placed? Do you know how close I came to snatching Unghard's soul for myself?"

"So you didn't?"

Ouch. That was a low blow. "You're really going to talk to me like that after you got on your knees and licked me out?"

"You fucked a *god*?" Kayl said, appalled.

"No need to be jealous, sister—"

"I'm bloody not! I didn't think you'd stoop that low."

"So it's fine for you to fuck your Time Boy, but I can't get a little loving?"

"How do you know about that? Were you *spying* on me?"

"Hard not to when you scream like a fucking Seren getting their wings plucked—"

"Do you both mind?" Edana snapped. "This is *my* court, and you make a mockery of it."

Kayl snorted. "Don't let me get in the way of your lovers' tiff."

Flame blazed in Edana's eyes. She didn't like being disrespected, huh.

That made two of us.

Serenity chuckled. "Edana, my love. Show a little grace to your guests. Chaos may speak colorful words, but it makes a refreshing change from the simpering of mortals."

Heat radiated from Edana's skin. She didn't like being chided by a statue, either, but she was smart. She knew she was outnumbered.

The temperature of the room dropped as Edana recovered her composure. "The Umber are no more," she finally said. "Regardless of allegiance, that is one less ally Dor can claim. But we cannot become complacent. Even alone, Dor is a threat to us. Only by uniting against him can we hope to succeed."

"Oh, so that was your master plan?" I rubbed my chin. "Bring us together so we can form a cute little prayer circle and take on Dor? You know what? I'm game. What do you say, sister?"

"Fuck you!"

I sighed. "See? This is the attitude I get. Edana's not wrong, you know. Together, we can defeat Dor. Alone, you don't stand a chance."

"Then let me go."

"It's for your safety I keep you. Don't you want to see Dru again? Or Vincent?" Sinder's breath hitched at the mention of his old lover. "They're all waiting for you in the clock tower." I dangled Kayl's Godless in front of her, and there *was* hesitation in her eyes. "And I could save your Time Boy."

She chewed her lip until it bled, and still she refused me.

What would it take to make her give up?

SHE'S NOT WORTH YOUR EFFORTS. FORGET HER AND DEAL WITH THE GODS.

No, Kayl was so close to bending. I was just missing one last piece.

"Look, we've all made mistakes," I said. "Some slightly more murderous than others. But what matters is Dor gets his arse handed to him and we make a better future where Chaos reigns. I'm not one to hold a grudge." I was *so* forgiving. "So let's keep the past in the past." I stood and opened my arms to Edana. "Kiss and make up?"

Edana hesitated. "Perhaps it is best if we focus on the task at hand—"

"Don't be like that!" I pouted. "One little kiss?" I edged toward her throne.

Sinder stepped in front of me. "My Queen wishes for respect."

By the look in his eye, I knew Edana was positioning him with unspoken commands, and he didn't look particularly comfortable with the situation.

I grabbed his wrist and yanked his soul clean out.

His body collapsed to the floor in a useless heap. And now I had another Godless in my pocket. Almost a full house!

"Sinder!" Kayl screamed.

She lunged at me, her fist swinging wide.

Really? My own sister was throwing a punch? That hurt my feelings.

Stone hands broke through the tiled floor and grasped Kayl's wrists, holding her still. Courtesy of my new best friend, Serenity.

Edana stood. Flame billowed across her shoulders, falling down her back like a cloak. "You *dare* attack my mortals in my own domain? After I welcomed you? Aided you?"

"Aided me by going behind my back?" I said. "All I wanted was a bit of loyalty, but apparently that was too hard. Maybe if you got down on your knees and apologized, I'd be more forgiving."

"I will do no such thing. You allow this mortal to disrespect us?" Edana asked Serenity.

"I'm sorry, my love," Serenity said with forced sympathy, though the gleam in her eye was positively cruel. "But you chose to act in this scene. Like all tragic plays, the curtain must fall... and it falls on you."

Edana snarled. "Then *burn*."

So much for love.

Flame burst across Edana's skin, sending her flimsy gown up in smoke. She resembled her immortals, only her black horns stood out. Fire spread from her feet across the floor, licking at Sinder's body.

Then the walls began to glow red.

Now things were really heating up! Oh, I tickled myself.

I switched to my Ember form. Whatever Edana planned to fling at me wouldn't do much damage, but I was curious to see her try.

"Jinx!" Kayl yelled.

I risked a glance. My dear sister was struggling to break free from Serenity's hold. She'd taken a Glimmer form to deal with the heat, though from my experience, it couldn't hold a candle to an Ember's raw flame. Sweat was already pouring down her face.

Serenity would release Kayl before Edana had a chance to hurt her. I didn't want my sister to burn.

But... Edana wasn't attacking me.

She simply stood with her arms held out, muttering words I couldn't hear over the crackle of flame.

"What *is* she doing?" I asked Serenity. If Edana wanted to fuck me to death, then sure, that would be great. Sweating to death seemed a little dull, though.

Serenity peered out the penthouse window. "Launching her finale, it would seem."

The fuck did that mean?

Something groaned above us.

Oh fuck!

Red-hot lava burst from the ceiling. It flowed down the walls like a waterfall, coming down thick and fast. Within seconds, it had already covered the floor between us by the throne room and the only door out of here.

"This is *my* domain, you impudent wretches," Edana hissed. "I will melt your skin off your bones!"

A chunk of lava sloughed off the ceiling and landed next to my feet. Fucking shit!

"*Jinx!*" Kayl screamed again.

"Can you shut the fuck up for a minute!"

Lava dripped around Edana like a fancy bead curtain in some Mesmer parlor, leaving little steaming patches. The curtain had fallen, all right, and it shielded her from my reach. Could I walk through *lava*? Not even my Necro form could heal that quickly.

I turned to Serenity, who was backing off as the river of lava surrounded her. Guess she didn't want to fuck around with it, either.

So that was Edana's plan—drown us in fucking *lava*, or let Serenity portal us out of here. We'd live to see another day, but we may never get another chance to take Edana down.

And honestly, I was starting to get a bit pissed off at her lack of cooperation.

All this hassle because she had to be a bitch.

Kayl switched to her new Umber form. She howled as the flowers on her brow immediately burst into flames, but what had she expected? Rapture wasn't made for Umber.

"Change form, idiot!" I yelled.

She ignored me. Instead, she used her Umber strength to break free from Serenity's hold.

And then she pulled out Corinth's pocket watch.

Aw fuck. "Don't let her get away!" I called to Serenity.

Kayl's form changed to Chaos. It had taken her weeks to finally understand how aether worked. Shame she'd figured it out right at this moment. A portal opened in the center of the room.

Water gushed through from the other side.

What the fuck?

She'd only gone and opened a portal into fucking Memoria!

A literal wave swept me off my damn feet! I screamed, or attempted to. Water splashed over my head, cutting my screams off midgurgle. Serenity grabbed my arm, stopping me from being dragged toward the lava.

And then the room *exploded*.

Water cascaded over the lava with an almighty hiss and went off like a gods-damn bomb! It erupted in a plume of vapor, showering the room with bits of molten magma and what was left of poor Sinder.

Serenity grew larger and sheltered me with her body. If not for her, I would have been blown to pieces—

Kayl.

Shit! Steam filled the room, hiding everything. I couldn't see where Kayl had gone! I couldn't fucking *see* her! "Kayl!"

Edana's shrieks rang out in response.

I wiggled from Serenity's hold and waded through a pool of warm water that sloshed up to my thighs. Smoldering lumps of black rock got in my way, and I had to hastily shuffle around them to avoid burning my feet.

Water had stopped rushing in, which meant Kayl's portal must have closed. The water level dropped as it evaporated, reduced to dirty pools around my ankles. As the steam finally dispersed, I found Kayl standing in the corner of the penthouse, panting, the pocket watch clutched in her hand.

Relief weakened my knees.

Smart move, sister.

But I'd deal with her in a second.

The penthouse was in a right state. That explosion had blown out the windows, allowing most of the water and steam to escape, but left the awful stench of sulfur native to Rapture to seep inside.

Edana sagged against her throne. Her fancy flames had receded, leaving her naked, shivering, and her teeth chattering. The water had completely doused her.

Wow. I hadn't even realized you could snuff out an Ember's flame like that.

"Ready to give up?" I said.

Immortals appeared in midair. Twirling dancers of flame with beautiful burning blue eyes. They materialized for an instant, and then they disappeared in a puff of steam.

Huh. The room was too damp for them to exist. Or was Edana tiring? Could gods tire?

"My mortals will protect me." Edana wheezed, her breath coming out all ragged. You'd think all that fucking would build stamina, but well.

She'd been a selfish lover, all in all.

Naked Ember popped into existence next. Six of them, all tough-looking males with sharp black horns and dangling dicks.

"Burn them!" Edana ordered, and pointed at me.

The Ember glanced between us, their shocked faces snapping between their beaten, pathetic god and Serenity.

They bolted for the door, splashing through puddles in their haste to get out.

What did you know? A selfish god bred selfish mortals. Who would have thought?

"Stop!" Edana reached for her mortals, her bare feet staggering against the still-smoldering obsidian rocks.

I approached Edana, almighty god of the Ember. "What's the matter? Your mortals don't love you? Your godly siblings don't love you, either. No one does. They've left you here to die."

"Aid me," Edana called to Kayl. "My mortals can be yours. Together, we'll face Dor—we'll save Corinth."

My dear sister had remained in this room the entire time, watching on with a sort of helpless fascination. The kind of morbid curiosity a mortal might have if they watched a Mesmer walking in front of a tram.

She wanted to fight me for Edana, but unfortunately for them both, Serenity blocked Kayl's way.

This bitch was *mine*.

And Edana knew it.

Edana's skin rippled with repressed flame. "This is *my* domain," she seethed. "I will destroy it and every last one of my mortals to bury you in their remains."

A crack splintered across the floor as the ground shook. Uh-oh.

That hadn't been an idle threat.

Fuck, she must be desperate—blowing up her own domain was a last resort.

"Jinx!" Kayl yelled. "You've got to stop her!"

My sister wasn't wrong. Kayl probably worried for all the mortals about to get pulped, but Edana could rebuild Rapture to keep us Chaos out, and then I'd never get her soul.

It was now or never.

"Do it!" I called to Serenity.

Marble hands burst from the tiles and reached for Edana. They clawed at her ankles and wrists, wrapping her limbs in solid limestone. Edana pulled them free, reducing them to rubble, but more and more appeared, overwhelming her.

Flame spilled out of Edana in frantic bursts, but could do nothing against Serenity's stone. It was entirely resistant to the Ember's heat.

Not even the Umber could boast *that*.

Edana drowned in marble until it encased her body completely, turning her into a living statue. Only her snarling face remained free.

"She's all yours," Serenity whispered into my ear. "But be quick, my love. She remains volatile."

Oh yes. Having Edana at my mercy would have made my hair stand on end, if Ember had any. The ground continued to shake, and outside, lava poured down the volcanic skyline. Serenity's fancy trick would only hold Edana for so long.

She was, after all, a god.

A god about to lose everything.

I lifted Edana's chin so we could see eye to eye. "We could have had something special, you know?"

She spat in my face.

"That's rude." I wiped my cheek clean. I actually enjoyed sharing saliva with her. Edana had been my first real fuck in this new body. I may have been there for all those times Kayl had fucked her Vesper, but without my own body, it wasn't the same.

LOVE ISN'T WORTH THE PAIN OF BETRAYAL. EVEN DOR WOULD WHISPER SWEET NOTHINGS IN MY EAR WHILE PLOTTING MY IMPRISONMENT.

I don't need to know the finer details of your relationship with Dor, Mother.

YOU UNDERSTAND HOW IT HURTS. MORTALS ARE MADE FROM OUR EMOTIONS. THE PAIN YOU FEEL, I SUFFER TENFOLD.

WHEN I AM FREE, I WILL BRING DOR TO HIS KNEES.

I WOULD HEAR HIM BEG FOR MERCY. IT WILL BE DELICIOUS.

Damn right it will. As would this.

I pressed my lips against Edana's.

One final kiss.

A kiss that would steal her breath away.

Edana tried to pull free. The marble holding her in place cracked.

My teeth sank into her bottom lip and tasted blood.

With that one drop of blood, thousands of voices exploded in my mind. The Ember were now mine, and they ran from their casinos and brothels in mass panic, scattering cards, poker chips, and bocs while shoving whores out of the way. When the end-times came, none of those pleasures mattered.

I withdrew from the kiss and wiped my lips dry.

Serenity wore a pitying smile. "All's fair in love and war."

"You're a fool if you think you can trust her," Edana said to Serenity. "She'll take your soul next."

Serenity sneered. "Unlike you, I've seen the end of this particular production. I know where my loyalties lie."

"Then enjoy your oblivion."

The marble finally fell away, allowing Edana's naked body to collapse and shatter into a clump of smoldering ash. Ironic, really, considering her whole domain was made of ash.

I clapped dust from my hands. "That wasn't too bad, was it?"

"Is this all a pissing game to you?" Kayl snapped. Her fists were shaking by her sides. "It's not enough you took Vincent and Harmony and Dru, but you had to take Sinder? Let them go!"

"They're my friends now. But if you want to see your precious Godless again, then you know what you have to do." I held out my hand.

She wound Corinth's pocket watch.

STOP HER!

Other than her Time Boy, there was only one thing that would stop my dear sister.

I plucked Harmony from the clock tower and dumped her right here in the penthouse. She stumbled on her feet, still not quite used to standing so tall in her Chaos form. Her eyes opened wide at the sight of Rapture falling apart.

Kayl paused, the watch clutched in her fist. "Harm?"

"You think I'm unpredictable and violent," I said. "But I'm doing what even you couldn't do—rebuilding the Godless and taking down gods. Harmony here's acting as my voice. All we're missing is *you*, sister. Go on." I nudged Harmony. "Tell her how great we're doing, but be quick. This place isn't gonna last long."

Harmony lifted her chin, though her legs trembled. "Run, Kayl. Stay as far away as you can—"

I snapped her soul back into the aether. Rude. Harmony was supposed to be *my* voice!

A portal opened in the room, this time to the Undercity. Before I could even blink, Kayl dove inside, and it closed behind her.

"That's unfortunate," Serenity commented.

Fuck!

STOP GIVING YOUR SISTER CHANCES.

She'll come to the clock tower eventually. I'd not left her much choice. Corinth had gone and gotten himself captured by the Diviner, and I needed him, or the souls he was carrying. Without Zyclone and Lionheart's souls, I couldn't unlock the chains around Mother. We wouldn't be able to free her.

There was no way Kayl could take on Anima or Dor on her own, and she wasn't crazy enough to try. If she wanted my help, she knew where to find me.

Though my next steps would be awkward.

DOR WILL HAVE ARRANGED FOR QUENTIN CORINTH'S IMPRISONMENT TO SPITE ME. TO KEEP YOU FROM COLLECTING THE SOULS WE NEED.

Which meant Corinth would no longer be in Memoria, but Krono. And getting into Kronos would be a pain in my arse.

What the fuck had he gone to Memoria for anyway?

For the Vesper. A different mess, because I needed Kayl's memories fixed in order to take back Valeria's soul. If Anima was buddying up to Dor, then Dor would likely learn of Kayl's memory issues and target her.

Unless Anima kept that juicy nugget secret.

Fucking gods and their traitorous plots.

RELEASE EDANA'S SOUL TO ME, Mother urged. *THEN I CAN RELEASE MORE POWER INTO THE CLOCK TOWER.*

I chewed my thumb. *Not yet. I'll need all the gods' power if I'm going to take down Dor.*

YOU HOARD THEIR SOULS WHEN YOU COULD GIFT ME A TASTE OF FREEDOM. DO NOT EMULATE YOUR SISTER'S SELFISHNESS.

That stung. I wasn't doing this to be selfish. *If I can't stand against Dor, then you'll never get your freedom. You know I'm risking everything for you.* Wasn't that what I'd always wanted? To hold my mother close for once in my mortal life?

THEN DO NOT SHOW KAYL MERCY. YOU HAVE A SOFT SPOT FOR YOUR SISTER, BUT SHE IS A LIABILITY. TAKE THE SOULS SHE OWNS AND BE DONE WITH HER.

But she's my sister—

I AM YOUR MOTHER. THE ONLY FAMILY YOU NEED.

"We're not family!"

DO NOT LET ME DOWN.

I won't, Mother. I'm sorry! Mother was right. I'd given Kayl enough chances.

If my sister wouldn't join me willingly, then I'd have no choice but to take her by force.

"I see your mind working hard, my love," Serenity said, bringing me out of my miserable thoughts. "Perhaps we should plan our next move in comfort?" She opened a portal to Arcadia's sweet gardens. I could already taste the wine waiting for me, and fuck, did I want to knock myself out for an hour or two.

I was tired. Mortally tired.

Besides, this place was toast. Literally.

Ash fell from the ceiling. Where the windows had blown out, I could see the strip. The once colorful casinos were now muted and gray.

I'd expected the Ember to still be panicking as their existence came to an end, but they weren't. Nope. Many of 'em were busy rolling their last dice, downing their last whiskey, or trying to rub one out before the curtain fell on their souls.

Living life to the fullest. What was left of it.

Rapture just wouldn't be Rapture without someone squeezing their pleasure out at the last ticking second.

I stepped through the portal and let Rapture collapse into nothing.

What happened in Rapture, stayed in Rapture. Forever.

XXXII

R: Do you understand why you've been summoned, Mr. Sterling?
N. Sterling: Well, to be honest, sir, I'm not entirely sure—
R: Our Father has chosen me to test each Diviner for sin. In our war against
Chaos, it is vital we guard ourselves against the temptations of sin and
avoid the corruption of Chaos. It states here in your personal file that you
regularly indulge in minor sins, yes?
N. Sterling: If downing a whiskey or two is considered a sin during these
uncertain times?
R: I'm afraid it is. But don't fret. Our Father is willing to forgive your sins
if you submit your soul to a holy baptism. Through this, I will redeem you.
—The Redeemer, *Transcript for the Redemption of N. Sterling*

AS MEMORIA'S GATE WAS no longer in service, Dor simply created a smaller portal within Memoria's Warden HQ. A marvel! It functioned exactly the same as Elijah and I crossed over to Kronos, and on the other side, we emerged from a miniature version of the Gate in the main plaza of Father's clock tower.

The Covenant prevented gods from traveling between each other's domains, but those rules apparently no longer applied.

"Why didn't we use our main Gate?" I asked Elijah as this smaller Gate powered down at our arrival.

"It's no longer functional."

That was shocking to hear. The Gate rarely went down. "Chaos damaged it?"

"No. We did, to prevent Chaos from using it."

That made sense. If Chaos was invading and destroying domains, then taking the Gate offline would be the logical course of action.

Elijah strode on ahead, and I hurried to keep up. Once a bustling hub for Kronos's administrative offices, the plaza was largely empty, save for Wardens in their traditional uniform, going about their duties. It was an eerie sight, when so many Diviner would normally queue here for their various needs.

War had already changed Kronos.

It had been too long since my last visit to my domain, but the atmosphere felt altogether different. As though it had moved on without me, and I found myself falling one second behind.

Was it Kronos? Or had I changed? Things were different, yes. I had an entirely new arm, for one. My time in Memoria had certainly relaxed me.

But I was still a Diviner, deep down.

Still a Warden.

I followed Elijah into an elevator and to the ambassador offices further up. I'd always been his shadow, serving him in whatever capacity he needed. That had been my path in life, and returning to that duty grounded me.

I expected him to enter his office, but no. He strode further on to a room guarded by two Wardens. They nodded at our approach.

What we stepped inside was no office, but more of a conference room. In fact, it reminded me of the Council chamber back in Chime, though I couldn't remember when I'd stepped inside—my memory was a little fuzzy on the details.

A circular table in the design of a clock took up much of the room. Like the Council chamber, the table was decorated with a map of the twelve domains, or had been, once. Most of the domains were crossed out with black tape. Marking them as lost. Otherwise, the room was empty, save for a tea stand opposite Heartstone.

Elijah took a seat by the designation for Kronos. "This is our war room." He gestured for me to sit.

I took the chair beside Heartstone. The Umber domain was also covered in black tape. Saints. "Heartstone was attacked? When?"

"Only hours ago. Rapture has also fallen, but we've yet to update our records."

"Edana is gone? How did you verify it?"

"We have men watching Sinner's Row. They reported the Ember vanishing in a wave of dust."

My heart sank. No, it plummeted into my gut and threatened to make me regurgitate my breakfast. "How could we have lost two domains in the space of hours?"

Elijah wore a grim expression. "This is why I've brought you home. The situation is dire."

Dire was too mild a word for this—this unfathomable disaster! I examined the table. So many domains had been crossed out, with only simple tape to mark their demise. Thousands of mortal lives wiped away in an instant.

Only a handful remained, if that. Memoria. Arcadia. Kronos.

Three domains. Three gods.

I didn't just want to be sick. I wanted to curl into myself and cry.

Never again would I hold a pleasant conversation with a fellow from Heartstone, or buy baked bread from an Ember stall owner, or drink tea in a Glimmer café. Everything I'd loved about Chime had been destroyed— the many faces from across the domains coexisting, sharing their lives, their stories.

All that time writing lecture notes and preparing lesson plans, and the universe had been falling apart without me. Why had I become a Warden, if not to protect mortals? I'd utterly failed in that duty.

I'd... I'd failed.

"Quentin," Elijah ordered. "Look at me."

I did so, and hastily wiped away the tear that had run down my cheek.

"Now is not the time to falter. Chaos has grown strong, and we cannot afford to show weakness, do you understand? Pull yourself together."

I sat up and cleared my throat. "Yes, Your Excellency."

"Good. It's imperative I bring you up to speed. While it is tragic to lose our allies, there will be time to mourn later. Right now, our priority is defending Kronos and our Father. We must do whatever it takes to keep our domain safe."

"What of the Amnae? They're our allies—"

"They are not our priority. I know you care for them, but they're on their own."

I clenched my fists in my lap. Of course our own domain and mortals were important, but surely we'd have greater success working together? "And the Seren?"

"Serenity has rejected Father's offer for peace. They remain our enemy."

Then we were alone?

Blast it all. Eli was right. I had to hold it together. The fate of Father, of all the Diviner, rested on our shoulders. "If the Gate is no longer usable, then how is Chaos invading domains?"

Elijah rubbed his chin. "We have theories, but no concrete evidence. One theory suggests certain gods aligned with Chaos are creating portals. Serenity, for instance."

"If that's true, then Chaos could enter Kronos..."

"Attempts have already been made to breach our domain."

Gods help us. "They didn't succeed?"

Elijah rose from his chair and strode for the tea stand. "Father sensed their presence and dispatched Guardians to eliminate any who tried." He turned his back to me and prepared himself coffee, by the smell. His spoon rattled against the cup. "We've caught Seren spies, some Ember. And a few Necro. The gods have at least their retained distance, instead sending their mortals to prod us. Thanks to the Zephyr, we can better protect Kronos from outside influence. They generously gifted us shields to ward against Chaos before their own domain fell." He returned to his seat, coffee in hand. I'd never liked the taste or texture, but it would be rude to make a cup of tea for myself.

"If Serenity is in league with Chaos, then we can expect more Seren spies," I mused. "What happened to those mortals you caught?"

"We submitted them to our soul-splitting machines."

I was glad I hadn't opted for tea, for I would have damn well choked on it! "I'm sorry? You—You destroyed their *souls*?"

Elijah took a slow sip of his coffee. "We couldn't risk them returning to their gods with intel. You may not approve—"

"No, I certainly do *not*—"

"This is war, Quentin." He set his coffee down and held me with those hardened brass eyes. "We do what must be done."

"There must be another way—"

"This is not debatable. Chaos could invade our domain at any time—we will take any and all precautions to protect ourselves. If that requires utilizing technology you do not consider morally sound, then so be it. Father approves of whatever actions I take for the good of our domain."

I sucked on my teeth. Elijah had commissioned these machines in order to destroy Chaos, though we'd apprehended the Glimmer and Godless using them for their own means. Yes, I found them morally reprehensible. But if Elijah had been responsible for their creation, and Father had sanctioned it, then could I judge their purpose?

No, but I still didn't like it.

"It's not enough to simply protect our domain," Elijah continued. "Chaos must be destroyed."

A shiver ran down my spine. "How do you plan to achieve that?"

He took another considered sip of his coffee. "By turning their power against them."

"Splitting their souls?"

"Think more ambitious. A god can throw as many of their mortals at us as they can conjure. To remedy this problem, we must destroy the source."

Oh my. "You mean..."

"We must destroy Chime's clock tower, and thus destroy Corentine."

I leaned back against my seat. "Is that even possible?" Surely it must be, if Chaos could steal the souls of gods.

"We've not been idle all this time." He took a deep gulp of his coffee and then stood. "Come. I'll show you our work, and you can see for yourself the plans we have in place."

I leaped to my feet and followed, my nerves a shaken mess. Did I truly want to know the depraved machinations Elijah had devised? But know I must, if I was to assist him.

Is this your will, Father? I asked in my mind.

He did not reply. Perhaps He was simply too busy to answer my prayers, which was perfectly understandable given the circumstances. But His silence weighed on me.

It left me with a void no tea could fill.

We headed back downstairs to the private laboratories in Father's tower. There were many Diviner here in lab coats, scribbling notes on clipboards. It reminded me of what I'd left behind in Memoria, though Doctor Burns's experiments had been entirely on harmless subjects. On memory retrieval.

Elijah stopped me beside a large observation window. "These are some of the spies we captured, and other prisoners of war." He gestured to the one-way glass.

Slowly, I peered inside.

The room wasn't some scientific torture chamber as I'd feared, but appeared to be a classroom. Inside were rows of chairs, and seated at each chair was a living mortal. Only they weren't Diviner.

There were Fauna. Umber. Seren. Ember. Mortals from domains that had apparently ceased to be, and yet here they were, all sitting politely, their hands in their laps. Their eyes staring at nothing.

My stomach churned with sudden dread. "Why are they sitting like that?"

"Their souls have been taken."

"But... how?" I spluttered. When the Godless machine split a soul, it literally ripped it from their body, leaving their sockets without eyes, and their body little more than an empty vessel. They were dead, in every gruesome meaning of the word.

"The Glimmer reprogrammed these devices to split a mortal from their god. It effectively destroys their souls without killing them. The result is as you see before you—willing slaves."

"Slaves?"

Elijah leaned into a microphone beside the observation window. "Stand."

His voice crackled through an electric speaker. All at once, they stood on command.

"Pat your head," he commanded.

They did so, in perfect sync, until Elijah ordered them to stop.

I sank against the wall, completely flabbergasted. It was one thing to rip souls from mortals, but to turn them into mindless drones? "What purpose does this serve?" I refused to believe we were so desperate we'd recruit soulless slaves!

"These were spies sent to attack us, Quentin. We needed to split their souls to prevent them from taking information back to their gods. That we have found a use for them means their sacrifice won't be wasted."

Wasted? Dear gods. It was bureaucracy at its deadliest! "And the Umber?" I found it hard to believe they would betray Dor!

"We required their intel. Unghard was none the wiser."

"That's hardly..." What? Fair? Was there any fairness in all this?

"We need to protect our own, which is why I am our Father's voice. He trusts me to make these difficult choices." Elijah carried on down the hall.

I dutifully followed. Did Elijah weigh the consequences of these decisions in his heart, like I did? Did it occur to him the Covenant was being torn to shreds by sacrificing mortal lives from other domains?

The Covenant was everything we Wardens stood for. What we believed in.

Elijah stopped outside another observation window and gestured for me to look. I stepped up tentatively, fearing the fresh horrors inside.

It was another classroom. Only the mortals sitting with unnatural stillness were all Diviner men.

"Eli?" My voice came out in a whimper. What justification could he have to split the souls of our own mortals?

"These were redeemed."

"*Redeemed?*"

"Father tasked me with routing out Chaos's influence from our own ranks. You know it manifests as sin. By purging their souls, we also cleansed them of sin. This is a concept the Glimmer understood well. Also, Chaos *can* steal the souls of our mortals—"

"So you thought you'd cut out the middle man?"

Irritation flashed in his eyes. "My taking the souls of Diviner gives us an advantage. Through our testing, we discovered soulless mortals have a natural defense against other domains' abilities. For example, a soulless mortal is immune to a Seren's song and a Mesmer's illusion."

Odd that he'd bring up the Mesmer. They were hardly a threat in war, surely? And they were gone... Weren't they?

"These men have been redeemed in Father's name to fight for their brethren," Elijah continued. "They have already proven successful. This is all part of Dor's plan."

Is that true, Father? No response.

What redemption was worth losing one's soul? Once again, we'd become arbiters of souls, judging which were worth saving, and which could be tossed to the front lines of a literal soul-sucking war. Where did Elijah draw the line? Which sins could be absolved, which ones only redeemed?

Why would he show me these things, knowing they horrified me? To warn that my soul could be 'redeemed' if I strayed too far into sin? Which sins? The minor sin of taking too many sugars with my tea?

The failure to protect our domain?

What point was there in saving Kronos if it came at such a high cost? If by splitting souls willy-nilly, we lost our own in the process?

If we defeated Chaos, only to become *worse*?

I dug my nails into my palms and let the pain ground me before I became hysterical.

Why was I the only one who saw this for what it was?

Utter madness?

No. I had to stop thinking that way. Father trusted Elijah to make these decisions. I needed to place faith in them both that they were taking the correct path.

This was a test. That was why Elijah had brought me here.

A test.

I rolled my shoulders and regained what little composure I had.

Elijah nodded at me, as though he understood the battle warring within my heart, and the effort it took to restrain my emotions. Perhaps I judged him too harshly. He knew me too well.

"This is the result of our efforts." Elijah gestured at another window.

I braced myself.

Two mortals were visible this time. Both strapped to a chair, though like the others, they didn't make a single movement and barely even blinked. They were male, identical twins. Their skin was a silvery blue, their hair shocking white with the tips of pointed ears poking through. They were unlike any domain, and yet I'd fought them already.

"You caught Chaos mortals?" Though these mortals had lost their souls, their eyes still brimmed with colorful aether. "Are they..." I gestured at them uselessly. "Dangerous?"

"They're subdued, but we're taking no chances where Chaos is concerned. We've run multiple tests on each. The first we dissected and healed thanks to a Necro who offered us their skills in exchange for a report on our findings to The Nameless One, though naturally, we allowed no such report to leave this building." Elijah lifted a clipboard from the wall and flipped through it. "Our research has allowed us to fine-tune our aether sensors—those that can detect Chaos energy—and also perfect our aether collars and soul-splitting devices. We have created portable versions of the device. A means of splitting a mortal's soul without needing to risk bringing them to Kronos first."

The ramifications of such technology were too much to bear. I had to focus on the positives. "Which would mean we can bring the fight to Chaos?"

"Correct. Chaos mortals can take the soul of a god through touch. Our plan is to utilize these mortals to destroy Corentine."

I glanced at the Chaos males. If they'd been reduced to mindless slaves, then they could be controlled—ordered into attacking their own god. My stomach churned at the moral implications of forcing a mortal to kill their maker... But it truly was the best plan.

Chaos had to go.

"How do we reach Corentine? Isn't she imprisoned in the clock tower?"

"We've made numerous attempts to breach the clock tower and believe we have a good assessment of its structural integrity. We have a plan. I want you to lead it."

"*Me?*" I stared over the rim of my spectacles. "Well, I—"

"Your Excellency!" called a feminine voice.

My jaw dropped. A woman approached—an actual female Diviner! She stood shorter than me, though dressed similarly in a tan skirt and jacket. Her silver hair curved around her face, with a single line of brass cutting through the silver.

My gosh. I couldn't remember the last time I'd met a female Diviner, if I ever had?

Though as she neared, I noticed something odd painted on her face, like lettering...

Saints.

That wasn't paint. Words had been carved into her skin. The red marks were wounds.

Who would do such a depraved thing? Chaos?

Elijah frowned at the interruption. "I specifically ordered that I was not to be disturbed."

The woman dipped into a demure curtsy. "Apologies, Your Excellency. Have you had time to read the report I sent you? It's a most concerning matter—"

"It's of no concern to me." His instant dismissal was rude. So unlike Elijah.

"Then perhaps Mr. Corinth may be interested?" She pulled a file from her handbag and held it out for me.

How did she know my name? Was I that well known as Elijah's shadow? "I'm sorry, have we met?" There was something familiar about her I couldn't place.

I went to take the file, but Elijah snatched it from my hand and glared at the poor woman.

"You have your duties," he snapped. "See to them."

Defiance shone in her silver eyes. That look was familiar, too. "They're being abused. It's not right."

"Who are?" I asked. Did it have something to do with those terrible scars? "What's this about?"

"The female slaves. Our men are touching them inappropriately—"

"Do *not* disobey me!" Elijah slapped the woman across the face. So hard, she lost her balance and fell to her knees.

Saints! I crouched and steadied the woman. She was shaking, and a streak of blood smeared her bottom lip.

"Quentin, stand," Elijah barked.

What had gotten into him? Acting as our Father's voice was a stressful duty, but he'd always projected a calm demeanor. It wasn't like him to lose it.

The woman grabbed my wrist, her fingernails digging through my sleeve. "Don't trust him," she whispered. "He's—"

"Now, Quentin."

I hurried to my feet, my heart pounding.

The woman stood slowly, her head bowed. "Apologies, Your Excellency. I'll take my leave." She strode out of the labs as I stared, completely baffled out of my wits.

Who *was* that woman?

And why had she warned me against Elijah?

He held the woman's file. A bubble of time surrounded it, and the paper fell apart into fragments as time sped up. Whatever secrets had been written inside were now lost to time.

A few Diviner men in lab coats, who had been watching the situation, returned to their work, ignoring us.

"Eli." I spoke softly. "Who was she? What was she talking about?"

Eliajah pulled a handkerchief from his upper jacket pocket and cleaned his hands. "Nothing of consequence."

"She said the—the soulless were being abused. Is that true?"

"It hardly matters—"

"Of course it matters!"

He turned to me with such hard metal eyes. "Her report is greatly exaggerated. These mortals are soulless beings. They do not feel pain. They have no emotions."

They were being touched inappropriately, that was what she'd said. What did that mean? That the Wardens were hurting them? Groping them? Worse?

Gods. I swayed on my feet with a sudden bout of dizziness. "Do we not owe them basic respect?"

"Their feelings are irrelevant, and this is a waste of our time. Come." He strode down the hall.

Clearly, I needed a different tactic. I hurried to catch up. "To seek pleasure is sin. If we're allowing our men to abuse our charges, then that is a distraction from the work ahead. Father needs every man at his best."

Elijah glanced at me. "I see your point."

Finally, a concession.

"I'll have them redeemed."

Blast, that wasn't what I'd intended!

Elijah stopped outside another room. This one didn't have any scientists milling about it, but was instead guarded by a Warden. What now?

This entire afternoon had been a showcase of misery.

"You've always had a soft spot for mortals, haven't you, Quentin?"

I nervously fiddled with my bow tie. "I'm a Warden. It comes with the job."

"You serve our Father, first and foremost. That is your path."

"I understand—"

"Do you?" He placed a hand on my shoulder, his grip tight. Possessive. "I have shown you the steps we have taken to secure our domain and protect our mortals. Spoken to you of what it will take to save Kronos and destroy Chaos for good. And yet you have shown me nothing but doubt."

I tucked my hands behind my back and avoided his gaze. "I'll admit your methods are a little unconventional—"

"Look at me."

I lifted my chin and met his brass stare.

"If we are to defeat Chaos, then you must have unquestionable faith in our Father. In me. There can be no room for doubt."

"But Father... He hasn't answered my prayers."

"When He believes your faith absolute, He will deem you worthy."

"How can I prove my faith?"

Elijah released my shoulder and opened the door to the room.

Today had been an exhausting flurry of surprises. A single Diviner was strapped to a chair, only this fellow was like no other Diviner I'd ever seen. He was simply humongous. A giant of a man. Bruising covered his face. His left eye was swollen, half-closed. He shifted uncomfortably in his bonds and let out a whimper.

This man was not soulless, yet he'd been condemned to imprisonment.

"Who is this?" I asked.

"A traitor. He allowed captives to escape Kronos, endangering our security and the lives of our fellow Diviner."

I eyed the giant warily. Clearly he'd been thoroughly questioned, though not in a way I approved of. "Has he revealed any motive?"

"None. He refuses to talk. But no matter. Father has decided his fate." Elijah lifted a helmet-like object from a table opposite and held it before me. "This man is an apostate who believes in a wild delusion that he was born under the wrong god. He is to be redeemed. You are to administer Father's judgement."

I stared at the helmet, at the odd wiring that curled around its back, and the glaring red button on top that screamed danger. Saints have mercy. It was a soul-splitting device. "Eli, I'm a Warden! I'm no executioner—"

"You asked for an opportunity to prove your faith. Prove your loyalty to me, and to our Father." He shoved the helmet into my hands. "Prove you have what it takes to destroy Chaos."

I almost dropped the horrid thing! It was far too light for the weight of damnation it carried. Could I really damn this fellow to a soulless existence? To rip apart everything that made him unique and toss it into the unknown?

This was the test. Was this what that woman had tried to warn me about?

What would happen if I failed? If I refused? By the hardness in Elijah's eyes, I couldn't possibly fathom the consequence.

Would he tut? Display his displeasure and demote me?

Punish me?

Redeem my soul next?

But should I acquiesce, then I'd destroy a soul. Could my own soul bear that?

I steadied my breathing and gawked at the man in shackles. An anomaly, for a Diviner. A traitor, Elijah had said. Could I justify my sympathy for a traitor?

"Quentin," Elijah ordered.

That one command snapped me to my senses. I gripped the helmet and approached the traitor.

He glanced up and forced a smile. "Sir. Glad to see you again."

I paused. "We've met?"

"You don't remember me, sir?"

It was possible we may have crossed paths in my capacity as a Warden, and those memories had been wiped for security reasons. "I'm afraid that's classified."

He grimaced with more emotion than most Diviner dared. "I understand, sir. I didn't... I messed up, sir. But not in the way you think. I tried to save Chance, and I... I failed."

"Chance?"

"The Chaos male."

One of the Chaos prisoners? Gods, then this man *was* a traitor. "Why were you trying to save him?"

"He's innocent, sir. They all are."

"Quentin," Elijah called.

I placed the helmet on top of the traitor's head and secured it. Judging by the apparatus, there was no need to switch it on or charge it. One press of that button would be enough to send an aether-powered pulse through the device. And then his soul would be gone for good.

"Did she make it?" the man asked in a whisper. "Kayl. Did she make it?"

I froze.

That name.

The woman from my dreams.

"Who—Who is she?" I whispered back.

"She's the only one who can save us, sir."

"Who are you? What's your name?"

"Benjamin Seasons, sir. But the Wardens, they call me Big Ben."

"Because of your height?"

"Because of my height, sir."

"Why do you keep calling me that? Sir?"

"Because I served you, sir, and I liked doing it. Dor always said I would die in service to our ambassador. I always thought... it would be you." His voice cracked. "And I wouldn't have minded."

"Quentin, you're wasting time," Elijah snapped.

Saints. I didn't want to do this. Hundreds of questions exploded in my mind, and here was the one man who could answer them. But time was not on my side. "I'm sorry. I can't..."

"It's okay, sir. I know what you have to do. I forgive you. But please... look in the mirror. Look at yourself, sir. Look at who you are. This isn't you."

I didn't know what that meant, but gods, those words would haunt me for the rest of my days. Who was I to this man?

Who was I?

My metal finger hovered above that odious button.

The traitor—Big Ben—closed his eyes, though his limbs trembled, his shackles clinking faintly.

I couldn't do this. I couldn't—

"Do it, Quentin!" Elijah urged. "For me. For our Father."

My finger pressed down.

A jolt of aether zapped through the helmet.

Big Ben's head lolled to one side.

His mortal body was still here, though his eyes stared at nothing.

For his soul was gone.

I choked back bile.

Elijah patted me on the back, and it took all my effort not to scream and shove him away. "Well done, Quentin. Father will be pleased."

I'd killed a man. Destroyed his soul. And for what?

"What—What now?" I managed to spit out.

"Now we do what must be done."

33

Serenity is not to be underestimated. On the surface, they appear little more than a bumbling fool, but behind their whimsical nature lies a devious intellect that plots behind the scenes. Their mortals, too, should not be underestimated, for their power of song can render any domain helpless, even our own. They must be approached with caution. I suggest we devise means to protect ourselves against their vocal manipulation.
—P. Bezel, *Personal Report on Serenity*

MY FEET WERE ACHING by the time we reached our destination. Grayford. It had been weeks since I last stepped foot here—since I was forced to abandon the depot and everything had changed. The Godless weren't the only ones who'd left in a hurry, but with the Fauna and Ember now gone, the streets were well and truly empty. There was nothing left but dust and grime.

The slums had always been a somber place, which was to be expected when you were surrounded by so many grumpy Vesper. But now it felt mournful. Walking through main street and avoiding the large dust piles that had likely been Vesper was like attending a funeral march. I could almost hear a dirge accompanying my every step.

I avoided the depot—returning there would have been too obvious—and instead found myself standing outside Varen's old office. The emotions it brought back were somewhat ruined by the Mesmer complaining.

"I'm tired," Cosmo whined. "Can we sleep now?" They cradled a bucket containing Sugar the fish. Why they insisted on bringing it with us, I didn't know.

For the same reason we'd brought the Fauna with us, I supposed.

We couldn't leave them behind.

We'd walked along the tram lines for hours, all the way from Sinner's Row. After what had happened in Rapture, it wasn't safe for us to stay, but that meant bringing all the soulless Fauna with us. At least the bigger Fauna helped carry the Mesmer when they started kicking up a fuss, while others carried bags of whatever we could bring with us—food, water, clothing. The essentials.

But how was I meant to feed and shelter a group of fifty-odd Fauna who needed to be told to eat and shit? They didn't complain about their lot because they couldn't.

One question played on my mind the entire walk here.

Why keep them alive, if they were soulless?

I'd thought about drugging their drink with laudanum and letting them go peacefully. If Jinx were here, she would have declared them husks and killed them already. At least an overdose would be a mercy. But I couldn't bring myself to do it. I had to believe their souls were still out there, somewhere. Floating in the vast aether.

Reve had once implied there would be a way for me to bring his soul back after it had been torn in half by the Diviner's machine. He'd looked at the far future and witnessed *something*. If he'd believed his soul would remain intact, then I had to believe the Fauna's would. That Autumn's soul could be saved.

It was ironic, really, for a Godless to grasp on to faith, but gods, I needed it.

Because the alternative was too terrible to accept.

"Yes, Cosmo, we can rest now. Let's get these bags inside."

Varen's front door wasn't locked. It was one of the few buildings in Grayford that actually had a door. I pushed it open with my shoulder, a bag of canned goods in one hand, a bag of biscuits and candy in the other, and another bag of clothing slung over my back. This old place had enough space to fit us inside, though it wouldn't be the same as a hotel. We'd have to make do. We had no other choice.

While Grayford's market and soup kitchen had been picked clean by scavengers, Varen's place was remarkably intact. The couches and armchairs in the reception were scuffed and covered in dust, but perfectly usable. The washroom even had running water.

I dumped my bags by the desk and left the Mesmer to help the Fauna settle in as I headed upstairs to Varen's office. It was something I needed to face alone.

The door clicked shut behind me. I rested the back of my head on the thick wood and caught my breath.

Fuck.

Just... fuck.

The office remained more or less the same as when I last stayed here, when Varen had let me sleep on his couch overnight. Only, the curtains were torn and there were papers scattered across the desk and floor. Someone had come here looking to dig up dirt, but what did that matter, when Grayford had died in the Vesper's absence?

I staggered to the couch and collapsed on it, sending up a cloud of dust.

So many of my years had been spent in this room, listening to Varen's instructions, laughing at his jokes, begging him for stories and advice. Stories he'd willingly shared with me as a captive audience. I'd always looked up to him as the father I never had. I'd thought he'd felt the same. But none of that had been true. He'd tolerated me for as long as I was useful to him.

Strange, how I remembered him and not the male I supposedly loved. They both existed in the depths of my subconscious. I could bring them back. Would I even want to rebirth Varen? Did he deserve that second chance at life after everything he'd put me through?

Varen, the man who'd half raised me and forged me into the Godless I became.

Varen, the man who'd lied and sold me and my family off to the Wardens.

All that good will ruined by a terrible choice. I couldn't forgive him, and yet I could forgive Sinder, though his betrayal to Jinx had hurt just as much. Sinder's sins were understandable, given his background with the Glimmer.

And now Sinder was gone.

Maybe Varen had been right about me all along—that my use was limited.

I'd fucked over the Fauna. Failed to save them and the Necro.

Then I'd lost the Ember. The allies I'd needed to save Quen.

And Dru. She'd been there within my grasp, and I'd lost her, too.

How could I get her back? How could I get *any* of them back?

I lay down on the couch and stared at the sliver of light coming in through the torn curtains. I didn't have the energy to cry over my failures.

I just wanted the universe to swallow me whole. If only for a little while.

Wasn't that what Reve had wanted?

At least I could say... I finally understood him.

I appeared in the depot. It was getting easier to tell dreams from reality, though my tram still swinging above the platform was a big giveaway.

This was my safe space, so naturally my subconscious had brought me here to scream and cry and grieve the plans I'd let die. If I could find a bottle of wine, then maybe I could get sloshed out of my mind and still wake sober.

There was a thought.

I headed for the stairs leading down to the kitchen.

"Hello? Is anyone there?"

Shit. That was Quen's voice!

I turned slowly in case my mind was playing some shitty trick on me, but it *was* him. Quen stood on the platform in his tan suit, looking lost.

"Quen?"

"Ah! It's you. Kayl, was it?"

And there went the last of my hope. This wasn't my Quen.

But he was still *a* Quen. The fact he'd appeared inside my dream meant something.

He took off his eyeglasses and rubbed them clean before putting them back on and squinting. "Where is this? Are we still in the Undercity?"

"You remember your last visit?"

"Well, I *was* hoping that was merely a dream. But... you're not a figment of my imagination, are you? You're not Mesmer either." His eyes roamed over me and then met mine. "You're Chaos."

I held up my hands. "You've got me."

His brow furrowed. "You're the enemy, though you don't appear all that threatening. I'll confess to being confused on the details. Answer me this: how do you pronounce scone?"

"Why?"

"I need to judge how wicked you are."

I laughed. I couldn't help it. It was such a ridiculous Quen-like question. "I call them scones." Scone like *gone*. "Though I'm told that's one of the unforgivable sins."

A smile quirked his lips. "Whoever told you that was right." He turned and examined the walls. "If this is the Undercity, then why are we both here? This *is* a dream. Right now, I'm taking a quick power nap between meetings."

"This is my dream. My home."

He turned back to me sharply. "Chaos lives in the Undercity?"

"No, but I didn't always know I was Chaos. It's a long story, but I grew up in Chime."

"Fascinating. I'm afraid I don't know much about Chaos—"

"Only that we're the enemy?"

"Precisely." His voice faltered. "Except I'm a... little lost on that point." He ran a hand through his hair. "I'm lost in general."

Oh, my poor Quen. Lost once more in his memories. I stepped closer to him, and he didn't recoil. That was a good sign. This may not be *my* Quen, but it was a version of him, and that was worth protecting. Even if I never got my Quen back, this Quen had the potential to be good.

To become my Quen.

There was still a chance I could sneak into Kronos and snatch him back. With his memory issues, that would have been too difficult before, especially if he thought I was trying to kidnap him or something.

But now? It felt possible. I had to earn his trust. "If I can help, I'm here to listen. I won't judge you. Even if you can't pronounce scone right."

He chuckled, but there was no warmth in it. Gods. Quen was upset. No.

He was frightened.

It pained me to see him this way. I wanted to grab him, hold him tight, but that might scare him off. What was that prick Karendar doing to him?

"It would be unwise to discuss my... *reservations*... with a Chaos mortal."

I stepped closer until he was within reach. "What happens in the dream world stays here. I promise."

He let out a sigh, though the tension clinging to him didn't loosen. "Does the name Benjamin Seasons mean anything to you?"

Oh shit. "Yes. Is he safe? Is he..." I trailed off at the guilt filling Quen's eyes. "Quen. He's a friend. *Your* friend. What has Karendar done?"

"You know Elijah?"

"Of course I pissing know him! What has he *done*?"

Quen's throat bobbed. "It was me. I... He ordered me to... I submitted him to a soul-splitting device."

No.

Gods. Not Ben.

Fuck! Karendar had tricked Quen into destroying Ben's soul. That sick bastard!

Quen tugged at his collar, his face paling. "Seasons said he helped you. He tried to help Chaos. *Why?*"

"He did, he... If you saw..." Wait. I could reach into my own memories and project them as an illusion. I could show Quen the truth. "I can show you everything. How we met, what Chaos really is. The real Karendar. All your questions will be answered." I held out my hand. "But you've got to trust me."

He stepped back. "What do you mean, the real Elijah?"

"He abused you. And you killed him."

"No. That's not possible, I would never—I don't believe you."

"I can *show* you—"

"You're the enemy! I'm supposed to be leading the charge against your kind—" He suddenly snapped his lips shut and glanced at me with guilt. "I should go."

Shit! "Quen, please—"

He vanished from my dream as though he'd never been here.

Gods damn it! I'd been getting somewhere!

Karendar was fucking with Quen's mind *again* while I napped and let it happen. If Quen was showing signs of doubt, then... I knew what fucked-up shit Karendar had put Quen through before. He was doing it again by making him kill Ben.

Shit. Ben had deserved better than all this.

But... if Quen was being forced into fighting Chaos, then he'd need to enter Chime at some point. Perhaps I could head topside and speed the process along—take a page out of Jinx's playbook and spread a little chaos. Then all I'd have to do was wait for the Diviner to appear.

And I'd get Quen back.

Offering myself as bait was a shitty plan, but it felt like hope.

Hope was all I had left.

I woke to Cosmo standing over me and staring. "You were yelling. It scared me."

Gods! I couldn't have been napping that long. "I'm sorry. Everything's okay—"

"And there're no pillows. I can't sleep."

That was the real reason Cosmo had bloody woken me. "Are there no cushions downstairs?"

"No. We searched, but Celeste only found whiskey—"

"She better put that whiskey back." I hadn't forgotten the time they'd gotten drunk and almost led to our capture by bloody Diviner.

"Castor found some crackers, but Sprinkles doesn't like them. Too salty."

"Sprinkles? I thought your fish was called Sugar."

"She prefers Sprinkles. She told me so."

I sat up and pushed my hair behind my ears. "She—what? You know what, it's fine." I really didn't want to know, nor would I let Cosmo's random weirdness of the day get me down. Not when I had a plan to enact. "Sprinkles is a great name. I approve."

"What about the pillows? The hotel had pillows."

I bit back a sigh. It had been hard enough walking all this way with pissing tins and bottles of water. Pillows weren't high on my priority list. "I'm heading topside. If the three of you promise to stay put and *not* touch the whiskey, I'll see what I can bring back." There wasn't likely to be much bedding left to scavenge nearby. Grayford had always been sparse on home comforts at the best of times.

"In Central? That sounds dangerous."

"I'll be fine. You know I'm only a prayer away."

If I could keep the Mesmer and Fauna safe here, the Diviner should leave well enough alone. Their fight was at the clock tower. Should I summon Hazelhearth to keep the trio in line? Gods, what an idea.

"Okay, Mama," Cosmo said. "Stay safe."

Did I treat Cosmo too harshly? They were sweet, when they wanted to be. I hoped I was doing right by the Mesmer, as Mesmorpheus wanted. Gods knew I'd fucked everything else up.

I ushered them out of the office and checked no one lingered in the street outside, but of course no one did. Then I pulled out Quen's pocket watch.

It was a beautiful thing. The more I held it, the more detail I discovered etched into the brass. He'd once described it as a comforter, so it was ironic that it now comforted me in his absence. But I had a practical use for it.

He'd programmed three of the domains to correspond to Chime. Solaris for the Golden City, Eventide for the Undercity, but I was struggling to remember which one for Central. Was it Phantasy? Witheryn? Tempest? Shit.

What would happen if I opened a portal to nothingness? I was about to find out.

Phantasy made logical sense, so I set the watch to two minutes past eleven.

A portal opened, except... Shit. I'd gotten it wrong.

There was nothing but white space and an odd keening wail, like a high-pitched ringing in my ears. I winced and wanted to cover them, but couldn't lift my arms.

The ringing took on meaning. Words.

A song.

Don't you move, please lower your inhibitions.

You'll spoil our groove, and dirty our ambitions.

Shit! That was a Seren song!

The portal blipped out, revealing Serenity seated at Varen's desk, completely naked as usual. Two female Seren hovered over her shoulder and hummed gently—whatever noise they were making kept my arms pinned to my sides.

Great. Just great.

Serenity clapped slowly. "What a delightful little trick. Where were you planning on running to, my love?"

"I don't see how that's your business."

"On the contrary. Everything you do is my business. Though I don't think much of the décor." She sniffed at the curtains. "Truly dreadful. *Noh-oct?*" she called out in a singsong voice. "Come here, my lovely, and sing the lady a song. Loosen her up a little."

Noct flew in through the window and offered me a sheepish smile, to which I responded with my best scowl. Shit, he must have followed us from Sinner's Row. He didn't have a choice but to obey Serenity's commands, but that didn't mean I had to like it.

I was trapped. Even without the Seren pinning me to the spot, there was little I could do against Serenity. I could put her mortals to sleep, but I'd still be at her mercy. Calling the Mesmer for help would only endanger them.

Unless...

Celeste, I called into my mind. *Don't panic, but Serenity is in the upper office. She's got me trapped. Order one of the Fauna to break down the door—the big one with the horn.*

Yes, Mama! she replied.

I couldn't endanger a mortal with no soul, and not even Serenity would be expecting a beast to plow through.

Noct drew a breath, his chest rising as he prepared to sing.

The door burst open, shattering its hinges into splinters. Just in time.

The Fauna roared. He was a hulking man with thick fists and a single horn protruding from his head. A rhino, I think Castor had called his animal form. He snorted and turned to Serenity.

The god appeared amused. "How interesting."

The Fauna charged at Varen's desk.

Serenity snapped her fingers.

The Fauna suddenly stopped, as though time itself had paused. Shit, was there a Diviner nearby? But no. Time hadn't stopped. The Fauna's skin had turned alabaster. Oh fuck! Serenity had turned the Fauna into pissing *stone*!

"How did you do that?" I spluttered.

"Simple. They don't own a soul. I always wondered if their physical forms were malleable in shape... Seems so."

Shit. Serenity had found some fucked-up loophole.

She leaned across the desk, her fingers steepled. "Now, where were we? Noct?"

Run, I urged Celeste. *Take Cosmo and Castor and get out of here.* I couldn't risk leaving them in Serenity's hands.

Where do we go?

Follow the tram tracks to the depot. Hide there. "Why are you even here? Did Jinx send you after me? You know she'll destroy you next, right? Edana was a warm-up!"

Serenity merely smiled at my attempts to stall.

And then Noct began to sing. Truly, I was getting sick of his voice.

Pretty lady, I implore, look into my eyes.

My dearest goddess yearns for such a pretty prize.

Offer her your soul and swear you'll always be true.

Whisper sweet things to her, and your heart will renew.

It belongs to my god, and no other mortal.

Please rise, pretty lady, and open your portal.

His words burrowed into the deepest caverns of my subconscious, luring me from a reality I knew and guiding me gently to a new one I'd always dreamed of.

My eyes met Serenity's.

The most beautiful being in all existence.

All this time, I hadn't realized what reward had been waiting for me. Those years spent building the Godless had been wasted on a foolish ambition. Oh, don't get me wrong, the other gods weren't worth my time, but Serenity?

She was perfection.

The curves of Her marble body. The way She brought art into this universe through Her mortals, Her domain. There could be no greater god than She, and I wanted to throw myself at Her feet and lick the salt and dirt from them. The fact She alone remained while so many gods had fallen was testament to Her cunning, Her bravery.

"My Goddess," I breathed, my heart aflutter. I lifted Quentin's pocket watch—a stupid thing, but a necessary tool for my god's service—and set the time to five past five.

The portal opened to the brilliance of Arcadia.

Serenity stood and smiled with such innate perfection. "Let us return home so we may drink and be merry."

I gasped aloud at Her words. "You're offering me your home?"

"For as long as you like, my love."

I could barely contain my glee as She wrapped Her arm around mine and we strode into the portal. Serenity had chosen *me*.

I'd never been so blessed.

A dark red sun dipped behind the ocean, casting rippling colors more marvelous than Eventide's across the crashing waves. Sunset in Arcadia was simply magical, and we'd arrived at a pavilion by the beach that offered the greatest natural show.

Seren fluttered by, delivering bowls of dates, grapes, and almonds as well as pitchers of wine to the pavilion. More Seren dressed in togas played the harp, their soothing melody accompanying the swell of waves and buzzing insects. Serenity knew how to play host, and I was Her only guest.

The god sprawled out across a couch, the mound of Her sex visible to all. None of the other Seren dared look, flitting away out of respect. All except for Noct, who hovered awkwardly nearby. Really, he should be on his knees in worship. The blatant lack of admiration grated on me.

How lucky he was to have been born under such a god.

I remained standing, unsure what worship would be appropriate. Should I touch a Seren and transform? Would She like that?

"You look uncomfortable, cherished one," Serenity said. "Take off your clothes. All of them."

I stripped down and kicked my bra and panties aside. The evening air was warm enough, though a slight breeze hardened my nipples.

Serenity sat up and patted Her thigh. "Come. Sit."

I approached with giddiness.

Noct swooped in front of me, blocking my way. That prick!

"Sublime One." Noct bobbed a series of frantic bows that sent him flying up and down. "I don't think it would be a good idea to, um, *entertain* this mortal."

Irritation flashed in Serenity's hard eyes. "Why do you presume to offer me advice?"

Noct's blue skin paled to a light gray. "Begging your pardon, Great One. I merely think of Your welfare—"

"Do you?" Her words came out blunt. Captivating in their power. "Then go ahead." She plucked a golden goblet and raised it close to Her luscious lips. "Offer your advice so I may weigh it and deem it worthy."

A line of sweat ran down Noct's brow. He glanced at me, lost, as though expecting sympathy, but what sympathy did he expect when he'd offended his own god? "Gre-Great One," he stammered. "You—You brought Arkey here to—to keep her out of harm's way. If—If Jinx learns—"

"If Jinx learns *what*? That I intend to keep my word so she may proceed with her plans without distraction? She has such a soft spot for her sister, the poor thing. As do I."

Noct lifted his chin and stared Serenity in the face. "Then—Then leave her be."

I wasn't entirely sure what power game was going on between them, but aether buzzed in the air. The entire pavilion seemed ready to burst with it.

"Jinx is vengeful," Noct hastily added. "I worry for Your welfare after what happened with Edana..." He trailed off.

Serenity took a slow gulp from Her drink and then set the goblet down. "I honor Lady Arkey by inviting her here, and I will honor her in all ways." Her smoldering gaze turned to me. "What do you say, my beloved? Would you allow me to treasure you and spoil you with delights?"

"Yes." The word burst from inside my gut. "Oh, gods yes."

Serenity gestured at me. "Your worries are ill-founded. She wants this. Who am I to deny her life's greatest gifts?"

"You don't want this," Noct whispered.

I shot him a glare. "Mind your own pissing business."

"Language!" Serenity chided. "You're upsetting my guest. Apologize, Nocturne. Make sure you grovel appropriately."

Noct landed on his feet and then bowed low, his forehead scraping the pristine grass. "I'm really, *truly* sorry, miss." He lifted his head. "May I return to Chime, Great One? I can be on hand should You need me."

"So you may betray me?"

The harp-playing suddenly stopped. My heart caught in my throat.

Serenity rose from Her couch. "You think I don't read your intentions? That I cannot see your thoughts, as plain as your precious white wings?"

Noct stumbled back. "No—No, Great One! Sublime One, *please*—"

"Nocturne won't allow me to treasure you, my beloved Chaos. He intends to fly to your sister and tattle. We can't have that, can we?"

Stone arms burst from the grass and grabbed Noct's legs, pinning him in place. He clasped his hands in prayer and whimpered. "I—I think only of *You*, Great One!"

Serenity approached with feminine grace. She turned to me, Her head tilted to one side, a wide grin bringing Her lips to life. "What do you say? Shall we make this one suffer? Or is he deserving of mercy?"

I examined Noct and his pathetic sniveling. Snot ran from his nose, and his eyes widened with unspoken pleading.

Once upon a time, I would have helped mortals like him against lesser gods.

But Noct had been born under the most perfect god of them all. Truly, I now understood what it meant to recognize divinity and worship the righteous. In a way, my past embarrassed me. Someone had to pay for my sins.

That someone was Noct.

"He's disrespected You. Make him squeal."

The gleam in Serenity's eyes was positively delightful. "It always disappoints me when one of my mortals misbehaves. But no matter. An artist can seek inspiration in pain—it is a true teacher." She clapped Her hands. "Let's have a little music to set the scene, shall we?"

More Seren appeared before the pavilion with an entire band's worth of musical instruments. Another group of five female Seren stood in a line. A choir.

Oh, this was exciting!

The band started off with a slow melody. Their music was timed with Serenity's every movement as She danced around Noct, Her limbs stretching in a soft ballet.

Gods. She was beautiful.

Noct continued to beg and grovel as the music climbed, and Serenity's dancing grew faster. The choir's song hummed alongside, their lyrics subtle but there.

Oh, maim him, our dear Great One.

Oh, bloody him, Placid One.

Serenity placed nimble fingers on the upper ridge of Noct's wings.

The music reached its crescendo.

"*Please!*" Noct sobbed, tears streaming down his cheeks.

Those tears turned to feral screams as Serenity crushed his wings and twisted them sharply, tearing feathers like wooden splinters.

Blood ran down Noct's back, his misshapen and bent feathers stained red.

Ah, so this was why so many mortals visited Arcadia. For the spectacle. *This* was art.

The stone arms holding Noct in place retracted, allowing him to collapse face-first in the grass. His limp body twitched, and he quietly curled into a whimpering ball. Serenity hadn't pulled his wings off, no, but they'd been warped in such a way that they were now painfully deformed. He'd never fly again.

Really, it was a fitting punishment. Harmony must also have deserved the fate that had found her. Gods, it filled me with such guilt, knowing I'd associated with someone like Harmony Arabesque. That I'd *respected* her.

"Can you forgive me?" I asked, my heart aching.

Serenity placed a bloodied finger under my chin, smearing the warm stickiness with Her touch. "You are mine, my beloved. There is nothing to forgive. But you may please me in your adoration."

Her touch withdrew, leaving me empty and cold. She returned to the couch and beckoned me to follow.

I slid onto Her lap.

Her smooth hands ran down my back, across my thigh, examining every inch of me. "I always wondered how you differed from your twin. If you were truly identical. Twins are a blessing among mortals. Gods rarely make the same one twice."

"I was an accident."

"The greatest art in the universe was made by pure chance. You, my love, are a miracle. A shining star. Though, tempting as you are, you do present *some* danger..."

"I would never harm You!"

"Don't fret." She cupped my cheek, and Her thumb rubbed my bottom lip. "While I'd like to indulge in that mouth of yours, I have other ways of taking my pleasure from you. Do you prefer males?"

"I prefer whatever form You do."

"Both male and female aesthetics please me. Though your twin refused my cock. You won't refuse me, will you?"

"I wouldn't dare!" The thought of Serenity fucking me was already making me wet, and I squirmed on Her lap, hoping the heat building within wasn't that obvious.

Gods, I was desperate. So, *so* desperate to be taken. Ravaged. Destroyed utterly.

Serenity could tear me in two, and I'd beg for more.

Her body shifted. She remained female, but a hardness pressed against my leg. I glanced down and almost squealed. She'd grown a cock. A large, throbbing stone cock.

It was *glorious*.

Her hand slid down to my breast and began teasing my nipple. Waves of pleasure pulsed through my cunt, and I swooned.

"But before we begin, my love, you must part with a few secrets."

"Anything," I gasped. Shit, it was hard to pay attention while She touched me like this. It was pure aether burning me from the inside.

"You were trying to create a portal earlier. To where?"

I bit back a moan. "To Central."

"What for?"

"To save Quentin." Such a stupid idea now I thought about it. What did I care for him when I had everything I needed right here?

"Tell me everything you planned, my sweet."

"The Diviner have him imprisoned in Kronos, but he came to me in a dream. Told me they plan to attack the clock tower again, with him leading the fight against Chaos. He doesn't remember, you see. Thinks he's a Warden again and Chaos is the enemy. So I was going to make a bit of noise in Central, catch the Wardens' attention. Encourage the Diviner to launch their attack so I could snatch Quentin back. Ridiculous, I know, but Quentin does have two god souls—Zyclone and Lionheart. That's power we can't let Dor keep."

Serenity hummed in agreement. "You're right, we do need those souls if Jinx is to progress with her plans. And that may give me a little leverage." Her fingers stopped caressing me. She stared out to sea, lost in thought. "It would be wise to seek additional collateral against Corentine."

"If we take Quentin, then those souls could be Yours."

She turned back to me and patted my head. "Aren't you clever. But your sister... Do you love Jinx? Or me?"

"You. Always You. Jinx means nothing to me."

"Would you do that for me? Defy her?"

"I'd do anything for You!"

"Then I'm afraid we must part for now, my cherished dove." She patted my thigh. "Up you go."

I slid off Her lap, my heart sinking. "You don't want to fuck me?"

"We must act before your sister learns of our plans. Lure Quentin Corinth back to Chime and deliver him to my domain. Then I will make you all mine." Her lips twisted into a smirk. "We can even let him watch. He'd like that."

I tried not to sulk as I gathered my clothes, and I glanced over at Noct's twitching form. He still bled and groaned. Those diamond pupils stared at me, pleading for mercy.

But what did mercy matter, when I served his mistress?

And what did I care for whatever Quentin liked?

I'd save him, all right, and then bring him to his knees.

All for the glory of my chosen god.

34

War. What is it good for? Inspiring lyrics, of course! I've never been more creatively charged than by coming up with power ballads for a battle or a tragic dirge for a lover lost to a stomping Umber. War and death have become my muse. Imagine the plays we can put on when all this blows over. It'll be spectacular.
—Anonymous, overheard on the Isle of Harps, Arcadia

CENTRAL WAS EMPTY. THERE was a slight chance I may have overestimated the success of my plan, which was to simply fuck shit up until a Diviner came calling. But how in Serenity's name was I meant to get their attention when no one was here?

Diviner operated on their own pissing timetable, whatever that was.

I stepped over a pile of debris and entered Central Station. I'd never seen it in such a state—the waiting-area chairs were knocked over, dust and rubble and scorch marks were everywhere, and of course the bits of metal and cogs that belonged to the Gate were scattered about. Even the tea stand had been smashed to smithereens. No wonder the Diviner had abandoned the place.

It was quiet. Too quiet, even if it was early evening. Only the hum of aether kept this place alive. I glanced up at the clock tower, where Jinx's silly shield was still protecting the clockface. It seemed almost pointless to keep Corentine locked away. What was she powering? A dead city.

Chime had once been my home, but now every part of me belonged to Serenity. Funny how these things worked out. I'd spent weeks worrying about the future of the domains and their stupid mortals, and now it was all so simple.

Destroy the gods. Allow Serenity to rise. Even Jinx would appreciate that.

But first... Quentin bloody Corinth.

Since the Diviner were so worried about Chaos stepping into their precious domain—worried enough to destroy the damn Gate, anyhow—there was really only one logical conclusion. I needed to open Kronos.

Though not even I was stupid enough to face the Diviner alone. The Mesmer had been coasting along on my generosity, so it was about time I put the trio to work.

I found their souls languishing in my subconscious. One quick yank through the aether, and I tossed them out into the station.

They appeared in thin air as naked as the day Mesmorpheus had created them.

Cosmo immediately started whining, because of course they did. "You promised never to do that, Mama!" They immediately hid behind Celeste.

Celeste looked confused. "Why are we here?"

Castor at least had the sense to gather some of the clothes nearby.

I stood over them, hands on my hips. "Listen up! We need to get Quentin back, and that means we need to get the Diviner moving. I'm going to open a portal to Kronos and lure them through. You three will be on standby to knock them out. Understand?"

"But, Mama!" Cosmo wailed. "That sounds scary! I don't want to."

"Cosmo. I don't give a *shit* what you want. You're a whiny little brat who needs to learn how to obey your god."

For the first time in their pathetic mortal life, Cosmo was stunned into silence. Thank Serenity for small mercies.

Castor exchanged a glance with Celeste. "She's under Serenity's control."

Celeste gasped aloud. "How do we snap her out of it?"

"Would singing help? I don't know how to sing—"

"Shut up, both of you!" I yelled, making them jump to attention. "You're giving me a pissing headache. Just do what I say." I stomped off toward the Gate, or what was left of it, and pulled out Quentin's pocket watch.

If the portal opened without being detected by Dor, then I'd need to draw Karendar's attention enough for him to send Quentin. How many

Diviner would I need to kill? Killing had never been my style. That was more Jinx's sort of thing. Should it worry me, that in serving Serenity I was unleashing the destructive side of Chaos?

Nah. I set the pocket watch to half past twelve and the portal opened to boring brass buildings so perfectly shiny, the walls reflected the dull, dark gray skies.

Gods, Kronos was dreary. Not even the evening brought color to their domain. We needed to destroy it to save the Diviner from themselves.

A Diviner male in a tweed suit and carrying a briefcase stood under a glowing streetlamp opposite, his mouth gaping like a suffocating Amnae.

I waved. "Hello, Chaos here. I hope you don't mind, but I'd like to pop on over and devour your soul. It's nothing personal." Oh, it was entirely personal.

The man dropped his briefcase and ran. How rude!

I tucked the pocket watch away and glanced over my shoulder. "Get ready to fight."

The trio had barely gotten dressed and were huddled together.

Pissing useless.

I'd set the portal to last a good thirty minutes. Surely that would be enough time for Dor to shit out his ambassador?

Marching footsteps echoed on the other side of the portal. It sounded like it would take less than that. Diviner Wardens gathered on the Kronos side. They lined up, presumably surrounding the entire portal.

Then the Wardens parted, and a familiar face positioned himself in front.

"Karendar."

Death hadn't changed him one bit. Hatred burned in those brass eyes. He still dressed the part in his pinstripe suit. Why had Dor brought him back now? To torture Quentin? Well, that was no concern of mine. I had a job to do, and this prick stood in my way.

"Kayl Arkey. You've made a name for yourself. Last we met, you had none at all."

That was right. He'd had me chained to a table in Warden HQ. "Why do you assume it's me, and not my twin?"

"Because your twin is smarter. I doubt even they would risk opening a portal directly into our domain. Especially with the few allies left to you."

"Oh, that's funny. What allies do *you* have? The Umber are gone. The Zephyr are gone. I can't see the Amnae fighting your battles for you. What do you have left?"

Karendar merely smiled. "Time."

I scoffed. "Time means nothing to me. Or have you forgotten when we first met?"

"I haven't forgotten your sinful nature." The way he looked me over with that slight sneer made my stomach churn. "Chaos has little respect for time, yet even gods must obey its laws. Can your mortal body outlast a millennium? We have the patience of eternity. You'll have turned to dust long before my Father grows tired."

"So, what? You'll sit and wait out the war *your* god started?"

"This war began thousands of years ago when Corentine was first committed to the clock tower. Dor foresaw this outcome. Everything that has unfolded has been by his design."

"Keep telling yourself that. Now stop wasting my time; where's Quentin?"

"Quentin is an asset. Did you really think we'd risk sending him to deal with the likes of you?"

"Your god sent *you*. Not much of an asset anymore?"

"On the contrary. Dor sent me to assess the Chaos threat, which I now have. You are of no concern to me. Though you have provided us with a valuable training exercise, so thank you for that. I'll stop 'wasting' your time, though really, Miss Arkey... you've wasted your own."

The portal suddenly went dark. Had it blipped out? No, it was still there. Aether ripped around the edges. Dor must have placed a barricade around it on his side.

Shit!

"Come back, you miserable—"

"Mama!" Cosmo screamed.

I spun. Oh shit!

Three portals had opened into the station. Diviner poured through, armed with pistols and tasers. They spread out through the concourse, blocking off exits as more Diviner marched right at us, weapons aimed.

Karendar had played me for an idiot, just stalling for time.

Shitting shit!

I ran to the portal and tried to step through, but it truly was blocked with some sort of shield. There was no way I'd get to Quentin like that.

Could I create another portal with one still active? I pulled the pocket watch out.

A shot blasted by my feet. Shit! I ran for cover behind the clock tower, shoving the watch away. More shots echoed throughout the station, ricocheting off the brickwork. Gods, the Diviner were shooting to kill.

I had to get back to Serenity. I had to—

Pain lanced through my skull.

I screamed and fell to my knees. Sharp heat burned a hole through the center of my forehead. I touched it with trembling fingers, expecting to draw back blood, but...

It wasn't my injury. What the shit?

"Celeste!" Castor yelled out.

I glanced around the clock tower.

Celeste was gone, leaving only a spray of blood, brain matter and dust. Her soul returned to my subconscious. Gods. The Diviner had shot her in the fucking head, and I'd felt it as clearly as though they'd pulled the trigger against my own skull.

They'd killed her.

They'd...

Oh my god!

"Mama, help me!"

Cosmo. Shit, Cosmo!

Diviner swarmed the station. There was no way I'd reach the Mesmer. Shit, I couldn't even *see* where Cosmo was, though I sensed them further ahead.

Castor ran for the station exit.

A Diviner pointed their pistol at his back and fired.

I yanked Castor's soul before the bullet could take him. It was a death, a different sort of death than being shot. A less painful one.

Cosmo didn't like it when I took their soul and rebirthed them, but I had no choice. I couldn't save them like this.

I searched for Cosmo's soul, but couldn't find it.

That didn't make sense!

"Mama! Please!" Cosmo begged.

My heart clenched until my chest ached.

The Diviner had Cosmo on their knees, an aether collar wrapped around their neck. With that thing on, Cosmo couldn't use their powers and escape, nor could I reach their soul to save them.

I couldn't let the Diviner take them. Even if it meant risking my own damn life.

Cosmo, can you hear me? I yelled into the void of my mind.

No answer.

Shit!

"Mama!" Their voice broke into hysterical sobbing.

Gods. I'd done this. I'd dragged them here. "Hold on, I'm coming!"

I ran from cover. Something buzzed by my side, missing me by an inch. A taser strike. Oh, *now* they wanted me alive? Shit, they were using Cosmo as bait, and it was working.

I leaped behind an overturned information kiosk, dodging more shots. If I could get close enough to summon a miasma and knock them all out...

I readied to run.

And my heart stopped dead.

The Diviner had placed a helmet on Cosmo's head.

A portable soul-splitting machine.

No. *No*, I was not letting that happen!

I ran for all I was fucking worth, my chest heaving as I summoned a miasma between my fingers.

Something sharp stung my side. I fell hard against an overturned bench.

The taser strike spasmed through me. Shit! I rolled to my stomach, my limbs numb and flailing, too useless to drag me up.

Diviner surrounded me, each pointing their taser. No life filled their eyes. No light or warmth or hatred or fear. Nothing.

They were soulless husks. Slaves for Dor.

"I'm scared, Mama," Cosmo whimpered. Tears spilled down their cheeks.

A Diviner pushed a button on their helmet.

Aether shrieked through the air, a scythe cutting through a soul.

It was a blip in time, in the grand scheme of things.

But I felt it. The absence of life. Of everything.

As it left Cosmo's eyes.

No.

"*No!*"

I blinked, and the next thing I knew, I was on my feet, my skin glowing with righteous gold.

Sunlight burst from my hands.

Heat and rage exploded around me in a fiery ball, like a deadly flower come to full bloom. The soulless Diviner didn't even scream as their flesh melted down to their pitiless bones.

Any Diviner who stepped near met a similar fate. Others retreated, though not through any sense of self-preservation. The portals into Kronos were closing, likely to protect their domain from me.

Those who remained burned.

Though... their bodies didn't fade, nor turn to ash.

They stood there as charred, fleshy stumps, their skin and bone sagging into grotesque statues of horror that stunk of smoked meat.

I stared at my shaking hands. Glimmer. I'd... I'd turned Glimmer and killed...

Oh gods.

Dizziness overcame me, my head swimming, and I staggered toward the Mesmer lying on the floor. Still. So still.

Cosmo.

I dropped to my knees, yanked the helmet off them, and tossed it behind me. Then I fumbled at the collar. I couldn't get the pissing thing off, but a jolt of heat burned through it easily enough. That, too, clattered behind me, and I sat Cosmo up.

Their eyes were open, staring at something in the distance.

"Cosmo? Can you hear me?"

I dove inside my subconscious, digging for the one soul I needed to find above all others.

But Cosmo wasn't there.

"I'm sorry." I wrapped my arms around their chest and held them tight. "This is all my fault, I'm *sorry!*" I buried my head in their shoulder and choked out the tears.

I'd brought them here, endangered them, all because of...

Serenity.

The heat of my grief was drowned by cold reality. Serenity had done this. She'd manipulated me, forced me into obeying her, loving her...

Gods. She'd touched me. Had almost *fucked* me. And I'd... I'd wanted it.

I laid Cosmo down and jerked to one side as bile erupted from my stomach. I retched, letting the misery and disgust of the past few hours splatter the station floor.

Serenity had turned me away from everything I loved. The Godless. The Mesmer.

Quen.

I'd lost Cosmo.

I'd almost lost *everything* to Karendar.

All because of one fucking god.

I wiped my lips clean, gagging not only at recent memory, but at the death I'd brought with me. If it weren't for Celeste getting shot, then I would still be under Serenity's influence. I may have happily handed myself over to the Diviner.

Would I have even cared that Cosmo... No, I didn't want to think about it.

My portal to Kronos had closed. I couldn't leave Cosmo here, so I opened another portal to the Undercity and lifted them, carried Cosmo over my shoulder to Varen's office, where I lowered them onto his old couch.

"Sleep. I'll return for you."

Cosmo closed their eyes at the command, though whatever sleep they'd find would be a mimicry. Cosmo wasn't a Mesmer anymore. They wouldn't demand sweets ever again.

I placed Sprinkles's bucket next to the couch.

The soulless Fauna were still here. I ordered them to remain and to watch over Cosmo. They accepted the order with silent acknowledgement.

And then I opened another portal to Arcadia.

I would never forgive myself for losing Cosmo, but right now I had only one goal in mind.

I was going to *destroy* Serenity.

I was going to fucking rip her apart.

Arcadia was arguably one of the prettier domains, especially at night when the stars came out. Beautiful beaches and gardens. Wonderful art on display wherever you turned. Amazing grapes. Oh, I loved the grapes.

But this whole damn domain would look a lot nicer on fire.

This past week had taught me so much, and for today's lesson, I'd learned Jinx may well have a point. Burning things *was* fun.

Sadly, I needed an Umber's face for my next role. Life was a stage, and I needed to pull off my greatest act—convincing Serenity I didn't utterly loathe her and wish her dead.

If I could infiltrate a Glimmer estate in the Undercity, I could manage this.

The portal opened a short walk from Serenity's pavilion, which was now lit with burning torches. A Seren boy with minty-green skin guided me back to where Noct remained twitching on the grass. Shit. The poor man was still conscious, despite Serenity twisting his wings so badly, they were a broken and bloody mess. I couldn't offer him any sympathy, not without alerting Serenity. Truly, I did sympathize. Yes, it was his song that had doomed me to Serenity's perverse whims, but it wasn't like he'd had a choice.

I'd get revenge for us both.

For Harmony and every Seren forced to bleed at Serenity's feet.

More Seren remained outside the pavilion. The band continued to play their harps as the choir sang a low humming chant that buzzed in my ears.

The god lay on her couch, exactly where I'd left her. Still in their female form with a stone cock dangling for everyone to see.

"You've returned empty-handed, my love." Her voice was a little muffled with my Umber hearing.

I feigned shock. "I'm so sorry I let you down! The Diviner completely outnumbered me, it was terrible." I stumbled toward her. "Please, let me beg forgiveness. I need to be close to you, to feel your safe arms—"

"Stop," she commanded.

I rocked back on my heels. "Yes, Great One? I would do anything for you. Name it."

She sat up, her nose scrunching at some distasteful scent. "Why are you an Umber?"

"Oh, this?" I twirled a string of vines around my finger. "It was the best form to face the Diviner—"

"It doesn't suit you. Change it."

The command came out like a whip-crack. No terms of endearment there.

Well, that hadn't taken long. The game was up. I wanted to burn Arcadia, but the only way I'd defend myself against the Seren's awful singing was by plugging my ears full of weeds. An idea that had been whispered to me from the depths of my subconscious. Who knew the Umber had such tricks up their sleeves?

Serenity stood, her stone form towering over me. "You assumed I wouldn't have my own little birds watching over Chime, my love? No matter."

Stone hands burst from the grass and grabbed my arms.

Really? We'd performed this act so many times, it was growing dull.

For a god of art, they should really change it up.

I kicked off my shoes, and the grass stirred beneath my bare toes. Unghard's power flowed through me, eager to punish Serenity for her transgressions, and I was merely a mortal conduit made of flesh and blood and raw aether. No longer did I need to think of how to use the abilities Chaos had blessed me with.

They simply acted on my will.

Vines erupted from the earth and wrapped around the stone hands. They squeezed tight, crushing stone until it crumbled into rock and dust. A trick I'd learned from Dru.

Serenity recoiled. "You wound me. I invite you to my domain, and this is how you repay my affection? I gave you my heart on a platter!"

"Oh, give over! Did Jinx put you up to this?" They were allies, though it seemed Serenity didn't trust Jinx as far as she could throw her. Not after what happened to Edana.

"I offered to watch over you in Jinx's stead for your own protection—"

"My *protection*?" Gods, I didn't know whether to laugh or cry. "Does Jinx know you brought me here to toy with me? *Rape* me?"

"You wanted this, my beloved. I merely unveiled the dark desires of your soul." Serenity opened her arms wide. "Join with me, and we won't need Jinx or Corentine. We can rule the domains together."

"Go fuck yourself."

Her lips twisted into a cruel smile. "Is that how it's meant to be? The greatest love story of them all begins with the lover chasing his unrequited love." Her form changed back to that of a male. "I will make you *mine*."

A dark blot covered the sky. I squinted—it was difficult to tell apart danger from clouds at this time of night, but...

Oh shit!

Hundreds of Seren descended from out of nowhere. Most were armed with harps and lutes, which they strummed on the way down. The others bellowed at the top of their lungs, their song growing louder as they neared.

Oh, love him, we beseech you! Please offer him your soul.

Obey him, we implore you! His love will make you whole.

I slapped both hands over my ears. Not even the plants stuffed inside could drown it out!

They were going to sing me into submission.

Then it would all be over. I'd be nothing more than Serenity's pretty puppet.

And I'd never get Quen back.

Two Seren dive-bombed me, their little grubby hands outstretched to grasp mine and yank them from my ears.

I commanded more vines to shoot out of the earth. They whipped at the Seren, thwacking them out of the sky. More came flying in. Vines surrounded me in a tangled mess, as though I were a seed trapped in a soundproofed bloom of my own making. But I couldn't hold them off forever.

Not unless I took down their god.

I wrapped vines around my head and ears in a makeshift set of earmuffs. Then I tore a hole through my green cocoon and ran for Serenity.

Stone hands burst from the ground and reached for my ankles. Each time, I countered with my vines, but they slowed me down, and the Seren were gaining on me.

Serenity laughed, though I couldn't hear it. It was all a pissing game to him. *Give it up, my love.* His voice echoed inside my mind. *Or don't. I quite enjoy the chase.*

Shit! My plan wasn't working. Serenity had me fucking pegged.

I could swap to my Glimmer form and start burning his shitty pavilion, but the moment I gave up my vines, I'd leave myself vulnerable to their singing.

Unless I could make them believe I was untouchable. Make them fear. But what did a god fear? Serenity didn't care about Dor. But...

Corentine. He was scared of Corentine.

It was time to pull off my greatest act.

I switched my form to Mesmer. Before the Seren could even blink, I projected an illusion, making myself appear taller as a Chaos god in the silver dress and hat I'd witnessed Corentine wearing in a vision.

"You disappoint me, child!" I yelled in imitation of Corentine's voice. "Serenity! I've come to collect what's mine!"

The Seren's song ceased instantly, their voices murmuring in collective confusion. I eased the vines from my ears, so as not to disturb the illusion.

Serenity recoiled. "What is this trickery?"

"You don't recognize the power that spawned you? Why would you? You only damned me to an eternal prison a millennium ago."

"Mo-*Mother*? This isn't possible! You're free?"

Oh shit, it was working! I swaggered up to the pavilion. "You underestimated my daughter. Jinx was able to use what few souls she'd gathered to break my bindings. And now, I have come to collect what is owed."

Serenity skittered back, almost tripping over his couch. "I'm a child of Chaos! I always have been! Jinx will tell you—we worked together to keep Dor at bay—"

"Yet Dor still exists—"

"We can face Dor together. You need me, my mortals—"

"Too little, too late." Though it was almost tempting to coerce Serenity into my battles, I doubted I could hold an illusion for that long. "What use are you?" I stepped toward the couch and stood over Serenity as he practically cowered at my feet.

"Of all your children, I alone held you dear." Serenity kneeled before me. "My domain embraced the art of Chaos. We rejected Dor's rule. I did it for *you*—"

"What do your platitudes mean to me?" I sneered. "Beg, you worthless piece of shit."

"Mother, please—"

I grabbed his chin, forcing him to look up.

The horror in his eyes sent tingles all over my skin. So gods did feel fear.

Oh, this was glorious.

This was power.

I let the illusion drop.

Confusion shone in Serenity's eyes, followed by a split second of rage. "*You*—"

I felt the tug in the palm of my hand and yanked Serenity's soul out.

He gasped and fell back against the couch. His flailing limbs knocked over his goblet, and wine spilled down his chest in a bloodied mess.

My body shrank to the size of a Seren, and I sprouted tiny wings. I stepped from my clothes before I could ruin them.

Voices sang inside my mind like a choir searching for the correct pitch. The Seren. They circled above the pavilion in a screeching mess. Some fell from the sky, crashing down with bloodcurdling screams. Others cried and tried to soothe themselves by singing gibberish, though their song no longer held any power.

"Great One!" a Seren yelled. They flew right at me, holding their lute like a weapon. "We'll save you, O Great One!" They swung their lute at my head.

I leaped up, my wings carrying me an inch from being pummeled. "What are you fighting me for? Your god is finished!"

Another Seren came flying at my side, this time holding a pissing cake knife. "We love you, Sublime One!"

I snapped their soul out of the air with a *poof*. "You pricks don't even deserve the salvation I've granted you!"

"They really did love me," Serenity said with awe. "How... tragic." He reached toward the sky, and then dust fell from his fingers. His entire form rapidly disintegrated until nothing was left but a pile of pathetic rubble.

Silence hushed the chittering insects and crashing waves as the curtain fell over Arcadia. Its song had ended. The music had reached its crescendo.

I glanced to where Noct had lain. Only his bloodied clothes and feathers remained.

The colorful splendor of Arcadia turned gray.

I drew a shuddering breath.

Serenity was gone. The Seren were mine. All but Harmony.

I dug through my new collection of Seren, swiping souls aside, and found her family—parents, siblings, aunts and uncles, cousins—so many cousins—and... Monica. The lover Serenity had once murdered.

But Harm's soul was nowhere to be found.

Shit. Jinx really had ripped the Godless from me. Joe. Vincent. Sinder. Dru. Harmony.

Who did I have left on my side?

Quen was unreachable. I'd... I'd lost Cosmo.

I hugged my chest and rubbed my upper arms.

What did I have left?

A soul knocked on the door to my subconscious. I hadn't even known that was possible, but this particular one was insisting on my attention.

I spat it out, and Noct appeared in the same spot he'd died.

He rolled onto his stomach naked, his chest heaving with shocked rasps, his wings—now shiny and new—were a fluttering blur. He was still Seren, though his dark Vesper-blue skin had turned a lighter Chaos shade. "Phew, lady. I thought I'd lost you back there."

Octavius Nocturne was his full name, though he hated it due to being nicknamed 'Oct Noct' by his peers, and thus went by Noct. Flashes of his recent memories burned in my mind. I didn't want to see them—I *never* wanted to see them. A mortal's mind was their own business, but then one recent memory snagged me.

Noct had been with Quen in Tempest. Shit. "You're the reason Quen lost his arm."

He stopped gathering his blood-stained clothes and pointed to the dust falling from the sky. "That's... It's—"

"Yes, I know. Arcadia is falling apart. Give me one good pissing reason why I shouldn't leave you here?"

"Because I have intel!" he blurted. "Serenity had me playing spy—watching you, most of the time! Me and Gast—"

"Quen lost his *fucking* arm!" Rage burned through me so quick and sudden, it begged to unleash Glimmer-style justice by ripping Noct's individual feathers from his wings, one by one.

But then, would I be different from any other shitty god? From Serenity?

Noct flinched. "I know I'm an arsehole, I'm sorry! Mother always said I'd end up with my feathers in the trash... I didn't know Corinth's portal would cut off his damn arm. I just wanted Serenity off my fucking back, okay? Do you have any idea what it's like serving a vengeful god?"

"I have an inkling." I was low on allies, and Noct could be useful, but he'd only gone knocking on my mind's inner door out of self-preservation. "You and Gast have been nothing but a pain in my arse!"

"You did sort of leave him in the Asylum, *not* that we're playing tit for tat, or anything! Uh, lady? That doesn't look good." He stared out to the ocean.

The gray nothingness that permeated my soul now rolled across Arcadia in one big wave of despair. This domain was dying, like so many before it. All the art and beauty of this world, destined to be wiped away.

Quen and I had once attempted to stop this from happening, until Mesmorpheus had assured me it was the only way to save the domains.

Were we really saving them by destroying them?

So many mortals had died. Was it worth it?

I knew I needed to have faith, but... I was Godless. Faith was anathema to me.

Had Mesmorpheus really given me their Mesmer, knowing there would be a future where I'd fuck up this badly? That I'd let the Diviner shoot them? Wipe Cosmo's soul?

That wasn't a future I wanted.

It wasn't a future to strive for.

And yet... it was here. I was living it.

What would happen if I let the nothingness of a dead domain wash over me? Would I feel anything at all?

"Do you have a death wish, lady?" Noct snapped.

"Oh. Right." I swapped my form back to Chaos and opened a portal to the Undercity. What was there left to return to, but the soulless? I *had* promised Cosmo I'd return.

It was the least I could manage.

35

Everyone dies. That's just what mortals do. But what happens to our soul when we die? Mesmorpheus says death is one big nap. Dying is like falling asleep. It wraps you up in a big black blanket of stars, and you drift off peacefully. Only, you never wake up.
But that's okay. Being awake for so long is tiring.
We all need that rest at the end.
—Reverie, *Is There Life After Death? A Mesmer Handbook*

COSMO REMAINED EXACTLY WHERE I'd left them, as did the Fauna. I'd changed back into my Chaos form and found clothing, as getting around as a Seren was far too awkward. Then I'd rested on the arm of Varen's couch and watched Cosmo sleep. Their body still lived. Their chest rising and falling with air in their lungs.

But they were still gone. Utterly gone.

There were about fifty soulless left over in total, including Cosmo and Autumn. I couldn't look after them all on my own, nor did I feel safe hiding out in Varen's old place. They needed a home. Somewhere they could be protected. Not just the soulless, but Celeste and Castor too.

"What now, lady?" Noct asked. He'd escaped Arcadia with me and now sat on the edge of Varen's desk, his legs kicking. "What's our next move?"

"Our?"

"I've got intel on Jinx. Whatever you need to bring her down."

"That's nice of you, but I don't think any of us will be bringing Jinx down."

"Then what's the plan? You've... got a plan, right?"

I shrugged. "I need to protect my mortals. You're free to leave if you want."

He stared at me. "And go *where*? In case you hadn't noticed, everything's fucked—"

"I had noticed—"

"It's the end of the fucking world! Serenity's dead, and I'm still alive for some godsforsaken reason. I never expected to survive the gods-damn *end-times*, so what do I do now? Hit Sinner's Row, raid the liquor stores? Actually, y'know, that ain't a bad idea."

"I'm not stopping you." Maybe I'd even join him once I was done here. Losing consciousness as a Mesmer wasn't quite as satisfying as destroying my brain cells.

Right now, I wanted a taste of oblivion.

Find some whiskey or brandy. The good stuff.

Toast the end of everything.

Could we bring the soulless back with us to Sinner's Row? There were plenty of spare beds now. I could tuck them in, let them sleep. Either the Diviner or Jinx would come for us eventually.

No.

Jinx would kill them, and then I'd never get a chance to fix this mess. Nor could I let the Diviner take them and turn them into slaves or fodder for their stupid pissing war.

Oblivion would have to wait.

I cradled Quen's pocket watch in my lap. He'd left Phantasy spare in case we needed it, and I needed it now, more than ever. But Phantasy was gone. There was literally nothing there but a blank canvas.

Though...

A blank canvas could be painted.

The Seren souls within me stirred at such an implication. They were true artists, capable of turning any material into something beautiful. Where anyone would see an empty, lifeless domain, I began to imagine something different. Something new.

A domain reborn.

Or... a new domain entirely. A fourteenth.

Yes! my imagination cried. Or was it the Mesmer? Their souls suddenly came to life within my subconscious, yelling out possibilities. A new domain wasn't something I'd ever thought possible, not until the power of the Seren and Mesmer came together inside my mind to dream it.

I carried the power of the gods. Jinx had once explained aether could be shaped. Chaos could take the gods' power and rebirth their mortals—to create instead of destroy. So surely the same theory applied to domains?

If Quen were here, he'd understand. He'd approve, I think.

I was sick of taking domains and damning mortals.

What else was this all for, if not to remake the universe? I had to begin somewhere.

I set the pocket watch to Phantasy, and the portal opened to nothingness.

My blank canvas.

"Uh, lady?" Noct jumped down from the desk. "What are you doing?"

"Something new." I stepped into the portal, and it snapped closed behind me.

Oh my god.

I stood in white space. I honestly didn't even know *how*. There was nothing below me, yet I wasn't floating, my feet were on solid ground, and despite the lack of wind, I was still breathing. It was as though I'd entered a square windowless room completely painted white.

Aether hummed in my veins, responding to the raw energy still present here, even after the gods had abandoned it. I lifted my hands, which crackled with static. I'd been so terrified of that rolling gray, of the nothingness of a dead domain, that I'd never stopped to appreciate it. To *feel* it. It was brimming with possibility.

This domain could become anything.

I could shape it into a haven for heathens. A home for the Godless.

A sanctuary for the soulless.

All I needed to do was let my imagination wander. That, I'd always been good at.

You could even say I was born for it.

Though... I was no artist, not like Vincent. Give me a paintbrush, and I wouldn't even know where to start. While I couldn't imagine myself painting, I could imagine a stage. That was what reality was. Theater in motion.

I drew a breath and closed my eyes.

What home would Cosmo want? What would suit the Mesmer?

Their suggestions came to me, intermingled with the Seren's.

A lush paradise with golden grass. Trees that grew candy apples and flowers that sprouted toffees, strawberry bonbons, and sherbet pollen. A winding river with fresh, sparkling water, but also fountains filled with chocolate milk. Pavilions full of bowls containing grapes, dates, nuts, hard candies, ice cream that never melted, jelly that wobbled for an eternity. And pillows. So many pillows and sheets so they could make their own pillow forts.

Soft grass pushed between my bare toes. I opened my eyes to the reality I'd created.

Exactly as I'd imagined it.

Shit. Was this how easy it was to play god?

It was... *intoxicating*.

A warm breeze stirred the many colorful trees that dotted the horizon on hills of golden grass. A few pavilions lined a marble pathway, but it still looked empty.

It could be better. It needed *more*.

I waved my arms as though directing actors, and my thoughts flowed fast, sparking with too many ideas all at once.

The river expanded, becoming an ocean. A beach sprouted bioluminescent seashells and pretty, shiny rocks. Teal waves crashed in a soft melody.

I twisted the hills, forming more rivers, a lake, and then I dragged the hill up to create a flowing waterfall. These waters weren't too deep. Enough for the Mesmer to wade in, if they liked. I placed edible jelly lilies throughout.

And then, behind the waterfall, I made space for a tram.

My tram. My home. Full of pillows and clothing and the trinkets I'd collected from Grayford over the years. I plucked it from my mind and recreated it here, exactly as I remembered it.

I dotted the empty space with more bushes and flowers, creating a garden even the Umber would appreciate.

Finally, I finished the scene by waving my arm in an arc across the sky, scattering a glitter of iridescent stars. They shone with the colors of aether, with bright blues and pinks. Bright enough that we didn't need a sun or a moon to light this new world, though I'd summon a few lamps, just in case.

It was missing only one thing.

Mortals.

I reached inside myself and found Celeste and Castor, though there was one other Mesmer I needed. Reverie.

The three of them burst through the aether into my new garden.

"Mama!" Celeste gasped in awe. "Look what you've made!"

Castor stared at the sky. "It's beautiful."

I quickly summoned a trunk of clothing. "Take what you need."

They rummaged through the trunk as Reverie watched, apparently unimpressed with my new ability to summon clothes from thin air. Playing god was easy. As easy as projecting an illusion. All I needed to do was tap into the swirling mass of godly aether brimming inside me, imagine what I wanted, and it appeared. Just like that.

Where had this ability been when I'd actually pissing needed it?

I summoned a black dress and held it out for Reverie. "I'm sorry to drag you back to reality. It's not what you wanted, I know." When I first took on Mesmorpheus's powers, I'd hoped the old Mesmer ambassador would lend me her knowledge and advice. Reverie would have been more useful than the trio. But she'd wanted a break from everything, and I couldn't blame her.

She took the dress with a grateful smile. "On the contrary. I believe it's now time."

"You... you've seen a vision of this, haven't you?"

"Yes."

Gods. What had Mesmorpheus neglected to tell me?

Reverie slipped into the dress and then beckoned me toward the beach, as though she'd lived in this domain her whole life and knew the layout. I followed, allowing my feet to sink into the soft sand.

"Is this it?" I asked. "The end?"

"Did you know each Mesmer is made after the stars that exist in the sky? Every soul as unique as those constellations."

Okay, that was a very Mesmer response to my question. "That came to me, I think. Since becoming a Mesmer."

She gestured to her neck, and the stars that decorated her skin. "These stars belong to a universe thousands of light-years away. Let me see yours."

A different universe? A different domain? I wasn't quite sure what she was talking about, but I changed my form to Mesmer. My skin was a dark purple dotted with silver and pink stars. Different patterns to hers and the trio's, though I'd assumed the pattern to be random.

Reverie pointed to the collection of stars on my wrist. "Your stars are yet to exist."

"What does that mean?"

"They come from a sky which hasn't yet been born. A future universe."

A shiver ran down my spine. Could that be the same future that Future Quen had come from? Or one of the many futures he'd spoken of?

"It means," Reverie said slowly, as though I were a simpleton, "that a future awaits you. This isn't the end."

I hugged my chest. "But I've failed. I lost... Cosmo is gone." The words caught in my throat. "Did you know I'd fuck it up? Did Mesmorpheus know?"

Reverie shared a sad smile. "It was a potential future—"

"There's a future where Cosmo lives?"

"There was. That timeline has gone."

"But why? How? Couldn't a Diviner roll back time—fix this?"

"Chaos is immune to time. Even if the universe rolled backwards, Chaos would remain in place. An immutable object."

That meant every soul I or Quen or Jinx had ever taken was immune to time. We'd turned them all into Chaos mortals.

"But..." I stared out across the ocean, as though a solution would crash over the waves. "Cosmo is still *here*. Their body, anyhow. If we can recover their soul, we can bring them back." It must be trapped in the walls between domains somewhere! A purgatory of lost aether or something like that. "Reve told me as much. He *told* me!"

Reverie placed a hand on my arm. A comforting gesture I'd never seen a Mesmer make. "Lost souls cannot return to their original body. They're gone."

"Souls are reborn all the time—I rebirthed *you*!"

"Because my soul belongs to you—transferred from one god to another. Those who have been ripped from their god belong to no one. I'm sorry. There is no way to recover them."

"Then... Cosmo is gone?"

They were all gone.

Every soul condemned to the Diviner's soul-splitting machines.

Reve. Quen's Amnae professor. The Fauna. Autumn. Any poor soul captured by the Glimmer or Diviner. Ben.

And Cosmo.

I'd failed to protect Cosmo—to keep them safe. The main bloody responsibility that Mesmorpheus had left me. Gods, it had been my idea to recover and rebuild the first of those shitty machines, thanks to Gloria and her Glimmer. I'd run for salvation and brought about the end of the domains.

Of everything.

Every shitty fucking mistake began with me.

"There's no point in keeping their... in keeping Cosmo's... body." A tear escaped, and I hastily wiped it away, as though I didn't have the right to cry when all of this had been *my fucking fault*.

Reverie turned to the ocean and said nothing.

It fell to me. This was my sin, my shame. My responsibility.

I had to do this. Let them go. Not only Cosmo, but the Fauna and Autumn, too.

I wandered further along the beach, away from Reverie, and used Quen's pocket watch to summon another portal into the Undercity. It opened to Grayford, outside Varen's front door. I stepped through the portal and it closed behind me a second later.

The upper office window opened, and Noct dangled his head out. "You're *back*? Where in the twelve fucking domains did you go?"

"I've found a safe place. A haven." I didn't want to let slip that I'd literally built a whole new domain on top of Phantasy, in case spying eyes lurked in the shadows. "You're welcome to join us." I didn't want to pry further into Noct's history. That was his private life, and his business. Whatever mistakes he'd made in the past could stay there. I trusted him with the Mesmer. At least, Gast vouched for him.

"Safe? Whaddaya mean?"

I ignored him and entered Varen's place, hopefully for the last time. A large Fauna woman in the form of an upright dog stood guard by the entrance.

"Can you gather all the Fauna outside, please?"

She turned to carry out the order without acknowledgement.

I headed upstairs, where Noct waited, his wings fluttering with nerves.

"Lady, are you gonna talk straight with me?"

"Not here I won't." I didn't need to gather any clothing or food, not when I could simply summon what we needed in abundance. But I rifled through the supplies and pulled out a small brown bottle.

Laudanum.

It shook as I shoved it into my pocket.

Noct caught my eye. He'd seen what I'd taken. He knew what it was. "Lady..."

"Shut up and help me."

"With what? Poisoning yourself?"

I pointed to Sprinkles's bucket. "Bring her with you."

"*Her?*"

"We're not leaving anyone behind." I bent beside Cosmo still sleeping on the couch. "Cosmo? Sweetie? Wake up. It's time to go now."

Their eyes opened, and they sat up, their movements stiff like a clockwork Guardian.

"Follow."

Cosmo followed me down the stairs as Noct waddled after us, the bucket in his hands. The Fauna waited outside on the main street, Autumn barely visibly among the taller ones, though there was no mistaking her red hair.

"All of you, after me."

I opened the portal once more to our new Phantasy. One by one, they followed me through. I'd never tried closing it manually before, but Quen was my clever boy. He would have programmed a shutoff into the watch, and it was so simple, I could kick myself. One click of the mechanism, and the portal vanished. Another trick I should have figured out by now.

I led Cosmo and the Fauna toward a pavilion I'd already prepared in my mind. Beds for each of them, and an open ceiling so they could gaze at the stars one last time.

"Go find a spare bed to sit on. Make yourselves comfortable."

I didn't think they understood what comfort meant anymore, but they did as ordered and sat waiting for my next command.

I summoned enough cups of juice for everyone except Cosmo. They got chocolate milk. Their favorite.

Then I pulled out the laudanum.

"That's your plan, huh?" Noct asked. He placed Sprinkles the fish by the entrance and lingered by the threshold.

I turned and met his eye. "They're living dead. This is the kindest thing I can do for them."

This wasn't to grant them a peaceful passage to the beyond—their souls had already departed. It was to give them dignity in death. To ensure their bodies would never be used or defiled.

Noct nodded, understanding sharpening his diamond pupils. "Can I help?"

"No, it's... fine."

It was my fault these mortals had lost their souls. I needed to do this.

"Then I'll stay nearby." *So you're not alone,* came his thought in my mind.

I choked back a sob. "Thank you." His company meant everything right now.

I popped open the laudanum and began to pour the tincture into each cup. Enough for a fatal overdose, though I'd help them along the way to make this as painless and easy as possible.

A dark part of me wanted to ready my own cup.

But I still carried the Vesper and Mesmer souls, and now the Umber and Seren. If I died, what would happen to them?

I went around the room and handed a cup to each Fauna. "Drink, now."

They did so.

I left Autumn and Cosmo for last.

The fire in Autumn's eyes had left the moment her soul had. She'd been so full of righteous energy, of anger and life. It reminded me of my younger days in Grayford. Surviving on the barest of scraps, and the rage whenever a Vesper was kicked to the curb by the Wardens.

Autumn had burned with so much potential. All the Fauna did. Would we create a better universe where they could finally be equal, as the Covenant had once promised? I didn't know.

It was a promise to strive for, but I lacked faith we'd ever get there.

"I'm sorry, Autumn." So, *so* sorry. "I'll get Freddie back and watch over him for you. We'll get him all the pasties and cake he can ever eat." I pressed the cup into her hands. "Drink this. It'll make you... feel better."

She lifted it to her lips and drank.

Gods. It hurt.

Autumn was wild, and soon she'd be free.

I then approached Cosmo. The one I'd saved until last.

Though this wasn't a decision I could make myself.

Celeste? Castor? I called out to them both. *I don't know if Reverie has explained, but... I'm letting go of the Fauna. Putting them to sleep so their bodies can find rest with their souls. I'd like to offer the same for Cosmo. But it's... it's your choice.*

They were a trio. Lovers, even though it was hard for me to imagine Cosmo that way. But Celeste and Castor held affection for Cosmo all the same. They had a greater claim to Cosmo's soul than I ever did.

We understand, Mama, Celeste said.

Wait for us, added Castor.

Even after everything, they still referred to me as their Mama. Truly, I didn't want to put them through this. It should be my burden alone.

But they needed closure. A chance to say goodbye.

They entered the pavilion a few minutes later with Reverie, who chose to wait a respectful distance by the entrance with Noct.

Celeste ran to Cosmo and wrapped her arms around them. "We love you, Cosmo."

Castor joined in, and the duo became a trio again. "We always will."

The cup of chocolate milk and laudanum shook in my hands. "Whenever you're ready."

They kissed Cosmo on either cheek, and then stepped back, each clasping the other's hands.

"We're ready," Celeste whispered.

Castor sniffed back tears. "I—I hope Cosmo finds Reve, wherever they are."

Oh gods. Why did he have to mention Reve?

My heart couldn't bear this anymore. It ripped in half, into jagged pieces that cut me and bled from the inside out.

But I had to bear this pain. *I* had to. For them.

I passed the drink to Cosmo. "Here you go. Your favorite. Please drink."

Cosmo took the drink and downed it in one.

"What—What now, Mama?" Celeste asked, her eyes brimming with tears.

"Now we let them sleep."

"Can we stay?" Castor asked.

I forced a smile. "For as long as you need."

I ordered Cosmo and the Fauna to lie down. Celeste and Castor climbed into the bed with Cosmo, snuggling against them as I'm sure they'd done so many times together. I sat beside Autumn and held her hand. Among the Fauna, she was the only child, and I didn't want to leave her alone.

The effects of the laudanum could take hours, so I summoned a miasma and allowed it to drift over Cosmo and the Fauna, lulling them into a gentle sleep.

I'd wait here with them until the end.

Until sleep swept them away.

"Lady?" Noct prompted. I hadn't heard him approach. He'd brought Sprinkles the fish and placed her bucket beside Cosmo. "You want me to sing them a lullaby? My, uh, mother used to sing it when I was scared or sad."

I nodded. My chest squeezed too tightly for words.

He cleared his throat.

When the night is dark and lonely,
And your god won't answer your prayers,
It seems so very frightful, but,
There is a mortal here who cares.
We will face your fears together,
Hand in hand, I will be right there.
My love cannot heal your heart, but,
Your tears and pain are ours to share.

Tears dropped into my lap. "Thank you," I whispered. "That was beautiful."

Noct sat beside me. "You're doing good, lady," he whispered back.

Was I?

We sat together overnight as the Fauna slowly stopped breathing. Autumn was one of the last to go, her heartbeat fighting until her very last breath.

Cosmo faded quickly, as though eager to head to the beyond and see what candies awaited them. Yet Celeste and Castor remained clinging to Cosmo's body. They'd say goodbye in their own way.

I released Autumn's hand and stood, my legs numb from sitting in the same position for so long. "I'll—I'll give you some privacy." I brushed a lock of Autumn's hair from her forehead and then collected Sprinkles's bucket.

The fish couldn't stay trapped in this tiny thing forever. Cosmo would want me to find her a new home.

I headed for the beach, each step impossibly heavy. By the time I made it, I was ready to collapse, and only just managed to toss Sprinkles into the ocean before my legs gave out.

My entire body deflated, the last of my hope gone, and I collapsed onto the sand.

"I'm sorry!" I cried between garbled sobs.

I curled into myself, my knees pressing into my chest, my arms wrapped around them so tightly, as though I could squeeze myself into a ball and pop out of existence.

Everything was my fault.

Mesmorpheus had set me this task—to save the domains and all their mortals—and I'd fucked it up in every way. I'd failed to protect the Mesmer. Failed to find allies and unite them. The few allies I had made among the Fauna, I'd also failed.

But I'd left behind a string of fuckups throughout my entire life, hadn't I? That was what Jinx would say, if she were here.

And Quen. I'd fallen in love with a Diviner—the Dark bloody Warden, of all mortals—and lost him before I even had a chance to tell him what he meant to me.

Was it even fair? That I'd fallen for Quen, when I still carried the Vesper inside me, and the lover I'd supposedly forgotten? Another group of mortals I'd fucked over.

It had all begun with Reve. Though, no, my failures had begun long before I'd lost him.

Harmony knew my true nature, and I'd failed her. Failed the Godless. Thanks to me, they'd suffered horrors I'd not wish on anyone. Now Jinx owned their souls, but they were better off with her than me.

I was the wrong twin. The one who should have never been born.

My shuddering sobs turned to hiccups and rasping gasps.

"Why did you leave me, Quen?" I asked the stars. "I need you... I *need* you, and you're not here."

Something fluttered at the corner of my eye. I wiped my cheeks clear and sat up as Noct flew on over. Shit, I appreciated his company, but not now.

"Sorry, I want to be alone—"

"The Mesmer found this." He held up an envelope and waved it. "It was tucked inside Cosmo's shirt pocket. They said to bring it to you."

What? Noct dropped the envelope in my lap and then flew back off to the pavilion.

The envelope was sealed, with my name written in ink.

Oh my god.

It was Quen's handwriting.

I tore through the envelope and unfolded a letter.

My Dearest Kayl,

It breaks my heart that I cannot be with you to comfort you right now. Please forgive me, for I am currently lost and need to find my way. I pray my past self will look at himself in the mirror and become aware of the suffering he causes—to himself and others.

You are almost at the end now, my dear. I know you will face it with dignity, for you are the strongest mortal I have ever been blessed to meet.

I have every faith in you. Please, have faith in yourself.

Until the end of time.

Your Quen.

I clutched the letter to my chest, soothing the ache that burned there. These words had been penned by Future Quen. Had he somehow slipped this letter onto Cosmo, knowing it would reach me?

Why not warn me this would happen?

Why not stop it?

Shit!

Great, Quen had faith in me. I was glad someone did, because I sure pissing didn't. He was frolicking in a future that may or may not come to pass, tossing hope like confetti while I remained here, suffered *here*.

Falling behind as I always had.

None of my plans for saving the domains had worked. My Quen—the current version of Quen—was lost to me. Likely being tortured by

Karendar as I sat and wailed. I had no means of saving him. Karendar would stop any attempt at rescue.

And then my soul would join Cosmo's, which honestly sounded lovely about now, but then I'd be damning the souls I carried.

Only one mortal could save Quen.

I'd entered this war wholly unprepared, and it had cost me.

Only Jinx could end it now.

I headed back to the pavilion where Celeste and Castor sat with Noct, discussing tales from their lives with Cosmo back in Phantasy.

But it was Reverie I needed.

She waited by a private alcove in the pavilion. Gods, she'd likely seen a vision of the conversation about to play out.

"You know what I'm about to ask, don't you?"

"Yes," she said, her voice dreamlike. "It can be done." She held up a tarot card. Solaris. The dawn. A new beginning.

One I needed to grasp.

If Chaos could take the power of a god, could rebirth mortals and shape souls, then it made sense such power could be transferred. Passed on to another. That was what Chaos had wanted to begin with—what Jinx wanted. To collect the souls of the gods and unlock Corentine's prison.

If I was to hand myself over to Jinx, that didn't mean I'd willingly hand over the Mesmer, Umber, and Seren. There wasn't much I could do for the Vesper. While they were buried deep inside my subconscious, they were untouchable.

Mesmorpheus had likely seen this turn of events.

They'd gifted me the trio. Three mortals. One for each domain.

Though now the three had become two.

"Take the Mesmer," I urged. "They're your mortals. They always have been."

"And the Seren? The Umber?"

"Celeste is into fashion and art. She'll be at home with the Seren. And Castor, he's a caring soul. He'll take good care of the Umber."

They didn't know it yet, but they were about to become demigods.

Though first, I wanted to bury Cosmo and the Fauna. Find them a nice spot under a tree somewhere, so they could be at rest.

"This domain is now their home. The Mesmer, the Seren, the Umber. Shape it into something for them, but don't let them leave." So long as they remained here, hidden in this domain, they'd be safe. I wouldn't let Jinx or Dor ever find them.

Reverie cocked her head to one side. "And you will go?"

"It's about time, don't you think?"

Harmony had warned me to run from Jinx, but I didn't have an alternative.

At least we'd be reunited.

I'd give it until midday. Staying up all night had left me exhausted and I needed at least a nap before I damned myself. Time held little meaning here.

"This is your home too," Reverie said. "You could stay. Let the stars fight their own battles."

She was offering me a way out. A chance to turn my back on Chaos, and war, and the whole pissing lot of them.

But I couldn't abandon Quen. I wouldn't.

"Mesmorpheus set me on this path. They saw where it went, and where I have to go. Fate, or whatever." I pulled out Quen's pocket watch. My ticket to destiny. "Besides. I've gotten used to running around as a Mesmer. I'll keep this form so I can return in my dreams and make sure the three of you haven't decided to conquer the universe yourselves."

Reverie chuckled. "It's a possibility. Before you go, this domain needs a name."

I supposed it did.

While it wasn't quite the sanctuary for sinners I'd envisioned, it was still the last refuge in the entire universe.

A home I'd protect with my very soul.

"Haven. We'll call it Haven." The fourteenth domain.

A haven for the lost, the godless, and the dead.

REMEMBER WHO'S IN CHARGE

Name: Sinder (No known surname), Ember
Known Affiliations: The Godless, Erosain, Edana, The Blue Flame
Cabaret Theater
Sinder is the Ember of the Godless, and while you would suspect him of
being the firepower of the group, he in fact plays spy by keeping track of
known targets such as Erosain. His natural charm has given him
connections all the way to Edana herself. He is, however, easily
manipulated, and was pivotal in our capture of the Godless and the
destruction of Solaris. Though he was killed during the Gate Closure
Incident, we believe he may have returned to Edana's side as a spy.
*—*P. Bezel, *Personal Report on Sinder*

SOMETHING BIG HAD GONE down in Central Station last night.

I changed into my magpie form and swooped over the station. Wowee, it fucking *stunk* of death. Diviner bodies were scattered everywhere, or whatever remained of them—half-burned corpses and the charred stumps of legs and arms. Smoke still rose from most of 'em, and the *smell*! It was a Necro's wet dream. I could send a bunch of them down here to finish these poor fuckers off, since clearly no one else had bothered.

They were soulless. Which meant the Diviner had come here to launch some sort of attack right under my nose. But none of my mortals had fought them off, and there were no Glimmer or Ember left to create this much devastation.

Which meant Kayl had been here. She'd done this.

But why? A failed attempt at rescuing her Time Boy?

Which also meant... Fuck! Fuckity fuck!

Serenity was *meant* to be fucking babysitting her! Not letting her run rampant across Central.

I took another tour around the station, and even flew inside the private waiting area, but there were no Diviner around. I didn't spot any signs of Kayl, either. She'd vanished along with her war crimes.

What if the Diviner had gotten her?

Gast! I yelled inside my mind. *The fuck's going on?* From the last report I'd received from him yesterday, Serenity had managed to lure Kayl to Arcadia, where the plan had been to keep her trapped until I was ready to come collect her sorry arse. It was a pretty simple plan; I didn't know how a god could have fucked it up.

Really, my dear sister had been *so* predictable, returning to Grayford. I wasn't even surprised she'd holed up in Varen's old office. She'd always gone crawling back to men who betrayed her. Malk. Varen. Sinder. Corinth, technically. No cock was worth that much effort.

Serenity's dead, came Gast's deadpan reply.

What! Are you fucking shitting me? How do you know? It wasn't like I could pop open a damn portal and go see Arcadia for myself!

I could sense Gast's glee all the way from the Undercity. *Noct confirmed it. Your sister took Serenity's soul and rebirthed him.*

God fucking damn it! Serenity'd had *one* job!

I checked Gast's recent memories and saw the truth for myself. Kayl had come back to Grayford through a portal, looking rough as shit, with Noct at her heel—rebirthed as a cute lil Chaos Seren and not as an actual Chaos mortal, which was how I liked to bring 'em back. I supposed it was easier to spit them out how they'd gone in. And then she'd popped open *another* portal and disappeared, giving Noct time to fill Gast in on what had happened.

Serenity had seduced Kayl.

No.

Tried to rape her.

...Fuck.

Could I be angry that Kayl had fought back and stolen the soul that was mine by rights? Serenity had always been a creep. I'd never liked them, not that I really liked any of the gods, apart from Edana.

I'd have taken their fucking soul, too. Even if I hadn't already planned to.

At least Kayl was safe, wherever she was.

"I've found a safe place. A haven."

Where the fuck could she have gone?

I WARNED YOU NOT TO TRUST SERENITY, Mother said.

I didn't think she'd betray me after she saw what happened to gods who betrayed me. And teaming up against Edana had been *her* idea! Well, whatever. I'd run out of gods to betray. All that was left was Anima and Dor, and I didn't see either of them extending the red carpet.

YOU MUST FIND YOUR SISTER. KAYL NOW OWNS FOUR SOULS. WITHOUT THEM, I CANNOT BE FREED.

I know, Mother. I'll find her. Though we had another problem. Corinth.

I would have to pay a visit to Daddy Dor sooner rather than later.

You might as well come back topside, I told Gast. *No point hanging about the Undercity.* There wasn't anyone left.

What if she returns?

She'll come back to Central, if anywhere. Because that was where the Diviner would be. *Make yourself useful and keep watch over the station.*

His irritation rang through our bond. I didn't see what he had to complain about. I was putting his skills to use *and* keeping him out of the madhouse that was the clock tower. It was getting a little crowded in there these days.

I APPRECIATE THE SPECTACLE. LONG HAVE I ENDURED THE BOREDOM OF MY IMPRISONMENT. MORTALS FIGHTING AMONG THEMSELVES AMUSES ME.

Are they fighting again?

THEY NEVER STOP, DAUGHTER.

I told them to quit it!

WHAT DO YOU EXPECT FROM MORTALS?

I clicked my beak. What would it take for them to get along? Chime's bakeries were fucked, so I couldn't order in some cupcakes.

I flew back up the clock tower. Sparks were flashing through the clockface window. Yep, they were going at it, all right. Harmony was supposed to be handling them!

The Glimmer and Ember were at each other's throats, and for some reason, even the Necro and Fauna were fighting. Problem was, both groups were opposites while also being alike in their abilities. Thrown together, it led to shit like this.

How the fuck had Chime ever worked?

It was Sinder and Gloria at the center of this mess. Sinder's fists were aflame as Gloria glowed with pure sunlight. They were locked almost head-to-head, so close Sinder could impale Gloria with his horns if he wanted, and he looked like he was about to.

Gawking onlookers surrounded them—Glimmer, Necro, some Fauna, but none of the Godless. They were too busy huddling in the corner, conspiring with Sinder acting as a distraction.

Didn't they know I could read their every thought?

I flew in through the upper clockface doorway and swapped my form to Chaos as I landed between Sinder and Gloria, forcing them both to back off. "All right, you fucks! Pack it in."

"Get this golden whore out of my face," Sinder spat.

"That's rich, coming from Edana's plaything," Gloria countered.

Their raw anger for each other ached inside my own gut. They sure hated one another, but their warring emotions were making me nauseous.

"We're all friends here," I said. "Both of you need to kiss and make up. Sinder, say sorry to Gloria—"

"I'd sooner fucking die than apologize to that... *thing*." Sinder's nostrils flared.

Gloria took the insult on the chin. "Why did you invite this useless male here? He clearly hates women—"

"I hate *you*," Sinder snapped.

"We've been making ourselves useful," Gloria said with an eyebrow raised. "What, exactly, will this male contribute that we cannot provide ourselves?" A flicker of light danced in her palm as an example.

I had to hand it to Gloria—she'd transitioned from ambassador to my personal prisoner rather quickly. Guess she knew how to cling to power somehow, even if that meant cozying up to me. But she did have a point. Sinder was volatile. I'd seen his memories—seen how the Glimmer had abused him.

But I'd also seen a darker side to him, no different from the Glimmer.

He couldn't go around calling the Glimmer whores when I'd seen his past—witnessed how he'd whored himself out to Erosain when working in a cabaret theater so he could work his way up to whoring himself out to Edana. And then he'd whored himself out to me—offering my dear sister on a platter—to get payback on the Glimmer.

That boy had more issues than the back catalogue of the Chime Courier. Clearly, hanging out with the Godless and indulging in wine and card playing hadn't helped him move on with his life. Nor had his relationship with Vincent.

What would help poor old Sinder? Making him apologize to Gloria wouldn't work. Giving him the reins to beat Gloria wouldn't either. Besides, Joe would only complain if I did *that* again.

Maybe what Sinder needed was a little perspective. A chance to put himself in the Glimmer's shoes and learn a little empathy.

I pointed at him, and his form changed from Ember to Glimmer.

His dark pink Chaos skin now shone gold. The horns of his head receded into a head of cropped golden hair that suited him. Sinder scrubbed up well as a Glimmer.

Shame he didn't think so.

He screamed. His reaction was so visceral, it was like a ticking bomb finally exploded. He collapsed to the floor in a fit of wailing howls and flailing arms, as though I'd zapped him. Honestly, his performance would put a Seren to shame.

"Change me back!" he shrieked. "*Change me!*"

The rest of the Godless finally noticed the commotion and ran over. All except for Green Girl, who remained curled up in the corner, and Vincent, who hung back, wary of approaching the lover who had betrayed their tight little group.

"What did you do?" Harmony demanded.

"Gave Sinder a little perspective."

Joe crouched beside Sinder, attempting to calm him. "Change him back. Can't you see this is torture for him?"

"He betrayed my sister to destroy a whole domain." Though technically I *had* encouraged him, but that was beside the point. "He needs to sit on his hands and reflect on what he's done." No one had yet discussed Sinder's betrayal of my sister. Despite making Sinder and Vincent share this cramped space, they'd avoided the subject.

Sinder crawled to his knees. His face was a sniveling, snotty mess. "The—The Nameless One had Vincent. I—I did it for him—"

"No, Sinder. You didn't do it for me." Vincent stood watching. He clenched his cane so tight; his knuckles were about to pop.

"Vince, please!" Sinder begged. "I never wanted to hurt Kayl—"

"Then you shouldn't have." Vincent turned his back and strode over to the clock window, leaving a trail of misery in his wake.

Sinder merely hung his head and sobbed.

Harmony glared at me. "If your goal is to unite us, then great job." She stomped over to comfort Vincent.

"All right, everyone." Gloria clapped her hands. "Back to work." She shuffled the crowd out of the way as though she were in charge, and flashed me a smug smile.

I wasn't on her side, either.

All that remained was Sinder, silently weeping in the center of the room, and a very pissed-off Joe, who marched right up to my face to complain.

"Do you listen to *anything* I say?" Joe ranted. "We're your mortals now, so you like to keep reminding us. That makes our well-being your responsibility."

"What do you think I'm doing?" I placed my hands on my hips. "This will be good for Sinder. He'll be forced to think about his shitty behavior. Besides, I've done you a favor. Now Vincent can be all yours." Matchmaking and gossiping was more Kayl's thing, but I understood why she enjoyed it. Oh, the scandal! The drama!

Joe glanced over at Sinder, the poor boy's face reddening. "I never asked you to do this!" he hissed. "Forcing him to look Glimmer is no different than changing my body without my consent."

"Oh, come on. You've always wanted a cock—"

"That's beside the point. You assumed what I wanted. You never asked."

"I didn't need to ask. Everything you've ever wanted is right here inside your head." I poked his forehead.

He frowned and swatted me away. "Don't you get it? Mortals have lived their entire lives at the whim of the gods, with no choice in the matter. You're no better by taking autonomy away from us. Wouldn't you want a choice in who you are? Wouldn't you choose to be different from your twin if you could?"

No. I never minded looking like Kayl. I liked that we shared the same face. "I could make your lives perfect, and you still wouldn't be happy. Why didn't either you or Harmony tell me about the fighting going on when I was away?"

"We didn't want to bother you—"

"Don't lie to me. I saw you conspiring in the corner—"

"We were comforting Dru!" Joe threw his hands up. "Do you have any idea how traumatized she is? You tossed her into our arms and left us to deal with it. Her god strung her like a damn puppet and forced her to kill other mortals. She remembers every moment."

Okay, that wasn't entirely a lie. Green Girl wasn't in a good state right now, and fuck if I knew how to handle that. Between Sinder and Green Girl, I should start running a damn therapy group.

Maybe I could find a bookstore in Central somewhere and bring back a self-help book.

But the Godless had *also* been discussing ways to break free of my hold, and I gotta say, that kinda hurt.

THEY WON'T EVER LOVE YOU, DAUGHTER. NOT LIKE I LOVE YOU. IF THESE MORTALS CANNOT BE USED AS BAIT TO DRAW OUT YOUR SISTER, THEN WHY BOTHER KEEPING THEM?

Kayl would come for them eventually.

THEY ARE A DISTRACTION. STOP HELPING THEM AND START SMITING THEM.

Smiting wouldn't make 'em any easier to handle. *They can be useful. The Glimmer are keeping the aether shield going—*

YOU KNOW I SPEAK OF THE GODLESS. DEAL WITH THEM.

Don't worry, Mother. They're under my control.

ARE THEY?

They just needed a little reminder of who was in charge.

I left Joe to play therapist and wandered off to the clockface window, where Harmony was staring outside. She'd finished giving Vincent her little pep talk and looked as though she'd aged a few years.

Harmony had fucked up my chance to recruit Kayl back in Rapture, and I'd been nice enough to forgive her for it. We stood side by side in silence until it irritated me. "You know I own your souls, right? There's no point in conspiring against me."

Anxiety rang from Harmony, who faced me slowly.

"I can see it from your perspective," I continued. "Kayl once stole the soul of a god. Valeria. In doing so, she'd freed herself from her god's grip and made herself immune to our mother's influence. Surely you or one of the other Godless could steal my soul and free yourselves, too?

"Except, you're not strong enough to do it. Neither is Vincent, not with his leg, nor is Green Girl in any fit state. Gast would willingly throw himself at the chance to take me down, which is why I keep him at a distance. I don't want the hassle. Which leaves either Joe or Sinder to volunteer. Have I about summed up your stupid plan?"

Sinder was too volatile. Joe had been putting on a friendly face and buttering me up all this time, likely waiting for the right time to strike. They were both a pair of arseholes.

Harmony sucked in a breath.

"It won't work, dumb arse," I said. "I own the souls of four gods. Do you know what that makes me?" I leaned close to her ear. "Fucking invincible."

A thrum of fear pulsed through Harmony's blood. She stepped back, squaring her shoulders as she regained her composure, quick as a flash. "Do you know why we formed the Godless?"

"Because you needed friends for your wine-tasting club?"

"Because we all had one thing in common. We'd all existed under the shadow of a cruel and merciless god. Each of us had lived through our darkest moments and come out of it alive. You don't scare us, Jinx. We've survived worse than you."

"Really? You haven't survived me yet." I examined my nails. "You're lucky I want your fleshy mortal bodies intact for when Kayl comes calling. And she will soon. But after then?" I flashed my sweetest smile. "All bets are off."

I didn't want to threaten them. I wanted to be friends, damn it! To make the Godless better. But threats were the only thing they understood.

When Kayl finally makes an appearance, they'll realize they need me.

Something tapped on the clockface window from the outside. The fuck?

I left Harmony staring and headed out through the door to the balcony overlooking Central. A brass clockwork bird sat perched on the handrail. Some sort of Diviner toy? Fuck, was it here spying on me?

It had something in its mouth—a tiny rolled-up piece of paper. It flapped its wings and trilled with a mechanical whirring, urging me to take it.

"A message?" I carefully pulled the note free and unrolled it.

I know how to reach Corinth. Meet me in office 313, floor 3, the steamworks, at twelve o'clock – P. B.

Oh shit. A message from Penny?

Why the fuck would she want to meet me in the steamworks?

And why give me intel on Corinth?

IT'S A TRAP, DAUGHTER. THE DIVINER GROW DESPERATE.

Maybe. Or maybe Penny was finally willing to defect.

Either way, we needed Corinth. I sure didn't fancy visiting Kronos without a sound plan. But that didn't mean I was dumb enough to walk into a Diviner's trap.

It was time I put my Godless to use.

I flew on down to the Undercity via the elevator shaft. It was still powered, but no one was using it. Besides, flying was much quicker. Since I'd taken Faen's soul, I'd unlocked a few of their secrets—including the ability to combine multiple animal forms within the same body. So now I could fly in my magpie form with an extra set of wings and sharper talons. It looked fucked up, but was sure effective.

The flight gave me time to reflect on dear old Penny. She'd sent me a vague note, assuming it *was* her, and here I was dropping everything at her beck and call.

What did that say about me?

The Undercity tunnels were quiet. No trams clattered along the tracks. It felt strange coming back here when the Undercity had been my home as long as Kayl's. Except, my home had been inside her head. Grayford and the rest of the Undercity never meant anything to me.

Now that I'd returned with my own body, my own eyes and nose, wow was it shit. The darkness, I'd expected. It was always dark down here, even during the day. But the air tasted horribly of soot and oil. It was like the more evil side of Kronos. The darker side. Why had Kayl ever thought of it as home?

The tunnel eventually opened to the tram station beside the steamworks. The station itself was empty, but a few Diviner stood guard by the main entrance to the steamworks.

It was still pumping smoke into the air. What were the Diviner even using it for? Could they be hiding soul-splitting machines inside? Making them there?

Is that what Penny was luring me to? It would make things interesting.

I flew into an abandoned tram and changed to my usual Glimmer form. Materializing clothes out of thin air came easily to me now, and I chose my favorite red dress, though I skipped the heels this time.

Then I found the souls of Harmony, Vincent, and Joe, and yanked them into the carriage.

They appeared in a naked heap as their Chaos selves and awkwardly pulled themselves apart. Joe's embarrassment burned the hardest. The poor man was blushing so much, he was flashing like a fucking streetlamp.

"Here you go." I waved my hand, and a pile of clothes appeared next to them. "Sort yourselves out."

They hurriedly dressed.

"Where are we?" Joe asked as he finished tucking his shirt into his trousers.

Vincent strode to the tram window. "The steamworks."

"Why have you brought us here?" Harmony demanded.

I wanted to sit and cross my leg over my knee, all businesslike, but the seats were filthy. Who knew what mortal had sat or pissed on those things. "We're having a little team-building exercise. I need to get inside the steamworks, so I need you three to watch my back."

"What about Sinder?" Joe said.

"Sinder can manage on his own for a while."

Harmony was still scowling at me. Honestly, I don't think she'd ever stopped scowling from the moment I'd taken her from Serenity. "What do you expect us to do? By your own admission, we're hardly fighters."

I rolled my eyes. "Did you even listen to what I said literally thirty seconds ago? I want you to watch my back. The key word being *watch*. You'll take a Seren form and fly up to the top of the steamworks and watch from there. Vincent will stay here and watch from the ground, no running about required. If you spot anything suspicious—more Diviner turning up or whatever—pray to me." I'd be slipping into their thoughts to keep an eye on things anyhow.

"And me?" Joe asked.

"Congrats, you're my new bodyguard." I slapped his upper arm. "It's time for you to step up."

I left Harmony and Vincent to their orders and hopped out of the carriage.

Joe rushed after me. "Step up and do *what*? Do you have a plan?"

"We need to sneak inside and find office 313 on floor 3."

"I'm not exactly cut out for espionage—"

"Course you are. You spent years hiding who you were from the Glimmer, sneaking under Gildola's shiny golden arse so you could dress like a man and smoke cigars."

"That was a bit different from this."

I spun on my heel and faced Joe. "What would have happened if you were caught?"

"Possibly reeducation—"

"Nope. Gildola would have tied you to a stake in her fancy cathedral and burned you to death in front of a shitty choir. Here, the Diviner will only destroy your soul. It's quicker and less painful."

Joe rubbed his neck. "*Only*, you say. Is this supposed to be a pep talk?"

"It's whatever gets you moving." I continued down the platform and eyed the main entrance to the steamworks. Joe dutifully followed.

Three Diviner waited by the doors. By the way they stared at nothing, these were soulless. A Seren's song had no effect on them, apparently. Would a Necro's abilities work? Of course, I could sneak in with a Fauna form, but Joe hadn't tried on a Fauna form yet, and I didn't want to put up with his complaints if I made him change into a ferret or something.

I'd brought him along because I wanted my enemies close, even if that made him a liability.

We could burn through the Diviner, but I didn't want to announce my arrival. "You ever wondered what it's like to be a Fauna?"

"Not really, no—"

"Then today's your lucky day! Try not to scream." I tapped him on the shoulder, and forced him to change form.

I expected him to turn into a mouse or something and disappear into a pile of clothes. But no, the fucker did the opposite, didn't he.

His clothes ripped apart as his body hunched over, his face elongated, and he took the form of a red-furred stag, massive antlers, and all. He stumbled back in surprise, his stupid hooves clattering all over the place. "Oh my gosh!"

"Take a smaller form, you idiot! Before the fucking Wardens see you!"

"How do I do *that*?"

Seriously? I slapped him on his rump.

Joe squealed, and this time he shrank into something more reasonable—a red squirrel. Fuck, even with a Fauna form, Joe always managed to look pretty. But then I'd never met an ugly Glimmer, and that was his soul. Handsome in a way he had no right to be.

I shrank to my magpie form and quickly checked the Wardens hadn't noticed a fucking *stag*. Luckily, they still stared into space.

Though if Dor was spying on the area through his mortals as I was, then we wouldn't have much time.

"Stay quiet, follow me, and move quick," I said.

Joe's whiskers twitched.

I fluttered above the Diviner and over to the main doors as Joe scurried under-foot. The Diviner didn't notice or react at all.

Head to the door, I ordered Joe telepathically. *Push it open a couple of inches.*

His anxiety spiked, but he ran on over to the door, his poofy tail bobbing behind him, and then nudged the door open.

I flew in through the gap, and he followed, letting the door close behind us.

We were inside the steamworks. Or some shitty reception, at least.

It was empty and quiet. Aether lights hummed overhead. The lights were on, no one was home, or at least not on this level.

"What now?" Joe whispered.

"We find this damn office."

I'd been inside this place, once. Well, Kayl had, and I'd hitched a ride, but I remembered the layout. Remembered the numbered offices and the stairwell that led downstairs to the reactor. This time, I was heading up to the third floor.

Again, I flew ahead as Joe followed. We moved quickly from one corridor to the next. But we didn't bump into any Diviner, and the offices we passed were empty, the door handles gathering dust.

Aether continued to churn through this monstrous place, groaning like the rotten guts of a city that had consumed something foul. The first time Kayl had brought me here, it had pulsed with Mother's screams. Kayl hadn't heard it, but it still haunted me. Still shuddered through my blood.

THIS FACTORY WAS DESIGNED TO BLEED ME DRY AND PUMP MY LIFE'S ENERGY THROUGHOUT THE CITY, Mother said. *I SCREAMED FOR RELEASE AND NO ONE TOOK HEED.*

We'll destroy it. Burn the whole place to ash.

I CALLED OUT TO MY DAUGHTERS. ONLY YOU ANSWERED. MY SWEET GIRL. ONCE TRAPPED, AS I AM.

Kayl didn't understand the bond I shared with our mother.

I AM NOTHING WITHOUT YOU, DAUGHTER. I NEED YOU TO BE MY WINGS.

It felt good to be wanted. Needed. *I'll fly for you, Mother.*

"I hear someone ahead," Joe whispered.

I heard it too. Shuffling. We'd made it to office 313.

I flew to the door's window, and there was Penny, alone, her back to the door as she rifled through a filing cabinet. The office looked like a generic Diviner one, with shelves full of dusty books and a few clockwork parts neatly placed. Only as I moved back did I notice the placard on the door: Doctor H. Bezel.

Getting here had been easy. Too easy.

DOR HAS ALREADY ATTACKED YOU THROUGH HIS MORTALS. HE WILL DO SO AGAIN. BE CAUTIOUS.

Don't worry.

"Stand watch," I told Joe. "Alert me if anyone shows up."

He bobbed his head and then hunkered in a darkened corner.

I swapped my form back to Glimmer, complete with red dress, and then pushed open the door.

Penny spun, a file in her hand. "You came."

The scars on her face were as prominent as ever, but a new one stood out, red and raw with the word *denier.*

But the aether collar around her neck surprised me most of all. "You've collared yourself?"

"So Dor will be unaware of this meeting."

Fuck me. She actually was defecting.

DON'T GET YOUR HOPES UP, DAUGHTER. THIS COULD BE A TRICK.

Desperation haunted Penny's gaze. I didn't think it was a trick. Not after the way Dor had abused her.

She placed the file on a desk. "This is my father's old office. He oversaw the god-splitting-machine project, designed to split a mortal soul from their god, though in reality, it also splits the soul from their body. This explains his original prototypes." She tapped the file. "To trap and destroy Chaos. Of course, the project has evolved beyond that scope."

I stared at the file. That entire shitty project was made to kill mortals like me, yet if the Diviner hadn't condemned Kayl to it, I would never have been freed.

Would never have gained my own body.

"Why'd you bring me here? If you wanted to plot treason, I'm sure we could have found a cute little café somewhere topside."

Penny slid onto the edge of the desk, her hands clasped in her lap. Ever the demure Diviner woman they expected her to be, but I'd seen her wild side. I knew her ambitions. Behind that calm demeanor lay a deviousness that had forged our temporary partnership and eventually led to the downfall of the Glimmer. And yes, I'd admit it had been fun meeting up with her in a Central café to make plans and scheme over blueberry pancakes and cream tea.

Dor had tried to crush her soul because a strong woman likely terrified him. But Penny carried her scars with a quiet dignity no god could destroy.

Those silver eyes no longer feared me.

What was there left to fear, when your own god was capable of splitting souls?

Of carving your own flesh?

"Service isn't what it used to be these days." She smiled, though there was no warmth in it. "I need to warn you of events in motion."

I crossed my arms. "And betray Daddy Dor?"

Her cheeks flushed. "What Dor is doing, is... it's beyond what my father envisioned."

That didn't sound good. "What's he doing?"

"He's judging us. Every single Diviner is being brought before his Redeemer to be judged worthy. Those who have sinned in some minor way, who have been deemed unworthy by his arbitrary rules, are being submitted to the soul-splitting devices. Forced to give up their soul and enter Dor's service as mindless slaves and weapons of war. The men you likely passed on your way inside here are a few such cases, only... the few have now become many."

Oh fuck. Dor was mass murdering his own mortals? Ripping their souls out? That was pretty fucked up, even for him.

IT DOES NOT SURPRISE ME. DOR NEVER HAD RESPECT FOR HIS OWN MORTALS. IT WAS I WHO WISHED TO CREATE MORTAL LIFE. HE SAW THEM AS CURIOSITIES AT BEST, ANNOYANCES AT WORST.

"Who the fuck is this Redeemer?"

"The old ambassador. Elijah Karendar."

I uncurled my arms. "No way! Dor brought Karendar back? I thought Corinth shot that prick in the head." Shit, that probably meant... "Karendar's got Corinth?"

"Yes. Quentin's memories have been wiped. He doesn't remember anything, not even me. I think Karendar and Dor plan to use him as a weapon, but..."

"They don't know what'll happen if they try to split his soul." Not when Corinth possessed Zyclone and Lionheart.

Plus, having a Chaos on their side and under their command would be useful to them, though it made Corinth a threat. Dor could brainwash him into believing any old shit.

"I've discovered plans," Penny continued. "To blow up the clock tower."

"They've attacked the clock tower before and gotten nowhere."

"You don't understand. They plan to destroy the clock tower from above and below—by dropping the Golden City plate and placing explosions in the steamworks. They've already begun setting them up. That's why I came here—to confirm it myself."

Fuck, really? "That would split Chime in half!"

"It could, yes."

"Fuck." Dor was willing to destroy Chime to get at us? Guess that meant I couldn't burn this place down. "You're betraying Dor by telling me this, you know."

She rubbed her forehead. "I—I know. I'm next to be judged. Karendar demanded my presence, so I—I stole a collar and ran."

"You don't think he'll judge you kindly, huh?"

"I'm a woman. We've been the purveyors of sin since the dawn of time, in their eyes. And they..." She rubbed her hands. "They abuse their soulless women. Those who can't fight back. I'm not letting them do that to me."

Not when they'd already done enough. Rage burned through my veins. Fuck, I wanted to rampage through Kronos. To find Dor and carve out bits of *him*. How could a god be so terrible, and yet have created someone like Penny?

"Join me. We'll destroy them."

She glanced up, defiance in her eyes. "I wanted to return and find a way to free Quentin—"

"Fuck Corinth." If Penny returned to Kronos, she may never get out. I'd find another way of freeing him. "Do you know how to stop these bombs?"

She grabbed the file. "It's all here. These explosives have been rigged to decimate the tower in a last-ditch effort to destroy Chaos. A fail safe, in case their tower-maintenance project didn't pan out. Using this, I can program the explosives to fail. But we'd still need to find and stop the ones hidden in the Golden City. There may be information on that somewhere in these offices."

Her excitement sent my clit tingling. Penny was willing to do all this for me? Okay, not for me—to escape Dor. But I was her way out. I could be. "We?"

Her silver cheeks blushed pink. "I wouldn't expect you to do this alone. Consider it a favor."

I stepped toward the desk until we were only inches apart. "I could free you from Dor. Permanently."

A flicker of apprehension shone in her eyes. "I'd rather keep my soul for now."

"It would be easier for us to communicate. And you wouldn't need to wear this ugly thing." I reached up and touched the collar, my fingers grazing her neck.

Penny took my hand, stopping me. "I've not experienced a godless existence. I'd like to enjoy my freedom for a little longer. But I will help you dismantle these explosives. You have my word."

"And after that?" I bit my bottom lip.

"After? I'd like to discover what it means to sin." She lifted my hand to her lips and pressed a lingering kiss.

Aether shot through my gut as though she'd fired a taser at me, but she was unarmed, and I was somehow still standing, despite my legs threatening to give out.

Fuck!

I wanted to fuck her.

Right here on her dead dad's desk.

Fuck Time and Chaos and everything in between. They could fucking well *wait*.

DAUGHTER! Mother's voice came through with alarm. *SHE'S HERE!*

What? Who's where?

YOUR SISTER. KAYL HAS RETURNED TO THE CLOCK TOWER. HURRY AND CLAIM HER BEFORE SHE CHANGES HER MIND.

Huh. What do you know?

Everything was finally starting to come together. The timing could be better, but whatever, I'd take it!

Soon, I'd have everything I ever wanted.

And then I'd bring time to an end.

37

We're living in fucked-up times. Never thought I'd see the end of the gods. Can't say I'll miss them.
I'm bound to another god, now. A crazy bitch named Jinx. She's had me running across Chime and doing what I do best, which is to say running into trouble and attempting to keep Noct out of it. As more and more mortals keep vanishing along with their domains, there isn't much I can do except keep Noct safe. Not even sure I can manage that.
I suspect we're not gonna last much longer, but I made a promise to a lady, once. When the end comes, I'll be there.
—M. Gast, *from the new personal journal of PI Gast*

I STOOD BEFORE THE clock tower in my Mesmer form, wearing a simple blouse and pencil skirt—the same outfit I'd worn so many times when running operations for the Godless. The tower loomed above me as it always had my entire life, forever judging me with the passage of time.

It was the origin of my birth. But it wasn't my home.

YOU'VE MADE THE RIGHT CHOICE, said Corentine. I'd opened my mind to her once more, and she was only too keen to enter. *MY DAUGHTERS BELONG TOGETHER.*

I hadn't been left with much choice.

From the corner of my eye, I caught Gast spying on me, his face twisted into a grimace. He likely knew what I was about to do and didn't approve.

Time ran out for us all, eventually.

Footsteps echoed behind me, and I faced Jinx.

She approached in her Glimmer form, still wearing that ridiculous red dress, and smiling like a Fauna after a meal. "Say it."

"All right, Jinx. You win."

She put her hand to her ear. "What's that? I didn't quite catch it."

I ground my teeth. "You. Win."

She bit her lip and moaned. "What I've always wanted to hear. It took you long enough, sister. I want proof this isn't a trick." She held out her hand. "Corinth's watch."

It pained me to hand over my remnant of Quen. "I'm only agreeing to this if you save him. Please. The Diviner have him trapped in Kronos, and I—I can't—"

"Relax. I'll save your precious Time Boy. He has two souls I need."

So long as she saved him, I didn't care. I pulled the pocket watch from my blouse and handed it over. "I wouldn't bother trying to open Memoria. Not unless you want to cause a flood."

She tossed it in her hand. "I'll think about it."

"So what now?" I'd handed myself over to Jinx's mercy and readied myself for what came next.

"Plans are afoot. But you needn't worry your pretty little head. You're carrying four souls. How greedy of you. It's about time you gave them back to our mother."

It was what she'd wanted all along.

To finally start pulling down the chains binding our god.

"Change into a Seren," Jinx ordered. "And we'll fly up."

"I can't fly that high."

"Fine. I'll carry you up." A pair of massive red feathery wings sprouted from her back, far larger than Zephyr ones. I couldn't even name the creature they belonged to, and her Glimmer form remained intact. How had she done that? Was it something she'd learned from Faen?

She opened her arms wide in a mocking embrace. "Come give your sister a hug."

I bit my tongue and positioned myself against her with as much awkwardness as I could muster. She was enjoying this far too much.

Jinx wrapped her arms around my waist, her breath heating my neck. "We used to be closer than this. We still could be, if you weren't so stubborn."

I stared down at my shoes. "Are you going to fly or not?"

"You know, a smile would be nice—"

"What do you expect from me, Jinx?" I glanced up and met her aether eyes. My eyes. "That everything will be rosy between us? We'll do each other's hair and nails?"

"Maybe when I've destroyed Dor, you'll finally appreciate me."

I chewed my tongue before I could say something I'd regret.

Jinx's wings flared open, and then we shot up to the sky. She swerved dangerously as we rode the wind up, causing me to tighten my grip around her neck. It was deliberate. Anything to remind me I needed her.

That my life was in her hands.

I tried not to let my fear show as my hair and skirt whipped behind me, rippling as we sped up. Moments later, we were eye level with the clockface window.

This close, it was huge. Despite Chime falling apart, the clock tower lived on and still kept time—its tall hands currently set to twelve thirty. Energy pulsed around it in an all-encompassing aether shield. A barrier designed to keep Diviner back.

Jinx flew right at it. I braced myself, expecting the shield to sting, but it only tickled with brief static as we passed through and landed on the rickety metal balcony outside the clockface. It had since been reinforced, and wasn't quite as unstable as the last time I'd been here—when I'd leaped from this damn tower to escape the fate I was now happily walking right into.

YOUR RETURN WAS INEVITABLE, MY DAUGHTER. THINK OF ALL THE STRIFE WE COULD HAVE SPARED YOU, HAD YOU JOINED WITH US FROM THE BEGINNING.

You threatened to kill the Godless.

"And now I've brought them all together in one big happy family," Jinx said, as though she'd been privy to my thoughts. She yanked open the clockface door and nudged me inside.

It wasn't the same as I remembered it.

The clock tower's entire interior had been repurposed into a home, just as the Godless had repurposed the depot. Each corner had been divided into rooms with cardboard and cloth sheets to ensure privacy, and they were clearly segregated by domain—Glimmer sat in one corner, while the others were occupied by Necro, Fauna, and Ember. All women.

Between each 'room' was space for makeshift toilets and seating areas full of cushions. It was cramped—there really wasn't enough space for four domains—but cozy. The exact sort of rooms you'd find in Grayford.

Had Jinx taken inspiration from our childhood?

By the clockface window stood a group of Glimmer, their arms outstretched as aether energy flowed from them and around the room. Shit. They were powering the aether shield outside.

Opposite them was the reason I'd come here.

Corentine.

The god of Chaos remained trapped behind her barrier and strapped to that horrible chair. Everyone avoided looking at that part of the clock tower, and I didn't blame them. Corentine was a horrendous sight. The chair must be an early prototype of the soul-splitting devices. Corentine's naked body was tied in place with worn leather cuffs around her wrists and ankles, and a helmet sat on her head—her hair shaved down to the scalp.

Wires protruded from the helmet and chair, pumping energy into the city. They fed from Corentine's veins. They were literally stuck inside her flesh, the bruises so black, they may well be rotting flesh.

Corentine had our face. Jinx's and mine. Except her body appeared weak, almost skeletal and malnourished as the city drained her. And her pupils rolled back, revealing the whites of her eyes, in a silent, desperate scream.

LONG HAVE I AWAITED MY FREEDOM. YOU AND YOUR SISTER HAVE DONE WELL IN GATHERING THE SOULS NEEDED TO FREE ME. YOU HAVE EXACTED THE VENGEANCE I DESERVE.

I hadn't done it for Corentine.

IT MATTERS NOT, IF THE RESULT IS THE SAME. BREAK MY BONDS.

There isn't much point until you recover the souls Quen has.

YOUR SISTER WILL FIND QUENTIN CORINTH. UNTIL THEN, THE BONDS YOU BREAK WILL LESSEN THE HOLD DOR

HAS ON MY PRISON, AND I CAN HELP DEFEND THE CLOCK TOWER AGAINST FUTURE ATTACKS.

"The Diviner are still a threat," Jinx said. It annoyed me that I couldn't say anything to Corentine that she wouldn't immediately tattle to Jinx. The two of them had always conspired against me.

NOT CONSPIRE, DAUGHTER. WE WOULD WELCOME YOU INTO OUR FOLD IF YOU ONLY OPENED YOURSELF TO OUR LOVE.

"Love." I snorted.

"We're your real family," Jinx said with a flare of irritation. "Not those bumbling idiots you found in the Undercity."

I scanned the room, but I hadn't seen any of the Godless. "Where are they? Jinx, I swear—if you harm them, our deal is off."

"That entirely depends on you, doesn't it, sister?" She waved her hand lazily through the air, and five naked figures appeared in the center of the room.

I sucked in a breath.

The Godless. My family.

They were forced onto their knees, almost unrecognizable in their new Chaos forms. On the far left sat Joe in his new male body; he met my eye with a determination I felt in my gut. Beside him was Vincent, who remained still as a statue, and Harmony, who sat far taller than the others. Then came Dru. Gods, Dru! She shifted uncomfortably as she averted her gaze from me and tried to hide her nakedness. In her Chaos form, she lacked her golden daisies and looked so vulnerable.

But it was Sinder who shocked me.

He was the only one not wearing the colors of Chaos. No, Jinx had forced him to appear as a Glimmer. By the way his body trembled and he hung his head, this must be pure torture for him.

"See?" Jinx said. "Not a hair on their heads harmed."

True, I couldn't see any bruising or injury, but she could have healed or wiped away those wounds, and not all wounds were visible.

"Give them clothes, for gods' sake."

"You want them clothed? Comfortable? Then you know what you need to do." Jinx pointed to the barrier surrounding Corentine. "Break the chains."

The barrier was made up of twelve magical chains across a spectrum of color representing the twelve domains. Each had been locked by one of the twelve gods. Only their souls could unlock the chains.

"What happens to the god's soul when the chain is broken?" I asked.

I WILL ABSORB IT, AS YOU ONCE DID.

"So it would be the same as transferring that power to Corentine?" I met Harmony's eyes as I asked. She said nothing—possibly because she couldn't. Harmony wasn't one for withholding her opinions, and by her frustrated expression, I was right. Jinx must have magically gagged her.

But the message in her eyes was clear. Harmony would risk the Godless to prevent Corentine and Jinx from gaining more power.

Could I really sacrifice them, knowing they were truly at Jinx's mercy?

"Stop stalling," Jinx snapped. "I've got shit to do." She grabbed my wrist and dragged me toward Corentine, and then forced my hand to press against the barrier.

Raw power tingled against my palm. This was the lingering power of the gods, caught here for thousands of years, and yet still strong. The thrum was almost overpowering.

But as I held my palm against the barrier, there was no reaction. No chain responded to my touch. Not even Valeria's.

I struggled to hide my glee.

Jinx frowned. "The fuck? Why isn't it working?"

WHERE ARE YOUR SOULS? Corentine screeched. *THEY'RE GONE!*

"What the fuck did you *do*?" Jinx shoved me hard against the barrier. "What did you do with them?"

I half shrugged. "Anima buried the Vesper inside my subconscious. I can't reach them." Which was honestly the best idea Anima had ever had. By suppressing Valeria's power, Anima had ensured I couldn't touch it or reach it, and neither could Corentine.

"And the other fucking gods?" Spit flew from Jinx's mouth and landed on my cheek. "Mesmorpheus? Unghard? Serenity? What did you do with them?"

"Oh, *those*! I didn't think I needed them anymore, so I gave them away. Extravagant gifts, I know—"

"Gave them away *how*? To whom? Where the *fuck* are they?"

I met Jinx's rage with cool detachment. "They're safe where you can't find them. Save Quen, release the Godless, and I'll return them to you."

Jinx screamed with frustration and shoved me aside. She stomped over to the Godless and grasped Harmony's hair, yanking her painfully. "*Or* I start cutting bits off your precious Godless until you give me what I want."

I clenched my fists so tight, my fingernails dug into the skin. "Do that, and I'll throw myself off this tower, and you'll never see me again."

Something tapped against the clockface window.

Jinx released Harmony with a smirk—her demeanor changed so quickly, it made me dizzy. "No need to be so damn dramatic, sister. I'm fucking pissed off with you, though. Dor is planning on blowing up the clock tower, and thanks to your little stunt, everyone in this tower is in danger. Even your Godless. But don't worry. I have a plan."

She strode over to the maintenance door and swung it open. A small clockwork bird flew in and landed on her shoulder.

Shit. I recognized that bird. It was one of Pendula's.

It carried a small rolled-up piece of paper in its beak. Jinx reached up, and the thing dropped it into her hand. She promptly unrolled it.

"And Operation 'Fuck Shit Up' is a go." Sunlight burst from her hand and burned the tiny note into ash. "I'll tell you what, sister. You make yourself comfortable here, and I'll go save the day."

"What about Quen?"

"I'll get to Corinth eventually. And when I do, you better deliver those souls, or we'll have a real problem." She left through the maintenance door, slamming it shut behind her.

It didn't take a Mesmer seer to work out she'd trapped me inside the clock tower.

But that didn't matter. I had my family back.

I ran toward them.

"Stop!" Joe called out.

I stumbled, confused by his outburst.

And then they vanished before my eyes, exploding into specks of dust. Each of them. Joe, Dru, Harm, Vincent, Sinder.

Snapped out of existence in the blink of an eye.

"No!" I screamed. I fell to my knees and thumped the hard metal floor. I'd only just found them again! "Bring them back!"

THEY COULD HAVE BEEN YOURS IF YOU HADN'T BETRAYED ME, DAUGHTER.

Fuck you, you vile bitch! I hadn't wanted to open my mind to Corentine, but without a god's soul to block her out, I didn't have a pissing choice.

IS THAT HOW YOU SPEAK TO YOUR SUFFERING MOTHER? ALL I EVER WANTED WAS MY FREEDOM—

No, you want destruction! Death! I rose to my feet and spat at the barrier. *So long as I breathe, you won't get your chance!*

THEN YOU WILL NEVER SEE YOUR LOVER AGAIN.

Quen will be no safer with you than with Dor. If it wasn't for you, none of this would have happened—the gods wouldn't have warred, the domains wouldn't have fallen—it's all because of you.

DOR IMPRISONED ME. WHAT POWER DO YOU BELIEVE I POSSESS?

Enough to start all this!

AND IF I HADN'T, YOU AND YOUR SISTER WOULD NOT EXIST.

Maybe that would have been for the best. What had either of us achieved, except to spread misery wherever we went? I'd destroyed Eventide and other domains. Jinx had done worse. If not for me, the Godless would never have formed.

They wouldn't be tortured by Jinx just so she'd get her own way.

DEFIANT UNTIL THE END.

I'm only what you made me.

HAH! I WOULDN'T HAVE CHOSEN TO DESIGN SO STUBBORN A MORTAL, BUT THE HAND OF CHAOS TOUCHES

ALL. PERHAPS DOR WAS CORRECT IN HIS RELUCTANCE TO CREATE MORTAL LIFE. YOU HAVE BEEN NOTHING BUT A NUISANCE.

We never asked to be made, but we'd be quite happy if the gods cleared off and left us alone. Go build yourself a universe elsewhere.

RELEASE ME FROM MY PRISON, AND I WILL GLADLY LEAVE.

Except I don't believe you. As soon as you're out, what's the first thing you'll do?

SMITE DOR.

And after that? Smite the rest of us?

Corentine's laughter echoed in my mind. She didn't need to answer. We both knew I was right.

What about Jinx? I asked. *Will she escape your smiting?*

SHE IS MY LOVING DAUGHTER, LOYAL TO THE LAST.

That's not an answer. Jinx still didn't realize the gods couldn't be trusted. Not even Corentine.

I hugged my chest and wandered off deeper into the clock tower. The few mortals there stared at me, some with apprehension, others with fear. Of course, I looked like Jinx, though in a form they'd likely never seen before. A Mesmer form.

The worst thing was I recognized some of their faces. The Fauna. The Glimmer. Even the Necro and Ember. Faces from my past. Faces I may have glanced at in passing.

All plucked from my mind—Jinx's mind—to create a familiarity more jarring than comforting. Among the Glimmer stood the worst of all. Gloria. Her smug smiles churned in my gut, and I turned away, pretending not to notice her.

Why would Jinx bring *her* back, of all pissing mortals?

I staggered over to a spare couch and collapsed onto it. Jinx may have trapped my physical body here, but my mind was still free to wander. I closed my eyes and let my own personal miasma wash over me, drifting me off into a deep sleep.

Haven had changed in the short time I'd been away. Celeste and Castor had been busy.

Mortals filled the domain. Seren lounged on the beach or within the pavilions, which had tripled in number to accommodate the growing population. Umber tended to the gardens and rose bushes that had sprung up. And Mesmer sat within the shade of the candy apple trees, stuffing their faces with all the sweets they could eat.

It was a paradise of happy, relaxed faces. Exactly what I'd wanted.

They hadn't let me down.

In my Mesmer form, I could astrally project myself back whenever. This wasn't just a home for displaced souls, but also a haven for me. While the tram I'd installed behind the waterfall was my home, I wandered to the memorial garden instead—a mound of beautiful glowing flowers I'd dug for Cosmo and the Fauna. Where I'd buried their bodies.

Reverie already stood there, waiting for me.

"You've done a great job," I said by way of greeting. "Seriously. Thank you."

She dipped her chin. "You were right to trust Celeste with the Seren. She enjoys hosting art classes with them and bringing their art to life. Castor has also become an accomplished gardener. He finds the work fulfilling."

"And you? Are you happy here?" I'd dragged her out of retirement to care for the Mesmer once more, and I knew from first-hand experience how troublesome they could be.

"I missed tending to their needs. Mesmorpheus always coddled their mortals. I was forever chiding them, asking them to give their mortals a chance to grow. Now they are under my care once more, I understand why Mesmorpheus coddled them so."

"They grow on you. Like children, I suppose."

"What of you? Are you safe?"

"Safe enough. Dor's planning on attacking the clock tower again. With only two domains still standing, I'm starting to feel..." What?

Nervous?

Like the end was finally approaching?

"Tired," I said. "I could do with a nap for an eternity or two."

"Be careful what you wish for. Mortal minds aren't meant for eternity."

Neither were god minds, if Corentine's madness was anything to go by. "Could I be alone for a little while? I'd like to spend some time paying my respects." At least until reality dragged me back to the clock tower. Who knew how much time I had left?

"Of course." Reverie curtsied and then meandered off to where a group of Mesmer were getting a bit too excited over a chocolate fountain.

I sighed and sat between the flowers.

They glowed such pretty colors, like starlight. I'd modeled them after Dru's daisies, and they were soft to the touch, with petals made of velvet. It still amazed me they existed at all. They lived in a domain I'd designed.

Yet none of this felt worthwhile. Where had this paradise been when the Vesper or Fauna had needed a home?

Why had it taken me up till now to do something actually useful?

I'd never operated on time's schedule, had I?

Air whooshed behind me, ruffling the flowers. I turned and gasped.

Quen stood in my meadow, looking utterly lost. The Present Quen, currently trapped in Kronos. Only his mind had traveled here, likely seeking comfort as mine had.

I scrambled to my feet. "Quen?"

He was staring in awe at the Seren paddling and splashing by the beach. "I don't understand. Our reports state the Seren are gone. The Umber and Mesmer, too." He finally turned to me. "Where is this? Another dream?"

"Not quite. But I'd rather not go into detail. Not while you work for Karendar."

He swallowed a lump in his throat. "I understand." His gaze then fell on the placards I'd made and scattered throughout the meadow. Each with a Fauna's name. His eyes scanned them until they landed on the last. "Cosmo. You... buried them?"

"You remember Cosmo?"

"No, but I..." He awkwardly adjusted his bow tie, as though struggling to breathe. "I witnessed your attack on Central. Eli—Karendar invited me to watch."

Shit. Had Karendar opened a portal to watch me burn Diviner? To force Quen to watch and make him fear me? "Your Wardens ripped out Cosmo's soul. They were a Mesmer—an innocent who wouldn't harm a pissing thing—"

"I know." He swayed on his feet, looking sheepish. "The Mesmer didn't deserve that fate, but neither did we—"

"Why are you here, Quen? Did Karendar send you to haunt my dreams?"

"You burned an entire unit."

"I wasn't in my right mind—"

"Who *is*?" He laughed hysterically.

Oh gods.

Something was wrong.

"Quen?"

He ran his metal hand through his silver hair, his fingers working almost seamlessly now. "You're—You're real and burning men, the same men we're damning to machines that devour souls, and I don't know whom to trust!" He paced, wearing a path into the meadow, and then suddenly stopped before me. "I'm lost." A single tear ran down his cheek, which he hastily scrubbed away. "You promised to show me your truth, so *please*. Show me the way."

Oh, my poor Quen.

A breeze lifted behind me, enough to grab my attention. Reverie had planted a single bench within the meadow. The same bench Quen and I would meet at outside Central Station.

Thank you, I whispered to Reverie.

I took Quen's hand and sat him down. "I can show you my memories." Or at least a projection of them. An illusion. "Everything I show you is the truth. Are you ready?"

His chest rose with a deep breath. "Yes."

"Then open your mind."

Images bloomed within a floating collection of clouds. Pictures from my own memories, as vivid as a vision and directed with the vigor of a theater production. I began from the beginning—the moment I met Quen within the Undercity. The death of a Vesper girl, and the elevator ride after.

From there, I zipped through to every encounter. Even the uncomfortable ones. The time he arrested me in the Glimmer mansion. When he questioned me at Warden HQ, dragged me all the way to Eventide, and we forged a partnership to discover the truth behind Chaos. I didn't want to miss a single moment, and so I laid it all out.

The naked truth of Quentin Corinth and Kayl Arkey.

Quen sat rapt, his hand clutching mine, as our shared history played out. His breath hitched at our awkward first kiss, and then seemed to stop entirely at the reveal of the soul-splitting machines.

When Varen betrayed me and Quen lost his professor.

"I'm sorry," I said. "There're a few blanks in my memories over Eventide. Anima wiped them, so I can't show you everything, but I remember the aftermath. It's... not pretty."

"Show me."

I did.

The moment Quen shot Karendar in the head.

The moment Dor took back his soul and I screamed his name.

Quen broke contact and paced once more. "I—I killed Eli? I... died? Then how am I here? Did Dor bring me back?"

"There's more to your story."

He sat again, grasping my hand tight even though touch wasn't necessary. The memories resumed, through our reunion during the ambassadors' ball, the rekindling of our partnership, and our ill-fated adventures across the domains.

His pearly cheeks blushed red as I recalled our visit to Rapture, and the moment we kissed again on this very bench after losing Vincent. And so the memories continued right until I took his soul.

I released his hand and slowly said the words that would either make him or break him. "You're no longer a Diviner."

He stared at his hands—one flesh, one metal. "But that's... Everything you've shown me is impossible."

"Everything you've seen with your own mortal eyes is impossible, and yet it's here. You visited Memoria to help restore *my* memories, and in the process, you've lost your own. Anima did something to you. Now Karendar is taking advantage. You can't trust him."

"I kissed you."

Trust him to get stuck on *that* detail. "A couple of times, yes."

"Who are we? What do I mean to you?"

"We're partners, Quen."

"In what sense of the word? Colleagues? Lovers?"

"In every sense of the word."

"How can I believe what you've shown me? You're a Mesmer. You could have conjured up a fake vision or be manipulating my emotional state. I know nothing about you, and yet you could be lying about what you know of me." The cogs were whirring in his eyes as he tried to make sense of it all.

"How else would I know that you take your tea with two sugars and a splash of milk? Or that your favorite biscuits are bourbon biscuits? Or that when you were a child, you wanted to be a tram driver, but Dor forced you to become a Warden?"

"You could have taken that information from my mind."

"Except your Warden instincts are telling you I'm speaking the truth, and don't deny it." I pulled the letter from Future Quen out of my pocket. "Read this."

He scanned the letter with a furrowed brow. "This is my handwriting."

"You wrote this in the future."

"Now *that's* impossible—"

"Well, I'm your impossible woman."

Quen blinked for a moment, the aether of his eyes sparking.

Then he grabbed the hem of my blouse and yanked me forward, our lips slamming together.

My mouth opened to the taste of him. Fuck, how I'd missed this, missed *him*.

He pulled back, breathless. "I'm sorry, I—it felt natural to kiss you."

"I'm not complaining."

"But I'm not the Quentin you know."

I took his other hand and squeezed it. "I don't care."

He pressed his forehead against mine. "You're right," he whispered. "My Warden instincts are telling me to trust you. That I believe you. And that I... I love you. Saints, I love so you deeply, it pains me. How can I love someone I don't remember? But I know it to be true. Whoever I am, whoever your Quentin is, that love is so infinite, so complete, it apparently transcends time and space."

Gods.

He'd never said those words. None of his future or past versions had ever uttered a depth to our partnership beyond attraction. Had my Quen felt the same?

Such simple words, yet they left a profound mark on my soul, as though this Quen had cut open my chest and branded my heart with a red-hot poker. Each letter seared with purpose and promise. A scar that time could never heal.

Words I'd carry close until the end of my days.

I wiped tears from my cheeks. "I love every version of you, Quen. Even the ones that don't remember." And now that the real truth of Quentin Corinth and Kayl Arkey had been laid bare, what was I to do with it?

I remained trapped in the clock tower, while he languished in Kronos beyond my reach. I'd hoped Jinx would save Quen, but could I trust her to? Apparently, she had other priorities, and if she was shacking up with Pendula, then that would only mean danger for Quen.

Not to mention the Godless were at her mercy. Jinx would only dangle them in front of me to force my hand.

Everything that had gone wrong was my fault, and yet I was the only one who could fix it. I couldn't afford to wallow in self-pity. The play wasn't over yet. The final curtain hadn't dropped.

There was still time to pull myself together.

"I'll save you," I said. "I'll find a way to enter Kronos—"

"No." He cupped my cheek. "I need to save myself."

"Quen. I say this with all love. Don't be a chivalrous arse."

"Is that something I do often?"

I couldn't help but smile. "Sadly." I reached over to kiss him once more, and he vanished, disappearing entirely from my bench in a blink. Shit. He'd woken back into whatever reality he faced. Karendar may not have tortured him yet, but...

Time was running out for us both.

I needed a new plan to save him, save the Godless, stop Jinx, stop Corentine, and ultimately stop Dor, and I'd not made it easy for myself by handing over Quen's pocket watch. Since I'd given up my god souls, I'd lost their power, including the ability to summon whatever could help me deal with this mess.

All I had left were my wits, determination, charm, and the power of love.

Oh, we were fucked.

"This is where you're hiding your souls, daughter."

Shit. No!

I slowly rose from the bench. Corentine stood in the center of my meadow, her silver dress ruffling in the slight breeze. She'd followed me into my dream and was now sniffing the bloody flowers.

If she learned about Haven, then Jinx could find us. "Get out of my dream."

She examined a pink flower. "You shouldn't leave doors open to your mind. Who knows what will walk through?"

Corentine's face warped. Her features melting. The petals drooping.

No. Haven was fading out, gradually morphing into somewhere else— an office.

Was I having a vision inside my dream? How was that even possible?

I tried to take a step, but the horizon swirled, sending me spinning in a dizzying rush.

Corentine watched from above as I crumpled at her feet.

I swore I caught her smiling, but then everything disappeared under a blanket of darkness.

"Explosives are in place, Your Excellency," the engineer said. "We're ready to proceed on your command."

"Good. Stand by and await my orders."

The engineer left my office, closing the door behind him. I shuffled my papers together and piled them neatly on my desk. Orderliness was next to godliness.

Soon, our attack on the clock tower would commence. We were aiming for total obliteration in this case. No mortal would be left standing—on either side.

When we were done, Chime would not be the same.

The city I'd watched over for so many years would be reduced to dust. Then we'd rebirth it once more in Dor's grand design. A city without imperfection.

A city without mortal sin.

During my time as His redeemer, it became clear to me—and to my blessed Father—that to be mortal was to sin. No mortal could escape it, not even I.

The solution to the problem of sin was therefore obvious.

The complete and utter eradication of all mortal life.

I approached the piano—the centerpiece of my office. The mortal side of me had insisted on installing it, on running my delicate fingers across the keys and summoning a melody that elicited mortal emotions. It was a remnant of sin. It would have to be destroyed.

My finger pressed a key. It rang with harsh finality. A period at the end of the sentence. At the end of all things.

The time was almost one in the afternoon. Quentin would soon wake from his nap to lead my cause.

"You're watching me right now, aren't you?" I spoke aloud to the empty room. Except... I wasn't alone. I never had been. "Did you not think I'd find Quentin's sudden interest in napping suspicious? You've been reaching him across the dreamworld, and yet, you've failed to realize I've sensed your presence, Kayl Arkey."

The vision warped and I found myself standing in Karendar's office. Shit!

Had these been visions or dreams? Had I been astrally projecting myself all this damn time without realizing? Fuck!

Karendar turned to face me. "There you are at last. Mesmorpheus truly made a poor teacher. Or were you simply a poor student?"

Honestly, I had no idea what to say. I didn't even know *how* I was standing here.

This was a dream. It had to be a dream.

He charged toward me, grabbed my neck, and slammed me into a bookcase.

My head bashed against the shelf, and the pain felt too real. But I couldn't be here! I was simply imagining the pain.

His fingers choked me, but my breathing steadied, and the pain faded. It *wasn't* real. He was trying to intimidate me, but I wasn't here, not really.

I wanted to push back and retort, but I bit my tongue instead. Better to let him monologue while he believed he had me at his mercy. If he wanted me scared, I'd put on the act.

"Let me go," I begged, and forced tears to well.

He cupped my cheek with one hand, the other still squeezing my neck. "Corentine bore such beautiful daughters. Both so full of sin, and yet you, Miss Arkey, simply radiate it. A magnet so powerful it lured Quentin from his god. You can cease your simpering, now."

I blinked back the tears and straightened. "What do you want from me?"

"From you? Nothing. I merely wish to judge you—"

"I'm not interested in your judgements."

"A shame. There's a chance for your redemption. All it will cost is your soul." He ran a thumb over my bottom lip. "And the souls of every mortal you ever loved."

I shoved him back with all my strength and seethed. "You touch me again, or any of my family, and I'll rip your soul out first."

He adjusted his cufflinks with a smirk. "How do you plan on saving Quentin's soul, hrm? You're rather conveniently trapped inside the clock tower. I know this, because while you've invaded my mind, I could glimpse inside yours. Thank you for providing the insight my Father and I needed to organize our movements. We'll be coming by to collect you soon... Should your mortal body survive."

Karendar snapped his fingers, and I fell through darkness once more.

I awoke to Corentine staring at me. Actually staring at me, those aether eyes red-rimmed and full of swirling madness. I yanked my skirt straight and sprinted up to Corentine's barrier so quickly, my nose pressed against the pulsing energy.

"It's Dor and Karendar!" I yelled. "They're coming—they'll blow up the damn clock tower!"

JINX IS ALREADY AWARE OF THEIR PLANS, Corentine drawled.

You don't understand! They've been spying on us—on me—through my visions! Whatever Jinx is heading into is a trap!

I WITNESSED YOUR VISIONS FOR MYSELF, DAUGHTER. WHY ELSE WOULD I LEAVE THE DOORS TO YOUR MIND OPEN?

You... you invited Karendar into my mind?

TO SPY ON DOR'S MOVEMENTS. YOU GUARDED YOUR WAKING MIND WELL ENOUGH, BUT FORGOT THE DREAMWORLD. I'VE SPENT ENOUGH YEARS WANDERING DREAMS TO UNDERSTAND MESMORPHEUS'S SECRETS.

All this time, Karendar knew what Quen and I had been up to. I'd thought those visions a blessing, but they'd been a damn curse. *You fucking idiot! You let them spy on* me!

I WARNED YOU AN OPEN DOOR WAS AN OPEN INVITATION.

I yanked at my hair in frustration.

The Diviner had always been one step ahead. They'd let us prance around the domains, taking down their enemies for them, one at a time, waiting for the right time to strike.

That time was now.

They were going to blow the tower to pieces, and then everyone in this room would be condemned to a fate worse than death.

I had no way to stop them.

XXXVIII

During uncertain times, it can be tempting to forgo the vows you made to your god. Many mortals mistakenly believe this is their opportunity to indulge in sin. Why not, when mortals are dying and you and your domain could be next?
To that, I say, hold faith with your Father. Trust in Him.
Trust in His vision to deliver you to safety. To nurture and protect your soul.
Only our Father can save you—physically and spiritually.
Seek comfort in Him. Should your mortality come under risk, know your soul will be redeemed.
—The Redeemer, *Hold Your Faith*

I STARED INTO THE mirror at my eyes.

The eyes of Chaos.

My entire life had been turned inside out, and my mind was refusing to process it. I sat down on the bed, my head in my hands. The little room the Wardens had granted me was serviceable enough, with a simple bed, privy, and wardrobe. I'd been so horrified by what I'd done—splitting a mortal's soul, one who claimed to know me—that I'd sought answers, been terrified out of my wits and run—only to eventually confront the truth. Or the truth presented to me.

I had no reason to believe the images Kayl had shown me were a lie. I'd felt their reality in my gut. Tasted it on the tip of Kayl's tongue.

It would be so simple to dismiss them as a dream, a flight of fantasy.

But Benjamin Seasons *had* known me. I'd known him, too, even though I couldn't remember.

I loved Elijah. *That* was the truth I knew.

And yet this Elijah wasn't the man I'd fallen in love with. Death had changed him.

Saints. Death had changed me too, apparently.

When Dor had opened a portal and I'd witnessed Kayl fighting Diviner in Central, I knew then that she was real and no longer a figment of my imagination. The scenes Eli had forced me to witness were meant to horrify me, and they did.

She was Chaos in its most devastating form.

I should have been disgusted. Bolstered in my hatred for Chaos. Instead, I'd felt sympathy. We'd thrown soulless men at her. Fodder for war. And we'd condemned innocent Mesmer who didn't deserve being thrust into this conflict.

The pain she'd screamed out at that Mesmer's death had broken me.

I knew then I was lost.

Truly lost.

Someone rapped on the door. "Master Corinth? Ambassador Karendar has asked to see you, sir."

I lifted my spectacles and ran my palm down my face. "Right you are."

Was I finally going mad? Was my mind so warped that I trusted lustful dreams over stark reality? I'd fallen in love with a woman I didn't even remember, and she was telling me to betray my god, my domain, the very man I owed everything to.

Could it be a trick of Chaos?

But then how could I explain the aether of my eyes?

The aching in my gut? The inappropriate hint of arousal?

No. I was Diviner. I'd been born Diviner, and I had apparently died a Diviner. I existed in the realm of logic, and therefore logic dictated I seek the truth for myself.

I needed to confront Elijah.

I reached for the door handle and hesitated.

What if everything was true, and I willingly walked into a trap?

Elijah was redeeming mortals and casting those he found sinful into purgatory. He knew of my struggles with sin, and right now, I threatened to burst with every perverse predilection I'd ever indulged.

Bugger and blast it. Kayl was right. I wasn't safe here.

How could I escape Kronos if the bloody Gate was no longer working? *You blithering fool*, it was obvious. Elijah wanted me to lead the fight against Chaos, and that fight led to only one place: Chime.

I needed to stop playing the prat and start playing the martyr. Only that would earn me a one-way trip to freedom. Then... then I would find Kayl and sort out this entire mess.

It was a solid plan. The only one I had.

I grabbed the handle and stepped into the hall with renewed purpose. I had to simply trust fate was steering me well, because if I didn't, I'd unravel into a complete mess from sheer shock.

Wardens hurried by, all heading toward the plaza. They were dressed in their uniforms and armed with a battalion of weapons. Were we readying an assault so soon? I joined the throng and followed them to where they gathered in orderly lines, awaiting their orders. At least fifty good men.

All of them soulless.

What had been their sins?

I swallowed my unease and continued through to Elijah's office on the third floor. A jarring clang echoed along the hall. I knocked on the door and waited outside. "Eli?"

"Come in."

I entered to Elijah seated at his piano, his fingers nimbly working the keys. He was an immensely talented player, almost unheard of in high society, yet these notes were discordant. All wrong.

"Are we preparing to march?" I asked, keeping my voice casual.

Elijah finished his playing and helped himself to a cup of coffee—the scent always made me nauseous. "Our plan is in place. We'll begin our assault on the clock tower at the turn of the hour. The first stage is to destroy the tower."

"Destroy? How?"

"We have explosives placed within the steamworks and within the top station of the Golden City. They're set to detonate remotely. Once triggered, the explosive shockwave will sever the tower from the Undercity and the Golden City plate."

"Sever?" I leaned against Elijah's desk, my hand brushing a letter opener. "But the tower holds up the Golden City plate. Destroying it would mean…"

Saints.

It would be catastrophic.

The falling plate alone would crush anyone remaining in Chime. The entire layer of Central would be flattened by falling debris, not to mention the complete and utter destruction of the Golden City itself. The Undercity could provide some shelter, but the resulting explosion would send fire and ash for miles.

The devastation would mark the end of Chime. The end of the city I loved, the city I'd called my home for most of my mortal life.

There would be nothing left worth saving.

Elijah observed me as the sheer horror of his plan dawned on me. "Once the tower has been exposed, our men will move in to capture any survivors. Our intel suggests a great number of Chaos mortals still reside behind the clockface."

"And they'll be judged?" As a sinner or saint?

"There'll be no need. There is no redeeming Chaos."

His brass eyes stared into mine.

Surely he could see it? Surely he knew?

"You've been slovenly lately, Quentin."

"*Slovenly?*" I blurted. Of all the traitorous things he could accuse me of, I'd never expected that!

"Your hair is a mess. Your bow tie is crooked. Pride is a sin, but our Father expects a certain kempt appearance. Not to mention the frequency of your afternoon 'naps.' This isn't behavior befitting a Warden."

"Well, I—I've only just returned from Memoria. The difference in air quality and pressure can leave one exhausted—"

"Don't lie to me."

My heart skipped a beat.

Elijah rose from the piano, setting his coffee aside. "Did you not think our Father would look into your mind and find the quality of your thoughts wanting? You have been judged, Quentin. And our Father is most displeased."

"Eli—"

"Take off your jacket and shirt."

Gods! "Eli, please—"

"You have sinned. This is the only way I know to redeem you." He undid his belt. "Let me save your soul."

What choice did I have? I was trapped here in Dor's domain, surrounded by hundreds of soulless Diviner. Possibly more. If I placated Elijah now, then perhaps it would appease him enough to spare my soul and send me on my way. I could handle a few lashings.

I shrugged off my jacket, draped it across his office chair, and undid my shirt buttons with difficulty. The fingers of my left hand trembled, whereas my metal hand still struggled with precise movement and grip, especially under pressure.

I managed the top button and then fumbled the second. "I'm sorry, my arm—"

Elijah grasped the hem of my collar with one hand and yanked my shirt open, ripping through the stitching and scattering buttons with tinny *clinks*. "There. Get on your knees."

His brass eyes hardened into something I'd never seen before in my memories, but had inside Kayl's. An emotion so full of abhorrence, I couldn't describe it.

I removed my shirt, tugging it carefully around where my metal arm connected to my residual limb.

And then I lowered myself to my knees.

"Clasp your hands in prayer," he ordered.

I did so, my heart thudding against my bare chest.

"You know I hate doing this."

"Then why do you do it?" The quip came out too quickly for me to bite back.

My soul must surely be cursed by Chaos, for my past self would *never* have dared.

Pain lashed across my back in answer.

I gasped as his belt seared my skin. It struck again before I had the chance to catch my breath, and again. Heavy blows rained across my torso, my shoulders, and upper arms without mercy. Each a harsh *thwack* that echoed through my bones, proving just how pitifully mortal I was.

"Eli!" I pleaded.

But his blows did not slow.

"This is what you make me do," Elijah said between grunts of exertion. "You continue to disappoint me and our Father, and yet we refuse to give up on you."

I couldn't take it anymore. I fell forward onto my palms, my arms shaking with the effort of stopping me from collapsing altogether.

My vision fluttered in and out of darkness.

Elijah leaned against me, panting. His groin pressed against my stinging back. "We do this because we love you." Something hard rubbed against my buttocks. Good gods. He'd sprung an erection!

Did my suffering—my whimpering and crying—bring him *pleasure*?

This wasn't love. It wasn't even a mimicry.

Elijah wasn't Eli. Not my Eli. Not anymore.

His hand rested on the back of my neck. A possessive touch. "You've made me angry, Quentin. I may have overreacted. But we will fix this."

The door to his office opened, and in stepped Brooke, the Amnae ambassador.

"You sent for me, Your Excellency?"

Elijah caressed my neck. "We'll ensure your loyalty is absolute."

Saints. Everything Kayl had shown me was true. Elijah had conspired to wipe my memories, and he planned to do so again.

I'd forget Kayl. The woman my past self had loved so fiercely, it reverberated inside me. And then I'd lead the Diviner into Chime's destruction.

If I ran from this room, there would be no turning back. But who would I be, if I allowed Elijah to keep rearranging my memories? To invent new backstories and situations to force my compliance? I wouldn't be me. To lose myself in memory once more would be no better than to lose my very mortal soul.

I pushed myself from Elijah's hold, using the strength of my metal arm to grab the side of his desk and launch myself onto my feet.

Before he could even react, I snatched his cup of coffee and threw the contents at his face.

He hissed and stumbled back. The beverage was cool enough not to burn, but it blinded him for the few seconds I needed.

I then snatched the letter opener and pressed the sharp edge against Brooke's neck. "Lift your hands where I can see them."

She raised them, palms up. "There's no need for this—"

"No need?" Had she so conveniently ignored the blood running down my back? Every movement hurt as my skin stretched. Sheer adrenaline kept me conscious right now.

For if I dared escape to my dreams, I'd wake up a different man.

Elijah wiped his face dry with a handkerchief. "Enough, Quentin. Release her."

"Restore my memories," I whispered in her ear with anxious desperation. "And I promise you won't be harmed."

"I don't possess your memories," Brooke whispered back. "Anima owns them now. If you want them, you'll have to take them the only way Chaos can." She touched my arm, and a memory bloomed inside my mind's eye.

Quentin, if you're witnessing this memory, then your memories have been taken. As have mine. All is not lost. We released your memories and my father's into the ocean surrounding Memoria. Many memories float in the waters—the fish feed on them. That was what my research focused on. I believe Anima releases these memories as a waste product when they're no longer needed. You are Chaos. You can transform into an Amnae and bathe in the waters. By doing this, the fish and their memories will come to you.

I sucked in a strangled gasp.

That was one of Ilona Burns's memories. Why had Brooke retained it? Why had she chosen to share it now?

"Quentin!" Elijah snapped. He held up his hand.

A bubble of time enveloped Brooke's head, and it popped like a balloon, showering me in blood and bits of brain matter. Elijah had sped up time so quickly, the pressure had imploded the poor woman's skull.

Brooke's body fell to my feet in a sprinkling of dust, her clothes fluttering to one side.

So much for a partnership between the Diviner and Amnae.

Elijah adjusted his cufflinks. "If we cannot resolve this matter civilly, then you leave me no choice."

The door opened. A Warden stood there, an aether collar in hand.

If I couldn't take the Amnae ambassador hostage, then another would suffice.

I leaped at Elijah. While he wielded authority like a pistol, he didn't have the Warden training or instinct I'd cultivated over the years.

Within seconds, the letter opener was pressed against his neck.

"This won't end well for you," he said between clenched teeth.

It was never going to end well. "Order the Wardens to back off."

He nodded, and the Warden blocking the door stepped away, giving me the opening I needed.

I clenched Elijah's upper arm with my metal hand and shoved him out of the office, walking with my back to the corridor wall so the Wardens were in my line of sight at all times, the blade still at Elijah's throat.

"Do you think our Father wants this?" Elijah hissed.

"I don't give a damn."

"You always fall into sin, don't you, Quentin? What are we meant to do with you?"

"My name is Quen." I dragged him into the elevator and punched the button for the first floor. The miniature Gate downstairs was offline. "Tell Dor to power the Gate."

"Tell him yourself."

I slammed Elijah into the elevator wall. "You know very well I can't."

Now that I knew the truth, it was obvious. Dor hadn't answered my prayers because he hadn't heard them.

Elijah sneered. "Will you kill me twice? I already died for *your* sins." The poison in his tone burned.

How had I ever believed he loved me?

The elevator door pinged open, and I dragged him out.

Wardens waited by the makeshift Gate, their forms unnaturally still. As soulless, they now depended on the orders of mortals like Elijah, and no longer on training and instinct alone. That gave me one advantage over them. It also made them unpredictable.

I pressed the letter opener closer to Elijah's throat. "Open a portal. I won't ask twice."

The Gate burst to life. Aether shimmered at the center, and within it lay Memoria. Was Elijah encouraging me to devour Anima's soul? Why? To rid Dor of a potential rival? Had that been his plan all along? If I failed, my memories were likely forfeit regardless.

But this was my best chance of restoring my missing memories.

I shoved Elijah aside and ran for the portal.

Dor could have closed the portal on me, but as predicted, he left ample time for me to reach Memoria. He wanted me here. I'd either become his unwitting servant or I'd stumbled into a trap.

Then why wipe my memories? Why carry on the charade at all?

Unless he expected any outcome to end in his favor. Mechanisms turned in the background, and I couldn't yet recognize the pattern of cogs and gears. Perhaps once my memories were restored, I'd gain a clearer picture.

Dor still threatened to destroy Chime. If I hoped to prevent that outcome, then I couldn't dally.

Memoria remained much the same as when I left it only days ago. Amnae went about their business completely oblivious to the chaos outside their domain. Mortals shopped. Children splashed within the water spouts that lined Memoria's streets. The shell-shaped gondolas ferried workers down the canals as more swam through the large glass pipes above the city.

It was hard to believe I'd imagined myself living peacefully here. That I'd gone from bumbling professor to traitor in so short a time.

An Amnae with green gills paused as they walked by me, their jaw slack.

Blast it. My presence here was noted. A Diviner in their city was odd enough, but I'd appeared out of nowhere, shirtless and bleeding. Now the adrenaline was wearing off, so came the pain, but I could do nothing about that now. Anima would surely be aware I'd entered their domain. How many bleeding Diviner with metal arms did they entertain?

I doubted Anima would simply hand over my memories. How else would I restore them?

Ilona Burns.

She and her Godless compatriot had tried to recruit me. Help me. And I'd damned them both. My memories regarding our encounter in the bookstore were hazy. Brooke must have manipulated them, wiped important details.

If the memory Brooke had shared was true, then there must be hundreds of errant memories within the ocean. Thousands. All stolen from Memoria's mortals. No wonder they were forbidden from touching the fish if they contained lost secrets.

But I didn't have time to go swimming after bloody fish.

No. I needed to bring the fish to me. Not just me.

To every mortal in Memoria.

The waters above turned dark and choppy, as though a storm brewed somewhere beyond. What could Anima possibly be afraid of? They were immune to time.

But their city wasn't.

I raised my hands in the air. I couldn't envelope the entire city in a pocket of time, but I could pinpoint structural weaknesses within the metal frames that formed Memoria's dome. Though brass didn't rust, it would still erode given enough time.

Say, a thousand years or so.

Time flashed with the sharpness of a knife. It cut through the integrity of the dome, the structures weakening and snapping.

Above, the glass dome cracked.

I forced pockets of time across the dome ceiling. Blood ran from my nose with the effort, pounded in my ears with the pressure, and I fell to one knee. Mortals screamed, pointing above.

There was an irony in destroying one city to save another, but the Amnae would survive this, in a roundabout fashion. They could swim.

I forced myself to stand. "Anima has taken your memories!" I yelled. "Find them within the waters. Touch the fish. They have—"

My words were drowned out by a thunderous *crack*.

The glass dome shattered.

Mortals ran, seeking shelter where they could, as a deluge of water and thick glass poured down in the greatest storm Memoria would ever see. The ocean itself invaded the city, bringing with it fish and other marine life.

Oh gosh, I'd made a slight miscalculation. I needed to become an Amnae!

I grabbed an Amnae fellow running past, my left hand pressing against their exposed wrist. He shoved me off, but not before the change took hold.

My entire arm transformed into a semitranslucent silver. The change continued throughout my body, until a tightness squeezed my chest. I breathed in, and the gills at my neck flapped open.

Oh my! I really was Chaos!

My entire life had been a well-scripted lie, but I didn't have time to ponder the philosophical implications or consequences. Water was pouring in fast. I braced myself for impact.

Memoria's ocean crashed in a punishing wave that swept me off my feet.

The sheer force of water thrust me backwards. I reached for a streetlamp and wrapped my arms and legs around it, hanging on for dear life until my metal arm threatened to snap off. Water cascaded over me, the pressure pushing down, drowning me.

The air was knocked from my lungs. Oh saints! Water invaded my mouth, stealing what little air I'd managed to gulp.

I couldn't breathe!

The gills at my neck worked overtime to adjust. For one frantic moment, my heart panicked as my new form learned how to breathe underwater, and the pressure swelling around me threatened to drag me into unfathomable depths.

But then, thank the gods, the water settled.

I released the streetlamp and floated. The entire city had been flooded. Warbled cries echoed around me, distorted by the volume of water. Amnae swam by, pointing and shouting, their mouths releasing a collection of bubbles. Debris bobbed all around us. Newspapers, coffee cups, someone's sandal.

And fish. Oh my. Colorful fish swam past the park benches and streetlamps, seeking out the seaweed grass as though they'd lived here all this time.

YOU HAVE DESTROYED OUR CITY! boomed a voice from the depths.

Anima.

The Amnae god emerged from the gloom, finally entering their city, perhaps for the first time. More mortals swam away at the sight looming above them. I'd wanted them to touch the fish and reclaim their memories, though right now, their sole concern was survival.

As was mine.

WE NOW SEE DOR'S PLAN, Anima continued. *TO USE CHAOS AS A MEANS OF DESTROYING HIS OWN CHILDREN. CORENTINE WOULD BE PLEASED.*

I'm not here on Dor's orders, nor Corentine's. You stole my memories. I want them back.

YOUR MEMORIES WERE PROOF OF YOUR TREACHERY. YOU INTEND TO STEAL THE SOULS OF THE GODS FOR YOUR OWN GAIN. TO BECOME A GOD YOURSELF.

I couldn't fathom the intentions of my past self, but I knew who I was, deep down. A Warden of Chime. *I have no interest in playing god.*

YOUR HATRED OF DOR BLINDS YOU. WE ARE THE LAST OF THE LESSER GODS TO STAND AGAINST THE OLD ONES.

My breath escaped me in a flurry of bubbles. *Old ones?*

WHOM WE REFER TO AS DOR AND CORENTINE. THE GODS OF TIME AND CHAOS ARE NOT THE ONLY GODS IN THE VAST UNIVERSE. THIS ANCIENT KNOWLEDGE HAS BEEN LOST FOR MILLENNIA, YET WE STORED THAT KNOWLEDGE FOR WHEN THIS AGE WOULD COME AGAIN.

THE AGE OF WARRING GODS.

Then where are these other gods?

BEYOND THE SCOPE OF THIS DIMENSION. DOR AND CORENTINE ABANDONED THEIR PANTHEON TO CREATE A UNIVERSE OF MORTALS. LIVING CREATURES CONSTRAINED BY THE RULES OF TIME AND CHAOS. THE PANTHEON DID NOT APPROVE. THEY FEARED IT WOULD LEAD TO THE BIRTH OF UNWORTHY GODS OUTSIDE THEIR JUDGEMENT. LESSER GODS.

Like yourself?

YES. THERE WERE HUNDREDS OF US. ONCE MORTAL AND GRANTED GODLIKE POWER. WE FOUGHT IN THE CONFLICT BETWEEN DOR AND CORENTINE. MANY OF US WERE DESTROYED. MANY MORE CHOSE EXILE. THOSE WHO REMAINED SUPPORTED DOR AND BANISHED CORENTINE TO HER IMPRISONMENT. BUT SHE IS AN OLD ONE. SHE CANNOT BE DESTROYED SO EASILY. NOR CAN DOR.

ONLY A GREATER GOD CAN END THEIR EXISTENCE. YOU WILL NOT WIN.

A greater god?

Or the power of multiple gods combined?

Then what was your plan? To see who won between Dor and Corentine and choose a side?

DOR WOULD DESTROY US, AS WOULD CORENTINE. WE HAVE OBSERVED YOU, CORINTH AND ARKEY. WE HAVE EXPLORED YOUR MEMORIES.

MORTALS ARE FALLIBLE. YOU ARE NOT OUR SALVATION. WE WILL SEEK IT BEYOND THESE STARS.

You're planning on exile? Was it even possible for a god to abandon this universe and run away? *What of your mortals? What happens to them?*

THEY WILL CEASE TO EXIST.

That was *not* an option.

Figures swam beside me. A familiar older woman I recognized from Bath's Books and Beyond. She held some sort of sea creature in her hands—a round, puffy fish the shape of a balloon.

She flapped her mouth, and an angry display of bubbles exploded around her head in a garbled collection of words I could barely make out, but that sounded like, "I forgot my son!"

More mortals surrounded us within schools of glittering fish. Another came to the old woman's side. Laguna, the book-store proprietor, if I recalled correctly. Their face was a mix of apprehension and anger.

They'd recovered their memories.

Your mortals deserve better, I called out to Anima.

One of their purple tentacles shot out and wrapped around the older woman's waist. She screamed as the god dragged her into their embrace.

MY MORTALS WILL FORGET.

I glanced at the growing crowd. Many of them were afraid, but if I'd learned anything of mob behavior during my time as a Warden, it was that all it took was one thrown brick to start a riot.

It was a risk, but I either died here a martyr, or returned to Dor redeemed.

Redemption wasn't all it was cracked up to be. Not if it made me into a soulless husk, or worse, a man like Elijah.

I kicked my feet back and swam with speed at Anima. The god's tentacles lashed through the water. I rolled to one side, but wasn't quick enough. A tentacle slammed into my side, swatting me backwards.

They didn't want me getting close, and for good reason, but that one action was enough.

I'd thrown my metaphorical brick, and now the Amnae surged forward.

They latched on to Anima's tentacles. The god writhed, attempting to whip them off. Mortals were flung into the depths with a blank face—Anima was wiping their memories with each touch.

But as soon as one tentacle became free, two more Amnae clung on like barnacles. They crowded Anima, drowning them in a sea of mortal bodies.

This was the only chance I'd get.

Though gods help me for what I was about to do.

I swam again, this time aiming for Anima's underbelly. The god was so distracted fighting off their mortals, they didn't notice me slip underneath.

I pressed my left hand against a fleshy mound. Static electricity rippled across Anima's skin, zapping me as though I'd been hit with a taser. Gods! I recoiled, shook off my arm, and thrust my hand out again.

Agony lanced through my wrist, and my metal arm spasmed out of control. I chewed my lip raw and held on until an odd sensation tugged at me.

It beckoned me, and I followed where it led.

Voices swam in my mind. Angry, accusing voices that shouted their hurt.

My mother! yelled one. *I forgot who she was, and she died alone!*

You made me forget my own wife! Why? Why would you do that?

Those memories were mine! You had no right!

I forgot my own son! That last one belonged to the old woman.

It seemed Anima had skimmed memories from all their mortals, and they weren't best pleased.

NO! Anima screeched. *THEY ARE OUR MEMORIES! OURS!*

Their tentacles writhed once more, flinging mortals across the water. I kicked out of the way and swam back a safe distance.

A MILLENNIUM OF KNOWLEDGE! WASTED! SEE WHAT YOU HAVE UNRAVELED, QUENTIN CORINTH! YOU WILL FAIL! AND YOU WILL BECOME NOTHING!

Ooze leaked from Anima's bulbous head. Thick gray tar melted from their skin and tainted the ocean. I'd witnessed the end of a domain through Kayl's memories, where everything turned to ash. But as always, Memoria had to be different.

Instead of fading to dust, everything fizzled into that same gray tar.

Mortals swam away in panic.

I'd done this. I'd engineered their destruction.

A whirlpool opened above us, on the surface of Memoria's ocean. Once more, the waters became choppy as the whirlpool pulled in fish, debris, mortals.

Oh gods! It was sucking in everything!

And yet I remained static, unmoving. The whirlpool had no effect on me. I floated and stared as the entirety of Memoria was dragged into the whirlpool's frenzy.

Something knocked inside my mind, as though a doorway had appeared and guests were now arriving. Not Amnae. Memories belonging to mortals from other domains.

My memories.

They were locked inside my subconscious—readily transferred from Anima's mind to mine—and I now held the key to unlock them.

Everything I'd lost was behind that door. Was I ready to receive it? To cast aside the man I was and become the man of Kayl's memories? That man had witnessed unspeakable horrors... Yet still carried love in his heart.

To leave one Quentin behind and become another was a form of death. But... I'd already taken the soul of a god. There was no turning back, now.

I opened the door, and memories washed over me, singing one blessed word.

Kayl.

My darling Kayl. How could I have ever forgotten her?

It took a moment for the memories to settle and for my mind to arrange the various versions of Quentin. A new one had been added to my collection—a Quentin who longed to follow Walter Burns's footsteps as a professor of mnemonics. It wasn't a terrible vocation, but it wasn't me. The real me.

More voices flooded my mind and mingled with the Amnae. Zephyr. Leander. A mix of familiar mortals.

What took you so long! Doctor Zachery Finch trilled with indignation. *Do you understand how frustrating it is to be trapped inside another mortal's head? Very!*

Apologies, Doctor. My initial plan to take Anima and restore Kayl's memories had ended in disaster. Thank the gods she'd steered me straight. Her memories were safely tucked inside my subconscious, ready to return.

Kayl. She—*Where* was she?

I'd foolishly confessed my love to her—or the other Quentin had. But I had no time to consider the implications. Memoria was being drained.

The whirlpool still spun. Most of Memoria's mortals were now gone, and the very ocean itself was being sucked out of this domain.

I needed to leave, posthaste.

I no longer possessed my fob watch, but thanks to the combined knowledge of the Amnae and technical prowess of the Zephyr, I felt confident I could rip a hole through the fabric of aether holding the domains together and escape to Chime.

In the jumble of my memories, I'd almost forgotten Elijah's plan to destroy the city.

Elijah.

The very thought of Dor naming him a redeemer filled me with revulsion. That Dor had brought him back, allowed him to capture me, to manipulate my memories into loving him once more, kissing him...

He'd made me kill Ben.

No.

No!

The fresh memory slammed into me with the force of a steam train.

"No!" I screamed into the ocean, my garbled voice choking.

I'd ripped out his soul. *Ben.* I'd destroyed him utterly! Not Ben!

Ben, the man who'd stood by my side as my bodyguard. Ben, the man who'd confessed his apostasy before sacrificing himself to allow my escape from Kronos, and for what?

I'd damned him to a fate worse than death and not even realized.

All due to Elijah's twisted manipulation.

There's nothing you can do for him now, Doctor Finch said, his inner voice bitter.

No. There was something I could do. I could ensure Ben's soulless body was never used as fodder by Dor.

And I could fucking *obliterate* the whole lot of them. Elijah. Dor. Every cursed Diviner who still retained a soul, for what use was their souls, if they allowed *this?*

Quentin! the doctor squawked. *Don't do anything hasty!*

I'm done being polite, Doctor.

I was *done.*

I held my breath and switched my form to Chaos. The churning waters threatened to drown me. Aether static snapped from my flesh, and I channeled it around my metal fist.

It took one punch to tear a hole through the fabric of space and create a portal into Kronos. A wonderful trick.

Water swelled through the gap, forcing it to expand as the ocean flooded into Dor's domain. I rode the wave through and appeared inside Dor's clock tower, filthy dark water lapping at my feet. The portal stitched itself together, cutting off Memoria.

An entire legion of soulless Diviner surrounded me in a circle, their tasers aimed at my chest.

My breath came in shuddering gasps. Exposed to Kronos's air, my damp skin shivered, and the salt of Memoria's water stung the wounds of my back, causing my limbs to tremble all over—or perhaps that was from pure rage pumping through my blood. "Where. Is. Ben?"

No answer.

"*Where is Ben?*" I yelled.

"Look at you," came Elijah's familiar voice.

I almost retched as the sea of soulless parted and Elijah walked between them, his arms outstretched like some parody of sainthood.

The man I'd once loved. I'd shot him in the head. I'd fucking do it again. Rip out his soul and reanimate his body just to put another bullet through his skull.

"Look at the state of you." Elijah sneered. "My poor Quentin. All I ever wanted was to save your soul from sin. I've given you chance after chance. It's clear Chaos has corrupted you, but your soul can still be redeemed."

"You're no redeemer," I seethed. "Sin is a concept concocted to control mortals and make them obedient. It means nothing. Now, where is Ben?"

"Always concerned with the apostates. He's a rather big, strapping man, is Benjamin Seasons. I'll be putting him to good use, don't you fret. As for you... Our Father is a generous god. He's willing to forgive you—"

"He's not my father!" I spat.

"He's willing to forgive you if you kneel and accept him as your god. Submit, and all this unpleasantness will end."

My heart hammered so fiercely, it bruised my rib cage.

I scanned the surrounding Diviner. All trained Wardens. Twenty, at least. Most had a weapon holstered at their hip—a pistol or baton, though others carried those horrid portable soul-splitting helmets. Their tasers were primed. In a normal Diviner, there would be a margin of error—a chance to misfire or aim wide. In these soulless men, the margin of error was effectively zero. Even if I tore another portal out of Kronos, I'd made any potential escape impossible.

The alternative would likely result in the destruction of my soul, and that of any souls I carried with me. The Amnae, Leander, and Zephyr.

Submission was not an option.

You've trapped us! Doctor Finch yelled.

Emotion had brought me here—pure pain and rage. It had always been my greatest weakness. Elijah knew that. He'd been waiting for my return, so certain of it. Could I blame Chaos for my feral soul? Or had I been born under the wrong domain, like Ben? For logic and reason had long since abandoned me.

I'd wiped Anima from the universe and cleared the way for Dor. There were no gods left to challenge his reign, save Corentine.

All that was left was a few Chaos to mop up. Dor had used me and Kayl to spy on the gods and weed out potential threats, starting with the Glimmer. Allowing Chaos to traipse across the domains and claim the rest of the gods came right out of his handbook.

Now that we were done, he was preparing his final move.

To destroy the clock tower and end Chaos.

"Kneel," Elijah ordered.

I wanted to scream and rage. In my mind, I'd transformed into my Leander form and torn through the whole lot of them. Teeth and claws ripping through flesh, splattering blood.

My fangs at Elijah's throat.

No.

I wanted to smash his skull into the wall. To rupture his brain, send teeth and blood flying with the force of my metal hand.

Or turn Zephyr, and fly to the very top of this tower and claim Dor's rotten soul.

But more than all this hate and death, I wanted to find Kayl.

I wanted to restore her memories, her heart.

Though the more selfish part of me wanted to forgo that. I wanted to tell her what my other self had been brave enough to say aloud. I wanted her to know.

But I'd never deserved what I wanted, had I?

I dove to one side and yanked a pistol from a Diviner's holster. They didn't even react as I took aim with my left hand and fired.

My shot went wide, missing Elijah and hitting some other poor fool.

Elijah tutted. "Shooting me won't save you."

He was right, of course.

Apologies, Doctor. We're out of options.

I placed the barrel under my chin and pulled the trigger.

Eternity blasted through my brain.

And then there was no more.

The Bell Tolls for Thee

In order to prove my usefulness to our Father and His chosen Redeemer, I have elected to prepare a series of reports on the gods and targets of interest which could help guide our efforts within this conflict. Starting with our natural enemies: Chaos. The so-called thirteenth domain, Chaos can steal the souls of other domains, effectively destroying the soul and gaining that domain's abilities. This makes them formidable and extremely dangerous in combat situations, however, Chaos also exhibits certain weaknesses. For one, Chaos are not immune to our aether tasers and collars. For two, Chaos are still mortal. They bleed. They can be killed.
—P. Bezel, *Personal Report on Chaos*

I HAD TO HAND it to the Diviner. Their plan to blow up Chime was mighty impressive. I hated this shitty city, so watching it go up in smoke would have been fun. But, when Chime did eventually go *pop*, it would be on Mother's terms.

Babel was our domain. It was ours to reshape, not theirs.

Penny had sent another message letting me know the steamworks had been dealt with and to meet at the other end of Chime—the Golden City. I flew on up the clock tower and squeezed through the gap our little explosion had caused when we tried to catch Edana's attention. Fun times.

The Golden City remained empty. If the Diviner planned to launch an attack soon, then where were they? They weren't the kind to turn up to the party fashionably late. What was I missing?

BE ON YOUR GUARD, Mother warned. *YOUR SISTER IS CONCERNED. SHE BELIEVES DOR HAS BEEN SPYING ON HER DREAMS.*

Huh. What did Kayl know that would be of interest to Dor? Besides hiding *three fucking* god souls somewhere the Diviner could find them.

Had she created a pocket domain? That was how I managed to store and instantly transport my clothes. But how the fuck had she even learned to do that? Mesmorpheus must have taught her.

Whatever. I needed those souls, even if I had to start poking out eyes to get them. Honestly, I didn't even *want* to torture the Godless. I'd kinda grown fond of 'em. But I'd do whatever it took to free my mother.

Though first: Penny.

I found her sitting by one of the fountains in the plaza. Water was still spouting out the marble vases, but algae spots and moss were spreading from neglect. A week had passed since mortals abandoned Chime, and time was already trying to claim it.

Not on my watch.

"It's taken care of," Penny said at my approach. She still wore an aether collar around her neck. Her pet clockwork bird perched on her shoulder and made an annoying clicking.

"You found the explosives?"

"Yes. They were gathered by the upper portion of the clock tower. I've since disabled and transferred them to a safer location. I can take you to them, if you don't trust me."

Did I trust Penny?

YOU SHOULDN'T. NOT EVEN FEMALE DIVINER CAN BE TRUSTED.

Penny wasn't a normal Diviner, though. Okay, she was as meticulous and neat as the rest of them, but she had an ambitious streak more akin to that of a Glimmer. I was pretty sure she didn't get excited over trains the way Corinth did, either.

And she was far, *far* sexier.

Was there something about Diviner that both attracted and repulsed Chaos? I hated them. *Hated* them. Yet, I found Penny alluring. Kayl had the hots for Corinth.

And you fell for Dor, I told Mother.

OPPOSITES ATTRACT, DAUGHTER. DOR AND I FORGED OUR OWN PATH TOGETHER. WE WANTED TO CREATE A UNIVERSE OF OUR OWN DESIGN, COMBINING THE FORCES

OF CHAOS AND TIME. WE BIRTHED GODS. DOMAINS. THERE IS PLEASURE IN CREATION. THEN HE BETRAYED ME.

I WILL TAKE PLEASURE IN HIS DESTRUCTION.

Maybe the daughters of Chaos were idiots, too.

"I'm good," I replied to Penny, before I totally lost my thread of thought. "Though, where are all the Diviner? You'd think they'd be guarding this place."

"I couldn't possibly tell you. With this, I have no means of spying on their movements." She tapped the aether collar. "But from what intel I stole on my way out of Kronos, it seems Karendar has been retaining Wardens on standby because of Corinth. Karendar is particular. He'll strike at the right moment."

"What's Karendar's deal with Corinth, anyway? Why not just zap his soul and be done with it?"

"They were lovers." Penny shrugged. "Sometimes, even Diviner let emotions get the best of them. We're still mortal."

Those who still had a soul, anyhow, and I wasn't convinced Karendar had been born with one. I tossed Corinth's pocket watch in my hand. "I've got the key to breaking into Kronos."

"What is that? A fob watch?"

"Corinth's. He programmed it to open portals." And what perfect timing. When Dor launched his attack, I'd use the distraction to rescue Corinth. Assuming he hadn't had his soul split already.

Then we'd bring all the gods souls together.

And Mother would finally be free.

THEY'RE HERE! Mother screeched. *DIVINER HAVE SURROUNDED THE CLOCK TOWER. MOVE WITH HASTE, DAUGHTER.*

The party was about to begin. "Diviner have turned up down below. Probably isn't safe to wait around here, either." I eyed Penny. If Karendar or his minions caught her, she'd be fucked. "I can bring you inside the clock tower, where they can't reach you."

Penny stood and straightened her skirt. "Absolutely not. Do you think me some weak woman who requires shelter? Bring me to Central Station. I can spy on them from there."

"Your life will be in danger. You know that, right?"

She flashed a sly smile. "When is it not?"

When she looked at me like *that*, how could I refuse?

Right, my new plan: get Penny down to Central, see what those fucking Diviner were up to, and then pop on over to Kronos for tea, crumpets, and a whole load of chaos.

"We'll take the elevator down." It would give me a sneak preview of Dor's forces on the way. They'd likely know someone had sabotaged the explosives in the steamworks by now and would be readying their plan B or C. At least, I *would*.

Diviner were twats, but they weren't amateurs.

We jogged over to the glass elevator. Despite our blowing up the entrance, the elevator had escaped most of the damage and had been parked here, unused, all this time. I'd considered dropping it to Central and smashing it to smithereens, but we'd already pulled off that trick once, and I so hated to repeat myself.

Carefully, we squeezed through the remaining gap and popped into the elevator. It swayed slightly, but held. Clothes were still scattered inside alongside piles of dust and abandoned copies of last week's Courier. Imagine what the headlines would be now—CHAOS REIGNS SUPREME! I'd even give an interview.

Penny strode to the window, stepping over dust that likely belonged to a Glimmer, judging by the outfit beside it. "How will you operate this? Someone blew up the control panel."

"It can't be that fucking hard." One bolt of aether would get it moving.

I changed to my Chaos form and summoned static electricity around my fingers. It burst around me in a cocoon of energy, filling the space.

The elevator rattled for a few seconds, the aether lights blinking.

And then the entire elevator dropped.

It fucking *plummeted*!

Penny screamed and was thrown backwards. I rushed over and caught her before she hit her head on a chair.

Time slowed around us. A bubble that surrounded the entire elevator and stopped us from hurtling down too quickly.

"I thought that collar blocked your abilities?" I ran my finger across the metal joint where the collar locked. "How are you slowing time?"

Penny leaped from my arms, her silver cheeks a lovely shade of Ember. "I modified the collar's design, of course. While I don't want Dor to find me, I couldn't leave myself vulnerable. I thought you could control the elevator?"

"I got it moving, didn't I?"

She tutted. "That's one way of describing it. I can only hold time for so long, so please—try not to kill us both." She brushed strands of brass-brown hair from her eyes, her fingers trembling a little.

"I'm Chaos, I can't make any promises. Admit it. That got your blood pumping."

"Plunging to one's death would get anyone's blood pumping, I'm sure." She faced the glass window, placing her hand on the pane to steady herself.

The elevator rattled down the clock tower at an infuriatingly slow pace. Infuriating when I could turn Fauna and fly down quicker.

"Anyone's?" I approached and leaned against the window next to her. Central was still far enough away, the buildings like tiny little blocks I could squash with my fist.

Penny turned to me again with that cheeky smile. The one I wanted to bite. Taste.

She'd kissed me back in the Undercity.

All right, she'd kissed my damn hand, but that was a signal as clear as any, wasn't it? What would Kayl do? Go for it? Gossip with Sinder over wine? If Kayl hadn't turned up at the clock tower, then maybe we could have explored it. Maybe we could have gone further.

Fuck it. I still had time.

"Do Diviner ever take chances?" I asked. "Or is everything running by a rule book? What you eat, how you dress, who you... fuck?"

"If you're speaking of arranged marriages, then yes, they are standard in Diviner society. There are so few women that we're effectively paired off. Men have more freedom to dally."

Like Karendar and Corinth? "Women have no choice in it?"

"Not really, no."

"That's shit."

"An understatement. Though... many women seek comfort with one another on the side."

"Oh?" My brows shot up. "You already know what it means to sin, don't you?" The little harlot!

Her cheeks flushed again. "How can one understand sinners without indulging in sin?"

"You're so prim and proper, I'm having a hard time imagining it." I brushed my knuckles down her cheek. Fuck, her skin was so soft, even along the bumps of her scars.

She grasped my hand, stopping me, and the smile left her lips. Had I hurt her? Was it her scars?

Something gold flashed amid the city skyline.

Those immortal brass clockwork fuckers gathered in Central below. Hundreds of them. Even from this height they were easy to spot thanks to their size and shiny brass bodies. Fuck. Dor was bringing out the big guns like he never had before. Was his plan B to rip the clock tower apart, piece by piece?

I needed to get back and prepare a better defense. "We've got company. It's too dangerous to reach the station now. We're better off barricading ourselves inside the tow—"

Penny pressed her lips against mine.

Aether exploded from my skin, causing the elevator to jolt sharply. Penny jumped, her mouth opening to my tongue. Fuck, she tasted like I'd always hoped—sweet as berries, and not metal like I'd expected.

She rose on tiptoes, wrapping her arms around my neck, deepening the kiss.

I pulled back. "I want you," I breathed on her lips.

Her eyes brimmed with lust. "Then take me."

Fuck!

I DO NOT ADVISE THIS, DAUGHTER, Mother warned. *SHE IS A PRETTY DISTRACTION, NOTHING MORE.*

Maybe that was what I wanted.

DOR'S ARMY GATHERS!

I don't give a fuck! I pushed Mother from my mind—the only time I ever had—and sucked on Penny's neck, above the collar.

She responded to my touch with a groan and tilted her head, letting me get closer. Though, fuck, that shitty collar was getting in the way. I worked at the top buttons of her blouse as she shrugged off her jacket. We had, what, ten minutes before this elevator came crashing down?

It wouldn't be the only thing arriving.

I popped the last button and ripped open her blouse, exposing a fucking gorgeous pair stuffed modestly in a lacy cream bra. I loved breasts, their mood and shape. Couldn't help myself. They were the only thing the gods had done right. Didn't care if they were small or large, though Penny's were perfectly hand-sized.

Just... *perfect*.

She reached behind her back and undid her bra as I slipped the straps from her shoulders, pulling it free. My hand rested against the glass, holding us both steady, as the other cupped her breast and squeezed. The skin of my palm lightly grazed her hardening nipple.

God, I'd give up a domain or two for *this*.

I bent, lowering my mouth to her breast while holding her waist. Penny's hips bucked, those delicate lips releasing oh so many sweet moans and sighs as my tongue encircled her nipple, switching between flicking and sucking. She jumped as I nipped it with my teeth. *Really* couldn't help myself.

The elevator suddenly jolted. Penny's hold of time slipped.

She gasped and yanked it steady. "Sorry," she murmured. "Got distracted there for a moment."

What would kill us quicker? If I licked out her cunt? Or if she got down to mine?

I wasn't sure we could survive her orgasm from this height, but I was dripping wet.

Really though, I wanted to see a Diviner on their knees.

I pushed her down. Her silver eyes widened in surprise, but she kneeled as we swapped places, ever the dutiful Diviner. I didn't even need to tell her what to do, she just *knew*.

Yep, she'd used that tongue of hers before.

Who knew Diviner women were so damn filthy?

I leaned against the window and lifted both my skirt and leg, giving her easier access.

That first lick could have taken my soul. Her tongue was *everything*.

Edana had been a good fuck, but this? This was something else. A technique only a mortal could create. Penny worked her tongue with methodical precision, exactly like a Diviner would, I guessed. But there was something about watching Penny on her knees, her tits out, her eyes fluttering as she busied herself with my pleasure.

Behind that prim and proper exterior was a slut. Was that what Kayl saw in Corinth?

What Mother had seen in Dor?

It fucking set me alight.

One, two fingers pumped inside me, stroking that oh so magical spot. Static bounced off my skin as Penny took me over the edge. The elevator screeched with my moans, and we plummeted again.

Fuck!

I wrapped an aether shield around us and pulled Penny up into my arms, bracing for impact. A second later, we crashed into Central Station.

We slammed against the floor. The glass window exploded into hundreds of flying shards. They bounced off my shield, but I held Penny close to my chest, just in case.

"Have—Have we stopped?" Penny asked.

I lifted my head. We'd landed right in Central.

The elevator's door was bent out of shape and completely unusable, but the window was wide open, shards of glass scattered everywhere. I stood, bringing Penny up with me.

A line of Diviner waited outside, their tasers aimed at the elevator.

Things were about to get a lot messier.

"Wait here," I told Penny, and headed for the window. My own juices had leaked down my leg, but whatever, I wasn't ashamed of how I looked or smelled.

Diviner surrounded the clock tower, and behind them hulked more of those clockwork figures.

But there, standing directly ahead of me with a smarmy grin, was Karendar.

What did that fucking prick want?

"You know how to make an entrance," he called, amused.

The first time we'd met was when he split my soul from Kayl. His mistake. I climbed out the window, careful to avoid catching the broken glass. "You know how to make an exit. Is Corinth not around to give you another one?"

That brought on a sneer. It hadn't taken long.

CAREFUL, DAUGHTER, Mother warned.

I'm not scared of this twat. "Quite an impressive number you've brought with you." I whistled at the crowd. "Are you compensating for something?"

"A Diviner is prepared for all possibilities. All possible outcomes. Did you really believe we'd destroy the clock tower with something as mundane as explosives? Miss Bezel? You may come out now."

What?

I snapped a glance over my shoulder.

Penny had quickly dressed and now hurried to Karendar's side.

He held out his hand, and she slipped him Corinth's pocket watch. Fuck. I hadn't even noticed her take it. The collar... She'd lied to me.

She may as well have slapped my fucking face. "Why?" I spluttered. "They've been abusing you!"

Penny avoided my eye, though her cheeks were red, her hair and clothes in a state. "He's my god."

That one simple fucking statement.

I WARNED YOU, Mother said.

They carved insults into her goddamn face! They treat her like a second-class citizen, all because she was born a woman! I should have taken her soul.

I should have freed her.

SHE IS DIVINER. HER LOYALTY IS TO DOR, NO MATTER HIS TRANSGRESSIONS. SHE HAS BETRAYED YOU. DO NOT PITY HER.

Another betrayal.

But this one hurt. It really fucking hurt.

"Quentin's fob watch." Karendar examined the watch. "I recognize the design. Interesting." He placed it in his upper jacket pocket. "Seasons? Please deal with Miss Bezel."

A large Diviner stepped out from the crowd. An absolutely massive man. Shit, I recognized him. Wasn't he Corinth's old bodyguard? His face had that blank soulless look.

He grabbed Penny's arm and roughly shoved her to the ground.

"No!" Penny screamed. "You agreed to spare me! I whored myself out for *you*!"

Karendar looked down on her with contempt. "We appreciate your sacrifice."

She lowered her head and sobbed quietly.

The Warden, Seasons, held a helmet in his hand.

A portable soul-splitting machine.

Penny may have fucked me over, but she didn't deserve that.

I switched to my Glimmer form. A burst of blinding sunlight hit Penny before she had a chance to scream. I let a whole wave of light blast over the Diviner, burning them to ash, stopping only at Karendar.

I'd left a smoldering line of charred feet in my wake. The remaining Diviner didn't even blink. Not even Corinth's old bodyguard, who stood there holding that helmet like an idiot.

Penny was nothing more than a shadow. I'd obliterated her in the blink of an eye. Dor could bring her back and finish off the job, but I'd bought her time. Was it mean of me to burn her? Maybe. She kinda deserved it, though.

Karendar brushed stray ash from his jacket, completely unfazed.

I pointed a glowing finger at him. "I'll burn you next."

"Go ahead. You'll find it changes nothing. Though I'm disappointed the only trick you have is a few sparkly lights."

"That's where you're wrong." I snapped my fingers.

My mortals appeared around me. Groups of Glimmer, Necro, Fauna, Ember. All ready to tear and burn through the Diviner. I may not have the Umber and Leander to fight with us, but I still had the advantage.

Though with an unlimited number of mortals on each side, this battle could drag on for eons. I needed this distraction to reach Karendar and get that damn pocket watch back.

And then I could finally take Dor and end this for good.

"Is that how you expect this to go?" Karendar said. "How insipid." He raised his hand like some shitty Glimmer preacher about to recite a sermon. "You have been judged and found wanting."

"Chaos is immune to your time tricks, idiot."

"You are," he agreed, matter-of-fact.

The clock tower struck one. A single *dong* echoed throughout the city, a signal to battle. Above, the sky rumbled with thunder.

Oh fuck!

Dor's hands reached through a portal, then his head. His long white beard dangled from the sky, peppered with streaks of lightning. What was he going to do? Shake the clock tower with those massive hands?

DOR! Mother screamed inside my head. *STOP HIM!*

If Dor wanted to come here and expose himself to Chaos, that was fine by me!

I swapped to my new phoenix form—red wings and all—and flew up.

Time shuddered around me.

We were caught in a bubble of time. Not only the clock tower. All of Central.

Fuck.

All of Chime.

The hair on the back of my neck stood on end as time leaped forward.

My clothes disintegrated in a heartbeat, leaving me naked. Below, my mortals cried out in alarm and confusion. Time was rushing forward, aging everything caught within it.

Even Dor's own mortals.

I landed on a streetlamp that was beginning to rust, and stared.

In the blink of an eye, the soulless Diviner had aged into older men, their skin sagging and spotty, hair growing long and gray. They stood there, letting time wipe them out. Their own flesh peeled back, revealing their bones, and they faded into dust.

All of them except Karendar and Seasons, who remained in the safety of their own pocket of time. The only mortals spared by their god.

My mortals ran. They couldn't be touched by time, so what the fuck was Dor doing?

What was his plan?

The streetlight blew beneath me. I flew off it and landed on a roof. Chime's infrastructure was falling apart. Hundreds and hundreds of years were speeding past, causing everything to decay. Weeds pushed between the cobblestones, bloomed, and instantly died.

An Ember screamed as a building collapsed on top of them. I felt their limbs crushed inside my own gut. More and more buildings tumbled over, unable to withstand the passage of time.

"The fuck are you doing?" I yelled at Karendar.

He remained with his arms outstretched, muttering in tongues, while Dor's hands hovered in the sky.

Fucking freaks!

An almighty crack echoed above.

THE CLOCK TOWER!

I glanced up.

Shards of metal and rust began to rain from the Golden City plate.

Oh shit. Karendar had said they didn't need explosives to bring down the clock tower.

They would let it collapse on its own.

But if Dor could do this all along, why not destroy the tower from the start? Why string us along with petty battles?

DOR WANTED CHAOS TO DESTROY THE GODS. ONLY WE HAVE THE ABILITY TO TAKE THEIR SOULS AND RESHAPE THEIR ENERGY.

So, what, we did the dirty work for him?

YES. AND NOW WE ARE DONE. HE HAS CALLED TO COLLECT.

Collect *what*? Was he going to capture Chaos, split our souls, and hope that did the job? Fat chance! We were still a threat. Dor had Corinth, but Kayl and I...

Kayl was still in the tower.

Time skipped forward. Thousands of years passing in seconds. Metal fell from the upper plate in large clanking chunks, thudding into Central and sending up clouds of choking dust. I flew out of the way and sought shelter against the tower as more debris crashed down and pulverized unlucky mortals below. Each death shuddered through me, taking my breath away.

Then the tower began to peel open like a fucking banana.

I flew up, heading for the clockface. "Kayl!"

The hands of the clock fell first. A large number *V* headed right at me, and I narrowly swerved out of the way. It took everything I had to weave through the sky, dodging steel beams and fuck knows what else.

Glass shattered from the clockface.

There was Kayl, looking down, still in her Mesmer form. Her hair flapped in the wind, her face a picture of pure terror.

"Jump!" I yelled.

But she didn't hear me over the clanging and smashing of metal colliding with the station below.

I zapped back my mortals—no point leaving them to get crushed—and thrust my wings up and up, heading straight for the broken clockface.

LEAVE HER! SAVE YOURSELF.

We need Kayl!

WE WILL FIND THE SOULS SHE STOLE. IF YOU PERISH, I WILL BE AT DOR'S MERCY, AND THEN WE LOSE EVERYTHING.

But Kayl!

I couldn't leave her!

SHE CHOSE TO DISOBEY ME, TO HAND HER LOYALTY TO MORTALS INSTEAD OF OUR FAMILY. CHOOSE WHERE YOUR LOYALTY LIES, DAUGHTER. WITH ME OR YOUR SISTER.

How could you make me choose? Kayl was my heart.

SHE HURT YOU. BETRAYED YOU.

She'd done many shitty, fucked-up things. Things I could never forgive. Words neither of us could ever take back.

But she was still my sister.

I flew to the clockface. "Kayl!"

She reached out. "Jinx!"

"Jum—"

The clock tower lurched.

And then it split in half.

Kayl was flung from the clockface, her screams swallowed by the roar of the tower coming down.

I dove for her. My lungs heaving, my wings flapping harder than they ever had.

Something slammed into my side with an almighty *dong*. That fucking bell!

I spiraled down, unable to correct my flight.

Dust and wreckage pummeled me from above. I couldn't see Kayl. Shit, I'd lost her!

The entire damn clock tower crashed down on my head.

I landed with a painful thump.

More wreckage fell on top of me. Heavy lumps of metal and debris crushed my bones. I tried to crawl free, but there was so much shit falling from the sky, it pinned me down.

I couldn't breathe.

The remains of the clock tower buried me until I couldn't see anything at all.

Tick Tock

Chaos is controlled by the thirteenth god, Corentine. Unlike other gods, Corentine is effectively imprisoned, which restricts her reach. She operates through her mortals, chiefly the Chaos creature known as Jinx. This mortal is extremely dangerous and unpredictable; however, I was able to study and learn of Jinx during my operation to destroy Solaris. I believe Jinx can be controlled. It would be in our best interest to study her further. The powers she wields could be an asset in the battles to come, though this will require a delicate hand. Given my experience, I willingly volunteer my expertise.
—P. Bezel, *Personal Report on Corentine and Jinx*

FUCK. MORTALITY SUCKED.

I pushed a sheet of metal off my legs and coughed out dust. My arm hung at an unnatural angle—broken for sure. Every inch of me was bloodied and bruised. Any movement sent spasms of pain and a real horrid need to vomit.

It could be worse. My limbs were mostly intact. I was still breathing.

I switched to my Necro form and let the power of The Nameless One flow through my veins, stitching cuts and mending bones. When I felt more myself, I stood slowly.

The clock tower was gone. Shit, even the Golden City above was gone.

Chime had been utterly destroyed.

I was surrounded by dust clouds, and debris so rusted and mangled, it wasn't recognizable. Large chunks of metal were scattered across what was left of Central. Some buildings remained, but it was almost impossible to see where everything was supposed to be.

Thousands of years had passed within seconds.

The Diviner really had done it.

"Kayl?" I choked out, my throat unbearably dry.

She had to have landed close by. Gods, she had to be all right.

"Kayl!" I climbed over broken brick and shards of glass, my bare feet crunching down and rewarding my efforts with sharp cuts. I used my Necro abilities to instantly dull and heal my injuries before I remembered to summon clothes and shoes. Not a dress this time. A more practical skirt.

An awful gurgling echoed nearby. I stumbled around the round metal lump that had once been the clock tower's bell, its song permanently silenced.

Oh fuck no.

Kayl was still alive, but barely. She'd landed on a metal pole. It had impaled her torso, and blood was gushing out of her stomach.

I ran to her side. "Fuck, fuck, fuck!"

She glanced at me, her eyes already turning glossy. "Qu—en." She coughed, spitting out blood, which ran down her chin.

I placed my hand on her torso and let my healing powers flow into her skin. The blood pouring from her gut receded, but while that pole was still fucking her up, I couldn't save her.

I switched to my Glimmer form and grasped the metal, heating it until the pole snapped. Carefully, I pulled her free, and she sagged in my arms, her weight forcing me onto my knees.

Kayl drew a ragged breath.

Then her head lolled back. Her eyes stared at nothing.

No.

No, I wasn't ready to let her go!

What would happen to her soul? Could Mother rebirth her? I didn't fucking know!

"Don't you fucking die on me, you selfish bitch!" I switched back to my Necro form and gave everything I had. First, stitching the wound in her abdomen, and then caressing her heart.

Nothing happened.

Fuck! Only one power in this universe would get her heart pumping again.

Pure aether.

I changed form to Chaos and sent a jolt through her nerves.

She opened her eyes with a strangled gasp, her limbs spasming.

I wrapped my arms around her waist. "I've got you."

Kayl buried her head in my shoulder and sobbed. "I'm—I'm—"

"Alive. Don't think I'd let you die, sister." Even if her soul joined the aether, I would never *ever* let her die.

She pulled back and stared at me, blinking away tears.

Her aether eyes. Mine. My sister. My heart.

HE'S HERE! Mother shrieked.

Mother!

I pulled Kayl to her feet and summoned her an outfit identical to mine. "Dor's here. He did this. We've got to protect our mother."

She said nothing as she dressed. Once she was ready, I guided her across the debris and approached the ruins of the clock tower.

It had been reduced to a smoldering stump. On top was Mother's chair, now a throne overlooking the chaos. Somehow, the shield surrounding Mother remained intact. She was still trapped, but the wires and cables running from the back of that horrible fucking chair had been severed. There was no Chime left to power.

A figure stood before the barrier. A familiar Diviner male wearing a pristine pinstripe suit, though his hair was silver, not Karendar's bronze.

"Corinth?"

Kayl took my arm, her nails digging in. "That's not Quen."

The man had Corinth's face, though he wasn't wearing eyeglasses, and he sported a neat silver goatee.

Shit. "Dor."

I'd only ever seen him as an older male, not as this—the mortal form Mother had fallen in love with.

"My precious Corentine," he said, his voice full of affection. "How long has it been? The years have simply fallen away. I'm sorry, my dear. Your time has come." He pressed his palm against the barrier.

One by one, the chains that made up Mother's prison snapped and fell apart.

What?

All this time, I'd been gathering the gods' souls, and he'd held a master key?

When the last chain broke—the chain for the Diviner—the barrier dropped in a spark of scattering aether.

Mother sucked in a rasping breath.

The first breath she'd taken in over a millennium.

More figures appeared behind Dor. Two Chaos males.

It was Chance and Lucky. The brothers I'd lost to the Diviner. They wore matching Warden outfits, and looked practically identical, as Kayl and I did, but their souls had been ripped out.

My stomach sank.

I knew exactly why Dor had dragged them here.

Why he'd kept them all this damn time.

Mother writhed in her chair, the straps still holding her in place. She didn't have the strength yet to break free.

Dor stepped back. "Take her soul."

No!

"Mother!" I ran across the space between me and my mother.

Something zapped my arm, and I fell face first into a pile of dust. I tried to scramble up, to stand, but my limbs had turned to jelly.

Chance loomed over me. A taser in his hand.

There was nothing in his eyes. Nothing.

"That's—That's our mother, you idiot!"

He didn't even blink.

And then Lucky approached Mother's chair.

"Stop him!" I screamed at Kayl. She just stood there, staring, her mouth gaping.

I hadn't come this far just to lose my mother!

Lucky placed his hand on Mother's shoulder.

No, no, *no!*

Mother stared up at the son about to betray her, then her eyes rolled back.

Aether burst from her skin. Brilliant blue and pink aether, the colors of the cosmos. Of Chaos.

Was it over?

Was that... it?

Eleven domains had fallen. I'd been responsible for four of 'em. Condemned four gods and thousands of mortals to the aether. To a life beyond death. It had been fun while it lasted, and now it was my turn.

What would Dor do with our souls? What would become of me?

I expected to feel something. To feel the dust fall from my skin, or anything.

But as I blinked back the stars of exploding aether, a tall woman in a tight silver dress emerged from her chair. She gazed at me with Kayl's face. My face.

"My beautiful daughters."

My heart pounded.

"Mother."

My mother was finally free.

Her limbs elongated as she grew taller, towering above the ruins of Central at double my height. She snatched Lucky by the throat and lifted him off his feet. Lucky tried to reach her, to grab her arm and take her soul.

Mother grasped his hair with her other hand and pulled his head free from his neck. His spinal cord was still attached and dangled beneath, dripping with blood.

She tossed both Lucky's head and body aside.

Quick as a fucking flash, Mother appeared over Chance. She lifted him clear above her head and tore his torso in two. Blood and guts rained over her face, running down her cheeks and staining her silver dress. She bathed in its glory.

Fuck, she was *magnificent*.

Everything I'd ever dreamed her to be.

She let Chance's body collapse at her feet and licked his blood off her lips. It hurt to see Chance reduced to nothing but Dor's slave—to see him tossed into the trash like that. But that wasn't Chance anymore. He'd stopped being Chance the moment Dor ripped out his soul.

Feeling returned to my limbs, and I stood, shaking off the remaining effects of the taser. "Where the fuck did Dor go?"

That idiot had freed the catalyst of his own destruction and then up and disappeared, leaving us alone in Central. I still couldn't believe Mother stood here in front of my own eyes, but now that she did, we could finally destroy the Diviner and reclaim Babel.

"He watches," Mother said. "Let us show him what Chaos means."

The sky darkened. A crack splintered above, breaking through the space between domains, wiping away the sun and the clouds until purple stars bled through.

Aether swirled into giant nebulae. The churning power of Chaos.

Then the ground shook.

Kayl staggered to my side. "What's happening?"

I hugged her tight. "It's Babel! It's our home! Mother is bringing it back!"

Kayl looked terrified, but I'd never felt so damn giddy!

A quake shook beneath, us and the ground split.

I clung on to Kayl as the patch of Central we stood on drifted away. Chime crumbled into the void of stars, leaving islands to float around us. Other shit drifted past; half-ruined town houses, a single streetlamp, a bench, a tram with its windows blown out. They all floated on by, exactly as Mother had once shown me.

This was Babel. At long fucking last!

Chaos mortals appeared on some of the individual islands, wearing similar silver outfits. My siblings. Some I recognized from the clock tower, like Flux, but others were new. There was no Chance or Lucky, though. There never would be again.

Mother stood on the largest of the islands, floating in the heart of our domain. "What do you think, my pretty pancake?"

I nudged Kayl forward. "She means you."

Kayl's legs were trembling. "Well, you've gone and destroyed the restrooms. Where am I meant to take a shit?"

I scowled. Mother had taken back our home, had even given Kayl a cute little nickname—which was more than I had—and she couldn't show *any* fucking respect?

Mother chuckled. "Ungrateful as ever, daughter. The reign of gods has ended, yet you're still not pleased. Isn't this what you always wanted? A godless world."

Kayl chewed her lip.

"You still mourn your mortals," Mother continued. "But they were never your family. I'm your family. Your mother. I birthed you from my own aether."

"And I *so* appreciate it—"

"Show me your appreciation. Where are the souls you're hiding from me and your sister? Serenity? Unghard? Mesmorpheus? Return them to me."

Kayl lifted her chin. "Why? You've got what you wanted."

"Why?" Mother's brows rose. "Because they are mine."

"Finders keepers."

"Daughter." Mother smiled. "This isn't a request. I am your god. Do as you're told."

"Kayl!" I whispered. "Fucking do it!"

Kayl glanced at me, her eyes full of sorrow. "No. You know what Corentine will do with them—destroy them, so they'll never come back. Can you do that to Joe? To Vincent and Harm? I can't." She faced Mother. "I spent my entire life living in fear of Valeria, only to learn she was never my god. But that fear... It shapes you. It hangs over every mortal like a shadow. I became Godless so I could stare that fear in the eye and refuse to allow it power over me. You can do what you want—I can't stop you. You may own my soul, but you don't own *me*. You aren't my god. You never were."

Why did Kayl have to be so goddamn stubborn?

Mother's brow twitched. "What a disappointment you are. You're my daughter—I wanted to give you a chance. But every time, you've spat back like an impudent child. I blame myself, of course. I wasn't there to raise you and your sister, to discipline and guide where necessary. And this is the brat you've become. Perhaps what you need is a good spanking."

Kayl stepped back until her heels were at the edge of our floating island.

There was nowhere for her to run.

Static surrounded Mother, and she flew over to our island. She grabbed Kayl's wrist, twisting it behind her back. Kayl's clothes vanished, leaving her naked as the day the aether had birthed us.

Then Mother bent Kayl over her knee.

"Ungrateful child!" Mother slapped Kayl's arse *hard*, leaving a red handprint on her cheek. "I suffered an eternity for you, and this is how you repay me?"

Kayl cried out as Mother slapped her again and again.

I giggled. I couldn't help it. The sight of a grown adult getting their arse spanked sent me into hysterics, and quite frankly, Kayl deserved it.

"Where are those souls?" Mother demanded.

Kayl yelped and writhed, but still refused to answer.

"Come on, sister!" I called out. "Stop being a shithead!"

"Fuck—you!" she ground out.

Mother whacked her harder. Faster. The red marks turned to purple bruising.

Then blood.

My laughter trailed off. It wasn't funny anymore. "Kayl, please."

Mother shoved her face-first in the dirt and kneeled on her back, her kneecap digging into Kayl's spine. "Do you have any idea what torment I endured? Let me give you a taste." She grasped a chunk of Kayl's hair and ripped it out.

Kayl screamed as our mother pinned her and tore the hair clean from her scalp. She kicked out and sobbed until her head was completely bald.

I swallowed a lump in my throat. My siblings watched from their various floating islands, completely unmoved by Kayl's torment.

They didn't give a shit, so why should I?

Mother flipped Kayl onto her back. "What next? Shall I pull out your teeth?" She slapped Kayl across the face. "Take your eyes?" Another slap. "Break every bone in your fragile mortal body?" She struck Kayl so hard, her nose snapped to one side and spurted with blood.

Fuck. Mother was taking this too far!

I leaped forward and caught her wrist as she readied another blow.

Mother shoved me off. I fell backwards onto my arse, and then she was over me, her hand raised. "You dare defend her?"

"N-No, she's an idiot, but—"

"Of course you'd defend your *dear* sister. The two of you are twins. You share the same mind, the same traitorous inclinations."

"What? No, you know I'd never—"

"Except you have! You hid Kayl's mind from my reach for *thirteen* years. You kept hold of the souls you carry, even when I asked for them, begged for them, you selfish cunt—"

"You can have them! They're yours!" I hastily shuffled back.

What was happening? I didn't understand.

"You *fucked* a Diviner. The pair of you. Disgusting. How could you betray me like that when you knew what Dor did to me?" Mother prowled toward me, leaving Kayl to roll to her knees and pant.

"I—I'm sorry!" Tears filled my eyes, and I blinked them away. "Mother, I love you! You know I do! I did all this for *you*!"

"You did nothing for me. You're a waste of aether." Mother slapped me across the face.

I recoiled, my palm instantly covering the sting of her touch. "Mo-Mother?"

The spark in her eyes turned cold, dead like a Diviner's. How had this turned so wrong? What had I done to upset her? She was my mother, she was—she was supposed to love me!

"Give me your souls," Mother demanded.

"Don't," Kayl groaned.

"The pair of you can suffer in my place." Mother grabbed my neck and squeezed.

Electricity zapped my skin. Fuck! It burned through my veins worse than a taser, my limbs flailing.

"It hurts!" I screamed. I writhed in her grip, but she didn't let go.

It was fire boiling my blood from the inside out.

I was dying. Gods. I was going to *die*.

"This is what I endured for thousands and thousands of years. Do you understand my pain now, daughter?"

"Mother, please stop! I'm sorry! *Stop it!*"

"Do you understand your own selfishness?" Mother laughed. A hacking, cold laugh. "All mortals are the same. They beg when it hurts them, when it pleases them. This is what you deserve."

I clenched Mother's arm to pry her free, to make her *stop*! If I could calm her down, she'd see we were loyal—misguided, maybe, but loyal!

My siblings watched, not a flicker of emotion passing over their faces, as though they were soulless, Diviner-cursed machines.

We were Chaos! We felt things! We *lived*. We...

Something tugged in my palm.

No.

No, no, no!

My instincts followed the tug—they latched on to the source of our pain, desperately wanting it to end. "No!" Tears ran down my cheeks. "Mother!" Agony burned my skin black, but she wouldn't listen.

Only the sweet release of that tug would make her *stop*.

Aether pulsed between us. Mother hissed and flung me aside as though she'd been stung.

I landed in a pile of dirt.

Kayl crawled over to me. "What did you do?"

I chewed my lip and squeezed my eyes shut.

No.

I couldn't have. I fucking couldn't have!

"Well," Mother said, calm returning to her voice. "I see I was right. Mortals really are a waste of aether."

"Oh shit," Kayl breathed.

I forced my eyes open, though I knew what I'd see.

Dust fell from Mother's skin.

She smirked at me. Manic. And yet, there was pride in her gaze. "You cunt."

I pulled myself to my knees, my breath coming in heaving gasps, my chest torn in two. I'd fucked it. I'd fucked *everything*. "I'm s-sorry! I love you!"

"Love." Mother tutted. "What mortal understands the infinite concept of love? Enjoy the ruins of what you've earned. You'll find godhood to be a disappointing experience."

"I don't want this! How do I fix it?" I stood on shaking legs. "There has to be a way! How do I bring you back?"

"You don't." Mother's voice came out bitter and cold. "I've had enough of this. Of *you*."

Her words eviscerated me.

They may well have.

Color drained from the sky. The purple stars turned gray. I frantically scanned the islands for my siblings, to see if they could save us, but they were already gone. Reduced to dust and returned to my mind.

There were so few Chaos mortals, and they barely spoke.

Only... *Always knew you were a fuck-up,* said Flux.

Jinx! Kayl screamed inside my head.

Oh fuck. That *was* her voice, and yet she still sat beside me. Why hadn't she returned to me, like the others had? I could feel her soul, but... it was guarded. Shielded by Valeria, still?

Kayl pinched my arm, and I glanced up.

Dor stood on one of the floating isles with an entourage of Diviner, including the big one—the bodyguard. Why had Dor returned? To gloat? Finish us off?

Mother brushed dust from her skin, so nonchalantly, it hurt my gut. "You got what you wanted in the end, didn't you, dear?"

Dor inclined his head in a respectful bow. "It saddens me. The pantheon has lost one of their greats."

"Oh, please. Don't act like you care when you orchestrated this from the start. You'll spend your eternity as a lonely old man. Not even your mortals will please you."

"They never did."

"Tell me one thing: did you truly envision this end? Or was it all a lie?"

"Your children were always destined to end you." Dor smiled. "I merely helped them along."

Mother rolled her eyes.

And then she exploded into a constellation of pink and blue stars.

"Mother!" I screamed. I tried to reach her, but Kayl held me back.

She kept me from teetering over the edge, as she always did.

Dor glanced at me with contempt. "Take them both."

The Diviner leaped down onto our floating island and advanced.

I couldn't move.

I didn't want to.

Kayl grabbed my shoulders. Blood smeared her face from where Mother had smashed her nose and ripped her hair out. "Jinx, we need to get out of here. I have a safe place we can go, but I need you to reach it—I don't have the power to open a portal."

I placed my hand over hers and let my form switch to Necro. Before she could even question me, I sent a healing burst of energy through her, enough to fix her nose and sprout hair across her head. "Then go, sister."

Four domains gathered in my subconscious. The Glimmer, Necro, Fauna, and Ember. Four gods. Four domains full of mortals.

They weren't mine. I didn't want them anymore.

I returned to my original form. The one I was born as. Chaos.

Then I shoved my wayward souls into Kayl. It turned out transferring godly power was easy, when you had the right recipient.

She gasped and stumbled back. "What have you done?"

"What you wanted. Now, fucking *go*!" Aether static gathered around my fingers.

My mother was gone. But I'd buy my sister some time.

Time.

I fucking *hated* time.

The Diviner pointed their tasers and fired. Fucking pricks.

It stung. Each shot was a little bite into my skin.

One of 'em tried to push past me, to shoot Kayl.

I charged into him and bit his neck. A Necro's fangs would have been more effective, but I didn't give a shit. I screamed and kicked and bit until the next taser shot me down.

As my vision darkened, I caught Kayl out of the corner of my eye. She'd managed to tear a hole in the space between domains. A portal. She'd somehow summoned an actual portal.

I always knew you had it in you, I whispered into her mind.

I'll come back for you, Kayl replied. *I promise.*

I didn't believe her. Why should she? After everything we'd been through together?

When it was always meant to end this way?

One of us had to live, to bring the Diviner down. It had to be Kayl.

The Diviner wrapped a collar around my neck, cutting off her voice. They didn't want to split my soul right away. Maybe I was in for some old-fashioned torture. Diviner loved that shit.

Pain spasmed through my spine once more.

And my mind fell to the toll of a clock.

Tick.

Tock.

XLI

There is much speculation on what it means to die. Death is the final destination for a mortal life. One cannot know the exact time or nature of one's death, and death itself is the purview of one's own god. The nature of death and the afterlife is different for each domain.
But where does the soul come from?
Each mortal soul is created by one's god. Your soul contains the energy—the aether—of your god, willingly given. That is why a mortal is made in the image of their god, and why the essences of two gods cannot be merged. Your god sacrificed a piece of themself for you. I can think of no greater love.
—H. Bezel, Philosophy for the Young Diviner

I'D DIED. AGAIN.

TRULY, death wasn't as terrifying as one would believe. Once you were gone, that was it. There was very little to worry about, and certainly no need to worry oneself with the mundane or the impossible. Had I left the stove on when I left my apartment? Had I remembered to wear matching shoes? Had society finally collapsed, leading to the destruction of all gods, mortals, and their domains? Trivial concerns, really.

None of it mattered anymore.

I floated in the blissful nothingness between domains, cradled by stars and silence. I was dead, but my mind conjured up a facsimile of my physical body. It was naked, yet it did not feel anything—no temperature, no wind. Nothing. It curled into itself. Its natural state.

Only... it was missing its right arm.

Vaguely, I recalled losing it in a past life. How interesting, that in death, my residual limb had become a part of me as surely as my terrible vision. As though the blueprint that made up 'me' had been updated, and this was now the default.

Enough aether soaked around me that I had the power to fix both. But... did they need fixing? They were simply facts. Aspects of my body I'd learned to accept. Perhaps my flawed vision was meant to keep me humble. And perhaps the aches and pains of my residual arm served as a reminder I had once been mortal, with a mortal body that hurt and bled.

A mortal body that had died. Many times.

Mortals were made in the image of their god, bound to the laws of chaos and time. If chaos were to end, then mortals would lose their free will. The creative spark that made all mortals individual and flawed. If time were to end, then mortals would effectively become immortal—they would never age or die.

As the great Diviner masters of the Academy would say, time was a teacher, a healer, and a gatekeeper. Only saints earned the promise of eternal servitude, and I was no saint. The rest of us needed to age and wither, for that was the path to progress. Without time, society would stagnate. That simply would not do.

To die, then, was to allow the next generation to step forth. To live beyond one's mortal means—except in the case of saints—was frowned upon.

By remaining in death, I lived—or died—in accordance with societal norms.

Should society continue to exist.

So that begged the question—who owned my soul in death? If my soul had been cast from the gods, for Dor surely didn't own me and Corentine no longer spoke to me, then whose aether did I swim amid? The very energy I bathed in felt familiar in a way my addled mind failed to recognize, and yet oh so different. It conjured more questions.

If Dor and Corentine had created the gods, then who'd created *them*?

And what lay beyond the white space between domains?

Was that where I found myself?

I supposed I'd never know.

Really now, none of these questions actually mattered. Not when this was the end.

Blissful nothingness.

Or at least, it would be blissful, if my mind would shut up.

The downside to death was it was a lonely place. There were no other mortals here to converse with. No one to listen to my philosophical ponderings. No god to cradle me in their arms.

There never had been, had there?

No god who ever cared for my pitiful soul. No mother. No father.

No one.

Lights blinked within the aether. The stars vibrated. Something was disturbing them, but what? Gods, don't let me be reborn again! I'd had enough of reality!

A black void sucked the stars away in a darkened silhouette. The figure of a woman.

And then a woman appeared before me. A naked woman with silvery blue skin and shocking white hair. Chaos.

"Quen!" She screamed my name and reached for me.

I blinked, and then everything rushed back.

"Kayl?"

The woman I loved. The woman I'd left behind. But how could she be here? Unless she'd also... No!

I swam through the aether to reach her, grab her, yet I didn't move an inch. How did one swim through the endless constellation of eternal death?

But then she vanished as quickly as she'd appeared.

That was good, wasn't it?

Fucking sod it!

I had to get back. Kayl needed me, and I was being a selfish prat enjoying my restful oblivion. But I was *dead*. No god had recalled me. Not Dor or Corentine.

Hello? Corentine, if you can hear me, please answer! I prayed.

There was nothing but the hum of the void. Had I shielded myself so successfully from Chaos that I was no longer attuned to it? I concentrated on the aether clouds surrounding me, and they slowly came into focus.

Oh my.

There were souls among the stars. Thousands of them. Tiny things compared to the space we occupied, swimming with no rhyme or reason and blinking with a multitude of colors. Zephyr. Leander. Amnae. They were gathered around my being as though I'd been stabbed and they'd bled out of me.

They were my souls.

But who was I?

I was of all of them, as they had become all of me. I examined my remaining hand. It wasn't the color of Chaos or Diviner, but a gold, almost tan color. And, rather oddly, I was suddenly wearing my Warden's uniform. Black and bronze.

Oh my gosh. I'd absorbed the aether of the domains and transformed it into something else, something new. A new god. Born of what I'd always been, deep down.

The Dark Warden.

If I could only laugh in death!

That accursed title had haunted me for years, and yet it fit the man I'd become. Only the Dark Warden would kill gods to protect their mortals. Only the Dark Warden would transgress life and death on an unholy quest to uphold the values of the Covenant.

I'd never wanted to become a Warden, but Dor had seen it.

He knew my path.

My duty to Chime and her mortals was not over yet.

I scooped the stars into my arms, gathering the many souls I was sworn to protect. With their aether, I'd rebirth myself as the Dark Warden.

Then I would save their universe.

With a *pop* I arrived back in Chime. It wasn't quite how I'd left it.

Both I and the city had been reborn. I stood on the concourse of Central Station as Diviner milled around me, queuing for the crossing. They drank tea from the kiosk or sat in the waiting room, reading the Chime Courier. They didn't even notice me, for I'd finally learned how to rebirth myself with actual sodding clothes. To them, I looked like any Diviner, in my tan suit, brass spectacles, and of course my metal arm.

Though to me, something was distinctly off about them. Something wrong.

The station had been fully restored to how I remembered it. As had the Gate.

The portal was currently set to Kronos. Above it sat the clock tower, which loomed over Chime and connected to the Golden City above. The hands of the clockface were set between twelve and one. Nothing looked out of place. In fact, it smelled distinctly sterile, instead of the usual trash and grime that tainted the city.

It was perfect. Too perfect.

Chime had been in ruins.

Had I accidentally traveled to the past, somehow?

Or the future?

Finally! Doctor Finch squawked in my mind. *Do you know how irresponsible it is for you to go flapping between dimensional states? Who knew what would have become of you—of us!*

Apologies, Doctor. I can't promise it won't happen again. Not now that I knew I could embrace death and quite literally rebirth myself. *The important thing is that you and Ilona are safe.* Ilona was also tucked into my subconscious, where I could finally fulfill my promise to her father.

Yes. Well. Safety is a matter of definition.

Indeed. And once it was safe to do so, I'd rebirth the good doctor, Ilona, Dandelion, Lyonelle and her cubs.

I'd do what I'd sworn to.

But first, I had to find Kayl. I needed to know she was safe.

A Diviner bumped into me. They wandered off without apology or acknowledgement.

Rude, the doctor said.

Not just rude. A Diviner would never be so impolite!

Oh fuck.

They weren't Diviner.

They wore the faces of Diviner and went about their business with clockwork precision, as though operating on preprogrammed commands befitting Guardians made of cogs and gears. But they *were* mortal, if you could call them that.

None of them had a soul. Every single mortal in the station was a soulless being. Their movements were all an act, a puppet show, though where was the master pulling their strings?

Sadly, my erratic, not-soulless movements had been noted.

A group of Wardens approached across the concourse and surrounded me in a circle, their tasers aimed. Each had the face of a Diviner male, but their expressions were slack, their eyes vacant. Acting on the command of Dor.

No, not Dor. I wasn't that lucky.

"Quentin."

Elijah stood at the head of the Wardens, next to Ben, who acted as his bodyguard. Ben being paraded this way made me swallow bile.

Though nothing revulsed me more than Elijah's hateful brass eyes.

This wasn't the past or future.

It was something else entirely.

Elijah opened his arms. "Welcome back to Chime."

Part Four

42

My god's dead. My god's dead! I—I don't know what I'm supposed to think or feel or say, but the Mesmer tell me I don't need to think or feel or say anything. What do I feel? Scared? Elated? I... I always hated having a god listening to my thoughts and prayers, like I always had to be careful what I thought, you know? But now you're telling me... I can think what I want? Feel what I want? Say what I want? So what am I supposed to think? Or feel? Or say? I don't know where to begin.
—Anonymous, *overheard in Haven*

CORENTINE WAS GONE, AND I was still standing.

I couldn't wrap my head around it.

Through sheer panic, desperation, adrenaline, and dumb pissing luck, I'd somehow managed to tear a hole between domains and stumble through to Haven. The portal or whatever it was had closed behind me, as though the wound I'd torn in the universe magically stitched itself together, but not before giving me one last look at Jinx.

At my sister.

The Diviner had swarmed her. Shot her with tasers and then collared her. For one brief terrifying moment, I'd feared they'd rip out her soul, but no, they wanted her alive for reasons I didn't understand.

And so I still stood, my mortal body continuing to exist.

Jinx had become my personal god, as she'd always threatened to. Her voice had spoken in my mind. But since I'd arrived in Haven, she'd gone silent.

Jinx? Do you hear me?

The collar must have cut her off from me.

She'd taken Corentine's soul. How was I still standing? How was my soul intact, when my Chaos siblings had faded to dust?

My feet brought me to the memorial meadow. The others avoided coming near. I liked to think they didn't want to disturb the ground out of respect, but it was more likely due to the literal bodies buried underneath.

No other domain buried their dead. They never had to.

A soft breeze caressed the flowers, spreading their sweetness throughout the meadow. I sat on the bench that had become mine and Quen's, my hand resting on the space he'd last appeared, as I stared at the stars twinkling above.

For one brief moment, I'd died. I'd fallen into the aether of the universe and found Quen there, waiting for me, which meant he'd died, too. Maybe Dor had finally gotten sick of him. It didn't matter. I'd failed to save Quen—another broken promise—and now I couldn't find his soul among the stars. What if Dor had taken his soul? What if I'd lost him forever?

Gods. I couldn't bear it.

Entire domains crushed my shoulders. Thousands upon thousands of souls. I couldn't carry this burden anymore.

Jinx had surrendered the Glimmer, Necro, Fauna, and Ember to me, as well as the Godless. It should have felt like a victory, yet their souls sat heavy in my gut.

There was a home for them all in Haven, but would they be happy? Would they get on? Would it be better to create a new version of Chime without their domains, their gods? That was the goal, wasn't it? To end the reign of gods. We'd achieved it, as we'd promised Mesmorpheus, though...

We'd lost the Amnae, the Leander, the Zephyr. They'd died with Quen.

The Vesper, too, would remain trapped inside me forever.

We were stuck here. I'd always hoped to restore the twelve domains, to bring everyone home without their shitty gods. This didn't feel like a victory. It didn't feel right.

Dor remained out there, beyond Haven. He'd find us eventually, and then the fight would start again. While he had Jinx in his grasp, the fight hadn't ended.

She'd sacrificed herself for me, and I couldn't even feel gratitude for that.

I'd lost my sister. Lost the love of my life.

Not to mention Cosmo, and Autumn, and the other lost souls.

They were gone, yet I was still standing and that wasn't *fair*.

Hey, lady, said a familiar male voice inside my mind. *If you're going to wallow in self-pity, why don't you let me out first so I can have a smoke?*

Gast? Of all mortals to come knocking at my subconscious, why did it have to be him?

Your guilty conscience, maybe?

I had more than my fair share to feel guilty about, and plenty of mortals I owed an apology. I supposed there was no better place to start making amends than with Mortimer Gast.

His soul lingered in the darkest reaches of my subconscious. Fitting. I drew him out, and he appeared naked before me. I summoned clothes and averted my eyes as he got dressed and then sat on the bench beside me.

"Interesting place you've got here." He pulled a packet of cigarettes out of his jacket pocket that I'd generously put there, and he went through the practiced motions of picking a cig out and placing it between his lips. "Got a light?"

I switched to an Ember form and summoned a spark to my fingertip.

"Cheers." He took a deep drag and let out a line of smoke. "Want one?"

"No, thank you."

"I've gotta say, lady, times have been interesting lately. Knowledge is my bread and butter, yet I've learned things these past few weeks I never wanted to learn. Things I'd rather scrub from my brain. You know?"

"I know."

"Way I see it, everything's fucked. All I wanted to do was get the Vesper back. Shit, I'd welcome the end if I could get them back. That's never going to happen, is it?"

I hugged my chest. "I'm sorry. I'm out of solutions."

Gast shook his head and chuckled. "Almost every gods-damn domain, rebirthed and brought here. And still no Vesper. Is Noct safe?"

Ah, that was the real reason he was cozying up to me, the big softie. I'd seen flashes of Noct's memories, enough to know he and Gast were close. Partners, though not in the same sense as Quen and me. A Necro and a Seren made an odd pair. "He's here, somewhere."

"He's a little shit at times, but I feel some sort of responsibility for him, as I'm sure you do your Godless." Gast offered me the packet of cigarettes. "Sure I can't tempt you? Not many sins left in the universe."

It was a disgusting habit, but so was I, truth be told. "Might as well."

We sat in companionable silence for a moment as I lit up and took my first drag in years. Smoking wasn't for me. It tasted far too foul compared to other, more pleasurable vices. There was a time when Sinder and Vincent smoked often, and even Dru gave it a try—arguing it was okay to try a plant-based substance, before giving it up—but Harmony couldn't stand the smoke. It irritated her smaller Seren lungs, so we'd quit for her. Though her singing voice sounded like she smoked ten packs a day, anyhow.

"Funny thing," Gast said. "I investigated the rumors of those electrical monsters back in the Undercity. Never expected it would lead to all this. Some cases I should have never touched, but I can't help myself. I see a damsel in distress, and I've gotta step up."

I cocked my head. "Is that what I am now? A damsel in distress?"

"I call it like I see it." He let out a cloud of smoke. "Why haven't you brought the Godless back? They're your team, and you need them."

Was this about the Vesper? Did Gast think the Godless could help me bring them back? Or did he see a pathetic woman in need of his counsel? Confessing to him couldn't make things worse.

"We're Godless, and I've become their god. What if they're scared of me? Don't trust me? I share the same face as my twin, and she practically tortured them. I wouldn't blame them for hating me."

"You freed them from Jinx. Why would they hate you for that?"

Because I'd fucked up.

Because this wasn't how it was meant to go.

I'd wanted nothing more than to save my family, to reunite them. I'd gone to all this pissing effort, even as Jinx had thwarted me at every turn.

But I'd failed to protect them from her. Failed to protect Cosmo, Quen...

Would my family be proud of all I'd done?

I sucked on my cigarette to avoid answering the question.

"Mortals don't trust a Necro PI," Gast continued. "Even a man with my handsome face. But they came to me for help because they were desperate, because they had no other choice. And then you Godless came along. Damn near put me out of a job."

I summoned an ashtray before he got ash all over my meadow. "You probably helped more mortals than we ever did."

"I don't know about that. Truth is, I've had cases that went bad. Cases with no happy ending, because what ending could we hope for when the gods and their Wardens were in charge? I couldn't save everyone. Those failed cases got to me. But for every mortal I failed, I helped two more."

"What are you saying?"

"Stop wallowing and bring back the Godless, lady. This case ain't finished yet." He tossed the stub of his cigarette into the ashtray and stood. "I'm off to find Noct before he swindles someone. Do what you need to do. We'll be ready to back you up." He flipped his collar up, shoved his hands into his pockets, and left me to my wallowing.

Did it matter how long I chose to wallow? Wallowing was all I was good at. But Gast was right. I had to get it together.

We weren't done yet.

I stubbed out my cigarette and magicked the evidence away.

Then I searched inside my subconscious for my family. I found their souls cradled around my heart. One by one, I pulled them out. Harmony first, back down to her original Seren size. Then Sinder, Vincent, Joe, and finally... Dru.

I'd summoned clothes for them too, and they got dressed without any hints of the awkwardness I'd expect at suddenly being rebirthed naked in front of one another. Whatever Jinx had put them through had apparently negated all that.

Then the awkwardness came as we stood here, staring at one another.

"Corentine's dead," I finally managed.

"And Jinx?" Joe asked.

"I don't know. Gone. You're safe here. This is... Haven. It's a new domain. Perhaps the only one left; I can't be sure Memoria is still standing."

And Kronos was still out there. "The Umber, Seren, and Mesmer are already here. There's food, beds—"

"The mortals I killed," Dru started, the golden flowers of her brow quivering on end, "Are they here?"

"I haven't brought them back yet—"

"Will they remember? Kayl, will they remember how they died?"

"I—I don't know. I'm not good with memories, that's an Amnae's thing—"

"Do you remember how you died?" Dru asked the others. "*Do you?*"

Harmony shared an uneasy glance with Joe.

"You do, don't you." Dru wiped tears from her eyes. "Of course you do." She tore away from the group and ran through the meadow.

"Dru!" I reached for her.

Joe took my arm. "Let her go. She needs time." He grimaced. "We all do."

I felt like utter shit as Dru ran off toward the beach.

This wasn't how I'd imagined our reunion. How could I comfort her, knowing what she'd done, that I'd failed her?

"Kayl, what do you plan to do now?" Vincent stood a distance from Sinder, avoiding his eye. "You'll bring back the souls Jinx took? Even the Necro?"

"That was the idea—"

"Then don't." His bloodshot eyes bored into mine.

"Vince," Sinder moaned.

Vincent ignored him. "You've a chance at creating a better world. Don't taint it with my kind. They'll prey and feed on the mortals living here—you know that's true! Save yourself the heartbreak. Don't bring the Necro back."

I swallowed a lump in my throat. What Vincent was asking wasn't how we Godless operated. "The Nameless One is gone—"

"The Necro haven't changed. Joe will confirm that. You cannot blame a mortal's actions on their gods when the gods no longer exist."

Shit, I didn't have the energy for a philosophical debate. "You know as well as I that you can't judge an entire domain based on a handful of mortals—"

"Can't we?" Vincent shot Sinder a telling look, the first time he'd even acknowledged Sinder. "I've witnessed for myself what a Necro will do without the fear of their god or a Warden's purview. Not even I—" He cleared his throat. "Not even I can resist the urges. A Necro *will* feed. If you're willing to subject mortals to that, then I want no part in it." He turned on his heel and limped away in the opposite direction from Dru.

Joe ran after Vincent to comfort him, or at least that was what all the anxiety and concern bouncing in my mind suggested. That should be Sinder's job.

Instead, Sinder just stood there. He sucked in a strangled breath.

"Are you going to demand I don't bring back the Glimmer next?" I snapped.

"I wouldn't dream of it, dearest. Bring them all back. What do I care? Don't forget Gloria. Your new domain is missing a workhouse or two. Now excuse me while I go find a way to get high out of my skull." He, too, splintered off, heading for one of the Seren pavilions.

Gods, my family was falling apart, and I didn't know how to fix it.

Only Harmony remained, and she wavered on her feet, both of her restored wings fluttering slightly.

"Harm?"

"Did you bring all the Seren back? My—My family? And..."

The unspoken name drifted in my mind. Monica. "I've not brought everyone back—we've not worked out the logistics yet—but I can bring back Mon—"

"No," she blurted. "No. I'm not—I'm not ready for that. For her. For *them*." She waddled over to the bench and climbed up to sit. She could have flown, but I supposed some habits took a while to shake off.

I slumped beside her. "The Godless need you, Harm."

"No, girl—"

"You're our leader. Quen's dead. We've lost the Amnae, the Zephyr, the Leander. The bloody Vesper. Dor is still out there and probably has Jinx captive—I can't reach her. I've got no plan. No idea what I'm pissing doing. All my plans fell apart because I'm *actually fucking useless*."

Everything I'd tried to hold together unraveled inside me. My heart. My soul. It all fell apart and spilled out in a flood of tears.

I needed Quen, and he was gone.

Even my own family had cracked into pieces.

Jinx? I called out. *Are you there? Sister?*

Still no answer. She'd been right, too. I couldn't do this without her, without Quen, without my family. On my own, I was nothing.

What had Mesmorpheus seen in me? Why had they trusted me to save the domains?

Too many souls depended on me, and I couldn't take it anymore.

I couldn't.

Harmony rubbed my lower back. "Girl. You've done the best you could with what you've had. No one can ask more of you than that."

"It's not—not enough!" The words stuttered out between fits and sobs, pushed between my fingers as I bent over and cradled my head in my hands.

"We're Godless. We pick up the pieces and recover."

I glanced up and rubbed my snotty nose. "How? Dru's traumatized, Vincent and Sinder aren't even speaking anymore, and I'm not doing much better. They need you, Harm—"

"You think they need me? I couldn't protect them, and I completely failed *you*. I failed to notice Vincent spiraling. I didn't even see Sinder's betrayal coming. I fucked up and let the Wardens take you and Joe—"

"Harm—"

"I hesitated because I was too scared to risk you, and none of that mattered in the end. I couldn't keep them safe from Jinx, and I left you to take the fall. Some leader I turned out to be."

I summoned a handkerchief and blew my nose. "Maybe we're both just shit at it."

Harmony snorted. "You took on *gods*, girl. You're far braver than I've ever been. Though I wish I could have been there when you dealt with Serenity."

"I made him beg."

"Have you been smoking?"

"Just one."

She laughed, a full-on belly laugh that sent her wings fluttering so fast, she almost bloody took flight! I grabbed her leg to stop her from falling arse over tit. "We're a mess. Not much has changed there." She fell back against the bench and wiped the tears streaming down her cheeks—from laughter or madness, I couldn't tell. "But we're still here. You need to speak with them and sort them out. Vincent, Sinder, Dru."

"You're our leader. They'll listen to you—"

"Kayl. The Godless wouldn't exist without you. You're the one that holds us together. You need to bring us back together again."

"And then what?"

"Then we'll come up with a plan. With wine and a packet of cigs if we have to. This fight isn't over, girl. Not until all the gods are dead."

I embraced Harm and squeezed her tight, careful to avoid her wings.

She returned the hug with a contented sigh. "We're home, girl."

Hope was all a Godless ever had, though I was afraid of what it offered. I didn't know for certain if Quen's soul still existed out there, but I dared not search... in case hope failed me, this one time.

That didn't mean I could give up on the Godless, on the mortals who still needed us.

Not when Dor remained.

Living a good life was the best revenge against shitty gods. That had to start somewhere. It was the only way mortals would heal.

Maybe I would, too.

Alone in the Dark

It hurt. Everything hurt.

The Diviner had tased me. Collared me. Slapped me across the face, punched me in the stomach until I vomited, and one even kicked me in the head until I passed out. There hadn't been any emotion in it. The Diviner beating me half to death didn't care either fucking way. They'd been given an order, which they carried out. It didn't make 'em happy to boot me in the face. It didn't make 'em sad when I cried. They weren't even disgusted when I pissed myself.

They were lucky. So fucking lucky, because they felt nothing.

And I felt *everything*.

I'd woken strapped to a chair.

Mother's chair.

The leather straps were tight around my waist, throat, wrists, and ankles, giving me no wiggle room or freedom to find comfort on the hard metal. They'd stripped me naked and shaved me bald, as they had my mother. The helmet on my head was damn heavy, forcing my neck to stoop and ache.

But that wasn't the worst of it.

They'd shoved thick tubes into my skin, in my arms, my thighs, and the back of my neck. The wounds they'd cut to insert them still stung and oozed with blood. They'd removed the aether collar, but the tubes leeched away my Chaos abilities, blocking them somehow... With my every inhale and exhale, those tubes pumped out energy. My own life force.

It felt like my nerves were being pulled out of my body, shredding my skin as they passed.

It hurt to breathe.

To exist.

I refused to scream, but I'd long since ran out of tears. The dehydration set in quickly. My mouth was fuzzy, my tongue cracked and sore. My head pounding. Thank fuck I sat in the dark, because my eyes couldn't take the light.

It was pure fucking *agony*. Mother had endured this for centuries.

How long would I endure it?

Unlike Mother's, my prison wasn't locked behind twelve gods, and that itself fucking hurt. My chair was bolted to the metal room behind the clockface window. The clock hands mocked me with their ticking and ticking and *ticking*.

Freedom was right fucking *there*, and I couldn't grasp it.

Couldn't move.

Couldn't slice my own throat to end this misery.

Couldn't do shit.

I didn't want to scream.

I refused to scream.

Not while I was still sane. Hah.

Well, I thought I was sane. Except I was inside the clock tower, and I'd watched the clock tower fall apart. Maybe that had been a metaphor.

I hated metaphors.

I'd been a god, once. Then I'd sent my mortals away. Sent my sister away. Did that make me a hero? I'd let myself fall into this trap for *them*, and yet they'd never loved me, never respected me.

"I'll come back for you. I promise."

That was a dirty fucking lie, wasn't it?

No one was coming for me. Why should they?

"We're not family!"

I was alone in the dark.

Alone for the first time, with no sister for company.

My sweet child, Mother crooned inside my mind. *You are strong. You will get through this.*

All right, I wasn't completely alone.

When I'd taken the souls of gods, they'd been trapped inside my subconscious in a much nicer state than I was now. But they were effectively dead. They couldn't communicate with me, or I'd assumed they couldn't.

But Mother could. She wasn't even mad that I'd taken her soul.

Why would I be mad? You took my place.

It fucking sucks.

It does. But only for the first hundred years or so. By then, your body will have decayed into numbness, and your mind will be thoroughly broken. Then all that's left is to enjoy your madness.

I thought Mesmorpheus had put you to sleep?

They had. It's a shame no one can offer you that peace. Madness it is!

She cackled. I didn't get what was so fucking funny.

A figure suddenly appeared in the center of the room. I wasn't expecting guests, so there was really only one twat it could be.

"Dor," I croaked.

The god of time looked so much like Corinth, it pissed me off. There he stood in his swanky pinstripe suit, with the same face as Corinth, but with a twisty little beard.

He approached the chair and examined the various tubes coming out of me. "How are we settling in? Your input is almost at maximum value. You should be pleased. You're providing energy for the entire city."

I tried to spit, but I had nothing to give.

Was I mortal enough to die of dehydration and starvation? I sure hoped so.

"Fuck you," I rasped.

He put a hand to his ear. "I'm sorry, what was that?"

He'd fucking heard me! "Fuck *you!*"

"Expletives are a waste of your energy and thus a drain on our resources. Refrain."

Had that fuck told me to *refrain*? "Was it worth it, you crusty old shit? You killed your own gods—your own children—just to have this city for yourself, and it's a shit city at that!"

"My children meant nothing to me. They were little more than an inconvenience, emotional beings who refused to obey. Chime will run in perfect symmetry without them."

He never cared for mortals, Mother hissed.

"That's it, huh? You want a universe without mortals? Without gods? Then what's the fucking point of running this city?"

He looked down his nose at me, as though I were some dirty, wretched thing incapable of understanding basic language. "The gods believed life to be sacred, but life is overrated. It is chaotic and filthy. It follows no rhyme or reason. It cannot be effectively controlled, not even my own iterations of mortality. This *experiment* has run its course. For thousands of years, I have studied mortals. I have watched generations age and die in the hopes they would evolve into something better. Alas. I remain disappointed. Not only in mortals, but the gods. Given a millennium, most chose to barricade themselves in their own domains and squander their gifts. Life was wasted on them."

This fucker liked to ramble almost as much as Corinth. "So Daddy Dor doesn't approve of how his children grew up? Or is it because they rejected you for being a miserable, lonely old fuck?"

"I have all I require. This city serves my purposes. All that remains is to collect the missing souls of the gods and destroy them. Unfortunately, they are in the possession of your twin. Therefore, to answer your previous query, I do not require your energy to power this city. I am a god. However, your presence will draw out the souls I need. Your twin's profile suggests a proclivity for dramatics."

I drew a strangled breath. Kayl, no. Not Kayl.

She'd escaped. She was safe. Dor couldn't reach her. He couldn't.

I could still sense her soul inside my mind... Is that what Dor wanted? For me to call out to Kayl? To trick her into coming here?

Fuck no.

Even if I had to suffer a thousand years, I would *never* do what Dor wanted. I'd never risk my sister.

It hurt to breathe, to swallow, to talk. My throat was so damn scratchy. "You'll never find her."

"I don't need to. Quentin will."

Corinth. Fucking Corinth. No, not even Kayl's precious Time Boy would betray her, but was he dumb enough to accidentally set himself up as bait? Eh, probably.

"Good luck getting Corinth to do what you want."

"If Quentin won't obey me, then I'll have no choice but to take his soul and force his hand one way or another."

Fuck.

As much as Corinth annoyed me, he was the only mortal left who could protect Kayl.

Who could bring Dor down.

But not if Dor took his soul. Then Kayl would be in danger, and there wasn't a damn thing I could do to protect her.

I shook at my bindings, desperately trying to rattle myself free. "Fuck you! Fuck you! *Fuck you!*"

Dor hastily stepped back. "Your appearance mirrors Corentine's, though your personality is somewhat abrasive. A pity. You do make an excellent energy source—you certainly have a lot of it."

I blinked, and he'd disappeared.

You scared him off, Mother pouted. *He could have kept you company during these lonely nights.*

Fuck that! I don't want your disgusting ex-lover putting his cosmic dick anywhere near me!

Dor gave me hundreds of godly children. Think what he could do for you, if you were only a little nicer.

He can do himself!

I didn't know what disturbed me most—that Dor was keeping me here like some fucked-up beacon to lure Kayl out, or that I could be trapped here forever. Alone.

You have an eternity to think about all your mistakes, daughter. Take your time.

My biggest mistake was not going into Kronos and ripping out Dor's soul when I had the chance.

No one is coming to save you.

I didn't want them to. I didn't want Kayl to.

Oh, daughter. Don't lie to yourself. You're so desperate to be loved, and yet no one loves you. No one ever did. Not your sister. Not the mortals who refused to respect you. Not even me. You'll be trapped here forever and ever until your name is lost to time.

Mo-Mother?

Was that true? She'd never loved me?

Did you think yourself worthy of love? Kayl is my true daughter. It was her body I created. You simply attached yourself to her soul and leeched her glory. You took the name I had planned for her, but I never named you—you didn't deserve one. You made yourself useful in the end, but now look at you, you worthless shit.

No, I was more than that, I was... "Mother!"

How does it feel? To be trapped with me for eternity?

Noise tore through my throat. It echoed off the metal walls and shook through the pipes pumping out the aether keeping me alive.

I screamed and screamed and screamed.

XLIV

Mortals who wander from their gods are lost. They are broken.
The relationship between a mortal and their god is fundamental to their
existence. To deny that connection is akin to cutting off a limb and naming
yourself whole. You need the love and presence of your god to be complete.
Otherwise, what is the point of your existence?
—E. Karendar, Commandments for the Diviner

THE WARDENS WRAPPED MY neck in an aether collar and even cuffed my wrists behind my back, so determined to keep me at their mercy. I was in no rush to escape. Dor had remade Chime, had damned his mortals to a fate worse than death, for every mortal we passed had that vacant soulless look about them. I needed to know his endgame.

I needed to know if he'd caught Kayl or Jinx.

Elijah paraded me through the station and out into Central's main square. Chime had been pieced back together with exquisite detail, only now everything was Diviner owned and Diviner made, even the Glimmer tea houses. The streets were perfectly clean and orderly. In fact, it all looked rather... sterile. Robotic.

It was hushed, too. No chatter or gossip. No Vesper paperboys shouting out the headlines or Ember stall owners selling baked goods. Even the trams and carriages moved past in silence, like cardboard set pieces in a play.

It was a version of Chime plucked from my worst nightmares.

I'd take the ruined version any day. At least that had character.

Though one difference between my Chime and this new one was that the Wardens, for reasons unknown, had set up gallows in the middle of Central.

Oh. Was this meant for me? Wonderful.

How fitting that I'd break my new body in by breaking my neck.

It was a simple wooden platform with a hangman's noose. There had been talk on the Warden Council years ago of introducing capital punishment to the masses. A spectacle to threaten the populace and punish the sinners and apostates. Thankfully, the Council had voted it down—only the Glimmer and Diviner had been in support, though even they agreed such matters should be handled privately by each god and their ambassador.

I distinctly despised what this new Chime had become.

"That's rather an eyesore," I said. "Rather unnecessary too. Do you have many rogue soulless?" Though killing them would be a blessing. Existence without living was no life.

Elijah stopped us before it. "It's a gift."

I tried to keep my unease off my face. "I've died a few times now. What's one more?"

"Not *for* you, Quentin. This is merely a demonstration." He clapped his hands.

Ben disappeared into the crowd and returned with a woman slumped against his side. Pendula.

Oh saints.

Ben's forever stare acknowledged nothing, least of all me, thanks to his absent soul. Pendula looked a state compared to the last time I set eyes on her, though the scars were still etched across her face—more this time, including an unfortunate *whore* above her right eyebrow. Ben dragged her up the gallows. She was conscious and alert—she still retained her soul, then—but her eyes were a different sort of vacant. Pained and hopeless.

I watched helplessly as Ben wrapped the noose around her neck and waited for Elijah's command.

Gods no. He was going to make Ben execute Pendula.

"Stop this!" I spat.

Elijah turned to me with such cold, cruel eyes. "Miss Bezel cavorted with Chaos. She betrayed our Father. This is the price of disobedience." He nodded a signal.

Ben shoved Pendula forward.

The noose tugged tight, cutting off her airflow. By some cruel twist of fate, it hadn't snapped her neck outright, leaving her to dangle mercilessly, slowly choking to death.

I wanted to tear my gaze away, but I forced myself to meet her eye, to show that while I could do nothing for her now, a time would come when I'd avenge her.

Pendula and I had never been enemies, but Dor had forced our paths to cross. She deserved better than me—better than this.

"If she betrayed you, then why am I not swinging from the gallows?" I asked.

Elijah's smile spoke the answer. Because Dor held nothing but contempt for women, and for some ungodly reason, he held affection for me.

Pendula continued to choke. It had been at least a full minute—why wasn't she dead? Was Dor keeping her alive, only to suffocate for all eternity?

"Does this make you uncomfortable?" Elijah asked.

The question was so absurd, I snorted! "What do you think?"

I blinked, and Central disappeared. I stood in an apartment living room. My old apartment. The large floor-to-ceiling windows overlooked the clockface, as they always had.

Elijah stood beside me, gazing upon Central. "Corentine is dead."

My heart skipped a beat. "How?"

"Father released her. One of her daughters took her soul, as he foretold."

Saints. Had Kayl taken Corentine? Could I reach into my mind and find her there?

And was that why mortals had suddenly lost their free will? No, it couldn't be. Pendula still retained hers. That meant the soulless I'd encountered had all been submitted to a soul-splitting device. Dor had manually destroyed their souls, one by one.

'Redeemed' them.

If Corentine no longer existed, then... "Dor is powering Chime?"

"No. We captured one of Corentine's daughters and installed her anew."

Installed her anew...?

Oh gods. Dor had taken either Kayl or Jinx and replaced Corentine. I stared at the clockface. Behind that, Kayl could be strapped to a chair, her veins being bled of godly energy to power this mockery of a city. The thought made me weak. Dizzy.

"Why—Why am I here?" I blurted.

"Because, for all your sins, I still love you."

"Love!" My voice rose in hysterics. "You've done nothing but hurt me! Torture me! What kind of love is that, when you must toy with my mind and memories to force some reciprocity?"

"Father loves you—"

"Dor expects devotion but does nothing to earn it! Look at the world he's created." I stared out at Central. "The domains are gone. There are no mortals left to occupy Chime. Those who remain have no fucking *souls*!"

"Language, Quentin—"

"Don't you understand, you ignorant prat? Your soul will be taken next!"

"I already offered my soul to Father."

"What?"

"There's little point in carrying on the pretense."

A man stepped out of Elijah's body. A man whose face was almost identical to mine, except he wasn't wearing spectacles, and a silver goatee framed his chin.

I blinked at the two men standing side by side, dressed in the same pinstripe suit. Elijah—or his body—stood still and vacant. His soul had been shattered.

And the man before me was no mere mortal.

"Dor." My voice cracked.

"My beautiful Quentin." He raised his hand to caress my cheek. "I've loved you since I first created you." Then his lips pressed against mine.

I stood completely stunned out of my wits as his tongue invaded my mouth. Nausea threatened to overwhelm me. This was wrong. It was all wrong!

I hastily shuffled back—my hands still bound—and gagged. "You're my father! I was made in *your* image!" How long had he been using Elijah's body as a puppet? When he'd last kissed me? Whipped me?

Gotten an erection, for gods' sake?

I'd long suspected Elijah had been twisted by Dor's constant presence in his mind. One didn't become voice to a god without changing. The gods held mortals in their hands to twist and pull as they pleased, but there was no torture quite like being their favorite.

Had Elijah's abuse been Dor all along?

Elijah had long ago stopped being the innocent boy I'd fallen for.

Dor licked his lips. "For centuries, I desired a son made in my image. It was the only reason I agreed to create mortal life. Thanks to Corentine's insistence, each mortal I formed became tainted with Chaos. None matched my desire. And then, by chance... Chaos gave me you. A perfect match."

"But Corentine... She said you named me to mock her. That I was named after the first mortal?"

"Corinth? He was the blueprint for mortal life. The first to age and die. Yet he was tainted by Corentine's touch. No other mortal has been worthy of the name. Only you."

"Then why do you hurt me?" The words came out in almost a strangled sob. "Why did you do all this?"

"Because you are broken, Quentin. You disobey and sin. I wish to understand your imperfections."

"I'm not some broken clock you can fix! Surely you understand the anatomical and chemical composition of your own mortals?"

"When Chaos took your soul, I ordered Pendula Bezel to retrieve your body. I had it dissected."

That was rather depressing, though unsurprising. "You cut open my brain to try and understand why I would sin?"

"It yielded no results."

"You can't stand the thought I may be flawed, can you? That I'm a sinner, and you made me wrong? That I was a mistake—*you* made a mistake in my creation."

Irritation was plain across his—my—face.

Gods didn't make mistakes.

Had my entire life path been born of the actions of a sexually frustrated god? How confusing must it be to uphold the laws of logic when feelings and emotions were illogical. That was love—or infatuation, perhaps. I couldn't call whatever Dor felt for me something as pure as love. He'd made me a sinner because he'd wanted me to sin. Did some part of him also desire sin?

The same part that had allowed Chaos to exist for as long as it had? That had courted Corentine?

Diviner were made in Dor's image, and we'd gained his particular proclivities. We desired sin, yet we feared that desire and attempted to tamp it out. The outcome was a domain full of frustrated men, and women in some cases.

"Did you gift me such devastating visions of death so I would be afraid to touch? So in doing so, my touch would be reserved for you only?"

He sucked in a breath.

I hated being right.

Dor wasn't mortal. How could he understand love? How could he expect that of me?

"What now?" I asked. "You've grown bored of your mortals, so you destroy their souls? Cast them out as nothing?"

He tugged at his cufflinks, the action so like Elijah, my heart ached. How much of Elijah had been Dor? The man I'd once loved? "I do not care for mortal life. Free will is illogical. There's little point in caring for beings that age and die."

To a god of time, mortals must only exist for the blink of an eye. Why bother getting attached? "Then why do I still possess my soul? Clearly, I frustrate you. Why not split my soul and be done with it?"

"You are no longer mortal, Quentin. You are one of a kind."

"Surely you can create better company than me?"

"You are all I require. Why else would I have bothered to rescue you from the clock tower the day you fell? I could have reclaimed your soul, rebirthed you as a saint. But I wanted you by Elijah's side, at his—my—command."

I swallowed my revulsion. Dor kept me alive because I fulfilled his perverse desires, and the very thought of him owning me once more sent my skin crawling. I could throw myself from my apartment window. Find solace in death. Even that would be better than allowing him to turn my body into his plaything.

"Then what was the *point* of all this? You alone stated Corentine was a threat, that you'd imprisoned her to prevent Chaos from destroying the domains. You've gone and damned them with your own hand! War could have been prevented—"

"It was Chaos who attacked first by taking Eventide—"

"Which could have been avoided had you not imprisoned them! What of Gildola? Don't deny you used Chaos to destroy the gods. Your own children."

"Gildola threatened my rule."

"Oh please. You're the god of time. Gildola was no threat to you. And what of your allies? The Umber? Zephyr? They were never a threat to your rule, but you let them die all the same." Anima had described Dor as an elder god.

The most powerful god of all the domains.

"They betrayed Corentine in my name. They would have betrayed me, given the opportunity. But they knew nothing of the greater universe. They were lesser. Unworthy of the power I'd granted them."

Wasn't I the same, by Dor's own definition? "You plotted against the gods... because they *annoyed* you?" A ridiculous notion! Though not even gods were above pettiness.

"I acted preemptively, as was logical. Corentine would have done the same in another timeline. She would have grown bored of this universe. At least I will it to continue."

Ah. So either Corentine or Dor could have waged this war, only Dor had the foresight to see the outcome and twist it. "Then congratulations.

You've bested Corentine, destroyed your own children and their domains. You've won."

Dor stared out at the clockface. "There are still matters to clear up."

"Such as?"

"The remaining child of Chaos."

One of them was still loose. Jinx?

"You'll recover her for me."

That was a bold statement. "Will I?"

Dor faced me again. "You will. You will obey me in this, Quentin. If you do not, then I have one of Corentine's daughters in my grasp. I can do with her as I wish."

I choked back bile. Pendula had been a demonstration. A warning. I knew from first-hand experience Dor could do far, far worse. "I need a little more incentive than threats."

Dor smiled, and I hated how it looked on my—his—face. One thing was for certain—I was never growing a beard. "I can offer you eternity by my side."

"Tempting." Of course it wasn't. What did eternity mean to me, if I couldn't share it with Kayl? But here I was, trapped in a nightmarish alternate Chime with a god who had worn my ex-lover like a blasted suit to manipulate my mind.

What choice did I have but to obey?

There were always choices.

I could refuse and let Dor torture and rape my soul for the next century or two, until he got tired and damned me to the same fate as his other children. But then whoever sat in that clock tower would surely face the brunt of his wrath. If that was Kayl, I would never forgive myself. Even Jinx deserved a better fate.

Or I could play this smart. Whore myself out, if need be. Play the good boy, as I had for so many years. Dor would eventually drop his guard.

And I'd damn his twisted soul to oblivion.

"All right. I'll be your bait. But you'll need to let me loose." I wiggled my cuffed hands behind my back and cocked my head, flashing the collar. Without that on, I could speak to whoever resided in the tower.

Dor took my chin, pulling me down so I was forced to stoop and stare up. "When you earn my trust. I know you are resourceful. I made you that way."

If it *was* Kayl who'd escaped, then... I knew where I'd find her.

In my dreams.

The aether collar followed me into the dreamscape, but hadn't prevented me from entering. Thank the gods for small mercies.

Back in reality, I napped in my armchair, certain Dor was watching me. But here, in the sanctity of my mind, I stepped into another world. Another domain? My past self had already visited, though to me it was an altogether new experience.

It was a paradise combining the energies of the Seren, Mesmer, and Umber. Golden fields full of flowers stretched across the horizon, meeting with warm sands and a dazzling ocean. Above, the stars were so bright and colorful, they provided enough light to rival Chime's sun. Sweet scents danced on the breeze, like breathing in a candy store.

Though odder still was the sight of varying mortals coexisting in this new plane. I caught glimpses of Seren and Glimmer within pavilions, Umber and Fauna within fields of rosebushes, Ember and Mesmer on the beaches, and even the odd Necro lurking wherever trees cast a shadow.

Kayl had done it. She'd saved them.

A stone path cut through the fields, and I followed it. If Kayl was here in this new domain, there was only one place she'd be.

As I came across the tram carriage hiding behind the waterfall; nearby sat a figure within a meadow.

"Kayl."

She turned instantly, standing on trembling legs. It was her, wearing the Mesmer form I'd gotten so used to and a tight black dress. "Quen?" She approached tentatively, and I met her at the edge of the meadow, giving her the space she needed. "Are you my Quen?"

That one innocent question almost undid me. It was *her*. My beautiful, darling Kayl. "Until the end of time."

She ran into my arms.

Together, we fell to our knees among the flowers. She clung to my chest, tears streaming down her cheeks.

"I thought—thought I'd lost you!"

I took her face in my hands, allowing her tears to flow over my fingers. "I *was* lost. You helped me find myself, as you always do."

"Corentine's gone. Chime, it's—"

"Dor has remade it."

Her eyes widened. "Then Jinx..."

"She's trapped in the clock tower." I shouldn't feel relief that it was one twin instead of the other, but that was the truth. "Dor has taken over Chime. He's... gods, he's split the souls of his mortals. All of them."

"And you?" She fingered the collar at my throat.

"Safe, for now. I'm his prisoner. He's dangling me to draw you out. I won't allow that to happen." The less she knew about Dor's threats and perversions, the better. I certainly didn't want to dwell on the subject.

"Quen—"

"We need a plan. I took Anima's soul, and I still possess Zyclone and Lionheart."

"Jinx, she saved me. She gave me her souls and sacrificed herself so I could escape here. I've got a full house, now. Gildola, The Nameless One, Faen, and Edana. She gave me everything."

"What of the other souls?"

"I gave them to the Mesmer for safekeeping. Celeste has Serenity, Castor has Unghard, and I brought Reverie back to handle the other Mesmer. I thought, even if I got caught and had my soul wiped, at least they'd be safe here."

I brought her fingers to my lips and gently kissed them. "You're a genius."

She smiled. A rare smile that burst through my heart. "I wouldn't go that far."

"What is this place? It's not simply a dream."

"No, it's a new domain. I've named it Haven."

Gosh. It really was an entirely new domain. She must have gathered the energy of the gods, same as I'd used to rebirth myself, only she'd created something incredible. Something so beautiful.

Dor would crush it, given the chance.

My eye wandered to the placards within the meadow, and my stomach sank. Names of lost souls. The Fauna. Cosmo. "I'm so sorry I wasn't there for you."

Kayl followed my gaze and squeezed my left hand. "The Mesmer miss you. They've been practicing their tea-making skills. They knew you'd come back. They've even got cake on standby."

I chuckled. "I look forward to indulging in less-stale cake."

"Oh! The Godless—they're back as well! They're staying in the tram. They've had a shit time of it."

"Did Jinx...?" Torture them? I didn't want to finish the sentence aloud.

"She tormented them, but, well, everything has been a bit much. That's a pissing stupid way of putting it. Harm has already thrown herself into plotting with Joe. The pair of them are getting no rest. Vincent has been trying to console Dru—she's badly shaken up from what Unghard did to her. Sinder's not in great shape, either. Oh, and Gast and Noct are here—"

"Mortimer Gast, the private eye?" I raised a brow. "You know I once booked him on suspicion of murder? And Nocturne is no gentleman."

"Yes, I know. You've got history. But you're no Warden anymore, and they've earned their place among the Godless."

Was I no longer a Warden? It was stamped into my very soul. But Kayl was right in that we couldn't afford to turn away potential allies. Gast and Nocturne had once been a thorn in my side, but they were resourceful, I'd give them that.

Honestly, it was good to know the Godless had returned to Kayl's side, albeit in a different state to who they'd been. War had changed us all in unexpected ways.

"I wish I could add to your rota, but this collar..."

Kayl slipped a finger underneath it. The thrill of her touch on my skin sent my pulse running.

And then with a burst of aether, the collar snapped in half and fell into my lap.

"How did you do that?" I rubbed my neck. Had it broken outside the dream world? I reached inside my mind and—there. The mortals I carried with me were waiting. Doctor Zachery Finch. Dandelion. Lyonelle and her cubs. Ilona.

I could bring them back. Leave them here with Kayl in her private sanctuary.

Kayl shrugged. "I don't really know how this works. You're the aether expert, you tell me."

"It's the magic of the gods. We're both infused with it."

"What does that mean, in reality?"

"In reality? That we'll kick Dor's fucking arse. But I... I can't do it alone."

I wanted to.

Dear gods, I wanted to. This battle between us was personal on every level.

But too much was at stake for me to risk it all by playing martyr. That was what Dor expected of me. Yet each time I'd taken on that burden, it had ended in disaster. I'd almost lost everything because of my damnable hubris. And... I didn't know if I *could* face him alone, knowing his true desires and what he wanted from me. "If we're taking him down, we need to do so together."

Kayl's eyes lit up with her smug grin. "Are you certain you're my Quen? Because *my* Quen would never swear. And *my* Quen is a certified chivalrous arse—"

"Yes, yes, no need to rub it in. I can admit when I'm wrong."

"Oh really? And how often are you right?"

"Nine times out of ten." Though now that I had Anima's power, there was a more pressing matter. Her memories.

My heart sighed.

Dor and Elijah had forced their 'love' upon me. It was so warped and depraved, did I even know what love was? Dor was my father. He'd created me—had cradled me in his palms when I took my first breath, spoke my first words. I'd considered his presence in my life that of an overbearing parent, but now...

There was no innocence in Dor's love. How many of his children had he abused in the same manner? Or was I simply cursed due to the likeness Chaos had granted me?

The Diviner didn't care for love. Marriage was a relationship of convenience. But the great Seren poets saw love as an honor and sacrifice. All the things I would have offered Elijah.

All the things I'd offer Kayl.

Love? Love was chaos. There was nothing logical about it.

Love couldn't be forced. It couldn't be controlled and tamed, not like Dor's version of love. I had no desire to control Kayl. She was a free spirit, and it gave me such pleasure to watch her soar. To become the best version of herself. A woman who didn't need me.

All this time, I'd been acting a prat. I was no gentleman. I'd kissed her, forced my lips upon hers without consent. I'd dumped my trauma at her feet. I'd ignored Malkavaan's plight in order to pursue my own attraction. No, I'd never been a gentleman.

But now I could make amends.

I loved her. And that was why I needed to let her go. She wasn't mine. She never had been.

If I could earn a chance at redemption, a chance to undo this mistake, then that would be enough. Perhaps I was still a chivalrous arse.

Elijah had made me a monster. Kayl made me a man.

I held her hands in mine. Such a wondrous thing, touch. A gift she'd given me. "Kayl. I've been guarding your heart, but it's not mine to own. I can deliver it where it belongs."

She frowned, confused. "Quen, what—"

"Please. Listen to me. I have your missing memories. Let me restore them."

She recoiled from my touch. "What if I don't want you to?"

"These are *your* memories—"

"What if they change who I am?"

I understood her fears all too well. "I've experienced many different versions of myself, and there is no greater torture than to understand that a piece of me is missing. That I'm not quite whole. Even if the missing pieces were flaws of my character, they're still me."

"But what if... it changes how I feel about you? I don't want that."

"Kayl." I took her hand again. "You're the most wonderful mortal I've ever met. Regardless of what happens next, or what you feel, I will *always* be here for you in whatever capacity you need me. I will see this through to the end."

The end of time itself.

She pulled away from my touch once more to wipe clear fresh tears. "You've always had faith in me. My mystery benefactor."

"I always will." I changed my form to Amnae. The air was a little tight, though it didn't constrict my lungs. If I brought Ilona here, perhaps Kayl could make an adjustment to her domain. "Whenever you're ready."

She closed her eyes. "All right. Do it."

I placed my left hand on Kayl's forehead, allowing the suckers at the tips of my fingers to take hold.

You're a good man, Doctor Finch said.

I aspire to be. Kayl's memories bloomed within my mind, and I located the strands of her timeline running through her subconscious.

It turned out navigating the river of memory as an Amnae wasn't much different from doing so as a Diviner. Of course, Diviner couldn't manipulate memories as an Amnae could. They were simply observers. But thanks to Walter, I had a rough idea of what I was doing.

Anima had cut away sections containing Malkavaan, though they'd left the rest undisturbed. They'd filled in the blanks rather artistically—essentially wiping all traces not only of Malkavaan and his mother, but also Kayl's involvement with Valeria's demise.

These were deep memories, embedded in emotions.

Though... the Kayl I knew had remained more or less the same even without them. Her compassion had shone through regardless.

That was why I loved her.

I located the blanks, the edited memories, and carefully began to revert them.

She wiggled under my grasp.

"Hold still, please."

"It tickles."

"It will feel a bit odd. You may be out of sorts for an hour or two. Nothing a good cup of tea won't fix."

"We've got wine in the tram."

"That'll do." The memories of Malkavaan and Elvira Byvich slotted in perfectly, like pieces of a jigsaw. The bigger picture came together slowly, and when that final piece completed the art, her mind shifted. A door opened. Valeria's power returned.

I released her forehead and smiled at Kayl the Vesper.

A persona I hadn't seen in some time.

She stared at her hands. At the wisps of shadow that twisted around her fingers.

"Bring them back," I said.

Kayl scrambled to her feet. "I—I've got to go." She ran from the meadow.

Will she be all right? the good doctor asked.

She'll be fine. More than fine.

She'd be brilliant.

45

Other than the unforgivable sins of apostasy and blasphemy, there are many minor sins, often wrapped up in temptations of the flesh. Unforgivable sins are named so because they are unforgivable. They must receive the harshest of punishments. Can minor sins be forgiven? No. Minor sins are the gateway to apostasy and blasphemy. When one indulges in a glass of wine, they are choosing pleasure over their god. When one sleeps in late, they are denying time that could be spent in worship to their god. No sin can be forgiven. Flogging is an adequate punishment for first-time offenses, but should a sinner continue to sin, then greater punishments are required. These are for the good of one's mortal soul.
—Ambassador Gloria, *On Sin and Divine Punishment*

MALK.

I RAN ACROSS the beach, lines of shadow trailing behind me. They poured from my skin as though I'd stored so much darkness inside, I could no longer contain it.

Malk.

I hear you.

Oh gods. It was him. His voice. Malk.

I remembered him. I remembered everything.

I remembered the way my hand fit into his. How his arms always made me feel safe. Our first kiss. Our first fuck. The nights we'd giggled as we tried to keep our moans quiet. The times we'd foraged together in the Undercity, searching for scraps. The chestnuts we'd shared. The errands we'd run for Varen.

When we'd created the Godless.

After we'd lost Elvira.

Anima had made me forget every interaction with Malk, but Quen had restored it all. My joy at Quen arriving in Haven now clashed with the warring emotions of my heart.

Malk had been my whole life. Two Vesper trying to survive.

"I love you with everything I am."

I'd killed him. Let him suffer at Valeria's hands and then wiped his soul, and all this time I'd been carrying him. Trapped inside my subconscious.

The guilt crushed me until I couldn't breathe, squeezing out more shadow.

I drowned in it.

No. I had to pull myself together. I hadn't been able to bring back mortals then, but I could now. The Vesper deserved more than I could give them, but I could at least give them life.

I sucked in a breath, and my shadows calmed.

Malk's soul rested near my heart. I pulled it out.

He appeared before me. Tall, dark, broody. His once midnight blue skin now a lighter Chaos shade, his luscious long locks white.

And he was naked. Shit!

"Sorry!" I summoned a pile of suitable clothes—slacks, shirts, and sandals for the beach—and then turned to give him privacy.

"You haven't changed," he said with that thick Vesper accent.

I risked a glance over my shoulder. "I've changed a little."

He'd dressed, but forwent the sandals, letting his toes sink in the sand. He flashed me a smirk that had once made me weak at the knees, though now, I really didn't know what to feel.

Part of me wanted to hug him tight and laugh. Another part wanted to cry.

A completely separate part wanted to run to Quen and seek solace in his arms. I hushed that thought.

"All right, you've changed a little. The Kayl I knew could barely keep her room tidy, and this Kayl's created a whole new domain."

My cheeks heated. "Well, uh... A lot's happened."

"I know. I saw everything you saw."

Oh shit, really? "Everything?"

Mischief glinted in his eye. "Everything. Come. Sit with me." He made himself comfortable on the beach.

I sat beside him on a warm patch of sand, an arm's length between us, and stared at the ocean. It didn't rise and clash the way Arcadia's did. My ocean was calm—completely at odds with the rise and clash of my heart. "I—I don't have the words to explain—"

"Then don't."

"I owe you *something*. An apology." A hundred apologies.

"It's me who should be apologizing."

I turned to him. "What could you possibly apologize for? I literally stole your soul! I destroyed the entirety of Eventide! If it wasn't for me, we wouldn't even be in this situation."

"Maybe. Maybe not." Malk shrugged. "We Godless were bound to run into trouble eventually, and it was always going to be you who found it. It's one of your greatest talents."

"Thanks. I think."

He tilted his head back and stared at the stars. "When Valeria held me captive, I wasn't myself. I hurt you—"

"That wasn't your fault—"

"No? I betrayed you to Varen. That fucking arsehole."

"Varen was a prick, but you were being tortured, and I didn't do enough to—to save you." My voice caught. "I'm sorry, Malk. It's me who should be begging for your forgiveness. I'm *sorry*." I sniffed back the tears that threatened to spill. He deserved a proper apology, not one tainted by guilt. "I know you must be angry and scared. Your soul belongs to me, now. But I promise I'll make amends."

"You're forgiven."

"Just like that?"

He picked up a handful of sand and let it trickle between his fingers. "This place is beautiful. Have you got a chestnut stall, somewhere?"

"Malk—"

"Being trapped inside someone's mind gives you a lot of time to calm down and reflect. I won't lie to you, Kayl. I can't... Things can't return to what they were. Valeria, Varen, everything... It's left a mental scar. I don't know if I'll ever get over it."

"Whatever I can do to help—"

"You're fighting the good fight. What we always wanted. So sign me up. If I can pummel some Diviner, that'll make me feel a whole lot better. Besides, I've missed the others. Harm, Vince, Sinder, Dru. I'm sure they're not expecting to see my ugly mug again."

"We've got new allies too. A Glimmer called Joe; he's lovely. Honest."

"I know. Saw him from inside your head, remember?" He tapped the side of his forehead. "You don't need to bring me up to speed, but I'd love a glass of wine. I'm fucking gasping."

I smiled. "I'm sure we can sort you out."

He stood, dusted sand off his slacks, and then offered his hand to pull me up. "You fell in love with Corinth, huh?"

I took his hand and cringed. I wanted to avoid the subject, but there was no avoiding it, and based on the scrutiny of Malk's gaze, he wasn't going to let it go.

Now that my heart had calmed a bit, the truth was...

I'd truly fallen for Quen, as crazy as that sounded.

Malk and I had been through so much together, and yet even that didn't compare to the absolute trials Quen and I had endured. It was odd, really. I'd known Quen for only a short time and yet I needed him in my life.

I couldn't explain the connection Quen and I shared, but it went beyond two lonely souls finding comfort in one another.

"I did. He's not the Dark Warden, you know. He's a good man."

"You deserve each other. I mean that in the sense you're both completely insane and only he's brave enough to put up with your style of crazy. Try not to kill the poor fella." He flashed me a mocking grin.

I lightly punched his arm. This banter was new, but it was something. An end to romance, and the beginning of a lasting friendship, I hoped.

Malk had meant everything to me. I still loved him and always would. "I mean it, though. If there's anything I can do for you—"

"There's one thing. Bring back my mother."

Elvira. "Of course." It was the least I could do.

This time, I summoned clothes in advance, and also a little beach changing room for privacy.

I'd had enough emotional reunions for one day, so I brought back Elvira and left her in Malk's care. The two of them had plenty to catch up on, and I'd check in on them later.

Besides, I had my own man to attend to.

I found Quen sitting on the bench overlooking the meadow. He'd since reverted to his natural state—his Diviner form—and was doing that contemplating thing he did so well.

Why had I fallen in love with a Diviner? It was a tale as old as time.

I sat beside him, and he jumped, startled.

"Is—Is everything all right?" he asked. "Malkavaan, is he...?"

"I think he'll need therapy after all this." We all would. "But he'll be fine."

Quen nodded slowly. "I hope you don't mind, but I took the liberty of bringing back Doctor Finch, Dandelion, Lyonelle and her cubs. Reverie is helping them get settled in. I'd like to bring back Ilona as well, but we'd need a few accommodations for her and any other Amnae, if you can. The air's a little dry."

Oh, Quen. Always thinking of others.

"I'll sort it, but first, we need to talk, mister."

"That sounds ominous."

I faced him and placed my hands in my lap. "Quentin Corinth, you beautiful man. I love you."

"But?"

"That's it. No buts."

"*But—*"

"*No* buts. Malk was my past, and you're my future. It could only ever be you, and I want *you*, Quen. All of you. The good, the bad. I'll even accept you being a chivalrous arse on occasion. In return, you get me. All of me. The good, the bad."

His face lit up with such a bright smile, he squirmed in his seat, as though struggling to contain it. "Are you—you sure? I'm a complete cad!

An ungentlemanly bastard! You know I cheated on Elijah with Dandelion and Erosain, don't you?"

"Yes, I know. That hardly counts when Karendar had been fucking with your memories. Besides, Malk and I had an open arrangement."

"Is that what you want?"

"Honestly? No. I want you to myself." Even though Malk had agreed on an open relationship so we could explore various sins, we'd never acted on it. "If that's acceptable. Though I must warn you—I'm a high-class lady with needs, expensive tastes, and I'm going to be late for *everything*."

"Well, *that's* nothing new—"

"And I want a man who knows his own worth." I gave him a pointed look. "You think you need to make these grand dramatic gestures to prove yourself, but you're already worthy, Quen. You always have been."

He lowered his chin, his bottom lip wobbling.

His past lovers had used him. Abused him. It broke my heart to see him think of himself as unworthy. I placed a finger under his chin and lifted it until our eyes met. "I promise I will always treat you with the love and respect you deserve."

"You've never given me any less. Kayl, I... Saints. I love you more than all the stars in the sky."

"You're such a romantic. Or a dork. I can't decide which."

"I *did* study at the School of Art."

"Whereas I spent my formative years learning how to pick pockets in the Undercity. What a pair we make."

"You stole my heart."

"Definitely a dork."

Quen chuckled. "May I kiss you?"

"Gods, I think you better."

He leaned in, and our lips met in a ballet to rival any Seren production. And my heart felt at home once more.

I straddled his lap and wrapped my arms around his neck, giving him easier access. He adjusted, and we slotted together. This was also new—the beginnings of a relationship we'd previously navigated in the dark. There was much I still didn't know about Quen, much I wanted to explore and learn. I wanted to take my time with him, but time wasn't on our side.

I ground my arse against his groin, and his cock stirred. His metal arm held my lower back as his other hand slid up to my left breast and gently squeezed.

We'd certainly feel our way through this.

I pulled back and placed a finger on his lips. "I'll stop you there. As much as I want to fuck your brains out, we're on borrowed time, since you're not technically here." This Quen had entered through a dream, and I was sure he didn't want to cream his pants in reality. "And we need to make plans."

He groaned his frustration. "Very well."

We broke apart, and I leaned my head on his chest, his heart beating out another performance, as he wrapped his arm around my shoulders. I could be at peace with Quen, and that was worth everything to me.

"We need to come up with something smart if we're going to save the universe," I said. "Remember what Mesmorpheus told me? About taking the domains and remaking them? That's still the plan, right? I've been putting in practice."

Quen squeezed my shoulder. "You have. But we're missing two vital ingredients—Chaos and time. We need Dor."

"And Jinx. If she's trapped in the clock tower, then we need to bust her out. Easier said than done. Though I doubt even Dor will be expecting a group of Godless to come knocking."

"Are the Godless prepared to fight?"

"Oh, they're itching for one." Even under all the layers of trauma, that undercurrent of action buzzed between them. "Other mortals as well. This is their fight too, you know. It's like you said—the only way we're taking down Dor is if we work together. If we don't, they'll never get their domains back. And Harm is desperate for action. I've never seen her so pissed off."

"Dor will be expecting an attack, but I can distract him. Give you and the Godless time to infiltrate the clock tower."

"Sounds like a plan. We'll get together in the tram and work out the details." This time, it would be Harmony's operation. She was the expert at these things, and I trusted her to place me where I'd do best. "And then we'll remake Chime into a truly godless city. Assuming we succeed and don't get our arses beat, what will you do after?"

"After?"

"There'll be no more gods to tell us what to do. You wouldn't need to be a Warden anymore. You could become a tram driver, like you've always wanted."

"You're right," he mused. "I could. What about you? If you could do anything, be anyone?"

"Oh, that's easy. I'll become a famous actress in Chime's most popular theater. Though I'd specialize in improv. No point trying to memorize my lines when I'd likely forget them. Would you come watch my shows?"

"Naturally. I'll sit in the front row, holding a single rose."

"Just one rose?"

"An entire bouquet of roses. Except..." Quen rubbed his chin. "As much as I'd like to drive trams, our new Chime will need Wardens. We can't change the world and wash our hands of the whole affair. Without the gods, mortals will need guidance. They'll need a new Covenant, new rules for society to live by, otherwise everything will go to pot. Chime needs Wardens. Good Wardens. As much as Chime needs heathens."

"You're right." I sighed. "Acting is a dream, but that's all it is. I promised Mesmorpheus I'd take care of the Mesmer. I still intend to do that. Though... are you sure Chime needs Wardens? They only ever acted in the gods' interests. So many of them used their position to abuse mortals, and did more harm than good. I can't think of many instances where they actually helped."

Quen squirmed in his seat. "Without Wardens, who would protect mortals from violence or theft?"

"Why do you think mortals commit violence or theft in the first place? Because they had little choice. Vesper were always being dragged up for stealing, but they only needed to steal because of Valeria's tithe. Without the gods, and with proper support systems, mortals will prosper and crime levels will dwindle."

"Those are good points. Violent crime was an issue within the Undercity, and rarely impacted the Golden City. Crimes such as apostasy and blasphemy should no longer exist. I'm not entirely sure what a Chime without Wardens would look like, but I'm willing to work toward it, with you as my partner."

"Is this a proposal, Quen?"

He kissed my hand. "Become my partner in all things. No caveats."

"Wouldn't I get in your way?"

"I rather think we balance each other out."

We did make an excellent team.

We're gathering in the tram to make plans, I broadcast inside my mind. A message to the Godless. *Get the wine out.*

I pulled Quen up from the bench, and we walked hand in hand over to the tram behind the waterfall. I'd since expanded it into a private carriage room for myself, and a larger meeting room for the Godless. Fairy lights gave the inside a cozy glow, and the water running past the windows was a nice touch.

In time the Godless could add their own personal touches. Dru could bring some potted plants. Maybe Vincent would paint again.

Harmony and Joe were already inside. Harm was back to her old Seren self as Joe remained a Glimmer. The two of them sat hunched at the table, poring over a whole pile of hastily written notes.

Harm glanced up, her eye darting to Quen's hand in mine. "It's about time."

"Time puns? Really?" I helped myself to a bottle of wine. A rare vintage, because now that I had the power to do whatever I wanted—within reason—I could drink what I wanted, too.

"You might be a god now, but you're not above a good pun."

"I'm hardly a god. More a woman with a taste for vengeance."

"Same thing."

Quen sat and made himself comfortable. "It's good to see you both safe." He nodded at Joe and Harmony.

Joe smiled. "Likewise. We've all been through a lot."

"I'm sorry I left you behind in the clock tower—"

"Don't be. You went where you were needed, and I remained where I was needed. Do you need a hand with the wine?" Joe asked me.

"I've got it." I popped open the stopper.

The tram door opened, and in stepped Vincent and Sinder. I almost dropped the pissing bottle! Vincent leaned on his cane, back to his Necro form. He gave a weary smile, but it was Sinder who shocked me.

After everything Edana and Jinx had put him through, I'd expected him to remain in his Ember form.

He hadn't. His skin had changed to the golden hue of a Glimmer. Long golden hair flowed across his shoulders.

"Are we making plans for a revolution or hosting a wine tasting, darling?" he said, more his old self.

I picked my jaw up off the floor. "Bit of both. Thought we could whet our appetite for chaos and destruction. Maybe play a round of cards later."

"Like old times." He sat on the other side of Quen. "Since you're dating Kayl now, I suppose I ought to be nice to you." Sinder held out his hand. "No hard feelings?"

Quen shook it. "Water under the bridge."

My heart burst with pride at seeing Quen so readily accepted by my family, because he *was* my family now. He always had been, as our mystery benefactor.

His place was by my side.

"Am I late?" Malk called from the door.

Everyone turned to stare at Malk and Elvira. Malk's mother was exactly how I remembered her when she escaped the Glimmer workhouse. She stood as tall as her son, her long black hair dangling freely down to her hip. They'd changed to the forms of Vesper and were showing off more skin than Valeria ever deemed acceptable.

I glanced at Quen, whose entire body had gone rigid, fear in his eyes.

He'd killed Elvira. The guilt he carried would never leave him.

"Fashionably late, dearest," Sinder said, breaking the tension. "What kept you?"

"You know, the usual," Malk said. "Shit gods, domain-ending disasters. We've all been there. Is that a new look?"

Sinder batted his eyelashes. He did make for an exceptionally pretty Glimmer, and their natural femininity sure brought that side out of him. "You know me, I like to try on different styles. But you're being rude. Who is that ravishing beauty beside you?"

"Behave, will you?" Malk wrapped his arm around Elvira's shoulder. "Everyone, I'd like you to meet my mother."

Elvira giggled. "I've heard so much about you all."

Quen stood slowly. "We've met."

The tension returned. Quen looked as though he may faint, which wasn't ideal—I needed him conscious to discuss our plans. But I didn't want to step in on his moment.

His heart needed this if it was ever going to move on.

Elvira stepped free from Malk. "Mr. Quentin Corinth."

"I—I need to apologize to you, to your son, for so many things, but mere apologies aren't enough to beg your forgiveness—"

"I don't need an apology, Mr. Corinth. What I need is for you to keep your promise of a godless world." She embraced him in a tight hug and whispered something into his ear, something only for him.

But her words echoed in my mind. *If any of us need forgiveness, it's you.*

He'd killed her on Karendar's orders, though through Elvira's eyes, Quen had been another victim of his god. There was nothing to forgive.

Quen broke away and lifted his eyeglasses, wiping back a stray tear. "Thank you." He regained his composure and faced Malk. "I also owe you an apology, Malkavaan—"

"Forget about it." Malk waved him off.

"Please, I insist—"

"You made sure she didn't forget my sorry arse." Malk pointed at me. He'd witnessed my interactions with Quen through my eyes and the extent Quen had gone through to restore the Vesper. Malk's emotions were bittersweet: a mixture of guilt, gratitude, and regret. There was a part of him that still loved me. But he'd accepted the role Quen now played in my life. "I should be thanking *you*. And hey, my name's Malk." He slapped Quen on the back.

Quen winced. "You're very welcome."

Elvira cleared her throat. "Are you pouring that or playing with it?"

"What? Oh!" I still held the wine bottle. "Right."

We could all do with a drink.

I poured out glasses as more came to the tram and we made space.

Gast and Noct turned up, offering polite nods to Quen, who returned them without comment. They were followed by Trixie and Wolfsbane. Since I'd brought them back, they'd kept a cool distance from me—Trixie still blamed me for losing her Fauna. But she held a grudging respect for me, at least, since I'd brought back her mate and restored his missing left eye. Respect enough to take part in the meeting.

Then Dandelion and Nelle came. She'd left her cubs to play with the Mesmer, Freddie, and Doctor Zachery Finch, who was apparently being tormented but said he'd catch up on the meeting later. Honestly, I think the doctor enjoyed cutting loose for once, or whatever his definition of cutting loose was.

Then Reverie stepped in and helped herself to wine.

Almost everyone I'd ever loved was here for this meeting.

Everyone but Dru.

As we were about to begin, the door opened once more.

And there she stood. Her golden daisies quivered slightly. "Is there room for one more?"

We'd barely spoken since she came back. Vincent had wanted to give her space, and so I had, even if it hurt to see her so withdrawn.

I'd not even had a chance to tell her about Ben. I couldn't do that to her. Not yet.

I shuffled aside. "Here."

Dru tentatively sat beside me.

"It's good to see you, Dru," Malk said.

She forced a smile. "You too."

I took her hand and squeezed it. "I love you, you know?" I whispered.

"I know," she whispered back, and returned the squeeze.

We'd be all right. All of us. So long as we had each other.

We'd survived the cruelties of our gods, the end of our domains, and we were still family. Whatever happened next, we'd face it together.

Harmony tapped the side of her wineglass with a pen. "All right, listen up. You've all gathered here so we can decide how we deal with Dor—"

"I thought we were playing cards?" Malk said.

"Let's worry about where our cards stack against Dor first. Kayl?"

I swirled my wineglass. "Quen and I are going to remake the domains. That was always the plan. We've gathered every god's soul except for Dor's and my twin sister's. She's taken Corentine's place and is currently trapped in the clock tower. Quen can tell you more about that, and what state Chime is in."

"Chime still exists?" Gast asked. "I was there when it blew up."

"It exists in a fashion," Quen said. "Dor has recreated it."

I let Quen explain everything as my mind wandered. Perhaps drinking wine before an important meeting wasn't the best idea, but it loosened everyone up.

And, honestly, I bloody deserved it.

Sister.

I froze. Jinx spoke inside my mind, the first time she had since I'd escaped Dor and returned to Haven.

Since Karendar had split her soul from mine.

Jinx? Where are you? The clock tower?

Good guess. Dor wanted a new battery for his shitty-arse city and plugged me in. It… it hurts, sis. It really fucking hurts. No—no wonder Mother went mad.

Pain laced her words. I believed her.

Shit.

We're coming up with a plan to get you out—

Don't. It's a—a trap. Dor wants to draw you out. He knows you're hiding in a pocket dimension somewhere, and he's dangling me and Corinth. When he's caught you, he'll split your soul—yours and Corinth's—and then your precious Godless, all the mortals you carry, will be gone. Poof. Destroyed.

What are you saying? That you don't want me to rescue you?

You get it, good.

You literally just said you're being tortured! And you want me to leave you at Dor's mercy? Not a chance.

Because Dor will kill you! For once in your mortal life, don't be a fucking idiot. You can hide from Dor. Keep your Godless safe—Joe and the rest of them. Live your best fucking life and forget about me.

You became my god the moment you took Corentine's soul. I'm tied to you.

We both know that's not true anymore. You've collected enough souls that you've become your own damn god now. Be free. Frolic. Whatever. Just stay the fuck away.

I chewed my tongue. This was so typical of Jinx. *No.*

For fuck's sake, Kayl—

You want to be a martyr? Is that it? You think sacrificing yourself will make up for all the shitty things you've done?

Won't it? I killed our mother! I never even let you have a relationship with her, because I—I was scared. She screamed so much. All the time, just screaming, screaming—which, you know, I get now. And I was trapped inside your mind for so long. You never even acknowledged me, even when I kept you safe. You drove me fucking mad! But you're my sister. I loved you. Even though you never... you never loved me back.

Jinx...

Mother wanted you to become a tool for her vengeance. She wanted to poison you, like... like she poisoned me, I guess. But I, I loved the way you smiled in the mirror. Your silly little thoughts. I didn't want Mother to ruin you. And now she's gone. This is what I deserve.

Her confession sat heavy in my heart.

We'd grown up together. Thirteen years where she'd helped me, guided me, kept me out of trouble as best she could despite my talent for it. All that time she'd been trapped inside my mind with no freedom of her own. I couldn't imagine what that was like. The only inkling had been when Anima had fucked with my memories, and when Serenity had forced me to act against my own will, and that had been horrifying enough.

But Jinx had hurt me. Had threatened and tortured my friends and family. Had turned them against me, in some cases.

I'd forgiven Sinder. Could I forgive Jinx?

Her warning was real, at least. If I tried to save her, I was risking everything. Quen, the Godless, every single mortal soul bound to mine.

But I couldn't hide from Dor and let others fight my battles for me. Hiding here wasn't even the logical option—Dor would come for us, especially since he knew how to navigate and spy on my dreams. We weren't safe here or anywhere.

The fact Dor was so keen to draw me out was an advantage we could use.

And, fuck it. Dor had hurt Quen. That alone meant I wanted vengeance.

You're my sister, I said. *I'm coming for you.*

Why do you have to be so damn stubborn?

You were inside my mind for thirteen years. You know how this goes.

"Kayl?" Harmony snapped. "Are you even listening?"

Oh shit, I'd completely blanked out for the past twenty minutes. "Sorry. I had Jinx talking in my ear. Everything Quen said is true—Dor's keeping her locked inside the clock tower."

Trixie scowled. "Considering everything she did, isn't that the best place for 'er? Can't ruin more lives from in there."

"Dor's practically torturing her—"

"And? What goes around comes around."

Quen placed his hand on my knee under the table where no one else could see. A calming gesture. He must have noticed me getting irate.

I met Trixie's feline eyes. "To stand any chance of defeating Dor, we need Jinx. Luckily, she can communicate with me from within—we can use that. So do we have a plan?"

Harmony shared one of her sly smiles. "We've got something."

She explained her ludicrous plan as I poured more wine. It was bold, ambitious, and had Harmony's signature all over it.

Everyone was in agreement.

Come tomorrow morning, we'd enact it. We'd save my sister. Save the domains. Save Chime. Kick Dor's arse.

Though I'd need to invent a hangover cure first.

As promised, we spent a much-needed evening playing cards. Even Dru took part. It was Quen's first time, and he was a dab hand at it, though I caught him losing deliberately to Elvira. He confessed later that he hadn't wanted to show off, that dork.

The whole night, I worried Dor would snap Quen back to his reality, but he didn't. That should have worried me, I supposed, but I clung to Quen. To the time we had left.

When everyone broke off to sleep or spend the evening reminiscing, I dragged Quen to the pile of cushions that made up my bed.

We didn't fuck. We made love. As slow and considerate as I knew Quen to be.

And then he vanished, like it had all been a dream.

Every mortal soul was depending on me to deliver them salvation, yet it was my friends, my family, who worried me the most.

I could see a future for us. For me and Quen.

For that future to come to pass, time had to end.

46

There's a new group in town. Call themselves the Godless. Picked up one of their fliers. They're spreading blasphemous propaganda. It's sending the Wardens into a frenzy—I've had one of 'em knocking on my door.
Love to see it, but it won't last.
Whoever's behind these fliers are going to face a one-way trip out of Chime.
A man can hope, though. Something's gotta change in this damn city.
—M. Gast, from the personal files of PI Gast

HAVEN WAS ABUZZ WITH activity as we gathered and prepared for Harmony's outrageous plan. We were splitting into teams, and team one consisted of Quen and my new doppelganger. They'd be handling Dor. I entered one of the pavilions I'd turned into a changing room and found Elvira already inside with Sinder doing her makeup.

"Almost done, darling," Sinder called over his shoulder. "Vincent's worked his magic, then you can work yours."

"Do I look all right?" Elvira asked.

I sat on a cushion beside her. "You look perfect."

Vincent had tailored the contours of her face to resemble mine and adjusted her hair. With Sinder's touch, and a little Mesmer illusion, Elvira should hopefully fool Dor into thinking she was me. We stood at roughly the same height, with a similar body composition. We needed someone to play pretend, and honestly, Elvira made sense. I had based my adult persona on her as my greatest female role model.

The closest I had to a real mother.

"I don't like it." Malk scowled. He sat on a stool opposite, his arms crossed, and two dark leathery wings protruding from his back. They were the same type of wings Valeria's Winged Twilights bore, without the feathers of a Zephyr. The same that Valeria had both gifted and ripped from Varen. They were my gift to Malk, which I'd specifically gifted to him last night so he'd have time to learn how to use them. "You're asking her to parade herself in front of a god and risk her *soul*. Do you really think we'll trick a damn god?"

"Deception plays on the ego, dearest." Sinder squinted in concentration as he finished applying Elvira's eyeliner. "Dor is a god of logic. Parlor tricks are beneath him. He won't even suspect Kayl of being that subtle. No offense, darling."

"See?" I said. "Sinder knows what he's doing."

Malk huffed. "I still don't like it."

"Oh, give over!" Elvira chided. "Do you think me that old already? I *want* to play my part."

"Playing your part may get you killed, Ma."

Elvira twisted in her seat and gave Malk a withering look—the kind that brought back memories of my childhood. "Malkavaan Byvich. I've died three times. The day Valeria killed your father. The day I entered that Glimmer workhouse. And for real, when the Wardens dragged me to their correctional facility. Don't presume to tell me what I can and can't survive."

Gods, I fucking loved her. "Quen will protect her." After everything Quen had been through, there was no chance he'd let anyone lay a finger on Elvira. That worried me most.

Guilt flashed across Malk's face. "Then he better not slip up."

"All done," Sinder declared, finishing Elvira's makeup.

Elvira admired herself in the mirror. "I look twenty years young! Thank you for this." She joined Malk for what I hoped wouldn't be a final mother-son conversation.

"Did you want me to touch up your eyes, dearest?" Sinder asked. "Nothing says 'god slayer' quite like smoldering eyelashes."

"Sadly, I don't think we have time."

"Ironic."

"Are you doing all right?"

Sinder sighed. "I don't need everyone to keep checking in on me. I'm not 'fine,' but who is these days?"

I took his hand. He'd painted the nails red to complement his new golden skin. "You don't have to punish yourself like this."

"By looking gorgeous?" He tossed his hair over his shoulder. "Working with hairstyles is such a pleasure. I've never felt so femme. It suits me, darling."

"Is that something you want to explore? Should I start referring to you as a she?"

"Truthfully, I don't know." He picked at his nails. "I've always hated the Glimmer for what they did to me, but part of it, I think, was envy. To be so feminine and powerful and cruel. Joe is helping me sort out my feelings."

"Not Vincent?"

Sinder glanced to the opposite end of the room where Vincent was meditating alone. "He's a little cool with me right now. I don't blame him. But don't worry about us. We're ready to do what's needed."

They were both joining team two alongside Joe and Wolfsbane, led by Malk. Their task was arguably the more dangerous one: to portal into Chime, scout the clock tower for potential weaknesses, and then create as much chaos as possible.

A distraction for when *my* team would break into the clock tower. We weren't quite sure what protections Dor would have placed on the tower—presumably something that could detect and disable Chaos—which was why my team included an expert on the subject: Doctor Zachery Finch.

The rest would protect Haven, if necessary. We had children here, now, and other mortals who couldn't and shouldn't be expected to fight.

I left Sinder to finish his preparations and wandered over to Vincent.

"You and Sinder aren't talking?" It was important I checked in on each of the Godless after everything they'd been through. While I could have dug into their minds for the answers, it was more personal to speak, and I didn't want to violate their trust.

Vincent grabbed his cane and slowly eased himself up. Since I'd rebirthed him, I'd been able to remove the pain in his legs, but he kept his cane nearby out of habit. "He betrayed you." His voice came out in a whisper.

So that was what it was about. "I forgave him."

"His actions damned an entire domain—"

"So did mine. In case you hadn't noticed, that's part of our goal."

"He was motivated by spite."

"Look. We all carry baggage where the gods are concerned. Sinder is trying to do better. You know he is."

Vincent ran a hand down his face. "Then how can I bear to look at him? I killed him. Back in Witheryn. I drained him of blood."

Oh. *That* was the real reason. "You didn't attack Sinder. You weren't in control of yourself. The Nameless One used you. They made you feral. Sinder understands that. He forgives *you*."

He gazed at Sinder with bloodshot eyes. "Can I forgive myself? No, I'm sorry. We don't need this right now."

"Do you want to stay here? With the others?"

"No! No. I'll be there. You can count on me." He smiled, though it was restrained and hid his fangs.

Did I trust him not to have a breakdown in the middle of our operation? He likely wasn't feeding, but I didn't want to push him. He'd work it out with Sinder. They always did.

A commotion rumbled outside the pavilion, and I headed out to greet it.

Leander appeared across the golden hills as Zephyr descended from the sky and landed among them, led by a familiar Zephyr ambassador with black feathers.

I strode over to Harmony, who was counting them. "Is that the ambassador? Colin? Crowley?"

Harm rolled her eyes. "Corvus. Pay attention, girl."

Dandelion and Nelle approached. "Leander warriors," Nelle said, her chest swelling with pride. "Finch says Zephyr also make good warriors."

"That we do," Corvus said, announcing his presence. "Lady Arkey. Quentin called to me in your hour of need and explained the situation. We'll protect this domain."

"Thank you." Having a bunch of fighters on our side would make all the difference. We were almost ready to begin. "Where's the doctor?"

"I'm here! I'm here." Doctor Finch ran out of another pavilion, juggling four shiny pocket watches in his talons. Portable portals. One for each team. "They're tested and ready to go."

Harmony nudged me. "Looks like we're ready to begin, then. You still remember the plan?"

"My memory's not *that* bad."

She gave me a look that suggested she didn't agree. Some things didn't change.

"You know, your plan is overly chaotic and dangerous," I said. "The kind of plan I'd suggest and you'd shoot down for being overly chaotic and dangerous."

"Maybe I learned a thing or two from you."

Gods, I hoped not. I needed this plan to actually succeed.

We wanted to avoid a direct confrontation with Dor's mortals and especially immortals, but a fight was inevitable. Since the Diviner were all soulless, we didn't need to worry about casualties on their side, but they had the ability to rend souls. That was the real risk of getting up close and personal.

And we needed a way to keep them and Dor occupied and away from the clock tower.

Everyone gathered outside the main pavilion on time. It was quite a number. Since Malk and I had begun the Godless all those years ago, we'd gained allies and grown. I'd never actually thought we'd end the reign of gods, yet here we were. Achieving the impossible.

If life was a play, then we'd come to the final act. It was time to take center stage.

I cleared my throat. "Thank you all for coming here, even if some of you didn't have a choice. I created this domain—Haven—to be a sanctuary for the godless. It's something I wished we had back when the gods were tormenting us. So many of us have suffered under the cruelties of our gods. A few of you may have been lucky enough to escape their attention. I've always believed mortals can do better, *be* better, without divine entities breathing down their necks and dictating their lives. Now I'll put that theory to the test.

"The gods are dead. Only one remains, and he hates mortal life. Dor would see us turned into soulless husks or wiped from existence altogether. But life belongs to those who live it, and the gods could never understand what it means to be mortal. I'll show him what mortals can do. Are you with me?"

A cheer rippled across the crowd. Many determined faces stared back at me, mortals I didn't know—Leander, Zephyr, even some Glimmer and Vesper. Volunteers. Among them stood Gast, Noct, and the leader of team four—Zorya. A Vesper ex-Warden who'd volunteered for the job, and Gast's lover. I'd brought her back last night at Gast's insistence, and they'd been inseparable ever since. Honestly, Zorya was gorgeous, and eager to help. I could see why Gast was so smitten.

But it was the Godless whose faces I sought.

My family.

As part of our defense against Dor, Harmony loved that I'd split my souls among the Mesmer, giving the Seren to Celeste and the Umber to Castor. But I'd taken those god souls back to divvy up among the Godless.

Faen's soul had gone to Trixie, who would summon Fauna to help fight.

Unghard's soul I'd handed over to Dru, even if she was a little hesitant.

Joe had taken Gildola, ready to use her powers for righteous burning.

Serenity was now in Harmony's hands.

I'd trusted Vincent with The Nameless One and hoped he'd keep it together long enough to keep the Necro safe.

Sinder had taken Edana and swapped back to his Ember form for now.

Reverie would keep the Mesmer safe.

Quen had kept Anima, Lionheart, and Zyclone for himself, for his defense against Dor, and to ensure the Amnae could never be used against him again. I needed to retain Valeria's soul, not only so I could use her shadows to sneak into the clock tower, but for another reason. Each team would be led by a Vesper—Elvira, Malk, Zorya—so I could reach into their minds and keep track of everything through their eyes.

In our effort to defeat Dor, the Godless had become gods.

The teams dispersed. Doctor Finch waited for me alongside Dru.

"I'm coming with you," she said.

That wasn't part of the plan. "The Umber are needed here—"

"I'm leaving the Umber behind. You can't seriously run off to fight a god on your own. I'm your bodyguard. You need me."

"I won't be alone. I've got Doctor Finch—"

"He needs a bodyguard more than you do." Dru sighed.

"I don't require supervision!" Doctor Finch huffed.

I took Dru's arm and steered her away from the doctor. "Dru, you know I love you, but you're not ready for this. We're going up against Diviner. It won't be pretty."

"I'm not a child. You don't need to parent me—"

"They got Ben." This wasn't how I'd wanted to go about telling her, but she needed to know. "He's one of the mortals who lost their souls."

Dru let out a breath. "I figured. I'm not... I'm not someone who makes a fuss. I get on with whatever needs doing, and sometimes others notice and thank me."

"Dru—"

She held up her hand. "I want to make a fuss, okay? I—I know it wasn't my fault for what happened in Chime, when I... did those things. I know it was Unghard. But they... they thought they were protecting us. The Umber. Our domain. They thought they were doing the right thing, and they were *wrong*. Dor twisted everything. And Ben..." She choked back a sob, and her flowers wilted. "Revenge isn't my thing, but I want it to be, for one damn day. Let me have this, Kayl. Let me be Godless for once."

I pulled her into a hug. "All right. You're with me."

She squeezed my lower back. "I always have been."

Finally, we were ready to begin Operation Break into the Clock Tower.

The clock struck eleven, and the first portal opened into Quen's old apartment, for some reason—he'd chosen the time and place, so I had to trust he knew what he was doing. Elvira nodded at me, then Malk, who stood brooding over my shoulder, and then she—looking almost exactly like me—stepped through.

Quen waited on the other side, his face grim, the aether collar still around his neck. We made eye contact. He licked his bottom lip, and the yearning behind those eyeglasses almost made me call off the whole thing.

You should, Jinx said inside my mind. *You're going to fail and fuck everything.*

Have a little faith.

I knew we could do this.

The portal closed. There was no going back now.

I opened Elvira's mind and watched from her eyes. My presence would be a gentle hum, enough for her to know I was with her. If the worst happened, and Dor threatened her, I'd snap her out of there. It wasn't ideal, but she'd volunteered. She knew the risks, even if Malk didn't approve.

Honestly, I wished we'd had more time to catch up before I threw her into danger, but that was how we Undercity folk did things.

From her perspective, I got a good view of Quen's living room. It was identical to how I remembered it. The window looked out to the clockface, where Jinx was held captive, and the first thing Elvira did was stare out across Central Station to grant me that vantage point.

It was like I'd thought. The Gate was crawling with Wardens and the station itself had a handful of those clockwork Guardians watching each exit. It was bizarre to see immortal beings casually hanging about.

Breaking into the clock tower from Central would be difficult, but I had other options. Plan A, B, and C if I got truly desperate.

Quen took Elvira's hand and guided her to his couch. "Please, sit. Would you like a cup of tea while we wait?"

"No, thank you." *He's such a gentleman,* Elvira commented.

He still feels guilty about what happened during the Grayford riot, I said.

I know. I told him the best apology would be this. Making the gods fear.

And I'd wondered where Malk and I got our godless inclinations from. Elvira really was the best choice to act as me.

"Inform Dor my guest has arrived," Quen said to someone out of sight.

Elvira turned, and in the corner was... Oh shit.

Karendar was seated at Quen's piano.

Only, he was as still as a statue. It was like Quen had described during our meeting. Dor had taken Karendar's soul. Or rather, the ex-ambassador had volunteered it, though who in their right mind would willingly give up their soul? I didn't want to feel pity for that prick, but I was sure he *hadn't* been in his right mind. He was another of Dor's victims.

Karendar's limbs suddenly spasmed, like a puppet become animated. He turned to Elvira—seemingly staring right through me—and I suppressed a shudder. Dor wasn't daft enough to face me alone, then. But that didn't matter.

I wasn't sure if Dor would detect us entering Chime. All Quen needed to do was hold his attention.

I withdrew from Elvira's mind. "Malk, you're up!"

Malk wound his new pocket watch, courtesy of Doctor Finch, and opened a portal into the Golden City. That would be Malk's first step—to scout the entrance to the glass elevator for a means of sneaking in. My plan B.

He disappeared into the portal, fading into shadow as it closed behind him.

Now, it was my turn. I opened another portal into the Undercity, where I'd scout the clock tower from the opposite end if needed for plan C. "Ready?" I called to Doctor Finch and Dru.

The doctor fiddled nervously with his sleeve. "If I could have only a few more minutes—"

"No." Dru shoved him forward. "It's now or never."

The doctor whined as he stumbled into the portal, and we stepped in after him.

Going from Haven's bright starry skies to the pitch blackness of the Undercity was a little jarring, but I swapped form to Vesper, and my eyes adjusted immediately. Not so for Doctor Finch, who bumped into Dru and flapped his arms in a panic.

"Calm down, it's only Dru."

"This is absurd! I can't *see!*"

Dru rolled her eyes. "Give it a minute, and you will. Kayl, where are we?"

Dor's new version of the Undercity was far cleaner than the one I knew, without the years of layered soot and grime, yet I still recognized it. "We're in one of the tunnels. Start walking that way." I pointed west.

"Which way?"

"Oh, right." I took Dru's and the doctor's wrist and let my shadow envelop them both so they could see. "This way."

We hurried along the tracks. I let my mind slip back into Elvira's.

"...no threat to you or your mortals. Release my sister, and we'll be on our merry way. You can have Babel, and we needn't speak ever again."

Elvira had launched her negotiation attempt with Dor. I didn't expect him to accept.

Karendar—or Dor pretending to be Karendar—stood by Quen's window, his back to her, as he surveyed the city. "You and your sister have orchestrated the demise of gods and their domains. How can I accept your word?"

"Oh, come now. You wanted the gods out of the way. I've done us both a favor."

He faced Elvira. "It's only a matter of time before you come for my soul."

"She's here in good faith," Quen said.

"If you promise to leave my mortals alone, then I'll honor a truce," Elvira added.

"Chaos and time are incompatible," Karendar said.

"Only if you're being stubborn about it."

"It is the nature of time to persist. As it is the nature of Chaos to cause disarray. This meeting is a waste of my time, and I have no need for a second Chaos mortal. Quentin? Subdue her."

Quen looked apologetic. "I'm sorry. I tried." He drew a taser from his belt and fired it at Elvira.

The shock wave kicked me from her mind. I stumbled and would have fallen if Dru hadn't steadied me. "Shit!"

"Everything going to plan?" Dru asked.

"Like pissing clockwork." I dove back into Elvira's mind. Quen had wrapped a faulty aether collar around her neck. Faulty, because I couldn't enter her mind if it worked. *Are you all right?*

Were you going to warn me he'd bloody zap me?

No, because he wanted your reaction to be real. It was hard to fake being tasered. Guilt flashed across Quen's face. He didn't need to fake his emotions.

What do I do now?

Call Dor a prick or something. That's what I'd do.

"You—You arsehole!" Elvira spluttered.

"Language," Karendar chided. "Quentin. Do what must be done."

Quen nodded. "Then remove my collar."

Karendar reached behind Quen's neck, drawing him close. The intimacy of it sickened me. "Make me proud, Quentin. Do not fail me."

The collar came off. Quen drew a breath, steadying himself.

And then he approached Elvira.

Just like we said, I told her.

I'm ready.

Quen straddled Elvira, pushing her against the couch as she pretended to flail. "I'm sorry," he said again with genuine remorse. "But you cannot be allowed to retain these souls."

He placed his hand against her chest and mimicked drawing out the god souls she supposedly carried.

Elvira let out a strangled gasp. "Quen, please! Stop!" A performance worthy of the Golden City.

Quen leaped back, his chest rising with his rapid gulps. "It's done. I have every soul except Chaos."

"Show me," Karendar demanded.

Quen changed form from Diviner to Leander and then Amnae. They were the souls he'd already owned, though hopefully his quick display would be enough to fool Dor. He approached Elvira once more and placed his hand on her forehead. "Chaos will hold no power if you forget."

Another trick. This time, he pretended to wipe Elvira's—my—memories.

Elvira leaned against the couch, her eyelids fluttering. "Where am I?"

"You're under my personal protection. Do you remember who you are?"

"I'm a Warden. I—I follow your commands."

"Wonderful." Quen turned to Dor. "She is now docile and will no longer prove a threat."

Karendar rubbed his chin. "The logical option would have been to take her soul."

"You chose to enslave Jinx. However, she is the more volatile twin. Keep this one as a spare should Jinx prove dangerous."

"A spare for me? Or to spare you? I know you have inclinations toward this woman. Would you fuck her?"

Quen recoiled. "Gods, no! I pity her, and all Corentine's mortals—"

"Corentine's mortals do not require pity—"

"I'm a Warden. I'm sympathetic to all mortals." Quen lifted his chin. "This is how you made me."

"A weakness, Quentin. One that will no longer be relevant when I end mortal life."

Quen swallowed. "Then what will you do with me?"

Karendar smiled. "Whatever I wish." He beckoned Quen close. "Prove your devotion."

Quen had no choice but to obey. Karendar's hands went to his shoulders as Quen leaned in to kiss him.

I wanted Elvira to turn away. I wanted to crawl out of her mind and break Karendar's pissing nose.

"Kayl!" Dru yelped, snapping me back to reality.

"Sorry, what?"

"You're crushing my wrist."

"Sorry," I mumbled.

"We're here!" Doctor Finch squawked, and pointed ahead.

The tunnel opened to the central chamber of the Undercity, where the tram station and elevator resided. Once, lines of Vesper and Ember would have queued up for that damn elevator. It was where Quen and I first met.

Now, lines of bloody Guardians stood in front of it. Shit!

Malk? I called into my mind. *Have you made it yet?*

Barely, he replied. *There are too many Wardens, and those hulking clockwork things.*

Shitting shit!

If Dor had every possible entrance into the clock tower locked down, then we'd have to fight our way through, and that wouldn't be easy.

Kayl! Elvira yelled. *Something's wrong!*

I threw myself back into her mind. Karendar had his hand around Quen's neck.

Shit, what had I missed?

"You offer yourself to me, Quentin," Karendar was saying. "But I've studied the patterns of your behavior. Logically, you will betray me."

Oh fuck. The game was up.

Quen sucked in air, as though about to argue.

Instead, he swung his metal fist at Karendar's hateful face.

Karendar suddenly morphed into Dor and caught Quen's fist in his own hand.

"Get out of there!" I screamed with Elvira's voice.

A bubble of time enveloped Quen's arm. It rusted in the space of seconds and fell in a sprinkling of parts.

Quen tried to grab Dor with his other hand, to snatch Dor's soul, but he wasn't quick enough.

Dor shoved him through the glass window.

It shattered into shards. Shit! Quen fell out of sight.

"Quen!" I forced Elvira to stand and rip off the aether collar. Shadows burst from her hands.

Dor glanced at me with a taunting smirk. "You aren't a child of Chaos, but you see me, don't you?"

"You fucking prick!"

He waggled his finger with a tut. "So vulgar, the pair of you. You must understand you cannot win this war—"

"You're not the only power in this city. So long as I breathe, mortals will continue to rise against you."

"I admit, I struggle to understand the mortal mind. Though, will you be able to comprehend immortality? If you choose to become a god, you will live forever, and watch your loved ones wither and die until you forget what it means to be mortal."

"Is that what happened to you? You lived so pissing long, you forgot how to care?"

"You presume I cared to begin with."

Wings flapped by the broken window. Oh, thank fuck!

Quen had switched to his Zephyr form, his jacket gone, his right arm missing, and his shirt now in tatters from the sheer force of growing wings. "Dor!" he yelled.

Dor spun.

I yanked Elvira's soul back from her body, tossing it into the aether of my subconscious. I'd not wanted to leave Quen, but I couldn't risk Elvira's soul falling into Dor's hands.

I'd barely opened my eyes back to the Undercity when Malk's voice came through.

We're spotted! Wardens are attacking. What's our next move?

We'll regroup in Central. I couldn't think of an easier way to get into the clock tower than a full-on assault.

And Central was where we'd find Quen.

Portals are opening! Zorya said. *It's the Diviner! They're here!*

Shit, not now! I dove into her mind and watched the chaos unfold.

Multiple portals opened into Haven. At least twelve that I could count. Dor's men marched through—all soulless Diviner armed with tasers and carrying those portable soul-splitting devices. Gods, they hadn't come to capture or kill.

They'd come to obliterate.

Through Zorya's mind, I watched as she readied the defense. We had Leander and Zephyr on our side, but the number of Diviner was terrifying.

Kayl? Malk said. *What now?*

I switched to Malk's mind. He, Sinder, Vincent, Joe, and Wolfsbane had portaled into Central and hid inside an alleyway behind the station.

I need a better look at the clockface. Can you fly up and scout it?

I'm on it.

Sinder and Joe ran from the alley and began flinging fire and sunlight at the Diviner. A distraction as Malk spread his wings and took to the sky. Through his eyes, I tried to catch a glimpse of Quen over Central, but Malk flew too fast for me to see anything except Chime pass by in a dizzying blur.

He slowed before the clockface. Aether crackled all around it. Worse, the maintenance door which had led inside no longer existed.

There went my plan A. We weren't getting in that way, either. Shit!

"Kayl!" Dru shook my arm. "They're moving!"

I returned to reality and swayed on my feet. All this head-hopping was making me nauseous.

The Wardens guarding the Undercity elevator were heading straight for us.

"What do we do?" Doctor Finch shrieked.

"I don't know," I said. "There're too many Wardens guarding the damn clock tower. Dor's got it locked down."

"I don't mean to rush you," Dru said. "But we need a new plan."

"I'm out of plans! We're fucked!"

I told you so, Jinx said.

Could you sound less gleeful? We're trying to rescue you!

I told you not to bother.

It doesn't matter now, does it? Dor's found our hideout. If I stand any chance of stopping him, I need you!

Oh, now you need me? There's nothing I can do. I'm as powerless as our mother was. Create another domain and save yourself.

"Shit!" I kicked the wall.

Noct! Zorya screamed. Her pain stabbed through my mind. For a moment, I thought she'd been hurt.

No, it was Noct.

Through her eyes, I watched as the Diviner overwhelmed Zorya, forcing her to retreat. Gast pulled her away from a taser blast, which hit Noct instead.

They swarmed him.

We both watched in horror as a Diviner placed a helmet on his head. His diamond pupils were wide with fear, his tiny wings beating frantically to escape.

I couldn't reach his soul to save him—I'd given it to Harmony.

With a pulse of aether, his soul was gone.

Fuck.

We'd lost Noct, and soon I'd lose the rest of them, because I had *no fucking plan*!

No. No. I had to think. *Think!*

Jinx and I had been born in the Undercity, yet our souls had traveled out of the clock tower somehow. Through the natural aether present in streetlamps, of all pissing things.

That was it.

"Doctor," I said. "Do you remember when we first met? Chaos was leaking from the clock tower and attacking Diviner."

"Yes, yes, but shouldn't we be *escaping*?" He pointed to the approaching clockwork immortals.

"In a damn minute! Listen, a Chaos mortal crawled out of a reactor in the steamworks. Remember? They escaped from the clock tower! What if I did the opposite? Entered the reactor and used that to enter the clock tower?"

He stared at me as if I'd finally gone mad. "The clock tower reinforcement project prevented Chaos from leaking out."

"In the old clock tower, yes. Dor destroyed that one. What are the chances he forgot to reinforce this one?"

"Can you really enter the clock tower that way?" Dru asked.

"We're all made of aether, so maybe. It's the only idea I've got." My plan D.

It was a long shot. Jinx was the expert at manipulating aether, not me, and Quen would surely stand a better chance.

I could do it. I *had* to do it.

Dru nodded. "Then we better run."

"What about *those*?" Doctor Finch said.

"I can slow them down."

"How?"

"Nature finds a way." Dru headed for the tunnel we'd come out of. As soon as Doctor Finch and I entered it, Dru kneeled by the entrance, placing her hands flat against the ground.

"What *is* she doing?" the doctor exclaimed.

I hushed him. The ground began to vibrate, and not just from whatever Dru was doing. Two Guardians were striding toward the tunnel, their heavy steps shuddering through the cobblestones.

Doctor Finch covered his eyes. "Oh gods, I'm going to die—*again!*"

Vines sprouted from cracks beneath us. They shot up and attached themselves to the ceiling and walls, spreading into an intricate web of weeds and flowers.

I nudged Doctor Finch. "Look!"

He uncovered his eyes and gasped.

One of the Guardians collided with it. Their metal arms ripped through the wall of weeds, but they quickly regrew and stitched the wall together again. Time sped up around us as the Diviner attempted to age and wither the plants, but as soon as they died, new vines grew—thicker than before.

They wrapped around the Guardian's legs, holding them in place.

Gods. There weren't many things that could counter a Diviner's time manipulation, but Dru was working with Unghard's power now. I honestly didn't know if the Undercity even had weeds lurking underneath the stone—or if Dru was powerful enough to conjure them.

"Let's go," she said.

The doctor was still staring as I dragged him along. We ran through the tunnel, Dru leaving a trail of weeds in her wake. It would slow the Diviner, but we didn't have time to waste. Not when Dor was attacking Haven.

"Let Quen know of the change in plan," I told the doctor. "Is he safe?"

"He's hiding in Central—oh no, Ben is searching for him."

Shit. I really didn't have time to fuck this up.

Dru and I ran for all we were worth. Like old times. When the doctor flagged behind, complaining of his feet, Dru scooped him up and carried him in her arms. The poor doctor didn't know what to make of it, but we couldn't leave him behind.

Chances were, I'd need him. He was the boffin.

Aether shit and reactors were his area.

Eventually the tunnel opened to the steamworks. I hunched over and caught my breath as Dru set the doctor down.

The steamworks hadn't changed in Dor's new Chime. It was as bleak and oppressive as ever. Thick piping connected the steamworks to the plate above. Was that how aether traveled? I'd soon find out.

A couple of Diviner stood guard by the main entrance, but no Guardians. Did Dor not expect us to attack the steamworks? Or did he not consider it worth protecting?

Or was it a trap?

It wouldn't be the first trap you've willingly walked into, Jinx said.

Do you have any other ideas?

Give up.

Fuck's sake, Jinx. You're the one who wanted to end the reign of the gods, so help me bring down Dor.

What's the point? I help you create a better universe, and then what happens to me?

What do you want to happen?

I wanted my mother. I wanted a family, like you have. But you won't give me that.

Shit, I didn't have time for this. "What do you think? Sneak in or rampage our way through?"

"Sneak in carefully," the doctor said. "We don't want to attract attention."

"Rampage," Dru said. "We don't have time to knock and be polite, and Dor probably knows we're here anyway."

Honestly, I loved this new Dru. "Rampage it is."

My Vesper form would be ideal for sneaking, but I needed something with a bit more oomph. Of all the souls I'd stolen since I became Chaos— which wasn't many because I wasn't a complete bitch—Whiskers's soul would give me the oomph I needed.

I gave his soul a poke and transformed into a Leander. *Malk? Keep the Diviner busy. We're almost there.*

You better hurry. The more we put down, the more turn up, and the bodies are starting to pile.

That was a mental image I didn't need. "Ready, Dru?"

She cracked her knuckles. "Ready."

I crouched on all four paws and ran. Dru followed me, and her form shifted, her arms thickening into massive Golem-like limbs.

As soon as I neared the first Diviner, I pounced.

My claws sank into his torso. I didn't even think of what I was doing as I let instinct take over and ripped apart his chest. Beside me, Dru launched at the second Diviner and pummeled him into the ground.

"You're both *insane!*" the doctor squawked as he stumbled after us.

Together, we burst into the steamworks. The reception was empty, but I didn't hang around to discover why. "Doctor, do you remember the way?"

"Follow the corridor to the maintenance stairs, then head down!"

"Right."

We ran through the same corridor Quen and I had once entered when investigating Chaos, and passed the room where a Diviner had been frozen on ice.

Those familiar metal stairs came into view, and we headed down them to another corridor lined with metal piping. "Which way?"

"Follow the signs for reactor A, pipe C."

It wasn't too hard to find. All the while I kept glancing over my shoulder, but no Diviner appeared.

I opened the door to the reactor, and aether whooshed over me.

The reactor was on. It was *alive*.

Aether swirled within the machine, a beautiful dance of pink and blue. The room itself was exactly how I remembered it from when Quen and I visited last, with brass piping running up the walls—a miniature version of the clockface room, now I thought about it.

Other than the reactor, the room was empty.

Waiting for me.

Dru and Doctor Finch stepped in after me.

"What now?" Dru said. "I know a thing or two about engineering, but this is beyond me."

"I assume I step in it? Doctor, any advice?"

The doctor sagged against the metal wall. "Any normal mortal would be instantly vaporized by that level of aether. I—I have no idea how you would survive it."

You wouldn't, Jinx said. *That's how aether works, idiot. The parts of you break down and rearrange themselves on the other side. It's how our siblings could travel through Chime. It's how Mother birthed us.*

That doesn't sound pleasant.

It's not. You'll die and come out different.

Was that any different from dying and being reborn? If Quen and the Mesmer could endure it, then so could I.

But I needed to warn Malk and Zorya. The moment I died, the Vesper would blink out of existence as well, their souls returning to me.

First, I checked in with Zorya. They weren't faring well. They'd lost Leander and Zephyr fighters to the Diviner and were now barricaded inside a pavilion as a Guardian pounded on the walls. Fuck. They wouldn't last much longer.

I pulled out and stepped into Malk's mind.

Malk? I'm almost at the clock tower, but I'll have to take your soul temporarily. At least, I hoped temporarily. *The battle in Haven isn't going well. Send the others back to help.*

On it.

I watched from his eyes as he flew above the station and sent a signal using hand shadows. From below, Wolfsbane caught the signal first. The raggedy wolf was soaked in Diviner blood and grinning like, well, a wolf. Clearly he'd been having the time of his life. He met with Joe, who'd since discarded his jacket and rolled up his sleeves, sunlight glowing from his skin. Gods, he had no right to look that handsome in the middle of a pissing battle.

"Vincent!" Sinder screamed below.

Malk swerved.

What's going on? I asked.

It's Vincent. He's... What the fuck is he doing? Malk swooped down and landed in the middle of Central next to Sinder, whose hands were aflame.

Vincent stood in a circle of dead Diviner, blood dripping down his chin and staining his waistcoat. He'd ravaged the Diviner—their necks were a twisted, pulpy mess.

He lifted one of the soul-splitting helmets, weighing it in his hands.

"Vince, we're done," Malk said. "Kayl's almost made it to the clock tower. We need to head back to Haven—they're suffering casualties. They need us."

Vincent glanced up, his fangs bared. "I can't go on."

"Dearest, put that thing down," Sinder urged. "We're almost at the end now. Then Kayl will make everything better—"

"I've always had faith in Kayl to do what is right. I've always believed she'd be the one to bring the gods to their knees. In that regard, the Necro do not belong in her new world."

"What are you saying?"

Vincent placed the helmet on his head.

Oh fuck! *Stop him!* I yelled into my mind. *He's carrying the Necro! Every single Necro! If he splits his soul, they all go!*

"Vince, listen to me," Malk said. "If you do this, you'll take the Necro with you. Innocent mortals—"

"Not innocent." Vincent's eyes were rimmed so red, they almost bled. "Look at me. At what a mess I've made." He examined the blood staining his shirt. "The Necro have committed atrocities that can never be redeemed. We rely on the blood and flesh of other mortals to sustain ourselves. Where do we fit in Haven? In Kayl's vision of a godless world? The universe would be better off without us—"

"That's not true, and you know it!" Sinder snapped. "You're healers! Artists—"

"We're monsters."

"You *saved* me." Sinder's voice cracked. "You healed me. Brought my soul back from the dead. You inked me so I—I could bear to look at my own skin again. You did all that because you're *good*. You've got a good heart."

"I killed you. I drank your blood."

"I don't care. I love you! Please, Vincent." Sinder held out his arms. "Come back to me. Make me complete again."

Vincent licked blood from his lip. "I loved you. I always said I'd give my soul so you may keep yours. *Live*, Sinder. For me."

He reached for the helmet and pressed the button.

Sinder's scream tore through the universe. It rang through my throat, forcing me out of Malk's mind.

Dru grabbed my arm. "What is it? What's happened?"

"It's Vincent! He's—He's gone."

Gods.

He'd destroyed his own soul and taken the Necro with him. An entire domain of mortals. How could he have done that? Why? Because he believed the Necro were evil? But he was Godless! He knew mortal cruelty was a result of the gods! He'd understood that when we fought the Glimmer at every turn, when he accepted Joe into our ranks!

I sank to my knees.

Was this my fault? Had I missed the signs? Pressured him? I knew he hadn't been doing well, but I'd never thought he'd do something this desperate.

If I'd known he truly felt that way... We could have brought the Necro back as other domains. Found some way to tamp their urges. Fuck, it hadn't needed to end like this!

Fuck!

Morty! Zorya's screams echoed in my mind. *Gast's disappeared! What happened? Why did he suddenly vanish?*

Shit. Gast was gone, too. Every Necro had been erased from existence.

I'm sorry. I didn't have the words to explain. *The Necro are gone.*

Gone?

Voices collided in my mind. Malk and Zorya demanding answers, help. Things I couldn't give.

Vincent was gone. An entire domain had been wiped from existence, just as Dor wanted. They were our healers. Mortals depended on them, despite their nature.

But Vincent couldn't see that. He'd only seen the monster within.

I'd failed to notice. To stop him. Help him.

I switched to my Chaos form, cutting off their voices, and dragged myself up.

"Kayl?" Dru asked. She'd been shouting about Vincent, and I'd totally blocked her out.

I shoved the pocket watch into her hand and stepped toward the reactor.

"Do we stop her?" Doctor Finch asked.

"No," Dru said. "She needs to do this."

The aether called to me with a song sweeter than any Seren's.

It's home, Jinx said.

No. Home was the world I'd make after this one. With my family. With Quen.

Without Vincent.

Without me?

I didn't have an answer for Jinx yet.

I thrust my hand inside the reactor. Aether wrapped around it, tingling all over my skin. It pulled me in, inch by inch, until my entire body glowed with raw energy.

The stars came alive in my mind, humming with raw potential.

Of everything that could be.

And then my mind exploded into a million galaxies.

47

Let your rage guide you.
In the face of the gods' injustice, they want you to tire.
They want you to give up.
Then you will be easier to subjugate.
Do not let them quiet your rage.
Simmer if you must to survive. But keep on burning.
—Anonymous, *Godless flier*

DEATH WASN'T SO BAD.

I bathed in a pool of stars. All sizes and shapes, blinking with a multitude of colors and scattered across a backdrop of night. Every time I moved, I sent ripples of stardust that cascaded into new colors. New stars. Really, it was a trippy experience, like when I'd gotten high off Vesper mushrooms.

It was pure aether, the building blocks of the universe. These stars could be shaped by Chaos. Turned into mortals or teahouses. Stars had always existed in plain sight, yet only the Mesmer saw them for what they were.

Gods. Each and every one of them.

No wonder the Mesmer were mad.

Some part of me knew I had to pull myself back together and return to reality, but this was honestly nice. Drifting amid the mighty cosmos gave me a peace I'd never known possible. Here, I could let go of my worries, my anxieties, my pain. I needn't feel anything except the warm contentment that came with a good glass of wine.

Life was the harsh place. It was loud and dirty and stuffed with exhausting emotion that tugged and demanded. Why bother making mortals at all, if mortality came with aches and pains? With needs that could never be truly satisfied?

I understood the Mesmer now. I understood Reve.

It didn't make me weak for wanting this. For needing it.

It made me mortal.

And all mortals died eventually.

Ugh. You get a new Diviner boyfriend, and suddenly you're a philosopher. Get a grip.

It took me a moment to piece together the voice inside my head. It sounded like me, but a far more sarcastic version, if that was possible. *Jinx. Can't you let me enjoy my pissing death?*

Why? It wasn't a real death. You didn't earn it.

What do I have to do to earn a real death? Jump in front of a tram?

Achieve something for once. Your Godless are getting pounded by Dor, and your Time Boy isn't faring much better, yet you're happy to float in fucking space.

I didn't think you cared.

Would you even notice if I cared? Or all the things I ever did for you? You owe me, and I need out of this damn clock tower.

Of course. It's always about you.

Oh, fuck off! When has it ever not been about you*? Everyone loves you. No one ever gave a shit about me! Stop being so fucking selfish and fix this mess you started.*

That I *started?* That was rich coming from Jinx!

You started the Godless. You got yourself noticed by Karendar and then captured by Corinth. You took Valeria's soul. I've always tried to keep you out of trouble, but everything that's ever happened was your fault.

Like you and Corentine didn't plan it!

Whatever. We're tied together, sister. I'm your mess. So fix me.

I was arguing with myself again. Apparently, I couldn't escape Jinx's shit even in death. If she was going to torment me for eternity, then fine. I'd give her what she wanted.

If she could even be fixed.

How do I get back? I asked.

Find my star. Focus on it.

How was I meant to find Jinx's star when there were millions?

But I didn't have to look far. Her star was next to mine.

I scooped her soul into my hands. It was warm and radiant with color. So full of potential. Jinx was smart. Far smarter than me. What could she achieve if she applied her mind? If she was free to live a normal mortal life? She could be someone incredible.

As could I.

The Godless had been shaped by the cruelties of their gods. Sinder had betrayed me, attacked the Glimmer, all because of what they'd done to him. Vincent had chosen to sacrifice himself and every Necro because of The Nameless One.

Jinx had done terrible things because of Corentine.

I could forgive Sinder and Vincent.

Jinx had been part of my life since my first breath. She was my mind, as I was her heart. In a way, she *was* me.

We'd both fucked up. Made mistakes. Hurt others.

All mortals deserved a chance. Deserved love. Jinx had been denied those rights from the start, and that wasn't fair.

If I deserved forgiveness for my failings, then so did Jinx.

I gave her soul a gentle squeeze. The stars brightened until they blinded me with color. Feeling returned to my limbs, and I sucked in a breath.

I stood inside the clock tower.

Without the makeshift camp and mortals filling it, the room looked sterile and empty. The clockface window dominated the space, and I ran over to gaze across Central. I still retained my Chaos form, enough to sense the aether barrier surrounding the clockface with a staticky buzz—this one generated by Dor.

A figure flew outside by the window, out of reach of the barrier.

Quen.

He remained in his Zephyr form. Gods, he'd lost his shirt and flew with his wings outstretched, his right arm still missing. The sight stole my breath. He stared at me with an odd intensity, and rather belatedly, I realized I was naked. Well, he'd seen it all before.

I placed my hand on the glass and nodded. A simple gesture that carried everything.

Quen dipped his chin. An acknowledgement.

He trusted me to do this. He'd wait for me.

And for that, I loved him.

"Sister," came Jinx's strained voice behind me.

I turned to where Corentine had once sat inside that odious chair. To where Jinx had now replaced her. There wasn't much difference between the two, only where Corentine's skin had been gaunt and hung off her bones, Jinx still had some life left in her. Where the pipes pumping energy out of Corentine's veins had turned black, the ones inside Jinx were still fresh, bloody, and raw.

The ragged expression of agony across Jinx's face was the same. Her eyes rolled back into her head, showing the whites.

"It hurts. Make it stop."

I approached my sister. My twin. There was no barrier to stop me from reaching out and taking her soul, claiming her once more, and all of Chaos.

The power I'd need to finally stop Dor.

He'd done this. He'd hurt my sister.

The gods were the real sinners of this universe, and they couldn't be redeemed.

I placed my hand against Jinx's chest. "I'm here, Jinx." *I'm here.*

Aether thrummed under my palm with the beat of my pulse. Our pulse. While I shared a connection with Quen, my connection to Jinx went far deeper. It was a connection I'd refused to accept until now, but Jinx *was* my responsibility.

The tug pulled at me. This was it. The end.

Screaming rang in my ear.

What the shit?

I recoiled, slapping my hands over my ears before I could finish taking Jinx's soul, but the horrid screaming was coming from inside my damn mind! It was the same screaming that had pounded my head with migraines whenever I stepped near aether before I knew what Chaos was.

DID YOU THINK YOU WOULD BE FREE OF ME SO EASILY, DAUGHTER?

Oh shit. *Corentine?*

Jinx had taken Corentine's soul! How was she alive?

The screaming eased, replaced instead by Corentine's laughter. *I EXIST IN YOUR SISTER'S MIND BECAUSE SHE WILLS IT. THROUGH HER, I WILL DEVOUR THIS WORLD.*

The metal room morphed, transforming into a vision of Babel. A crack splintered the floor before me, and I crouched, steadying myself as the floating rock I stood on tore away from Jinx, taking her out of my reach.

Was this a vision? A dream?

Had I somehow fallen inside Jinx's own mind?

She remained strapped to the chair, her eyes rolled back in delicious delight as Corentine emerged from her, standing at full height in her silver dress.

As though Jinx had never taken her soul.

Shit!

But if this was only a projection, an illusion, then Corentine couldn't hurt us. I just needed to reach Jinx.

"Let Jinx go," I demanded. "Can't you see she's in pain?"

Corentine patted Jinx's cheek. *WHAT GREATER COMFORT IS THERE THAN A MOTHER'S LOVE?*

"What mother tortures her own daughters? Jinx deserves better than you."

BETTER THAN A SISTER WHO WOULD CAST HER ASIDE? JINX HAS EARNED HER REST. SHE WILL ALLOW MY SOUL TO FLOURISH AS I TAKE OVER HER BODY. THEN WE WILL DESTROY DOR.

Shit, could Corentine *do* that?

I'm tired, sister, Jinx said, her thoughts coming through distorted and wrong. *I never meant to take Mother's soul. But she can return—I can let her return.*

No! Jinx, listen to me—we can end Dor together. Quen and I have enough god souls between us that we stand a chance! If you let Corentine out, she'll destroy everything!

It's the only way I can earn her love—

Don't you see? Corentine's pitting us against each other! She hurt you!

And you didn't? You said you hated me, remember? That you'd never forgive me. That we weren't... family.

I couldn't deny there were times Jinx had pushed me to my limits, but whatever angry words I'd said had been just that—shouted in anger and fear. *Please, Jinx. I'm sorry for being a shitty sister. I don't want to lose you to Corentine.*

If you take my soul, what then? I remain trapped inside you, as I always was? You hate me forever for everything I've done?

We can start afresh. Become what we were meant to be. Sisters.

Why should I believe you?

Lightning flashed across the skies of Babel. Dark clouds gathered around Jinx, each sparkling with stardust. A reflection of her heart, or a barrier to keep me out?

Corentine remained in the center. She took Jinx's chin with a tenderness that was forced and completely unnatural. We were Corentine's daughters, but she wasn't our mother. She'd never loved or cared for us.

That was what the gods had promised their mortals. The illusion of parental love. Unconditional love that came with such conditions as worship and unquestionable devotion.

Love was often messy. Sometimes it hurt. Even mortal parents weren't perfect.

But they wanted the best for their mortal children.

The gods did not.

I can't heal your soul or offer you empty promises, I said to Jinx. *I can't say that all is forgiven and we'll become best friends overnight. But we can work at this. And slowly, piece by piece, we can reach a place where we can paint each other's nails or do each other's hair. Is that what you want?*

I... I want my mother.

Corentine isn't your mother. She's nothing more than a cruel god who views her mortals as disposable. But I can be there for you. I promise I'll try.

She—She's so strong. In my head. Always screaming...

She only has power over you if you give it. Let her go, Jinx. Let her go.

Corentine snarled. *HER SOUL IS MINE!* She gripped Jinx's chin tight, her nails digging into skin and drawing blood.

Kayl! Jinx screamed.

Shit, now I'd done it.

I swapped to my Vesper form and gifted myself a new pair of lovely wings, courtesy of Valeria's power. Flying wasn't my talent, but if I wanted to reach Jinx, I didn't have a choice.

My wings flared and the wind billowing in Babel wrenched me off my feet. I corrected my course and flew straight for Corentine.

Toss her out of your mind! I yelled.

I can't!

Of course you pissing can! This is your *mind! Don't let her control it!*

Corentine released Jinx and stood to face me. *I'LL DESTROY YOUR SOUL NEXT, YOU INGRATE.*

"Fucking try it!"

I slammed into Corentine with my elbow and we both tumbled to the ground. She grabbed my wing and yanked it.

Fuck! I screamed as agony ripped down my spine. This might be Jinx's mind, but that pissing *hurt*!

I backed off, tucking my aching wings behind me, though one hung lower than the other—I wasn't flying away from this.

Corentine's nails extended into claws. If that was how she wanted it, then fine.

This fight was long overdue.

She swiped at me, those claws slashing at a speed meant to gouge out my eyes. I summoned shadow to throw her off and blind her, but it didn't slow her assault.

Her claw snagged my neck and left a nasty cut that trailed blood across my collarbone.

I shoved the heel of my palm into her chin.

It wouldn't do any damage, but it knocked her back a few steps, enough for me to catch my breath. Fighting wasn't my thing, but I had a few self-defense moves up my sleeves if I needed them.

Right now, I needed a lot pissing more. Corentine was going to rip me to shreds.

No, this wasn't a fight I could win alone.

Corentine circled me. *YOU SHOULD NEVER HAVE BEEN MADE.*

"That was your second fuck up."

WHAT WAS MY FIRST?

"Believing Jinx would choose you over me."

Corentine glanced over her shoulder.

Jinx stood there in her Chaos form, glowing radiant with aether. She'd finally regained control of herself, her mind, and freed herself from the chair.

I AM YOUR MOTHER! Corentine screeched.

Jinx snapped her fingers.

Corentine vanished like an unwelcome afterthought.

The billowing clouds of stardust receded, leaving us with the clear skies of Babel's constellations.

I switched back to my Chaos form, and we stared at each other.

Twins. Sisters.

Tears burst from Jinx, and she fell to her knees. "I'm—I'm sorry."

I ran and fell beside her, pulling her against my chest. "I've got you, Jinx. I've got you."

She buried her head in my shoulder and sobbed. "Take my soul. Take it."

I rested my hand on the small of her back and held her, letting her heave and shake in my arms. Giving her the comfort she'd been denied these past thirteen years. I owed her that much.

The tug pulsed underneath my palm, ready and waiting for me.

Gently, I pulled her soul into my subconscious.

With it, a smattering of Chaos souls followed. Siblings I barely knew. Only some I recognized, like Flux. And, oddly, an old soul. The very first mortal to be born, in fact. Odder still, Corentine had named him Corinth. Was that just a coincidence?

And then, Corentine's soul.

YOU'RE A FOOL, she said, eager to get her parting shot in. *MORTALS CANNOT EXIST WITHOUT THEIR GODS.*

I beg to differ—

MORTALS ARE THE IMAGININGS OF A GOD'S MIND. WE WILL THEM INTO BEING. SOMEONE WILL NEED TO RETAIN THAT POWER IF YOU WISH FOR THEM TO EXIST. WILL THAT BE YOU? DO YOU TRULY BELIEVE YOU HAVE THE TEMPERAMENT TO RULE OVER MILLENNIA, DAUGHTER?

TIME WILL TAKE ITS TOLL, AND YOU WILL BECOME LIKE THE GODS YOU HATE.

In the depths of my own soul, Corentine's words rang true. Mortals couldn't exist without a god's power.

But I'd worry about that when the time came.

BE WARNED. YOU ARE NOT ALONE. THERE ARE WORSE GODS IN THE GREATER COSMOS THAN DOR OR ME.

I'll face them, too.

Corentine laughed. *THEN GRANT ME ONE FINAL REQUEST FOR YOUR BRAVE NEW WORLD.*

What else could Corentine possibly want?

NAME A STREET AFTER ME.

I buried her soul deep. There was no chance I'd risk Corentine trying to escape again. But her power was within me now, raw and brimming with aether.

The power of Chaos. Of destruction and creation.

Jinx crumbled to dust in my arms with a parting sigh. I blinked, and found myself standing once again in the clockface room.

Dust covered that horrid chair. Jinx was now free.

Sister. Her voice spoke inside my mind as it always had.

I can remake your body, if you'd like? Bring you back so we can face Dor together.

I... I want to stay inside your mind a bit longer. Where it's safe.

All right. But say the word.

I wouldn't want to get in the way of you and your Time Boy.

Oh shit, Quen! He was still out there fighting Dor!

I ran to the window.

Gods. Chime had shut down.

The streetlamps were no longer lit, and the trams had stopped running. I couldn't tell from this angle, but the Gate must have switched off, too. Without a power source, Chime had simply powered down in a way I'd never seen before.

Even the clock hands had paused, resting between twelve and one.

At the thirteenth hour.

I couldn't see Quen flying along the skyline, nor could I tell what state I'd left Haven in. To end this, I needed to destroy the source.

We needed to destroy Dor.

In leaving my god souls behind with the Godless, I'd put them at risk. I'd lost the Necro. And now I needed them more than ever. Fighting without the Necro's healing abilities would make things difficult, but we could still win this.

I needed those souls back, if only to protect them from Dor, but I had no way of reaching Haven to get them—I'd given my pocket watch to Dru.

What do you think happened to your new domain when you died, huh? Jinx said. *It went poof!*

Oh shit. I hadn't thought about what would happen to Haven once I stepped into that reactor. But then... What had happened to the Godless? To the gods' souls?

They returned to the aether, where they're swimming around. But Chaos is connected to everything. You're their god, now. You can bring their souls back into you.

I thought owning a god's soul shielded me from Corentine's power?

Only if you want it to. Corentine was limited by Dor and being trapped in the clock tower, but you've got everything now. The full chaotic package. Look inside. Find their stars.

Could it be that easy? I reached into my subconscious and...

There they were.

The bright and beautiful stars of my friends and family. Dru, Harmony, Sinder, Joe, Reverie, Trixie. Each glowed with the god souls I'd gifted. The only ones missing were Quen's souls. They *were* shielded from me, for some reason.

Because Quen had evolved into something else. Something beyond Chaos and time. But Quen's soul was still connected to me, bright and beautiful. Waiting.

I tugged at each of my friends' souls, and they unraveled like a thread, folding into me.

Their souls returned, along with the souls of gods I'd gifted. Faen, Unghard, Gildola, Serenity, Edana, Mesmorpheus. They filled me with aether until I wanted to burst.

You did it? Dru asked.

I pulled her soul into mine, as well as the rest of the Godless, safely tucked away from Dor. *We're just getting started.*

As though on cue, the clockface window shattered.

Shards of glass flew in all directions. One flew right at my face, but I didn't flinch. I had nothing to fear.

It sliced across my cheek, leaving a trail of blood. I no longer had the Necro to heal me, but a Glimmer's power worked well enough to bind the cut back together and heal the wound across my collarbone.

I wrapped myself in a black dress and faced the now broken clockface window.

Hundreds of clocks floated outside. So many different types. They echoed with ticks and tocks of varying pitches and chimes, a maddening melody that belonged to only one god.

And there, hovering among the clocks and glass shards, was Dor.

He tugged at the cufflinks of his pinstripe suit. "I see we've run out of time."

XLVIII

Of the thirteen gods, Dor is the most powerful. He alone controls time.
There is no standing against Him.
The remaining gods have no choice but to accept His rule.
And through Him, their mortals can be redeemed.
—The Redeemer, *Speech at the Plaza, Kronos*

THE STREETLAMPS FLICKERED OUT. She'd done it. Kayl had rescued Jinx.

I'd been forced to abandon Kayl and take refuge in Meridian Park. There wasn't much I could do to help her from outside the clock tower, not when Dor had sent his Wardens after me, led by Ben. Each carrying tasers and collars. Their intent was clear—to pummel me into submission.

The park had adequate cover, and I crouched underneath the bandstand. There were hardly any soulless here, because why would a mortal without a soul take pleasure in the local greenery? It did, however, give me time to reforge my metal arm. I'd been operating it enough by now to understand the mechanics, and through Zyclone's power, and my new ability to summon objects, constructing a new appendage didn't require much effort.

If only I could summon myself a blasted cup of tea. Hrm, perhaps I could?

Kayl has recalled her mortals, came Doctor Finch's urgent voice in my mind. *I suggest you do the same, Master Corinth. Haven is no more.*

The domain was gone? What had Kayl sacrificed? But if she'd recalled her mortals, then it was time.

I reached inside my subconscious and pulled at my connecting souls. The Zephyr and Leander came back to me, as well as Doctor Finch and Ilona. A few souls were missing. Mortals who had been caught by the Diviner.

Among them was Dandelion. He'd sacrificed himself to protect his sister. Nelle's pain ached in my own heart.

We'd lost so many to Dor's damn machinations, though not all our losses were by his hand alone. Vincent had damned the Necro. I'd sympathized with him, but that... that was unconscionable. Despite how I felt about my own domain, there were good among the Diviner, as there were good among the Necro.

I'd ensure their names, and countless others, would never be forgotten.

Thank you, I said to Corvus and the many mortals who had fought to protect Haven. *You've played your part. Now Kayl and I will finish this.*

There was only one god soul left to collect, and oh, would I enjoy collecting it.

Unfortunately, the bandstand had gained an audience.

Ben and his entourage had found me and surrounded the bandstand. It was unnerving, as they stood in synchronized silence. In their black-and-bronze Warden uniforms, only Ben stood out at his height, his once expressive face now blank.

"Give yourself up, and this will all be over," Ben said. Or at least, that was Ben's voice, but those words were all Dor.

"Order your men to back off, and I'll consider it," I called over my shoulder.

"You delay the inevitable. You know I have no wish to harm you, Quentin—"

"I'd find that more believable if you hadn't sent my ex-bodyguard to capture me." I summoned a pistol in my metal hand. It wasn't my prized pistol, just a standard-issue Warden weapon. And it certainly wouldn't be enough to kill all these.

There was only one kill I wished to make.

Even if it would hurt me to do so.

I rose from my crouch and took aim.

A single bullet pierced Ben's head.

He tipped backwards and landed on the grass as though he'd simply fallen into slumber, cushioned by the nature he so loved. His body didn't fade like it was meant to, for his soul had long since vacated it, but Dor could no longer animate it and use Ben for his own ends.

It was the only mercy I could grant him.

That Dor had forced me to this… It left me empty. Cold. My metal fingers tightened around the pistol's grip, crushing it and rendering the trigger useless.

All at once, the Wardens turned their tasers on me. "You disappoint me," they said in unison, their voices merging into one.

I flapped my wings and took off into the sky.

Their tasers fired. I swerved over the bandstand, using it as cover, and their shots fizzled out, unable to reach my height.

I'd had ample time to practice flying, and although the fear of heights no longer held power over me, the thought of accelerated falling still threatened my bowels. I tossed my useless pistol and flew over Chime, the Wardens beneath fading into pinpricks as I headed back for the clock tower.

At my approach, the clockface window shattered, sending shards of glass raining down on any unsuspecting soulless below. Was that Kayl's doing?

No. Dor hovered by the window, surrounded by a curtain of clocks.

Fuck.

He blocked the way between me and Kayl.

"Dor!" I yelled. "You've had your time. It's over!"

He turned to me with an unnerving smile. "Quentin. Do you forget I'm a god?"

"You're the god of nothing! Without mortals, what claim do you have to godhood?"

He opened his arms. "I claim Babel and Kronos. I claim the laws of chaos and time."

The faint ticking grew louder with each passing second, joined by more ticks and tocks and bells and dongs.

Saints.

Thousands more clocks materialized in the air around the clock tower. The same clocks that dominated Dor's domain were now here, chiming in and out with their horrendous clanging. I covered my ears against their discordant harshness.

Dor vanished, replaced instead by Elijah's body, which he wore as armor. A pair of bronze wings stretched from his back, composed of a metal spine pieced together with cogs and levers, and feathers made of pure brass.

Guardians rose beside him, also sporting brass wings.

This was how Dor wanted to play it. Very well.

"Make this easy on yourself, Quentin," Elijah said. "Mortal minds are fragile. Their bodies equally so. Bow before me, or I shall shatter you into a thousand pieces and rebuild you from the shards."

"Mortal bodies may bend and break, but my thoughts will always remain mine and mine alone!"

Dor no longer owned my thoughts. No god would ever lay claim to my soul.

Only one woman.

Kayl emerged from the clock tower a dark goddess. She'd switched back to her Vesper form and now bore the same black wings as Malk.

As I'd become the Dark Warden, she'd become something else. Something so utterly terrifying and beautiful, I'd have thrown myself to my knees if I hadn't been flying.

And she was mine, as I was hers.

She flew to my side with silent acknowledgement. Not as my god, but as my partner. My equal in all things.

Together, we'd take on the universe.

"You seemed to have this in hand, sweetie, but I thought you might appreciate the company," she said.

Gods, I wanted to kiss her. "Always, my dear. I couldn't end the world without you."

Elijah sneered. "Why do you continue to worship Chaos? She'll destroy this universe, Quentin!"

"And I'll stand by her side as she does!"

He's going to do the predictable villain thing and send his flying minions after us, Kayl said inside my mind. *So let's make sure we coordinate our counterattack.*

Gods! My gaze snapped to hers. *How am I hearing you?* Was it because she'd taken Corentine's soul? Had Kayl become my god after all?

She smirked. *We have a connection. And yes, owning Corentine's soul means I can sense yours.*

You're reading my thoughts.

Your thoughts are yours, Quen. I won't pry. But it'll be easier to take down Dor if we're not shouting battle tactics or whatever at each other.

She made a good point. And, honestly, I didn't mind the intrusion.

I trusted Kayl implicitly.

Ah. Elijah had been monologuing the entire time Kayl and I had indulged in our secret conversation, and I had no idea what the man was blathering on about.

I cleared my throat. "Can we get on with it? I'd like to have this wrapped up in time for tea."

One of the Guardians flew at me.

"Is that better, sweetie?" Kayl said.

"It's a start. Would you do the honors?"

"My pleasure." Her form changed to Ember, yet she retained her Vesper wings.

I blinked, but no, her body had morphed two separate domain personas into one. How in god's name was she doing that?

It's a trick Jinx taught me. Chaos really can do anything. Kayl blasted the incoming Guardian with a torrent of flame.

The Guardian's brass body began to melt. Saints! I never knew an Ember's flame could burn that hot. *You continue to surprise me, my dear.*

Just you wait until I get you back in my bed. She winked.

Oh my.

The misshapen remains of the Guardian fell in a molten lump. Gosh, I felt giddy at what Kayl could possibly do next. In comparison, I could either fly or turn Amnae or Leander and crash down to Central. Neither of which were that impressive.

But I did have a rather dapper metal arm, and thanks to the imagination of the Zephyr, I'd installed a few upgrades.

Four Guardians now flew at us at a wide berth, presumably to avoid being melted and to split us up. Kayl took on two by wielding her flames.

The other two came for me.

One charged with an outstretched fist, its body clicking and whirring as it moved. I flew to one side and grabbed its fist with my metal hand. With a simple flex, I crushed it with ease. Tiny cogs and pieces of metal splintered off.

Behind you! Kayl warned.

I turned in time to intercept the second Guardian. It reached for my neck.

I caught its wrist, pulled it free from its body, and tossed it aside.

A bullet hit my metal arm, ricocheting off the casing.

Below, the soulless were aiming at us with pistols. I tutted. How ineffective.

Kayl switched from Ember to Chaos and cast an aether shield around us both. As soon as their bullets hit her shield, they fizzled into nothing. Really, did she even need me?

More Guardians materialized out of nowhere. Dor would keep throwing them at us until we tired.

This is growing dull, Kayl agreed. *Let's fly to the source.*

Elijah. He still hovered above Central Station, his brass wings a blur.

I'll make you a path through, Kayl said. *Go get him.*

She changed back to her Ember form while still maintaining her aether shield and lobbed fire at one Guardian. Then, in the blink of an eye, she swapped to an Umber form and summoned a bloody plant pot from thin air! Vines burst from the pot and whipped at the Guardians, tangling their limbs together.

Stop gawking and fly! she chided.

Yes, dear. I tucked my wings close and thrust forward, flying with speed.

Kayl dragged the Guardians out of my way as promised, though I flapped my wings as I passed, sending a gust of air in their direction to push them out further. All the while, Kayl's aether shield continued to follow and protect me against the potshots from below.

A circle of Guardians materialized around Elijah. A circle of protection. Didn't he understand yet?

Kayl had become a god. An almighty god who wielded the powers of many. Dor couldn't hope to stand against her.

I'm turning off the lights, Kayl warned. *Be ready.*

The way she controlled this entire situation gave me goose bumps, and I'd admit, the excitement thrumming in my blood was heading south. Did I err on the submissive side? My past relationships certainly hinted so.

Something to consider another time.

Right now, I had one goal in mind: to destroy Elijah. Destroy Dor's mortal tether to Chime.

Then I'd utterly obliterate his soul.

And we get tea and scones for afters? Kayl said, her inner voice amused.

You do tempt me.

She was rather enjoying this as much as I was, but she'd also given me a gift by clearing my path. Elijah was mine.

Though while Dor continued to use Elijah's body as a shield, I couldn't take his soul. I needed a way of getting Dor out.

As I neared Elijah and his collection of flying clockwork abominations, the lights did indeed go dark. Kayl had changed to her Vesper form and flung a cloak of shadow over Central. I'd never known a Vesper capable of *that*, either, but when one possessed the power of the gods, anything was possible.

The Guardians' heads spun, clicking and whirring with confusion as they lost sight of me, yet I could still see perfectly clear. Another gift bestowed on me by my beloved.

And then multiple versions of me appeared in the air. Illusions cast by a Mesmer's power. The Guardians readjusted their vision and simultaneously launched themselves at the various fake Quens.

Elijah, however, was staring right at me. Could he see me, still? Sense the real me? It was Dor staring through those mortal eyes, so I didn't doubt it.

I could summon another pistol and blast his brains out from this distance.

Or take a Leander form and crash into him, sending us both tumbling down as I ripped him apart, limb by limb.

But what I wanted was to grasp his throat. To wrap my metal fingers around his windpipe and choke the life from him.

He lifted his chin, as though he read the murder on my face and braced himself for the inevitable.

The wind ruffled my feathers as I soared toward my destiny.

Elijah's form changed back to Dor.

"Quentin." He smiled again with my face. If he thought that would stop me from throttling him, he was sadly mistaken. "I grow impatient with these games. Would you have made it this far without your Chaos whore? Shall we remove her from the board?"

I almost faltered, and I glanced back at Kayl.

Saints. We'd separated so I could reach Elijah, but in doing so, we'd given Dor the advantage.

"You dare touch her," I seethed.

I'm safe! she said. *These clockwork pricks have nothing on me. He's trying to unnerve you. Don't let him!*

Dor raised his hands.

Time began to flow backwards.

Below, the Wardens' movements grew erratic, working through the motions of the past twenty minutes, but in reverse. Bullets fell from Kayl's shield, returning to their pistols, and then their owners retreated into the station.

"What are you doing?" I yelled. "You can replay this fight over and over, and it won't change a damn thing! You have no power over Chaos!"

"Quentin," Dor repeated with a tut. "The laws of time are mine."

Buildings fell. Time stripped them away, deconstructing them brick by brick.

The city's infrastructure followed. Trams, streetlamps, gutters—all collapsed to mortar and blueprints, the entire city flattening in a heartbeat.

Above, the Golden City plate receded, piece by piece.

And then the clock tower itself.

Kayl was still holding off a group of Guardians. Immortals were immune to Dor's time manipulation.

While he was busy destroying Chime once more, I could strike. I could end this.

I flew, pushing my wings until they ached along my spine.

The clock tower vanished, sending with it a shock wave of aether, which blew me off course.

Chime became ruins. The same state Kayl and I had left the city in, before Dor had reclaimed it. It rebuilt itself, the clock tower realigning until even the Gate was restored to its natural state.

Before the gods had warred and destroyed it.

The clock tower rang out, its harsh *dong* screeching in my ear. The hands of the clockface whirred out of control, speeding through seconds, hours, days. Bell after bell rang into one continuous drone that throbbed in my head.

"Stop!" I yelled, but my voice was drowned out.

What is he doing? Kayl asked, her concern now stark.

Reversing time.

The Gate flashed with a new domain every second, cycling through them with each blink. I swallowed a lump as Eventide rejoined the rotation.

How far back was Dor pushing time?

To when I met Kayl?

Before?

Time was moving so quickly, I couldn't keep track of the years flowing by. Storefronts changed—new ones, old ones. But Chime had remained static for much of its history. I couldn't even sense where in the timeline we were.

The drone of the bells turned into a keening wail.

I pushed through it and reached for Dor.

Then a crack splintered the sky with a blast of raw aether.

Oh gods!

Reality itself had torn, leaving a gaping hole of stars above Central. It leaked shimmering aether in blues and pinks.

Dor was ripping reality apart.

No.

We'd gone so far back in time... We'd reached the beginning of creation.

"Imagine, Quentin!" Dor roared over the screaming bells. "A better reality. One without Chaos. Isn't this what you always desired?"

Quen—

Kayl's inner voice cut off.

I turned with horror. She no longer floated in the sky. *Kayl? Please, answer me!*

Dor clapped his hands. Another shock wave of aether exploded in the sky as time lurched forward, hurtling now to the future—an alternate future.

It was so dizzying, I struggled to keep airborne.

My wings finally failed me.

I fell parallel to the clock tower and out of reality.

XLIX

*Is it possible for multiple timelines to exist? The answer is complicated.
When a Diviner manipulates time, it casts a minor ripple in the pond of
time. Eventually these ripples stabilize and the surface of the pond steadies.
If a Diviner causes too many ripples, such as by abusing time, it could create
turbulence that forces the pond water to spill out entirely and form a new
pond—a new timeline where a mortal soul exists simultaneously.
We refer to this as a paradox. We are forbidden from creating paradoxes,
as this disrupts the natural flow of time. While an ordinary mortal may
not notice the difference, it is additional work for our Father to fix.
Better to avoid playing with time, as the consequences can be dire.*
—H. Bezel, *Horology and the Laws of Time*

REALITY CAME BACK INTO focus slowly. I groaned and lifted my spectacles,
rubbing my eyes.

"Steady on, chap. You've had a rough time of it."

I froze.

That voice was mine.

I put my spectacles back on and blinked away the blurriness. I was
seated on a bench outside Central Station—the same bench Kayl and I
would often meet at—back to my Diviner form and dressed in my usual
tan suit, though my right arm was still metal and ached. Chime looked and
smelled exactly as I remembered it, only...

Saints. Mortals strode by on their way to the station. Vesper. Glimmer.
Ember. All went about their business as though the events of the past few
months had never happened.

As though the gods and their domains still existed.

"Jelly baby?" offered the man seated beside me.

It was me. Future Quen. Or an alternate Quen?

"No, it's me—or rather you—from the future," he said. "Remember not to get too chummy. Paradoxes and all that."

I sat up. "Kayl." The clock tower and Gate were present in this reality. Was Corentine still hidden behind the clockface window? Did Chaos still *exist*? Something was powering the city—the streetlamps, the trams.

Everything was operating as it should be... before Chaos had been unleashed.

"Before you panic, run off, and get caught by a suspecting Warden lurking around the corner, please calm yourself and remember the facts," Future Quen said. "Chaos is immune to time."

My chest was heaving with ragged breaths. It was all very well, telling me to calm down when I was about to hyperventilate! "Meaning what?"

"Meaning, my dear boy, that Chaos cannot be affected by the simple manipulation of time. Is your mind still addled? Do you require me to explain further?"

My future self was a prat, and I shot him a glare. But no, I didn't require further clarification. It came down to metaphysics, really.

Dor had created an alternate timeline and left Chaos behind. In other words, my timeline still existed, somewhere. Wherever Kayl remained, she was trapped. As was I. Separated by a multiverse of sorts.

Kayl? I called into my mind, but there was no answer. Nothing.

"You can't communicate across timelines," Future Quen said. He dug out a purple jelly baby from his candy bag. A licorice Vesper. "Unfortunately, she is out of our reach."

"If Chaos is immune, then how am I here?"

"Isn't that an interesting dilemma? I believe some part of you—of us— is still Diviner, and therefore sensitive to the manipulation of time."

"Wonderful. I'll just toddle on over to a tram and fucking throw myself in front of it, then."

"That would be dramatic, but ultimately pointless. You're bound to this timeline, now. You'll only rebirth yourself back here."

I wanted to punch myself in the face. "Then I'm trapped here, no thanks to you. Are you aware of what your advice has done? Mortals have lost their souls. The Necro… We've lost them all. Did you know my path would lead me back to Elijah when we met in the steamworks?"

"There's no need to be angry with me. You may as well be angry at the stars." He popped the jelly baby into his mouth. "Yes, I knew where your path would lead. And I allowed it—"

"You *allowed* it?" My metal fist clenched around the bench armrest, crushing it with an indent of my palm. Everything I'd endured at Elijah's hands in Memoria could have been avoided!

"I *allowed* it because I've witnessed various future scenarios, and your timeline is the only one that matters. You needed to make the choices that brought you here, even if those choices caused you pain and suffering. I won't apologize for that."

"What of this timeline?" I eyed a Necro who walked past. A sodding Necro. "Could this future be salvaged? Could we return the soulless?" The damned?

Vincent, Gast, Dandelion, Nocturne, Cosmo, Walter, Reve.

Ben.

All of them?

"That's up to you. Right now, we're caught in a branching timeline. A reflection of our own. An echo, if you will. What you are looking at is more of an illusion than reality, a product of Dor's mind. He knows he cannot fully recreate this universe without Chaos, and any soul reshaped by Chaos or the soul-splitting devices no longer belongs to our reality. They cannot be reborn, only imitated, and a poor imitation at that."

"And if I take Dor's soul? This is the power of gods we're talking about, damn it!" Surely, I could return to my timeline and pluck the soulless out before they ever lost their souls?

"The soulless are no longer part of our universe. When their souls were split, they were effectively cast out. No god lays claim to them. Not even you or Kayl."

Outside our universe? Was that even possible? "How do you know all this?"

"I've seen it. The many timelines Dor creates will vanish as soon as he does, which means the fate of the universe will rest in your hands. We sit here on the precipice of time. Corentine would have seen time end, but without time, there can be no mortals—soulless or otherwise."

"Are you trying to talk me out of destroying Dor or simply philosophizing?"

"I'm preparing you for what comes next. To return to your timeline and find Kayl once more, you must break time. Though it's your choice, if you'd rather stay here and live in blissful ignorance under fake gods. Kayl cannot restore her version of Chime without you—without time. Which Chime do you choose? A Chime where the domains remain intact, as they should be? Or a Chime where the gods and soulless no longer exist, but Kayl does?"

Even if the gods, their mortals, and domains existed happily in this timeline, could I remain in a Chime where Kayl did not exist?

Was my own happiness worth more than every citizen in Chime?

More than every Necro? Every soulless Diviner?

Except it wouldn't be real, not entirely. My mind had been manipulated enough times, would I even recognize reality for what it was?

"Before you decide," Future Quen continued, "I'd recommend visiting a dream parlor. There's a lovely one in the Market District only a block away from here. The Daydream Domain. They'll show you what I've seen—alternate timelines. Possibilities. They may even have a solution to your soulless problem."

"Then I'll be ready to face Dor? I'm having a bit of bother dealing with him." Who knew a Chaos-fearing god would be so skittish? He'd tossed me out into this timeline to stop me from getting my hands on his soul.

Future Quen pulled out another jelly baby. A white vanilla Diviner. They were rare. "You'll never beat him in a physical confrontation. He'll keep on tossing you between timelines until he wears you down. You want to get close to Dor? Then give him what he wants. You. All this?" He gestured around him with the jelly baby. "Is an attempt to win you over. To show you a world restored without Chaos." He offered the jelly baby to me. A minor peace offering, all things considered.

I opened my palm and caught the jelly baby. Could it be so simple? That all Dor wanted was me brought to heel?

For so long, I'd blamed myself for the demise of the domains, for the actions of my Father. Even if I condemned Dor's actions, and that of the gods, I'd still willingly served as a Warden and upheld injustice in their name. There was always a choice, and every time, I'd chosen the coward's way.

Until I met Kayl.

I'd died for her, for her cause. Numerous times now.

I'd die again.

"You're Godless," Future Quen said. "And despite who we may be now, we're mortal, deep inside. Give yourself some grace."

He was right.

We'd been victims of Dor. Victims of the gods, as the Godless had. No different. No better. I owed an apology to myself—quite literally. "I'm sorry, Quen."

"You're forgiven, Quen. Now, do get moving. We're both on a schedule and have places to be, but I'll be waiting here if you need someone to hold your hand." He glanced over the rim of his spectacles, as though I was meant to understand the hidden meaning behind his words and lacked the foresight to do so.

I stood and stretched. Despite being thrown into an alternate timeline, my metal arm still worked. If anything, flexing my various artificial fingers had gotten easier. "Stupid question, how do I break time?"

"Simple. You create a paradox."

Simple, he says.

Future Quen waved me off as I strode for the tram that would take me to the Market District and the Daydream Domain parlor. He was waiting for a future I wasn't yet privy to, and I didn't want to tempt fate by prying.

This version of Chime was the city I'd known and loved before I met Kayl—twelve domains coexisting. Diviner waited for the tram as Seren gossiped nearby. A Vesper paperboy ran past, waving this afternoon's edition of the Courier. Walking among them didn't require an act on my part. I simply belonged.

It wasn't perfect, but it was home.

No. It could never be my home without Kayl.

My beloved waited for me in a timeline that housed pain, but that was the nature of reality, wasn't it? I had to find my way back. I had to finally confront Dor.

But first, I needed answers.

As Dor's alternate Chime was near identical to the Chime I knew and loved, it didn't take long to traverse the Market District and find the Daydream Domain memory parlor.

It was in decidedly better condition than the Dreamcast memory parlor of the Undercity, the place I'd taken Kayl to explore her memories and had instead indulged in lurid dreams of her carrying my progeny. A fact I'd forgotten until this very moment. There were aspects of our new relationship we hadn't had an opportunity to discuss, and which, honestly, weren't so pertinent when the world was ending.

But should everything work out for the best, what then?

Another time, Quen. Quite literally.

What worried me most was I'd quite easily hopped onto a tram and ridden it all the way here without being accosted by a Warden or a Diviner. Dor must surely sense me inside the city, so why hadn't he come to claim my soul?

If I understood Dor by now, he didn't leave things to chance. Was he allowing me free rein so I'd see the city for myself and wish to make this timeline my reality? It was a safe gambit, for he knew I held a soft spot for mortals and could easily bend.

But he also knew I was an irredeemable sinner where lust was concerned.

There was no greater threat than a fool in love.

I pushed open the door of the Daydream Domain to a soft singsong chime instead of a bell. The wallpaper was a dark purple dotted with stars, like the painted wooden sign outside. Soft aether lamps gave the reception a cozy glow. One could certainly fall asleep easily inside such a place. Indeed, the Mesmer slumped over the reception desk was completely out of it.

Why had I come here? Mere curiosity? Because my future self had suggested it?

"Look! It's our second papa!"

My jaw dropped.

The Mesmer trio stood by the door leading to the parlor rooms. All three of them. Celeste, with her pink bow. Castor, with his blue tie.

And Cosmo, who was grinning widely and pointing at me. In this timeline, the trio looked exactly as I remembered them. More importantly, Cosmo was here. They were *alive*.

That wasn't fair. What next? I'd bump into Walter and Ben?

"You—You know who I am?" I asked.

"Of course we do!" Celeste said. "Papa told us all about you. They've been waiting."

"Mesmorpheus?"

Celeste wrapped her arm around mine and dragged me into the corridor. "This way."

"We'll get you nice and comfy," Cosmo said.

"Would you like tea?" Castor asked.

Could I trust the trio of this timeline to make an adequate cup of tea? After being flung through time, I sorely needed a drink. "Please. Two sugars."

They led me into a vacant room where lavender incense wafted overhead. Much like the memory parlor of the Undercity, this room contained a large bed, coatrack, and little else. Only, the painted stars on the ceiling were the same design and color of Haven's. A coincidence? Or was I truly awaited?

Mesmorpheus wished to commune with me, and yet their soul had been taken in my timeline. Were they aware? Had they seen it? Did they still maintain their godly powers in this universe, or were they bound to Dor? So many questions, and only one way to get answers.

I hurriedly kicked off my shoes and hung up my jacket, tucking my spectacles into the inner pocket. The Mesmer's giddy energy infected me, and they followed me all the way to the bed.

Cosmo plumped a pillow and placed it ready for me. "There. All comfy."

"We'll help you nod off," Celeste said.

"And keep watch in case Wardens show up," Castor added.

"Thank you. All of you." I lay my head on the pillow and closed my eyes.

The last time I'd lain on a parlor bed had been my first. When Kayl had lain beside me.

It had been at that moment I'd realized how much I enjoyed her company.

That I'd fallen for her.

My consciousness dipped in and out as Celeste hummed a soothing tune.

"That's it, second Papa," Cosmo crooned. "Sleep now."

Hearing their voice hurt. If I could save Cosmo... save them all...

I stood in white space.

The walls, the ceiling. Everything was a sterile white. Even the ground beneath me was simply blank. It was an absence of everything. A place of nothing.

A domain that had long since died.

Stars sparkled before me and took the shape of a mortal man. A figure stepped through, their faceless head a collection of varying dark nebulae. They dressed in a black suit.

Mesmorpheus. God of the Mesmer.

QUENTIN CORINTH. They spoke aloud. *I'VE BEEN EXPECTING YOU.*

"I have to admit, this is all rather new." Mesmorpheus had only chosen to commune with Kayl in the past, except for a dream they'd implanted in my mind when Corentine had claimed my soul. That had been a vision of their conversation, enough for me to go by. This was more direct. "Are you aware you shouldn't exist?"

I AM NOT REALLY HERE. I AM SIMPLY A SHADOW OF MY FORMER SELF AND CANNOT SEE BEYOND THIS TIMELINE. THE VERSION OF MYSELF IN YOUR WORLD GIFTED ME WITH

VISIONS, AWARE ALTERNATE TIMELINES EXISTED. I HAVE SEEN THEM ALL.

"In this timeline, the gods exist? What of Corentine?" Of Chaos?

THE GODS ARE NOT AWARE OF TIME'S MANIPULATION. THE CORENTINE WHO SITS WITHIN THE CLOCK TOWER IS A FACSIMILE. A SOULLESS REPLICA THAT EXISTS TO POWER CHIME. YOU KNOW THIS. CHAOS CANNOT CROSS THE TIMELINES, NOR CAN ORDINARY MORTALS. ONLY YOU CAN.

"Only me?"

YOU ARE NO ORDINARY MORTAL, ARE YOU, DARK WARDEN?

Just what had Mesmorpheus seen? "There's no way I can merge the timelines and save Cosmo or the rest? What if I took Dor's power? Couldn't I reverse time, like he has?" Stop the gods from ever abusing their mortals to begin with?

YOU CAN. YOU WILL BIRTH AN ALTERNATE TIMELINE, LIKE THIS ONE. AND CHAOS WILL STILL NOT EXIST WITHIN IT. YOU MAY BE ABLE TO TRAVERSE THE TIMELINES, BUT KAYL ARKEY IS THE HEART OF THIS UNIVERSE. ONLY TOGETHER CAN YOU REMAKE IT, WITH CHAOS AND TIME COMBINED.

LET ME SHOW YOU THE RESULT OF DOR'S MACHINATIONS.

Mesmorpheus waved a hand. A clump of clouds appeared, sparkling with stardust. And within, a vision played out of the Godless in this timeline. A timeline where Kayl didn't exist.

Without Kayl, the Godless never formed.

The vision began with me. A whole other life. My alternate self still fell into the clock tower, but in this timeline, Corentine never awoke. Kayl was never born. I continued my life as a Warden, devoted to Elijah and Dor, punished whenever I strayed.

Harmony was still abused by Serenity. Her single wing ripped off; shunned by her family and exiled to Chime. Without the Godless to channel her rage, she became an alcoholic and killed herself with an overdose of laudanum only five years later.

Vincent remained employed by The Nameless One. His experiments eventually drove him mad, forcing him to turn feral. He spent the rest of his life locked away in Witheryn Asylum.

Sinder escaped the Glimmer workhouse, and the Grayford riots still happened in this timeline. But instead of joining the Godless, Sinder was captured by Wardens and returned to the workhouse, where he suffered until he died.

Dru continued her labor within the steamworks and was forced to return to her family after a tragic accident resulted in the amputation of her legs. While she was still able to join her family's smithy, she fell into a deep depression and endured an arranged marriage with an Umber man who showed her no patience or respect.

Joe never became the man he wanted to be. Gildola forced him to carry a child. Both died within the year.

Elvira and Malk entered Chime. Elvira was still forced into a workhouse, thanks to Varen. She too was caught during the Grayford riots—alongside Malk. They were both brought to a correctional facility and sent back to Valeria as illegals. The Vesper god tortured and killed Elvira as Malk was forced to watch, and his fate ended in one of Valeria's cages.

And Reve. He'd tried to end his life multiple times. With no soul-splitting device to grant him the peace he sought, he continued his campaign, over and over again.

"Why didn't you stop him?" I yelled at Mesmorpheus. "Why continue to rebirth him, only to let him suffer so?"

WHAT DOES IT MATTER, WHEN NONE OF IT IS REAL?

"It was real to him!"

The vision of this timeline ended, and new ones bloomed.

Alternate futures.

Timelines where different domains held political sway over Chime or the Golden City. Where Valeria came out on top and the Glimmer were destitute.

Timelines where the gods failed to create a Covenant, allowing them to freely enter Chime and make their mortals' lives a misery.

Timelines where mortals had no freedoms at all.

Timelines where the gods didn't exist, but without them, neither did their mortals, and Chime became a second home for the Diviner.

A timeline where not even Corentine existed, and mortals were copies of themselves with no free will, acting like machines as the soulless did.

And in none of them did Kayl exist. In none of these timelines were mortals free or happy. Dor could have created a paradise, a timeline where mortals could find peace, and yet he'd not chosen that path in any of the worlds I'd witnessed.

Nor could I create that reality, apparently. Not without removing mortal free will.

"Stop it. You've made your point."

The visions vanished. *YOUR CHOICE SHOULD BE CLEAR.*

It was. The timelines couldn't be merged. There were no happy futures. Only a choice between terrible outcomes. Without Kayl, mortals would never find their freedom, and the cost for them to do so was the soulless and the Necro.

THIS IS REALITY, QUENTIN CORINTH.

I lifted my spectacles and ran my hand down my face. "Reality is overrated. My future self stated there could be a way to save the soulless. A way to travel beyond our universe?"

OUR UNIVERSE IS SEPARATE FROM THE OTHERS FOR A REASON. WE ARE SHIELDED BY AETHER. BREAK THE BOUNDARIES OF THIS UNIVERSE, AND YES, THE SOULLESS CAN BE REACHED. BUT DO SO, AND YOU OPEN OUR UNIVERSE TO OUTSIDE FORCES. OTHER UNIVERSES. OTHER GODS.

Other gods?

YOU DO NOT UNDERSTAND THE CONSEQUENCES.

A different vision bloomed of a dark primordial void beyond the stars of aether. It wasn't of our universe, but of a time before.

Mesmorpheus had once explained to Kayl that other gods had existed before the thirteen. Hundreds of gods who were destroyed or cast out of our universe when time and chaos warred.

The vision revealed only glimpses of them. Different gods from different domains. Perhaps gods who could have existed in our universe.

Gods who came in different states of matter—gases, liquids, and even stardust. One could shift through various elemental forms at the blink of an eye, wielding those elements as surely as an Ember could wield flame.

Gods who took on grotesque and horrifying forms. Another was made of multiple limbs and a carapace reminiscent of the scorpions of Obituary.

Gods so warped, so incomprehensible, I couldn't even perceive them without going insane.

They looked dangerous. Threatening.

THESE ARE THE GODS WHO REJECTED DOR'S VISION. BREAK THE BOUNDARIES OF THIS UNIVERSE, AND YOU INVITE THEM IN. DO YOU WANT TO LIVE THROUGH THESE BATTLES AGAIN?

No, I didn't want to contend with more gods, especially unknown entities, but it wasn't my choice alone to make. "You also have a choice. This is your chance to shape reality how *you* want it."

WHEN YOU TAKE DOR'S SOUL, MY SHADOW WILL FADE.

"You don't have a sense of self-preservation, do you?"

WE GODS HAVE RULED FOR LONG ENOUGH. THERE IS ONE FUTURE I HAVE NOT WITNESSED AND NEVER WILL. THE FUTURE YOU AND KAYL ARKEY WILL CREATE. A FUTURE BEYOND DOR.

IT WILL NOT BE PERFECT. SUCH IS MORTAL FREE WILL. BUT IT WILL BE YOURS.

"Well said." It was a pity I couldn't have spent more time with Mesmorpheus. Of all the gods I'd conversed with during my tenure as Warden, they were by far the most interesting.

YOUR KAYL IS LOST WITHIN THE TIME STREAM, TRAPPED BY DOR. SHE CANNOT NAVIGATE IT AS YOU CAN. TO FIND

HER, YOU MUST BREAK TIME AND TRAVEL THROUGH HER PERSONAL TIMELINE.

"*How* do I find her?" Traversing an entire timeline would be no easy task. Where would I even begin?

FOLLOW HER VOICE. SHE IS CALLING FOR YOU. BUT BEWARE. DOR WILL SENSE TIME FRACTURE. HE WILL HUNT FOR YOU. MOVE QUICKLY THROUGH TIME AND DO NOT REMAIN IN THE SAME STREAM FOR LONG.

YOU WILL HAVE ONLY ONE CHANCE TO FIND HER. DOR WILL NOT ALLOW YOU ANOTHER OPENING.

Wonderful. As if playing with time wasn't complicated enough.

THIS IS THE NATURE OF TIME, QUENTIN CORINTH. NOW GO. RETURN TO YOUR TIMELINE AND END DOR.

I wanted to thank them, but the room darkened as Mesmorpheus threw me from the dream world. I supposed they didn't need my thanks.

Though, now I was ready to do what must be done.

I opened my eyes to Cosmo standing over me. "Did you meet our papa?"

Celeste pulled them away, giving me space to sit up. "I did."

The guilt was still there, knowing Cosmo's soul was lost and there wasn't a damn thing I could do to save it. No matter what timeline I chose, some mortal would suffer. One could argue existence was precious, and even a life of suffering was better than no life at all. Reve would disagree.

But the timeline Kayl and I belonged to had destroyed the gods while freeing their mortals. It was the only timeline worth saving, even if we lost Witheryn and so many others.

Celeste fetched my shoes and jacket for me, and I quickly redressed.

Castor brought that much-needed cup of tea.

I took a tentative sip. My gods! This was the best cup of tea I'd ever had in my mortal life! The correct balance of tea leaves, sugar, milk, all brewed to a moderate temperature. "How did you make this?" I spluttered.

Cosmo beamed a wide smile. "You taught us. We practiced." They pulled a brass fob watch from their pocket. "You misplaced this in your timeline. Papa modified it for you."

Good gods! It was *my* fob watch! The same broken glass and marred design. I cradled it in my palms. "Modified it how?" I couldn't tell simply through examination. "I'd previously modified it to travel between domains."

"Papa says you can use it to travel accurately through time."

Ah. When Dor had unceremoniously tossed me through the aether, I'd had no control over where I landed. My modified fob watch would make it much easier to find my way. That knowledge came to me as though I'd always known it. As though it made perfect sense.

This simple watch had now become my compass. My guide.

It would lead me home.

"You'll also need this." Celeste handed me a small notebook. "It contains a list of your encounters through time."

The notebook was filled with detailed commentary akin to a personal diary. "How would you know of these?"

"We watched them."

"Like watching television!" Cosmo said. "We don't have television, yet but Papa says the Zephyr will invent it in fifty years, and it works the same way as watching dreams."

"Use it to find our mama," Celeste added.

"Then I shouldn't keep her waiting," I said. "Thank you for your help, and for the tea."

I tucked my watch and notebook away, and then the trio embraced me in a hug. Was Cosmo aware of their fate? Saints. I squeezed them tight and bit back the tears. The Mesmer were Kayl's charges, which also made them mine. I'd always held a fondness for them.

We broke apart, and I rubbed my eyes clear. Cosmo handed me a bag of jelly babies for my trip—the same bag my future self had carried only half an hour before.

Gosh. I suddenly realized what I needed to do.

I needed to close that particular time loop.

I bid my farewells and caught a tram back to Central Station.

My past self lay slumped on the bench, unconscious. I made myself comfortable beside him and pulled out the bag of jelly babies. We used to sneak bags of these into our dorms back in the Academy. The masters didn't approve of candy, but I daresay they helped shape my sweet tooth. The red raspberry Ember were my favorite. There was something naughty about popping one into your mouth.

My past self groaned and slowly woke up.

"Steady on, chap," I said. "You've had a rough time of it."

It was amusing to see myself struggle. In only the space of half an hour, I'd become the man I needed to be to step into my future self's shoes. Though no, I'd always been headed for this path.

"Jelly baby?" I offered.

He reacted as I expected because I'd already lived through this conversation. I knew his thoughts, and exactly what he planned to say next. I'd considered my future self a prat, but really, it was amusing to play this scene again.

Unfortunately, his timeline was about to end.

Young Diviner were warned of paradoxes during our early horology classes. An accidental paradox would shatter one's own personal destiny, effectively canceling out an entire timeline. A bogeyman, really. To create a paradox, one simply needed to interrupt one's own time loop with a single blip.

My soul was now Chaos, which meant I was immune to time. I'd assumed that also meant I couldn't create a paradox by merely getting handsy with my future self, except...

Time had already broken in his reality.

He'd said it himself—some part of our soul remained Diviner. Enough for us to do *this*.

I pulled out a white Diviner jelly baby and offered it to my past self. He opened his left hand in naïve expectation. Instead of dropping it, as my future self had, I grasped his palm and yanked his soul—my soul—from his body.

He vanished instantly, wiped from time. If the horror stories of my youth were true, then I should have disappeared with him, erased from existence.

But my timeline, my memories, remained.

I'd become an aberration, and time was not pleased.

Aether cracked through the city with thunderous finality.

Clocks rang out erratically. Time itself shuddered to a halt. The very gears of the universe were grinding with a painful shriek, the machinery congesting and failing.

The timeline fell apart, swallowing me into aether once more.

L

Time. An interesting concept. All mortals obey the laws of time. Indeed, none of us can escape it. Even when a Diviner pauses time, it still catches up with us. It's odd, then, that mortals seem to experience time differently. An Ember states they can make time go faster when in the throes of pleasure. An Umber states they can make time go slower when engaged with work. And a Mesmer states they can stop time entirely by staring at the wall.
—Chairman, *The Timekeepers Guild of Kronos*

TIME WARPED AROUND ME, dragging me through the aether. It wasn't the same sensation as a mortal death—I wasn't floating through stars, but rather hurtling past them. Gods, I fell so fast, I could barely scream!

I fumbled for my fob watch and pushed in the crown twice.

Time paused. Or rather, I paused. My free fall came to a complete stop. I floated within the time stream, and my mind opened to a million possibilities.

Various timelines appeared before me. Amnae swam through the rivers of memory, so I'd half expected time to be a series of interconnected threads. But no. What I envisioned was more a jumbled map of various train tracks. Some of time's tracks ran parallel to each other, others crossed over, touching briefly before heading in different directions.

There were so many tracks—so many timelines—I couldn't tell which one was mine and Kayl's.

What's happening? Doctor Finch's voice returned to me now I'd escaped Dor's alternate world. Wonderful. I wouldn't be traversing the timelines alone.

Welcome back, Doctor. We're going for a trip through time and space.

Oh no. Do you know what you're doing?

Not entirely, but we'd figure it out as we went along.

My task was to navigate through the timeline and find Kayl, and the clock was ticking. Mesmorpheus had advised me to listen for Kayl's voice. In the void of aether, all I could hear was my own damnable heartbeat. But thanks to the Mesmer, I at least had a starting point.

I wound the watch and focused on my first destination. Grayford.

Time once again flung me through the aether, and I appeared in darkness dotted by bright aether lights. The Undercity. Specifically, the main square in front of Varen's old residence. It was eerily quiet, the streets abandoned except for piles of clothing and dust.

This was the correct timeline. But when?

I flipped open the notebook Celeste had gifted me. It contained events I'd not lived through, but that Kayl had. Points in the timeline to help guide me back to her. My first stop wasn't meant to be here, and it was one memory I did recall.

A flash of aether caught my eye. A short figure with wings moved across Varen's upstairs window. Nocturne.

"Uh, lady?" he said. "What are you doing?"

"Something new." That was Kayl's voice. It was full of pain, though I didn't recall this particular memory.

"*And* she's gone. Where the fuck did she go? Ugh, women! You might as well come out."

A door creaked. And then… "Whatever Arkey just did, I don't need to know." Gast's voice. "It'll go back to Jinx, though she'll learn of Serenity anyway. There's no hiding that. You better fill me in on what the fuck happened in Arcadia."

"Gonna dig around and find some whiskey first. I'm not recalling all that shit without a drink. I bet that old twat Varen had something stashed for those miserable days. Like, you know, every fucking day down here. You want in?"

"You know I don't drink on the job."

"Everything's a bloody job to you. How are you handling your urges?"

"Diviner. Plenty of soulless around for a snack. Don't give me that look, they're already dead."

"I'm saying nothing." Nocturne sighed. "What do I do now?"

"Stick with Arkey. She's safe, and... I get the feeling she needs a friendly face on her side."

"Shame it had to be mine."

Typical Nocturne. He and Gast had both lost their souls in this timeline, which meant what I was looking at wasn't entirely real, but an echo, as my future self had described it. Despite the history I shared with the pair, I never wished for this outcome.

It also meant I couldn't simply snatch this version of Kayl and be done with it. No. I needed to find 'my' Kayl.

Nocturne and Gast headed downstairs and out of sight of the window. This moment of the timeline came after Cosmo lost their soul. I hadn't been there for Kayl, during what had become her darkest hour, as I suffered mine.

It hurt my heart to know how much this pained her. But I'd written her a letter—my past self had read it. I could leave it here for Kayl to find.

Since Walter had restored my memories, I discovered my capacity for memory had become almost perfect. Eidetic. I summoned a pen and ripped a spare page from my notebook for the letter I could recite from memory. I considered adding more terms of endearment, but while this letter was meant for Kayl, it was also a message for my past self.

I waited until Gast was occupied by Nocturne's recounting of Kayl's time in Arcadia and snuck my way upstairs in Varen's house.

Cosmo lay napping on the couch. They looked peaceful, but that too was a facsimile. I slipped the note into their shirt pocket, certain someone would find it.

Where next? Doctor Finch asked.

Good question. We didn't have time to dally, not if Dor had eyes on the time stream. Perhaps I could avoid exploring Kayl's entire timeline by going to the source of her birth. But if Dor *was* waiting to pounce, then I needed to be armed.

I returned to the timeline and threw myself back a year into Past Quen's apartment. It was roughly two in the afternoon, which meant my past self would be performing his Warden rounds, leaving his apartment empty.

The perfect time to steal from myself.

I'd expected his pistol to be under his bed, as it always had, but it was gone, replaced instead by a letter. Blast it! I'd apparently traveled too far. I opened the letter. It wasn't addressed to me, but to Kayl. Ah. It was the letter I'd written before Solaris fell, warning her of Gloria's intentions to split Jinx's soul.

The memory of that day burned. I'd been fully prepared to sacrifice Jinx to save Kayl, and had almost lost Kayl in the process. I'd not wanted to damn Jinx, but Dor had pushed me, leaving me no choice.

There had always been a choice.

I resealed the letter with silver wax and wrote another note for my past self, reminding him to check for it later. I then stole the last of his bourbon biscuits for good measure. Time travel was hungry business.

I hopped back to an even *earlier* point of my timeline to retake my pistol. *Do remind me to put the darn thing back where it belongs.*

Is this safe? Doctor Finch asked. *All this time hopping? What if you accidentally change something you're not meant to? And trigger a rippling effect through time that fundamentally changes the future? What* then?

I'm a Diviner, Doctor. Firstly, you need to learn to panic less. Secondly, it would take greater change to affect the timeline. Though perhaps if mortals banded together more and made smaller changes, they'd have greater control over their future. That was Diviner philosophy. The power of many outweighed the few.

I wound my fob watch and flung myself through the timeline, arriving inside the clock tower. My past self had already fallen, landing painfully on the metal platform. Logically, I'd arrived here not for myself, but to witness Kayl's birth. It was the starting point of her personal timeline.

However, before events could unfold, I sensed another presence with me. Dor?

I braced myself as a figure emerged from the darkness in a rippling cloak of stars.

"Mesmorpheus." This was a surprise. "What brings you to this part of the timeline?"

Mesmorpheus stared at my fallen and broken body. *YOU, QUENTIN CORINTH. I SENSED YOUR MANIPULATION OF THE TIMELINE. THIS WAS DESTINED TO BE.*

The unfortunate part of time travel was I didn't know which Mesmorpheus this was. Were they aware of the task they'd set me? "Time's a little broken, I'm afraid."

THE TIMELINES CONVERGE. Mesmorpheus breathed in. An oddly mortal gesture I'd never seen them capable of. *THE ERA OF GODS IS ALMOST OVER. YOU HAVE ACHIEVED WHAT I DARE NOT. YOU HAVE AWOKEN CORENTINE.*

"I dare say I've done a bit more than that, but I need you to play your part in this brave new future."

They cocked their head. *YOU WISH FOR MY ASSISTANCE?*

It had occurred to me if the events of this timeline were to continue, then someone would need to ensure they were set in motion. "Shortly, Corentine will birth two daughters. In just over thirteen years, one of them will take my soul. I'll need a soul-splitting device installed in your temple somewhere out of sight to get it out."

I SEE IT. MY MORTALS WILL ENSURE IT IS DONE. They produced a key from their jacket pocket. *THIS WILL OPEN THE WAY.*

I took it and shoved it into my own inner jacket pocket. "Thank you."

REALITY IS BUT A DREAM OF THE GODS. REMEMBER THAT AS YOU SEARCH THE TIMELINES. CORENTINE'S DAUGHTER DREAMS. SHE REACHES OUT FOR YOU.

Mesmorpheus suddenly vanished.

Kayl appeared inside the tunnel. Just as I'd visited Haven inside my dream, she'd somehow bled through reality to find me. Was it a dream? Or was it reality? The two were often one and the same, as I'd discovered. A difference in semantics.

My heart soared at the sight of her. I wanted nothing more than to pull her into my arms, but this wasn't my Kayl. Not yet. I should have fled back into the timeline, but she'd already spotted me, and gods take me for a fool, I needed the comfort of her smile.

She slid to my side. "What's going on?" she whispered.

"He's just fallen," I whispered back.

My past self was now conscious and rolling around in agony. The poor boy had broken his ribs, but I could do nothing to ease his discomfort. Paradoxes and all that.

"I'm dreaming again, aren't I?" Kayl said.

"You're dreaming. I'm watching history unfold. This is where it all began."

"Where what began?"

"My downfall. Your birth."

"I have a lot to thank you for."

I slid my arm around her waist, pulling her close. "I have more reasons to be thankful." Gods, I wanted her. Needed her. "I'd kiss you right now, but I wouldn't want to disturb ongoing history. Doing so tends to have catastrophic consequences."

She placed her hand on my chest, above my heart. "I can be quiet."

"I know from experience that you can't." I nuzzled against her neck and breathed in her sweet scent. It took all my willpower to resist her, but she *wasn't* my Kayl. We hadn't performed this dance yet.

Her cheeks flushed. "And how would you know that, mister? Are you from the future?"

"I can't reveal all my secrets."

"How are we both here? *Why* are we here?"

I sighed. "I'm trying to find you. The future you. My Kayl. Let's say that the timeline is... complicated. Mesmorpheus knows this. They've brought you to me for reasons yet unknown to you."

"Could either of you be any more infuriating?"

I squeezed her hip and chuckled. "It'll make sense, I promise. I'll be taking my leave shortly. I just need to ensure events unfold as they should."

She glanced at my younger self. "Are you my Quen?"

"That depends on my past self. Right now, he's suffering at the mercy of Dor's whims. While Dor is in my mind, I have no choice but to obey his orders—to deny you."

"But you're here?"

"The timeline is fragile. This future is not set in stone. Whatever decisions you and Past Me make could change its path. I exist now, but should the timeline change, then this version of me will also change—or fade away entirely."

Weariness darkened her aether eyes. "Then what future do you represent? What man do you become?"

I cupped her check. "I'm the Quen who adores you. Who will fight by your side for a future that glorifies all mortals."

"Does this version of you swear?"

I couldn't help but smirk. "He fucking does."

She grabbed my jacket and yanked me to her lips. Saints, I wanted to melt myself into her touch, to feel this bliss for eternity, but it wasn't our time yet, and some rules needed to be obeyed.

Sadly, I'd overstayed my welcome. I pulled away and placed a finger on her lips. "In time, my dear."

"How do I save you?" she gasped.

"If you want this future, then you'll need to fight for it. I'm sorry. It won't be easy." I pulled out my fob watch. "My time's up. But before I go, remember this: my past self has placed a sealed envelope under our bench. Don't forget it."

Time opened up, flowing over me with blinding aether.

"Don't leave me!" she cried. "I *need* you!"

"We'll meet again. You're my salvation."

I merged back into the time stream, and a voice whispered.

Find me, Quen. Find me.

It was Kayl. She was calling me.

Finally, the hunt could begin.

I hopped between the tracks of time, searching for her voice. It led me to a version of Central that had been destroyed by Dor, and I appeared on the bench outside the station.

Kayl was seated beside me, and she jumped, my sudden arrival startling her.

This time, I'd entered her dream. At least I could take a moment to get my bearings. I pulled the bag of jelly babies from my jacket. "Would you like a jelly baby?" I offered.

She looked absolutely bamboozled. "Where in god's name did you get jelly babies?"

"Cosmo was saving them. They said the purple ones are your favorite. Licorice flavor, I believe?"

She picked out a purple jelly baby in the shape of a Vesper. "This is a dream, isn't it?"

Once upon a time, the Amnae jelly babies came in green tea flavor. I did so miss those limited editions. I helped myself to a blueberry Amnae. "It would appear so."

"This isn't the first time you've entered my dreams."

I raised a brow. "Is it not? How many other times have you dreamed of me? Let's compare." I put the jelly babies aside and flipped open my notebook. Perhaps her own memories of my future self's visitations would match up to my notes. Anything to track my version of Kayl helped. "Where did you dream of me first?"

"In Grayford, when I was a child."

"That makes sense. Where else?"

"Grayford again, a few times."

"Have we met inside the clock tower?"

"No. Should we?"

"In my timeline, we already have." I tapped my notebook.

She strained over to catch a glimpse. Naughty. I snapped the notebook shut with a tut. "No spoilers."

She pouted. "If this is my dream, shouldn't it bend to my will? Where are we? Is this the future?"

"It's *a* future. A potential one among many."

"Shit." She grabbed the jelly babies and picked out an orange Leander. "How do we prevent this one? That's what you're trying to do, isn't it?"

"That depends entirely on you."

"On me?" She choked on her jelly baby.

"What are you willing to sacrifice to prevent this future? Whose soul are you willing to take?"

"Are you speaking of Jinx?"

Our conversation had veered too close to reality for my liking. It was time to move on. My Kayl waited for me out there, somewhere. I just needed to find her.

I wrapped a small bubble of time around the streetlamp and shoved time forward. It blew out, plunging us into darkness, allowing me the escape I needed.

The stars welcomed me, but something was off about them. Something wrong.

Two silver orbs floated in the aether.

QUENTIN!

Oh fuck. Dor! He'd already sensed me infiltrating the time stream.

Giant floating hands pushed past the stars and reached for me.

I wound back my fob watch, returning me to the safety of Kayl's memory. But instead of me landing back at the scene, reality shifted, dragging me through flashes of her past.

Saints. I no longer traveled through Kayl's timeline, but through Kayl's dreams.

In Kayl's mind, I was altering her reality. Appearing in places important to her. Important to me, too. It was her soul that beckoned me.

In one such dream, she'd tried to trick Edana into believing in a false future.

In another, I'd become the Godless benefactor, and Kayl had run after me, tripping over wreckage and almost impaling herself—she would've if I hadn't stepped in and caught her.

Then I entered another version of Grayford. One where Wardens tore through the streets and Vesper ran and hid. Saints. I'd arrived at the Grayford Incident.

My hand went to my pistol on instinct. I held many regrets about my personal timeline. The events of the Grayford Incident were high among them. It was the first time I'd killed a mortal, and that had led to a catastrophe of consequences: defying Elijah, the execution of Elvira, my incarceration in the correctional facility, and the efforts I went to afterward to suppress my own memories. The creation of my nickname. The Dark Warden.

I could change the timeline.

But the Grayford Incident was a fixed point in time, for without that moment, the Godless would never have existed.

Kayl found me here, but there was nothing I could do to protect her from the trials to come. Not without risking another paradox.

The dreamworld thrust me out, and I stepped from one riot to another, this time arriving in Meridian Park.

Kayl's cries tore through me. She ran across the park, a trail of blood dripping from her coat.

Gods. She'd been shot during the riot.

My past self had held a memorial for the loss of Eventide and he'd gone and fumbled the entire thing, leading to this situation. Could I be angry at my past self for making these grievous mistakes? Yes, I sodding well could.

Kayl was *bleeding*.

She and Dru had sought shelter against the park's walls, but the Wardens were closing off the exits. They wouldn't be able to get out.

Then I caught sight of Ben. Wonderful Ben. How I'd missed him, but I had no time to mourn. He was giving orders to a group of nearby Wardens to lock the park down.

I approached and caught his attention. "Ben! Change of plans."

"Sir?" He looked confused. "Are those different clothes?"

"Focus, Ben. We've got more important matters to deal with. We need to gather the Wardens back to the cricket hut."

"But the gates, sir? You told me to—"

"Sod the gates. If a few undesirables slip out, then so be it. The safety of the ambassadors takes priority. Or do you intend to keep wasting my precious time?" I raised a brow.

"No, sir." He saluted me. "Sorry, sir."

I watched as he strode off and recalled the Wardens by Kayl and Dru's hiding spot. They were understandably wary, but eventually made their escape. I followed at a slow pace to ensure no Wardens caught them. At least they had the sense to avoid the crowds and head for the nearest alley.

"Oi! You there!" a Diviner Warden called after them. "Halt!"

Blast it. Kayl and Dru ducked inside the alleyway.

"I said *stop*!" The Warden paused time. Dru was instantly frozen. Her arm was wrapped around Kayl's, trapping her too and forcing her to remain still.

I drew my pistol and stalked closer.

The Warden tapped Dru's arm with his baton before returning it to his belt and facing Kayl. "What do we have 'ere, then? Two lovely ladies running from the law? You don't look great, love."

He took Kayl's hand and rubbed it against his groin.

That degenerate!

I could barely contain the rage that threatened to erupt. How *dare* he? I would blow his fucking brains out, but I needed to angle myself without attracting attention. This wasn't a dream—I was certain, based on my interaction with Ben—which meant exposing myself to Kayl now would only create complications within the timeline. Doubly so if Dor discovered my future self had come back to kill Diviner.

This particular wanker deserved worse than the quick death I was about to grant him.

"I wonder what we have under 'ere?" He began to undo the buttons of Kayl's blouse.

Perhaps not all souls were worth saving. This one could drown in aether for an eternity for all I cared. I aimed my pistol with my left hand.

My shot pierced his head, decorating the alley wall.

Lovely. My aim *had* improved.

Kayl was staring down the alleyway at me. I needed to leave, but I couldn't afford to dally inside the time stream in case Dor waited for me.

I wound my watch to the next hop in Kayl's timeline and appeared outside Central Station, early afternoon. Mortals busied themselves with the lunchtime rush as the clock neared one o'clock. The Gate still operated with all domains except for Eventide.

Which part of the timeline had I stumbled into now? I was about to pull out the notebook and check when I noticed my past self and Kayl sitting outside a café and enjoying tea and scones.

Soon, Kayl would enter Memoria alone and Anima would alter her memories of Malk, effectively blocking Valeria's powers.

Ah. I remembered the role I needed to play.

Was it necessary to alter her memories? Doctor Finch asked.

A good question. I peered into the time stream, at the many tracks branching from this moment.

If I'd accompanied Kayl into Memoria as planned, Aberforth wouldn't have dared touch her. She would have been under my protection and thus retained her memories and abilities. In this alternate world, Kayl wouldn't have learned how to harness her Chaos powers. It wouldn't have been my soul that came out of the soul-splitting machine, but Malk's, and the entire timeline would unravel as a result.

For this timeline to exist, I needed to become Chaos.

It was selfish of me, then, to manipulate the timeline for the desired outcome. By placing my own soul first, yes, we'd end the reign of gods. But I'd also come between Kayl and her lover. Should I feel guilty for that?

In another timeline, they'd reconciled.

In that timeline, I'd married Pendula. What a terrible outcome.

But it was a moot point, since that timeline would end with Dor winning.

Then this is one of those moments where one action cascades and causes ripples in time? Doctor Finch pointed out.

I suppose it is. And it began with a tragedy.

In order to stop my past self from following Kayl into Memoria, I needed a distraction, and nothing distracted him more than mortal suffering.

I merged with the crowd parallel to the tram platform outside the station. The clock tower rang out one o'clock, and the Gate switched over to Memoria.

A tram came down the tracks, like clockwork. I focused a pocket of time around it, forcing it to speed up.

You'll injure mortals! Doctor Finch yelled into my mind.

Unfortunately, yes. Mortals would die.

I was still the Dark Warden. Death followed me.

My past self attempted to slow the tram, effectively popping my bubble of time with his own. Sadly for him, my mastery of time had evolved somewhat. I slammed the tram forward.

He fought me. It was a valiant effort, but not even he could stand against the Dark Warden.

The tram jerked forward and plowed into a crowd of mortals. Their personal timelines ended with a blip, their futures wiped in an instant.

You couldn't have distracted your past self with a telegram? Doctor Finch demanded.

Blame my past self for being a bleeding heart. The good doctor needn't fret. Once Kayl and I restored the universe, I'd ensure the lives I'd taken would get a second chance.

Death was not the end.

The resulting carnage achieved the desired result. I headed into Central Station, where Kayl had finished speaking with the stationmaster and had regrouped with Dru.

Kayl spotted me and rushed over. "Gods, what do we do now? Do we call this off?"

"No, no. We'll leave this incident in the Wardens' hands. There's nothing more we can do, and we're still on a tight schedule. I'd rather not keep Aberforth waiting." I glanced over my shoulder to check my past self was still out of sight. "Can you go on ahead and queue for the crossing? I'll collect Ben and join you shortly."

"All right." Kayl fetched Dru and headed for the queue.

Once again, I merged with the crowd and observed as my foolish past self inadvertently waved Kayl on, and she and Dru stepped into Memoria.

I couldn't afford to let him follow.

I encased the station in another pocket of time and forced the clock to jump forward, skipping an hour. The Gate switched over from Memoria to Juniper. No other mortal had noticed the lost hour, not even the Diviner Wardens nearby.

None except for Past Quen and his bodyguard.

They both looked dumbfounded. Good. My work here was done.

The timeline would progress as it should. If Mesmorpheus had done as I'd suggested, then the soul-splitting device would be ready to receive me. It was a slight detour, but I needed to take the steps required to convert my soul to Chaos.

Timelines, eh. Weren't they wonderful?

I stepped out of time and into the Mesmer temple, appearing in the halls below.

"Quen?" Kayl asked, surprise in her eyes.

"Oh bugger." I'd gotten my timing completely wrong. This was far too early.

I ran and dove inside the closet. The key Mesmorpheus had given me worked, as promised, though the room had not yet been prepared to my specification.

"Quen!" Kayl thumped on the door. "What are you doing? Why are you even here? What is going *on*?"

"I'm sorry. I'm going through a strange time in my life right now—"

"You're not the only one!"

"Be patient with me, please. I know I'm insufferable, and I suffer for it." I wound my watch and leaped back into the time stream.

QUENTIN! Dor's voice echoed through the aether. *DO NOT RUN FROM ME. YOU WILL LOSE YOURSELF TO TIME. I CAN PULL YOU TO SAFETY.*

Whatever safety he offered came with caveats. I'd sooner take my chances.

The time stream spat me out into the temple district of Chime. Abandoned clothes and piles of dust were scattered everywhere.

Diviner Wardens were on the prowl, armed with tasers. Had Dor sent them after me? But no. These weren't soulless. Their eyes were alert, and they were hunting with a purpose.

Heart-wrenching screams echoed from the Glimmer temple. Kayl's screams.

It caught the attention of two Diviner nearby. They headed for the temple.

Gods. I remembered now. This was the moment I'd come for.

I followed the Diviner at a safe distance as they entered the temple. Kayl was crouched over my dead body. Her sobs were torturous.

I don't remember any of this happening, Doctor Finch said.

You were already dead at the time.

Oh.

"She's here!" called out one of the Diviner. They stalked toward her, their tasers aimed.

One of the Diviner leered over Kayl. "You're done for, you unholy whore." He raised his hand, as though to strike her.

Rage seethed through me. I aimed my pistol with my metal hand, and my shot rang true, piercing his head.

The second Diviner spun to face me, and I blasted his brains out next.

Their bodies faded, leaving their clothes to float to the ground.

"It appears I've arrived in time," I said.

Kayl's eyes darted between me and my past self lying on the ground. "But you're—you're *dead*!"

My relief at finding Kayl was short-lived. This wasn't *my* Kayl, but this was where it began. My past self was trapped inside her mind. For the future to happen at all, I needed to get him out. He needed to become Chaos.

"I've died quite a few times now, actually. It doesn't get any more pleasant." I peered over at my dead past self and grimaced. "Oh my, what a state I'm in. I best not get too close. Paradoxes and all that. Can you walk? Or are you going to faint?"

"You're an arse!" She pulled herself up and thumped my chest. "You've just *died*, and you're standing here joking about it?"

I wished I could spare the time to comfort her, but if I recalled correctly, more Wardens would be on their way. That, and I didn't wish to waste time when Dor was searching through the time stream. "I'm not joking. But we *are* on a tight schedule."

"*What* are you talking about?"

I pulled out my fob watch. "Wardens are on their way, and worse besides. You've met the Guardians by now, haven't you? Immortal creatures. Best we don't tangle with them. You're carrying my soul, and I need to get it out."

"I—what?"

I tapped her head. "In there. Hello, Past Quen."

Her eyes went wide at the private conversation she was now having with the version of me occupying her mind. I could recall the conversation—recall the sensation of being trapped inside another's head. It was an altogether surreal experience.

Tell me about it, Doctor Finch huffed.

Was that sarcasm, Doctor? Are you learning?

He harrumphed inside my mind.

Emotions clashed across Kayl's face, ranging from grief to elation. Alas, we really didn't have time for a reunion. I cleared my throat. "Time, please."

"So why are you here?" she asked. "What's your plan?"

"I thought that was obvious." I examined my pistol. The chamber could only hold six bullets, and I'd already spent three, but there was nothing stopping me from summoning more. "Follow me but stay close. We need to get into the Mesmer temple."

"Why there?"

"You'll see."

"I don't know why I trust you."

I bit back a smirk. "We're both grateful you do."

Thanks to my past self, I'd already lived this moment and knew exactly where to guide Kayl, when to stop, when the Wardens would attack, and when the newly rebirthed Joe would make his appearance to distract them.

I led Kayl into the abandoned Mesmer temple. The sight of scattered clothes made Kayl react with unease, but soon, the Mesmer would become hers. She just didn't know it yet.

The less I explained, the less chance I'd accidentally reveal something I shouldn't. We arrived outside the closet I knew would now be ready to receive us and pulled out the key. "Trust me."

True to their word, Mesmorpheus had managed to procure one of the soul-splitting devices. It sat ominously in the center of the room. I so detested those things, but it was a necessary step in securing the future. Without my rebirth into Chaos, none of this would be possible.

"What is this?" Kayl entered behind me with some apprehension.

I approached the console. Bugger. I didn't know the start-up sequence. *Doctor?*

Must I? he whined.

For this timeline to exist, yes.

He sighed internally, and then the sequence flashed in my mind. This wouldn't be pleasant for any of us, but again, it was quite necessary. "You can't remove my soul from your body without help. Reverie recovered this device and rebuilt it to my specifications with Mesmorpheus's guidance. Please. Take a seat."

Kayl, however, did not sit. "Jinx was able to bring back Joe. Why can't I do the same?"

I glanced over the rim of my spectacles. "Jinx didn't tell you everything you needed to know. She has the power of Gildola. A god. Without that same power, any souls you take will remain inside you."

"But—I own Valeria's soul, don't I?"

"You do. However, Anima rather conveniently blocked you from accessing Valeria's power, which is why you're struggling to remember certain details. They're buried in your subconscious where you can't reach them."

My past self made the connection that I'd derailed the tram in Central, thus ensuring Kayl would enter Memoria. "Yes, I caused the crash. That was my—your—abilities you felt, Past Quen."

"It was you who told me to enter Memoria knowing Anima would fuck with my memories," Kayl accused. "Why?"

"Because if you'd retained Valeria's powers, then this moment in the timeline wouldn't have been possible." My past self was not pleased with this revelation. Specifically, that I'd ended mortal lives to ensure the sanctity of the timeline. "Sacrifices had to be made."

Kayl's nose twisted, as though she were swallowing something sour. It was my past self's emotions bleeding through her, manipulating her expressions without Kayl even realizing. He didn't yet understand mortal death wasn't the end.

That we'd die many times to come.

No, he had to be a prat and compare my actions to Elijah's, because that was his default, wasn't it? We always compared our sins, but we were better than that. "Stop being so dramatic," I said. "We're nothing like Elijah."

"I forgot the truth of Eventide," Kayl said. "Of Malkavaan."

"And I won't apologize. You'll both understand why soon enough. Now, I must reiterate that we are on a *tight* schedule. This is the only way I can save you." I'd already wasted enough time here. I gestured to the chair. "You're wondering if you can trust me. Unfortunately, I don't have time to fully alleviate your fears. Just know that if your Quen dies, then so do I, and I'm not feeling particularly suicidal right now."

Kayl finally conceded and allowed me to attach the headpiece that would ultimately rip out my soul. Aether burst from the machine. I took my opportunity to dive back inside the time stream, rather than watch my rebirth into Chaos.

From that point onwards, everything would change.

A giant silver hand hurtled toward me through the time stream. Fuck! Dor was getting closer!

I threw myself back through time, narrowly avoiding his grasp, and landed inside a dark, dusty room underground.

The workshop! Doctor Finch exclaimed.

Ah, yes. This was the workshop beneath the steamworks. In exactly two minutes, my past self would be arriving to collect his new arm. Luckily, I'd learned how to make a spare, though I'd have to leave my pistol behind, too. That would put me at a disadvantage.

How was I meant to follow Kayl's voice and find her with Dor on my tail? He was forcing me to hop from one time event to another, but I couldn't keep this up. Soon, time would run out.

The workshop door opened, and in stumbled my past self looking rather disheveled and, honestly, like a complete disaster. What did Kayl see in me?

"Good afternoon, Past Quen," I greeted him.

His jaw dropped. "Future Quen?" he spluttered.

We'd already performed this dance, and once again it amused me to torment my past self a little. I truly was a bastard. But he needed to understand the gravity of what was to come. He needed to be clear in his devotion to Kayl.

She was a goddess. Our goddess.

And saints, did I ache to worship at her feet. The last time I'd gotten on my knees before her had been a dream, and there was nothing more frustrating than ruining one's briefs for an act that wasn't technically real.

Your thoughts are deeply troubling at times, Doctor Finch said.

You're the one who insists on playing voyeur.

I do not! he squawked.

Relax, Doctor. Perhaps my sordid thoughts would inspire the man to loosen up a little. I'd wasted so many years of my life, attempting to resist sin, only to flourish as an apparent pervert regardless. I could have been enjoying myself all along.

Alas, I had more pressing concerns.

I finished setting my past self up with his new arm and my pistol. He'd need it for the battles to come, and soon.

We thought the steamworks were empty because you'd taken care of the Diviner, Doctor Finch said. *If not you, then who?*

Wasn't it obvious? *Pendula laid a trap for me. Anything to deliver me to Dor.* The steamworks were her father's domain. She knew the layout.

It was my domain, too, he lamented. *Now I don't know who I am anymore, or who I want to be. I never really fit in anywhere. Not with the Zephyr. Not with the Diviner. Probably not with the Amnae. I never thought myself Godless, but... This, all this, has given me a purpose I didn't know I lacked. Oh no, I'm suffering emotion—*

Zachery. For all the madness I've put you through, I'm glad you chose to accompany me. The good doctor had been an unlikely companion. A friend.

Thank you, Master Corinth.

Call me Quen. Unto the breach once more?

You need to complete your personal time loop.

How silly of me, I'd almost forgotten.

I needed to return my pistol to Past Quen first, and I did so in the blink of an eye by collecting the pistol I'd left with Kayl in the Fauna hotel, that she'd also conveniently forgotten in her haste to abandon Sinner's Row.

Time. What a blessing and a curse wrapped in one.

Are we ready, Quen? Doctor Finch asked. *We must find Kayl.*

Yes. Before Dor found me.

I returned once more to the void.

Find me, Quen. Kayl was louder now. Was I getting closer?

Kayl? Where are you?

Where I needed you most.

I followed her voice further back into the past as it beckoned me on. The time stream's track became bumpy, and it spat me out once more into the Undercity.

A streetlamp flickered above. I'd arrived in one of the tunnels near Grayford. All this traveling through time had taken its toll. My residual limb ached from wearing an artificial arm for what felt like hours, but alas, I wasn't yet ready to rest. With Doctor Finch's guidance, I summoned myself an additional arm, one that looked far more real, and slotted it back into place with gritted teeth.

The streetlamp gave enough light for me to quickly flip through my notebook, but according to Celeste's careful annotations, this was it.

I'd run out of time.

"I don't want to hurt anyone," a young voice whimpered. A girl's voice.

I glanced into the tunnel. A girl was seated there on a mat, naked and dirty. In this low light, her skin looked Vesper, except it was the silvery-blue of Chaos.

A lost child? Doctor Finch squawked. *We must help her!*

Those familiar eyes shone bright, even as the timid girl tried to shy away. Good gods.

It was Kayl as a child before Elvira had found her. The timeline squeezed around me, as though hugging me with its presence. I was witnessing Kayl's first moments in this world.

She'd only just been born.

That knowledge shocked me to my core. This was a pivotal moment in Kayl's life, and I was truly privileged to be a part of it.

I took a few slow steps closer so as not to frighten the poor girl and wore my most charming smile. "Don't be afraid. I'm not going to hurt you."

"What—What are you?" she croaked. Her lips were cracked and dry, for she'd never had a glass of water in her life.

"I'm a little lost, like you. I shouldn't be here—this isn't my time—but luckily fate has brought me to you." I summoned a flask of water inside my jacket where she couldn't see and offered it. "Go on. It's clean water."

She snatched the flask and eagerly drank mouthfuls. Water dribbled down her chin.

"Slowly now," I warned. "You don't want to choke."

She spluttered and tried to pass the flask back.

"Keep it." I shrugged off my jacket and laid it before her. "Cover yourself in this. It's a little big, but it will keep you warm until help arrives."

"Help? I don't want—"

"There's no shame in accepting help, and you need all the help you can get." I gave her a stern look over the rim of my spectacles. Elvira would come soon—I'd seen those memories from Malk. She'd be all right, but I didn't want to tempt fate by remaining here longer than I should. I flipped open my fob watch. "My time is up, I'm afraid. Listen to me; a Vesper woman is going to find you shortly. She's a nice lady, and she'll look after you, so please listen to her, will you? She has a son, and he's going to be grumpy, but be patient with him. He's suffered a lot."

Kayl draped my jacket over her shoulders. "What happened to him?"

"His god was mean to him and his family."

"Why? Didn't his god love him?"

"Sometimes the gods are cruel."

"Do you have a god?"

I instinctively ran my thumb over the marred brass of my watch. An old habit. "Not anymore."

I stood back on my heels and prepared myself for one more jump into the time stream, though where it would lead, I had no idea.

What existed beyond this memory?

She reached out and grasped my wrist. "Don't leave me. Please." Tears welled in her eyes. "Don't go."

Truly, I didn't want to leave her. It pained me to see her so small, so frightened. But to travel through time and witness Kayl's life was truly an honor. I'd seen her future—had so gladly shared it. I knew the woman she'd become.

A woman who made me a better man.

I gently pulled myself free. "You're a brave girl. The bravest girl I know. And you're going to be fine. More than fine; you're going to be brilliant."

Time wrapped around me with its familiar comfort, and then the tracks of Kayl's timeline came to a sudden end. A terminus.

All that remained was a dark tunnel leading nowhere.

What now? Doctor Finch asked.

I suppose we enter the tunnel and see where it leads.

The doctor's anxiety wasn't enough to override my curiosity. I stepped into the tunnel and walked.

And walked.

It seemed to stretch on for an eternity. One foot plodding in front of another.

Then, at the end of the tunnel... Light.

I emerged into white space. It wasn't entirely what I'd imagined.

The tracks had led to a station almost identical to Central Station. A replica stranded in the white space. It even had its own Gate and clock tower. The Gate rippled with churning pink and blue aether, like a reactor in the steamworks, and the clockface was set to the thirteenth hour—the actual thirteenth hour, for this clock went all the way to thirteen, for some bizarre reason.

Mortals wandered within the station. No, not mortals.

They were Diviner, Necro, only something was distinctly wrong with them. Their skin appeared as white as the space around them, almost translucent. Was this the effect of being soulless? Would I find them all here?

Ben? Walter? Cosmo?

Sitting in the waiting room of time's end? Waiting for salvation?

I wanted to search, but I hadn't made this journey for them alone.

There was only one place I'd find Kayl.

Even here, at the end of all things, our bench existed outside the station.

And there she sat, radiating pure aether. A spark of color against the drab backdrop of white. Her twin lay curled across the bench, Jinx's head resting in Kayl's lap as Kayl ran her fingers through her sister's hair and crooned soft words.

They both glanced up at my approach.

Kayl whispered something I didn't hear and stood. Jinx vanished in a sparkling burst of aether, merging with Kayl's body and soul.

The two of them together as one once more.

Kayl's aether eyes carried the weariness of a thousand timelines. "Are you my Quen?"

"Beyond the end of time."

She leaped into my arms.

I pulled her tight, burying my nose in her shoulder. "I almost lost you."

She laughed, her chest vibrating against mine. "You always find me."

"I always will." I wanted to kiss her. Gods, I needed her so badly. No matter where time brought me, I was home where I belonged—in her smile. Instead, my hand slipped into hers, as natural and precise as the tick-tock of a clock.

QUENTIN! Dor's voice boomed across the spectral station. His hands materialized above the clock tower, his large silver eyes staring down.

While his cursed soul persisted, this battle would never be over. The timeline would remain fractured. Kayl would never find comfort.

And I'd never be free.

It was time to end this, and I knew exactly what Dor wanted.

Me.

01000100 01101111 01110010

How does a god's mind work?
That is a blasphemous question. You are not to understand the
machinations of our Father, as you are not meant to understand the inner
workings of the gods. Know Father has created you for a reason. Our Father
has a divine plan for every one of us.
To demonstrate faith is to place trust in Him.
For there is no greater love than the love of our holy Father.
—H. Bezel, *Philosophy for the Young Diviner*

MY SON HAD SURPASSED Me. The emotions it elicited were a complex enigma of shame and pride. He stood hand in hand with Chaos, a bastion of Time, as I once had at the very beginning of all things.

Quentin wore My face, but He was not Me.

He, who rejected Me.

Corentine was gone. Cast outside time, where she would be forgotten. Her daughter wrapped herself in Chaos, yet she was only a shadow of Corentine's beauty and power.

They did not understand eternity.

They did not understand its price.

I lowered Myself to their level, wrapping the aether of My form into a mortal shell. It unnerved them. They did not understand where they stood. The nexus. The terminus. The very end of all things. Soulless mortals hid within the facsimile of Chime's station. They were no longer part of this universe. They could not interact with it.

Beyond the Gate's portal lay infinite potential.

A world beyond eternity, where no mortal belonged.

YOU ARE THE LAST MORTALS IN THE UNIVERSE.

It was Corentine's daughter who replied. "You know we're no longer mere mortals." She gripped Quentin's hand, her chin lifted in petulance. "The gods are dead. You've nothing left. No allies. No mortals to serve you. Your time is over."

The ire of her voice was familiar. Mortals were often impatient.

I could wait another millennium for her to age and die, if I was certain she would.

Both she and Quentin had absorbed the aether of the gods. It was how the Pantheon birthed new children according to their laws. Energy could not be destroyed, only transferred and transformed. The Pantheon chose which gods to sacrifice to bear gods anew. A logical, iterative process ruined by emotional decisions.

They believed mortal life would taint the covenant of the gods. Disrupt the flow and balance of aether. Corentine had wanted to birth a new universe free of their influence. Birth new gods. Mortal life. Such were the whims of Chaos.

The Pantheon had denied her. I had not. I had chosen to abandon them for her. That was My choice. My sacrifice.

In the end, the Pantheon was correct.

The children we'd birthed were lesser gods. They could not match the power of the Pantheon. Mortal life was a mistake.

And now, two new gods defiled the nexus. The Anarchy of Haven. The Dark Warden. My Quentin.

One was a chaotic entity sharing two souls.

The other... There could be a place for Him within the Pantheon, if only He would *obey*.

TIME IS INFINITE, AS I AM.

My Guardians appeared before Me in a perfect, symmetrical line. Their clockwork forms would continue to obey My laws endlessly.

Mortals burst from Anarchy. They were an unsymmetrical and imbalanced mismatch of domains in the guise of apostates. Godless mortals My voice had once attempted to hunt and destroy. Though they were born of the energies of various gods, they all brimmed with the color and aether of Chaos.

A tall, dark man with the black wings of Valeria's Twilights.

A severe woman with the thick stone arms of Unghard's Golems.

A large wolf man bearing Faen's sharp fangs.

A lioness standing proud with the deadly claws of Lionheart.

Other, less threatening mortals stood by Chaos's side. Each wearing the likeness of My children. Anima. Gildola. Serenity. Zyclone. Edana. Mesmorpheus. All except The Nameless One. There was an irony to their omission.

The Nameless One had invented the death these mortals sought. Of all My children, they alone understood the need for decay and death. Without Time to strip mortals of their mortality, there could never be progress.

These mortals would fight. They would die. Time would not stop them, but they were still mortal. For every Guardian they destroyed, ten of them would be crushed. Their guts and bones reduced to pulp with the tick and tock of wondrous repetition.

Quentin understood this simple law. Emotion warred across His face.

That had always been His weakness.

It had always been My prize.

My Guardians lumbered forward. Anarchy's mortals charged.

If I needed to kill Quentin again and again for Him to learn, then so be it.

Time would bring Him to His knees where He belonged.

He transformed into a Zephyr. An inelegant form. Wings spread across His back, tearing through His shirt. He took flight, hurtling over Anarchy's mortals, and landed in the space between us.

"Stop this madness!" He called, His hands outstretched to halt our march. "Haven't we fought enough?"

Was He finally ready to comply?

I paused My Guardians. Anarchy's mortals slowed to a stop.

"What will this take to *end*?" He yelled. "We cannot keep fighting this battle across the timelines. You know this universe requires both Chaos and Time to exist! Surely, we can find a way?"

"What are you saying?" Anarchy demanded. "It was Dor who started this when he imprisoned my mother!"

While His voice carried conviction, Chaos was tainted by madness. Quentin straddled the line between emotion and logic. He would see reason.

CORENTINE WOULD HAVE DESTROYED THIS UNIVERSE UTTERLY—

"And you haven't? The gods and their domains are gone. At least Corentine cared for mortals. Chaos gave us free will. What has Time given us, but aging and death? There's no place for Time in our new world. Every mortal deserves a chance at becoming something more. At reaching godhood."

A mad proposition. Mortal minds could not comprehend the eternity of godhood. My own children could not. They'd become twisted. Enraged and insane. The Covenant had been created to keep them in line.

To keep them away from Chaos's influence.

SHE SPEAKS MADNESS. MORTALS CANNOT AND SHOULD NOT BECOME GODS. IMAGINE THE CHAOS THAT WOULD CREATE. THE BATTLES THAT WOULD BE FOUGHT.

The emotion roiled across Quentin's face. He understood.

"Don't listen to him, Quen. He wants to control us—*you*. But he doesn't have that power anymore. Mortals are free to dictate their own fate, and we choose this."

CHAOS CANNOT BE CONTROLLED. IT CANNOT BE CONTAINED. IT HAS NO PLACE IN A LOGICAL UNIVERSE.

THINK, QUENTIN. THE COGS AND GEARS OF THE UNIVERSE MUST BE BALANCED IN ORDER FOR IT TO EXIST. THESE ARE THE FUNDAMENTAL LAWS OF THE COSMOS THAT ALLOW AETHER TO FLOW. CHAOS DISRUPTS THAT BALANCE—

"Stop it, both of you!" Quentin yelled. His talons pulled at the feathers on His head as He paced in frustration. "How are we meant to find peace if you both act this way?"

CORENTINE GAVE ME HER GREATEST GIFT. A SON IN MY IMAGE. RETURN TO MY SIDE, QUENTIN, AND THIS WAR CAN BE OVER. WE CAN REBUILD CHIME ANEW.

"How could I possibly trust you after everything you've done? You used Elijah—my own lover—to abuse me! No, *you* abused me through him. Even now you continue to wear his face like a damn costume."

ELIJAH WAS MY CONDUIT. MY MORTAL EYES. I USED HIM TO GUIDE YOU WHEN MY WORDS WERE NOT ENOUGH.

Once, I would have felt Quentin's emotions. Heard His warring thoughts. Among My many mortals, His inner voice and prayers were the loudest. His emotions intoxicating. They often confused and frustrated Me. Was He not happy to serve as My Warden? My son?

I'd tried to gift Him everything He'd ever wanted.

I'd tried to guide Him.

To show Him My devotion as a mortal would.

Elijah had been a means to that end. Through him, I'd experienced Quentin. His mortal body. To touch Him as a mortal touched another.

Not as a god.

"You didn't guide me. You hurt me!" His voice cracked, as it so often did when His emotions exhausted Him. "I'm not your mortal anymore. You want me to obey? Then meet me as an equal. You want me to confess and repent? Then let me hear *your* sins, Father. Let me hear your confession."

I had no sins to confess.

I CREATED YOUR SOUL, MY SON. YOUR BODY. YOUR ORGANS. THE VERY SYNAPSES THAT CONNECT YOUR THOUGHTS. ALL OF YOU BELONGS TO ME.

"He's not yours!" Anarchy snarled.

No. Quentin was Mine.

"Then there can be no way forward. There can be no peace between us." His form changed to Chaos. The colors of aether on His naked chest were perverse. I had not designed Him that way, but Corentine had corrupted Him, as she'd corrupted all My children against Me.

He summoned an object in His hands. A headpiece.

A soul-splitting device.

"You can own my mortal body. But no god will *ever* own my soul."

He secured the device over His own head.

That would destroy His soul. I could make another Quentin. Hundreds of Quentins. But none would ever be Him.

QUENTIN, I ORDER YOU TO STOP.

I launched My Guardians to wrench the device from His grasp.

He stared at Me. Those eyes were not My silver, but Corentine's.

It filled me with another of Quentin's emotions. Anxiety.

I abandoned Elijah's physical form and reached for Him with My own hands.

STOP!

He pressed the button.

Aether pulsed through the nexus. It tore His soul from the perfect body I'd designed. He remained standing, staring at white space.

I glanced at the gathered soulless of the nexus. A new soul stood among them.

MY QUENTIN.

He was lost to Me, beyond the reaches of this universe. The walls could be destroyed, but to do so would expose Me and My creations to the Pantheon.

Was His soul worth that risk?

The Pantheon knew Me as a traitor. Logically, I would not stand against them.

An unpleasant ache filled Me. Emotion that Quentin would have described as angst. The gods had invented emotion, yet mortals evolved them. I found it distasteful. Corentine had stirred emotion within Me. I'd felt something for her, once. Love, perhaps. Without her, I would never have left the Pantheon. I would never have created life.

I'd held Him in the palm of My hands. I'd asked Him for the time, as I did with all My newly created children. A test to analyze their mental state.

His answer, then, should have been a warning.

"It's thirteen o'clock."

Once again, Chaos had stolen from Me. It could not be abided.

Anarchy did not react. Her mortals did not mourn. No, she smiled. The madness of Corentine affecting her mind.

She did not care. Chaos had never loved Quentin.

A new emotion replaced the angst. One Quentin had also suffered.

Rage.

DESTROY HER.

My Guardians attacked. They smashed into the Chaos mortals as Anarchy laughed.

We would rend her asunder.

In Quentin's name, we would finally purge this universe of her sinful taint.

Force tore through My back. The searing power of aether ripping through the physical form of My flesh. It blinded Me with heat. A sensation I'd experienced through My mortals.

Pain.

It broke through My rib cage, eliciting more emotions that I only recognized through the lens of mortal understanding. Panic. Shock.

The quickening of a pulse.

A moment in time not paused, but stretched for eons.

I turned to Anarchy standing behind Me. She held the clockwork cage that protected My vital organ. My beating heart. "Ew, it's fucking shriveled in there."

Blood and oil dripped from the hole in My chest. How could that be? Anarchy still stood behind her mortals.

Which made this... the spare. The Abomination.

"Forget we were twins, you dumb fuck?"

STOP HER!

My Guardians changed course and charged at the Abomination. I reached for My heart, but its absence weakened Me. My limbs moved at only sixty percent of My maximum capabilities.

The heart was My engine. My aethereal core.

No mortal should have been able to take it, yet Chaos...

Should Chaos open the clockwork cage, My dominion would be at risk. Chaos must be destroyed.

"Don't worry, old man. I don't want it." The Abomination tossed the clockwork cage.

Into the hands of Quentin.

He blinked, His aether eyes alive. His soul whole.

A Mesmer illusion.

Anarchy had tricked Me.

"Thank you, Jinx," He said. "Though I've received better gifts." His metal fingers bent the brass cage containing My heart, shaping it until the pulsing organ was exposed through a gap large enough to fit His left hand.

I swallowed Him in a bubble of time and forced it backwards. Time flickered around us. The gaping wound of My torso stitched itself together, time reversing the damage, yet Quentin still grasped My heart in His hands.

As Chaos, He wielded a natural immunity to time.

He did not let My heart go.

QUENTIN, DO NOT—

"I grant you the only mercy a mortal can. Death." He grasped My heart and squeezed it until it burst. Dark blood and tissue oozed between His fingers.

The tick-tock of My core stopped.

My aether, My energy, leaked from My physical form.

I attempted to reverse time, to save it.

My aether did not return. Quentin was absorbing My energy.

My soul.

It left My physical form empty. Cold.

Few of my mortals remained. I reached out to them, to Kronos. The domain I had built for Myself hundreds of thousands of years ago.

The skyscrapers disintegrated into dust. My soulless mortals paid no heed as reality warped around them. The few Diviner who could contemplate their mortality screamed and ran as a wave of gray nothingness rolled over the city.

Clocks rang out erratically, chiming in and out of time.

My precious clocks, created with harmonious symmetry. Now ruined. Ruined!

Father!

Only one voice called to Me. Only one mortal who prayed.

Pendula Bezel.

I'm sorry! I failed you, Father! Forgive me.

Her thoughts turned to the Abomination. She did not mourn for Me. I did not answer her prayers as her mortal body collapsed to dust, her soul leaving My subconscious.

I searched My mortals' memories for a name to place the emotions swirling where My core should have been. Anger. Fear. Regret. My mortals faded as their souls did.

I was alone with nothing left to feel.

Even My Guardians had faded, leaving Me surrounded by the ghosts of the soulless, Anarchy and her mortals, the Abomination, and the Dark Warden.

Quentin.

My physical form withered, My skin aging to that of the form I'd worn when conversing with My mortals. I coughed, and a cloud of dust spilled from My breath.

It hurt, as it hurt My mortals when they shed their physical form and returned to the aether of My being. Death should not faze Me. What was death, but the turning of a clock? The coming of a new age?

But this was illogical.

YOU'VE DAMNED THIS UNIVERSE, QUENTIN. WITHOUT GODS, MORTALS WILL HAVE NO MORAL GUIDANCE. THEY WILL BECOME DEGENERATE, ABUSING AND KILLING WITH NO CONSCIENCE. LOOK WHAT BECAME OF THE FAUNA WITHOUT FAEN'S HAND TO GUIDE THEM.

Quentin cast aside the brass cage of My heart and wiped His hands clean with a handkerchief. "Mortals were already abusing and murdering each other even with guidance from the gods. Many of the gods were doing the abusing and murdering themselves."

WILL YOU GUIDE THEM? WILL YOU BECOME THEIR GOD?

"Mortals don't need gods to set rules. They can manage that themselves."

YOU'LL SOON SEE HOW WRONG YOU ARE. THIS UNIVERSE WILL NEED A VESSEL. THE VESSEL YOU CHOOSE WILL BECOME CORRUPTED WITH THE POWER OF THE GODS.

AND YOU WILL NEVER KNOW PEACE.

"I never have."

The last of My aether fell from My skin in a smattering of dust.

I, who had crossed the void between universes to forge this one.

I, who had sired gods and entire domains.

I would not be consigned to history.

What were My sins? To create mortal life that experienced emotion? Through Quentin, I had learned what it meant to love, and it was irrational. Chaotic.

My sin was that I'd loved an imperfect being.

For that sin, this universe was no more.

The void welcomed Me, as it had welcomed My children.

But this was not the end of the gods.

52

I once asked my Diviner colleagues if they ever thought about life outside the domains, and they hushed me. Diviner imagination is limited to our own universe. They consider it blasphemous to even discuss it.
It makes logical sense that life must exist beyond the walls of our domains. The very existence of the gods posits many questions. How did the gods come into being? Did a greater god create them? Who created that god?
Thinking about it sends me into a spiral of maddening thoughts. I assume this is why my Diviner colleagues drink so much tea and avoid the question.
—Doctor. Z. Finch, *Ponderings on the Universe*

QUEN SAGGED IN MY arms. Jinx ushered the Godless away to give us a little privacy, and they wandered off to the haunted version of Central Station to explore. We couldn't get inside before, not with Dor's immortals watching over the place. Dor couldn't beat me or take my soul, so he'd done the next best thing and thrown me out of reality altogether with no way back, the petty little bitch.

But now... Now we were finally free.

We'd done it. The reign of gods had come to an end.

For all Dor's protests about hating mortals, he'd fallen in love with one. Karendar had once told me he feared the gods were at risk of being influenced and changed by their mortal subjects, and perhaps that was what had happened to Dor. Quen's emotions defined him, unlike other Diviner.

I rubbed Quen's back, his arms wrapped tight around my waist. He needed this comfort after everything Dor had put him through.

Dor had been his father. A terrible one, but still.

"You're free," I said. "Dor won't ever torment you again."

Quen sighed onto my shoulder. "He was rather unhinged by the end. I'm glad you weren't there to witness it all. Dor... Saints. He'd so decimated his own mortals that only a few thousand souls passed over to me. Those who had previously died over the years and returned to the aether."

Gods. Almost all living Diviner had been submitted to his soul-splitting machines. They were lost, as the Necro were.

Lost here in the middle of god-knows-where.

Quen collected himself and, sadly, summoned a clean shirt. After quickly redressing, we strode hand in hand toward the station.

"Is she all right?" He gazed in the direction of Jinx.

"She'll be fine. We've reached an understanding."

He nodded, satisfied with that. Quen always knew Jinx was my responsibility, and despite everything, she was still my sister. There wasn't any point in holding a grudge for the past when the past likely didn't exist anymore.

"Has time finally ended, then?" I asked. I'd never had a sense of time, including no sense of whether time was still ticking.

"The timeline has shattered. We'll have to rebuild it, along with everything else. I'm afraid we've got our work cut out for us."

Shit. I didn't even know where to start.

The Godless waited for us in the station. Dru, Harmony, Sinder, Joe, Malk. Even Wolfsbane and the Lioness. They'd joined me for the final confrontation, and we were together again for whatever this was.

Jinx had taken her magpie Fauna form and flown off on her own. I sensed her discomfort. The Godless didn't trust her, and she didn't want to outstay her welcome or start a fight. It was best if the two groups kept their distance, but she *had* helped us defeat Dor. That counted for something.

The station was identical to the Central Station I knew back home, with the same waiting areas, tourist information, and tea stand. Only, it was made of a translucent white. It was eerie, too. The soulless flittered through, though they made no sound, nor really left any impression on the station.

It was desolate in a way Chime had been when the gods had recalled their mortals, only Chime had still been alive, beating with a pulse of aether.

This really was a void, and the emptiness made my ears pop. It even smelled of literally nothing.

Quen leaned on the tea stand counter. "Oh my. It's still corporeal? Physically here," he added at my confusion.

Harmony sat on a chair within the waiting area. "I can still park my arse."

"You can't touch mortals," Sinder said. "I tried to get the attention of a Necro, to see if Vincent…" He swallowed a lump in his throat. "My hand went straight through them, as though they aren't really here. Do you think Vincent is somewhere nearby?"

It was likely.

"Then what is this place?" Malk said. "Something isn't right. Look." He pointed at a group of loitering Diviner shuffling in circles and staring at nothing. "What's wrong with them?"

"Some mortals seem more lucid than others," Joe confirmed. "I think they're aware of where they are, and the others have sort of checked out?"

Quen rubbed his chin. "If the nexus is a type of purgatory, then some may recognize it as an afterlife and dissociate from that association. Others may well be traumatized. Losing one's soul isn't pleasant."

"You would know," I said. "What's the nexus?"

"It's the name of this place. The void between domains. Dor's memories revealed it to me when I took his soul."

"Does that mean the soulless are here?" Dru asked, hope lighting up her face. "Everyone who lost their soul?"

We'd only passed Diviner and Necro so far, no one I recognized, but if our lost loved ones had arrived here, then they had to be somewhere.

Ben. Cosmo. Autumn. Gast and Noct. Shit, we could find them.

We could find them all.

Apprehension flickered across Quen's face, and I immediately knew why.

Karendar could also be here.

Head to the private waiting room, Jinx said inside my mind.

What do you see?

Find out for yourself, sister.

"The inner waiting rooms," I declared. "Let's go there."

I squeezed Quen's hand, and then we strode for the private waiting rooms, the Godless following. More of the soulless languished on the chairs. Some napping, some with their heads in their hands, curled up in despair as they waited for either judgement or salvation. They were a mix of Diviner and Necro, though other domains lingered in the station—Ember, Fauna. Those Dor and the Glimmer had forced into their soul-splitting machines.

"The dawn suite?" Quen commented as we reached the most private of the private rooms.

"I'll stand guard," Malk said. "You know, in case of trouble."

"Thank you." I chewed my lip as I pushed open the doors.

I had no idea what we'd find inside.

"Mama! Papa!" Cosmo squealed. They immediately ran over and tried to tackle me in a hug, but they ended up falling right through me. "Oh right, we can't do that yet."

Oh gods, I was going to start crying. Only Quen's tight hold of my hand kept me grounded as we both took in the room.

Chance and Lucky, the two Chaos brothers Dor had taken, were in the back, attempting to arm wrestle each other. They laughed, enjoying their afterlife a little too much, but then they'd spent most of their lives trapped in a clock tower with a crazy Chaos god. This meager amount of freedom must be a novelty. Jinx sat on a chair, watching them. Still in her magpie form.

Quen's Amnae professor, Walter, and Dandelion sat with Autumn, telling her stories. They waved at us cheerfully. Nelle bounded off to join her brother as Wolfsbane ran for Autumn.

Vincent sat huddled in the corner. He'd always been deathly pale, but here, in an actual afterlife, he'd shrunk within himself, the consequences and guilt of his death eating away at him. Both Sinder and Joe immediately raced to his side, with Harmony waddling after them.

A tall Umber man approached us. "It's good to see you, sir. Well, maybe not here, but you know what I mean."

"*Ben?*" Dru gasped. "You're an Umber?"

Ben wore a sheepish grin. "Yes, ma'am. I said my soul wasn't Diviner. Seems the universe agreed."

Tears ran down Quen's cheeks, and he fell to his knees. "I'm sorry! I'm so, *so* sorry—"

"Quen, it's all right." I crouched and hugged his shoulders as he physically shook against me, his entire body racked with sobs. "We'll fix this."

I didn't know how we'd fix it yet, but we would.

"But I killed you." Quen glanced up at Ben. "I did this to you."

"And I forgave you, sir. You weren't in your right mind—"

"That doesn't excuse what I've done!" His voice pierced the chatter of the room, stunning everyone into silence.

"There he is," came Walter's voice. The Amnae professor strode on over with a grim smile. "Pinning the world's woes on your shoulders as usual, are we, Quentin?"

Quen rose to his feet, wiping his eyes with his jacket sleeve. "Pro—Professor?"

"Cosmo has been telling me all about your adventures, of what the pair of you have been getting up to while I've been stuck here. It was kind of eerie at first, I'll admit, but I had company. Weird little fellow, but what Mesmer aren't? Er, no offense." He winced at Cosmo.

Cosmo grinned. They probably took it as a compliment. "None taken!"

"I owe you an apology too, Professor," Quen said. "I failed to save you—"

"Nonsense!" Walter waved him off. "You didn't strap me to that chair."

"If I hadn't come to you regarding my memories, you would never have been placed in that position."

"I could have turned you away. It was my choice to help you, and I'd do it again. I've always been fond of you, Quentin. You took care of my daughter. Whatever debt you think you owe me has been paid in full."

Quen placed a hand over his heart. "She's in here. Ilona misses you terribly."

"Thank you, Quentin. There's something you should know..."

"Elijah is here."

I took Quen's hand again and squeezed my reassurance.

"Yes," Walter confirmed. "It wasn't what we expected. Neither was the influx of Diviner and Necro. We've got Elijah locked away in the private kitchen—"

"In the *kitchen*?"

"It was either that or the restroom. Even separate from Dor, we don't trust him. We've got two volunteers watching over him. A Necro and Seren. Odd pair. The Necro calls himself a private eye—"

"Gast and Noct?" I said. Bless them. Even in death, they were still making themselves useful.

"That's them. Lovely chaps."

Quen rubbed the back of his neck. "I—I don't think Elijah is the same one we knew. Dor manipulated and abused him. How is his manner?"

"He seems remorseful," Walter said. "Quiet. Honestly, I've more important things to care about than the quality of his soul."

"Understandable. I'll, ah, keep my distance for now."

"Mama, there's someone who needs to speak with you and Papa," Cosmo said. "Someone who's been here from the start and knows what this place is all about."

Gods. There was only one mortal who could understand the beginnings of the universe. "Reve?"

"He's waiting by the Gate," Cosmo said. "He wants to show you it."

We left the Godless to reminisce, with Malk still on guard as Quen and I left the waiting room and strode for the station concourse.

"I'm sorry." Quen pulled out a handkerchief and blew his nose. "I thought I had better hold of my emotions. The last few weeks have taken their toll."

I wrapped my arm around his and leaned against his side. "Don't apologize for having emotions. It's one of the reasons I fell for you."

"Because you enjoy my suffering?" He was joking, but the joke came out awkward.

"Because you're not afraid to express your feelings, you dork. Even when living under a god who considers it a sin. Sometimes, all mortals have is expression. To feel something that's meant to be wrong is the ultimate rebellion."

"I can't believe everyone is here. I thought we'd lost the soulless for good, but they've been waiting here all this time?"

"That's what I thought, too." Or what Reverie had explained to me, at least. I'd wanted to hold out hope we could save the soulless, but she was right that they'd never return to their original body. They didn't have a body we could grasp, but there must be a way.

"There's so little we know about how our universe works," Quen mused.

We'd come to the right place to get answers.

No one else dared approach the Gate, as though the soulless were afraid of it, and I could understand why. It was every bit as ancient and terrifying as I had once thought.

This version of the Gate rippled with aether, the only color in this drab place. Whatever lay beyond the portal wasn't our world, no. Sometimes the light shifted, revealing glimpses of other worlds. Domains that weren't ours.

A lone boy stood waiting before it, exactly as I remembered him—a fragile young boy in his dressing gown, his Mesmer skin a smattering of stars.

"Reve," I gasped.

"Welcome to the nexus," Reve said with the booming voice of an older male. "You have arrived as I have foreseen."

The way he stared and spoke always sent a shiver down my spine. It was so at odds with the physical form he chose to present, and I meant chose, because sometimes I wondered if Reve had ever been mortal at all, or if he was some unknown god in disguise.

But no, he was a boy who'd simply seen too much of the universe and decided that was enough for him.

"Hello, Reve," Quen greeted. "It's been a while. Are you keeping well?"

"No. I came to the nexus to seek comfort in the dark, but then other souls appeared. More and more. Most avoided me, except for Walter, who would not stop asking me questions. And then Cosmo, who would not leave me alone."

I forced a smile. "Cosmo can be a bit much, but they mean well."

"They are incessant. You are here to relieve me, to take the souls away."

I swallowed a lump in my throat. "How do we do that?"

Quen slipped from my arm. "We can't. When Dor threw me out of the timeline, I entered an alternate one where the gods and Mesmorpheus still existed. They showed me potential worlds and timelines, but in none of them could the soulless be saved. Their souls have been ripped from our universe. They're beyond our reach."

"But they're here! We can see them, talk to them—"

"But not touch them."

"You control the pissing timeline. We can hop to a time where the soulless still retain their souls—"

"I'm sorry. It doesn't work that way, and gods, have I examined every angle! The soulless belong to a different dimensional frequency, now. They cannot be brought back into our universe. Even if I traveled through the time stream, their souls cannot be manipulated. They exist as an echo, and their souls would fall between our fingers."

"No." I shook my head. "There has to be a way to bring them back!"

"What Quentin states is true," Reve said. "You both carry the power of the gods, but the soulless were split from their gods. You can recreate Chime, but the soulless will remain here, within the void between domains—"

"I'm not leaving them behind!"

"There are choices, Kayl Arkey." The intensity of Reve's stare gave me goose bumps.

"What are they? What have you seen?"

Reve gestured to the portal behind him. "This leads outside your universe, to universes unknown. Dor and Corentine were not the first gods. They came from a realm where elder gods are born. An entire pantheon."

"When Dor and Corentine warred, some of their children were cast out of this universe," Quen said. "They left through here?"

"Yes," Reve confirmed. "The portal is warded against gods from outside this universe. No one can enter, but you and the soulless may leave."

Then this portal was the porch to our universe. "Wait, you're saying Quen and I can leave?"

"I do not know what you will find, but if you leave, you may never return. Without a god to rule it, this universe will be destroyed."

I heard what he was saying. We could abandon this universe for another, for better or worse. New domains. New gods. It would be a whole new adventure. But we couldn't leave our mortals behind. Would they want to start over in a whole different universe?

Would it be worth the risk?

"If the soulless stepped through," Quen was asking, "would they become whole again? Corporeal?"

"They would exist within a new universe. You could join them, or remain here, behind the safety of our universe, and leave the soulless to find their way."

They could move onto the next life without us, if they wanted. I didn't like it. "Between us, Quen and I have the power of gods. You're saying we can't use that? I don't believe it."

"There's... another option," Quen said.

I gripped his wrist. "What is it?" I'd take anything!

"You destroy the portal," Reve said. "A bold move."

"Okay, I'm confused. What would that do? Is this some metaphysics thing?"

"Somewhat." Quen grimaced. "When Dor and Corentine created this universe, they also created a set of rules that all mortals and living things must abide by. Aging, entropy, death, gravity. That sort of thing. When we remake Chime and the domains, we'll follow similar rules, I would assume, but I digress. We have the power to shape this universe however we will it. We can break down these walls, break the portal, and allow the soulless in. The implications are we will lose whatever protections the portal offers."

"In other words, we'd no longer be warded against stray gods?" Huh. Had this inspired the Covenant?

"Precisely. Mesmorpheus showed me a vision detailing some of these gods... They don't appear pleasant." Quen shuddered.

Shit. We'd had enough trouble fighting off our own gods, let alone an unknown number of whatever pricks existed beyond the portal. "How likely is it a god will stumble upon our little universe?"

"I cannot see a future beyond this universe," Reve said. "It could be instant. It could take a year. One hundred years. One thousand. Time works differently for timeless beings. But make no mistake. They *will* discover us."

"So that's the choice?" I said. "We either abandon the soulless here to an eternally dull waiting area, we kick them out of our universe and leave them at the mercy of whatever's out there, we go with them and possibly end up trapped in another universe with another bunch of cruel gods, or we throw open the walls and invite god knows what inside?"

Quen ran his metal fingers through his hair. "We'd be risking millions of lives over a few thousand."

"You'd leave them here? All the Diviner, the Necro? Ben?"

"I'm simply stating the facts."

So you may have to deal with some shitty gods, Jinx said. I glanced over my shoulder. A magpie sat on the streetlamp above the Gate, watching us. She'd been listening in on our entire conversation. *We've done that before. We can do it again.*

You think we should risk it?

You're Kayl Arkey, god of Anarchy. This is your thing. And Time Boy is the Dark Warden, protector of mortals. Between the two of you, you've got this covered.

Trust Jinx to pick the chaotic option. *I thought you were the smarter one between us? Shouldn't you be trying to keep me out of trouble?*

Since when has that ever worked?

Good point. "We took the souls of thirteen gods to get this far. Us. Mere mortals. If other gods want to knock on our door, then let them. We'll destroy them, too."

Quen stared at me over the rim of his eyeglasses, the aether of his eyes so intense, I couldn't read the emotions warring inside. "We could be fighting this battle for the rest of our lives."

"We're Godless. This is what we do. As long as you're by my side, we can face anything."

"Then whatever exists in our future is ours to make."

Gods, I loved him. Loved that he'd be willing to make this sacrifice for me, for the soulless.

Reve sighed. "You'll make me return with you. Even after I asked you *not* to."

I placed my hands on my hips. "What's so bad about existence?"

"It's too loud and painful. It hurts me."

"Would you rather be left here to face an army of gods on your own?"

"Maybe."

"Reve. I know life can be hard, but I'll be there to help you. I promise. Whatever accommodations you need to make your life easier, we'll sort it." The Zephyr could invent something that blocked noise, for a start. "I'm not leaving you behind."

He sighed again. "I know you won't."

I turned to Quen. "How do we do this?"

"We destroy the Gate. Then the soulless should become corporeal once more, allowing us to reclaim their souls. However, our timeline has been fractured."

"Meaning what?"

"Meaning we'll need to rewrite the entirety of mortal history from the beginning. We're not only restoring what was lost. We're creating a timeline where the gods never existed at all."

My palms tingled. "You do say the sweetest things."

"There are some caveats. Any Chaos mortals will need to choose a domain—we can't allow Chaos to exist freely with their powers."

Chaos was only a handful of mortals, but they should have a say in their future. *What do you think, Jinx?*

We'll do it. Chance and Lucky always knew they'd have to, eventually, and they'd appreciate a new start. The rest will follow.

"That's fine. What else?"

"If we create a society where the gods never existed, then it stands to reason that mortals would have no knowledge of them. That would mean manipulating their memories on a global scale—to effectively wipe their memories of the gods. I'm... hesitant to force such a memory wipe on mortals without their consent. Therefore, I propose a referendum."

"A referendum? Really?"

"Mortals should have a vote in the future we create, otherwise we're little more than cruel gods ourselves."

"You don't need to twist my arm."

"We'll also need to ready ourselves for the worst-case scenario once the portal is down."

"Leave that to me." Jinx flew down from the streetlamp and transformed into her Chaos self, complete with her crimson dress. "I'll shield you both and keep watch in case any nasties drop by to fuck with us."

Quen nodded. "That would be appreciated, thank you. We should gather and warn the soulless—"

"The soulless will automatically return to where they belong," Reve said.

"Very well. Then we must prepare the Godless. What we're about to undertake is infinitely more complex than what you did to create Haven. As soon as you're ready, we'll begin."

I'd never been more ready in my life.

We'd ended the reign of gods.

And now we were about to birth a truly godless world.

We warned the soulless what was about to happen and recalled the Godless. Neither Quen nor I knew how rebuilding the universe would affect mortals standing in the middle of it, and we didn't want them to be harmed or to get in our way.

Then we were ready.

Quen approached the portal.

"How will you break it?" I called.

"Simple. I'll bend the timelines, forcing them to snap, which will in turn create a feedback loop that triggers a paradox, thus destroying the clock tower and portal of the nexus, exposing us to the aether of the universe, and returning the soulless to their corporeal form so we may then take their souls."

"Wowee, that's a mouthful," Jinx said. "Oh wait, that's Kayl's line."

I rolled my eyes. "Why not describe it as fucking with time? That's what you're doing, isn't it?"

"Fine. I'm about to fuck with time." Quen rolled up his sleeves. "Ladies, if you don't mind?"

Jinx and I shuffled back with Reve.

Time shifted. I couldn't really explain it, but something had changed. Quen possessed Dor's powers now, and they were near limitless. Honestly, it made me fucking *wet*.

Ew, yuck, Jinx said.

You don't have to read my thoughts.

Hard not to when they're so damn loud.

You know I can hear your thoughts too? Quen said.

Yes, and I'm not sorry, I said.

I know you're not. His amusement warmed my stomach. When all this was over, I was making a man out of him.

The clock tower cracked. It literally split in two right down the middle, breaking through the glass of the clockface. How many clocks and towers had we broken now, real or otherwise?

It collapsed in a *whomf,* sending a gust of air and stardust across the station and forcing me to shield my eyes.

The station completely vanished, as though it had never existed, leaving us in pure white space. The soulless stared around, suddenly exposed. They were whole again, back in color, or corporeal as Quen would put it.

And then they too vanished in a cloud of dust. All of them.

"What the—"

Aether slammed into me. I staggered back, half collapsing into Jinx, as energy fled into my blood, pumping through me at such speed I thought it would burst from my chest. I wheezed and glanced over to Quen, who was having the same reaction.

"What's—What's going on?" I managed to spit out.

It's the soulless, Reve explained from inside my mind. *They have returned to you, as have I.*

I searched inside, and there they were. Cosmo, Autumn, Noct, Chance, and Lucky. Even Reve's soul. Gods. Walter and Dandelion must have returned to Quen, alongside the entire Diviner.

Which left the Necro.

Vincent stood as the only other mortal possessing a god's soul. The Nameless One. The Necro including Gast had all returned to him.

"I—I can't go back," he said.

"Look, if Reve can—"

"I killed them all! Take the Necro if you must—I don't have the right to judge their fate—but leave me. Swear it."

I reached out to touch his shoulder, and he bared his fangs.

"Swear it!" he snarled.

Quen approached, his brow furrowed in concern, but I waved him away. I didn't want to scare Vincent, not when he was so vulnerable. Jinx remained still, scared to move an inch and set him off further.

Neither Sinder, Joe, or Harm had been able to convince him to return to reality. I wouldn't waste my breath.

"I swear it." I held out my hand.

Vincent tentatively took it, and I yanked his soul clean out, dragging him and thousands of Necro with me. And then I shoved Vincent deep into my subconscious, where he could stay buried for now.

I wasn't leaving him behind. We'd get him help, therapy, whatever he needed, but I refused to leave him. If that made me a dirty oath breaker, then I didn't give a shit.

"Then it's done," Quen said. "All that's left is to recreate Chime and twelve entire domains. How hard can this be? You created Haven, so I'm relying on your expertise."

"*My* expertise?" No one had ever asked me that before. "Well, it's like painting a picture." I gestured to the white space surrounding us. "This is a canvas. Though I'm no good at art, so I see it more like a play. I know how to set a scene."

"Mortality is the most ambitious play of them all."

"And we've got a show to put on."

Quen took my hand and pressed his lips against my knuckles. "Reality is ours, my dear. We can bend it to whatever we will it to be." His clothes suddenly changed to a black suit, matching my own black dress. "Though before we begin, a little lubrication is in order, I think." He let go of my hand and summoned a cup of tea and saucer. He took a sip. "Ah, perfection."

Show-off. I summoned a bourbon biscuit and dunked it into his tea.

"You wicked thing!" he gasped with mock shock.

Half the biscuit fell into his tea. I ate the other half and playfully batted my eyelashes. Aether sparked my blood once more, threatening to spill over and create a few new worlds of its own.

What if we fucked at the end of time?

Jinx cleared her throat. "I'm still here, idiots. Did you forget we could have stray gods visiting the neighborhood?"

Shit, I had.

Quen put his tea and saucer aside, allowing it to float in midair. "Jinx is right, unfortunately. There'll be time for frolicking later."

"So you keep promising me."

He flashed me a wry smile, and then rolled his metal arm, stretching the joint. "Are we ready to begin?"

Jinx clapped her hands together, and a static bubble of aether bloomed, growing larger and larger until it completely surrounded us. "I've got you covered."

I offered my hand to Quen. "Shall we dance?"

His metal fingers wrapped around mine. "Lead on."

We pressed our foreheads together, and our minds became one.

Between us, we held the souls of thirteen gods.

Thirteen domains to restore. An entire universe to piece back together.

It was a chaotic mess, but I could make sense of it. This was what I'd been born for. And Quen—since Walter had restored his memories, he could remember everything. Every little detail of Chime and the domains he'd researched and traveled to as a younger Warden. He was as ready for this task as I was.

Chaos had the power to destroy, but also create. I'd taken that role, now, as Quen would apply the rules of logic and time to make it work together.

I don't want things to go back to exactly the way they were. I spoke to Quen in my mind. It was quicker than actually speaking.

Oh?

Mortals should have a say in their domains, if there's any changes they'd want to make to their home. But Chime... Chime should be a city where mortals are made equal. Like the original Covenant promised. That means everyone should be on the same level. No Undercity. No Golden City. We'll make Central larger to accommodate the changes, with room to grow, with equal space for mortals of all domains.

That sounds wonderful.

I closed my eyes and imagined what that would look like. Twelve domains. Twelve districts. All centered around Central Station. The clock tower would be the centerpiece, but the tower would no longer hold up the Golden City, allowing the sun to finally shine upon Central's streets.

The usual districts would remain. The Market District, tower blocks, Warden HQ, Meridian Park. Everything Central had housed before, but with the Academy, theaters, art galleries, and museums of the Golden City, and the factories of the Undercity. The only thing we'd leave behind in our new Chime would be the Temple District and the Glimmer's workhouses. There'd be no place for them.

What of Sinner's Row? Quen asked.

We'll find a nice quiet spot for it. Our Chime wouldn't be perfect. There would be criminals and sinners, and they needed a place to go.

And Grayford?

The Vesper deserve better than a slum. They deserved a whole mushroom forest of their own.

We could even call it something nice like The Meadows.

Good idea.

We had a blueprint, but something felt missing. A spark of chaos that only my twin could provide.

Jinx, I called. *We need you for this.* I opened my other hand to her.

Are—Are you sure?

You're part of me. We can't create the universe without you.

She took my hand as Quen held her spare, and together we formed a triad of Chaos.

This was how it was meant to be.

Aether flowed through our veins. It spun around us, sputtering with glowing stardust. This was the power of thirteen gods, and their souls flashed in a pulsating nebula of color. It was a power that could never be destroyed, but in our hands, it could be reshaped.

While Dor and Corentine had provided the fundamentals of time and chaos, the other gods had touched upon this universe. The dawn of Gildola. The night of Valeria. Nature, sex, death, art, music, dreams, memories, technology. These were all gifts of the gods.

Now they belonged to mortals.

As my ideas took shape, Quen built the foundations, the structures that would hold Chime together, from the brickwork of a tavern to the pipework underneath the streets and the patterns of clouds above. Jinx was there to sprinkle in the details. The colors of individual flowers. The tastes of various flavors. The spice of life.

The world shifted underneath my feet. We were rising. I opened my eyes and gasped.

We stood inside the clock tower, in a room that had once held a chair.

Jinx ran to the clockface window. "Oh fuck! We actually did it!"

I dragged Quen over and stared outside. Chime had been remade. Our Chime. Sunlight shone across Central Station, on the empty cobblestone streets.

All it needed was mortals.

I reached inside myself and gathered the souls of my friends and family. They were the ones I trusted to relay this message to their domains.

You've all experienced much, but the way home is in sight. We'll restore your domains. Chime will always remain free and fair. Everyone gets a fresh start. A second chance at life free from the influence of gods.

We'd bring everyone back—the saints and sinners.

But we ask you to make a few choices. First, a wish, if any, for how you'd like your domain to be. Secondly, you must choose an elected ambassador to represent you. All of you. They'll form the new Council of Chime. And third, the biggest choice of them all... to forget your gods, and begin life anew.

The Godless spoke to the mortals in the depths of my subconscious.

Walter spoke on behalf of the Amnae, and they were happy to return to Memoria without a god manipulating and stealing their memories. Some wished to remove their power for memory manipulation altogether, but ultimately, they decided to keep it for its useful applications. None wished to see Aberforth return to power, and so they chose someone I wasn't familiar with—Ambassador Brooke.

Trixie and Wolfsbane spoke with the Fauna. They weren't sure what kind of domain they wanted Juniper to be yet, but they wanted the freedom to figure that out. They voted Trixie as their new ambassador, and she gladly accepted. She'd be perfect.

Dru spoke to the Umber, and as I would expect of them, they were eager to go along with whatever was needed to rebuild Chime. They were happy to keep Hazelhearth as their ambassador.

Joe spoke with the Glimmer. They weren't so happy, and made outrageous demands that, quite frankly, didn't fit with my vision of Chime. They'd get what they were given. Though, some expressed the desire to be male, and Joe wanted to be there to support them in that transition. I refused to name Gloria as ambassador, so they chose someone new. A young woman named Clara who Joe knew from his past.

Harmony spoke on behalf of the Seren, who were a mixed bag of outrage and placidity. They wanted greater social standing than the Glimmer, but more than that, they wanted the freedom to sing. They chose Sonata to return as ambassador, which was fine by me.

I chose Gast to speak with the Necro, as Vincent wasn't in the right frame of mind. Most were happy with the status quo, but others wanted a better way of living. They were tired of constantly battling their urges and feasting on the blood of others. We came up with a way of suppressing both. They couldn't name an ambassador they trusted, nor did Gast want the job, but they eventually settled on a newcomer.

Zachery spoke with the Zephyr. They were only too keen to return to how things were. Too much change was stressful for them, and they agreed to allow Corvus to lead as ambassador.

Dandelion spoke to the Leander. They, too, pushed for more power and influence, but again the message was clear—all mortals would be made equal. Even in Obituary. None of them cared who represented them as ambassador, so Dandelion retained the job.

Sinder spoke with the Ember. So long as they kept their casinos and Sinner's Row, they didn't care for politics. They voted Erosain in as ambassador again, and honestly, he wasn't my first choice, but Sinder didn't want the job, and Erosain promised to be on his best behavior. We'd give him a chance, and *only* one chance.

I chose Elvira to speak with the Vesper. They wanted a quiet life, free from Valeria's constant scrutiny. No more tithes. Not ever. While Varen would come back with the others, no one wanted him as ambassador. Elvira accepted the role.

Reverie spoke with the Mesmer, and they exploded with ideas for new play parks and candy stores within Chime. They were only too happy to keep Reverie as their ambassador.

Sadly, Chaos couldn't be allowed to return as they were. Corentine had only ever created a handful, and Jinx spoke to them, letting them choose a new domain they could be reborn as. Chance chose to become a Zephyr, which didn't surprise me. I hoped it made him happy. Truly.

And then Quen spoke with the Diviner.

I was expecting them to be as fussy and demanding as the Glimmer, but no. After everything they'd been through, they too wanted peace, and a chance to make amends.

But Karendar would not be returning as ambassador.

Quen summoned Pendula. "The Diviner stand on a precipice. Of all the domains, they alone have powers that can dominate the rest. Without the firm hand of godly intervention, that power could very well cause chaos. They need a leader who will guide them in their introspection, to allow them to feel empathy and emotion. I'm asking you to fill that role."

Pendula's mouth fell open in shock. "After everything I've done?"

"I don't believe you to be lost, Penny. I believe you, like most of us, were dealt a bad hand. Do you understand the world I'm leaving you with?"

"Yes. I... I accept. Will—Will you return my father? Hector?"

"I will. One condition—Elijah must *never* be allowed near public office."

"You're letting him live?"

"Everyone gets a second chance. Even Elijah. Prove to me that my faith in you isn't misplaced. Make the Diviner better, for all our sakes."

Pendula curtseyed, and her gaze fell on Jinx.

The two of them shared a longing I felt in the depths of my gut, and their emotions flittered across our bond. I could barely contain my surprise. Did Pendula love Jinx? Did they share a connection as deep as Quen and I? I dared a peek into Jinx's soul, where longing mixed with guilt. In another time, things could have been different.

Jinx dipped her chin. It was a parting gesture. Whatever they had wasn't destined to last, and they both understood that.

Pendula returned the gesture, and then she was gone.

I placed my hand on Quen's arm. "Are you sure about Karendar?"

Quen rubbed the bridge of his nose. "We cannot be the arbiter of souls."

"I think we can make an exception in his case."

"No. Everyone gets a second chance, even him. Let Elijah become the man he was meant to be, free of his god."

"And what if he becomes an even worse prick?" Jinx asked.

"Then he'll face judgement through mortal eyes. Any mistakes he makes from here on out will be his alone to bear." Quen didn't want to confront Karendar, to see if his ex-lover really had been corrupted by Dor. Regardless of whether Karendar was another victim or not, he'd used Quen. Abused him. He wasn't owed forgiveness.

Quen drew a steadying breath. "Let's return our mortals home."

Each domain had voted in Quen's referendum with a clear result. Mortals chose to forget their gods. They'd suffered so much trauma at the hands of their gods, and through being killed and rebirthed, that they no longer wanted to remember it. Or at least most of them did.

The Glimmer didn't want to forget Gildola, and the Umber wanted to keep Unghard in their hearts. Unsurprisingly, the Amnae were hesitant to forget. They alone had suffered greater memory loss than the other domains.

Everyone else wanted to move on. They wanted a fresh start.

For that to happen, they all needed to forget, and the Amnae conceded.

With guidance from Walter and Ilona, Quen altered the memories of each mortal on a massive scale. They would no longer remember the gods, and other details needed to be changed or created to fit their new reality.

"Memory is a river," Quen explained. "Each change could alter its course and create ripples or branching streams. We must ensure the waters remain calm."

Through every mortal's memory, we recreated their domains. A near replica in most cases. Then together, we returned mortals to their homes.

Everyone except the Godless.

I summoned my family into the clock tower. Dru. Harm. Malk. Sinder. Vincent. Reve. Even Joe, Ben, Gast, and Noct, our newcomers.

Dru immediately ran to Ben. "Your flowers. They're beautiful."

He tugged on the vines of his hair, embarrassed. Chamomile flowers sprouted from his brow, like large daisies, and Dru busied herself straightening them.

Quen and Jinx stood by my side as I addressed everyone. "We've come far, all of us. This is the world we always wanted—a world without gods, where mortals can finally be equal."

"It won't be that easy, girl," Harmony said. "Even without the gods, mortals are selfish and fickle. The work is never done."

"But you have a choice. We can create whatever life you've ever wanted. You can forget about us, the Godless, and everything the gods put you through." My voice caught. I didn't want to lose my family, but I had to give them this. It was the least they deserved. "This is my gift to you, if you want it."

"Not a chance, lady," Gast said. "I'm not forgetting *any* of this. You think I survived all this shit to move on like that?" He snapped his fingers. "No. This new world of yours will be rife with trouble as soon as it starts. You'll need mortals like me."

"And me, unfortunately," Noct agreed.

"There's a nicer way of stating it, but I agree," Joe said. "Gildola put me through strife, but I don't want to forget it. Not a second. And..." He turned to Jinx. "I'm grateful for the body I have. I'd rather like to keep it, thank you."

Jinx blew him a kiss. "You're welcome."

"Did you decide on a name, in the end?" Quen asked.

Joe rubbed his chin. "I've always been known as Joe. I suppose it's now short for Joseph."

"Then Joseph Brightwell it is."

"I'm with them, darling," Sinder said. He was back to his Ember form, but I wasn't sure what form he preferred, and based on his clashing emotions, neither was he. "It would be too easy for me to forget the things I've done... to forget my hatred of the Glimmer. But I don't want that. I want to do better." He glanced at Vincent, whose bloodshot eyes were rimmed red.

"I—I'm not sure I can do better," Vincent said. "What use am I to this world?"

"Become a doctor," I said. "That's what you always wanted to do, isn't it? That's why you studied medicine at Memoria University—to heal mortals. The Nameless One wouldn't let you pursue that path in the old world, but you can in this one."

"You'd make a fantastic doctor," Sinder added. "The Mesmer love learning from you."

Vincent squeezed his eyes closed and tilted his head back, as though the weight he'd been carrying had finally lifted. "Then I'll... I'll try it."

"Dru?" I prompted. "Ben?"

She was still straightening his flowers. "Huh? Oh, um. I don't want to forget. I'll find a job or something."

"I don't mind staying with the Wardens," Ben said. "It's the only thing I know."

"You could become a gardener," Quen pointed out.

"Won't you need Wardens, sir?"

"Kayl and I have a few ideas of what Chime may need."

"You're bringing everyone back?" Harmony asked.

"Everyone," I said. "Even Monica." I knew that was what she was asking. Would I bring her lover back?

"Would it be fair of me to rekindle that old flame? A lot's changed since then. I've changed. And if she can't remember—"

"We don't have to alter her memories."

"But that wouldn't be fair, either. Serenity..." Harmony hugged her chest. "No. It's time I moved on. Maybe start dating again... I want my old job back," she demanded, both her wings quivering. "At the Courier. Promoted to lead editor, if you please. With a *fat* paycheck and a fancy apartment. Don't wipe my memories, I need to be in the know."

"A fancy apartment, right."

"With a view!"

Malk shook his head. "You arseholes. Here I was, happy to wipe my memories so I can forget Valeria, but now I'd be the odd one out, and you'd all gossip behind my back."

"You can have a fresh start," I said.

"I want my ma and da to be happy. I want them reunited on our old farm. I want at least a damn *week* to myself growing fucking mushrooms and getting dirt under my fingernails, and *then*..." He drew a breath. "Then we'll see what your new Chime holds."

Sinder slapped him on the back. "We'll start a therapy group, dearest."

Malk smirked. "We'll need one."

"Reve?" I called.

Everyone turned to the young Mesmer boy who stood there, clutching at his dressing gown.

"I would like to forget," he boomed. "But that is impossible for me. I see challenges ahead. I see myself..." His brow furrowed in confusion. "Eating jelly babies?"

I laughed. I couldn't stop myself. "We'll get you a bag." If there was one thing our new Chime needed, it was a return of traditional jelly babies.

My family gathered, and I hugged them in turn. "I love you all."

Harmony squeezed my waist. "We love you too, girl."

Malk kissed my forehead. A kiss born of years of affection, and hopefully years of friendship to come. "See you on the other side."

Together, Quen and I ensured the Godless were returned to Chime, to where they needed to be.

And then we were alone with Jinx in the clock tower.

Three Chaos who also needed a home. A new start.

Jinx scuffed her heel against the metal floor. "A happy ending for everyone, huh? What happens now?" *What happens to me?*

I took Quen's hand and stared into his eyes, so beautiful and filled with glowing aether. "Corentine warned me mortals could only exist within a god's mind because, as Mesmorpheus would put it, reality is but a dream. So it's time for us to sleep."

Jinx stared between us both. "What?"

Quen kissed my hand. He knew my mind. My heart. "There should never be another Dor. Another Corentine. No mortal should wield the powers of a god."

"We're Godless," I continued. "Which means if we keep this power, we're going against who we are, and we risk becoming another pair of cruel gods. But we can't just give away this power either, not without undoing everything we've done. Quen and I have already decided—we'll recreate Haven and exist in our sleep. We'll dream this reality so Chime and the domains can go on without us."

Our combined aether would power Chime and the domains, as Corentine once had, only it would be willingly given.

"You'll just fucking *sleep* for the rest of eternity?" Jinx said, appalled. "What about the Godless? You're leaving them to deal with whatever mess your new world will make?"

"They'll manage without us," I said.

"It would be my honor to share eternity with Kayl," Quen added.

An eternity where we could exist within each other. Where we could find our own peace. Quen surely needed the rest more than me, but even I wanted a few hundred years to breathe after everything the gods had done.

After all the killing. The deaths. The rebirths. It was a lot.

"And *me?*" Jinx yelled. "You expect me to manage on my own?"

"You can have whatever life you want, Jinx," I said. "Everyone gets a second chance, even you. I'm offering you a fresh start—"

"While you'll be trapped in a prison of your own making!"

"Not a prison. We'll have all the time we want to enjoy each other's company, play billiards, eat scones—"

"Drink tea," Quen said.

"And what if gods turn up and attack Chime!" Jinx demanded. "What then?"

"We'll leave protections. A method of detecting unknown energy outside our universe." Quen had the clever idea of building a clock tower in each domain to keep watch over them, powered by the souls of their old gods. "If beings from outside come to call, we'll awake to deal with them."

Jinx shook her head. "No."

"We'll be happy," I said. "And you'll get to live the life you always wanted, as a mortal of any domain—"

"What's the point if I don't have *you?*" Tears welled in her eyes. "You're my sister, and you're abandoning me *again!*"

"Jinx—"

"No! I won't fucking let you!" She grabbed my wrist.

Aether pulsed between us.

"Jinx, stop—"

My soul was yanked from my body.

I won't let you go! Jinx screamed into my mind. *Not now. Not ever!*

Stars exploded inside the clock tower.

You're my heart!

And then my mind went silent for the first time.

I Did it For You, Sister

Reality is but a dream of the gods.
It's time to wake up.

LIV

We, the standing ambassadors of the twelve domains, do pledge to serve Chime's citizens and all citizens of the free domains to the best of our own limitations. We ordain this Covenant as a record and warrant between every citizen and their domain.

The Council do pledge:

1. *The right to life, liberty, and security for all citizens.*
2. *The freedom of thought and expression for all citizens.*
3. *The prohibition of physical punishment and degrading treatment.*
4. *To provide a domain [Chime] where all citizens are equal.*
5. *To allow citizens free and safe passage into their own domain.*
6. *To not interfere with the liberty of other domains.*

In turn, the citizens of the free domains do pledge:

1. *To respect and follow the ordinance of Chime.*
2. *To treat citizens of all domains as equals and with respect.*
3. *To never cause harm to another citizen except in self-defense.*
4. *To bear a mark identifying citizenship to Chime.*

All citizens shall be treated with equal fairness and be granted the same privileges and opportunities on Chime. Should a citizen fail to uphold these laws, they are entitled to a fair trial by a jury of equal domains.

Signed by the twelve standing ambassadors.

—Chime City Council, *The Covenant of Citizens and their Domains*

I JOLTED AWAKE. "KAYL?"

I lay sprawled upon a four-poster bed, fully clothed in my tan suit. My metal arm ached where it connected with my residual limb, as though I'd worn it for days.

As though I'd carried the weight of thirteen domains.

I sat up, my heart pounding, and I lifted my spectacles to rub my eyes clear. The room was a cozy bedroom. It certainly held a woman's touch. Strings of golden lanterns stretched across the bedposts, and the room was decorated with keepsakes, trinkets, and tiny potted plants. Clothes were scattered haphazardly on an armchair by the floor-to-ceiling windows. The room held a touch of Chaos, too.

"Kayl?" I stumbled to the window, my legs a little wobbly, and yanked open the curtains. Light spilled inside—it was day—though rain pattered the window in soft splotches. Saints. It was raining. The cobblestone street outside looked familiar, but not.

This wasn't Haven.

Where in god's name was I?

I wandered into the hallway. "Kayl?" No answer.

It was clear I'd woken in some sort of town house. The second-floor landing led to a bathroom with a large bronze tub. Another door opened to a nursery. A child's nursery? It contained a crib, a bookshelf, and an aether-powered train set that ran around the room making cute little toots. The wallpaper was surely inspired, too. It was painted in swirls of blue and pink stars.

My wanderings brought me to the first floor, which held an office and a library complete with reading nook and a well-stocked whiskey cabinet. The rooms looked lived in. Homey. But they were empty.

"Kayl?"

I ventured downstairs to a spacious living room and kitchen area that overlooked a walled garden outside, which also held more potted plants and fairy lights. The entire town house was generously sized, yet Kayl wasn't in it.

Kayl? I called into my mind. Still no answer.

For the first time in weeks, my mind was silent. No mortals. No gods.

I tried to reach my godly powers and summon an object—a cup of tea, a pistol, a blasted shot of whiskey, *anything*—but my powers were gone.

No. Not all of them. I knew the exact time. Quarter to eleven in the morning.

I could still pause time.

The mirror in the hallway caught my eye. My hair was back to its usual cropped silver, my skin a pearly shade. My eyes no longer glowed with aether, but were as Diviner as the day I'd been created.

I was mortal again. How?

Was this a dream? It couldn't be. My right arm spasmed with pain when I flexed my artificial fingers. Kayl and I had agreed to return to Haven together, to live out the rest of our immortality without the risk of becoming as corrupt as the gods we'd defeated. But this couldn't be a dream of our creation.

I would never exist in a world without Kayl.

The last I remembered, we'd been inside the clock tower. We'd been explaining the situation to Jinx, and... *Jinx*. Fuck.

She'd grabbed Kayl and taken our souls. She'd done this.

I shoved open the front door and stepped outside to the cobblestone street and the baptism of rain. Trees lined the rows of town houses similar to the one I'd left. There was a placard by the front door.

The Corinths

13 Corentine Avenue

My heart caught in my throat.

A man emerged from the house next door, and I did a double take!

"Morning, Quen!" squawked Doctor Zachery Finch with actual cheer. He was back in his Zephyr form, dressed in a casual turtleneck sweater, and clutching a copy of the Courier in his talons. Yet he still didn't own wings. "You off to pick up the missus?"

"I—what?"

"From the station? Didn't she take an overnight trip to Phantasy? Visiting the relatives?"

Gods. "Yes, you're right. I'm sorry. I just woke from a nap. I'm a little discombobulated."

"I'm not surprised! She must be keeping you up all night. Are we still on for dinner? Ilona's making the crossing at one, and Walter and Gillian said they'd be free from the Academy by five. I hate to impose. I understand how busy you both are."

Gillian? Walter's wife? I forced a smile. "I'm sure we can manage."

Bells rang across the city. It had turned eleven o'clock. If this Chime was the one Kayl and I had made, then the Gate would be opening to Phantasy.

"Apologies, Doctor. I better get going."

He waved me off. "See you later!"

The rain had slowed to a faint drizzle. I turned up my jacket collar regardless and strode down the street, occasionally gazing above. The clouds were a swirling gray, but they were here. There was no plate above Central, exposing us to glorious sky.

My shoes splashed through puddles. I didn't know where I was walking—except I did. Slowly, details came to me. New memories. I came to a tram platform only a few yards from my doorstep, and I hopped onto a tram as one pulled up, as casually as if I'd lived this reality my entire life.

Mortals filled the tram, forcing me to stand by the doors. Mortals of all domains. Glimmer and Seren took most of the seats. A Leander in a top hat stood opposite, reading the Courier. The headline: *DOES CHIME NEED A MAYOR?*

Did it? Gosh.

We'd barely created the new world, and it was already making its own decisions.

The tram made a few more stops along the way, picking up Umber, Necro, Diviner, and then soon it pulled into the stop outside Central Station. Mortals rushed out, some heading into the station, others toward the many cafés, shops, and businesses dotted around Central. Everything was so busy, so *alive*.

It was the Chime I knew and loved.

I merged with the crowd heading into the station. Diviner, mostly. Presumably they weren't here for Phantasy, and indeed, they headed straight for the waiting areas and tea stand. As predictable as ever.

A few Mesmer loitered around the concourse leading to the Gate. None I recognized, and not Kayl. Diviner station staff were on hand to guide the more confused-looking Mesmer tourists. That certainly hadn't changed.

I searched around the station, the waiting rooms, but Kayl was nowhere to be found. Each passing second ached inside my heart and only fueled my anxiety.

The clock struck quarter past the hour. Where was she?

The tower was the same design I remembered. It stood taller than any other building or skyscraper in the city, dominating the city skyline with its large clockface staring out across Chime. It no longer connected to the Golden City above, for the Golden City no longer existed. No great glass elevator rode up and down the tower. A shame. The views had been spectacular, even if they made me nauseous. No mortal queued for the Undercity elevator, either.

Were Kayl and Jinx trapped behind the clockface? Were they fighting? Had they chosen to toss me out and leave me here alone?

My chest fluttered in panic.

I considered buying an overpriced cup of tea from the station's tea stand, as nothing grounded me in reality quite like terrible tea, but instead I meandered out of the station, feeling like a lost boy once more.

Wait. There was only one place Kayl would be.

I jogged around the corner for the bench with the broken streetlamp.

A Mesmer woman sat on the bench, hunched over a wrapped bundle.

"Kayl?"

She glanced up. Tears stained her cheeks. "Quen?"

I ran to the bench. It was *her*. It was Kayl! Reborn as I'd been, as a Mesmer and not a Vesper, though her eyes were still the silvery blue of aether that I adored. I wanted to embrace her, to hold her forever as the most precious being in the whole universe, but the bundle in her arms let out a cry.

I stopped dead in my tracks.

Oh my. "A—A *child*?"

Kayl rocked a baby in her arms. It was swaddled tight, only its tiny scrunched face visible. A Mesmer child, of all things. "It's Jinx. She... took our souls. Remade us as mortals. She wanted a fresh start, so she chose this. To be reborn as our daughter."

My legs went weak. I slid onto the bench before I could pass out. "*Our* daughter?"

"She always wanted a mother. It's fucked up, I know, but... she chose you to be her father. I understand if that's too much, if you want out—"

"We're married, I think." I lifted my spectacles and rubbed the bridge of my nose. "We've got a house. Doctor Finch is our neighbor." I wanted to laugh at the absurdity of it all!

"She altered things a little. Memories. Timelines. She made sure everyone forgot who we and the Godless were, and what we'd done. And that no one would remember her as anything but what she is now. I'm sorry, I—"

"Kayl." I breathed her name. "I was prepared to spend an eternity with you in my dreams. I'm more than honored to live a mortal life with you as your partner. As a father."

A tear slipped down her cheek.

I pressed my palm against her cheek, catching her tears.

We were both mortal, and yet... I could touch her without being tortured with a vision of death. A gift. I was finally free of the curse that had plagued my mortal existence, and that alone made my heart soar.

She sighed against my touch. "Do—Do you want to hold her?"

"Please."

Kayl handed me the baby—Jinx. She was such a tiny thing.

To become a father was another gift I'd thought I'd never earn, one I was sure I'd never deserve. How could I become an adequate paternal figure when my own father had so thoroughly abused me? When I'd struggled to even recognize love for what it was?

But as she slid into my arms, new memories slotted into place in my mind. They didn't overwrite my memories, but coexisted in this new world. A memory of meeting Kayl and inviting her for tea and scones—our first date. Of marrying her, with Ben as my best man and Dru as Kayl's maid of honor. Of reading books in Meridian Park with my heavily pregnant wife.

I'd dreamed that memory before, back in the Mesmer memory parlor of the Undercity. Had it been a vision of my future? Or had Jinx simply taken inspiration from my desires?

I would never know.

Baby Jinx stopped squirming and opened her eyes. They were my eyes. The pure silver of a Diviner. The implications included one I hadn't fully realized.

Her birth heralded a new age of children born of multiple domains. Jinx was a hybrid of Mesmer and Diviner, completely unheard of until now. Other such children would likely be born in the near future.

We were heading for interesting times indeed.

"She's beautiful." Already, memories of the old Jinx were beginning to fade. This was my daughter, and she always had been.

"What am I supposed to do?" Kayl groaned. "I don't know the first thing about being a mother."

"You managed with the Mesmer."

"The Mesmer didn't need their diapers changed."

"We'll figure it out. Wait. If she's here, and we've been rebirthed as mortals... what happened to the gods' souls?"

"Oh, well. She has them. In there." Kayl gently poked Jinx's head, and the baby giggled.

"Are you telling me our newborn child possesses the powers of multiple gods? Power that can be used to shape the entire universe?"

Kayl cringed. "Yes?"

Oh dear gods. I was going to faint. "We'll need books on parenting, immediately."

Kayl laughed. "It's fine, Quen. She'll grow up with a whole family of uncles and aunts. Dru, Ben, Harm, for a start. Don't forget the Mesmer. They'll watch over her. I'm apparently still responsible for them in this universe, too."

Then that was our role. To guide our all-powerful child into growing up and becoming a kind god, and not a cruel one. To protect her from forces that could threaten our entire universe. We still didn't know what existed out there.

But would our universe be ready for Jinx?

"Tea?" Kayl prompted. "Maybe it's my new Mesmer body, but I could demolish an entire plate of blueberry pancakes right now."

We were going to be fine. "I thought you'd never ask."

One Week Later

QUEN

AFTER A WEEK OF adjusting to our new lives—an exhausting week of sleepless nights and far too much tea to cope—we couldn't keep ignoring the letters piling up on our doorstep. Especially the one from the Bank of Chime.

Thus, I made the pragmatic decision of setting up an appointment. It would behoove us to learn of our finances if we were to build a life together.

Sadly, we arrived late, no thanks to my wife. "Apologies for our tardiness."

A Seren man dressed in a tiny tweed suit and even smaller spectacles welcomed us into a private room decorated in antique furniture. "That's no problem, sir. Can we get either of you a drink?"

"Tea for me, please. Two sugars and a splash of milk."

Kayl slumped in a plush armchair, Jinx in her arms. "I'm good, thank you."

The Seren flittered off to the doorway.

"Tweed," I mouthed.

Kayl rolled her eyes.

An Umber brought my tea as the Seren pulled up our file. "Ah yes, Mr. and Mrs. Corinth. We're sorry to drag you in like this; it seems you've got your hands full with your little one, there. We won't keep you long. Your accountant wanted to assure you that your investments have now been transferred to your main account. With the amount in question, we recommend further investments to safeguard your finances."

"The last few weeks have been a whirlwind, as you can imagine." I smiled at my wife. No one ever prepared you for how demanding babies were, and in our case, there'd been no preparation at all. "How much is our account worth?" I took a sip of my tea.

"A little over thirteen million."

I spat out my tea, spilling it down my jacket. "What did you say?"

"Thirteen million in your account—are you okay there, sir?"

"Apologies." I choked, my eyes watering. I placed my tea down with my metal hand and accidentally spilled it across the man's desk. Even with practice, I occasionally got the grip wrong. "I am *so* sorry."

"It's quite all right, sir. Let me fetch an attendant." He flew out of the room again.

I dabbed at my jacket with a handkerchief. "*Thirteen sodding million?*" I couldn't believe my ears!

"Language," Kayl chided. "We don't want the baby learning such filthy words."

"How do we have *thirteen million* bocs?"

"Clearly our daughter didn't want us to live in poverty. You're a good girl who wants Mama to shop for pretty dresses, aren't you?" she crooned.

"My wage is hardly poverty. What are we meant to do with thirteen million?" I had enough suits to last, and Kayl always looked stunning in her floral dresses.

"Spend it on biscuits, private school. Oh! We could pay for Sinder's hair transplant! I'm sure you'll find a few worthy organizations that need a mystery benefactor. Besides, New Haven bleeds money. This will pay for its upkeep."

"And then some." Saints. Thirteen million. I could quit my job, except I enjoyed my job. I didn't do it for the money.

Chime's Council wasn't perfect. They needed mortals like me to serve as advisors and guide their way. Though I needed to stop thinking of mortals as mortals. With no gods and immortals left, mortality was now the default. Chime's mortals were citizens. People.

We finished at the bank and headed out into the Market District. It was a lovely sunny morning, and a variety of citizens from across the domains sat outside for brunch. I spotted two familiar faces getting breakfast at a nearby café—Gast and Zorya. They were seated together, nursing coffee, deep in conversation. I nodded, and Gast returned the nod with grudging respect.

Sadly, Kayl and I both had places to be, and we headed for the nearest tram platform, hand in hand, as Kayl carried Jinx across her chest in a shawl. For once, my precious girl was sound asleep, a smile on her tiny face as she dreamed.

It was remarkable how quickly we'd settled into a domestic routine, and how quickly this week had flown by. I squeezed Kayl's hand. "You're heading off to Eventide?"

"For a short trip. We'll be back within the hour."

. "Pass on my regards to Malk."

"I will, don't worry."

We waited by the tram stop. She'd be going the opposite direction to the Gate as I headed for the embassy to catch up on work. I'd had little time to fully integrate myself with the Council, but my memories and that of my new colleagues had been adjusted to reflect my sudden mortality. They expected me to be on leave with my wife and newborn, but that hadn't stopped me from investigating a few cases.

The Council had replaced the Wardens with community officers who focused on rehabilitation rather than corrective punishment, but we were still working out the fine details. Occasionally, a firm hand was required.

My new role hadn't stopped me from testing the limits of my abilities, either. While I no longer suffered visions of death through touch, I could still examine a person's history, like any Diviner. Though my touch wasn't as sensitive. Another gift to be thankful for.

Sunlight caught the glittering stars on my wife's face. Gods, she was so beautiful. Every day I woke up and couldn't believe my luck.

"What's going on in that mind of yours?" she asked. "I can see your cogs whirring."

I bent my head close, my voice dropping to a whisper. "I worry this is all a dream." This perfection. This bliss. "I'll wake up and you won't be here. I'll lose you again." I swallowed a lump in my throat.

"You always find me. I'll always be waiting."

"Don't you worry it's a little too good to be true? I have a wonderful wife and daughter, and apparently, we're now millionaires. What if—"

"You deserve happiness, Quen. It's okay to want it."

How often would I keep reminding myself of that? I lifted my spectacles and lowered my lips close to hers.

Kayl held her breath in anticipation.

But then my sodding tram pulled in.

"Sorry, dear. I best be off." I gave her and my daughter each a peck on the cheek and turned for the tram.

"You're not leaving me with that!" Kayl grabbed my arm and pulled me back.

I swallowed my surprise as my wife pushed me against the tram shelter and kissed me. A deep kiss that warmed my blood.

"Now go save the world."

I hurried for the tram before the doors could shut and found a seat at the back. Kayl waved me off as the carriage pulled away.

Someone had abandoned a copy of this morning's edition of the Courier on the empty seat beside me. It was the usual gossip. I flipped through the pages idly with my metal fingers. My arm still ached, even on good days, though my level of control *was* improving with practice, this morning's little accident aside. Living next to Doctor Finch also proved useful for the bad days.

I turned the page, and my heart stopped.

There was a photo of Elijah next to an article on his latest performances in Chime's most prestigious orchestra. With his new life, he'd become a talented pianist. A novelty for a Diviner, which explained his growing fame. Seeing his name and face still shocked me. He had no idea who I was—he'd forgotten I even existed—but I still lived with those memories. I didn't want to erase them, but I'd booked myself an appointment with an Umber therapist to help deal with it.

My hand instinctively went in my pocket and searched for my fob watch, but I no longer carried it with me, for I no longer required its comfort.

It was time to heal and move on.

A Seren woman got on the tram at the next stop and looked around for a seat.

I patted the cushion next to me. "There's space!"

She shot me a dirty look and turned her back to me. Oh well. She squealed as an Umber in a navy suit barged her out of the way.

"Sorry, ma'am," Ben said. "Excuse me." He squeezed into the seat beside me, and I could swear the entire carriage shook. "Morning, sir."

"I've told you a hundred times. You don't need to keep calling me sir. We're colleagues."

He flashed a sheepish grin. "Force of habit. You thinking of running?" He pointed to the front page of the Courier.

The headline was on the mayoral race. The good citizens of Chime, with the backing of the Council, had decided Chime needed its own ruler—a mayor—so leadership didn't automatically fall to a Diviner. It wasn't something I'd thought of, but it was a welcome idea. We didn't need another Elijah, and Chime had its own affairs separate from the twelve domains.

"Me? Oh gods, no. The paperwork would be intriguing, but I'm barely getting enough sleep as it is." Between a newborn and Kayl running me ragged. That woman had *needs*.

"How's Mama doing?"

"Eating all my favorite biscuits, as usual." Kayl had fully embraced the Mesmer lifestyle, and that meant spending a fortune on cookies and candy. I supposed we could afford it. "The Mesmer are helping to care for Jinx during the day, and I'm taking on the nightly feedings and changes. You wouldn't *believe* how much babies defecate." A Diviner standing nearby cleared their throat with disapproval. "How is Big Ben this fine morning?"

"Well, um." He tugged awkwardly on the vines that made up his new hair. "I wanted to ask your advice."

"Oh?"

"It's about Dru, you see. I, um, I want to ask her out on a date, but I don't know where to begin, sir."

"What makes you assume I'm qualified to assist?" I hardly had the best track record!

"You know more than I do. I know women like flowers, but do Umber women find that offensive? Where should I take her? A bakery? The theater? Is that too much?"

"Calm down. We'll head to the office and hash out a plan."

The tram shuddered to a halt. Everyone jerked forward, losing balance, and fell atop each other with confused cries.

Ben was on his feet. "What's going on, sir?"

I had my hand on my pistol. "Someone is fucking with time."

We'd had a few cases of a Diviner gone rogue, and this was my chance to finally catch them before they caused a serious injury. "Come, Ben!" I leaped from the tram carriage.

This was the path I'd chosen. The path I'd walk until the end of my days.

Only now, I no longer walked the path alone.

KAYL

IT WAS ODD VISITING Eventide without feeling utterly terrified. I made the crossing in good time, for a change, and rode in a wooden carriage down the main road. Once, this road led to Valeria's dark purple castle, but now the horizon was full of mushroom trees, a singular clock tower, and the beautiful purple skies of dusk. The road had been lined with cages and bowls full of tithes. In this reality, the road was lined with various carved pumpkins, gourds, and turnips, each lit with varying odd faces. I supposed it was an improvement.

My carriage veered off the road into the dirt. It shook all over the place and woke Jinx, who started crying.

"Can't you go a little slower?" I called out.

The carriage driver was an older Vesper man. "Can't, love."

I'd love to say Vesper had truly come out of their shell now that they no longer lived under the oppression of their god, but they were still as grumpy and broody as ever.

I cradled Jinx. "Hush now, or I'll need to find the right mushroom to knock you out. Your papa will be upset if I murder you." I could have left her with the Mesmer, but honestly, I didn't trust the Mesmer not to kill her accidentally by feeding her gobstoppers. "Why couldn't you have been a cute little Leander cub, hrm? Though I suppose that would raise questions. Think of the scandal!"

Jinx wailed, and I suspected the real scandal was coming out of her rear end.

We entered a wooded area lit by glowing mushrooms. Jinx stopped crying as a firefly flew overhead. I'd never had the chance to appreciate Eventide's beauty, though even without a god, there were still dangers.

Eventually we pulled up to a ramshackle cottage hidden in the woods. A mushroom farm. And there was Malk toiling away in the middle of a meadow.

I slid down from the carriage awkwardly, with no help from the driver, though I paid him a generous tip anyway because I wasn't a bitch. Then I wandered over to the meadow and waved Malk over.

He wiped a dirty hand across his sweaty brow, smearing soil. "I didn't think you'd make it."

"Why? Didn't you get my telegram?"

"You're usually late for these things."

"Maybe I'm a changed woman." Being married to a man who was fastidious about time counted for something.

"Huh. Maybe you are. I never took you for the mothering type."

"Dru helps with the babysitting." When she wasn't fussing over the Mesmer or Ben, anyhow.

Truth be told, motherhood was awful. Truly awful. Especially at twelve, three, and then five in the morning. But I was told Jinx would eventually settle down into a napping routine, as Mesmer children enjoyed their naps, or so Reverie promised me.

Jinx was also half Diviner. An interesting mix I was sure would bite me in the arse when she became old enough to discover what powers she possessed.

I'd wanted eternal peace, and I got a screaming baby instead. It was hardly a fair trade. But no, I supposed motherhood had its moments. It was odd at first to accept Jinx as my daughter and not my twin sister, but those memories had slipped in so easily, I couldn't imagine her as anything else. It was cute when she giggled, and for some reason, she found everything entertaining. Especially her Mesmer cousins.

Though Jinx *had* robbed me of a wedding. The memories were there of a beautiful day, but they technically hadn't happened. When everything had settled down, I was going to insist on a do-over. Or at least a lavish party. Something.

"What's with all the pumpkins?" I asked.

"On the main road? It's a contest the locals are having. Can you believe I came *third*?"

"Third's not bad."

"It's shit. It took me a whole week of carving pumpkins to get the design right."

"You're being productive, then?"

"I am, actually. Farm's doing well. Got some fancy mushrooms growing. Chanterelle. Really rewarding, you know?"

"You're bored, aren't you?"

He sighed. "I am *so* fucking bored. It's nice spending time with my ma and da, but the cottage is tiny, and I can hear 'em going at it every night. I'm traumatized. But what else can I do? Get a job at the Courier as a paperboy again? Maybe Harm will let me have a go at writing the sports column. Can't be that hard."

"Come work for me at New Haven."

"Doing what? Cleaning bedpans?"

I waggled my brow. "Espionage."

He leaned his arm against the fence. "I'm intrigued. Oh fuck, that's vile!" He wafted his nose and gestured at Jinx. "I think she needs changing."

I lifted Jinx and caught the whiff of something truly awful. She giggled. "What a chaotic creature you are."

The front door to the cottage opened, and Elvira stepped out. "Malkavaan Byvich! You didn't tell me you were having guests? Do come in for tea, dear!"

Malk waved her off. "Be right there, Ma!"

"She doesn't remember anything from before?" In this reality, she'd never been forced to flee Eventide. Elvira had never become my mother.

"No, and neither does my pa. It's awkward, sometimes. I have to be careful what I say, and I... I can't tell them why I get nightmares. They worry, but I'd rather they didn't, you know?"

"I know."

"Come in for tea, and I'll introduce you to Eventide's ambassador."

"I need to be back before the hour's up."

"I'll scrub up and come with. Then you can tell me all about this proposal."

"Deal."

I spent the rest of the afternoon in New Haven.

While Quen dealt with the Council, New Haven was my personal project. It was a home for Mesmer and others who struggled with reality. A nice stately building around the corner from Meridian Park back in Chime. Functionally, it served much like the Mesmer temple of old, and while I didn't live there, I spent most of my time running it along with Dru, who helped maintain the estate's gardens, and Vincent, who'd taken up residency as the home's doctor and ran weekly art therapy sessions. Occasionally Sinder would drop by and volunteer his services as a masseur, though lately he'd taken up baking. Zachery also helped maintain our aether lamps.

Mesmorpheus had tasked me with protecting the Mesmer, and it was a promise I aimed to keep, with Reverie's approval.

Our main residents were Mesmer, including the trio and Reve, though we also took in Fauna who found Chime confusing, orphans, and abused women. Trixie donated bocs and supplies to our cause, and Nelle acted as our main bouncer. Her cubs lived in one of the upstairs rooms with Autumn and Freddie, and they frequently played with the Mesmer trio.

They were helping me get an amateur theater production running.

While I liked to believe we did good work, New Haven was also a front for more nefarious activities.

Down in the basement, we hid a secret room that resembled the depot of old. It had a meeting table, armchairs, and a wine cabinet for when we broke out the cards.

Malk slumped in one of the armchairs. "When were you going to tell me you had a secret base?"

I leaned on the table. "If I recall, you said you wanted a week to grow mushrooms."

"Uh-huh. Honestly, I'm surprised you managed to keep a secret this long."

"The Godless wouldn't have lasted long if I couldn't."

"Is that what this is? You're bringing back the Godless? Didn't you kill all the gods?"

"Yes and no. We destroyed the gods of this universe, but more could be lurking out there in the wider cosmos. Personally, I think it's important we prepare just in case. But also, Chime will have its issues. Harm didn't want her old job back for fun, you know. Being head of the Courier means she has contacts and a network of spies. She's helping run our admin and fundraisers while also providing us with intel about any social issues. Corruption, inequality, that sort of thing. We've also got Joe helping with the legal side. He's training to become a lawyer, of all pissing things."

"You don't let up, do you?"

"Perhaps I feel a sort of responsibility toward Chime."

"That's your mothering instincts kicking in."

"Don't make me fetch Nelle. She *will* pummel you."

"What about your husband? Does he approve of all this?"

"Actually, yes. Corruption can affect the Council, too, and Quen appreciates being aware of issues they may miss or ignore. We're a team." While he worked his charm in a forward-facing role, I preferred working in the background.

Malk crossed his arms. "So you want me to become one of Harm's spies?"

"It pays well."

"How well?"

"Give me a figure."

"One hundred bocs an hour."

"Done."

He sat up. "Are you fucking with me?"

"Just don't spend it all on booze and mushrooms." I winked.

Jinx had believed in my cause. Thanks to her foresight, I had the funds to ensure Chime would be protected for generations to come.

When the clock struck five, my Godless family and friends gathered in New Haven for wine tasting and scheming. Harmony brought the latest gossip from her day job with her, though Sinder only turned up for Vincent, and Dru waited for Ben.

Quen and Ben were a double act now. Partners. I knew Quen would have preferred if I'd taken up the role, but really, this was more my sort of thing. Someone needed to look after Jinx and the Mesmer during the day, and I wasn't the best with authority figures.

He arrived after his shift and immediately came to my side for a quick kiss. "I missed you."

"You say that every day."

"Because it's true every day. Where's Jinx?"

"She's with Celeste and Castor upstairs. They're fine, don't worry. They're playing dress-up." I offered him a whiskey.

Quen took it with a grateful smile and slipped into a seat beside me, watching with restrained amusement as Ben and Dru awkwardly sat together, both too shy to start a conversation.

My family converged in the room, and I beamed at them.

They weren't aware of what I knew.

When Jinx rebirthed me as a Mesmer, I'd been gifted a vision of the near future.

Dru and Ben would eventually date. They'd take it slow—painfully slow—but they'd make it work, and I'd be the maid of honor at their wedding. Malk didn't think I could keep a secret? Well, this one was killing me.

Sadly, Sinder and Vincent wouldn't make it work. Both had too many issues to get through on their own, but there was a silver lining. Vincent would thrive as a doctor, and he'd grow close to Joe, of all people. Sinder would be happy for them. In fact, she'd go on to find herself and change her name to Sindy, with new tattoos to match her new identity.

Then, in the strangest twist I never saw coming, she and Malk would grow close, thanks to their shared therapy sessions. They'd always been friends, so it was only natural, and I truly couldn't wait to see them glow.

Harmony would move on. She'd suffer date after failed date and never feel satisfied. Until she decided to betray us and begin an illicit relationship with a certain Diviner ambassador behind our backs. Except Pendula would join our ranks, and we'd all learn to live with it. Even Pendula deserved a second chance.

As for Quen and me, challenges would be thrown at us through the upcoming years. The only certainty was we'd face them together.

He'd make a good father. I wasn't sure what kind of mother I'd become yet, but for the sake of Chime and the domains, I'd need to figure it out.

Jinx needed me to. Now, I could honestly say I loved her.

The Godless made themselves comfortable as I fetched a wine bottle. "Anyone for a drink?"

The door burst open, and in came a ragged-looking Joe. Gods, even when his suit and hair was a mess, he still lit up the room, though that was mostly his golden skin. He slammed a briefcase onto the table. "You won't believe the day I've had. It's only bloody Gloria again! She's trying to get tax breaks for her new church, only it's not an actual church, of course— it's another workhouse."

The Godless shared a collective groan.

"Chime still needs godless heathens," Quen said.

Though now, the gods would leave us to our fate.

Author's Note

Thank you for reading! If you enjoyed THE END OF TIME, then please consider leaving an honest review. Reviews mean the world to me and help support your favorite authors.

Want More from Chime?

Not ready to leave Chime yet or want to know what other projects I'm working on? Then join my monthly newsletter and you'll receive an ebook copy of **TALES FROM ACROSS THE DOMAINS**, a short story collection set in The Cruel Gods world:

TrudieSkies.com/Newsletter

Visit my website for signed copies of my books, domain map posters, character art, appendices, pronunciation guides, and other extra goodies:

TrudieSkies.com

Domain Glossary

A list of the twelve domains in order of their designated crossing time:

Memoria

Home to the Amnae.

An underwater city. Ruled by Anima, the god of academia, books, history, memories, and water.

Juniper

Home to the Fauna.

A treacherous jungle. Ruled by Faen, the god of animals, creatures, metamorphosis, and sacrifice.

Heartstone

Home to the Umber.

A mountainous region with valleys. Ruled by Unghard, the god of craft, discipline, earth, nature, servitude, and trade.

Solaris

Home to the Glimmer.

A golden city of cathedrals. Ruled by Gildola, the god of birth, dawn, femininity, piety, spring, and sunlight.

Arcadia

Home to the Seren.

A series of tropical islands. Ruled by Serenity, the god of art, beauty, creativity, song, and summer.

WITHERYN

Home to the Necro.

A frozen wasteland. Ruled by The Nameless One, the god of blood, disease, flesh, healing, and winter.

TEMPEST

Home to the Zephyr.

A sky world made from floating airships. Ruled by Zyclone, the god of air, machines, science, and technology.

OBITUARY

Home to the Leander.

A desert plain. Ruled by Lionheart, the god of battle, challenge, domination, legacy, masculinity, strength, and trials.

RAPTURE

Home to the Ember.

A volcanic strip of casinos. Ruled by Edana, the god of depravity, flame, pleasure, and sensuality.

EVENTIDE

Home to the Vesper.

A land of glowing mushrooms. Ruled by Valeria, the god of autumn, dusk, moonlight, and shadow.

PHANTASY

Home to the Mesmer.

An observatory of stars. Ruled by Mesmorpheus, the god of dreams, nightmares, stars, and visions.

KRONOS

Home to the Diviner.

A clockwork city. Ruled by Dor, the god of bureaucracy, justice, law, logic, order, and time.

ACKNOWLEDGMENTS

And so we've reached the end.

Coming to the end of a series is bittersweet. The Cruel Gods is my first completed trilogy, though it won't be my last. While I'm eager to move onto new adventures, I'm also not ready to leave Chime behind. This world and its characters have become my lifeline after living inside my head for the past four years. We authors pour parts of ourselves into our characters, and that's certainly true of Kayl and Jinx. I'm just as scatterbrained as poor Kayl, and I see Jinx as the personification of female rage in the face of enforced politeness.

Then there is Quen. My beloved Quen, who came out of nowhere and stole my heart, which is why I torture him so. Perhaps an acknowledgements page is an odd place to confess, but Quen encouraged me to question my gender. I wanted to BE Quen. It's no coincidence that The Cruel Gods has so many trans and non-binary characters.

I'm not sure where my personal journey of self-discovery will take me, but thank you, Quen, for setting me on my path.

While this may be the end of Kayl, Jinx, and Quen's journey for now, we will return to Chime. Until then, there are more stories to be told, and I promise they too will be full of trans and non-binary characters.

As the curtain falls, there are many wonderful people I must thank.

First and foremost, a big THANK YOU to the readers and fans who have joined me on this journey through Chime and the domains. Without your love and support, I may never have made it this far. Thank you to the bloggers and reviewers for your passion and dedication to indie books. Thank you to everyone who ever supported my Kofi, shared my books online, replied to my newsletters, or supported me in other ways I deeply appreciate. Thank you to my beta readers, past and present, for being honest. Thank you to my Friday night D&D group for keeping me sane. Thank you to the regulars in my Daydream Domain Discord server for keeping me company.

All of you have made this journey worthwhile.

Thank you, then, to A. Kwiatkoski, Ade, C. Holford, Cal Black, Catherine Bloom, David G, G. Banks, J. E. Hannaford, Jamedi, Jo, Joyce Gee, Kriti Khare, L. Fitzjohn, L. Winch, Lucy A. McLaren, M. Higgins, Maria Z. Medina, Melissa Bowlin, Nils Ödlund, Peter Hutchinson, Olivia Hofer, R. Pybus, Rari, Rowena Andrews, Sue Bavey, Tessa Hastjarjanto, T. M. Kohl, T. Wolff, Tyra Leann, Y. Marjot, and many more.

Thank you to Before We Go Blog for choosing The Thirteenth Hour as your SPFBO 8 finalist, and to Mark Lawrence for shining a torch on indie authors. You made me proud to be an indie author.

Thank you to the lovely Zack Argyle and Bookborn for believing in my work and supporting me via the Indie Fantasy Fund.

Thank you to editing god Nia Quinn for your diligent edits. I will be knocking at your door for future projects!

Thank you to legendary cartographer Soraya Cororan for your incredible map of the domains. I will forever treasure it.

Thank you to James T. Egan of Bookfly Design for bringing these books to life with your amazing covers. You really outdid yourself this time!

Thank you to RJ Bayley for the fantastic audiobook of The Thirteenth Hour. I hope we get to work together again in the future!

Thank you to Butchy the Border Jack for taking me on walks, and to Benji the Jack Russell who was there at the beginning but didn't make it to the end. You are both good boys.

Thank you to Bayley the cat who joined the adventure late and is the real reason why this book took so long.

And thank you to Jack for always being there.

Finally, **THANK YOU**, dear reader, for joining me. I hope your journey through the domains has been kind to you.

This isn't the end of the gods.

About the Author

Trudie Skies is a non-binary author based in North East England, though they have been living inside fantasy worlds ever since they discovered books and refuse to return to reality. Within Trudie's daydreams you'll find SPFBO and BBNYA finalist The Thirteenth Hour, a gaslamp fantasy described as obnoxiously British and best read with a cup of tea.

When not conjuring new worlds, Trudie spends their free time exploring the realms of indie books and video games, staring at clouds, and chasing after their fluffy companions.

Follow the Author:

TrudieSkies.com
TrudieSkies.com/Newsletter
Bookbub.com/Authors/Trudie-Skies

ALSO BY TRUDIE SKIES

The Cruel Gods Series

Adult Gaslamp Fantasy

Book One: The Thirteenth Hour
Book Two: The Children of Chaos
Book Three: The End of Time
Tales From Across the Domains: A Short Story Collection

Cruel gods rule the steam-powered city of Chime and demand worship from their mortal subjects, but when soul-sucking creatures prey on Chime's citizens, it'll take godless heathens to save them—before the gods take matters into their own hands.

The Chosen One Con

Adult Gaslamp Fantasy

A televised contest of mages to find the 'chosen one' in a world of designer enchantments and celebrity-branded potions.